ERIKA McCORKLE

MERCHANTS OF LIGHT AND BONE

THE PENTAGONAL DOMINION

Merchants of Light and Bone

First Edition: August 8th 2023

Written by Erika McCorkle

Cover design © Jessica Moon

Cover art © Bear Pettigrew

Map © Dewi Hargreaves

Published by Shadow Spark Publishing

www.shadowsparkpub.com

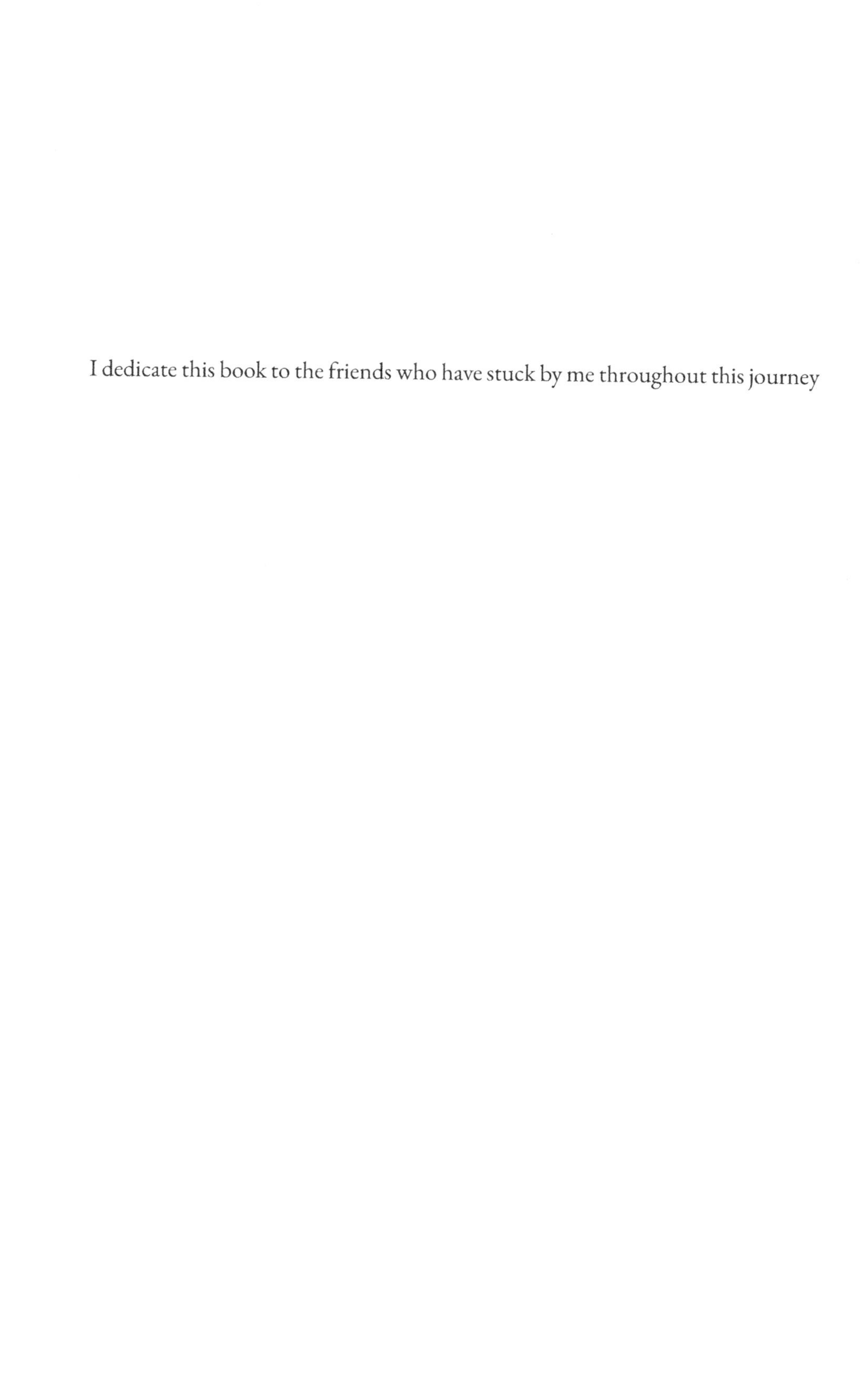

I dedicate this book to the friends who have stuck by me throughout this journey

AUTHOR'S NOTE

The world described in this book is a fantasy world connected to Earth. In the lore, people of Earth have occasionally found their way to the Pentagonal Dominion and vice-versa. As such, there are some cultural and linguistic similarities. Please note that any mention of the language called "English" is not an error. Their understanding of this language is that it came from a mysterious Land of Eng in the Terran Dominion.

The Pentagonal Dominion is a large fantasy universe with content that cannot be contained within a single book. This book includes footnotes and extra 'Codex Dominex' pages with additional worldbuilding information for readers who are interested. They are not required to understand or enjoy the plot. Feel free to skip them if you wish.

An online list of footnotes can be viewed here:

An online list of the Codex Dominex entries can be viewed here:

Please note that this is a Dark Fantasy novel with themes that may be unsuitable for younger audiences. It also contains content that some readers will find disturbing. Reader discretion is advised. A full list of potentially-troubling content can be viewed here:

TABLE OF CONTENTS

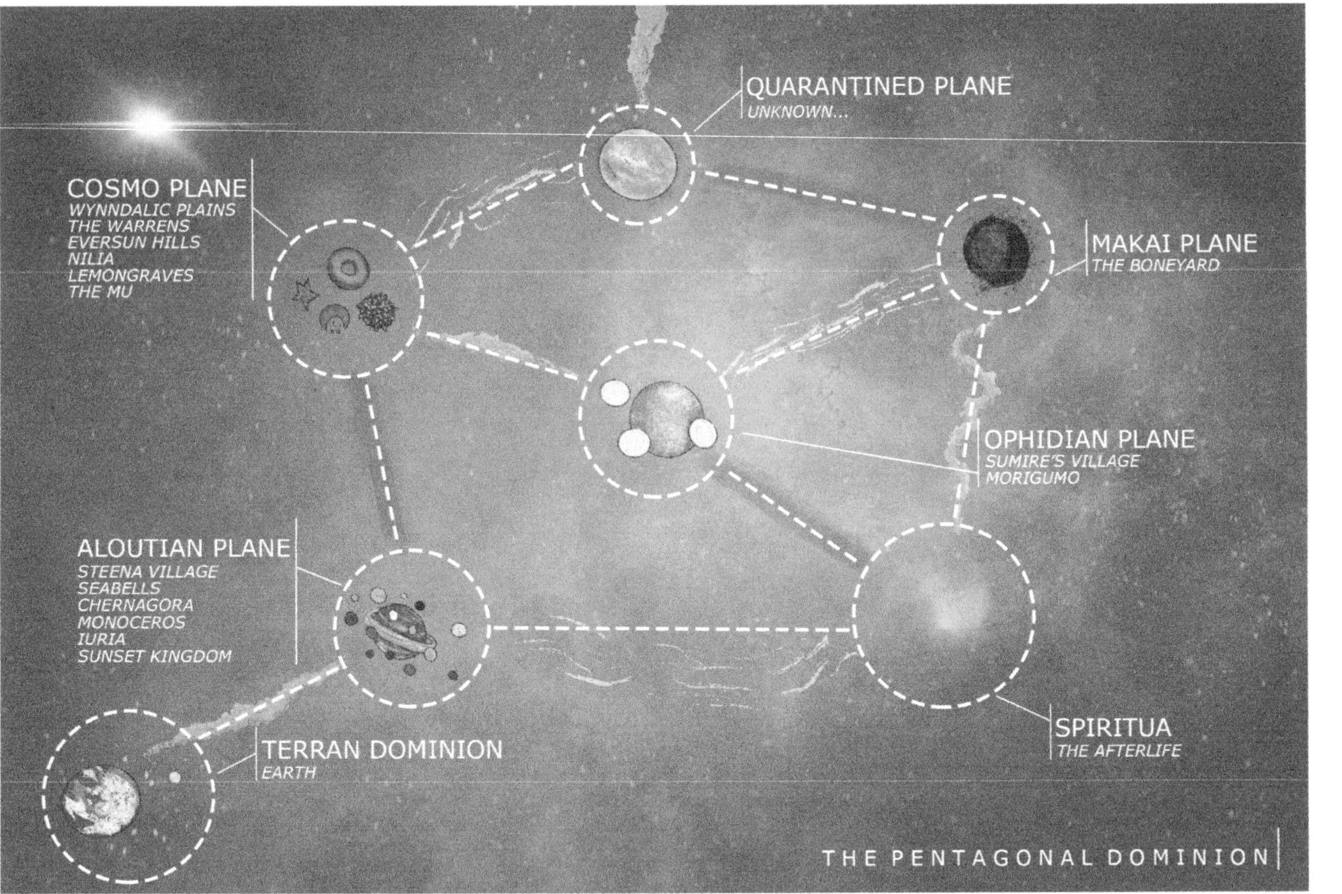
QUARANTINED PLANE
UNKNOWN...
COSMO PLANE
WYNNDALIC PLAINS
THE WARRENS
EVERSUN HILLS
NILIA
LEMONGRAVES
THE MU
MAKAI PLANE
THE BONEYARD
OPHIDIAN PLANE
SUMIRE'S VILLAGE
MORIGUMO
ALOUTIAN PLANE
STEENA VILLAGE
SEABELLS
CHERNAGORA
MONOCEROS
IURIA
SUNSET KINGDOM
TERRAN DOMINION
EARTH
SPIRITUA
THE AFTERLIFE
THE PENTAGONAL DOMINION

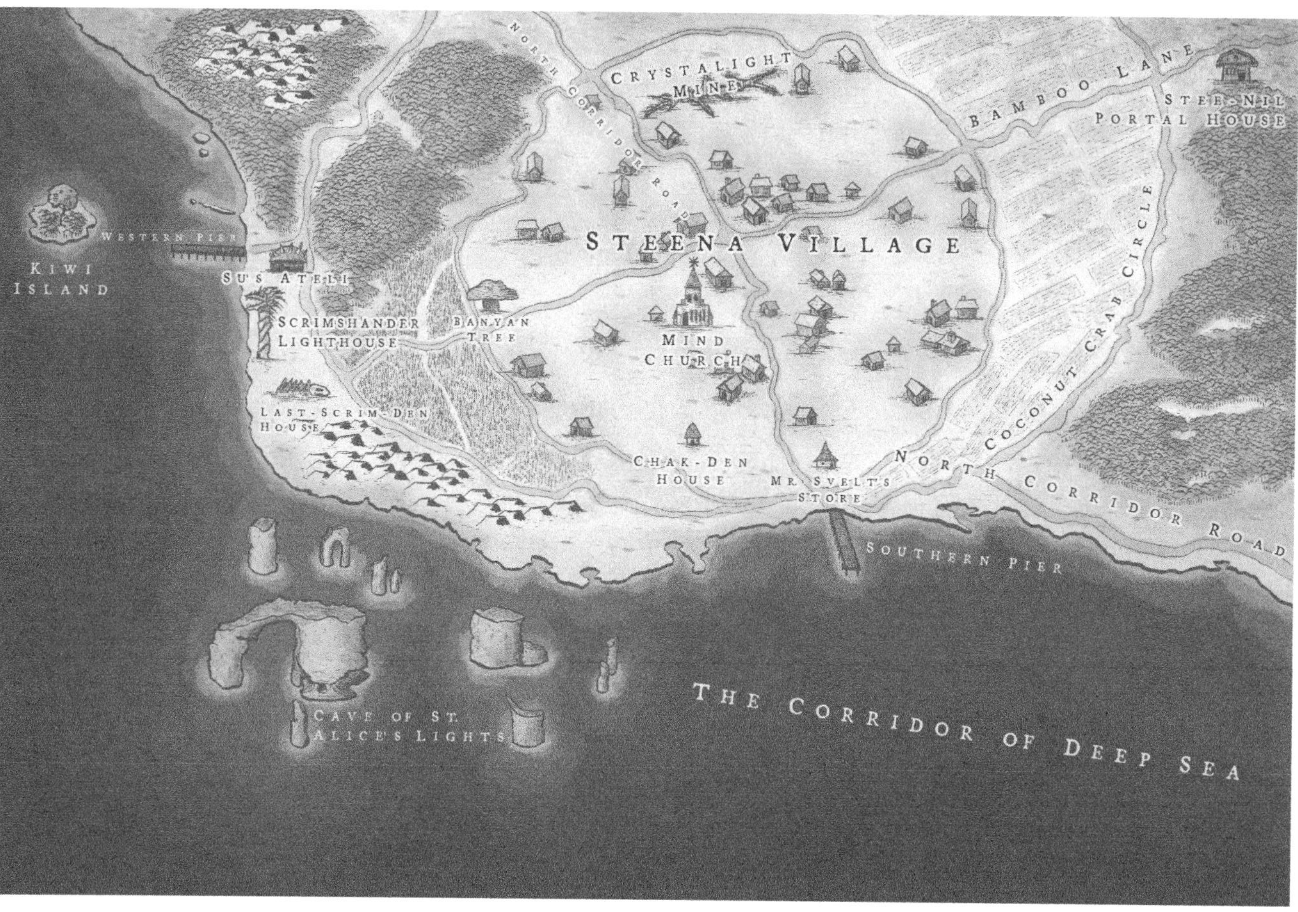
Crystalight Mine
North Corridor Road
Bamboo Lane
Stee-Nil Portal House
Steena Village
Western Pier
Kiwi Island
Sus Ateli
Scrimshander Lighthouse
Banyan Tree
Mind Church
Coconut Crab Circle
Last-Scrim-Den House
Chak-Den House
Mr. Svelt's Store
North Corridor Road
Southern Pier
Cave of St. Alice's Lights
The Corridor of Deep Sea

DRAMATIS PERSONAE

The Last-Scrim-Den Family:

AMIERE LASTERAN, 36 years old, merchant of light, biological father of his children. Yellow mane and skin with spots, yellow spark on tail. Wynnle-Nilian.

SU SCRIMSHANDER, 38 years old, merchant of bone, a Godblood of unknown element and sex (uses he/him pronouns). He has no biological children. Brown hair, brown skin, four arms, can transform his legs into a fish tail of any color or shape. Species unknown.

LIESLE DENWALL, 37 years old, merchants of faces, biological mother of her children. Blue mane, purple skin with stripes, blue wings, blue spark on tail. Wynnle-Winyan.

ERUWAN DENWALL, 14 years old, daughter. Blue mane, purple skin with a mixture of spots and stripes, blue wings, blue spark on tail. Wynnle-Winyan-Nilian.

FIONN LASTERAN, 12 years old, son. Yellow mane, blue skin with a mixture of spots and stripes, blue wings, blue spark on tail. Wynnle-Winyan-Nilian.

COHAKU DENWALL, 9 years old, daughter. Yellow mane and skin with a mixture of spots and stripes, yellow wings, yellow spark on tail. Wynnle-Winyan-Nilian.

HELIODOR LASTERAN, 9 years old, son. Quadrupedal and furry. Yellow fur with stripes, yellow wings, blue spark on tail. Wynnle-Winyan-Nilian.

TAWNY DENWALL, 7 years old, daughter. Yellow mane, yellow skin with a mixture of spots and stripes, no wings, yellow spark on tail. Wynnle-Winyan-Nilian. Deceased.

NIO DENWALL, 5 years old, daughter. Blue mane, purple skin with spots, yellow wings, blue spark on tail. Wynnle-Winyan-Nilian.

The Chak-Den Family:

ORIENNA DENWALL, 40 years old, merchant of song, sister of Liesle Denwall, biological mother of Nell and Demitris. Wynnle-Winyan.

PIOTR CHAKTON, 41 years old, apiarist, biological father of Demitris, adoptive father of Nell. Gluckan.

NELL DENWALL, 14 years old, daughter, biological daughter of Orienna Denwall and Miltico Svelt. Wynnle-Yosoe.

DEMITRIS CHAKTON, 7 years old, son, biological son of Orienna Denwall and Piotr Chakton. Wynnle-Gluckan.

The Svelt-Dem Family:

MILTICO SVELT, 36 years old, shopkeeper's assistant, biological father of Nell Denwall and Usana Demiu. Yosoe.

LAVINA DEMIU, age unknown, unemployed, biological mother of Usana Demiu. Lagodore.

USANA DEMIU, 8 years old, daughter. Yosoe-Lagodore

PHOEBUS SVELT, 67 years old, shopkeeper, biological father of Miltico and Tico Svelt. Yosoe.

TICO SVELT, deceased for 14 years, would be 39 years old. Brother of Miltico Svelt. Yosoe.

The Iolono Family:

GIORVI ONORETTI, 52 years old, merchant of light legal liaison, biological father of Beatrice Iola the Daughter, adoptive father of Oboro. Yosoe.

BEATRICE IOLA THE MOTHER, 53 years old, linguist, translator, and operatic singer, biological mother of Beatrice Iola the Daughter, adoptive mother of Oboro. Yosoe.

BEATRICE IOLA THE DAUGHTER, 12 years old, daughter. Yosoe.

OBORO, 14 years old, son, ex-slave rescued from Ophidia, bodyguard. Sasorin.

The Pavomusen Family:

LUNGIDUS PAVO, 34 years old, Mind Godblood, Captain in the Godblood Brigade, father of Tynan Pavomusen.

TYNAN PAVOMUSEN, not yet born when this story begins, Mind and Death Godblood, merchant of dance, genderless child of Lungidus Pavo.

Chapter One: Sorrow

In the briefest interval of time upon waking up, I was at peace with the world.

And then I remembered.

My breath left my lungs. I'd never be at peace again. My soul sunk into a fresh pit of sorrow, smothered by muggy tropical heat and crowned by a cloud of mozzies[1] . The songbirds and the ocean waves crashing on the beach outside my window, usually so calming, failed to pierce the grief that swallowed me whole.

My daughter died yesterday. It was the harsh and brutal truth from which I could neither escape nor bear.

I turned to my left. My wife, Liesle, slept soundlessly on her back, one hand protectively over her pregnant belly. I envied her ephemeral tranquility.

I turned to my right. My husband, Su, made quiet noises as his four arms twitched. With his back to me, I couldn't tell what horrified expression he might have worn. Did he have nightmares? Blessed folk didn't have nightmares, but no one knew if Su was blessed. He usually slept peacefully, but our daughter's death had shattered a piece of him.

I may have had the Gods' blessings, but as sure as slugs come out after rain, I didn't feel blessed. The Mind God protected against nightmares, but not depression or anxiety. I couldn't breathe; sorrow made a lump in my throat more stifling than the hottest, most humid days I'd suffered.

---

1. mosquitoes

Tawny. My beautiful, amazing girl. I knew every hair in her golden mane, every spot on her face. Was your soul sleeping? Were you awake in Spiritua? Volkhvs[2] said children weren't put into centennial sleep after death, but rather put into a temporary sleep, during which a servant of the Mind God would wipe their memories of the last few moments before death.

The scene repeated in my mind: the ground opened up, a fissure trailing like a snake toward Demitris. The Death elemental boy, all external stones and a heavy exoskeleton, couldn't move quickly if he wanted to. Piotr and I were too far away, too confused by what we were watching. How could the ground have cracked open like that? But Tawny—brave, quick Tawny—dashed toward Demitris and pushed him out of the way just in time. The ground swallowed her. She fell backward. The bell she wore on her tail chimed. The electric spark tip of her tail flashed brilliantly white before it was extinguished forever.

I had screamed her name and almost ran to the crevice, but Piotr's powerful stony grip on my forearm stopped me. Now, I was grateful for his intervention. If I had seen Tawny's corpse... I didn't think I could go on. I likely would not be alive this moment. The bell's ringing echoed forlornly in my memories.

Careful not to disturb my sleeping spouses, I stood from the reed mat bed. I stretched my arms and tail, but the mere act of moving my body was opposed by my soul that wanted to crawl into a corner and cry. I *had* to keep going, though. Tawny might be gone, but I still had five children who needed breakfast. Soon, it would be six...

Next to the door, a scapula set horizontally into the wall held our bone earrings. I would not need to wear them today...

I pushed aside the leaf-curtain door. The blue drapes over our crystalights washed the hall with an ambient cerulean glow. No longer concerned about waking my spouses with light, I uncovered the leaves around my tail. The electric spark on its tip flared to life, emitting a gentle yellow glow.

Across from our bedroom was the youngest kids' room—now just Nio's room. Damn, maybe we should move her to the older girls' room. I didn't want Nio sleeping alone.

Pale blue light exuded from the leaf door, a slight tinge lighter than the crystalights in the living room. She didn't like to cover her blue-sparking tail at night. I peeked in to make sure she was safe. Of course she was safe. A father's worries were never over. What was I worried about? A fissure erupting in the middle of our house and swallowing her, too? Nio would have survived, anyway, since she had wings. She could have flown out. Out of all six of my children, Tawny was the only one who hadn't inherited Liesle's wings. Only she had taken after me,

---

2. Gender-neutral word for a priest/priestess of Spiritism, the primary religion of the Pentagonal Dominion

wingless. Only she could have suffered such a fate as falling to her death.

The older kids' rooms were dark and quiet. The girls' room was for my daughters, Eruwan and Cohaku. Fionn and Heliodor lived in the boys' room, along with Maika, a female Wintershade shroomhound[3] who slept next to Fionn.

I always woke up first. Always the first to fall asleep, always the first to start breakfast. The quietude of morning before my spouses and children swarmed over me like mozzies had once been serene, but this morning, I was plagued by an ominous dread. I would have cut off an arm to have Tawny jump on my back and braid my mane again.

The rhythmic beat of Deep Sea's fingers[4] on the shore reminded me that life went on, no matter what trauma pinned my feet in place. Standing here and reminiscing over Tawny wouldn't get breakfast done. I headed outside to our ground oven.

I went around the circular vertebra table with nine reed mats laid out. I supposed we'd put one away soon. The table centerpiece, our fruit rotary made of six painted dolphin skulls, bore fruits in each skull—pitayas[5] in the red skull, kumquats in orange, mangos in yellow, kiwis in green, bright açaí[6] in blue, and steenas[7] in purple.

This had become so routine, I could do it without thinking, but now all I could think about was Tawny. At the leaf-door, I stifled a cry, recalling how Tawny had once tripped over the femur we used as the threshold. Su had stopped the physical pain with a sprinkling of magic, but my little girl wouldn't stop crying until Daddy kissed her knee.

I had to stop at the threshold, put my hand on the whale-bone door frame, and brace myself for a wave of existential dread. My world became unreal. This wasn't true. This must have been some God's cruel prank. A Demon Lord's game.

No. I was deluding myself. The only Demon Lord within a thousand miles was the ocean fifty feet away from the house, and he went on his journey the same as

---

3. A breed of domesticated dog that hosts fungi. The Wintershade variety features blue and purple fur and mushrooms.

4. Deep Sea is the Demon Lord of Despair who possesses the ocean. Colloquially, the waves are his fingers.

5. Dragonfruits

6. A sky-blue açaí berry, much more tart than the dark açaí berries on Earth

7. Mangosteens

always, stopping only to leave seashells and dominion shells[8] on our sandy shore. Lord Deep Sea had no interest in my plight.

I struggled to get to the ground oven, but eventually, one step at a time through this unnatural reality, I made it. Every evening, we put freshly-heated rocks, charcoal, and coconut fronds into the brick-lined pit and wrapped a fish in leaves—or several fish, if they were small. We covered the pit with leaves and soil, and let the fish cook slowly overnight. Sometimes we cooked taro, ube, and breadfruit, but since all of us except for Su were Wynnles[9], a species who primarily ate meat, the fish was the only certainty.

I didn't remember last night. Had we put a fish in there? Or had we wailed in sorrow until we fell asleep, so overcome with our grief in the moment that we hadn't concerned ourselves with our empty bellies of the future?

I bent down to scrape the soil off the ground oven, and once again had a flashback of the ground opening up beneath her.

I removed the thick, green tropical leaves and found a purplefin[10] fish below. It was big enough to feed us all. I had no recollection of preparing it. Maybe Su or Liesle had found the wherewithal to do our parental duty. Cooked meat, dead eyes... I wondered if Tawny's eyes looked like this right now. Her body was at the Death church in Seabells, but it was only Agneus, the Day of Fire. Moru, the Day of Death, when shinigami[11] come to turn bodies into sawdust[12], wouldn't be for another six days. Until then, her body would just lay there, rotting... Mud and sludge[13]; I couldn't think about that!

I turned to go back into the kitchen to retrieve a board so I could prepare the fish for cleaning and slicing.

---

8. Sand dollars

9. Leonine and tigrine sapient species. All members, including women and children, grow manes.

10. Pentagonal Dominionist fish that lives in tropical waters.

11. Servants of the Death God, Sawyer. Shinigami are ghosts from the afterlife, and cannot be seen or heard.

12. Sawdust is a euphemism derived from Sawyer's name. Shinigami erase bodies from existence; not even dust is left behind.

13. Pentagonal Dominionist expletive, equivalent to 'shit.' They do not defecate and have no concept of excrement.

Su stood at the doorway wearing a grass skirt and his ribcage-and-grass chest cover. He rubbed his eyes with his upper hands while his lower hands crossed over his abdomen.

"Amiere, I... I just can't..."

I stepped closer to him and he caught me in a tight embrace. Su was a full foot shorter than me, and buried his face into my chest and mane. He clutched at my back with all four hands as he howled in despair.

"I don't know how we'll keep going," I said, my voice straining through tight cords. The first real tears of the day trailed down my cheeks, soaking into the mustache that merged with my mane. "I'm so distressed, I'm going to puke." It was going to happen eventually. The stress continuously tumbled my stomach. Perhaps it would be best to get it over with before breakfast, then maybe I could retain *some* nutrition today.

Su pointed toward a palm tree growing in the shrub hedge. "Over there. I'll make it happen."

Better to do this before the kids wake up and see. I knelt by the shrubs, extended my claws, and dug a small hole.

"Ready?" Su asked.

I swallowed on instinct, but that would prove pointless in a moment. "Any time."

He put a hand on the back of my head and did... something. I didn't know what. Su was a Godblood[14] with magic powers, but he'd never said which element his powers belonged to. We all had our theories, based on his abilities. Amongst others, he could soothe physical pain and induce vomiting, as he did now, but which element had *that* as one of its powers?

I felt better after the expulsion was over, at least physically. My whole torso still swirled with anxiety. I buried soil and sand over my mess and stood up. My mane and mustache needed a wash, though.

"What do we do now?" I asked, referring vaguely to life in general, but if Su chose to interpret it for the here and now, I would not correct him.

"We keep going," Su replied. "One day at a time. One chore at a time. I'll get the purplefin deboned. You go wash your face in Deep Sea."

He patted my back and gave me a sympathetic smile before heading back inside. The look he gave me was enough to fuel my life a little longer. His large brown eyes, long lashes shivering in the wind, shone with a light no crystalight could match.

Shaking, I walked to the ocean. The white sand beneath my feet was a welcome softness. My body, abused by powerful emotions, could not tolerate hard surfaces today. A crab scuttled out of my way. Our house was on the beach, far enough

---

14. The descendant of a God, down to three generations.

inland to not be touched by Deep Sea's fingers, but close enough to use his body for all our water needs. Bathing, washing, cooking, anything we needed... Despite being a Demon Lord, Deep Sea's very existence allowed so many families to live in comfort.

He was calm today. His fingers were blue with white-crested knuckles, spots glittering in the sun as it rose behind me. Our house sat on the southwestern shore of Tsagwa. With the continent and its thick jungles to our east and Deep Sea to our west, we didn't see the sun until it rose above the lush, green canopies, but we were blessed with the most intense scarlet sunsets. As close to the equator as we were, planet Aloutia's rings were naught but a thin strip of light stretching overhead from one horizon to the other. Three moons hung over Deep Sea this morning: purple, silver, and lime-green.

I crouched beside the ocean's lapping waves and put my hand in him. Deep Sea curled a tentacle of water around my wrist. Coagulated into a slightly more solid form, the tendril felt like gelatin.

"Is this despair pleasing to you?" I asked. I didn't expect an answer. I wondered if he was even aware of me. Deep Sea was the entire ocean on all planes. His consciousness was probably preoccupied somewhere else.

Deep Sea let go of me. Our greetings complete, I waded in waist-deep and splashed water on my face. I scratched at my beard and the rest of my mane until everything was out. I let a few waves come and go, then took a drink. Deep Sea was made of fresh, pure water, and he allowed people to take portions of him for their personal needs. He was also the Demon Lord of Despair, and I had no doubt he enjoyed the taste of my despair seeping into his waters.

When I returned to the house, the whole family was awake and sitting around the vertebra table. We didn't use chairs, but rather a cushion for each of us to sit on. They all had their tails free and sparkling with electric light, save for Su who was the only non-Wynnle among us.

I'd never seen my family so devoid of joy before. Even Maika the shroomhound dog knew something was wrong and lay quietly beside Fionn. Liesle stared forward, her green feline eyes blank. Eruwan had her head down, crying. Fionn held a kiwi between his claws—kiwis had been Tawny's favorite. Fionn only ever went to Kiwi Island to get them for her. Cohaku tried to hold her tears in, while Heliodor let his pour freely. Nio showed no emotion, but that was normal for her. What wasn't normal for her was the state of her hair—down, uncombed. Nio liked to wear a bone keeping her bangs out of her face, but Liesle had not bothered to fix her hair yet.

All my kids resembled me and Liesle. Eruwan, Fionn, and Nio had Liesle's purple-skin and blue hair, but my spot patterns. Cohaku and Heliodor, the twins, had my golden skin—or fur in Heli's case—with Liesle's striped patterns.

"Ami-honey, come help me," Su called from the kitchen.

My sorrow made me lose my balance. I caught myself on one of the whale ribs serving as a frame to the kitchen entrance. Su held two patella plates with fish meat in two hands, and a boning knife in the other. He was about to hand the plates to me, but stopped when he saw my distress. With his remaining free hand, he reached around to my back to help me stand.

"Are you going to fall?"

I shook my head. "No, I'll be fine." I took the plates out to the vertebra table. Since Eruwan and Fionn were closest, they got the first two. Back in the kitchen, Su loaded two more plates, which I set in front of Liesle and Nio. As I went back for a third trip, Su came out with the last four in his hands. Two for the twins, and two for us.

"That's all, Ami-honey. It's just... eight... plates." His eyes watered and he sniffed back a wretched sob. He brushed past me to set the plates down so he could wipe his face. After he sat down between Eruwan and Cohaku, the two girls embraced him and wailed. Su held each girl with a lower arm while covering his own face and keening into his upper hands.

Liesle stabbed her claw into a piece of her fish and ate it. Nio watched her mother's every move. She had never seen the family in such a state and must have wondered if her routine had been thrown for a loop. She glanced at the empty seat where Tawny used to sit. Only after everyone had taken a bite did she eat, too.

Fionn extended his claws and stabbed the kiwi repeatedly, squirting its juices meaninglessly over the plate and staining his reed-and-leaf vest.

"Stop that," Liesle growled. "Eat it or leave it alone. Don't take your anger out on it."

Fionn's ears lowered. "Sorry, Mom."

Heliodor tried to eat without Cohaku's help. He was a quadruped, with no hands with opposable thumbs. He struggled with many tasks, and usually his twin sister helped out, but she had her face buried in Su's side. Like most quadrupeds, his body was covered in a coat of fur, so he didn't have to wear clothes. Dressing was one less task he had to struggle through, at least. Though in the hot, humid days of the rainy season, drying his fur was like bringing a towel to Deep Sea.

Tawny usually sat to my right, so... there was a spot available. I patted the cushion Tawny had kept exclusively to herself. "Heli, bring your plate here. Let Dadda help you."

Heli hesitated, a look of consternation painted on his visage. When nobody objected to him taking Tawny's seat, he grabbed his plate in his mouth and brought it closer. I put fruits from the rotary on his patella, slicing some that required dexterity.

It was the most painful breakfast of my life.

When Eruwan was done crying, she stuffed herself full of food as hastily as her paws could shovel it into her mouth. We Wynnles never used cutlery. Only Su used knives, forks, and spoons, handmade from bones and only meant to be used for a short time.

"We need to hurry," Eruwan said between bites. "We'll be late for school."

Liesle grimaced. She'd barely eaten. "Don't go today. I don't think any of you will be able to focus. I'm sure the volkhv will understand. And if she doesn't..." She didn't have to complete the sentence. Not that our children's teachers were bad—contrarily, they were the best teachers we'd ever had in the village—but Liesle still bore grudges against the volkhvs who'd been our teachers when we were kids. Mandatory prayer, bigotry toward Wynnles, and a switching on her behind once had left Liesle with a lifelong hatred of religion and those who preached it.

Eruwan swallowed a large bite. "Thanks, Mamali. Can I at least go to the Mind church and see if we have any homework?"

"If you want."

Fionn clutched at his mane. "Um, I didn't finish my homework last night. It was due today."

"We can work on it together, honey," Su said as he stroked Cohaku's mane. She had not eaten a single bite.

Eruwan finished her meal, scrounged around for her sandals in the little area before the door where we stored our footwear, and ran out. Her loudly flapping wings indicated she'd taken to the skies.

"I ought to try working today," I said with words devoid of energy—not a good outlook on my odds of success. "I might not be able to focus, either, but... gotta try."

"Don't force yourself, honey," Su said as I got up and left.

I sat on a stool of bones inside my ateli[15], holding a crystalight in one hand while my other hand's claws chiseled at the mineral. My workshop was big enough for myself, my desk, supplies, a bookshelf to my right stacked with crystalights ranging from raw to finished, and a few skulls for decoration on my left. Two baskets of incense hung from the ceiling. One burned cinnadyme[16] to help repel

15. A workshop, derived from 'atelier.'

16. Bark of an enchanted tree related to cinnamon. It smells like cinnamon and the scent repels insects, particularly mozzies (mosquitoes).

mozzies while the other burnt lemontine[17], a Fire-enchanted substance that kept its surroundings dry if it burned constantly. As soon as it was left to burn out, the white, lemon-scented cloud it produced would dissipate, and moisture would finagle its way in. Raw crystalights wore out more quickly in humid environments, lowering their value, though once I applied snowbark resin[18], the decay would be minimal regardless of the humidity. Although lemontine was expensive due to its rarity, the profit I made selling high-quality crystalights made it worthwhile. My decision to be a merchant of light living in the tropics was not the best choice I'd ever made, but this was my home, and carving crystalights had been my calling. Now, even if I *wanted* to leave or change my job, I had to consider how it would affect my family. The only thing that could uproot me now would be some catastrophe that forced my family to move away.

My current commission was for a statue of a little girl. A Lagodore[19], not a Wynnle, but when I put my claw to her neck, I could only see Tawny. I imagined putting my claws up against Tawny's neck and—*slice*.

That wasn't even how she died. Why... why did my skull torture me like this?

I set the statue on the table and tore off my visor to dry my eyes. The lemontine incense did a fine job of that by itself. Gods, maybe this was the best place to cry. The smoke absorbed my tears as soon as they escaped my eyes.

My ateli was close to the house, but not connected. From the entrance of our house, you had to walk around the whale's skull. The walls were solid mud brick and bamboo between massive whale ribs on the outside. Inside, it had wood paneling for décor. The door was lockable with a key only I had. Well, Su had once made a bone key that could open it, just to prove he could. He'd worn a victorious smirk on his face for a week afterward. The structure was not exactly soundproof, but any sound that came through would be muffled at best, then drowned under the music of Deep Sea's knuckles rapping at the beach.

One had to wear a visor when inside lest the crystalights damage one's eyes. I kept the ateli locked so kids wouldn't accidentally barge in and get blinded. Or so nobody would steal them. That was unlikely—only the most reckless fool would steal from a Wynnle. Even still, crystalights were one of the world's rarest objects. They were mined underground, exclusively in a small part of the world called Iuria in the far south, where a giant sapient species called the Iurion dwelt in their massive underground abodes.

Merchants of light such as myself had no part in the mining process. Typically,

---

17. Magical plant that produces lemons and absorbs moisture.

18. A substance from a tree known for its preservative qualities.

19. Species of sapient people who resemble rabbits.

when a deposit was discovered, the upper administrators in the guild divided the rights among themselves and hired Domovye[20] to extricate the crystals. The administrators sold raw crystalights to us merchants, as well as the occasional detailed commission order. The ones that came without orders could be carved however we desired and sold to any market in Aloutia. The real money came from commissions. As individuals were limited to a certain amount of wealth, these orders came from groups—a church, a city, or a community, for instance. My job was to carve the crystal into the requested shape. Raw crystals were brilliantly, blindingly white, but could be dyed. Certain chemicals soaked in as if the crystals were sponges. Whether color was added or not, several layers of snowbark resin had to be applied to the finished product. Skilled merchants could add intricate color details. At my age, having sculpted for twenty years, I was considered a master of the trade.

Yes, I was a master merchant of light. I had the skill to carve and dye crystalights into any shape and color, so long as it was physically possible and the color could be created with my dyes. So why... *why* was this little girl with rabbit ears giving me such trouble? The memory of Tawny falling repeated again in my head.

The last thing I'd seen of her was her tail's spark. In terror, she blasted the light brighter than she ever had before. I'd heard that a terrified Wynnle would instinctively brighten their tail, but I'd never seen it for myself. It was too similar to the white light of a raw crystalight.

My hands trembled. My claw nicked a mark into the girl's neck. Mud and sludge! How could I be so careless? In a fit of rage, I almost threw the whole statue across my ateli.

I imagined the statue was Tawny, and... Oh fuck, how could I have hurt her? My skull made me imagine myself throwing Tawny across the room. What the hell was wrong with me!?

I choked back a sob and held in my tears. I retracted my claws before they could do any more damage, set the crystal Lagodore down, and stepped outside. Liesle was right—nobody could focus today.

I returned to the whale-bone house and collapsed on the bags stuffed with cotton which we relaxed on in lieu of couches. Furniture used by Wynnles had to be easily

---

20. An underground-dwelling species of sapient people who resemble slugs. They do not have 'normal' eyes, and cannot go blind by looking at crystalights. Singular/adjective: Domovoi. Plural: Domovye

repaired after accidental clawing. Stuffing cotton inside a cloth and sewing it back up was easier than repairing wood or upholstery.

Our house was far from normal, even for the area of the world we lived in. The structure was supported by the bones of a giant Deep Sea megawhale[21] and a latticework of bamboo. The walls started with several layers of mud brick, rounded for the oval shape of our rooms, then comprised of reeds, leaves, and bamboo. It was light and airy, especially with the bamboo windows in the slanted roof open. A gentle sea-scented breeze wafted in through the roof windows and tousled my mane. Cinnadyme incense burned from censers hanging from the whale's spine that crossed the length of our living room and the hallway leading to our bedrooms. Even if it didn't keep all the mozzies away, every little bit helped. Any mozzy daring to get through the cinnadyme would be zapped by our tails instead. We didn't need the windows for light, given the sheer number of crystalights on bamboo and bone shelves that covered our walls. All of them had been made by me over the years.

Our house was made from materials that often needed repairing or replacing, but that was our way of life. Our clothes, too, made from leaves, grasses, and bones, didn't often last more than a season. The people of Seabells and its outlying villages, including our Steena Village, embraced the transient nature of life. The grass skirt I wore now would come and go. The pillow I laid on now would come and go. The bamboo pole holding the window open as I laid back and gazed wistfully out at passing clouds would come and go just like that cloud.

My children, too, were destined to come and go.

Su and Fionn sat at the vertebra table, working on homework together. Usually, Su talked the kids through the questions and had them find the answers on their own, but Fionn was in no mood to work today, so Su did his homework for him.

"Where's Liesle?" I asked.

Without looking up from Fionn's homework, Su answered, "In the bedroom, crying. Nio's with her."

Cohaku and Heliodor came to me as soon as I sat down.

"Daddy, can I snuggle?" Cohaku asked. She spoke with a lisp; it was more prominent when she was sad.

"Me too," Heli whined.

I opened my arms. "Of course."

They lay on opposite sides of me, resting their heads on my chest. I had to take care when I brought my arm down on Cohaku. I was so much bigger than her, and she was so brittle... she was hurt by the slightest touch. No, it was more than that. Certain textures and sensations bothered her in ways they didn't bother other people. I could be rough with Heli. Even ruffling up his wings didn't

---

21. A very large, long-lived whale

bother him. But Cohaku couldn't tolerate anyone touching her wings or mane uncomfortably.

Eruwan came through the door, feathers rustled, her tail shining white. Nervousness.

"Um, Papami? That, uh, new Yosoe[22] neighbor is here. Says he wants to speak to you... and only you."

Yosoe neighbor... Miltico Svelt. He was an absolute piece of garbage, more deserving of being tossed into Deep Sea than being called a man, but I wouldn't want to pollute Deep Sea with his filth. I stood after the twins shuffled away. Su put his pencil down and gave me a deep frown. If anyone had a worse opinion of Miltico than me, it was Su, and since Su was a Godblood, his anger could be downright dangerous.

"I'll handle it, Sugar. Stay here with the kids."

Miltico... Milti, we used to call him. Liesle and I had grown up with him in Steena Village. Once a friend who we'd go on adventures into the jungle with, now the only reason he'd go into the jungle was to look for the leaves to make crazy sugar[23] . He'd been in a relationship with Liesle's sister for a few years and had a daughter with her, though if you asked Nell who her father was, she'd say it was Piotr. Milti left Aloutia ten years ago, but now he was back.

He stood a good distance away from the house, leaning against a palm tree. A short man, not even five feet tall. Yosoe were descended from goats just as Wynnles were descended from lions and tigers. Milti was a sapient biped man with hooves for feet. He bore a goat's face as well, with curved horns, horizontal pupils, and a scruffy beard. He had claw marks across the left side of his face which had blinded that eye. I'd always assumed the scratch was from his ex-wife. Their parting had been anything but amicable.

"Just you, Ami?" he asked.

"Just me. What the hell do you want?"

He spat. "That fucking man-wife of yours isn't here, is it?"

"Don't," I growled. "Liesle and I both chose Su. Leave us alone."

"Or would you rather I call it a woman-husband?"

"Did you have anything worthwhile to say, or did you come to get your ass beat?"

Milti chuckled, almost losing his balance until he put a hand on the tree. "You wouldn't touch me, Ami. You wouldn't fucking dare. I *did* come here to tell you something, though. I wanted to be the bearer of good news. That crack that opened in the ground yesterday?"

---

22. A species of sapient people resembling goats.

23. Cocaine

Another flashback of Tawny falling inside... I swore to all the Gods, I couldn't handle rage and sorrow at once. The lump returned to my throat, pressing on the hyoid...

"It's filled with crystalights," Miltico finished.

What was his goal? Why was he telling me? I'd have heard about a new mine of crystalights eventually. It would be big news to the merchants of light.

"I just wanted to be the one to tell you," he said, shrugging his scrawny, brown-furred arms. "That crevice is one hell of a gift. It gave you a lifetime supply of money *and* got rid of one of your parasites. You should consider yesterday to be the greatest day of your life."

Su Interlude

Oh Ami-honey, my darling husband. No one should hear such words. No one should endure such pain. Su wished he could apologize for not asking for Amiere's consent first, but he had to act quickly. If he hadn't, he was afraid his husband's rage would have gone too far.

Please forgive me. Su swore to make it up to Amiere one day, however he'd like. He'd make him the best dinner of his life, or make a beautiful necklace made from the finest teeth, bones, and pearls. He'd kiss every spot on his skin, caress his tired muscles, and tend to his baculum in a way no other merchant of bone would ever do, if that was his desire.

Chapter Two: The Sea of Despair

The absolutely vile, unspeakable words Miltico had said so astounded me that I had no recollection of what happened immediately after. I would have killed the man, except the next moment I recalled, I was sitting on the bags in the living room. Cohaku and Heliodor snuggled next to me the same as they'd been before I left. The rest of the family was gathered around the vertebra table, eating a dinner of fish, rice, and fruits.

That wasn't a dream, was it? Had I hallucinated those awful words from my worst enemy? Had I hallucinated the crystalight message, too? Because that news made no sense. Crystalights never grew anywhere but Iuria, thousands of miles away.

"Are you back with us?" Liesle asked after licking fish meat off her claws.

I rubbed my eyes. It didn't feel like I'd been asleep. My body was far from rested, and another flashback of Tawny falling to her death made my heart jump again.

"What happened to me?" I asked. "I was talking to Milti outside and now I'm here."

Su looked like he was dressed for battle, wearing bone armbands, pauldrons, tassets, and an antlered deer skull over his head. He had his back to me as he ate dinner, and based on his stillness, I thought he was angry. He left his cushion to join me on the cotton-stuffed bags. When I saw his face, I relaxed. Su was worn out from crying, but his gentle smile convinced me he was staying strong for all of us.

"You blacked out," he said as he arranged himself on the same side as Heliodor. He picked up our son in his lower hands while wrapping his upper hands around my shoulders and stroked my mane lovingly. "I don't want that man near our house, and no matter what he wanted, I didn't want you to deal with him alone. He ran away when he saw me. You were... not well... so I brought you back inside."

"I have no memory of that whatsoever."

Su pushed back his deer skull above his head and nuzzled my mane, kissing my neck. "That's probably for the best, Ami-honey. Your soul is burdened with enough pain right now."

Cohaku sat up. She wasn't normally so affectionate, so it was no surprise that she was done with touching. Su's kiss may have grossed her out. "Um, so, it says on the calendar that after dinner today, Tawny was gonna make grass skirts with Mapa Su, and I was gonna clean plates with Mommy, and Heli was—"

"Stop trying to push your chores on Heli," Liesle snapped. "You get upset when the dishes aren't cleaned to your liking. If you want it done right, you have to do it yourself."

Cohaku curled her lip. "I—I wanna help Mapa Su! I wanna make grass skirts!"

She *never* wanted to make grass skirts. It was her most despised chore.

"I'll help with the dishes, Mamali," Eruwan said in a low, diplomatic tone.

"Today was your day to relax," Fionn said. "Don't you want to scrimshaw?"

Eruwan shrugged. "Of course I do, but... I think it's best if we let Cohaku do what she wants today."

Liesle opened her mouth to protest, but let out a sharp exhale and resumed eating instead. Cohaku didn't have the best relationship with her mother. I assumed she was trying to get out of doing chores with Liesle specifically, not get out of chores entirely. She loved Su so much, though... all the kids did. Although we parents would never say we had a favorite child, we knew all the kids had a favorite parent: Su.

I couldn't be jealous. I was just as enamored with my husband. Su was perfect. Kind, gentle, understanding, easy to talk to... and from my vantage point, the sexiest person in the Pentagonal Dominion.

Cohaku went to the chore board to make the changes official. It was a chalk board, framed with femurs crosswise and tibiae lengthwise, hanging on the wall near the vertebra table. Our initials labeled the rows, and the days of the week were the columns. We went in order of age, so Su's schedule was at the top, then Liesle's, then mine, followed by each of the kids in hatching order. Cohaku and Heliodor hatched from the same egg, but we counted Cohaku as being older because it was her hatching horn that pierced their shell open. We joked she was uncomfortable being touched by Heli for so long and needed some space to herself.

Most of us wrote our initials in the local Fleur[1] script. Our language was a patois combining Ebon[2]—language of the Ebonoir—and English—language of the mysterious Land of Eng in the Terran Dominion. Su's name was in a different script. He used Orochigo[3] characters—muji—starting with 'su' which he felt fit his mood best. I didn't know much Orochigo; honestly, all I knew were the muji he used for his name. He hadn't changed it since hearing the news about Tawny.

---

1. Language of the Flora, resembling a mixture of French and English

2. A language resembling French

3. A language resembling Japanese

Currently, it was 'suzu,' meaning 'bell.' Each kid had a different name for Su. He was Papa Su to Eruwan and Mama Su to Fionn. Cohaku and Heli combined Mama and Papa but flipped the order: Mapa Su to Cohaku, Pama Su to Heli. Tawny had always called him Suzu-bells. Su had changed his name on the board to 'suzu' to amuse her.

Her bell. When the ground had rumbled, I'd heard the bell on her tail ringing as she dashed toward Demitris. The bell Su and I had made for her. The bell which would never ring again. It was probably destroyed... Well, I supposed it would depend on how Tawny died. If a rock fell on her afterward...

I shook my head. Why did my skull conjure such accursed imagery? I didn't want this!

"Should we erase Tawny's name?" Cohaku asked, eraser in her hand hovering over the 'T.'

"No," Liesle said, so quickly I assumed she'd anticipated this conversation and had prepared her answer. "I'm not ready."

No one argued. I was glad Liesle voiced her opinion since I didn't have the emotional strength to even talk about Tawny. I feared I'd collapse into a mess of tears and vomit if I so much as spoke her name.

Cohaku changed the chores for herself, Heli, and Eruwan.

"What about you, Daddy? It says you're supposed to work on crystalights tonight, but if you black out while inside your ateli..."

"If I force myself to work, it'll be shoddy," I said. "I'd better relax tonight."

"Umm, so what does it mean to black out?" Heliodor asked. "Has it ever happened to you before?"

It had, long ago. Numerous times, in fact, but I had nothing and no one to blame except myself and my own stupidity. It was a shameful time in my life which I didn't want to mention around my children.

Su scratched behind Heli's ears as he answered. "It means his vision went black and he doesn't remember anything. It's like going to sleep."

"Why did it happen?" Fionn asked. "You were just talking to... what was that fellow's name? Milti?"

"He's calling himself 'Miltico' now," Liesle said as she set down a bowl of rice. She hardly looked dignified with grains in her mane, but as anxious as she was, I doubted she cared what she looked like. "I don't think I'll get used to that. He'll always be Milti to me. Tico was... never mind. It's all ancient history now."

"I can't bear to say what happened today," I said. "Fionn, I promise I'm not hiding anything from you, but it's too painful right now. Ask me again in a few days."

"How did you know him?" Eruwan asked. "I know he's Nell's dad, so Auntie Orienna must have been with him, but they don't talk about him much."

Liesle closed her eyes. "You know the shopkeeper, Mr. Svelt? Milti is his son. He grew up with me and Amiere. We played with him when we were kids. He wasn't a bad person back then."

"He changed after your mother and I went to art school together," I said. "I'm not sure why. Maybe he was jealous of us." I knew exactly why he'd changed, but I didn't want to say it in front of all the children.

Su, with his arms around me and his mouth next to my ear, whispered, "Crazy sugar."

Milti's older brother, Tico, had produced and sold crazy sugar, an addictive white substance that made people erratic. Milti had gotten addicted. We didn't think Tico partook of the drug, but after his untimely death, the investigation declared it had been an overdose.

"Milti wanted to be with me and Orienna," Liesle said. "After I came back from art school, I saw the changes he'd gone through. He was disgusting. Perverse. Cruel. I told him I didn't want anything to do with him. Orienna didn't see it, though. She was involved with him and had Nell. It took about three years, but she finally got rid of him."

"Was that when he moved to Cosmo[4] ?" Eruwan asked.

"No, he lived with his parents, planning to wait until a house became available," Su said. "His father asked me to build a house, but I was so busy with my own work at the time."

We were currently in the midst of building a house for Eruwan. It would not surprise me if Miltico was angry at us for that, too.

"Why did he move away, then? I don't remember his mother, but Mr. Svelt the shopkeeper is a nice man."

An uncomfortable silence pervaded the room. Liesle and Su looked at me to answer. Their expectant gazes suffocated me more than the humidity. On second thought, I was the best one to explain my own actions.

"I told him to leave," I replied. "I told him to gather his belongings and go through the portal to Cosmo. I never wanted to see him again and if I did, I couldn't guarantee his safety."

Eruwan stared at me with hurt eyes. Blue, inherited from her mother's stunning emerald eyes. Though not the same color, those eyes reminded me of Liesle's. Strong, feline... passionate and *com*passionate. She was much like her mother was at that age. Was she feeling sympathetic for Milti? If a large Wynnle like me were to fight a small Yosoe like him, not a soul in the dominion would cheer for me. I made for the obvious winner. People, even other Wynnles, were naturally drawn to stories where the weaker man overcomes his bullies, and it was too easy to paint me as the bully. "Why, Papami? What did he do to you? Did you get into a fight?"

"With me? He wouldn't dare touch me. I was two feet taller than him, with

---

4. One of the planes of the Pentagonal Dominion comprised of many small countries and a few colonies of the two large nations, Aloutia and Ophidia.

claws, fangs, and a body of pure muscle. Nothing like the flabby belly I've got now."

I shouldn't be so self-deprecating. My body wasn't as old as I made it out to be. Perhaps I was only trying to win back my daughter's sympathy by making myself look weaker now than I used to be.

Liesle cracked a smile, albeit briefly. "You're still handsome, Mo Ami."

Her words made me blush, but not as ferociously as the silvering[5] of her own cheeks.

"You don't remember Milti, do you, Eruwan?" Su asked.

She shook her head. "No, I just knew that was the name of Nell's dad."

"I'm glad you don't remember him from when you were a toddler," I said. "You asked what he did to me that was so terrible that I made him leave Aloutia for ten years? Nothing. He didn't do a single thing to me. He wouldn't dare. What he did was hit *you*."

She gasped, eyes wide. "Really? That tiny Yosoe man hit me?" Any shred of sympathy she'd once had was gone, quick as lightning.

"You were so small," I said. "I don't remember what you'd done. Nothing you should be ashamed of. Regular toddler stuff. We went to the shop together, where he was living with his parents and helping restock items. I think you'd touched some of the merchandise. Milti said if I couldn't keep you under control, he'd do it for me. He struck you across the face."

"Oh! Was that when he got the slash over his eye? Did you return the favor?"

I chuckled. "I wish I could say I'd been the one to do that, but no. Although she won't admit to it, we think it was Orienna who did that when she made him leave her house. When he hit you that day, he'd already gone blind in his left eye."

"Well, if he tries to hit me again, I'll hit him back." Eruwan scowled. She was a good, gentle teenage girl, but we'd raised her not to accept trouble from other people. "Maybe scratch out his right eye."

"If you ever do, come straight to me," I said. "You can bite my arm. Don't let your rage become more violent."

Us Wynnles, the descendants of lions and tigers, were born to kill. If we drew blood—sometimes if we even *smelled* enough blood—our skulls and sternums would flood with an uncontrollable desire to hunt, kill, and consume the source of that blood. There were a few ways to stop the urges, including biting a biological relative or achieving orgasm. The urge to kill never triggered if a Wynnle hurt their own blood relatives, though. Likewise, if it occurred during sex, it would inspire us to perform as more potent lovers so we could orgasm instead.

"I know. Thanks, Papami."

---

5. Non-magical people in the Pentagonal Dominion have clear blood, and when they blush, their cheeks turn a silvery glow.

"I'll hit him if he ever hits me!" Cohaku announced. "I'll bite him, too. I don't care!"

"No biting," Liesle said. "Wynnles are already viewed with suspicion and many towns would love to banish us. If not for Aloutia's anti-discrimination laws, we'd be forced back to the plains of Starsine. Don't give them a reason to think we're wild, uncivilized brutes."

"I don't care about Aloutia. I'm going to go live in Ophidia[6] when I grow up." I hated when she brought that up. We were trying to teach her not to say it, but progress was slow.

"That's great for you, brat," Fionn said. "Meanwhile, after all us men and Mama Su are banished to Starsine, we'll have no choice but to eat Cosmonite lizards and bathe in mud."

Cohaku realized too late how hurtful her statement was. "I didn't mean..." She faltered, sniffed, and looked to me for acceptance. "You wouldn't be banished to Starsine, would you, Daddy?"

"If the Aloutians thought we were dangerous, we could be."

Politics were outside my area of expertise, but judging by the current political climate, I had no fear of being banished. I assumed Liesle used the threat as a tactic to scare Cohaku into behaving, but I wasn't knowledgeable enough to disagree with my wife. Aloutia was welcoming to all species. Excluding anyone based on their species was antithetical to Spiritism, the predominant religion which ruled our lives... and the lives of our rulers. The country's full name was the Holy Empire of Aloutia. The Emperor, Ivan, had been chosen by the Mind God Lucognidus to rule us. The Emperor's closest aides were Godbloods, the magic-using descendants of the gods. Religion and politics were intrinsically tied in this nation, and for that reason, I did not doubt that Lucognidus's law of love, acceptance, and diversity would be upheld in perpetuity.

Cohaku grimaced. I knew that look—she was on the verge of crying. "I... I didn't mean to say I wanted you to be banished."

"I know that."

"Are you mad at me, Daddy?" She wiped her teary eyes with the back of her hands while her claws retracted in and out involuntarily.

"No, of course not. Just be sure to think about what you're saying before you say it."

She broke into an all-out wail.

"Cohaku, it's okay. Please, come give me a hug." I held my arms out to her.

"I'm sorry, Daddy!" Instead of running into my arms, though, she ran out the door.

---

6. The Women's Republic of Ophidia, a plane and planet in the Pentagonal Dominion where women have enslaved all non-women.

Liesle sighed with audible frustration. Nio, silently observing, as usual, arched an eyebrow as she tried to assess what had just happened.

"I don't think any grass skirts are gonna get made tonight," Su said. "Might as well put it off till tomorrow."

He patted my cheek before rising to change the chore board once again. After erasing the changes Cohaku had just made, he held the eraser over the character he used for his own name—suzu/bell.

I thought he would erase it, but he couldn't. His hand hovered over the chalk lines, steady at first, then shaking. I wondered if his mind was playing the same cruel pranks that mine did. Could he hear Tawny's voice calling for him? *Suzu-bells! Suzu-bells, save me!*

With his back to me, I couldn't see his expression. He sobbed, dropped the eraser, and covered his face with his upper hands.

I set Heli aside so I could stand and comfort my husband, but by the time I got to my shaky feet, he was on his way out.

"I need some fresh air," he said between muffled sobs.

I watched him step outside. Having just stood up, I didn't want to sit down again. My wife put her head in her hands, looking more angry than sad.

"Go," she said. "I'll stay here with the kids. Go cheer up Su or Cohaku or... whatever you want to do."

Whatever I wanted to do? I *wanted* to reverse time and prevent this tragedy from ever occurring.

I stepped outside. A cool oceanic gale chilled the sweat on my brow and rustled fronds from the hundred palm trees between here and the wall of koa trees demarcating the jungle. A toucan sat on a high branch. We kept the area around our house fairly clear of trees so the kids could find our house as they flew along the coast, but Su had insisted on keeping the coconut palms where they were. He liked sitting in their shade. A few fruit trees grew nearby, if only so we didn't have to walk so far to pluck their produce.

Cohaku was throwing a fit in her tree house, nestled in a grove right at the jungle's border across Coconut Crab Circle. Made of bone and bamboo, we'd built it for her a few years ago, high in the branches of steena trees, a tamarind, and big, leafy monsters that bore no edible fruit, but grew leaves large enough to use as clothing. When she was this emotional, talking to her only made the problem worse. It was better to let her get her tears out now and talk later.

Su sat on the beach at the fringe of Deep Sea's fingers. The sun, intersected by the planetary rings, approached the horizon. My husband had removed the deer skull and most of his clothes, except for the binding over his chest. He'd also transformed his lower half into that of a pink-scaled fish. He never told anyone how he did it, but there were a few options—if he was a Rubaiyan like the God of Fire, it was part of his natural biology. If he was a Death or Life Godblood, he could manipulate his genetics, though he'd only ever changed his feet into a fish tail. If he was a Water Godblood, he could grant himself aquatic biological traits, such as the ability to breathe underwater or grow appendages typically seen on fish or marine mammals.

"You going for a swim?" I asked as I approached. Wet sand crunched under my feet as waves rolled over Su's tail, scales glittering with pink in the sunset. So much like the stars—like starlight, the essence of joy. Ironic, as we were two souls enraptured by sorrow.

"It's hard to do anything right now," he replied in a melancholy voice that would have brought me to tears if I weren't there already. "In Deep Sea, only he can tell when you're crying, but I don't want to swim alone in the ocean of despair."

I sat beside him. I understood that pain, the feeling of hopelessness, like I might as well just die. Deep Sea lapped at my feet, solidifying into gooey tendrils to absorb my despair.

"Do you think Tawny's alright now?" I asked. "She's not... in pain, is she?"

"Of course she's not in pain. All dead souls are healed in Spiritua, but children get priority since they aren't put into centennial sleep. Their sleep is temporary."

"How long is it? Is she awake now?"

Su shrugged his shoulders and raised all four arms. "I don't know, Ami-honey. Days? Hours? What would it matter?"

"Because I want to *know*, damn it!" I punched the sand beside me, disrupting a sand flea. "I want to know if she's awake and lonely. Maybe... maybe I need to join her. Keep her company. Tawny—"

Su pushed me into the sand, two arms on each of mine. He was strong for his size, but I could have easily lifted him off. Tears trailed down his cheeks, yet he continued to hold my arms down rather than wipe his face.

"Don't you *ever* say that! *We* need you. Here. Alive! Besides, you know what would happen. Since you're an adult, the shinigami who comes for your soul would put you to sleep for one hundred years. The next time you see Tawny, she'll be one hundred and seven years old and she won't need her parents to keep her company."

"I know, Su." I pushed him off. But rather than letting him hit the sand and get fleas in his hair, I reached out to catch him, then pulled him closer, holding him gently. "The logic is in my skull, but my sternum wants me to die."

My sternum... What little I knew of anatomy, I had learned from Su, a merchant of bone. I knew bones weren't responsible for thoughts and feelings, but I did not know where else these sensations came from, so I referred to them by the nearest bone. Heart? Brain? Those soft, squishy organs were too fragile to carry the weight of my soul. Su knew what I meant, anyway. With him, I didn't need to be anatomically correct with my words.

"Bonehead Ami-honey." He slapped his fishtail on the sand and turned them back into legs. As always, bone formed around his crotch to prevent me from seeing his genitals. Su's biological sex was a mystery to everyone, even me and Liesle, his spouses of sixteen years. No, that wasn't quite accurate to say. After years of consuming shubin marrow, he had become 'neutral,' his personal favorite term for himself. There were many terms and labels for a person who defied being strictly male or female. Not all marrow-eaters approved of the term, but that was what Su wanted to use, therefore we used it on him. The truth of his sex was simply that we did not know what organs he'd been born with. His use of he/him pronouns was not meant to be a clue, either; he'd decided to use masculine pronouns based on his bad history with the Women's Republic of Ophidia.

He crouched beside me, holding my head in two arms while petting my mane and ears with the others. "Stay with your living family. We need you." Su nuzzled my cheek and kissed me. Just a quick peck, but it sent my sternum fluttering like a kaleidoscope of pili-palas[7] had been let loose inside me.

For the briefest moment, I remembered happiness. The weight lifted off my chest, I didn't think about Tawny, and my skull felt dizzy. I experienced a giddiness I hadn't felt since I was a teenager first falling in love with Liesle.

"I'm so sorry," Su said as he pushed away. Ashamed, he stood and turned to face the scarlet sunset sky. "I should not have done that when you weren't wearing an earring."

I took a deep breath, calming my pili-palas. "True, but... well... that's the first time I've been happy in the last two days. You can do it again if you'd like."

As he stood facing away from me, I had a beautiful view of his backside. His shapely back, four perfect scapulae, that long luscious brown hair, his gorgeous buttocks with a slender bone down his crack to hide what was in front. My baculum rose and stretched.

"I can't bring myself to do much right now," Su said as he turned toward me again. "Just hold me and kiss me."

He sat on my lap and I wrapped my arms around him. "My sweetest Sugar."

We watched the second sunset since the death of our daughter. I pressed my lips to his shoulder and cheek. He stared off into the horizon, with no concern for the blinding light as it plunged into Deep Sea. The ocean's fingers washed away our misery, if only temporarily, and the sun delivered our pain into the depths of Hell.

---

7. Butterflies

Chapter Three: Steena

A few days of mourning passed in which little work got done. I barely made five dents in my Lagodore crystalight. Liesle hadn't bothered to attempt painting. Su made fruit-flavored gelatin as a treat to cheer us up, but otherwise hadn't done much work, either.

When the kids were ready to go to school, we sent them off with a donation of food and gelatin to their teacher, the Mind volkhv. On the order of their God, Mind elementals weren't allowed to use money, so parents were expected to donate to their kids' schools. I was more than happy to perform my civic duty for the woman raising and teaching my kids six hours a day, for six of the ten days in a week. I'd even given her a crystalight with which she could have traded for a year's worth of supplies, but she'd kept it, bringing it to her classroom every day.

On school days, we packed lunches for the kids. Fruit slices, rice, and fish, usually, though on days after making gelatin, we packed that for them, too. At least, for the ones who liked it; Cohaku couldn't stand the wobbly nature of gelatin.

Tawny used to pester us endlessly about what we put in her bag. If we had any kiwis, we *had* to give her one. And the fish had to be in with the rice—opposite of how Cohaku needed everything to not touch.

The silence now was maddening. My soul screamed to fill that soundless void. Gods, what would I have done to hear her voice one more time?

Eruwan was old enough to accompany the younger kids to school without an adult, so I no longer went into the village to escort them, though part of me was nostalgic for the years I spent trekking down Bamboo Lane to the village with my kids, there and back twice a day.

Nio was still too young to attend school. Liesle retreated to the bedroom after finishing packing the kids' lunches. Nio carried her favorite bone mane-ornaments into the bedroom, chasing after Liesle.

Su stood by the chore board, once again trying to find the courage to change his name. He erased the character for 'bell' and made it 'vinegar.' I barely recognized it, so infrequently did he use it. A sour name for a sour mood. He erased it as quickly as he'd written it and wrote one I'd never seen.

"What's that one mean?" I asked.

"'End,'" he answered. "Gods, now that I've said it aloud, it's too sad." He erased it and put 'bell' back on the board.

I rubbed his upper shoulders. Bare, with his chest binding made of ribs and grass that wrapped between his lower and upper arms. He wore numerous pieces of bone jewelry including a goat skull on his head. "Do I need to accompany you everywhere today to make sure you don't do anything you'll regret?"

"Maybe. We need to gather fruit. Go tell Lisi-honey. I'll get the baskets."

I pushed aside the leaf door to our bedroom. Liesle had covered the window with leaves and put black drapes over the crystalights, allowing minimal light into the room. She lay curled up, facing away from the door, her tail also covered. Nio stood over her, curious, then walked up to me. She made a motion with her paw like an upside-down 'V.' She always did that when she wanted my attention. With her other hand, she held out her bone ornament.

"Come into the light where I can see better, Nio."

I crouched and gathered the bulk of her mane that had blocked her face. She hated her bangs covering her eyes. I had done this so often that it was second nature. In seconds, I had the bone wrapped and clipped to her hair. The tuft sticking out made her look like she had blue leaves growing on the top of her head, but she liked it, and everyone thought it was cute. Nio smiled and went back into the dark bedroom, holding her tail in front of her for light.

My chest hurt, worrying about Liesle. She had never ignored Nio before. I couldn't blame her for wanting to hide and cry over Tawny's death, but she had to keep going, if only for the other kids' sakes.

Su held two reed baskets for himself and one for me. I opened my mouth to ask what we needed to gather when Maika, our shroomhound, started barking up a storm from outside. We rushed out.

The dog's mushroom-hackles were raised and her morel-tail pointed straight. An aggressive stance, directed at Miltico and a crying Lagodore-Yosoe hybrid girl with him. They stood where Bamboo Lane and Coconut Crab Circle met, which was as close to our house as Maika would let a stranger come. Milti carried a long reed basket filled with fruits. No doubt he was collecting them for his father the shopkeeper, but why had he come here?

Milti grabbed the girl by the horn and pulled her away from our territory. She fell, unbalanced by his sudden movement.

I knelt beside Maika and pet her sides to calm her down. She sat on her haunches, excited for attention.

"If your dog bites my daughter, I'll kick it," Milti said.

"If you kick my dog, I'll kick out your teeth and string them on a necklace," Su said. "Then give it to your girl as a present." He took a good, long look at the crying child.

Half Lagodore, half Yosoe. I had seen Milti's new Lagodorian wife a few times in passing, but this was my first time seeing their daughter. She had hircine hindquarters and horns, curled like her father's, but a leporine upper body, arms, face, and long ears that flopped over the horns.

Miltico yanked the girl to her feet. "Get up."

She wore very little—just a leaf skirt. Tradition in our village was for biped girls to cover their upper halves, though perhaps they hadn't done so in Starsine, where Miltico's new family had come from.

The girl was alarmingly skinny. If I put both hands on her waist, my fingers would have touched. "Is everything okay?" I asked. "Are you getting enough food?"

Milti snorted. "Don't patronize me, lion. We have plenty of food. These fucking rabbits, though... they can eat their weight in grass and still be skinny."

Was that true? I'd never heard that about Lagodores, but Wynnles had a similar capacity. I could eat half my weight in one meal and be fine, though I wouldn't eat for a few days after.

Su crouched to the girl's eye level. "One, two, three, four..."

The girl hid behind her father's legs.

"What are you doing? You're going to make me trip." He held her horn and pushed her away.

Su stood to his full height with upper arms crossed and lower arms akimbo. "I can count her ribs."

Milti sneered. "What kind of pervert counts an eight-year-old's ribs?"

"She's too skinny."

"I know! We moved back to Aloutia for that reason. Not enough food on Cosmo."

My husband plucked a steena from a nearby tree and held it out to her. Our village had been named after the fruit which grew in wild abundance all along the tropical North Corridor. It was a cute fruit, stereotypically feminine, with a purple shell protecting six white edible slices.

It brought back a memory. Right after Nio had hatched, Eruwan had scrimshawed in a scapula a cross-section of a steena. The six slices were labeled with the names of the six kids. Our names were etched into the shell. Now we had a seventh child on the way, but Tawny was gone, so we were still at six.

I hated thinking of myself as a father of six instead of a father of seven. It wasn't like she had stopped being my daughter. I was *still* her father, even if she was in Spiritua now. No, no matter what anyone said, I was a father of seven.

"What's your name?" Su asked as he held the steena out to Milti's daughter.

Cowering behind her father, she lowered her head.

Milti rolled his one good eye. "I told her not to talk to strangers. Maybe your kids should be taught the same."

"Steena Village is too small to have strangers," I said. "She ought to know everyone who lives here. It might take some time, but if she's going to live here, she can't think of us as strangers."

"Fine. Take the damn fruit."

Cautiously, with her skinny goat-legs trembling as she walked closer, she took the steena from Su, then scurried back behind Milti.

"This girl of mine is named Usana. Usana, this is Mr. Lasteran and... um, are you a Mys or a Mister?" Milti could barely hide his disgust at Su's existence.

"I'm a Godblood," Su replied, not-so-subtly hinting that he could kill Milti with a blast of magic. "You may call me 'Your Luminance' or 'Master Scrimshander.' Avoids ugly gendered words entirely, doesn't it?"

"There you have it, Usana. The big, scary Godblood wants you to call it 'Master' like an Ophidian slaver."

"*Him*," Su corrected, taking a much gentler tone than I could have mustered in the same situation. "I am not an *it*."

"Oh, you decided you had a penis after all?"

I nearly choked on my own spit hearing him say that word at all, let alone in front of his daughter.

"Do you always use such words around your daughter?" I asked.

"Why would I hide it? Kids grow up to resent parents who hide things from them. If I don't teach her about sex, she'll find out on her own when she's eleven or twelve. That's about when Lagodores start fucking. I'm sure she'll be just like her mother."

I patted Maika's side before I stood. Slowly, so as not to startle the girl, I walked toward the two of them. "I don't want to hear you talk like that in front of a child ever again."

Usana clutched Milti's legs for dear life while her own shook so badly I thought she'd fall again.

"Is that a threat?" he asked. "Are you trying to scare my daughter?"

"I'm not going to hurt the girl, but I won't make any promises about you. Why are you here, anyway?"

Milti motioned to his basket of fruits. "Gathering fruits. What's it look like?"

"Why so close to my house? We don't want you anywhere near here. There are fruits all over the damn place. Go pick them from the other side of the village."

Milti scowled, but couldn't find an argument. His poor daughter was on the verge of tears.

Su crouched to the girl's level again. "That only goes for your father, Usana. You are welcome here any time."

She opened her eyes. Big, round, bunny eyes, glistening with tears. "T-thank you, Master Scrimshander."

"Let's go," Milti said. Guiding his daughter by the horn, he stomped away down Bamboo Lane toward Steena Village.

I put a hand on Su's shoulder. He shook, just enough that I wouldn't have noticed if I hadn't felt him calm at my touch.

I whispered in his ear, "If Milti causes problems again, I'll make him leave the village for good."

He was quiet for a long moment, watching the two head down the road. Milti never took his hand off Usana's horn, even though the angle he held it made her head twist so she couldn't see where she was going.

"I could see her ribs, Ami-honey. She's starving."

"There's plenty of food here."

"Here. In Aloutia. We have the Green Moon to spur our crops and trees to produce excess food. No child in Aloutia starves. But on the Cosmo plane? On planet Starsine?" Su shook his head. "If we make them leave, that girl won't get the food she needs."

"How is there not enough food on Starsine?" I asked. "Plenty of people live there without problems."

"If you're not integrated into a society, it can be difficult. The stereotypes that Lagodores eat grass and Yosoe can eat anything are both false. If Milti and his family were cast out of every society they tried to join, it's possible they couldn't find edible food."

I couldn't fathom having insufficient food. Why would anyone ever live in a place like that? I couldn't imagine my children starving. I'd let them eat *me* before I let them go hungry.

Steena Village, Seabells, the North Corridor, hell, all of Aloutia, was blessed land. Though the region around Seabells was perhaps *more* blessed than other regions of Aloutia. This was soil touched by the Gods. The ancestors of the locals had scoured this land clean of sin during the Greed Wars, and their ghosts could smile happily down upon us for preserving their legacy. They won the Gods' favor, and we reaped the rewards. The hands of Machenerate poured nutrients into the soil. Liqua's rains came frequent and fierce, keeping the vegetation lush and verdant year-long. And holy Cherribell, the Goddess of Plants herself, ensured the edible fruits, rice, sugar cane, anything we put into the ground, would blossom for her glory.

Su wrapped an arm around mine and tugged me toward the beach.

As he led me away, my feline ears picked up a faint sound. I turned my head in time to see Miltico hit Usana across the face. The first sound must have been him hitting the steena out of her hand, now rolling to the side of the dirt path where it landed amongst the bamboo.

From this distance, he was barely audible, and I knew only my ears would pick up on it. Su had average hearing for his species, which was far inferior to my own Wynnle and Nilian ears. Milti growled at his daughter, "I didn't give you permission to eat that."

The rage boiling in my sternum spiked. My pupils became thin, vertical strips. I resisted the urge to extend my claws. Su kept pulling me to the beach, even after my muscles tensed. He must have felt *that*.

"Ami-honey, shall I give you a massage before we collect fruit?" He wormed his way under my arm and rubbed my back with his two left hands.

Su... Su exerted some kind of power over me. I turned away from Miltico and Usana and promptly forgot about them. Su was my everything. His bright brown eyes challenged me to look anywhere else. Why would I want to?

Among the copious amounts of jewelry Su wore today were earrings made from wolf teeth. I hadn't put any earrings in today. I couldn't muster the mood. "Just a massage, Sugar. Nothing more."

In our family, the adults wore earrings to indicate when we were interested in having sex. Liesle and I were Lightning elementals—Su did not say what element he was, but he played by our rules anyway—and it was illegal and immoral for the other elementals to initiate asking a Lightning elemental for sex. The Lightning God, Sparkato, was to blame for that. He was such a bitter, sex-obsessed man that he believed that anyone who refused sex ought to be punished. According to stories, he had been rejected by women repeatedly when he was mortal, then became a rapist upon his ascension to Godhood. Some stories claimed the other Gods had him under control, locked away where he could cause no harm. And yet Lightning Godbloods existed, so he conceived children *somehow*.

In any case, he only had power over Lightning elementals. All people were born with the full complement of the Gods' blessings including immunity from nightmares and intense heat. If not for the latter, I'd have been a fool for living in this hot, tropical environment with a full mane of hair. People could lose their blessings after their fifteenth hatching-day, however, if they disobeyed their God's commands. In our case, we would lose our blessings if we declined sex when an adult requested it.

The workaround was for sexual partners to find ways of telling each other when it was okay to ask for sex. My partners and I used the bone earrings as our signals.

Lightning elementals didn't worship Sparkato. Not in the way other elementals lavished their Gods with reverence, holidays, and prayers. The gentlest, most forgiving Lightning elementals saw him as a nuisance—an entity we had to cater to so we'd keep our blessings. The more critical amongst us saw him as a foul rapist who *should* be disobeyed. There was no shame in a Lightning elemental losing their blessing. In some societies, it was even a mark of maturity and confidence, a sign that one had stood up for themselves when asked to do something against their wishes. Liesle and I took a different approach, though we had the benefit of being Wynnles, descended from lions and tigers. We had sworn that if someone we disliked asked us for sex, we would do it... and we'd make it *hurt*. Only other Wynnles and Nilians could handle my barbed penis, and *no* species could take our claws digging into their flesh. Unblessed non-Lightning elementals could also be cooked by the lightning on our tails.

Su nudged me toward the beach. His hands on my back and his cool cheek against my side as he pushed me felt nice. Too nice. My paws enjoyed the warmth of the soft sand. Deep Sea crashed rhythmically amidst the call of pink seagulls and the songbird trio—vily, gamayuns, and alkonosts. It could have been a perfect, idyllic day if not for the tumultuous storm brewing in my sternum. Sorrow over Tawny, concern for Liesle, and a bit of shame that I would lust over Su instead of worrying about those who needed help.

We sat on the sand. Su instructed me to lay on my belly. He straddled my back, just above my tail. As he was only wearing a grass skirt and bone thong, I felt the excellent skin of his buttocks on my back. Even before his hands could massage any tension out, my baculum pressed into the sand and my eyes rolled back into my skull.

As he eased my tense muscles, I wished I had worn my earring. I had refrained from wearing it not only because I'd woken up depressed, but also because I didn't want Liesle to judge me harshly. I feared that if I wore it so soon, she'd think I had gotten over Tawny's death already. Or maybe she would feel pressured to put her earring in before she was ready.

Su's fingers worked their way to my neck, digging through my thick mane. I turned my head so he could massage a different spot, and in doing so, I faced the house.

Liesle stood by one of the whale rib supports, watching us with a blank expression. She displayed no obvious emotion, and yet I felt a surge of shame, like I'd disappointed her somehow.

She went back into the house. Perhaps she, too, had not wanted to be seen.

I held back a sob which I could not explain. Why was I sad? I buried my face in the sand and let Su knead my anxiety out, though it grew faster than he could rub away. My family was falling apart around me, and all I could do was cry.

Heliodor Interlude

On Heliodor's first day back at school, he was scared he'd start crying in the middle of class. The kids' teacher, a woman they only referred to as Mys Volkhv, was a nice lady who'd never shame them for crying, but Heli didn't want to interrupt her lesson.

Like most buildings in Steena Village, the Mind church was constructed of bamboo, reeds, and enormous leaves. The bipedal students sat on bamboo chairs with cushions while quadrupeds like Heli had a bamboo mat with a soft blanket on top of it. A cinnadyme candle hung in the open window to keep mozzies out.

He glanced at the empty seat at the table that used to be assigned to him, Cohaku, Demitris, and Tawny. With Tawny gone now, he needed someone else to help him put on the quill-hold[1] . Cohaku was clumsy and Demitris was rough, but his cousin managed to get it on Heli's paw somewhat comfortably.

Heli believed Cohaku to be much stronger than him, emotionally speaking. She'd bury her nose into her notes or book, scowling, and never looked like she was about to cry. Meanwhile, Heli wanted nothing more than to hide his face behind his wings so no one could see his tear-stained eyes. Just seeing the empty chair where Tawny used to sit made his chest hurt. Demitris didn't hide his feelings. He'd openly weep, biting down on his hand's exoskeleton so he wouldn't make any noise.

Mys Volkhv left the room briefly when Eruwan and Fionn's teacher came in and said there was a problem.

"What's going on?" Heli said under his breath.

"None of our business," Cohaku mumbled. She disliked the volkhvs after they'd complained about her being too nosy, so now she made a point to never ask them anything. She tried to stay away from them as much as possible, and never went into their office after school hours. "Let's just finish up so we don't have to do this at home."

---

1. A device that allows quadrupedal people to hold a pen or pencil. Most are quite rudimentary in design.

Heli tried to write a few sentences, but... maybe it was the quill-hold. He wasn't very good at using it. No quadruped was, except for the few prodigies, but Heli had never met such a person. He couldn't delude himself for long, though; Heli knew his issues were because he was morose.

When the teacher came back in, she held the hand of a girl the kids had never seen before. Part Yosoe, part Lagodore. She was dressed for cold weather which Heli thought was weird. If she was a kid like them, she would have the Gods' blessing, so she wouldn't be overheated, but she surely wasn't comfortable. She had a lump on her head like she'd gotten stung by a gwenynen[2].

"Class, we have a new student joining us today. Please give a warm welcome to Mys Usana Demiu."

Heliodor strived to be friendly to all, so he was among the first to say hello, and he was proud of it. Cohaku kept her face buried in her book.

Usana was shy, Heli thought. She pulled her long Lagodore ears in front of her face and hid. It reminded Heli of how he sometimes wanted to put his wings in front of his face when he was embarrassed. *Poor girl.*

"We have a seat for you next to Heliodor and Demitris, Usana. Will you sit there, please?"

Tawny's seat. Heli didn't mind her sitting there. It would have been rude to make her keep standing.

"No!" Cohaku yelled. "Tawny sits there!"

Mys Volkhv started to speak, but closed her mouth. "Cohaku, I know you're going through a tough time, but Usana needs this seat now."

Heli tried to calm Cohaku back down. "It's okay, Sis. I don't think Tawny would mind letting Usana use her chair."

Cohaku bit her lip and did her usual thing with her claws. Heli didn't know what to call it, but his twin sister did it so often, it had become a trait he associated with her. She would extract and retract her claws, back and forth. Sometimes, it didn't seem like she could control it.

"Come sit next to me, Usana," Heli said with a big smile, trying to look as friendly as he thought he was on the inside.

Instead, Usana collapsed on the floor, screaming. "Lion! It's a lion!"

Confused, Heli tilted his head. The teacher tried to help Usana back up, but her legs were so skinny and shaky.

"What's wrong?" Heli asked. "I'm not a lion. Lions are animals and I'm a sapienti."

"Lions eat rabbits and goats," she said with a sniff. "Daddy told me. Daddy..." She broke out into a wordless wail.

Demitris jumped up and yelled at her, "Your daddy's a liar! Heli's the sweetest

---

2. A bee. Plural: gwenyn

boy!"

The teacher took Usana out of the classroom. The kids didn't see her for the rest of the day, so Heli supposed her father took her back home. He hoped her father was able to comfort her.

Chapter Four: The Shopkeeper

Moru, the first day of the week, the day belonging to the God of Death, finally arrived. Steena Village was too small to have its own Death church, so Tawny's body had been taken to the nearest big city, Seabells. It was a few hours' journey by ship or Daga[1] up The Corridor, and Liesle and Su needed to work after being lethargic the last few days, so I went alone.

I sat outside the church's double doors engraved with an image of the Death God Sawyer and his wife Laynie, the Demigoddess of Mercy. The church's circular saw emblem was embossed between the heads of the two figures.

Sitting on a bench too small for my species, I kept my head low to hide my tears. There weren't many Wynnles in Seabells and I didn't want to scare anyone who thought I might go berserk. It obviously wouldn't happen on purpose—not here with me—but people had good reason to keep their distance from a Wynnle. From me.

In my grief, I had forgotten to put on a kamen[2]. While it wasn't enforced, most people in big cities wore one when out and about. Hopefully, nobody would look at a crying Wynnle anyway.

Most of the townsfolk were Flora, an herbivorous species of people who changed their shape and colors in ways resembling the foods they ate. A man who ate rose petals would gradually grow rose-petal hair, thorny arms, and emit a powerful odor. A woman who ate rice would soon have braided hair resembling a rice stalk and pasty white skin. Florae may have looked dainty, but they were as sapient as any of the other sapienti species. An individual could be kind and loving, or a brutal murderer. They'd proven the latter true during the Greed Wars. The northern part of Seabells that had once been the so-called 'noble's quarters'

---

1. A sapient species of people resembling gigantic turtles. Many will ferry people, for a fee.

2. A mask that covers the whole face, worn in many urban parts of Aloutia, but less common in rural communities and small villages.

was a field of wildflowers now. To this day, nobody dared claim noble descent in Seabells or its surrounding villages. None dared try to *instate* nobility. The town was run by an elected mayor; I had voted in the last election, but couldn't even recall the woman's name. The outlying villages were often leaderless, as Steena Village was. We had no kindness in our souls for tyrants. We had no patience to test if someone would *become* a tyrant. True, we were ultimately ruled by the Aloutian Emperor, who sent his tax collectors to Seabells every year, and we complied if only to keep the peace. But the few lawkeepers in Seabells were a token force, and they never came to Steena Village.

Every twenty feet along the shore stood a tall post with ribbons, wind chimes, and strings of bells that sang in the ocean breeze. Each post was topped with a light, usually a lantern to protect the flame from the wind, and some stocked with cinnadyme candles, though that didn't stop clouds of mozzies from overrunning the city. If only the mozzies had nobility, then the people here might find the hatred within them to eradicate the damn pests.

Seabells had invested in a few crystalights as well. One of mine was somewhere along the coast, carved to resemble one of their famous bells. Even now, as the wind tousled my mane and blew away my tears, the bells sang, just like the bell Tawny always wore on her tail. A requiem for remembrance of my lost girl echoed along the shore.

My skull repeated that memory for the millionth time. Tawny fell, her bell chimed, and a blast of white light emanated from the crevice.

"Mr. Lasteran?"

The Death volkhv's voice stopped the next flashback. He was a Gluckan man with stony black skin with curling white bones for an exoskeleton. His face had the appearance of a painted-on skull. It was what I imagined Demitris would look like as an adult. Gingerly, reverently, he held an ebonwood[3] box out to me.

"She has been sawdusted entirely." The volkhv lowered his head in a bow and spoke solemnly. "Her body and soul shall forevermore be out of reach of demonkind."

I tried to thank the volkhv. I opened my mouth, but all that came out was a pathetic whimper. Trembling, I took the ebonwood box and held it close to my chest.

"Be safe on your way back home, Mr. Lasteran." He lowered his head again and went back inside.

I sat and cried for what felt like an hour, but in reality was probably only a few minutes, before mustering the courage to open that box.

Her clothes. A shirt Eruwan had made. A grass skirt Su had made. Leg wraps I had made. The bell that had been wrapped around her tail. Su had taken the head

---

3. A tree related to Terran ebony, but which also has black bark and leaves.

of a femur and sliced it in half. I'd coated crystalight shavings on the inside and strips of copper. Su had put a little ball inside, cut a slit for the sound and light to escape, then sealed the two halves together. Wherever Tawny went, bobbing her tail as she ran, her bell would announce her presence and shine light. It had been her most precious possession. She would put it on first thing in the morning—if she remembered to take it off the previous night. Wherever she went, her starlight went with her, singing the joy of her life.

With an ache in my sternum and salty tears stinging my eyes, I went back home.

Travel down The Corridor was much quicker than the journey up since we went with the flow of Deep Sea. I hired a Daga to carry me aboard a raft yoked to their enchanted, bejeweled golden shell. Daga shells were made of gold, enchanted with Water elementrons that kept them afloat. Farther up The Corridor, they had entire cities on islands made from shed shells and the shells of deceased Dagas, though I'd never been there to see it for myself. Odd that the shells of the dead weren't sawdusted...

I watched Scrimshander Lighthouse come into view. Su had built it from a coatl[4] skeleton, layered with vertebrae and crowned with the animal's skull. We were in the process of building a house attached to it; it would be Eruwan's house when it was finished. Inside the coatl's mouth, it bit down on a brilliant white crystalight, carved by my own hands. The light served not only to warn ships and Dagas about the rocks ahead, but was also Steena Village's Godlight. So long as its holy light shone down on us, no demons would dare get too close. No *weak* demons, at least. Demon Lords such as Deep Sea were immune.

The raft continued onward, past the beach where my kids played with their cousin Demitris and the dog Maika. The Daga veered away from the shore so they wouldn't hit any of the stone stacks ahead. The rock formations were large enough above the surface of the water, but were downright monstrous below, and held massive caves. Liesle had told me about small pockets on the tallest stacks that could only be reached by flight, and Su had hinted at some undersea entrances he knew about. As a wingless air-breather, the only caves I could access were the ones at surface level.

I had business in the village proper, so I let the Daga driver go on their normal route. Typically if I asked one of the giant turtle-people to take me to shore right by my house, they would oblige.

---

4. A gigantic, feathered serpent native to the jungles of the Mu, on Cosmo.

I wasn't sure how Su knew I was nearby—he had magic to detect people, though how it worked, I did not know—but he breached the water and swam closer. He wore a beautiful purple betta fish tail, more elegant and sinuous than any fancy lady's ballroom gown, and clambered aboard the raft.

"Ami-honey, are you alright?"

I let out a tired sigh. "As well as I can be while holding our daughter's remains."

He stared at the box, trying his best to suppress his emotions. "When you return home, watch out for Liesle. She's... not well. I think I'm going to hide in my ateli for the next few days. Work on Tawny's memorial. Meet me in the cave of St. Alice's Lights later. Don't tell Liesle. I'll tell her I'm going to my ateli."

"You want to *hide* something from her?"

"We agreed to respect each other's privacy. You don't ask about my sex or element. Liesle doesn't show us her ateli. You don't tell anyone about your mother's secret. So yes, I want to hide this from her. Meet me in the cave, if you want." Su made an exaggerated display of ensuring I noticed he was wearing furculae earrings.

Part of me felt it was ridiculous, utterly *sacrilegious*, to discuss physical intimacy as I carried our daughter's remains back home. Another part of me wanted Su in ways I'd never had him before. My baculum stretched; I blushed with shame as I clutched Tawny's box to my chest.

"It's just an offer, Ami-honey. If that's not what you want, you don't have to come. Or if you come without earrings, I'll know." He dove into the sea.

The Daga continued towing the raft around the stone stack archipelago, then toward the village pier while I battled my conflicting emotions. By the time we landed on the small dock, shame had won the war. I held my head low as I trod toward the store of our local shopkeeper, Mr. Phoebus Svelt.

Since he dealt with imports, his store was not far from the pier. Various dry goods were kept outdoors; he did not worry about theft in this small village. Racks of imported clothes made from cotton, silk, and linen, as well as hats, mostly for heads smaller than mine. Gardening and farming tools lined against upright boards. Baskets of candles and incense—one of them burning cinnadyme. Small, decorative objects made of driftwood and seashells. Barrels of fruits, though most locally picked. I wouldn't be surprised if the rambutans had come straight off the tree growing right next to the shop, its branches poised ponderously over the roof. A ladder leading up to the roof where a branch had been stripped bare of its hairy red fruit suggested I was right.

The shopkeeper was a timid man whose wife had died shortly after their son Tico died. Milti left soon afterward—I wasn't sure if Phoebus knew why, or that I had been the cause of it. Poor Phoebus had never been the same since losing his family. At the time, I'd been so hateful toward Milti that I had no sympathy for his father. Now that I was older and had experienced the loss of my daughter, I understood why the old Yosoe became eternally sullen.

The shop had a tall door specifically made for us Wynnles. Phoebus had enlarged the entryway after the hatching of his granddaughter Nell, my niece. The Mantodea[5] attending Nell's hatching predicted she would inherit Orienna's height rather than Milti's.

Nell was here now, actually, helping her grandfather with inventory stocking. "Good day, Uncle Ami. Um... are you here for supplies?" Half Yosoe and half Wynnle, Nell had Milti's goat-legs, curved horns, and horizontal-pupil eyes, but Orienna's electric tail, wings, tiger face, and striped patterns. The girl was a mish-mash of traits.

"I'm here for Collembola mucus[6] and snowbark resin. Where's your grandfather?"

She looked askance. I had difficulty reading emotion in Yosoe eyes. Even though I knew Nell was a sensitive girl, something about those horizontal pupils gave off no emotional energy to me. I had struggled reading Milti's emotions too, back when we were kids playing in the jungle and along the beach. I wondered if I had ever alienated him by misjudging his feelings.

"He's in the back with... Um, so you know my dad is back in the village, right? My biological dad. Not Piotr."

"I'm aware." For her sake, I tried not to sound too disgusted.

"And he has a new daughter, Usana?"

"I've met her."

Nell pressed her hands together. "Uh, well, Usana was supposed to start school today, but she had a crying fit and had to be taken out of class. Dad was angry about it and gave her a spanking when they got here. Grandpa tried to calm him down, but it only made Dad angrier. Dad left to do his job and Grandpa stayed in the back to talk to Usana. They're back there now, still. Usana was crying for a long time."

A sickness rose in my chest, mixed with a burning hatred. I couldn't imagine how anyone calling themself a man or father could hit *any* child, let alone their own. Milti had better stay away from me, or else I might show him what it was like to be hit by someone bigger and stronger. My claws extended involuntarily; I slid them back in, hoping Nell didn't notice.

Nell cowered away from me, bumping into a rack of spices in jars. She hurriedly grabbed it before any fell. "Uncle Ami? Are you okay?"

---

5. A sapient species of people who can 'read' genetics. They are hired by Life churches (nurseries) to report a child's biological parents and any other pertinent genetic information the parents should know.

6. The mucus of a Collembola, a sapient species, can be used as glue.

I forcibly eased my expression. "I'm sorry if I scared you, Nell."

"You looked... like you were going to go berserk."

Dizziness swept over me. I put my hands on Phoebus's cashier desk for balance. Was my niece scared for her life? I would never...!

She bolted into the backroom where she'd said her grandfather and sister were. Phoebus came out a moment later, wiping sweat off his brown-fur brow with a handkerchief. He'd lost his blessings many years ago; by day he was tormented by heat, and by night he was tormented with nightmares. I could not begin to guess why he continued to live in Steena Village. He could have moved someplace cooler, with no family tying him down. I supposed he loved his store too much. Or maybe he was closer to Nell than I thought.

"Ah, Mr. Lasteran, I've been waiting for you. Eruwan was here before school and told me what you needed. You have some mail from Mr. Onoretti, too. No doubt about the..." He paused and licked his lips. "I'm so sorry, Ami. It really is impossible to put into words the pain we've gone through."

"I owe you an apology, too," I said. "I was young and stupid, all those years ago. I barely gave any thought to how Tico's death affected you."

Phoebus opened his mouth to speak, but closed it and bent under his desk to rummage for my supplies. He sighed as he set the objects before me—a bottle of white Collembola mucus, snowbark resin, and an envelope sealed with wax and stamped with Giorvi Onoretti's business seal: the crystalline emblem of the merchants of light with his surname around the perimeter.

Mr. Onoretti was my commissioner, though he performed many other duties for the guild which went over my breadth of understanding. He dealt with the political and business side of the merchants of light while I focused solely on sculpting. It was illegal for anyone to buy raw crystalights except for the higher-ups in the guild. He had the power to purchase extraction rights, hire Domovye miners, and write up contracts between the merchants and customers.

I had no doubt this letter was to inform me that he'd purchased all the crystalights under the village and that he would be pleased to sell me as much as I wished. I also had no doubt he knew nothing of Tawny's death, and this letter would be strictly about business.

It wouldn't be his fault if this letter were impersonal or devoid of sympathy; he couldn't have known. Mr. Onoretti was a loving and devoted father himself.

Phoebus clenched a fist. "May I ask you something, Mr. Lasteran?"

"Of course."

He hesitated. "Maybe I shouldn't."

"Well, now you've got me curious."

"This may be insensitive. As a father who has lost a child, I want to know your opinion about... something. But it might upset you."

"I won't be upset, Mr. Svelt. It's important to be open about our feelings, isn't it? How else are we supposed to heal?"

"Yes, that's true. Okay, so about my son, Milti. You know he's going by Miltico now. Part of me wants to respect his wishes to go by a new public name, but part of me hates that name. Like he's... stealing Tico. Does that make sense? How would you feel if one of your kids changed their name to include Tawny's name?"

Eruwany. Fiawny. Cohawny. Heliawny. Tawnio.

Each one felt like a sculptor's pick assaulting my skull and sternum.

"That's fucked up," I replied. "But I can see it from his perspective, too. It's his way of keeping his brother's memory alive."

Of all the names I conjured up, I could definitely see Fionn taking Tawny's name as part of his. They were—had been—so close.

Phoebus's hands shook. He pressed them against the desk to steady himself, but still he trembled. "I am suffering, Mr. Lasteran. I was so happy to have my son back, but he's hardly the son I once knew."

"Milti stopped being the same man the first time he took crazy sugar and hit a child. Forgive me if I sound cruel, Mr. Svelt, but I have no hope of your son ever being a good person. All I ask is that you protect Usana. *She's* the one suffering."

He blinked to hold back the tears. "I know. You're right. Usana needs me... but I'm just an old man, Ami. When Milti comes back to take her home, I won't be able to stop him, even by force."

I didn't know enough about Milti and Usana's relationship to judge. Usana was starving, yes, but like Su had said, that was the unfortunate truth about life on Cosmo if you weren't in a community. Now that she was here, she should fatten up on Aloutia's bountiful fruits. Usana had been spanked, but spanking wasn't illegal or considered child abuse in Aloutia. It was an issue decided by each vassal nation, and Seabells allowed corporal punishment. Yet another outcome of the Greed Wars. To purify this land of the avarice that had once contaminated it, the Seabellers' ancestors needed validation to exterminate all nobles, including children. Although my partners and I disagreed with the idea of spanking, there were many parents throughout Aloutia who would hit their kids in the name of discipline. Since it wasn't against the law in Seabells, taking the complaint up with the lawkeepers would do no good.

Worse, if I threatened to get lawkeepers involved without evidence, it might cause Milti to retaliate by claiming *I* was abusing my children. He might claim Tawny's death was negligence, or that Cohaku's quirks were a result of emotional or mental abuse, or that Nio's silence was a result of abuse. No doubt the lawkeepers would find *something* wrong with a family of Wynnles. Any excuse to banish us to Cosmo.

I wore an antelope skull on my belt which Su had fashioned into a coin purse. I put a few coins on Mr. Svelt's desk; more than enough to cover the cost of my purchase, but I could afford it. All he had was this shop. I had my spouses to fall back on, and my job paid the maxima[7]. Taking Mr. Onoretti's letter in my hands, I suspected I'd never run out of crystalights again. Perhaps his letter would offer me work for the rest of my life.

All it cost was my daughter's life.

As I emerged from Bamboo Lane, I saw the kids playing down on the beach, minus Fionn and the shroomhound Maika who were by the house. Fionn had made a basket of reeds wrapped around bones, with a strap meant to go around Maika's chest. When he put the basket on her, it rested on her back-mushrooms. Maika wagged her morel-tail, probably thinking this was a game. Fionn scowled, about to lose his temper.

"You alright, son?" I asked as I traversed the interval between us.

"I can't get it to stay on."

"You could ask Su for help. He's good at making things like this."

He grimaced. "I wanted to try it on my own. To see if I wasn't a failure at everything I ever attempted."

What on all the planes was he talking about? Fionn had never mentioned feeling like a failure before... Was this just the anxiety talking through him, or was there an underlying problem I'd been too dense to notice? If it were the latter, the only failure here would be me, failing to be a good father.

Maika scratched her side with a hind leg, breaking one of the reed straps.

Furious, Fionn took the basket and chucked it aside. Maika thought he was playing fetch and retrieved it.

"Fuck it. I don't need it."

"Hey, don't use that kind of language," I chided, then immediately regretted it. Fionn had bigger problems than swearing. "If you want to make anything, it takes practice. My first sculpture was awful, too. Don't be afraid to ask for help. You're a kid; it's okay to not know how to do something."

"Everyone else is good at doing things! Eruwan can scrimshaw, play piano, and do all her homework without help. Cohaku can write so well. Heliodor is social and loved by everyone. Tawny is—*was*—better than me at sports when I was her

---

7. The maximum amount of money a person can earn in a given time period. The system was implemented after the Greed Wars.

age. Nio is a master of troika[8] and she's only five! I can't do anything!"

My hands were full with the bottles and letter, but I managed to get them all tucked under one arm. I grabbed Fionn's shoulder, where he wore a deer skull. "You have your skills. You're strong, athletic, good at fishing, and cooking the fish afterward. I never thought you were the basket-weaving type, but if that's what you want to learn, you have to practice it."

"I don't want to learn it. I just wanted to make something for Maika so she could help carry fruit."

I understood now. In the past, Fionn and Tawny would go looking for fruit they could only find in the jungle. They'd always gone together for safety and company. Maika was the replacement.

"Maika might not want to follow you far from home, anyway." She didn't like going into the jungle. When we'd first gotten her, we were concerned about her running away and getting attacked by tigers, but the poor dog wouldn't venture into the jungle even with treats and bones within range. "Don't worry about collecting as much fruit as you used to. Just carry what you can. Nio might be old enough now to accompany you."

Fionn scratched his mane. "Hmm, maybe. Anyway, I'm going. I'll get some fruit before dinner. Probably chop it up myself since Mom's not awake."

He grabbed his own basket and flew off into the jungle before I could ask any further questions.

Su had also warned me about Liesle being in a mood. I had to go inside to drop off my purchases and Mr. Onoretti's letter, so I decided to check up on her, too.

The inside of the house was disturbingly dark. Liesle had covered all our crystalights with drapes. The animal skulls adorning the walls stared down ominously in the shadows like they were in a creepy demonic cultist hideout. This was not what I wanted my home to look like.

I set the items down on the vertebra table and went into the bedroom.

Liesle was laying down on her side, facing away from the door, with grass wrapped around her tail to swathe her in complete darkness.

"Lisi? Everything okay?"

She roused and sat up. What little light penetrated the room made her tigrine eyes glow verdant green. Sucking in as much light as they could, her pupils became thin, threatening slits. "What the hell do you care? You and Su seem to be alright if you're well enough to fuck on the beach."

My sternum felt like it gained twenty pounds. A shiver ran down my vertebrae. I'd never been more afraid of my wife than I was in that instant. What was *wrong* with her? I knew she must still be suffering from losing Tawny, but this behavior

---

8. Three-player strategy board game similar to chess, meant to symbolize the three-way cold war between Aloutia, Ophidia, and the Makai.

didn't make sense.

"Sorry to bother you," I said. "I'll come back later. You want me to wake you up for dinner?"

"I can make dinner. My kids need to eat."

I couldn't understand her thoughts and feelings or why she referred to them as 'her' kids when she'd always referred to them as 'our' kids previously. She lay down and turned back around before I could find a response.

Since she wasn't watching me anyway, I took a pair of shark-tooth earrings from the scapula shelf next to the door. Without another word, I let the leaf-door fall back into place as I left Liesle well alone.

As I put in my earrings, my fear turned into indignation. How could Liesle think I didn't care about her or the kids? They had been at school when I had my moment with Su, and she had been acting cold and distant the whole week.

Liesle wanted me to feel guilty. She thought I was 'over' Tawny's death.

I made sure the earrings were visible and secure so Su would have no doubt in his mind when I entered the cave that I wanted his entire body and soul. If Liesle was unwilling to support me, I would turn to the comfort of my other spouse instead.

Chapter Five: The Cave of St. Alice's Lights

It had been several months since I last went into the cave of St. Alice's Lights. Although it was close to our house, buried among the sea stacks between our house and the Steena Village pier, it was difficult to reach due to the inconvenience of the entrance. It faced Deep Sea, but was also behind another rock formation. A land-dweller wouldn't know it was there unless they dared traverse the narrow passage between the two rock formations. The entrance was flooded, with no place to walk, until you were fairly deep inside. Su could swim in, and my winged family members could fly, but the only way I could get in was by boat. I paddled our koa-wood fishing boat through the narrow entrance while swinging my tail in front of me for additional light. St. Alice's Lights[1] would not glow if they sensed a disturbance. They would remain dark until I landed my boat and turned my tail light off.

Many years ago, Su had stuck some large animal's femur here to serve as a pier. I moored the boat and climbed out. Inside my antelope skull purse, I kept a leaf wrapping for my tail. By law, Wynnles were supposed to keep their tails covered in public. Since no lawkeepers came to Steena Village, I only did it if I thought I'd be near people who could be hurt by my electricity, but I carried a covering, just in case.

Deeper into the cave, the bioluminescence of St. Alice's Lights painted the walls in a soft, melancholic blue. This was another blessed place, touched by the hands of a God. On a deep, spiritual level, walking under the lights enhanced any emotion I was feeling. If I was sad, the cerulean glow made me sadder. If I was hot for my spouses, the mood lighting put me in an even more sexual mood. If I was happy, the sparkling was like the radiance of starlight shining upon my path.

Su sat up when he heard me coming. I was surprised by how much he wore. Usually, when he came in here, it was via swimming, and he rarely bothered putting on a grass skirt if he was going to get it wet. He was adorned in countless

---

1. Pentagonal Dominionist name for glow worms, named after a human woman whose Terran home had been near a glow worm cave.

other bone ornaments: armlets, anklets, necklaces, hair accessories, and of course earrings. Furculae, the V-shaped bone in a bird's chest. In Su's earring language, it meant he wanted to kiss and caress, but not much more.

His smile brightened the room more than any insect's glow could ever do. "I'm glad you decided to join me, Ami-honey."

I sat beside him. The cave floor was cold and rough, though on hot days like this, the cold floor was nice.

"You were right about Liesle," I said. "There's something wrong with her. I understand she's depressed. We all are. But she's..." I couldn't find the right word, so I left it hanging.

Su leaned against my arm. "Everyone reacts differently to trauma. I don't think there's anything we can do. Some people can only be healed by time."

"How long are we supposed to wait? She could be like this for months. I don't want to tell her to get over Tawny's death—Gods, I'd never say that! None of us will ever get *over* it—but I don't know if I can tolerate her being so cold to us or our kids."

"Give her all the time she needs. We need to support her."

I laid down with my arm stretched so Su could lie over it. He did as such and snuggled close. He took my hand in one of his, whilst also rubbing my leg and stroking my mane. The lights above twinkled like stars if stars were blue instead of pink.

Even though it was dark, I closed my eyes. I knew it was psychological, placebo perhaps, but closing my eyes helped me focus my other senses. I relished in the sensation of Su's hands on my body, his warm skin pressing close to mine, his hair tickling my arm, and his hard bone ornaments which were so... *him*. All bones were intrinsically *Su*. Skulls, femurs, humeri, vertebrae... all Su. When I saw a skeleton, I thought about what Su could do with it. When I ate around a T-bone steak, I thought of my mouth on his skin. When I felt bone, I felt him. Soft skin, hard bones. He was a being of many seemingly contradictory elements. Sweet kisses, strong teeth. Gentleness and kindness, wrapped in a Godblood who could shatter a planet. Femininity and masculinity in one sensual body. Sometimes a submissive who liked when I held his head down as he sucked my cock, sometimes a dominant who preferred to sit on my chest and glare at me with those big brown eyes, his mouth curled in a haughty expression.

Although Su was not in the mood for oral sex now—I knew because he wasn't wearing the jawbone earring to tell me so—just fantasizing about it made my baculum rise.

I opened my eyes. St. Alice's Lights were shining, transforming the cave ceiling into a mystical night sky. Clumps of white light at the center, with faint blue stalactites following the path of the cave like a river. I turned to my lover, to join his lips with mine. Su's brown skin and hair were tinted an oceanic cerulean.

I started to turn, so I could hold him in both my arms, but he moved first.

He got on top of me, legs spread, straddling me. The bone between his legs kept me from feeling whatever private parts he had. St. Alice's Lights formed a bluish aureole around his head like he was a saint. Gods, he might as well have been. His Luminance, indeed.

"Does this make you happy, Ami-honey?" He laid flat and kissed my chest. His upper two hands massaged my arms while his lower two reached for my hips.

"So very happy, Sugar."

He scooted up, moving his upper arms to my mane. He grabbed the sides of my braided mustache and kissed my mouth. My heart thundered, my penis went erect, and my brain went wild with erotic fantasies. With my hands freed from his grip, I caressed his back. I slid my hand down his skirt to grope his ass. I traced my fingers down the crease where his buttocks met his legs. Such a sacred spot, perhaps my favorite place on his body.

We only went as far as kissing and holding, but I was satisfied. For several minutes, my entire universe—my mind, my body, my soul—was nothing but Su. I was his meat and bones, and he was mine. My sternum swelled with pride over my possession, my conquest. This Godblood belonged to *me,* a mere clearblood mortal. I was unable to climax, partially due to my dick's inability to stay erect... a problem I'd had ever since I was a teenager. Sometimes Su was willing to help with this final part, but today he was in no mood for it, and I couldn't blame him.

He sat with his legs up, two hands on his knees, two over his chest, breathing heavily. Had I managed to give him an orgasm? Although we hadn't done much, Su claimed he could achieve orgasm merely by the act of giving pleasure to others. Who was I to question how he satisfied himself?

Su transformed his lower body into an aquatic tail. I assumed that process effectively cleaned anything secreted from his body.

Gods, he was magnificent. More than a Godblood, he could have been a God himself. So beautiful, perfect, and kind. His bone jewelry was regalia for a deity. I hadn't felt this way about Su in years. It was like I was falling in love all over again.

"How do you feel now?" he asked.

"Like a teenager."

Su giggled in a womanly voice. He had three distinct laughs, one feminine, one masculine, and one that was neither. He used them interchangeably, depending on the situation. His feminine laugh was when he was playing coy. "Oh honey, don't say that! I still feel thirty-eight, and I don't want to make this weird."

"Sorry. My body feels thirty-six, but for a moment, I had the same sexually-charged thoughts as when I was younger."

"Before I made you my honey?"

"I was wild for Liesle before I made you my Sugar. Just now reminded me of those days."

Our pet names went deeper than the sweetness they were made from. In our North Corridorean dialect, the word 'honey' was pronounced identically to the

Orochigo word 'hone' which meant 'bone.' When Su called us honey, he wasn't just referring to the sweet, golden liquid made by gwenyn, he was calling us his bones. He would also pronounce bon—meaning good—like bone, but that was a pronunciation specific to him, not to our dialect. Likewise, the first syllable in 'sugar' was pronounced the same as 'Su' in North Corridorean Fleur.

I sat up and took one of his hands. "How about you? Are you okay?"

He gave me a forced, wan smile, and eyes trying to hide an inner turmoil. "Yes, I am happy right now. Perhaps I am well enough to return to work."

Mud and sludge. I hadn't tried to work since the day after Tawny's death when I nearly tossed the crystalight against my ateli wall.

Fuck, what if *that's* what Mr. Onoretti's letter was about? To remind me of my upcoming due date?

"You look worried," Su said as he brushed his fingers through his hair.

"It's nothing. I got a letter from my commissioner which I haven't read yet. I initially thought he might want to talk about the crystalights in the crevice, but now I wonder if he's gonna chew me out for not working."

With a scowl, Su yanked his hair. "If he complains, he can talk to me. I'll chew *him* out."

I grimaced. "Sugar, please don't kill my boss. I doubt I could get any other job. Not one that pays the maxima anyway."

"Don't call him your boss. The only bosses you have are me and Lisi-honey."

"You know what I mean." Honestly, I wasn't sure I knew what I meant. The relationship between me and Mr. Onoretti was complicated. There was a significant degree of formality—I'd never call him by his first name to his face, and I knew I had to answer to him for any professional mistakes. But he had been kind to me and my family, helping us with financial matters during tax season, inviting us to fancy dinners, and helping with legal problems. Not that legal problems happened often, but... well, it *did* happen once, after Tico Svelt died. Although his death was ruled to be drug-related, some suspicions had come over me and Liesle for being Wynnles. It had been an utterly ridiculous accusation. A murderous Wynnle would have left their victim as a bloody pile of viscera and bones. Tico had died because his heart gave out in his sleep. Regardless, we were eternally grateful to Mr. Onoretti for taking care of the issue.

"Shall we go read the letter to find out for sure what he wants?" Su asked. "Better than speculating, yes?"

"Yes. And if Liesle is making dinner, we should help out."

Su glanced downward, ashamed. "Yes, we should. Perhaps we should have done that before sneaking off here."

The shame settled in my chest like cormorants come to roost. I did not want to face Liesle. I could not bear her disapproval. Those menacing emerald eyes haunted me...

Our kids needed us, though. They needed dinner, and it wasn't fair to put the entire burden on Liesle. This was what Su meant when he said we had to support her. It wasn't just about giving her space and talking to her when she was emotionally pained. We had to do our part in keeping the family moving forward.

When we came back home, Liesle was preparing dinner. I didn't want to anger her by reading Mr. Onoretti's letter while there was work to be done, so I decided to read it after we ate.

Liesle sliced fruits in the kitchen and set them into the dolphin-skull rotary, all without speaking or making eye contact with anyone. Su deboned a large fish which I cooked outdoors. He also kept an eye on the rice wok. The scent of cooking fish meat made my mouth salivate.

When she was done with her part, Liesle sat on the pillows, staring blankly upward like there was something of interest on the whale-rib rafters. I had replaced the cinnadyme candle an hour earlier, so she couldn't have been thinking about changing it.

Grief. It sucked energy and willpower out of a person like lemontine sucking the moisture out of the air. I wondered if Liesle had the same dreadful thoughts I did. Did her limbs also hurt to move because the sheer weight of living had become more than she could bear?

When dinner was ready to be served, I fixed her a patella with all her favorite fruit—steenas, mostly—and a generous portion of fish so she'd have enough for herself and the baby inside her.

"Are you able to eat, Lisi?" I asked, holding her patella. For the moment, Su had gone to get the kids. We were alone for once.

She struggled to her feet. Her eyes were strained and puffy from crying, but she hadn't cried when I was around. Her hands trembled, leading me to doubt she could hold the patella without spilling rice all over the floor. Maika would have liked that.

"Is that for me?"

"Of course. Would you like to eat with us or alone? I'll carry it to the bedroom if you'd rather eat there."

Liesle closed her eyes, fighting tears. "I'm sorry, Mo Ami. I can't... I can't be a good mother or wife today. I don't want our children seeing me like this."

Our children this time. I wondered if she regretted calling them *her* children earlier. I brushed those harmful thoughts aside. I couldn't let minor things like that bother me. If I couldn't forgive her for something said in the depths of despair, we'd never get through life.

I nudged my head toward the bedroom. "I'll tell them you don't feel well."

She followed me through the leaf door. I set her patella on the reed-mat bed and let her eat in peace, with nothing but the light from her tail. That was what she wanted, though.

Back in the living room, the kids came in with their cousin Demitris. We always prepared extra food than needed in case either of the Chak-Den kids were playing with ours, or if our kids brought any other friends home. We didn't worry about waste. This blessed, fertile, lush land produced more food in a day than we could eat in a month, and nothing went to waste when Deep Sea was more than happy enough to grind our unused food into marine snow for his abyssal pets.

Demitris had the overall shape of a Wynnle, with claws, tail, and mane, but he was covered in a Death-Gluckan's exoskeleton with bones wrapped around some parts of his body. A swirl over both arms, ribs over his chest, and specks of bone on his face. Black skin, white bones. His mane was like a wheel of fangs. He had the same hatching-day as Tawny, though that was no spectacular coincidence since they had been born on Egg Day, a holiday when many eggs hatched in the light of the Life Moon. Their eggs had been next to each other at the Life church and they'd broken out around the same time. Also like Tawny, he did not have wings. If she hadn't pushed him out of the way of the crevice, he most certainly would have fallen to his death instead.

"Uh, is it okay for me to be here?" he asked.

The question confounded me. "Of course, Demi. Why wouldn't we want you here?"

He sniffed and wiped tears from his eyes. "I... I thought you hated me."

"Oh, Demi-honey!" Su knelt and embraced the boy. "Throw away any such thoughts! Why would you think such a thing? None of us here could hate a sweet boy like you."

"Yeah, you're family too," Eruwan said, patting one of the fangs growing out of his head.

"Even if you weren't, you'd still be welcome here," Su added. "Everyone is welcome to eat at our table, as long as they're a good person. A sweet, darling boy like you shouldn't worry about what adults think."

Demitris sniffed and rubbed his hand over his nose. "But—but Tawny... If I hadn't been in the way—"

Su pressed him close, muffling him and silencing his words. "You *can't* think that way! Tawny knew you were in danger, and she knew she was putting herself in danger. She chose you to live because she loves you."

"*Loved*, you mean," Demitris sobbed.

"No, *loves*. Present tense. She's in Spiritua now, but her love is as strong as ever. She does not regret her choice."

Demitris broke out into a wail. I put my hand on his shoulder. The kids all touched a part of him, too. Together, under the somber bones of a long-dead megawhale, we lamented Tawny's untimely passing.

Liesle Interlude

She heard them all crying. Amiere, Su, all her babies, and Orienna's son Demitris, too. She should have been out there. She should have joined her tears with theirs. She should have... been a good mother...

Liesle ate a slice of steena. It took all the energy she had.

The baby inside of her needed nutrients, and yet she wondered if she was poisoning them with her sorrow. If a mother's depression—that endless gnawing feeling in one's gut, the dread that sank from chest to belly—could damage her baby, she'd never forgive herself.

Chapter Six: The Ateli

After dinner, the kids went outside to play kiwi-batte, a team-based ball game. I asked them to walk Demitris home before sunset since he was not old enough to travel the roads on his own yet. There was nothing and nobody dangerous in the village, and the largest animals living near Bamboo Lane were capybaras. But it had been a tradition since the Greed Wars, back when rich people abducted children for their sick amusement, that kids shouldn't go too far from their houses alone. Oh sure, we all had broken the rules when we were kids. I recalled plenty of times I'd left the company of Liesle, Milti, and other village kids to explore the jungle alone. But still, as a parent, I had to at least provide a means for the children to obey. I expected Eruwan or Fionn would fly him; they were swift fliers, and old enough to be on the roads alone.

Su joined me on the pillows as I unsealed Mr. Onoretti's letter. I recognized my commissioner's handwriting. Only Su had prettier handwriting, lush with curls and perfect forms. Liesle was a master painter, but tended to write sloppily. I seldom needed to write anything more than my name, which was barely legible in my script.

I read it aloud for Su. "Mr. Lasteran, I hope this correspondence finds you well. You've no doubt been inundated with news of the crystalight deposit found under your own village. It's been several days and still our hands are tied in bureaucratic mud and sludge, so we haven't been allowed to even survey the site, let alone mine it."

"Mud and sludge?" Su repeated. "I thought this was a business letter, not personal. The Mr. Onoretti I know would never put such foul language in a business proposition."

"Maybe he's reached an age where he doesn't care, or he knows he can get away with it." He'd been with the merchants of light for so long and done so much for them, they'd *never* get rid of him.

Su shrugged and rested his cheek on my arm.

I continued reading. "The upper administration of the merchants of light have been frantically trying to resolve any legal disputes. The Iurion are furious that this deposit was not found within Iuria. They are accustomed to profiting off mining extraction rights. The Imperial Aloutian courts are still arguing over who owns the deposit, though I suspect their ruling will go to the vassal nation of Seabells. I've contacted your Representative to let her know I'd pay a higher price than usual for extraction rights. I even brought up your name and mentioned you were a respected citizen of Seabells and one of the merchants of lights' master sculptors. From a purely monetary perspective, it would be more cost-effective to pay a little extra to ensure I acquire the mining rights if it allows us to save on transportation and security fees. Hiring you as the primary sculptor is an obvious move. This letter is to inform you that I am happy to sell you as many crystalights as we can extract, assuming all my plans go through and I do end up purchasing the mine. I will be arriving in Steena Village on Veter Thirty."

Su jolted up. "That's tomorrow!"

I checked the chore board where we wrote the calendar dates. He was right. Damn, the days had flown by...

I finished the last few lines of the letter. "I hope to see you in person to discuss details of the arrangement, though I will not burden you for hospitality. There is no need for you to host me or my apprentice, as we will not be staying long. I will be surveying the mine if you wish to find me. Best regards, Giorvi Onoretti."

I leaned my head back against a pillow. "He'll be here tomorrow."

"Shall I make sure your business attire is ready?"

I rubbed my hands over my face, frustrated and anxious. "I'll do it." The idea of dressing in hot, stuffy business clothes made me miserable already. At least I still had the Gods' blessing, or else the heat would be insufferable.

Mr. Onoretti never mentioned Tawny. He must not have known. It wasn't like news of her death would be important to anyone outside the village, anyway. Whoever reported about the crystalight mine to the merchants of light wouldn't have cared.

I wasn't sure if that was better or worse. On one hand, it hurt to think no one outside the family cared about the one event most distressing in my life. On the other hand, it was a private matter and I didn't think I could bear the public attention.

"Are you going to tell him?" Su asked.

He didn't have to clarify what he meant.

"I think I should. It'll be obvious, anyway. You know I can't hide my emotions."

"Nor should you. Still, I'm not sure how appropriate it would be. I'm not very good at talking to bosses, Ami-honey. It's hard for a Godblood to play submissive."

Had I been in a more playful mood, I would have joked about how he sometimes played submissive to me. I didn't have any humor inside me. Not now. It was too soon.

The flapping of wings outside indicated one of the kids was about to enter. Su had opened his mouth, perhaps to say one of the many dirty jokes I'd thought of, but was unwilling to make, but the words died in his mouth. Our sons entered.

Fionn sniffed and rubbed puffy eyes. Heliodor was staying strong.

"Do you need anything, son?" Su asked.

"No. I'll be fine. It's just..." He sighed. "Never mind. You'll both just get upset."

Su rose to embrace our son. I followed, but was slower in getting up. Su held his short-haired mane and kissed his forehead. "Fionn, you know that only makes us *more* worried about you. If you have something on your mind, you should tell us. We can't heal as a family if we keep our thoughts bottled inside."

He extracted his claws. Usually a sign of aggression in Wynnles, but Fionn did it when he was nervous. "I'll keep it bottled up if I have to. I want to say it, but... well, if you get mad at me, I'll never share again."

"I won't get mad," I said. "I promise." I was too exhausted to feel such heightened emotions anyway.

"I could never be mad at you," Su said.

Fionn wiped the tears from his eyes. "Back when Tawny... was alive, I used to carry her to Kiwi Island."

All three of us had explicitly forbidden the kids from flying Tawny over Deep Sea. I had suspected a few instances of disregard for our rules, but I'd never pressed them since I had no proof. The only reason I had the hunch was because Tawny would occasionally come home with a basket full of kiwis. The only nearby kiwis were the ones on the island.

"And Demitris," Fionn added. "He and Tawny liked to play together, so he'd ask me to carry him to the island, too. They'd pick so many kiwis we couldn't carry them all back home. Well, Demitris just said that he never wanted to go to the island again. He only ever wanted to go if Tawny could go with him."

I patted my son's shoulder while Su held him close. Fionn released his pent-up emotions in a deluge of tears and cathartic wailing. All we could do was be there with him, to bear witness to his grief.

I had to work on my commission. I'd gone too long without working on it. Already I knew it would be late, and I knew I'd be forgiven due to the circumstances, but if I could finish just a little bit tonight, before Mr. Onoretti arrived tomorrow...

Su walked with me to my ateli and looked out toward the beach. The shore was littered with driftwood, palm fronds, washed-up debris, and the kids' balls and clubs. A flock of pink gulls scavenged for the remnants of dinner. Deep Sea would take and absorb any remaining biological material later.

"I'm going to clean up after the kids," Su said. "I'll get their equipment before Deep Sea takes it. I'll wash your pretty, yellow business outfit tonight and let it dry in the lemontine room of my ateli. It won't pick up any odors there, I promise."

"Wait, Sugar, before you go..." I sighed, not wanting to ask the question I was about to ask. "I think Liesle still needs some space. Should we sleep in the living room tonight? Let her sleep alone?"

He frowned. Even when he was displeased, his face was perfection. Fuck, I wanted to kiss him repeatedly, and all over his body. Perhaps pinch his butt, too.

"That's a good idea, Ami-honey."

I'd forgotten what I'd said, then got lost in my own fantasies. For a second, I thought he was suggesting that it was a good idea to pinch his butt.

"I'll sleep on the pillows," he said. "If you come in after I've fallen asleep, you can cuddle with me."

Oh, right, sleeping away from Liesle...

"Same to you. If I'm in first and fall asleep, you can lay close to me."

Su smiled ever so sweetly and went on his way to clean up the beach.

I kept the key to my ateli in my antelope skull. I reached for the visor hanging just to the side of the door before opening it all the way. I hated being blinded by such bright light.

The visor sat comfortably around my head, cushioned by my mane. The dark-tinted glass over my eyes blocked the harmful effects of looking directly at a raw crystalight.

The figure of the Lagodore girl shone as brightly as when I last saw her. She was going to shine for seventy more years, according to Mr. Onoretti, and probably wouldn't start to dim for sixty. Like most crystalights, it originally had an eighty-year life span, but it had waited ten years in a storeroom somewhere before a merchant of light became available. I had heard whispered rumors that the mine discovered ten years ago had been fully extracted, but the last crystals in storage were almost all carved and sold. Had the mine under Steena Village never been found, I might have run out of crystals to carve. Not that I would have been out of a job; merchants of light supplied light in all its forms—growing glowlight lotuses, chandlery, oil production... I had dabbled in chandlery when I was younger. It wasn't much to my liking, but it was a worthwhile skill to have. We produced gwenyn wax right here in Steena Village, too—Piotr himself was the apiarist providing wax and honey—and scents, wicks, and cinnadyme were easily made with local materials.

I sat at my desk and extended my claws.

I scratched tiny pieces away. Even the tiniest flake was valuable. I brushed them into a container hanging off the side of the table. I could sell those back to my commissioner. Not that it would matter since I made the maxima, but it would provide material to other merchants of light who specialized in making miniatures or who used crystalights as tiny ornamentation on a bigger project.

Aloutia was a country of economic equity. No matter how much I worked, I would only be paid the maxima for the month. After I hit my quota, I might as well stop. Some people didn't like the implementation of the maxima. They wanted to make enough money to sneer down upon their neighbors while sitting comfortably on a silver throne in a bejeweled castle. Aloutian morals taught that such greed was filth. The greatest of sins. Mind elementals went to the extreme and were forbidden from ever using money. Anyone who wanted to make an obscene amount of money was welcome to leave for Cosmo. Or Ophidia, if they were a woman, where you could put a price tag on anything from a bean to a man's life.

But Aloutia was safe. No one starved or died to random acts of violence. As bitter as I was about Tawny's death, it couldn't be blamed on a person. A God maybe, but that was beyond my comprehension.

No one starved...

The statue in my hand was one of a Lagodore girl.

Usana. So skinny Su could count her ribs.

Was Miltico starving her? Su said Usana should get healthier now that she's in Aloutia where she could get plenty of food. Perhaps I should wait and see what Usana looks like in a week or two... How long would it take for the weight gain to become noticeable?

And if she didn't get healthier, what would I do? I had to get her away from Milti, and if I confronted him, he might take her back to Cosmo where she'd be in worse danger. I needed to get the lawkeepers involved. They may have avoided Steena Village on principle, but surely they'd come to help a starving child.

What if I was wrong about everything? Maybe Miltico *was* trying to be a good father and he brought Usana here to become healthy. As far as spanking... well, it's not something *I* would have done, but it wasn't illegal. I did not know if corporal punishment was child abuse or not. Su would have said it was and condemned it as cruel. Liesle's parents had believed in it, and she had a more ambivalent attitude toward it.

Soon after Eruwan hatched, the topic of discipline had come up. Liesle had said she was spanked as a child and 'turned out fine.' Su had then told her: "you didn't turn out fine. You turned out thinking it was okay to hit a child." We agreed then and there that we'd never hit our children. Sometimes it was difficult finding ways to teach them. Sometimes I couldn't do it myself, nor could Liesle. Su used to take Fionn aside and talk with him, even if it took hours. Cohaku had different kinds of behavioral problems which Su couldn't always fix. We built her a tree house made of bones where she could hide when she was overwhelmed, and it had worked well for her so far. It was her safe space, where no one would pester her.

As for me, I was never spanked as a child. My own mother could not have done it even if she'd wanted to. She was a quadruped with no hands. I went into fatherhood with no strong opinion on the matter.

If it hadn't been for Su, would Liesle and I have spanked our children? I wasn't certain. Perhaps. While it didn't bring me any great joy to think of now, I may have grown into a different kind of father if I hadn't met Su.

I never knew my biological father. He knew my mother long enough to conceive me, then left. I didn't even know his name. My surname, Lasteran, came from my mother. Per Aloutian custom, boys took the father's surname and daughters took the mother's surname, but for lack of knowing my father, I took my mother's surname. My sons were Lasterans, and their sons would be Lasterans. What was once a matrilineal name had become patrilineal. My daughters were Denwalls like Liesle.

Su did not have biological children, so none of our children were born Scrimshanders. For one, he did not wish to tell anyone what his sex was. If he made Liesle pregnant, or if I made him pregnant, it would be obvious whether he had a penis or a uterus, and he didn't want that knowledge announced to the world. Secondly, he did not want anyone to know his element. He was a half-Spirit, the child of a God, and his biological children would be quarter-Spirits. A young quarter-Spirit developing their magic powers wouldn't understand Su's desire for secrecy and might accidentally use magic in a way that would reveal the element.

Su was not born a Scrimshander, either. He claimed to have been born with the surname of whichever God was his parent. He had changed his public name when he moved to Aloutia, taking the name of his occupation. A scrimshander was one who scrimshaws, the art of carving images into bone.

He had shared with me in private that he dreamt of having a lineage by name, if not by blood. He'd be the happiest person alive if one of our kids became a Scrimshander. Anyone could change their name legally upon turning fifteen, though it was usually done in cases where a child wished to be perceived as the opposite sex from the one they were at hatching, or if they despised their same-sex parent strongly enough that they wished to be rid of that parent's name.

If nothing else, Su had the lighthouse named after him. He'd built it, so he had naming rights.

Chip, scratch, scrape...

The sculpture was almost done. Had it not been for the week's events, I would have finished it a few days ago. I doubted Mr. Onoretti would be too upset with me. Still, I was in a better mood than usual, so I felt I ought to get some progress made. For once, I didn't have that lumpy feeling in the back of my throat threatening to strangle me. That sensation had rarely left since Tawny's passing. I'd started to think that lump would become my third spouse, so often was it my faithful companion.

Su. Think of Su.

Yes, that improved my mood. The lump on my hyoid vanished; my baculum rose instead.

Just keep thinking about Su. Nothing else. No one else.

Chip away at the crystal. I'd done this so often, I could carve while my mind wandered. I didn't need to focus on my work. I could think about my Sugar instead. His lovely brown eyes, his flowing hair, his sweet kisses...

I was happy.

It was late when I left my ateli. Several moons and Aloutia's rings shone, reflected in Deep Sea, but even without them, my tail lit the way. Surely by now everyone else would be asleep.

I pushed aside the leaf door, expecting to see Su curled up on the pillows. At night, we put nio-blue[1] drapes over our crystalights to dim them, but it had the added effect of making the room resemble an undersea cavern aglow with azure serenity.

Liesle was asleep on the pillows instead, sleeping on her back, with an arm around Nio. My wife's belly protruded; she was due to lay her egg soon.

I pet Maika's head as she came to sniff me. She'd been sleeping in the living room, too. Usually, she slept in Fionn and Heliodor's room.

Why was Liesle out here instead of in the bedroom? Did she have an argument with Su? I went into the bedroom and found him laying on his side, facing away from the door. His backside was a sight to behold, but he was asleep. I wouldn't do anything uncouth. I lay beside him and fell under Somniel's influence[2].

1. Neon blue. Nio's name comes from this word, though she is not actually nio-blue.

2. Aloutian poetic way to describe sleep. Somniel is the Demigoddess of Sleep.

Su Interlude

Liesle sat in the darkness with her tail's light extinguished, curled against the wall. Her pregnant belly prevented her from curling as tightly as she might have otherwise. Su entered and sat on the end of their bamboo mat. He'd been gathering the courage to speak to Liesle for a few hours, to ask her if he could do anything for her, but now that he was here, his courage fled. Heart racing, he dreaded saying words that would ruin their relationship forever.

"Lisi-honey, can we talk?" He could not hide the quaver in his voice.

Silence pervaded the darkness.

"Please." Su scooted closer so he could touch her knee. "I don't understand—"

"Don't touch me!"

His hand froze an inch away from her knee. Cautiously, he drew back. "Okay. I won't touch you."

Her hands tensed, clutching her legs. "How dare you think you can play with my mind like you've been doing with Amiere."

Su's breath caught in his throat. When he tried to speak, nothing but a pitiful sob came out.

Liesle raised her head, glaring with vicious eyes, pupils thinned in rage. "Go. Go use your mind-control powers to seduce him."

"I... have *never* done that! Amiere has grown obsessed with me all on his own."

"He's different after you touch him. You hypnotized him to stop him from killing Miltico, so what's preventing you from hypnotizing him to get whatever else you want?"

"A moral code," he replied. "I have *only* ever used my powers to control him when it's been to stop him from making a mistake that would ruin everything. If he killed Miltico, all of our lives would be changed for the worse. He'd be jailed, if not exiled, and we'd be lucky if we weren't exiled to Cosmo, too."

"How do I know you're telling the truth?"

Su shrugged, slapping his knees as he brought his hands back down. "I don't suppose there is any way to prove it, but if I have to *prove* myself to you, perhaps this arrangement wasn't for the best. If I am in the way of your love with Amiere, I will go."

"Stop it." Liesle's demanding voice came out as a growl. "I'm not telling you to leave. I may be angry with you, but I still love you. But you need to stop what you're doing with Amiere."

Su took a deep breath to calm his nerves and collect his thoughts. "Like I said, Ami-honey's thoughts toward me are his own. I suspect he's become obsessed with me as a way of coping with Tawny's death. His mind is swimming in despair and sorrow, but if thinking of me can bring him a moment of joy—a brief escape from his pain—then why deny it to him? Don't you want him to be happy, too?"

Liesle closed her eyes, fighting back tears. "I want nothing *but* his happiness... but I want to be happy with him."

"I don't know what to tell you, Lisi-honey," Su said. "If you want to join us, I'm sure Amiere would love that."

"No. Not right now. I don't even want to think about sex. I don't know how either of you can, so soon after..." She trailed off, unable to say the most painful words in the dominion.

"Everybody copes differently." Su put his hand over his heart, still thumping so wildly. "He copes through physical touch."

Liesle's mane bristled. "I know how it works, Su. I... I need to be left alone. Just give me some space."

Fearing an argument would break out again if he did not leave her alone, Su obliged. He paused after pushing aside the leaf door. "Please, at least get some sunlight. And if you want to sleep alone, I'll stay out. I'll keep Amiere out, too."

"No, I'll sleep out there. You two can have the bedroom." Her voice didn't signal any anger—just exhaustion.

Su had no desire to push her on the subject. "Alright. If you need anything, just ask."

Liesle buried her head in her knees and stayed silent.

Cohaku Interlude

Earlier in the evening, as her father worked in his ateli, Cohaku and Eruwan took Demi home together. He rode Eruwan's back, but Cohaku went with them so Eruwan wouldn't be alone on the way home. Even though Eruwan was old enough to go alone, Cohaku didn't want to be around Fionn. He had started crying, and she didn't know how to cheer him up. She didn't *want* to cheer him up. Cohaku hated him; even thinking about what he said to her in the past made her want to grind her teeth until they were as flat as herbivore teeth. It wasn't like he would ever truly be a good big brother. Cohaku believed with all her soul that he'd only gotten close to Tawny because he wanted the parents to believe he was nice. He was never nice to Cohaku.

They flew above the treetops so as not to get in the way of anyone below, but close enough to the ground that they heard a loud, painful wail from a ground-dweller. It came from the tamarind grove close to a house that had once been empty. Previously, it had been a guesthouse. Now Mr. Svelt—not the kindly old shopkeeper, but his mean, grouchy son—was living there.

Eruwan stopped in midair, letting the magic in her wings hold her aloft without having to flap them. Cohaku had to flap a few times until she found balance.

"You hear that?" Eruwan asked.

How could she not? It was loud and annoying, like a baby screeching. Cohaku hated babies. She was glad Nio had never screamed, else she wasn't sure she could like her little sister.

Eruwan descended into the tamarind grove.

"Wait for me, Sis!" Clumsy Cohaku made more noise than she wanted to admit as she brushed through thick leaves, entwined branches, and swooping vines and lianas.

It was Usana, kneeling by a tamarind tree, holding a long, thin branch that had fallen off. Sparks danced on her horns when she let out loud sobs.

"Are you okay?" Eruwan asked.

Usana startled. Cohaku was surprised Usana hadn't heard her falling through the canopy. With those big ears of hers, she should have been able to hear a gwenynen buzzing in Lek[1] . Maybe her own crying had drowned out the noise. She dropped the branch and stood, though her goat-legs were so skinny and shaking that Cohaku thought she'd fall over again.

"L-l-lions!" she screamed. "Stay back!" Her horns flickered. Little strings of electricity twirled around them. Her big, floppy ears, held up by her horns, absorbed some of the sparks. Did she think Wynnles could be hurt with electricity? Maybe she didn't know they were Lightning elementals. The two girls had their tails wrapped in leaves since they didn't want to hurt Demi, and the only other time Usana had seen them had been when she was introduced to the class—another place where they kept their tails covered.

"You're the girl in my class, aren't you?" Cohaku asked. The time she'd seen her had been brief. She had never seen a Lagodore-Yosoe hybrid before her, but maybe the girl in her class had a sister. Cohaku was face-blind. Unless she knew a person well, most people of any given species looked the same in her eyes. To her, Usana just looked like any Lagodore with Yosoe horns and hooves.

"Yeah, that's her!" Demitris said, peering over Eruwan's shoulder.

"We're not lions," Eruwan said.

Cohaku puffed up her chest and crossed her arms. "Yeah! Besides, it's rude to call people by the name of the animal they came from."

Usana bolted, wailing. She dropped the tamarind branch as she fled.

Eruwan chased after her. "Wait! It's dangerous here!" Demi clutched onto her shoulders to stay on. Cohaku followed but was nowhere near as fast as either of them.

"Lions!" Usana cried as she fled. "Lions! Daddy, save me! Lions! Daddy!"

Cohaku's wings, arms, and face got disheveled by foliage as she tried to keep up with Eruwan. She got a few small cuts, but the only other Wynnle around to smell it was Eruwan. Blood-related family members couldn't make each other go berserk.

They broke through a line of koa trees near where a bold carambola tree spread its branches over the guest house where Mr. Svelt lived now. The Yosoe man, sitting on a wicker chair on his porch with a drink in his hand, watched his daughter race up the creaky, rotted wooden planks serving as steps to the porch. The Wynnles had approached from his left side, and since his left eye was scratched and milky white, Cohaku didn't think he could see them.

"Daddy! Save me!" Usana dove between his legs as he stood up.

Mr. Svelt nearly stumbled as the girl knocked him off balance. "The fuck is wrong with you? Where's the switch I told you to get? If you make me fall, you know what'll happen to you."

---

1. City on the opposite side of planet Aloutia from Steena Village. An idiomatic expression stating that a person's senses should be spectacular.

"I'm sorry, Daddy. I'm sorry. Lions! Save me!"

Mr. Svelt turned and saw them with his one good eye.

"Go hide in your cage."

"Yes, Daddy." Usana scurried into the house. A dark, depressing structure—no lights shone through the windows. Even though they had drapes over them, Cohaku thought she should have been able to see a little light coming out from the sides. The whole place smelled funny to her, though she did not know what the smell *was*. At least it wasn't a durian...

Cohaku shook, terrified. She just wanted to help Usana. Eruwan stood, strong and brave, clutching Demi's legs around her torso. Even Demi wore a fearless, scowling expression.

"I'm sorry we scared your daughter, Mr. Svelt," Eruwan said. "We heard her crying and—"

"Fuck off!" he yelled. "She's none of your concern. Stay away from her."

"Hey!" Cohaku called, finding her courage. "I'm in her class, so I have to be around her no matter what you say."

"Yeah! Me, too!" Demi added his support to his cousins' words.

"Does this look like a fucking Mind church?" Mr. Svelt raised his hands, waving chaotically toward the trees. He was still holding his drink, some of which spilled out. "No? Then you have no reason to be near her. Go back home to your ugly woman-dad."

What was he talking about? Who was a woman-dad?

"Don't ever talk about our parents like that," Eruwan said. Her voice was low, threatening. Cohaku wondered if Eruwan would actually hit Mr. Svelt. If she drew blood, she'd go berserk... Would Cohaku have to let Eruwan bite her to calm down? Wynnles could only stop their berserker rampage in a few ways, and the only safe way for children was to taste the freshly-drawn blood of a relative.

"That fish-freak isn't your parent. Don't pretend it is."

"Su is our dad just as much as Amiere is," Eruwan said sternly.

"You *call* him Amiere?" Mr. Svelt sounded shocked.

"What? No! I call him Papami. I'm only calling him by his name so *you* understand."

"Disgusting. You know what the name Amiere means, don't you? Is he molesting you?"

Eruwan went silent. Demi swallowed nervously.

Mr. Svelt turned to Cohaku next. "What about you? Does your *Amiere* molest you, too?" He said his name in such a... *weird*... way. It made her uncomfortable. But what did 'molest' mean? She had never heard that word before.

Eruwan grabbed Cohaku's hand while hefted Demitris up with her other hand. "Let's go, you two. We've heard enough."

Codex Dominex: Wynnles' Berserker Phase

Wynnles will enter a 'berserker' phase if they:

- draw blood from prey using teeth, claws, or a wielded weapon
- taste blood
- smell a significant amount of blood (a small cut or scrape will not trigger berserker phase)

All of the above conditions assume the blood belongs to someone they are not related to. A Wynnle will NEVER enter a berserker phase if the blood belongs to a close blood relative (parents, grandparents, children, grandchildren, siblings, uncles, aunts, nieces, nephews, cousins.) Their 'prey' can be anything that bleeds, whether it's a sapienti person, an animal, or a demon.

During berserker phase, a Wynnle's mind becomes obsessed with one of two thoughts, depending on the source of the blood:

- killing and eating (prey)
- achieving orgasm (with a sexual partner)

A Wynnle can be difficult to reason with while they are in berserker phase. The intensity of their rage will determine how much they must consume of their prey before calming down again. If they are truly enraged against someone they despise, they may not be satisfied until they've eaten the whole body. If they kill an enemy they do not have any personal feelings for, such as a combatant in a war, a single bite can turn them back to normal. Often, when hunting or slaughtering animals, a Wynnle will take a single bite of raw meat to satisfy their craving, then take the rest home to cook or share with their family/community.

One of the most important caveats to remember is that Wynnles are, and always are, sapient. They never truly lose control of themselves. They can be reasoned with and calm down on their own if they see the logic in doing so.

A Wynnle's berserker phase ends if one of the following conditions are met:

- their prey is killed and at least one piece has been eaten.
- they achieve an orgasm. Obviously, only feasible for adults. In some communities, individuals are encouraged to masturbate if they go berserk on accident.
- they bite (lightly, non-fatal) a relative. This can still cause damage to the bitten individual, thus Wynnle families will rarely use children or smaller members except in an emergency. Due to a lack of alternative options for children who go berserk, children are instructed by their parents to bite them.
- they ingest certain drugs or are afflicted by mind-altering magic.
- they fight the urges through sheer willpower.

Note:

the term 'berserker' comes from a word meaning 'bear shirt' which, in Pentagonal Dominionist etymology, originated in the Kreuz Dominion alternate timeline, then went to the Nureshian and Slevan Dominions. There are no bears in the Pentagonal Dominion timeline. Present-day Wynnles sometimes invent myths about what they think bears are.

Chapter Seven: Light Rain

The next morning, I woke up entangled with Su.

Every morning, the first taste of the day was the ever-renewed dread of Tawny's death, then a longing for those good old days, and a wish—a hope, a prayer—that it was all a terrible nightmare, and that *this* time I would wake up and she'd be home.

This day, my dread subsided, quickly replaced with shame and guilt. My face was buried in Su's luscious brown hair while my hands held tight around his torso, my legs wrapped around his, and my penis stood erect against the bone between his buttocks.

Ugh, how could my body make such lewd movements and yet still betray me by making me think of my child first thing in the morning? Shameful. Disgusting. I hoped Tawny, wherever she was in the afterlife, never heard about this...

"Are you finally awake, Ami-honey?" Su asked. He reached behind to scratch my leonine ears and pet my mane. My ears twitched; only then did I notice the pattering of rain on our leafy roof. Fuck, was it rainy season already? I hadn't checked the weather calendar in a while... not since Tawny's passing. We hadn't insulated the whalebone supports for rain recently.

"I'm awake," I replied. "Do you want me to move?"

"No, you can stay like this." He pushed against me with his hips. My penile spines brushed against his skin. Gods it felt good. To me, at least... but was he okay? It didn't poke or hurt, did it? I did not draw blood; I would have known, as it would have triggered my berserker phase.

I needed to get up, get breakfast started, get the kids ready for school, and do some work, but... this delicious mass of meat and bones was all I could think about. No... he had no earrings in. I couldn't do that to him. I pushed myself away and sat up on the reed-mat bed. The scent of cinnadyme wafted in from the living room. Liesle must have been awake already and lit a stick of incense.

"If you want to put in an earring, do so," I said. "I'm ready for anything."

"Are you sure?" he asked. "Do you believe you want to have sex of your own free will? Or am I hypnotizing you?"

It was too early in the morning for mental exercises. "I know it's my own free will, Sugar. If you were going to hypnotize someone for sex, why would you pick a Wynnle man?"

He giggled. "Perhaps the pain is part of the pleasure."

"You've never enjoyed pain in any other context. No, I know you aren't controlling my mind or sexual appetite. I'm fully capable of loving you on my own."

"In that case, I am ready for your love, too. You can pretend I'm wearing any of my earrings. I'll put them in once I'm dressed."

I nestled on top of Su, pinning his upper hands to the reed-mat bed, the contact of our flesh warming each other, bringing our souls closer together. His lower arms embraced my head and pulled me in for a kiss. The taste of his lips rang a nostalgic bell, a memory of happier times. Cinnadyme and the aroma of Su's sexuality invaded my nostrils, daring me to go further, to press my tongue into him, to grip his wrists with all the strength I was worth, to pummel his thighs with my thick, thorny cock.

Raindrops hitting our leaf roof disguised our noises from the rest of the family. Thankfully, Su was quiet during these activities. Liesle had always been the loudest of our triad, but that was common for Wynnle and Nilian women, for whom the scratching of a male Wynnle's penis inside them was like scratching a year-long itch they couldn't reach.

We delighted in each other's affection for quite some time, but eventually, guilt drove me to break away. As much as I wanted to spend the whole day loving Su, I had other jobs. I wasn't just a husband; I was a father and merchant of light.

"We need to get going," I said as I stood up. My cock was erect but faltering. Weakening. It would be flaccid in a moment, then I could put a grass skirt on without concern.

Su touched it, running his fingers up my shaft so as not to prick himself on the spines. "Wait." He crawled on his hands and knees to a drawer where he kept his bone jewelry. Even though I'd just been grabbing his ass, seeing it was another delight. Beads of sweat dotting his rear glistened in the crystalight. The way the bone sat perfectly down his crack was captivating. How I wished my baculum was in that bone's spot.

He took out a specific earring: a jawbone. I wasn't sure what animal it had once belonged to, but I knew its symbolism: oral pleasure.

"If you want, Ami-honey?"

"Oh yes I do, Sugar."

He crawled toward me. His lower two hands grabbed my ass, and one stroked my tail. His upper hands held mine. And his mouth... oh Gods, Su's mouth...

I never understood how he didn't get poked by the spines. I felt his tongue and lips, the gentle bristling of his teeth tickling my barbs, yet I never drew blood. I never went berserk. However Su managed to perform oral sex on me without bleeding in his mouth, I wouldn't complain.

My gorgeous Sugar. There was something empowering and gratifying about seeing a Godblood on his knees before me, servicing *me* instead of the other way around. Whoever Su's parent was could have me condemned to Hell or Solitude or wherever Gods sent blasphemers, but for these glorious, ephemeral moments, I was the God here. The God of the Bedroom, holy and mighty. Oh, who was I kidding? If it weren't for Su, I'd have been impotent. No man who couldn't even keep his dick up could claim to be a God of Sex.

He brought me to climax and swallowed the evidence.

Sweat drenched my mane. I'd have to bathe in Deep Sea after this. Or at least take a step outside. The rain pounded harder.

"Better?" Su asked as he stood. "Ready to work hard today?"

"If I have the stamina for it."

He patted my chest. "You'll have energy today, I promise. I'm going to work in my ateli, then meet with the Chak-Dens to discuss the upcoming fire feast. Shall we go into the village together? You can go to the mine and meet with Mr. Onoretti. We can walk together for a while, anyway. Share an umbrella..."

"I *do* need to talk to Mr. Onoretti. Tell him about... what happened."

Su dressed in a grass skirt and more bone jewelry. "I have your formal business attire ready in my ateli. I'll bring it back to the house when I'm ready to depart."

"Thanks. First things first, though. Breakfast. The kids will be pestering us soon enough if we don't get it started."

"Of course. Let's go." Atop his head, he put on the skull of an animal called a susi[1], which we often joked was his full name.

"Susi-Su," I said. A tinge of regret pained my sternum; that had been what Tawny would call him when he wore the susi skull.

Su grinned a big, wide smile. The bones framing his face—the jawbone earrings, the fangs and vertebrae choker, the susi's tusks—made him look like a king. An oddly happy king surrounded by symbols of death.

"You're not upset?" I asked. "Calling you... that?"

"Why would I be? I'd like to keep her memory alive. I am working on a memorial for her, you know. I'd like to place it in the living room when I'm done."

I lowered my head, unable to find the words that properly expressed my emotions. Hell, I didn't know what my own emotions were.

With nothing else to say, we left the bedroom and moved on with our day.

The living room was awash in its usual daytime colors, reds and blues and yellows, mixing and turning to white. The blue drapes had been removed, but it had not been Liesle who'd done it, as I had thought. Eruwan and Fionn worked together in the kitchen, slicing fruits while Liesle and Nio continued to sleep.

---

1. An animal like a wild boar, known for its massive tusks. It is against Spiritism to domesticate them, as they will become near-sapient (and thus ineligible to be eaten) if they become pigs.

They must have been the ones to light the cinnadyme incense, too. The kitchen was typically only used to slice fruits or prepare plates, but when it was raining, we used the hearth to cook. They had the giant rice wok cooking over the coals now.

"You two are up early," I said.

"Mamali hasn't been well," Eruwan said as she sliced her claws through a steena. "We thought we should do her job until she's better."

Fionn glanced downward. "Uh, I know Cohaku's favorite fruit is a pitaya. Do you think she'd eat one if she knew I'd cut it?"

"Just let her cut it," Eruwan said. "She likes pitayas because they're so easy to open and eat without making a mess. I think the rice is done. Can you fill up the plates?"

He set the large, spiky fruit in the red dolphin skull and went to the cupboards where we stocked our patella plates. I supposed we'd have to reapply snowbark resin to them soon, too. If Su planned to put resin on our house's bones for rainy season, he might as well get some extra so we could coat the other bones we used in our daily life. Some of the patellae would have to be tossed into Deep Sea soon, though. Resin could only do so much before the bones had to be recycled.

The other kids woke up while Su and I got yesterday's fish out from the ground oven—an ahi nearly half my height. The leaves had prevented most of the rain from getting inside, but I'd have to put our proper rainy season covering over it today. We had a tarpaulin in storage, and it was easily constructed.

Liesle slept through breakfast. We considered waking her up, but ultimately decided it was best to let her sleep if she was this exhausted. The rest of us sat around the vertebra table, eating today's fish, rice, and sliced fruit. Rain continued to pour outside, but the conversation had grown lively enough, I barely heard it.

Eruwan and Cohaku told me Liesle had been asleep here in the living room when they'd come in after taking Demitris home.

"Mamali was asleep while Nio played with toys," Eruwan said. "I didn't want to wake her up. She's been... angry, I guess, lately. Papa Su and Papami were in their atelis. Fionn and Heliodor were in their bedroom."

"I wasn't doing anything weird," Fionn said with a tone of defensiveness I rarely heard from him. Usually, he was the one provoking others.

"No one said you were," Cohaku replied in a snide voice, trying to belittle him, though at least she didn't outright insult him. She used to call him an idiot. I couldn't blame her for being upset, after the bullying he'd put her through. I wished they could both put the past behind them. If Cohaku could only forgive Fionn, who was trying so hard to be a good big brother now... And yet I understood her feelings, too. It would be like asking me to forgive Miltico. Some things could never be forgiven.

During a moment of quietude, I let the melody of rain lull me into a meditative state. Liqua's holy waters washed away a layer of sorrow and cleansed my soul of a portion of guilt, but some sins couldn't be wiped away. Not even if Deep Sea tore my soul from my body and crushed my essence into marine snow. My hatred for Miltico would remain in the final particle of my being.

Fionn usually argued back when Cohaku spoke in that voice to him, but today he was resigned. Or maybe Tawny's death had broken him. Maybe he decided that being a good big brother was forever out of reach.

"I wanted to talk to you, Daddy," Cohaku said under her breath as she plucked out a chunk of pitaya. "But I didn't want to interrupt your work."

"I'm sorry I wasn't around," I said. "But I want you to know you can always interrupt me if I'm in my ateli. You can knock on the door, or put a letter down by the opening if you don't want to talk in person."

She blushed. "I-I know." Cohaku was sometimes scared to talk face-to-face, even to her family. No, 'scared' wasn't the right word. It was more of a discomfort, or a general inability. Like how Nio never spoke, even though she physically could if she wanted. Cohaku had moments where she preferred to think about her words carefully and write them down in a letter.

"We heard Usana crying by herself," Eruwan said. "We wanted to ask what was wrong, but she ran away when we approached."

"Mr. Svelt is a jerk," Cohaku added. "Usana's daddy, I mean. Not the nice shopkeeper." Due to her lisp, she pronounced 'shop' as 'sop.' She would have a temper tantrum if anyone tried to correct her.

"Yes, he is," Su said. "I'd like for everyone to stay away from him and his house."

"He works for his father now," Eruwan said. "I might bump into him if I'm with Nell since she likes to help out at the shop."

"I trust you to use your best judgment," Su replied as he set down his fork. "You should encourage Nell to stay safe, too. Perhaps it would be best if you went to her house whenever Miltico is at the shop."

Eruwan nodded in agreement.

Cohaku stared at me. She did that sometimes when she was lost in her thoughts. She'd stare at anyone or anything, but the other family members would ask her what was wrong. I was the only one who ignored it. I thought it would make her more comfortable if I pretended not to notice.

Heliodor nudged her hand with his head to get her attention. She ignored him, her gaze locked onto me.

"Sis, we gotta go to school. Are you gonna eat your fish?"

Cohaku scarfed it down in a few bites. "Okay, I'm ready."

"Will you ride on my back and hold the umbrella for me?"

"Duh!" She jumped up and searched the closet for one of our many bone-and-baleen umbrellas. She put on one of her usual sandals before I suggested otherwise.

"Why don't you wear your boots today? Help keep your feet from getting muddy."

"Oh, good idea."

We didn't have boots, but Gods save you if you ever referred to any piece of footwear as 'shoes' around Cohaku. The first time she ever lost a shoe and asked where it was, we thought she was asking where Su was. The fit she had as we tried to tell her Su was in his ateli was legendary.

Once the kids were properly dressed and had their lunches packed, we watched them fly to school.

Su put the dirty patella plates in a basket so he could carry them to Deep Sea for cleaning later. "I wonder what Cohaku wanted to tell you."

"She'll tell me when she's ready. She might have been scared to talk while everyone including Fionn was around."

"I suppose you're right," Su said in a dejected tone. "Anyway, you go to your ateli. Make some progress on your sculpture if you're so worried about Mr. Onoretti thinking you've been slacking. I'll have your clothes ready in an hour."

"And they won't get wet again in the rain?"

"They will stay dry, Ami-honey." His voice was exasperated. "Please, go do some work."

Before I headed out, I set out some coloring books and colored pencils for Nio, who was sitting in front of sleeping Liesle, watching her pregnant belly. Nio extended a claw like she was about to pop a balloon.

"Nio!" I roared, perhaps louder than I should have. Her tail flared in surprise.

She pulled her feline ears down, making a miserable face.

"Do *not* hurt your mother," I chided. I swallowed, taking on a gentler tone. "Come over here and color this picture for me."

Liesle stirred, and I hoped she would wake up, but all she did was roll to her other side.

My daughter wasn't listening. She stayed crouched down, tugging her ears.

What was I going to do? I couldn't take her into the ateli with me. I wasn't sure if she would keep the visor on, and it would be a dreadfully boring place for her. Was it safe to leave her alone with Liesle? I had to ask Su to watch her.

I picked Nio up, which she did not like. She didn't scream or cry—she never made noise—but she did wiggle to get away.

"Stop it. If I can't trust you to be nice to Mommy, you're going with Papa Su."

I carried Nio in one hand to hold the umbrella in the other. Nio would get even more temperamental if she got rained on.

She must have realized I was about to take her outside. She did something she'd never done before: she bit my arm.

"Ow!" Her sharp little predator teeth drew blood. I put her down and, holding her shoulders firmly, made her look me in the eyes. "That hurts! Never do that again!"

Tears welled in her eyes, though I suspected it was less from my scolding and more from the biological response. When Wynnles were lions and tigers, we had evolved not to hurt our own family. If we tasted the blood of a family member, we'd experience a sensation that I would confidently describe as 'trauma.' If we were in a berserker state from drawing an animal or non-relative's blood, then the taste of a family member's blood would knock us back to our senses, but it left powerful, emotional, *depressing* aftereffects.

Liesle sat up, groaning, and glared at us.

"Sorry to wake you," I said.

"It's okay, Mo Ami." Her voice was low and gravelly. "What happened?"

"Nio bit me. Nothing big. I'll—"

"She *what*?" Her pupils thinned. "Nio! Did you hurt your father?"

Nio crouched down and pulled her ears down. Her tail's spark went out.

"Are you bleeding?" my wife asked.

Nio hadn't bitten hard. Two small dots marked my arms, both disguised by my skin's natural brown stripes. A minute amount of clear blood had escaped, but the pinpricks were already clotting.

"It's nothing worth getting excited about," I replied. "I'll wash myself off in Deep Sea and be fine. I was going to have Su watch Nio while you slept."

"Don't worry about her," Liesle said. "I'm awake now. I'll calm her down."

"Thanks. Um, we made breakfast already. Would you like me to get you a plate?"

Liesle sighed and laid back down. "I'd appreciate it. The egg is getting to a size where it's difficult to move."

I filled a patella with rice, fish, and fruit. "It must be close to coming out. For every other pregnancy, whenever you got to this point, the egg would be out in a few days."

"Yeah. I hope... I want this one out."

I couldn't fathom what was going on in Liesle's head. Maybe some complex thoughts about children which she'd never had until Tawny's death. Would this be our last child? The thought had occurred to me that Liesle was getting old and would be unable to have more kids soon. Maybe Tawny's death was the Gods' way of telling us it was time to stop having kids.

Maybe... *I* wanted to stop having kids. The thought had never occurred to me before, but perhaps we had enough children. The idea of creating *another* child, only to watch that child depart this plane before me again, made me so sick I couldn't think straight, but there was a new aspect taking root in my skull. Would the baby inside Liesle now, or any future children, think they were meant to be replacements? Would we give them Tawny's old clothes and furniture? Would we feed them kiwis in hopes they would come to love them as much as she did? Would we make a little bell and put it on their tail?

I did not want to replace Tawny. I wished to find satisfaction in the family I had *now*.

That thinking was problematic in several ways, but I was in no mood to contemplate it. I'd rather think about Su. Or getting my commission finished on time. Or Su.

I handed Liesle her plate and went to my ateli to work.

The rhythmic pitter-patter of rain on my ateli's roof helped me concentrate. The Lagodore girl's features were coming along nicely. Her fingers had life-like detail.

When my mind wandered, it always went to Su. I imagined him in the rain, laying on the beach, sand clinging to his wet body. I pictured raindrops landing on his skin, on his ass, in his hair... the medley of bones he wore getting soaked. Then him smiling at me, inviting me to join him in the sand.

At least my distractions were pleasant now. I thought about Tawny less and less. And when I *did* think about her, my body's response wasn't to freeze and grow a lump that sat on my hyoid and made breathing more difficult than the most humid of days. Was this what it meant to cope? To heal? I still missed her. I still would have put myself through unbearable torture if it meant she'd be brought back to me. But thinking about her wasn't *painful* anymore. Tears didn't flow unbidden.

Life went on, and I had survived.

I wondered who had ordered this Lagodore crystalight. Was it for a small Lagodore child? Would she grow old enough to watch it dim one day? And then maybe... go out for good?

Dead crystalights lost value, though they were still worth the price of their artistic merit, assuming the merchant of light sculpted them skillfully. One might think they'd be common as family heirlooms or decorations, but that was not the case. The higher-ups in the guild encouraged customers to resell dead crystalights back to them. For years, rumors spread of former Guildmasters hiring ghostly Poltergeist[2] thieves to reclaim them. Such rumors were unfounded, without a single verifiable occurrence, but everyone had heard the tales.

What did upper administration do with dead crystalights? I'd never heard of them being resold. As far as I knew, they couldn't be recycled or otherwise made to light up anew, either. The only person I knew who might have an answer was Mr. Onoretti, but I didn't want to bother him with such silly ponderings. I recalled he had some dead crystalight sculptures in his office, but even if all the members of the guild's upper administration had an office full of dead crystalights, that

2. A species of sapienti people. They have historically been unfairly maligned as thieves due to their ability to become invisible and incorporeal.

would account for naught but a small fraction of all crystalights that had ever been created.

The rain brought out the strangest thoughts in me. I discarded my musings about dead crystalights and resumed thinking about Su instead.

I remembered he had asked me if my love was genuine or if I believed he was enthralling me with magic. With all my soul, I loved him. I adored him. Thinking about him helped ease the pain. To accuse him of seducing me through unethical means invalidated my feelings and volition.

I continued to fantasize about Su, as doing so made me remember what joy felt like. Ooh yes, beautiful Su...

Fionn Interlude

Fionn and his siblings flew to school together. He flew side by side with Eruwan, Heliodor bounded up and down like a dog, if dogs could fly. Cohaku could fly, but she wanted to ride on Heli's back. Fionn thought she was weird for doing it, and rude to Heli. Didn't she realize it made flying more difficult for him?

In the past, Fionn had always carried Tawny to school. He'd fly lower to the ground, in case he dropped her. He didn't want her to fall and get hurt. Gods, fate was sick and twisted. He swore inside his mind. He still missed her. How long would this pain last? Fionn wondered if he was the weakest one in the family for still wanting to cry.

"Is that Usana?" Eruwan asked, pointing forward and down to the path below them.

Fionn had good eyes but hadn't been looking down. Sure enough, Usana was there, wearing much thicker clothes than anyone should be wearing in the tropics. She was headed for the Mind church, alone and without lunch.

"I wonder if she'll just cry and have to go home again," Cohaku said. "Her Daddy's not with her, so he can't take her back home."

"What would happen to her then, Sis?" Heliodor asked. "Would one of the Mys Volkhvs have to watch her in a separate room?"

"Maybe. Or maybe they'd take her to the shopkeeper Mr. Svelt."

Fionn didn't feel right letting her walk alone. "I could go pick her up. Carry her to school."

"Wait, Fionn," Eruwan said. "Yesterday when Cohaku and I tried to talk to her, she flipped out about us being lions and ran back home. You might scare her."

"Oh... Maybe one of the volkhvs should talk to her about what Wynnles are."

They continued on their way.

Chapter Eight: Giorvi Onoretti

Su crossed the wet sand in his tall-heeled sandals, carrying my fancy business outfit in his lower two hands while his upper two hands each held an umbrella getting pelted in the downpour. The scent of petrichor mingled with cinnadyme. There was an energy in the air—an electricity unrelated to the spark on my tail which I'd have to cover soon if I intended to go into the village.

Traditional Aloutian business attire was meant to be colorful, vibrant, and so constricting that it was obnoxious to wear. Mine was a gaudy yellow with orange fur trim and tropical flower patterns. The flowers depicted on it were common here in Steena Village, but would have been an alluring foreignness to the stuffy businesspeople in Chernagora who never left their snow-capped mountains. The few times in the past I had worn it had been to guild meetings in Chernagora, where the Summershade shroomwolf[1] fur lining the collar and cuffs was pleasantly warm in the cold. Wearing it here, where my sweat slicked the fur as surely as it did my mane, it only made me more gracious to be blessed by Lord Flamboil.

I dressed with Su's help. The garments were a tight fit. They always had been... or perhaps I was getting chubbier.

"You're packing more meat on your bones," Su said as he patted my flabby belly. "Gonna make me work harder to get to your bone, hmm?" He laughed in his masculine manner and I hadn't been so aroused in, well... a few hours, honestly. Being around Su, surrounded by his infectious liveliness, was enough to make me wish I could kiss him and grab his ass.

He helped me arrange my mane, too. It was an absolute mess. He stood behind me, combing the top of my head while I braided my mustaches into my beard.

"I've heard that depression is like a seagull," Su said. "You can't stop it from flying overhead, but you can take care not to let it make a nest in your hair."

I snapped a bone bead into place on a braid beside my mouth. "The seagulls almost got me this time."

---

1. A fungal wolf with orange, red, and yellow fur.

"We will fight them off together, Ami-honey."

With Su's help, I acquired a more publicly-presentable appearance, and my soul felt more at ease. I was grateful to have Su here to fight away those pesky nest-making seagulls.

We walked into the village together, a pleasant stroll between the nearly impenetrable wall of bamboo stalks to either side of us, with koa trees and other green giants stretching their boughs to the sky. I held an umbrella in one hand while Su clung to my other arm. On our walk, the canopy prevented most of the rain from falling on us, but once in a while, a leaf would be unable to carry its burden, and it would unload a glob of water the size of my fist. I could not blame them; some days, I, too, could no longer hold the tears welling inside my lacrimals. The rainyday flowers[2] had opened and spread their roots so wide to absorb this precious moisture that some roots protruded out of the ground, even intruding on our dirt path. And as sure as slugs in rain... there were slugs. We took care not to step on any of them. Su practically danced and tip-toed to get around the slimy friends. He may have jumped away from me at times, but he always came back, wrapping his arms around mine and pressing his cheek close.

Was he as in love and obsessed with me as I was with him? Or was I just a foolish man projecting my fantasies? Surely if he wasn't infatuated with me, he wouldn't rub his cheek up and down my arm like he was doing. It was the same arm Nio had bitten earlier, but I'd nearly forgotten about that incident already.

Su released my arm when we reached the crossroad at the village proper, marked by a massive banyan tree. Signs had been posted on the low-hanging aerial roots pointing in the direction of various important buildings in the village. The Chak-Den family's house was down the right path, the same path one would take to go to the shop, as indicated by the sign. But my destination was to the left... to the once-beautiful park where Tawny had taken her last breath.

"If you finish your meeting early, check on me at the Chak-Den house," Su said. He stood on his toes to kiss me. "And don't be afraid of Mr. Onoretti. He's just a small Yosoe, and if he's angry at you for not working while you take time to grieve... well, that says a lot about him, doesn't it? If he doesn't sell you any crystalights, it's not the end of the world. Liesle and I can work extra to make up for any lost income."

"I won't let that happen." What kind of a failure of a husband would I be if my spouses had to work longer and harder to compensate for my weakness?

Su grimaced, leaving any hurtful words unspoken, and went down the path to the right of the banyan tree. I kept the umbrella so I could keep my clothes dry. Su could have brought an extra umbrella if he'd wanted, but the rain didn't bother

---

2. A tropical flower of the Pentagonal Dominion that opens its petals during rain

him or mess up his clothes. He took good care of his bone ornaments, periodically bathing them in snowbark resin.

Most people stayed indoors during the rain, but a few saw me walking by from their windows. Pitiful glances. Everyone in the village knew about Tawny's passing. Being that I was dressed for business, however, they probably knew what I was going to the crevice for.

I wondered if they thought I was 'over' her death. Did they think I had forgotten about my daughter, and that I was only interested in money and crystalights now?

I stopped in my tracks with a peculiar desire to correct everyone. As inane and time-consuming as it would have been, I felt like I owed all of Steena Village an explanation. What was I supposed to do, go to every house, crying, and show them how much I missed her?

No, that's what the fire feast was for. Su was managing that. *Just keep walking. Get to... that place. That place. That cursed place.*

The lands around Steena Village were blessed by the Gods? Laughable. This was accursed land now. Dead, forsaken, despised.

Maybe that was why I stopped. I hadn't been to the park since Piotr dragged me away, saving me from looking down into that Hell pit and seeing Tawny's body. I didn't want to face that fear again. That abyss terrified me; what if I looked down and saw something of hers? A spot of blood, a torn piece of cloth, a lock of hair? Did the folks who recovered her body really get everything? Was everything of her sawdusted? If a demon found a strand of her hair, could they reanimate her from that?

My breathing labored, my pulse quickened, and my eyes watered but at least I could blame that on the rain. Gods, I was a mess.

I pushed onward. The only way to calm my tempestuous mind was to go into the abyss. I had nothing to lose. If I found any of her remnants, I'd keep them and ensure they were sawdusted. If there was nothing, I'd be at ease, knowing the rescue team found her intact.

The park had once been a playground for children, but now it was barricaded. Military personnel in Aloutian red[3] uniforms watched for intruders. Many soldiers carried weapons, mostly halberds. Railings and scaffolds had been set up along the perimeter of the hole—a long scar in the ground, like the planet Aloutia was also damaged by this grievous sin. The scar was some two hundred feet or more long and thirty feet wide. I couldn't bear to consider its depth—how far Tawny had fallen. Its length penetrated into the thick jungle. Several trees had been knocked down, though they were cleared away now.

For centuries, lawkeepers and their ilk had not been welcome in Steena Village.

---

3. Burgundy

I supposed when and where money was involved and the land has lost the Gods' favors anyway, even ancient traditions were tossed out with yesterday's dinner.

When one lady halberdier approached, I assumed she was going to shoo me away.

"Mr. Lasteran?" she asked.

"Yes. Amiere Lasteran, merchant of light."

"Come on through." She spoke a dialect different from ours. Less Ebon influence, more pure Aloutian-English. I understood it perfectly when I heard it spoken to me, but speaking it from my own mouth was difficult. She guided me to the edge of the crevice where a ramp had been installed, descending into a shaft full of light. "Mr. Onoretti told us you might come here and instructed us to let you enter. Be careful around the fissure, especially in this rain. It's getting muddy and slippery. We don't want you falling in. Mr. Onoretti is surveying the mine currently."

I didn't have the heart to tell her that I knew far too well the dangers of falling into this accursed pit. Besides, I wasn't confident in my ability to speak her dialect. I thanked her for guiding me to the ramp.

As I descended into the abyss, I passed through clouds of lemontine burning in censers dangling from supports. I had never seen so much lemontine in one area. I supposed it was necessary when the cave beneath was full of raw crystalights that were prone to damage by humidity.

Most of the people coming in and out of the mine were Domovye, a species of genderless, legless slug-like people who grew to a length of twenty feet and a height nearly matching my own. The ramps had been constructed by them, for them, and could effortlessly hold their weight. I had always been one of the larger people in Steena Village and had gotten accustomed to treading lightly around houses made for smaller people. I didn't need to worry about being heavy where Domovye lived and worked.

There was no need for torches or lamps inside a crystalight cave. The crystals themselves provided lights so blinding, I was not surprised to be handed a visor by one of the Domovoi miners. "Protect your eyes, drook."

I did not fully comprehend the biology of the Domovye, but I understood they could control how much light hit their seeing-organs. I wasn't sure if they called them eyes, nor was I sure which of the stalks emerging from their faces had these organs.

They had a mouth for eating which protruded from their chest like a loose-jaw shark[4] . Miners ate rocks, gemstones, and minerals, to be made into glass or deposited elsewhere. A dozen Domovye were busy at work when I entered, consuming the stone walls around the crystalights. They did not speak through

---

4. A goblin shark

that mouth. They had not evolved to speak, having been mere animals in the age before Spiritism. Lucognidus made them sapient, then Entomothy[5] granted them speaking apparatus in the metal pipes from whence they breathed. Their pipes were located on their back, some thin, some thick, some curled, some straight, and all of varying lengths.

One Domovoi led me into a room they'd carved out. "It has regular lighting," they said, with different words echoing from different pipes. "You can rest without a visor there. Mr. Onoretti and his bodyguard are there now."

"A bodyguard?" I asked. "I didn't know he felt the need for one."

"A Sasorin boy. Not yet an adult."

Curious. I wasn't sure if that was legal, but... well, Mr. Onoretti knew the law better than I did. Children could work, if they were close to fifteen years of age, and agreed to it, but even that was usually for small, safe jobs. Why on all the planes would he hire a *child* as a bodyguard?

The chamber was small, supported by wooden beams. Giorvi Onoretti sat at a plain wooden table, pouring over documents and a map of the cave with a pen in hand. Two Domovye stood to his right. The quadrubrachial Sasorin bodyguard loomed over him ominously. Golden chitinous claws crossed his chest, and his lower two hands rested on the pommels of swords to each side. The room was lit by a covered crystalight, bright enough to illuminate the documents on the table, but not so bright that we had to wear visors.

"Mr. Lasteran! I'm glad you're here. Drooks, I will finish this conversation later. I have business to discuss with my merchant of light."

Mr. Onoretti was a Yosoe, the same species as Miltico, but they were different races. The man before me had white fur and corkscrew markhor horns. His face resembled an upside-down five-pointed star, the representation of the Pentagonal Dominion: the two horns, his long goat-like ears, and his scruffy white beard each being a point on the star. As I expected, his clothes were exquisite—scarlet-red robes, purple cuffs, a black sable mantle, and fine black boots fitted for a Yosoe's hooves.

The two Domovye left. Mr. Onoretti tapped his pen against the right side of the table, and the bodyguard took a few steps closer.

"I'm very happy to see you, Mr. Lasteran. Please, have a seat so we can discuss business. Forgive the rough interior. This room was only finished yesterday."

"Is it safe?" I asked without thinking about how such words could be interpreted. All I had on my mind was Tawny. I didn't want anyone else to get hurt, whether by fall or cave-in.

My boss glowered at me. Yellow eyes with emotionless, horizontal pupils. The only hint I had of his dissatisfaction was his creased brows and a slight frown. The

5. The God of Life

emotionless eyes were scarier.

The Sasorin looked even more emotionless. I may have had trouble distinguishing emotions in Yosoe eyes, but they were downright exaggerated compared to a Sasorin's face. Insectoid, with wide mandibles and solid golden eyes that rarely blinked. Three spikes protruding from near his eyes resembled perpetually-angry eyebrows, but they were solid, unmoving parts of his body. The boy could have been having the best day of his life and he'd look enraged to me. Not just his face, but his whole body was comprised of layers of golden spiked chitinous plates. What little clothes he could wear were leather carefully arranged around his spikes.

"Do you think I'd come down here unless I was completely confident in my own safety?"

I swallowed. "I'm sorry, Mo Senya." A term of respect for an older man in our patois. Although it wasn't from the language Mr. Onoretti spoke, I'd used it for him often enough, he probably knew what it meant.

"No need to apologize. I would not put myself in danger while my daughter is still dependent upon me. I'm sure you feel the same way with your kids."

My chest sunk; my sternum felt hollow. "Of course. It's why I asked."

"On the topic of danger, before we talk, I want you to meet my bodyguard and apprentice. Mr. Lasteran, this is Oboro. Oboro, this is my best merchant of light, Mr. Lasteran." Leaning closer to me, he asked, "Would you be opposed to the title 'Signore?'"

"Is that related to 'Mo Senya?'"

"My love partner is the linguist of the family, but yes, I believe so. Oboro only knows Orochigo and some basic Ophidian-English. We're teaching him Aloutian-English and Caprise. He's got 'Signore' and 'Signor' down. I don't want him thinking he needs to learn Fleur or Ebon, yet. Maybe in a few years."

"I have no objections, but why does he know Orochigo? Is he from Ophidia?"

"Yes. Rescued in the guild's charity project. It was an emergency and we had to rescue him before we were able to learn his age. Turns out Oboro's still fourteen years old, so the adult social services couldn't help. Legally, they can only help integrate adults into Aloutian society. I gave him the choice to go to a Wind church or to become my apprentice. This is what he chose. He believes an apprentice should also be a bodyguard. He is... happy, in a way, doing this."

He was the most terrifying fourteen-year-old I'd ever seen. He was shorter than me, though still taller than Mr. Onoretti, with a slender but muscular build. His claws could have snapped my arms in half, then speared me with the spiky protrusions on a backhand slap. His expression was unreadable, calculating. I'd have never guessed he was a child. Perhaps such an appearance was common in Sasorin; I had not met many in my life. Oddly, his segmented tail ended on a blunt piece, rather than the wicked stinger Sasorin were known for.

Mr. Onoretti said something to Oboro in a language I assumed to be Caprise.

The language of the Yosoe came from the same language family as Ebon, so I recognized a few similar-sounding words.

"I am honored to meet you, Signor Lasteran," Oboro said, bowing his head low like an Ophidian slave. His accent was thick and difficult for me to parse.

"You don't need to bow," Mr. Onoretti said. "Your words carry a sufficient degree of respect."

Oboro stiffened. "I apologize, Signore."

"Don't worry about it," I said. "I'm more worried about why you think you need to protect Mr. Onoretti. Does he have many enemies?"

Oboro's mandibles separated, which I thought meant he was about to speak, but he did not.

Mr. Onoretti laughed. "I'd rather have a bodyguard I don't need than to be caught in a dangerous situation without one."

I nodded. "Understandable, Mo Senya. What did you want to talk about regarding business?"

He patted the map in front of him. "The survey isn't complete yet, but judging by the size of these raw crystalights, we believe it'll be a small deposit."

"That's unfortunate," I replied.

"Perhaps not. These crystals have a lifespan of one hundred eighty years."

I stared, mouth gaping open.

"Do you understand what this means for business, Mr. Lasteran?"

"I'll be honest, Mo Senya, I'm happy handling the artistic side while you handle the economic side."

Mr. Onoretti grinned. "That's best for both of us. It means we have a scarce quantity of very high-quality crystalights. The price we can demand for them will be... well, I can be selective with our customers. City mayors only, for the purpose of becoming Godlights. Few of these can be wasted on individual vanity, though I intend on setting aside a small portion for myself. But we will not throw them away like the last crystalight vein we found ten years ago."

"Ten Selachi, one soul.[6]"

He responded to my idiom with another: "We wear bright colors to warn others we're poisonous." In Aloutia, people who dealt with money were put on the same tier as spiders, snakes, and bolotniki[7]. Money was seen as a 'necessary evil' after

---

6. Idiom about resource scarcity. The Selachi are a species of sapient people resembling sharks. Each of their eggs is produced with numerous babies, but only one (usually) will live after eating the others. That one will acquire a soul.

7. Poisonous frog, some growing as large as thirty feet tall

the Greed Wars—it was an evil that was gradually being phased out. In mimicry of those poisonous animals, traditional attire for those who worked in business and finance were bright colors.

The merchants of light were in the privileged position of being the only distributors of crystalights. If a city wanted one to use as their Godlight for the next eighty years—or one hundred eighty if they bought the ones here—their only option was to negotiate with our administrators. Mr. Onoretti was known to be a shrewd, ruthless negotiator. He had sold crystalights for prices beyond what they should have been worth.

Some might consider his practices immoral, but in the end, we all made the maxima. He wasn't any wealthier because of it. The extra money he'd squeezed out of city treasuries went to charity functions, such as freeing slaves from Ophidia.

If Mr. Onoretti hadn't sold previous crystalights for such a high price, perhaps Oboro wouldn't be here now. Maybe he'd be slaving away on his master's plantation instead.

"We might get a few disgruntled mayors upset that I didn't select them. They may try to disparage the artistic quality of the crystal. It would just be to make themselves feel better, but their toxic words may have unintended consequences."

"For whom?"

Mr. Onoretti laughed again as he steepled his fingers. "For everyone. If a mayor whines about your sculpting ability, I will forbid their city from receiving a crystalight for as long as I live. Placing sanctions doesn't make the guild look good, however, so some cities may refuse to buy crystalights in that time period. And if the sculpture *is* mud and sludge... well, that's on you." His hircine eyes narrowed in warning.

"Have my sculptures ever disappointed?" It wasn't a question asked in arrogance. I was genuinely curious. Mr. Onoretti was the middleman between me and my customers. If they had complaints, they told him.

"Never," he answered. "It's why I say you're my best merchant of light. And it's why I want you to work on as many of these ones as you can. If these become artistic masterpieces, it will give less validity to the fuckers who want to disrespect us." He shook his head and turned to his bodyguard. "Oboro, I expect you to speak cleaner than I do. 'Mud and sludge' and 'fucker' are words you do not use."

"Yes, Signore."

He turned back to me. "I apologize, Mr. Lasteran. The older I get, the less I find myself caring about my language. If it upsets you, you can find a different commissioner."

There were only a few dozen commissioners in upper administration, and if Mr. Onoretti told the others that I was a bad merchant, they'd blacklist me. We both knew it. My only option was to accept his apology.

"Please, go on, Mo Senya. I'm not bothered."

"Good. I expect the highest quality work from you on these crystalights because if anyone wants to disrespect us, I want to defend you with every ounce of my passion, which I can only do if *I* think the sculpture is a masterpiece."

"Of course. I will not disappoint. Um, but on that subject, Mo Senya... I must apologize. The current commission will be late."

"The Lagodore? I don't care about that one. We're making yellow coins off that compared to what we'll be making soon."

Yellow coins were the smallest denomination of currency in Aloutia. They were so insignificant I thought nothing about giving my youngest children buckets full of them. Tawny used to put them in her hair, along with her bell...

"Um, I know this may be bad business etiquette, but I need you to know. The reason I've been slow finishing it is because my daughter passed away and I've been grieving."

I wasn't sure what emotion Mr. Onoretti would show. Worst-case scenario, he'd scold me for letting my emotions get in the way of my work. Best case, he'd offer words of forced sympathy. I knew he had a daughter, so perhaps he could see things from my perspective.

I wished I could see the emotion in his eyes.

"How did she die?" he asked bluntly.

"She was playing in the park above us. When this crevice opened up, she fell to her death."

Slowly, one breath at a time, I watched Mr. Onoretti go from being a savage businessman to being a loving father. He dropped his hands to the table and opened his mouth, although no words came out... and his hircine eyes welled with tears. A sob escaped. Oboro's hands clutched his swords. I wasn't sure if he intended to stand still or attack me.

I was taken aback. I'd never seen him cry. I had never thought him capable of it. "Mr. Onoretti? Are you okay?"

"Am *I* okay?" he repeated in a strained voice. "What the hell do I matter? Are *you* okay? What about your family? Has she been sawdusted? Is this place too painful for you?"

I couldn't comprehend why he was so upset. "Um... right now? Yes, I'm alright. I've been depressed and anxious, but... Mo Senya, why are you so distraught about it? You never knew my Tawny."

"I'm so sorry, Amiere. Can I call you that?"

"Y-yes, of course, Mo Senya."

"I didn't know such a thing had happened! No one told me. Why didn't anyone tell me? Oboro, bring the chief miner in here."

Oboro saluted with his lower right hand to his chest. "As you command, Signore."

As the Sasorin left, I wondered what I was supposed to do. I had prepared myself to be in a vulnerable position, but instead, Mr. Onoretti took that role.

"I'm so sorry," he said again, wiping the tears from his eyes. His hands trembled.

"Please don't apologize. You had nothing to do with it. It was a freak accident, that's all. Perhaps the curse of a God or Demon Lord."

He sniffed. "I can't believe I let you see me like this. I imagined it happening to my little Beatrice and..." He let out a deep exhale. "No father should ever go through that."

"I wouldn't wish this pain on any parent. When you go back home, give Beatrice a hug and tell her how much you love her. Play with her. Buy her something she wants."

Mr. Onoretti composed himself and gave a half-hearted chuckle. "Oh trust me, my girl already gets everything she wants." He wiped one last tear from his eye. "This is unlike me."

I remembered words of advice he'd given me many years ago about maintaining composure. "The calmest person in the room is the most feared and respected."

"Precisely." He rubbed the spot on his forehead below where his horns met. "Just as I'm finding it harder to control my language as I grow older, so too am I finding it harder to keep calm."

Oboro returned with a Domovoi in tow.

"Is there a problem, Mr. Onoretti?" they asked.

"Is there a problem?" he repeated, incredulous at the miner's audacity to ask such an obvious question. "Yes, there's a problem. Why wasn't I informed of the death of a Wynnle girl that occurred here?"

Domovye didn't have faces or eyes, making their emotions even harder to read than a Yosoe's. "There was nothing to be gained by spreading a story about a deceased child," they replied. "At best, the project would be delayed while superstitious people insisted on conducting... various obscene rituals. Not all our miners are proper worshippers of Lord Lucognidus. Since this mine appeared so close to Deep Sea, some believe he was involved. I don't know any of Lord Despair's rituals; frankly, Signore, I don't want to know. Gives me chills thinking about it. But if the miners thought the child was a sacrifice to him? I can imagine some of my people refusing to work until they felt Deep Sea was satisfied."

I had not thought about the ocean's role. Did he have something to do with the crystalights being here, so far from Iuria? Had he ferried them across The Corridor? Did the ground open up because he slammed so many crystals into the ground nearby?

I stole an inconspicuous glance at Mr. Onoretti's map, but it was drawn in such a way that only the miners could comprehend it. It was less of an actual, visual map and more a diagram of abstract lines and symbols relevant to a Domovoi.

"Your objections are perfectly good reasons not to talk about it to the *miners*," Mr. Onoretti said in a low, calculated voice. "But I heard nothing as to why *I* was not informed."

The Domovoi hesitated. "My apologies, Signore. I thought the issue was irrelevant at this point."

Tapping his forefinger on the table, he said, "I expect full disclosure of everything that happens in this mine from now on. Am I understood?"

"Yes, Signore."

"Good. Is there anything else you want to tell me? Anything else you thought was 'irrelevant'?"

The Domovoi answered in Caprise. I didn't know enough to understand. Mr. Onoretti replied in the same language, and after a few exchanges, the chief miner left.

"What was that about?" I asked.

"Some small issue with a crystal being difficult to extract. Nothing you need to worry about, Mr. Lasteran. In regard to your daughter, I told them to be on the lookout for anything that may have been... left... down here. If we find anything of hers, I will ensure it is returned to you."

"Thank you," I replied.

"Just so you know, I'll be here frequently for the next several weeks. I decided to take a more hands-on approach to this crystalight deposit. I plan to oversee more than I usually do. I know I said in my letter I wouldn't impose myself on you, but I would appreciate any advice you have regarding lodging or food. I may have to spend a few nights here. I would pay, of course."

I scratched my mane. The house Miltico was in now used to serve as a guest house. There was another empty house which would be Nell's when she grew up and had been constructed specifically for Yosoe feet. It was built last year, and it would be another year before Nell was ready. It wasn't my place to offer it to a guest, however. I would never betray Nell like that. "Ask the Chak-Den family about lodging."

"Den? One of your partner's family?"

"Yes. Orienna Denwall is Liesle's sister. She has a half-Yosoe daughter. Maybe she'd be kind enough to let you borrow the house she'll be moving into next year. For food, we're a small village, so we don't have any restaurants, but if you're not opposed to taking fruit from the trees, well, they're for everybody. You're always welcome at my house as well. We make big meals since we're never sure how many of the kids' friends are going to be over for dinner. And our shopkeeper and grocer, Mr. Svelt, is a Yosoe, so if there's anything in particular you want that we don't serve, he'd probably have it."

He smiled. "Since you've already seen my soft side today, I might as well be honest. I also want to bring my life partner and daughter here. My partner wants a romantic vacation, and my daughter has never been to the tropics."

"Ah, of course. You're welcome to visit my house any time, Mo Senya. I hope you have a lovely time at the beach. If you bring your daughter, I'll make sure my kids know to play safely with her."

"You're too kind. Since I'll be here frequently, there's no need to share everything today. I planned on going over all the details of your first commission, but, oh Amiere, I could never do that to you now that I know you're grieving. Please, take a break for a week. Don't even think about that Lagodore commission, unless you think working on it would be therapeutic. We'll talk again in a week and see where your mental state is at then."

His compassion and sympathy were unexpected, but entirely welcome. I had not expected a man dressed in the poison-colored robes of a businessman to shed tears on my behalf. But I, too, wore colors symbolizing aposematism. Perhaps he cried for me because we were the same animal—not lions or goats, but fathers who adored our daughters.

Eruwan Interlude

During the break between classes, Eruwan usually ate lunch with Nell and their small circle of close friends, mostly Florae whose parents worked in food production or up in the sugar plantations, but today she had a matter to discuss in private with Nell. They sat alone in the library, scooping rice and fish into their mouths sans eating utensils.

Nell sat on a bench in the library, swinging her Yosoe legs back and forth while stuffing her face with rice. A grain stuck to her lips, which she licked up. She had stripes on her face like a Wynnle, but eyes like a Yosoe.

Eruwan wondered… "Is Usana afraid of you?"

Nell cocked her head. "No?" The rising intonation turned the answer into a question. "Why would she be? I'm not the one dragging her by her horns and spanking her."

"She called me and Cohaku 'lions' and ran away in terror. I wondered if you were also a lion to her."

"It must be the mane. Maybe the eyes. I'm a Yosoe in both those aspects."

"Yeah, you look like your dad. Maybe Usana is comfortable with that."

"I don't see why," Nell said with her mouth full. "Our dad is a jerk. He spanks her. I'm glad Mom kicked him out before I got old enough to remember him. I don't know if he ever spanked me when I was young, but if he tried it now, I'd bite him."

How did Wynnle biological immunity work? Eruwan knew if she bit Papami or Mamali, her body would nearly shut down. They always said it wouldn't happen if she tried to bite Papa Su, but why would she want to hurt dear, old Papa Su? She wondered if it worked for a half-Wynnle child biting the non-Wynnle parent.

"Would your body freeze if you bit Miltico?" she asked.

Nell tapped her chin in consideration. "Hmm, maybe. Well, I'd bite him anyway, no matter if my body tried to stop me." She scowled. "I won't let any jerk spank me, even if he claims to be my father!"

As if on cue, Usana slipped in through the door on the far side of the room from the two teenagers. Nell had her back to the door. Usana surely saw Eruwan, but didn't make eye contact. Sticking close to the wall, she ran behind a bookshelf.

"There she is," Eruwan whispered.

Nell turned, but Usana was already hidden. "Is she looking for me?"

"Maybe she wants to eat lunch with us—or you, rather. Oh, you think she's not approaching because she thinks I'm a lion?"

"That's fucked up," Nell said in the quietest voice possible. She wasn't supposed to say curse words, but only the adults cared. Around Eruwan, she swore frequently.

"What if I wear a kamen?" Eruwan asked. "We have some that go over the entire head and can hide my mane."

"You think that would work? Wouldn't she assume it was you since she saw you talking to me?"

Eruwan shrugged. "I don't know. Cohaku is her age and she can't tell people apart."

The girls decided to try it out. The Mind church had a few kamens in storage. In Steena Village, no one bothered to wear a mask when the only people who ever saw you were your neighbors. The purpose of a kamen was to keep one's face hidden from potential merchants of faces who could summon the Demon Lord Vinoc to torture them. But if anyone's face was painted in Steena Village, they would know it was Liesle. Everyone knew everyone else in the village; there was no reason to keep one's face a secret.

The one Eruwan found went over her head like a helmet, covering her mane in its entirety. Since her blue hair was long, it was still visible at the bottom, but no one could tell it was a mane—it could have just as easily been a non-Wynnle's long hair. It also hid her eyes, so if that scared Usana, she would hopefully feel secure.

The two walked carefully around the bookshelf as if Usana were a wild animal. Eruwan asked herself what they would do if she bolted. Would Usana be in trouble with the volkhvs? Would Miltico spank her again?

Eruwan thought Usana had come in here to eat lunch, so she expected to see food, but remembered only after seeing her that she hadn't brought anything with her. Usana shivered, huddled in a corner, tugging at the long sleeves of her thick clothes.

"Are you hungry?" Eruwan asked.

She stared at the masked Wynnle with her big, innocent Lagodore eyes. Gods, she was adorable, Eruwan thought. Usana trembled, teeth clattering.

Nell went closer and sat next to her. "Hey, Usana, you remember me?"

"Sister Nell," she said, so quietly Eruwan barely heard.

"Yep. Are you hungry?"

She lowered her head. Eruwan wasn't sure if that was a nod of affirmation or a shameful confession. Either way, she didn't reply.

"Do you know who this is?" Nell asked, pointing to her cousin.

Usana studied the masked person, but if she was afraid, she didn't show it.

"No."

"This is our cousin, Eruwan."

"Cousin Eruwan?"

"Yep. Well, I guess she's only my cousin. You have a different mom than me, and I'm her cousin because our moms are sisters."

Eruwan sat down, too, feeling confident Usana wouldn't bolt. "I heard you met my parents the other day, Usana. Do you remember meeting Amiere Lasteran and Su Scrimshander?"

Her ears perked up. They were such cute ears! But so, so long... The way they draped over her horns, Eruwan wondered if they were too heavy for her.

"Master Scrimshander gave me a steena," she said.

"Did you like it?"

She blinked. "Daddy said I shouldn't take food from strangers. He made me throw it away."

"We're not strangers, anymore. Maybe you can come over and eat more steenas with us."

"I don't know. Daddy doesn't like your parents very much."

"Oh..." Eruwan didn't know how else to reply to that. "Hey, aren't you hot in that thick shirt? There are spare clothes here. We can—"

"Daddy said I can't take it off."

Silence. Why would a parent care so much about what their child wore?

"Cousin Eruwan," she said again.

"Oh, just Eruwan is fine. We're not related. Nell just got mixed up for a moment."

Usana wiggled her Lagodore nose. "Sorry. Eruwan... Scrimshander."

"Huh?"

"Your name is Eruwan Scrimshander, right? Mr. Lasteran is your daddy, so Master Scrimshander must be your mommy."

"Oh! No, my mother is Liesle Denwall, so my name is Eruwan Denwall. Su Scrimshander is my parent, but he's..." Would Usana understand? The way she tilted her head, confused, suggested she wouldn't.

"A third parent?"

"Yeah. He's... well, he raised me and my siblings."

"He's not a mommy or daddy?"

"He's both and neither. I call him Papa Su, but the others all call him something different."

Eruwan Scrimshander. It felt... right.

Mamali would be furious if Eruwan said that. But when she thought about Mamali, all she could see was her angry face, pupils vertical, claws extended. When she thought about Papa Su, she saw him happy and smiling; she could feel his four arms hugging her. She imagined him kissing her forehead in genuine paternal love.

"I didn't know you could have three parents," Usana said.

"Of course you can! However many people raise you, they're all your parents."

Well, they weren't all biological parents, but that didn't matter. For them, family was about love and support. The Last-Scrim-Den family had always emphasized the importance of 'us' and, as Su always said, you couldn't spell 'us' without 'Su.'

Usana blinked. "I only have two parents."

"Mm. Hey, can I ask you something? You said you met my father, Mr. Lasteran? Were you afraid of him?"

She wiggled her nose. "Yeah, he's a lion. Daddy said lions eat rabbits and goats, and I'm a rabbit-goat, so I'm twice as tasty."

Eruwan had a lot of work ahead of her, teaching Usana the difference between animals and sapienti... She would keep the mask on a little longer.

Chapter Nine: Funeral Arrangements

With a sensation of pili-palas fluttering in my sternum, I went to the Chak-Den house to meet up with Su. I knew we had to talk about the fire feast eventually, but damn I hoped he had the wherewithal to hammer out the finer details. I sure as hell didn't.

A fire feast was a gathering of all the villagers, who'd come to the beach, set up a bonfire, and eat roast goat, sheep, fish, okoes[1] , chickens, raptors, horned rats, and of course all varieties of the bountiful fruit in our area. While most fire feasts were happy, celebratory occasions... they served as memorials for the dead, as well. It was the custom of people in tropical, seaside towns to honor their dead with a grand feast. Whether the deceased was elderly or an infant, herbivore or carnivore, male, female, or anything in between or outside the concept of gender, they were sure to be remembered honorably by the ones who loved them.

Tawny had loved playing kiwi-batte, a team sport where we hit a ball resembling a kiwi with a thick, paddle-shaped bat. When I was younger, I had dreamed of having enough members in my family to have my own kiwi-batte team—eleven. Me, my spouses, and eight kids. Gods, I was an idiot... Regardless, Tawny had enjoyed the sport. I intended to set up a game during her fire feast if Su hadn't arranged it already. It was what she would have wanted to do, if she could have arranged her own party. She was only seven, but she'd insisted on playing kiwi-batte for her previous two hatching-days and all other fun holidays.

Hatching-days... Her eighth hatching-day was coming up, soon. Fuck, how was I supposed to deal with that? Moreover, it was Demitris's hatching-day, too. He and Tawny had been born on Egg Day, the day when the Life Moon comes closest to Aloutia. Statistically, more eggs hatched that day than any other day, so it wasn't much of a coincidence, but it would still make for a sad day, especially for Demitris. They always played on the same team when playing kiwi-batte because Tawny didn't want to compete against him.

---

1. Aquatic animal resembling jellyfish, but with a meaty interior around a ring of vertebrae.

What were we going to do on Demitris's hatching-day? Would he be able to cope without his best friend playing with him? Gods, it was going to be a miserable day...

The Chak-Den house was a bamboo-and-leaf structure with open windows, though no rain got inside as the bamboo shutters opened upward. As always, their abode was lively with the ever-present whistling of songbirds. Vily, gamayuns, and alkonosts were the trio of birds trained by the merchants of song. I announced my presence as I passed through their leaf door, but I was unsure if they heard me over the birds' singing and the dulcet tones of a piano. I made my way to the piano room.

The entire Chak-Den family was there, along with Su. Nell played the piano while Orienna stood behind her, hands on Nell's shoulders. Piotr, Demitris, and Su were in the early stages of a troika match. As usual, Su played with the bone pieces.

"There you are, Ami-honey," Su said as he moved his double agent a hexagon closer to Piotr's corner. "How was your meeting with Mr. Onoretti?"

"Good," I said. "He... was more sympathetic than I thought he'd be."

"Tha's a relief, aye," Piotr said in his thick, Gluckan accent. He had only lived in Steena Village for ten years. He would repeat his whole life story and the tale of how he came to Steena Village if anyone asked, but the telling would take all day, and I would only understand half of what he said. Ten years, but he still spoke like a Gluckan. "Scrimmy an' I bet arm bones on if he 'as gonna be a prick o' no'."

"And you lost," Su said. "Pay up, Piotr."

Piotr, a Stone elemental Gluckan with rock-hard skin and curling bone-fragment ornamentation, took a chisel to one of the bones embedded in his skin. It didn't hurt him to remove them. He did it about as frequently as some bearded men shaved.

"I tho' someone with as pompous a title as 'merchant o' light liaison ta the Aloutian Empire' would be a fockin' knob."

Orienna scowled at her husband for his language. More specifically, for saying it around the kids.

"Ope, sorry 'ove. Meant ta say flippin' cob."

"Actually, I wanted to ask you something on Mr. Onoretti's behalf," I said. "He's planning to stay in the village for a while to oversee the mining operations. He was hoping to rent the house we built for Nell, just for a few days."

My niece abruptly ended playing her piano. "What? I don't want some stranger Yosoe in my house!"

"Rent? So he's offering to pay?" Orienna said.

"Yes, he's a wealthy man. Makes the maxima."

"There's no reason to refuse, Nell," Orienna explained to her daughter. "He's offering you money, which would be a nice bonus for a new adult. You could buy a new instrument with that kind of money, or some birds to launch your career as a merchant of song. Besides, you want to develop a reputation for hospitality. No one is going to buy from a merchant of song known to be rude."

"But… what if he…"

"What? What would he do?"

"I don't know… some gross Yosoe thing?"

Orienna scowled. "You are a Yosoe, Nell. What gross things do you do?"

She tapped a key. "I thought pure Yosoes did weird stuff like… rub themselves on furniture and eat pillows."

"Where the 'ell didja learn 'at from?" Piotr asked. "Ya mom might talk poorly o' Milti, but we don't pretend 'e's all o' Yosoe-kind. What would your gran'pap think? 'E's a pure Yosoe, ya?" Piotr played his piece—an archer to intercept the double agent.

"Mr. Onoretti is a distinguished man of dignity," Orienna said. "He will absolutely not do anything of that nature in your house. If he does, we can fix it. New pillows don't cost much. We can make our own."

Nell shrugged her shoulders. "Fine. If you want to let him, let him."

Orienna shook her head and turned her attention to me. "Nell's just being moody because Milti is back in town. I'll convince her Mr. Onoretti isn't bad. Anyway, we've been discussing the fire feast."

"What'll it be, Scrimmy?" Piotr asked. "We talkin' 'bout the fire feast 'round ya Ami? Or's it bother 'im?"

Although the question was addressed to Su, I could answer for myself. I opened my mouth to tell them they could talk about the funeral arrangements around me. And yet… a lead weight sunk from my hyoid to my sternum and deep into the abyss of my stomach. I was supposed to be a responsible adult, but all I wanted to do was scream and cry and run away. I couldn't lose my focus in front of Piotr. What would he think of me? But if they really did talk about it… Fuck, he'd think I had the emotional maturity of a child.

"We got everything planned out," Su said. "You don't have to worry about it."

"W-well, I was hoping… maybe we could play kiwi-batte? Tawny would have—"

Demitris covered his face to hide his tears, but no amount of his stony skin could disguise the sob.

"I think that's a great idea," Orienna said as she let go of Nell's shoulders and came to stand beside me. She was such a tall woman. Not as tall as her sister, but every bit as intimidating. She looked a lot like Liesle, though she had more tigrine stripes on her face and neck, and her skin was a bit of a darker shade of purple compared to my wife's.

Having seen Demi's reaction, I had second thoughts. "Are you sure? I didn't mean to—"

"She's right," Piotr said. "A kiwi-batte game a'd be the perfect way o' sayin' farewell ta her. Demi, don'tcha 'gree?"

The boy gave no indication that he'd even heard the question.

Orienna tugged at my sleeve and pulled me into the hallway. While the birds quieted and Nell's piano-playing ceased, the only noise was the pitter-patter of rain. They had put their tarpaulin up on time; the raindrops resembled distant echoes.

"Is Demitris alright?" I asked. "I didn't mean to upset him. If kiwi-batte is a bad idea, we don't have to do it."

"He'll be fine. In fact, I think playing a game of kiwi-batte is just what he needs to move on. It'll hurt now, but I think it'll be good for him in the long run."

"If you say so..."

"I do. He's young, so this tragedy won't hurt for him as much once he's older." Orienna turned to me and looked at me with jade eyes that could have drilled holes in metal. "Now, I also need to ask about my sister. I tried to visit a few days ago and she was... abusive, to be honest."

"Abusive? To our kids?" The shiver that ran down my spine was colder than any I'd ever felt in Chernagora's winter.

Orienna must have seen the concern in my eyes that I'd immediately assumed she was referring to the kids. "Oh, Gods no, she'd never hurt your kids! I shouldn't have used that word. I apologize, Ami. She was rude to *me*. I want to know what we can do to help her cope. I'm thinking back to when Tico died... his mother couldn't handle it, and she died two years later. She was only in her fifties! Gods, I miss Tawny, too, but I don't want this grief to kill Liesle, either." Orienna wiped a tear from her eye.

I froze, silently contemplating her fears. I hadn't considered how the death of our child might affect our own life spans. There had certainly been times when I wanted to lay down in Deep Sea and let him turn me into marine snow, but I had always gotten back up. I had to, because I had other children who needed a father.

"I'm as clueless as you," I replied in a dry voice. All my emotions had been drained; this was the best I could manage. "I've been taking it one day at a time. I give her space. I help her with chores. I prepare her dinner and take her plates to her when she can't even get out of bed."

Orienna sighed. "Anyway, I know it's not much, but I made her some steena pudding. There's enough for your whole family, but make sure she gets her fair share, alright?"

"I will. Thank you. I'm sorry if I have said or done anything rude. My head just hasn't—"

"You don't need to make excuses. I can't fathom the pain you're going through. You know, for a while after Milti left, I had nightmares about him coming back to kidnap Nell."

Nightmares... Orienna was a legal heretic, so she had nightmares and could be hurt by fire. Although she didn't discuss the details of how she lost her blessings, she was a Lightning elemental. I assumed Milti asked her to have sex at one point, and she refused. Maybe that was when she scratched his eye blind.

"I'm sorry. At least now, Nell's pretty big. I don't think Milti could force her anywhere."

"Absolutely not! That girl of mine is even more stubborn than Liesle. Come with me." Orienna headed into their dining room, where they ate from a table with a giant marble slab for a top. Like us, they ate on the floor, on reed mats. The marble top table was not normal for Steena Village, but was standard in Glucka, where Piotr was from. He had inherited it from a distant relative, but that was yet another story that would take hours to hear him explain.

Atop the table was a massive bowl of steena pudding. Orienna thrust it into my arms. "Tell me if Liesle doesn't eat any. She... she is eating, right?"

"She is. Not as much as usual, but she's forcing herself, when necessary."

Orienna glanced downward. "Not enough for her baby, either. She should be popping that out soon, shouldn't she?"

"Any day now."

She nodded. "I've heard depressed mothers sometimes..." She hesitated, taking slow and controlled breaths. "I've heard they do bad things to their hatchlings. Ami, please, if you don't trust Liesle with your baby, let me take care of them. It can be just a short time. Until Liesle recovers."

I stood with my mouth agape. "Liesle would kill me if I suggested that, but I appreciate your concern."

"I'll tell her myself, then. You're so afraid of her being angry at you, but what if she were to kill the baby? You'd claw your own throat, thinking back to this very conversation and telling yourself 'I knew this would happen, but let it happen anyway.' Don't claim ignorance. Liesle is dangerous. If you know something bad might happen, you have to stop it."

"Can't we tell a Life volkhv? Maybe the Life church will agree to watch the baby for longer."

"Don't count on it," she said. "The Life church of Seabells is so crowded, they want to get babies out as soon as they can. And besides, they can't handle a mother's depression. Best you could do is get a social worker, and... Well, they don't have the time or resources to deal with a case in a small village like ours—a village that chases away any lawkeepers who dare come through. We have a stereotype here. Nobody comes snooping in our business, but that also means they won't help anyone here. In any case, they have enough work dealing with issues in the city. No one's gonna take the hours-long ride on a Daga to investigate a rumor."

"You seem to know this for sure."

"I tried to get help when Milti..." She trailed off, leaving the most painful words an implication in the humid air. And just like the air, the suggestion clung to my mane and made me feel filthy. "One person laughed at me because I was a Wynnle.

They thought I should be able to handle him on my own."

"What the hell did they want you to do?" My own rage spiked. Everyone seemed to think we Wynnles were immune to abuse just because we were tall and daunting. "If you hit him, you'd have gone berserk."

"They're a bunch of idiots," Orienna said. "And that's why we can't rely on them. Any problems in this village, we gotta solve ourselves."

Her words burrowed deep in my skull. I hadn't given it much thought previously, but she was right. I hated asking for help from authorities in Seabells, partially because help always came too little and too late, if it came at all. She was right—lawkeepers avoided Steena Village. Ever since the Greed Wars, when our ancestors put lawkeeper heads on bamboo pikes, this had been a place of anarchy. This was a community where peace was maintained by the villagers.

If we were going to do anything, we could only count on ourselves.

"I'll keep an eye on Liesle's behavior," I said. "And if I think she's getting worse or would be a threat to the baby, I'll let you know."

I'd talk to Su about it first, of course. Neither of us would so easily give our baby to another person to raise. Not before we lost Tawny, and certainly not afterward...

"Thank you, Ami." Orienna patted my arm. "Now, go take that pudding to her. Maybe it'll put her in a better mood."

Chapter Ten: Bullies

Su and I visited Phoebus Svelt's shop on our way back home to pick up a few things we'd need for the fire feast, namely herbs and spices. Even though it would be a somber memorial, there was no reason the food had to be bland. Tawny would have wanted the tastiest roast goat she could sink her fangs into.

The rain had slowed to a gentle drizzle, but we still walked under the same umbrella. I shared with him some of what I'd spoken about with Mr. Onoretti, as well as the news he had a Sasorin bodyguard who was a freed Ophidian ex-slave. Su always enjoyed hearing of boys who'd been freed. He would not tell anyone if he had been raised as a boy or a girl, back when he was a child on Ophidia, but if he was a boy, he was once a slave, too. That wasn't to undermine the abuse he went through if he was a girl...

Su stopped outside the store, a step before we reached the canopy of tarpaulins Phoebus had set out to keep his outdoor merchandise dry, including a pile of rolled tarpaulins for those of us who hadn't properly prepared for the rainy season.

Su held the steena pudding bowl in one hand, the umbrella in another, and pulled me in for a kiss with his other two. While I was bent down to his level, he whispered in my ear, "I think Miltico is here now, and I'd rather not listen to the mud and sludge that comes out of his foul mouth. I will stay out here. I don't care that it's raining."

Agreed. Putting Milti and Su in the same room together would only lead to trouble. Best I go in, get what we need, and leave.

The fact that Su knew Milti was inside did not surprise me. It was one of his Godblood powers. It wasn't always accurate at identifying the individual, but he could tell *someone* was nearby, and usually what species they were. He likely could have sensed two Yosoe. Since many of the Gods had powers relating to the detection of souls, minds, or some other living signature, it was worthless as a clue to his heritage.

I went inside with just my coin purse. Miltico was indeed in here, stocking the shelves.

He scowled upon seeing me. "What do you want?"

"If that's how you greet customers, don't expect to get any."

He huffed. "If you want to go to another store, fucking feel free. Nearest store with the mud and sludge we sell is in Seabells."

"Eruwan has an entrepreneurial soul. Maybe I'll convince her to open up a competitor to this store once your father passes away."

"I thought Eruwan wanted to be a merchant of bone like your man-wife."

"How the fuck would you know what Eruwan wants? Also, if you ever fucking call Su that again, I'll tear your ribs apart." All I wanted was to get my supplies and leave... Why couldn't I just keep my mouth shut?

"Ooh, a Wynnle murderer! You want to get yourself and your entire family banished from Aloutia? Go on, Ami. I dare you. Kill me." He spread his arms out and grimaced. "See what happens to your family when they're driven out of Aloutia because you proved Wynnles can't be trusted in society. Go back to your barbaric, lizard-hunting tribe, where your sons have to circumcise themselves before they're considered real men and your daughters have to break their own hymens before they're considered real women."

He wanted me to hit him. He was baiting me. If I hit him, if I drew his blood, I would go berserk, and I might actually kill him... and everything he said would come true. My family would be forced to Cosmo, exiled. I clenched my fists, keeping my claws inside.

"Tawny's the lucky one," he said.

"Don't you fucking dare say her name," I growled with a voice so low, but powerful, it felt like thunder in my chest.

"Oh, fuck off. I'm right, though. Even if your other kids get banished to Cosmo, at least she won't have to fuck herself to prove she's a real woman. I suppose it's easier for women like your mother who have sex before then. Maybe Tawny will be fucked by Sparkato before she is even pressured to 'become an adult,' as those wild Wynnles would call it. Maybe he's already gotten to her. He likes 'em young, I hear..."

"The other Gods keep Sparkato locked up and away from children," I said, trying my best to stay calm despite the intrusive images planted in my skull. "You're trying to rile me up, but I won't let it happen."

"Am I? I'm just pointing out facts. Like the fact that it's your fault Tawny died."

"How do you figure that?" Why was I even talking to him? I should have just demanded to see his father, finish my business, and leave.

"Liesle has wings. All your other kids have wings. But you don't. Tawny inherited her body shape from you, including her lack of wings. Just think, Ami, if only you had wings, she would have been born with them, too. Then she could have flown away when the ground opened beneath her. The ground, by the way, at the park *you* took her to. She'd still be here if you'd kept her by the beach."

"What kind of fucked up logic is that? You don't have wings, either. Usana would have fallen to her death, too. And how the fuck could we have known a hole would open up at the park? A hole could have opened up on the beach, too."

"You've never lived in a place where danger could swoop down on you at any time. Death could happen in an instant, anywhere. You could kill me right now."

Gods, how I wanted to. In the steadiest voice I could muster, I asked, "Do you care about Usana at all? If she died, would you cry?"

"Why? You planning to kill her to find out? I'll make a new daughter with Lavina. Maybe the next one will fucking obey me."

"Maybe you'll fucking feed the next one." My claws came out on their own.

The door opened and Su strode in, not even bothering to lower the umbrella.

Miltico's ears lowered, slinking below his horns. He scurried into the back room without a word.

"Amiere..." Su said as he put one of his few remaining free hands on my back.

"What is it? I'm about to teach this fucker a lesson in—"

I blacked out.

The next thing I knew, I was back at home, laying on the pile of pillows with Nio cuddled up against the arm she'd bit earlier.

Liesle sat on her own pile of pillows nearby, eating a small bowl of Orienna's steena pudding.

I blinked, uncertain. "Wha—? I was just at Mr. Svelt's shop. What am I doing here?"

"Su said you were acting funny, but you walked home on your own. You were... I don't know how to describe it, Mo Ami. Like you were sleepwalking. You didn't respond to anything we said."

"Did I buy what we needed at the store?"

"Yes, you got cumin, garlic, and kyamo[1]."

I looked around as if something in my house could give me a clue as to why I'd lost my memory of the last several minutes. What had happened with Miltico? Had I beaten the fucker within an inch of his life? Had Su? Had we walked away? I couldn't even recall walking home down Bamboo Lane. I had been careful not to step on any slugs, hadn't I? Judging by the lack of droplets hitting our roof, the rain had ceased.

"This is the second time it's happened. It hasn't happened since..." I hated to discuss that time before Eruwan's hatching, when I would snort crazy sugar, then not remember a thing. Oh fuck, did Liesle think I was ingesting crazy sugar again?

---

1. Culinary and medicinal herb, magically enchanted with Lightning elementrons. It's considered an important ingredient in Lightning elemental diets.

Her tigrine, slitted eyes glared at me, threatening to eviscerate me if I spoke a lie... or if I claimed to have been on crazy sugar.

"What have you eaten?" she asked menacingly.

"I-I'm not on crazy sugar!" I insisted. "I swear I'm not, Liesle. Please. If there's something else I've been eating that has been doing this to me, I don't know what it is. We haven't eaten anything different than what we've always eaten."

She softened her expression. "I believe you. I don't know why it's happening, either. Maybe it's a stress response. Something about Tawny's death may have triggered something in you. Maybe it's related to us being Wynnles and has something to do with going berserk. If we can lose our minds to rage at the scent of blood, perhaps we can lose our minds and... forget things... when we're filled with sorrow."

"How would that work? You think when I get furious, instead of going berserk, I black out?"

She shook her head. The bones in her blue mane braids clacked together. "I don't know anything for certain. It was just a guess. Perhaps we'd know if we lived in a society full of Wynnles. It's nothing my mother ever experienced. Would your mother know?"

"I'll ask her about it when I see her next."

My mother lived in the village, quietly and happily spending the winter years of her life with her best friend, a woman she'd met after I had grown.

I rubbed Nio's head, making sure not to disrupt the tuft of hair on the very top. "Well, blacking out is safer than killing. I'll take that curse if I must."

"It's not safe if you black out as the ground opens up beneath you."

"I'd be killed regardless if it's faster than I can run. I can't fly. I don't have wings. I... I'm so sorry, Liesle. It's my fault Tawny died. If only I had wings, all our children would have inherited them. I'm a failure of a—"

"Shut up." She shot up, imposing her size and willpower over me. She was so tall, even her protruding, pregnant abdomen was above my head. I shrunk back against the pillows. If Nio had been awake, she'd have probably run away. "Don't say such mud and sludge. I won't let you say those things about yourself. It's a bit odd so many of our kids inherited my wings. It should be a fifty-fifty chance, shouldn't it? But five out of six got wings. That's just the way of percentages, though. They don't always work out perfectly. Wynnles are supposed to have sons and daughters at fifty-fifty odds, but we had two sons and four daughters, rather than three and three. My parents had two daughters and no sons. Some parents have *ten* daughters and no sons. It's chance, Mo Ami. You couldn't have controlled what genetics our children got."

"You would have been happier having kids with a winged man," I said. "Then your kids would have all been safe. I don't deserve to be a father. I shouldn't have—"

She lunged at me, to the side so she wouldn't disturb Nio. Had our daughter not been there, Liesle would have pounced on me like a tiger onto her prey. She pressed her mouth against mine, forcing me into silence.

Liesle held the back of my head and thrust her tongue into my mouth. Her sweet scent overwhelmed my nostrils. Had she put perfume in her mane? Her wild tongue and seeking lips sent my skull spinning. I only regretted that I could not match her excitement; I hadn't expected it, and I could not force my body to take actions that my mind hadn't embraced. I tried to kiss her back with equal heat, for her sake, but it was not enough.

I hadn't experienced such passion from her in so long. I had feared she'd lost it forever. And yet it only made my sternum cry out in pain, as I knew she had forced herself to do it. Liesle had not kissed me because she wanted to show her love for me, but because she'd wanted me to shut up. For its lack of genuine desire, the kiss ended up only making me more miserable.

It was my fault. I wanted to be the powerful lover and strong man she craved, but I couldn't get the disgusting things Miltico said out of my mind. While Liesle kissed me, I had intrusive thoughts of... of the Lightning God... and my daughter who was at his mercy...

Unable to satisfy Liesle, and uncomfortable with this act of intimacy while my traitorous skull forced those images into me, I slid my face aside.

"I'm sorry," I said. "I... I can't right now." I let her down as gently as I could. After the bout of depression she'd been through, it was nice to see her in a kissing mood again. I just wished I could have shared that mood.

I wasn't just a failure of a father, I was a failure of a husband, too.

Liesle glanced downward, dejected, as she went back to her side of the pillow pile. "I should not have done that..."

After gently slipping Nio off my arm, I told Liesle I was going to help Su prepare dinner. It wasn't just an excuse to be with Su; I had a responsibility to help with chores. I had always helped prepare the meat portion of dinner, and I wasn't about to stop now. I may have been a failure of a husband and a father, but I didn't need to make the situation *worse.* I wouldn't give up on the people who needed me.

The rain had stopped for the evening, but this time of year, it would start again in a few hours, probably after we'd all gone to sleep. We ought to get the tarpaulins set up before it rains again... As I had that thought, I turned to the megawhale's skull to see the task had already been done. Tarpaulins covered our roof, stretching across the whale's ribs the whole length of its spinal column.

The kids had taken this moment of dryness to play on the beach. They'd often played a modified form of kiwi-batte that only required however many people they had. I expected to see them playing it now, but instead, Fionn sat on the sand, hands over his face. Su, Eruwan, and Heliodor stood in front of him. Even Maika stood there with her morel tail downward, a sign she was sad. I heard nothing over the crashing waves and the wind rushing through palm fronds, but I knew my son must have been crying.

Cohaku was further down the beach, throwing a coconut into Deep Sea.

As I approached, Fionn's crying overpowered the noise of the wind and water. I made my presence known, so I wouldn't startle him. My footsteps crunched in the wet sand and my tail's electricity crackled in the wind. I stood beside him as he explained what was on his mind.

"And—and—I know it's been half a month now, but I can't..." He hiccupped. "I can't stop thinking about her!"

"Fionn, please don't be ashamed," Su said. "We will *never* stop thinking about her."

"I know. I'm not saying I need to 'get over her.' But... why am I still crying? None of you are still crying. Why am I the weak one in the family? What's wrong with me?"

"None of us have 'gotten over her,'" Eruwan replied softly.

"You had a unique bond to Tawny, Fionn," I said. "You played with her more than anyone else. It's only natural you'd feel a different kind of loss. Besides, I still cry. I cried earlier today, but it was while you were at school."

I hadn't actually cried today, but I said it so Fionn wouldn't think there was something wrong with him. Or think it was unmanly. In Cosmonite Wynnle society, crying was shameful, especially for men. We may have been Wynnles biologically, but culturally, we were North Corridorean Aloutians. We had more in common with the herbivorous Florae, who encouraged outward and powerful displays of emotion. There was nothing unmanly about crying, but there was something unmanly about pretending you were strong because you hid your emotions.

Fionn sniffed and rubbed his puffy eyes. I sat beside him on the wet sand, and put my arm around his shoulder. He leaned into my chest and bawled. I rubbed his shoulders and mane as he released his frustrations:

"I miss her so much, Dad! I want to play kiwi-batte with her! I want to take her to Kiwi Island! I want to tease her about her silly bell! I want... I want to... talk to her again. She was just seven, but she was so funny!"

"You'll see her again," Heliodor said. "When you go to Spiritua."

Su ruffled the top of my head. "Stay with him, Ami-honey. I need to check on dinner. It's almost done. Don't worry about the meat. I've got it cooking, too."

I held Fionn until he was ready to go. I'd be here for him, my poor son who'd lost his best friend.

I wondered if I would black out again. If so, would I fall over onto Fionn? He was getting bigger and stronger; he could push me aside if needed. Both times it had happened was when I was speaking to Miltico. It must have had something to do with that bastard...

We gathered for dinner. Fionn had collected his emotions, but his eyes were still pale silvery and puffy.

Dinner was the usual—white rice, oko, a fish Su had traded with Deep Sea, and whatever fruits we'd gathered. The oko and fish were flavored with sprinkles of the cumin and kyamo I had apparently bought earlier. Or maybe Su had bought it. I had no recollection of events after Su entered the shop. It was a rich, flavorful taste. The scent of kyamo alone could make me salivate. To actually eat it... oh, it was divine! I'd heard from heretics who'd lost Cherribell's blessing that kyamo made food taste as good as it had been when they were blessed. Although I had no intention of losing my blessings, it was nevertheless a comforting thought that kyamo would always grace my taste buds.

The bowl of steena pudding sat on our table, too, with enough portions remaining for everyone to enjoy for dessert. The bowl, made of porcelain, looked humorously out of place with our bone tableware.

Cohaku scarfed down her oko with gusto, ate her rice, then moved to take a portion of steena pudding. She had many quirks when she ate, but one of them was that she would finish one food before moving on to the next. If she had meat, rice, and a steena on her plate, she would eat them in that order, and she wouldn't *touch* one until the first was done. She only made exceptions for drinks, as she'd take a drink of fruit punch after every few bites.

Liesle shot a look at Cohaku, but our daughter was not paying attention. She rarely looked at people's faces, and she certainly wouldn't have made eye contact.

"I heard you ignored your brother when he was crying," Liesle said.

Su and I both looked at Liesle with cautionary eyes. I wished to convey through my expression 'Leave her alone. Let her eat. Don't shame her for it'... but Liesle was stubborn and wanted the children to get along. If only she could see that her pushing of Cohaku had done more harm than good. The more she pushed, the more Cohaku pulled away.

"You need to apologize to Fionn. He needs our support. You can't just brush him off."

"Yes, I can," she said. "Eruwan and Heliodor were there. Then Mapa Su and Daddy. Even Maika was there. They can support him. He doesn't need me."

"Everyone needs to pitch in," Liesle said. "Including you. You're a part of this family. You eat at this table, so you need to get along with everyone."

"No!" she shouted. "I hate Fionn! He bullied me!"

"Two years ago!" Liesle cried. "And he has apologized for it *countless* times. When are you going to forgive him?"

Cohaku scowled. "I remember the pain. I won't forget what he said to me."

"You don't have to forget about it, but you *must* forgive him."

"No, I don't. I refuse."

"If you eat with this family, you forgive this family."

Cohaku bared her teeth and rose. "Fine! I won't eat with you, then!" She threw her portion of steena pudding on her plate and stormed off outside.

Liesle sighed, took a drink of fruit punch, and set it down with harsh finality.

"I'm *trying*, alright?" my wife said, almost on the verge of tears.

"You've always had difficulty communicating with Cohaku," Su said. "I'll talk to her after dinner."

Fionn had shrunk into a ball of shivering silence and stopped eating during the confrontation. I was not next to him to comfort him, but Heli was. The younger brother rubbed his head on Fionn's arm.

"You alright, son?" I asked.

"Not really," he mumbled in a low voice. "I just... I might as well stop trying to be nice to my sisters. Every time I try, I fuck up."

"Language," Liesle said.

Su waved two arms at her in a calming motion. "Let it slide. There are more important things to discuss."

Liesle scowled, but by the way her expression eased, she knew Su was right. "Cohaku is just a brat, and it's not your fault Tawny passed away. You don't have any problems with Eruwan or Nio, do you?"

Eruwan looked back and forth to me and Su, expectantly, like we needed to come to her rescue. What did she need rescuing from?

"I don't know," Fionn said. "Ask them. Or ask Eruwan, since Nio won't give you an answer."

"Just drop the subject," Su begged. "This isn't helping anyone."

Silently, we took his advice and finished our dinner with naught but Deep Sea's crashing fingers and the clacking of our claws on bone plates.

Chapter Eleven: Cohaku

After dinner, Su went out to Cohaku's tree house. He was brimming with confidence, sure that his irresistible charm and sweet demeanor would win our daughter over. He came back looking like a deflated balloon, all four of his arms hanging limply to his side and a pathetic frown staining his face. Still I wanted to kiss him... Ugh, this was not the time.

"I even promised to make her some cupcakes," he whined.

"I suppose I'll talk to her next," I said. "I'm going to my ateli afterward, so if you need me, I'll be there. You better make good on that cupcake oath."

I bumbled my way out of the house, wondering what the hell I was supposed to say to her. Of all my kids, Cohaku was the one I was most awkward with. I could talk to the others like a normal dad and they'd respond to me like normal children. Well, Nio would respond in her own way, but I knew what she was communicating most of the time. Cohaku, though... her brain worked differently.

The sun was halfway into Deep Sea. Golden light threw long shadows. The shade of palm trees on the beach reached all the way to Coconut Crab Circle, where its namesake crustaceans scavenged for fruit dropped in the heavy winds. One bright blue crab had claimed a coconut and was hard at work drilling its claw for the sweetness inside.

Cohaku's tree house had been built into a thick, lush tree with branches growing in a wide circle. Its dark green leaves grew from thinner branches that drooped down like hair. The tree house had no ladder; the only way up was to fly through the curtain of leaves or to climb the trunk. As a winged Wynnle, Cohaku could use either method, depending on her mood.

The draped leaves cloaked the tree house in darkness, but I usually knew if Cohaku was there because she typically took off her tail's covering when she was at home. Her electricity flickered and waved, like she was swinging it to and fro. She swung her tail when she was angry.

"Cohaku," I called in the most neutral voice I could muster. I didn't want to scare her by sounding angry or upset. I couldn't blame her for not forgiving Fionn for the bullying he'd done. Her tail went still, but she didn't say a word in response.

What the hell was I going to say? I hadn't planned this at all.

Oh, fuck it, there was nothing I could say that would have made her feel better. I might as well not bother. It would only push her away from the family more if I tried to pressure her into getting along with the boy who'd once bullied her.

"I'm going to be in my ateli for a few hours. If you'd rather lock yourself in there with me, you can. No one will bother you. You'll have to wear a visor the whole time, though. I don't want your mother and Mapa Su eating me alive because I let you go blind."

I stood in silence, giving her ample time to respond if she wished, but when she did not, I left her alone. The scuttling crabs down the road might as well have been my only audience.

Although Mr. Onoretti had given me his blessing in regard to taking a break, I genuinely wanted to carve tonight. Despite the trauma, despite the drama—or perhaps *because* of it—the serenity of my ateli put my mind at ease. Here I was lulled by the crashing of waves into an almost hypnotic trance. Here everything was in its proper place. Here I was in control. Nothing out of the ordinary would happen in my domain. If the ground opened up beneath me, I would accept it as the will of Gods who hated me.

I finished the Lagodore statue's carving stage. Next came the dyeing process. Dyes were cheap and plentiful in Aloutia. Various colors were scooped out of the Dye Rivers[1] half a planet away, but easily traded, thanks to portals. The guild kept me supplied with dyes and other tools. We merchants were instructed to only use dyes given to us by the guild. I was sure they had some business agreement with the Republic of the Dye Rivers, but it was also true that some dyes would block light from emanating from the crystal. A merchant of light experimenting with their own dyes risked turning a priceless work of art into a caliginous chunk of worthless rock.

A soft, almost inaudible knock came from the door. Cohaku? Had she decided to take me up on my offer? Liesle's knocks were far stronger, and Su liked to use all four hands at once.

I cracked the door open so as not to blind whoever was on the other side. Cohaku was indeed there, looking down so all I could see was her golden mane entwined in a dozen tiny furculae. Her tail's spark had dimmed—shyness.

I doubted she wanted to talk. She probably just wanted to be someplace where

1. Several rivers at the Twenty Thousand Rivers transformation circle, where water becomes a different liquid. In their case, many different colors of dye.

no one would yell at her to come down from the tree house. The sad part of the matter was, we'd initially built the tree house to be her safe place. If everyone kept pestering her while she was up there, it would lose all meaning.

"You want in?" I asked.

"Yeah," she mumbled.

I had a small visor in the ateli, made to fit over a child's head. I'd bought it from another merchant of light when Eruwan was younger and had wanted to watch me work. I handed it to Cohaku and let her in once it was safely over her eyes.

She wandered to the shelf of raw crystalights, but just looked at them. I didn't need to remind her to be careful; she knew.

I sat at my desk and resumed the dye job. Cohaku stood to the side, hands on the table, watching in silence. Her tail's spark livened up again and she waved it playfully, though in her case I believed she considered studying akin to playing.

Crystalights had the curious trait of being absorbent. Liquid applied to a spot for a decent time would soak inside. Merchants of light used a special kind of brush that we loaded dye into similar to a syringe, then held over a spot on the crystal to slowly embed the liquid deeper. Getting it back out if you fucked up was damn near impossible. The only method I knew was to ask Deep Sea to reclaim any liquid inside, but summoning the Demon Lord of Despair, the mind of the ocean, to erase an artistic mistake? It was a bold choice and would require a big enough sacrifice to make it worth his time. Su had only performed that particular ritual once, back when I was an apprentice merchant of light and he'd wanted to prove to me that he could summon Deep Sea with impunity. He'd only done it to show off being a Godblood... and being raised by Demon King Susan.

Yes, he had been raised by one of the three Demon Kings between the ages of eight and eighteen. When asked about his past, Su had two stories: one where he was born a girl, and one where he was born a boy. He always told both stories, so no one would assume.

In the girl-Su story, King Susan had shared her own pain at being a woman in Ophidia who was expected to be powerful, to not fall in love with men, and to enslave men. And to be betrayed by her fellow women when she decided she wouldn't play their game of oppression. In that version, Su chose to become neutral because he did not want Ophidia to even *want* him back as a noblewoman.

In the boy-Su story, King Susan had warned him that Ophidia would only ever see him as a tool. A Godblood to be hypnotized into obedience, and a dick to produce Godblood babies with their noblewomen. In that version, Su chose to become neutral as a means to mutilate himself, so he could never be forced to have children. If the Ophidians captured him, he might become their Godblood puppet, but he would at least deny them the pleasure of his seed.

The Demon King was also the source of Su's bone obsession. King Susan herself was a bone-based entity, though I had never seen her. Su described her as having only a skull for a head and riding astride a shortfur monoceros[2] whose head was likewise only its skull and horn.

"Daddy," Cohaku said.

She broke my reverie. I blinked away my thoughts and loaded dye into the pen. "What is it?"

"Is that for Usana?"

Gods bless my daughter. She could be so clever at times yet so naive at other times. I hadn't even known Usana existed when I'd received this commission. Milti sure as hell couldn't afford a crystalight, and even if he could, I doubted he'd get one for the daughter he barely bothered to feed.

"No. I don't know who it's for."

"Mm. Would you make one for her?"

"I would love to, Cohaku, but I buy all my crystalights from Mr. Onoretti, then sell them back to him. If I were to take one for my own projects, I'd lose out on a lot of money."

"Is it stealing?"

"Legally, no, because I bought them from him. They belong to me now. But the understanding is that I'll make a profit when I sell them back to him. Then he'll make a profit when he sells it to the customer."

"Is that why you've never made sculptures of us? Do we have to buy it from you?"

"It's illegal to sculpt a living child," I said, reciting words from art school I'd learned by rote memorization. Only at that moment did I realize... I could sculpt Tawny.

"Why's that?" Cohaku asked.

"Those are the rules of the merchants of light guild. You can only sculpt a specific person's image if you have their consent, but kids cannot legally consent. I can sculpt a nonspecific person, though, such as this Lagodore, or a deceased child. Perhaps I'll make a crystalight of Tawny to remember her by."

Cohaku cupped her chin in her hand. "Hmm..." She said nothing else for several minutes. Whatever she was wondering, she must have come to a satisfactory conclusion with her own critical thinking skills.

"Could I buy that Lagodore from you instead of you giving it to Mr. Onoretti?"

"If you had the money for it, you could."

"How much?"

I wanted to laugh, but I knew it would only annoy her. When anyone laughed in response to her ignorance—even if it was something I couldn't expect a child to know—she interpreted it as mocking. She wanted everyone to think she was as

---

2. A unicorn

smart as an adult.

"Five hundred red coins," I informed her.

Her tail went still. I glanced at her face without turning my head; through the visor, she wouldn't be able to tell I was looking at her. As expected, her mouth hung open. I'd have bet her eyes were wide open in shock, but she was dutifully wearing her visor as well.

"One red coin is one hundred lime coins. One lime coin is four yellow coins."

"That's correct."

"I only have six lime coins and eleven yellows."

"You're nine years old, Cohaku. When you become an adult, you'll get a job that pays you in red coins."

"Five hundred of them?"

"You'll have to save up. Crystalights aren't supposed to be cheap. There aren't many of them in the world. If one person could buy them all and hoard them, cities throughout Aloutia wouldn't have Godlights."

"Mys Volkhv says everyone should have one crystalight. One to be their lifelong companion. But only one. Any more, and they risk the wrath of L-Lu... Luco... the Mind God."

Cohaku had always had difficulties saying Lucognidus's name. It wasn't related to her lisp, which only messed up on the 'sh' sound. Something about the Lord Mind Spirit's name just didn't come easy for her.

"Can you say his name?"

"Yes."

"I hope you're telling the truth. I won't ask you to demonstrate, because I know how much you hate it. But if there's one thing you need to pronounce correctly, it's his name. Some silly people believe demons cannot say his name, and you may be asked to prove whether you're possessed or not based on if you can say his name." We were lucky we didn't live in a place with such superstitions. Su had told us stories about places on the other side of Aloutia where children were taught the names as early as possible, and some of the so-called "holy" cities made guests recite the Gods' names before allowing entry.

"Luc—Lucog..." she huffed in annoyance. "Lucognidus. If he's such a great God, why couldn't he give himself an easier name?"

That... *might* have been blasphemy. "Don't say that in public, especially not around your teacher." Cohaku wouldn't be punished for blaspheming at her age, but *I* could be punished for not raising her correctly. Thankfully the volkhvs didn't use corporal punishment in this day and age, but if I were to acquire a reputation for blasphemy, that might be enough to get the lawkeepers into Steena Village for the express purpose of arresting me and taking me to Hydra Island, the prison island.

"I *know*," Cohaku said in a smart-ass tone. She'd definitely picked it up from Su. Her inflection was just like his. "I don't talk about the Gods in front of her."

"What about when you do your daily worship?"

"What's that?"

I was taken aback. "Does Mys Volkhv not make you pray to Lucognidus every day at school?"

Cohaku went silent in her noncommittal way, like she was afraid of incriminating herself or upsetting me if she gave an answer I didn't like.

"I suppose the Mind church's policy changed since I was a kid," I said. "Or maybe your volkhv is more lax than mine was. When I was in school, our volkhv made us kneel in front of the statue of Lucognidus every morning before classes began and recite a prayer asking him to grant us knowledge, wisdom, all that mud and sludge."

"Did it work?"

"No. And being forced to do it only made me despise the dumb rituals of religion. Still, most people are religious, including people in positions of power over us, so I have kept my thoughts private."

"Power over us? Who's that? Mapa Su is the child of a God. Can't he beat up anyone who tries to bully us?"

"It's not that easy. There are other Godbloods who could beat him up." That probably wasn't the best thing to tell her. On one hand, I didn't want to upset her. On the other hand, she needed to know the truth about authority. "Besides, he hates religion as much as your mother and I do. It's why he chose to live a quiet, peaceful life with us. He could have become a merchant of dance or joined the Godblood Brigade, but he didn't want that kind of life."

"That's why we don't do any demigod prayers, isn't it?"

"That's part of it," I said. "The other part is that most rituals don't reach the demi you're praying to. There are billions of people in the Pentagonal Dominion. At any moment, thousands of people might be begging the same demi for help, and they can only help one person at a time. And that's only if they're working. Demis are people, too. They have to sleep and take breaks." Growing up, my mother had kept an offertory vessel to Ashen Soul, the Demigod of the Hearth and Home. When Liesle and I moved into the megawhale house with Su, I'd thought we'd have a vessel for Ashen Soul in our house, too. It wasn't something I had done out of devotion, but simply because it was our community's way of life. Everyone, everywhere, said their daily prayers. But Su asked why we should ask Ashen Soul to bless our homes when we could manage it on our own. Thereafter, we rarely prayed to any demigods. I had occasionally performed the ritual to Haolu, Demigoddess of Creativity and Artistry, when I felt my well of creativity had dried up. It was a trick we'd been taught in art school, but Haolu must have been busy with so many people praying to her, she had never inspired me. I had not performed her ritual in many years now.

"If you hate rituals, do you hate the fire feasts and sacrifices to Deep Sea, too?"

"I don't hate fire feasts. Those are fun. Even if there are religious aspects, you have food and games, too. And... Deep Sea's rituals are practical. He will always answer a summons, unlike the demis. Deep Sea has given us food and promises of safety."

"And our house."

"And our house," I agreed. The giant megawhale skeleton acting as the support for our house was given to us by Deep Sea. Well, given to Su. As he told it, after he left the care of King Susan, Su journeyed through Aloutia for a few years as a traveling merchant of bone, specializing in dentistry since many rural folks didn't have a dentist nearby. When he decided to settle down, he made a massive sacrifice to Deep Sea and asked him to give him a whale carcass, but to put it on the closest beach to wherever it was at the time. Su would make his house wherever Deep Sea put it. At the time, Su was on a distant continent, but didn't want to live there. He wanted to gamble on fate, or perhaps on the whim of the Lord of Despair. Deep Sea must have been in a jolly mood, or perhaps Su's sacrifice had been remarkable, because he put the whale in our tropical paradise. He could have given Su a whale near the ice caps.

Lucky for me. Without Su, where would I be in life right now? How miserable would I be?

Cohaku watched me work for a while, saying nothing. Just watching me apply drop after drop of dye onto the Lagodore.

"Um, can I ask a stupid question?" she asked.

"There are no stupid questions," I said. I was just repeating something Su had said once. I wasn't so clever as to come up with that pithy saying on my own.

"What does 'molest' mean?"

The entire world stopped.

I froze. My blood went still. My breathing halted. I set the Lagodore down before I let too much dye get into a spot it wasn't meant to be in.

What the fuck? Where had she heard *that* word?

"Who said that word to you?" I asked in a voice that had lost all warmth.

She shrunk back. "I'm sorry. I knew it would make you angry. It took all my courage to ask." She put a paw under her visor, making no effort to hide that she was crying.

"No, Cohaku, please. I'm not angry at you. But if someone said that word to you... Was it one of your siblings?"

"No."

"Was it someone at school?"

"No."

The face of Miltico came unbidden to my skull. "Was it Usana's dad?"

"Yeah."

I swore I would choke that bastard. I wouldn't draw blood. I wouldn't go berserk. Calmly, controlled, I would choke him until he passed out.

I had to remain calm around Cohaku. I wanted to ask so many more questions for context. When did she speak to him without me around? What else did he say? Was she alone with him? But all those questions would scare her away. She'd close up like a jealous oyster guarding a pearl when I needed her to *open* up.

"I'm sorry you had to hear that word," I said. "It's not a good word."

Gods, what if she heard that word because he threatened to do it to her? I needed to know! How could I ask without scaring her? I had no idea. Su would know. Su was the better parent. He always knew what to say. He knew how to talk to kids about their problems. Maybe I could get him to have this discussion with Cohaku instead.

"Oh, okay. Um, can I say why Mr. Svelt said that word?"

"You can tell me anything," I said calmly while internally screaming *'Yes! Please, tell me more!'*

"He said it was something to do with your name. I don't get it. I know I call you 'Daddy', but if someone asks me what your name is, what am I supposed to say if 'Amiere' isn't good?"

I understood now. Part of it was my fault for continuing to use the name Liesle had given me when we were young and hopelessly in love. In our patois, 'Ami' was 'love', and adding 'ere' to a word made it figuratively belong to someone. My public name meant 'my love.' We had only intended it to be used by Liesle and Su, who both went back and forth between calling me Ami and Amiere. Liesle even used Mo Ami most of the time, which was just another way of saying 'my love.'

But foolish me, I hadn't anticipated that my kids would grow up thinking of my name as 'Amiere' instead of 'Ami' and that I should be introduced that way.

"Next time someone asks, tell them my name is Ami. That's what the other villagers call me, right?"

"Okay."

I expected another question out of her. Maybe curiosity about why I didn't have my name changed legally. Maybe she thought I'd be mad if she kept up the conversation.

The primary reason why I kept the name Amiere at this point was because it was tied to my professional life. All my files and records with the merchants of light listed me as Amiere Lasteran. If I changed my name now, it would be a bureaucratic mess. They might think Ami Lasteran was my son or brother. I was at an age now where I figured it didn't matter what the legal documents said. Hell, most people with access to those files wouldn't know our patois and wouldn't know it meant 'my lover.'

Cohaku stayed with me until it was time to go back home and go to bed. I had the impression based on her restless pacing around that she was bored, but was too afraid of Liesle to go back to the house alone.

Everyone else was under Somniel's influence when we trod inside, using our tails to light the way.

At the door to Cohaku and Eruwan's room, I held the leaf-door open for her. "May Somniel give you good rest." Funny that after all my thoughts about how we didn't perform demigod rituals, we still spoke their names. It was done easily enough, I supposed.

"You, too," she replied.

Invoking the Demigoddess of Sleep's name like that was a standard phrase throughout Aloutia, wishing a person a good night's sleep. Traditionally, the other person would then invoke Yume, Demigoddess of Dreams, but Cohaku had a poor grasp of idioms and phrases.

Liesle and Su slept close to each other tonight. Liesle's arm rested between two of Su's arms. There was just enough room for me on the side. I was glad to see them close, physically at least. They must have talked and come to an understanding while I was at work. Good... good... maybe things would go back to normal soon.

Chapter Twelve: Farewell

Every parent must contend with the sobering reality that there were two possibilities laid before them: either they would not stay on this mortal plane long enough to watch the end of their child's journey, to protect them and love them as they grew older...

Or they would. They would bear witness to that tragic ending and be left standing alone on the shore of the sea of despair.

The day of the fire feast had arrived. The weather calendar said this would be a perfect day with the only rain being in the early morning and late evening. As the funeral was held in the mid-afternoon, I could not use the excuse of rain getting in my eyes to hide my tears.

Su bought five goats and three susi, butchered in a religiously-approved method, for the entire village to feast upon. We might not have been religious, but we followed the Spiritist laws of animal slaughter out of kindness. To go against the Gods, in this case, was to be needlessly cruel. On certain days, shinigami traveled to designated spots where farmers and herders took their animals meant for slaughter. Shinigami could kill without causing pain. They severed the animal's soul, if it had one; goats and susi did not always have a soul. If it had a soul, the shinigami would take it to Spiritua to live in everlasting peace and joy. If it did not, the animal at least did not have to suffer in its final moments.

With help from everyone else in Steena Village, we set out several tables encircling the bonfire. The fire was long—we placed kindling in a line so the fire would cover more area. It roasted all three animals at the same time. The aroma of garlic and kyamo hit my maxilla. Had I not been in a somber mood, the smell would have excited me.

As it was, this was Tawny's farewell feast. I thought of nobody else except my precious girl.

But I was at peace. She was in Spiritua. She was alright. She wasn't in pain or crying. I was sure there were people in Spiritua who took care of children. As much as I resented Lucognidus because his volkhvs had made me pray to him every day when I was a child, I at least respected the Mind God for setting up afterlife services for children. Or so the volkhvs preached. It wasn't like I could stroll up there and see it for myself.

I *had* to believe Tawny was safe and happy. If I didn't have those thoughts to comfort me, I'd have lost my soul to sorrow. I would have drowned myself in Deep Sea and begged the Lord of Despair to swallow me, to grind my body into debris and free my soul.

The whole village was here—nearly five hundred people. My mother and her wife were curled up by one of the roasting goats. I had visited my mother the previous day, mostly to make sure she knew the fire feast was today, but also to ask her about my episodes of blacking out. She had never heard of such things happening to Wynnles. In all the years she'd spent on Cosmo before being exiled to Aloutia, she had not once heard of any berserker state other than the one triggered by blood scent.

My mother and her fairly-new partner were both quadrupeds. I never knew my father, but I had clearly inherited bipedalism from him. But my mother's quadruped gene was still in me... and had been passed down to Heliodor.

I should have never had kids. I should have known after Heliodor that my genes were flawed. If I had stopped at Heli, then Tawny wouldn't have ever been born. This whole tragedy could have been averted. What was wrong with me? Why did I want so many kids? Just to fulfill my own fantasy of having enough kids to have my own kiwi-batte team?

When I was a young man, I'd envisioned my future family differently. I pictured more sons like Fionn. Fit, athletic. I hadn't foreseen the girls whose brains worked differently than mine. I hadn't foreseen the pain of losing a child.

Miltico was also here, taking pieces of mango from a plate. Why that that fucker here? I didn't want him anywhere near me, but especially not when this was an event for Tawny. He could have at least brought Usana so she could eat.

I approached him, making no effort to hide my displeasure at his presence. My tail's electricity crackled as it swayed.

"Milti!"

He startled and nearly dropped the mango.

"Ami! I'm not here to spoil your sad feast."

"Too late. I *was* sad, now I'm sad and angry. Why are you here? Who invited you? Did you come because we asked your father to come?" I had seen the shopkeeper wandering around. He was welcome here. Hell, most of the supplies came from his shop.

"Just wanted to get my share and go. I'm not going to stick around to watch you eat that goat. I'm not a fucking cannibal."

"Your share? You deserve nothing. Where's Usana? Where's her share?"

He frowned. Gods, I could have punched his stupid goat nose. "She'll get hers."

"I want to watch her eat," I said. "Go home. Get her. Bring her back and let me watch her eat. Bring your wife, too. Where is she? I haven't seen her much since you arrived in the village. Or are you starving her, too?"

"My wife? She's right over there." He pointed behind me.

I turned, only to feel like an idiot when I realized he was pointing at Orienna, standing with her daughter Nell. They were having a conversation with Mr. Onoretti, guarded by his giant Sasorin bodyguard. I hadn't even realized they were in the village today.

But moreover, this fucker still thought of Orienna as his wife? How delusional was he?

When I turned back, he was gone. He had escaped down the road, going as fast as his hoofed feet would take him. I could have caught up easily, but I didn't care. Let the coward flee.

I joined Orienna, mostly so I could talk to Mr. Onoretti. I had not expected him here. He was dressed in formal business attire, this one a bright blue with yellow fur trim.

"Mr. Lasteran," he said. He was so short in comparison to me, he had to make his horns nearly parallel to the ground to make eye contact. Or at least to make most of his face meet mine. Yosoe eyes could turn in such a way that they could look up without lifting their whole head, but other species found it unsettling. Uncanny, untrustworthy. Most socially-conscious Yosoe would turn their heads to avoid unnerving their friends. "My deepest condolences. I wish you and your family the best in these trying times. You have my sympathy."

"Thank you, Mo Senya. I didn't know you were here. I'd have sent a formal invitation."

"I hadn't expected to be here so soon, but the lovely Mys Nell Denwall agreed to let me stay in her house for a while."

Nell grinned up at me. Quite a different reaction than she'd displayed when I'd first pitched the idea of letting Mr. Onoretti stay in her future home. Perhaps a few coins had changed her attitude.

"I hope there's something here for you to eat. I, uh, wasn't expecting a Yosoe other than Mr. Phoebus Svelt to show up, and he always brings his own meals."

"I'm quite alright. Thank you for your concern. I'm already drooling at the scent of these roasting goats. I'll take a piece from the one you've seasoned with kyamo."

"You can eat goat?" I asked.

Mr. Onoretti tilted his head as if I'd just asked the dumbest question imaginable. "I'm not a goat, Mr. Lasteran. Not any more than you're a lion. Of course I can eat goat. It's delicious!"

I blushed, embarrassed. I was going off what Miltico had told me mere minutes ago. I thought *that* at least had been truthful, even if every other word out of his mouth had been mud and sludge.

"I apologize. Another Yosoe told me it was cannibalism, but that Yosoe is an idiot. I should have known better than to believe him."

He chuckled jovially. "No offense taken. By law, cannibalism is when a sapient person consumes another sapient person. We can eat the animals we became sapient from, so long as it doesn't go against Spiritist dogma. Goats and lions are both mid-sapient, so we're morally fine eating either. Truthfully, it would be more cannibalistic for you to eat me than it would be for me to eat that goat."

I scratched behind my head. "You would know. You're the law expert."

Nell listened with great interest. "Wow, that's the legal definition of cannibalism? What's the punishment if someone were caught eating a sapient person?"

Mr. Onoretti stroked his beard. "It would depend on many factors. If it had been done out of necessity for survival, all charges would be dropped. If the defendant was repentant and had made amends to their church, they could possibly get a thirty percent life sentence on Hydra Island, though probably lower. If they had no conscience? That could be a life sentence to Hydra Island. If it was a particularly vicious case, the prosecutor might even petition the Emperor for execution."

Even I shivered at the thought. Execution was unheard-of in Aloutia. Only the Immortal Emperor Ivan could pass that judgment, and I didn't know of any recent instances of it being carried out. The last time I knew of it happening was during the Greed Wars, when he condemned several noble families to execution for their excessive decadence.

"That's so cool," Nell said in a breathy voice full of awe.

"If you want to know more about law or business... or punishment... come visit me at your house later." He chuckled, perhaps at the irony of a person visiting him in their own house. "Better yet, do so after tomorrow. My daughter will be here, then. She's about your age. Maybe you'll get along."

"That'll be a good time," Orienna said, putting an arm around her daughter's shoulder. "Let's not talk about such dark topics here, though. Ami doesn't want to hear that kind of thing."

It hadn't actually bothered me any more than I was already bothered. Seeing Miltico here had ruined any hope I had for a day that had already promised to be terrible.

I tried to salvage the conversation and be a good guest by changing the subject. "Are you hungry, Oboro? I don't know what Sasorin eat, so I apologize if we don't have anything for you, but let us know for next time."

The bodyguard had not expected to be spoken to. His eyes went wide, his mouth fraught by a tight frown, mandibles opened. His lower two hands, always on his two side-swords, gripped them even tighter.

"Um, Signore?"

"You don't need my permission to answer, Oboro," Mr. Onoretti said. "Or are you just nervous around adults?"

The Sasorin nodded ever so subtly.

"Very well." Mr. Onoretti faced me again. "I promise you Oboro has plenty to eat. Sasorin *prefer* different foods than any species here, but they *can* eat goat and susi."

That was a relief. "I'm sorry if I scared you, Oboro. You're doing a diligent job as Mr. Onoretti's bodyguard."

"Th-thank you."

The golden-skinned Sasorin had the look of a bodyguard perfectly. His claws, scorpion tail, the swords to his side, and the massive khopesh across his back gave him an appearance that would intimidate all but the largest species. And yet when he spoke, and when he glanced nervously at his employer, it was easy to see the boy in him. Oboro was only fourteen—the same age as Eruwan. I couldn't imagine this weary child living the same amount of life as my precious Eruwan.

"I've been quite lucky to have him around," Mr. Onoretti said. "Although he hasn't had to protect me yet—and let us thank the Gods for that—he has been useful in other ways. He's a good cook. He's already won over my partner and daughter with his scrumptious dishes."

"Perhaps we could show him how to make Steena Village delicacies," Orienna said. "I don't know if Sasorin eat steena, but I know Yosoe do! You'll make Mr. Onoretti and his family quite happy if you learn to make steena pudding."

Oboro gulped, twitching the fingers on his lower hands as they gripped his side-swords. "I... will do my best."

"You and your family are welcome to dinner at my house any time," I added. "You said they're arriving tomorrow? Why don't you give them a day to rest here and get settled in, then eat with us the day after tomorrow?"

Mr. Onoretti smiled. "That's a wonderful idea. I look forward to it."

"Oh, Su's here!" Orienna announced as a cheer swelled from the onlookers. "Come, Nell. Let's get to our drums." Mother and daughter went to the table where their instruments awaited. A few other villagers were proficient enough with instruments to participate in the fire feast's musical parts. Eruwan was there, too, looking concerned. She hadn't played her drum in many fire feasts yet, so she was undeniably nervous that she'd mess up. Besides, she'd yet to play for any of Su's dances.

"Master Scrimshander?" Mr. Onoretti said. "Is he performing a bone dance?"

"He is," I said. "He's going to summon Deep Sea, too, to answer a few questions."

His brow creased. "Questions? What kind?"

I didn't want to elucidate the details. It was difficult enough thinking about Tawny. I couldn't imagine being Su, asking the ocean whether he was responsible for her death.

"Apologies," Mr. Onoretti said solemnly. "I let my curiosity get ahead of me. Obviously, you wouldn't want to talk about it now. You're probably eager to just get this over with."

The performance was about to begin. I held my breath as I turned toward where everyone else was looking.

Su came from the direction of his ateli, dressed in his bone dancer costume.

Gods, he was gorgeous and powerful. And yet, this was to honor our dead daughter. A war waged in my skull, in my sternum, in the marrow of every bone of my body. My urge to love Su battled with my need to cry for Tawny.

His headdress was made of the skulls of the three animals known as susi in various languages—the boar-like susi we ate, a wolf, and tiny fish skulls sprinkled throughout his hair. Blue parrot feathers adorned the tops of the bigger skulls. His chest was covered by scapulae and elephant tusks. Bracelets of vertebrae sat on his wrists, connected by sinew to his chest armor. Hanging from the sinew were ulnae, radii, fibulae, and tibiae. He stretched his four arms as he approached, letting the bones dangle and clack together with the swaying of his movements.

Su jumped on top of a table. "Thank you for coming today, everyone. I wish we could have gathered for a happy event. It's my great honor to dance at festivals, holidays, love celebrations, hatching-days, and fertility rites. Although I am honored to dance for my deceased daughter, it does not give me pleasure. Let us celebrate the life of Tawny Denwall, lost to us at only seven years old, but living forevermore in Spiritua. Tawny Denwall!"

Per custom, we all shouted her name. "Tawny Denwall!"

Finally, the war was won. My grief defeated all other feelings and left me a shivering, bawling mess. I hid my face in my hands and howled with pain and tears. Liesle came to me and put an arm around my shoulders.

"Hatched on Egg Day, Zhizn 22, 553. Taken from her family on Veter 18, 561. Born to Liesle Denwall, Amiere Lasteran, and myself, Su Scrimshander. We give her to you, O Gods. As she is but a child, let her not fall into centennial sleep, but learn and play in Spiritua. Grant her the patience to await us as we take our time reaching her side. Great God Sawyer, watch over her soul and save her from demonkind. Great God Lucognidus, watch over her mind so she might grow into a mature adult. Please, O Lord, Great Conqueror God, The Infinite Wisdom, protect this child from the one who is her rightful God. Born a Lightning elemental, she is subject to the cruelty of Sparkato. Please save her, Lord Lucognidus. Watch over her soul with one of your Twenty Thousand Eyes. As you conquered the world and saved us all from demonkind, may you conquer Sparkato and save our daughter."

As dark as those words were, they were the standard prayer following the death of a Lightning elemental.

"I surrender up now her magic name!" Su covered his mouth with his four hands and whispered her magic name. The name we gave her upon hatching. The name which was to be kept secret forever, even in death, as demons could torment dead souls as easily as they could torment the living.

Shiara Denwall. She had been given the public name 'Tawny' based on her light-brown mane. Colors inherited from me. Perhaps in another lifetime, I would have been named Tawny. She had inherited so many traits from me... Out of all our children, she had resembled me the most. You had to look hard to even find a trace of Liesle in her. What sick cruelty, that her death had occurred because she'd inherited my winglessness...

Liesle pulled me closer, allowing me to lean on her shoulder. I wanted to turn and cry. Cry and cry until my tears numbered greater than the droplets of water in Deep Sea. But I could not. I wanted to watch this ceremony. If Su could maintain his composure for this ceremony, I could do the same.

Su clapped his hands—his upper two, then his lower two—in rapid succession until the drummers took over the beat. It was a fast rhythm, punctuated by deep thumps from Orienna's timpani that made my sternum reverberate and sent shivers down my vertebrae.

Su jumped off the table and danced toward the raging bonfire, swinging his arms so the bones clacked together to the tune of the drum. He took an enormous humerus—probably from a Cosmonite lizard[1] —placed there specifically for his dance and twirled it above his head. He never ceased dancing. His lower arms kept swaying, his legs hopping and kicking to the beat in beautiful, enthralling movements. He twirled across the sand, around the bonfire, and picked up a second humerus.

Another lap around the flames, and he caught a femur tossed at him from Nell. At fire feasts, the drummers often played additional roles. I glanced toward Eruwan, getting her femur ready. Bibrachs couldn't perform the same bone dance as quadrubrachs. Usually, the ceremony involved a single femur and humerus, but Su, with four hands, excelled at using four bones.

He hit the humeri and femurs together, one then the next, as he went around the bonfire again. The drum beat picked up, with more ominous thuds from Orienna's.

At the sound of one loud hit on the timpani, Su slammed all four bones, then juggled them. He danced into the fire. Flames consumed him, licked his body as delicately as I wished I could have done, and toyed with his hair like a far gentler lover than I could ever be.

Su was immune to fire and smoke, of course. He was either blessed, or he was a Fire elemental holding his breath to avoid smoke inhalation.

Embers sprang from the bonfire as he swatted them with his bones. The smoke swirled in elegant designs as his hands wove in circles.

My beautiful Su, dressed in only bones, shrouded in an aura of burning orange and yellow, looked like the God of Fire himself. Or herself. No one in this village knew Flamboil's sex or gender, just as no one knew Su's gender. It was an all-too-apt comparison.

At the climax, he twirled and hopped in such mad circles while amidst the flames, juggling bones, that I was amazed he could still stand.

---

1. General term for animals known on Terra as dinosaurs

Su leapt out of the bonfire, next to one of the roasting goats. He dropped the two humeri so he could heft the goat over his shoulder and carried it to the ocean.

"What's he doing now?" Mr. Onoretti asked.

"Deep Sea's summoning ritual," I replied. I had dried my tears enough that I could speak without sniffling. "We intend to ask him if he was involved in the crystalights appearing beneath the village."

"What? Why didn't you tell me first? This is merchant of light business!"

Liesle scowled at him. "Sure, because it involves crystalights, but we need answers for Tawny's death, too."

Mr. Onoretti's arm twitched. He hesitated when everyone else went with Su as he marched toward the ocean.

"Is it wise to summon a Demon Lord so... casually?"

"Su has summoned Deep Sea many times," my wife replied. "He was raised by Demon King Susan and is a Godblood. I don't think he's as scared of Demon Lords as normal people are."

I turned back to look at Mr. Onoretti. I wished I were better at reading Yosoe faces. Were his horizontal pupils smaller than usual? Oboro must have sensed something amiss, too. His eyes drifted back and forth between us two.

"Something wrong?" I asked.

Mr. Onoretti forced a smile. "Something must be wrong if we're resorting to summoning Demon Lords."

Ah, was that his concern? Spiritists weren't supposed to summon demons. I wasn't religious in the slightest, so I had forgotten how taboo the act was. I was so accustomed to Su's rituals, it hadn't occurred to me that others would be unnerved by them.

"I didn't know you were religious," I said. "You're a Lightning elemental, aren't you?"

"I... I don't worship Sparkato, if that's what you're asking. But I acknowledge the Emperor's ban on summoning Demon Lords. Well, most Demon Lords. I know Deep Sea is one of the exceptions."

"You can stay away from the ceremony," Liesle suggested. "We won't think ill of you for leaving now, if you wish."

"No." The answer came alarmingly fast and with an annoyed tone. Mr. Onoretti seemed offended by the words. "Oboro, what Mys Denwall said applies to you, as well. I will not need a bodyguard for a few minutes. I'll be on the beach, surrounded by hundreds of people. If you feel it's better for your soul to stay away, you may."

"My soul would be crushed under Deep Sea's weight with despair if anything were to happen to you and I had done nothing to save you. I go where you go, Signore."

"You're too good, Oboro. Very well. Let's go together."

We headed toward Deep Sea to witness the summoning ritual.

Chapter Thirteen: Lord Deep Sea

Su waded knee-deep into the ocean, far enough for oncoming waves to go above his waist. After one of Deep Sea's fingers converged over his legs, they receded to reveal Su had transformed his legs into the tail of an orange fish.

"Ocean, hear my plea!" He spoke a prayer under his breath. I knew how this worked. He said the real words to the summoning first, which utilized his magic name—the name nobody could ever know. It was either Sunao or Sumika, though Su would never say which one was his true magic name. He repeated himself aloud so everyone could hear, saying his public name instead. "I, Su Scrimshander, hereby summon Deep Sea, Demon Lord of Despair. By my sacrifice of this biological material, you have found me worthy. Appear before me!" He tossed the goat into the next wave. Deep Sea curled his fingers around it, disintegrated it into dust, and carried the particulate into his cerulean body.

The next wave carried upon its white, foamy crest a small fish. An Anemone's companion—an orange fish with three vertical white stripes. They got their name from their tendency to live in the hair of Anemones.

"Lord Deep Sea, will you answer my questions?" Su asked.

The fish's face transformed. Its two black eyes grew into perfectly round circles, much larger than before. Its mouth morphed into a crescent, a wicked grin in a shape impossible for the fish's mouth to have formed naturally.

The face of Deep Sea. Two round, black, endless abysses for the eyes, and a smile shaped like the crescent moons of Ophidia.

The voice that came from the fish was also impossible. No creature smaller than my hand could have made that powerful, rumbling, slow voice, as deep as his deepest trench.

"My summoner... my friend... Su Scrimshander. We have many witnesses."

"Please let them hear you, Great Lord of the Oceans." As Su answered, the ocean lifted him in his hand. Su sat on a throne of pure water, his orange tail glimmering in the golden sunlight.

The waves stilled, stopping to hold Deep Sea's avatar in place. The beach had never been so quiet. Even the seagulls, cormorants, and songbirds, seeming to know this was a solemn ritual, flew away to give us a moment of peace. The crescent smile of the Anemone's companion did not move as the Demon Lord spoke; the voice came from no mouth, but rather some ethereal, unseen source. "Very well. Ask your questions, Su Scrimshander."

"Many days ago, the ground opened up beneath our village. Was this done by you?"

"I have no power over the ground beyond the reach of my fingers."

"Did you, perhaps, place something into the ground beneath you, near these shores? Something that might have transmitted an energy wave beyond your fingers? Like a ripple, but traveling through the ground?"

"Had I struck something into the ground below me, the resulting ripple would have been minuscule to your perception by the time it reached you. I do not permit tidal waves or tsunamis, if those words even exist in your language anymore."

Su nodded. I had no idea what they were talking about—literally, I'd never heard of a 'tidal wave' or a 'tsunami', whatever those were—but if it made sense to Su...

"There are crystalights beneath our village now. Did you transfer crystalights from Iuria to here?"

"I did not," Deep Sea replied.

"Do you know how they got here?"

"I do not. The Iurion—"

"Wait!" Mr. Onoretti shouted and stepped closer to Su and the Anemone's companion.

I could not imagine anyone expected the summoning to be interrupted, but I especially never thought Mr. Onoretti would intrude on a ritual. Oboro's face went pale as he hesitantly followed him toward the ocean's edge. The poor boy gulped, fearful. I'd be scared out of my wits, too, if I were the bodyguard of a man getting between a Godblood and a Demon Lord.

"Please, Master Scrimshander, you could have asked me these questions first," he said, waving his hands around desperately. "Lord Deep Sea, the matter of the crystalights is..." He hesitated as the face of the ocean turned upon him. "I apologize. My public name is Giorvi Onoretti."

"Insolent Yosoe!" the ocean roared. "If you would interrupt my conversation, at least offer your magic name and a sacrifice."

Without hesitation, Giorvi gave him what was demanded. "My magic name is Buongiornovici Onoretti. The sacrifice with be yours. Name your price."

"You are bold. You, a puny Yosoe, whose size barely matches that of the goat I consumed? Whose blood is as clear as my skin? Whose age is younger than many of the tortoises and megawhales within me? Are you certain you wish to interrupt this ritual?"

"I am."

A gasp echoed from the crowd. My eyes were wide. I half expected the ocean to crush Mr. Onoretti right then and there, and drag whatever remained of his body into the abyss, so he might feed whatever freakish fish lived inside him.

"Feed me a worthy sacrifice, Giorvi Onoretti, and I shall hear what you have to say. Let it be as worthy as the goat this Godblood has given me."

He glanced at Oboro and pointed back to the fire feast. "Bring me another goat. Hurry!"

Oboro nodded. "Y-yes, Signore!" He nearly tripped over his own feet in his rush to grab a goat from the bonfire.

"What are you doing?" Su asked the Yosoe. "We could have spoken later and compared information."

Mr. Onoretti scowled. He clenched his fists at his side and ground his teeth. I had the same curiosity as Su—what could possibly be on his mind?

"We were gonna eat that goat!" one of the villagers hollered.

"I'll pay you back for it!" Mr. Onoretti shouted back. "On my honor as a merchant of light, I'll pay for an entire fire feast for you."

That pacified the villager—I wasn't sure who had complained, but the promise of a feast would have been enough to calm anyone's temper.

Oboro returned with the goat in all four arms. "Um, do *you* have to give it to him, Signore? It's quite heavy. If you'll allow me, I'd be happy to..."

"Lord Deep Sea, will you answer my questions if the sacrifice is handed to you by my assistant?"

"Yes, if he agrees that he is here as an assistant. If he wishes to ask a question, he must feed me his magic name."

Mr. Onoretti glared at Oboro with eyes and creased brows that would have terrified me, but Oboro's face showed no fear. "Put the goat in Deep Sea. Do not speak a single word to him."

Oboro's face hardened into a stern expression, eyebrows furrowed. "I understand, Signore." He laid the goat down in the ocean's still waters. His mandibles quivered as he retreated behind the Yosoe. As with the first goat, the second was crushed into pieces too small to see. Even the scent of it never reached me, as the ocean consumed any particles that could have reached my maxilla.

Mr. Onoretti stepped closer to the Anemone's companion. "Lord Deep Sea, it's in the best interest of the merchants of light if the crystalight issue is kept between the guild and Iuria. If it has inconvenienced you in any way, I will pay for compensation."

"I have not been inconvenienced," the ocean said.

The whole village looked at him, confused, waiting for an explanation. Why was he getting involved? And to jump in suddenly—even taking one of the goats we'd brought for the feast—was a suspicious action. Why did he want to silence Deep Sea from talking about Iuria?

Su must have had all the same questions I did. With a nonplussed scowl, he asked, "Why are you so eager to stop us from talking about Iuria or the crystalights? Are you hiding something?"

"The Iurion are in the process of pressing a legal claim for all crystalight mines in Aloutia," Mr. Onoretti said. "We'd previously believed they claimed only the crystalights in the Chthonic Family Estates of Iuria, but since this is the first deposit ever found outside their estates... We have a team of legal experts looking into the matter. I fear if Steena Village got involved, you could get dragged into legal disputes."

"Good, let us!" Su raised his arms skyward. "They're under our village; we ought to own them! Actually, you've already bought them, haven't you? Who did you buy them from?"

Mr. Onoretti brushed his fingers through his grey beard. "Both Iuria and Seabells agreed to sell them to me. The merchants of light guild put the money in an escrow that will go to whoever is declared the legal owner."

"Is it not a bit presumptuous for everyone involved? Both sides agreed to sell them to you?"

"Raw crystalights can only be sold to the merchants of light," Mr. Onoretti said with absolute certainty and authority. "There's nothing presumptuous about asserting my right. We don't know how long the dispute will last. In that time, the crystalights are going to waste. These need to be turned into Godlights *immediately*."

"Why the rush?" Su asked. His tone softened, like he was about to take Mr. Onoretti's side, but needed a little more information. "Are Godlights burning out?"

"Yes. A great deposit was found eighty years ago which we turned into Godlights. Many of Aloutia's cities use crystalights from that deposit, and some have already lost their blessing. We found another deposit ten years ago which... unfortunately, due to mismanagement by our previous Guildmaster, was not allocated properly. Those crystalights ended up as trinkets or, worse, sold outside Aloutia."

Selling crystalights to Ophidia was against Aloutian law and the Makai rarely saw a need for them. They could be sold to Cosmo, but it was typically assumed that any purchaser in Cosmo intended to resell it in Ophidia.

"Lucky we found this one..." Su mumbled.

"Indeed. That mistake cost the previous Guildmaster his position, but by the time Thousand-Diamonds had taken over, the pieces were already sold and they didn't want to sabotage our reputation by recalling them. The crystalights under Steena Village, though? It could very well be a... well, I don't want to blaspheme here, but I believe the Gods intended for it to be a gift, but... messed up. I refuse to believe they intended to hurt your daughter."

Su rubbed his chin. "Machenerate is known to mess up when using her powers."

"Perhaps a Godblood such as yourself is more confident blaspheming, but I would never suggest the Lord Stone Goddess accidentally killed your daughter when she put crystalights in the ground."

Su's face relaxed. "Ah, yes. Of course, *you* would never suggest that, because you're a good man, Mr. Onoretti. But you think it. You believe it. You just won't say it."

"Some places in Aloutia will flog a person for blaspheming. I know Seabells is a more liberal nation than that, but I wouldn't want rumors going elsewhere that I am a blasphemer."

"I understand. Thank you for the advice, Mr. Onoretti. May I resume my conversation with Lord Deep Sea now?"

The Anemone's companion had not moved an inch amidst the swirling vortex holding it up. I suppressed a chuckle. Though Su and Giorvi were powerful, competent people, I had not in my wildest dreams imagined they could have pushed Lord Deep Sea aside in a conversation.

Su turned back to the fish. "Is what he said accurate, to the best of your knowledge?"

"Yes," Deep Sea replied. "I know not how the crystals came to your village. It was not my doing."

"And you didn't do it to harvest despair from us?"

The ocean laughed. Low, ominous, rumbling laughter. I felt it in the marrow of my every bone. "You conflate sorrow with despair. So many do. Are the spheres of myself and Hollow Void so easily mistaken for each other? No, there has been no *despair* in this village. If anything, the crystalights have filled your souls with hope. You who are grieving over the loss of your daughter... that has been sorrow, mostly. The few times I tasted your despair, it was not enough to satisfy me."

Su closed his eyes. "True. I apologize for my mistake, Lord of Despair."

"And if I were so concerned with harvesting despair from mortals, do you truly think I'd go through all the work to kill one child in a village of less than a thousand people?" The vortex holding the fish lifted, higher and higher, towering over Su. "Foolish Godblood..." Deep Sea's voice filled my mind with dread. I shivered and nearly fell to my knees. "If I wanted to kill someone—" Deep Sea grew higher, the fish emanated an evil, grey aura "—I'd smash an entire nation under my arm!"

A wall of water rose several dozen feet and hovered over Su menacingly.

Villagers panicked, though only Su appeared to be in any danger—not that I would expect Deep Sea to hurt him. Cohaku jumped into my arms. I hadn't even known she was so close. I hugged her, hoping to ease her fears.

"Daddy! Daddy! I can't swim!"

I watched the enormous wave looming over Su who looked remarkably nonchalant. Perhaps he also knew Deep Sea would not hurt him so long as Su had a contract with him.

I scanned the beach for my family. Eruwan clutched her drum and fell to her knees. Nio and Heliodor ran up to us. Nio tugged on Liesle's leaf-skirt, a sign she wanted to be held, and so my wife carried her. Fionn stood tall and brave against the rising wave. Some people ran screaming. I wondered if they realized that if

Deep Sea truly wanted to kill them, he would. According to legends, his hands could reach a hundred miles inland.

"Cohaku, are you okay?" Liesle asked. She put a hand on our daughter's shoulder. She wasn't in a mood to tolerate her mother and swatted her hand away.

Liesle opened her mouth to protest, but decided now was not the time or place. She grimaced and put her hand over her belly. "Damn, I think the startle he gave me may have..." She let the sentence go unspoken. The hint of her hand over her pregnant abdomen was enough.

"Imbecile mortals," Deep Sea growled. "Lest you conflate the other Trifecta's sphere with mine, what you're feeling now is terror! May Vinoc feast on it! Do not ever accuse me of a petty murder! If I wanted to kill you, I'd kill every last one of you. A single land-born child isn't worth my time! *You* aren't worth my time! If I wanted to feast on despair, I would destroy Monoceros, Seabells, Seashells, Labyrinthis, Ruby Heart, and every other city you mortals thought to build within range of my fingertips! Cry! Scream! Beg for mercy! When millions of you have perished, *then* you may ask if I am to blame."

The wall of water receded, back into the ocean... back into his body.

I let out a heavy sigh, relieved. Every bone in my body felt exhausted beyond comprehension, and I hadn't even panicked as *some* had. Cohaku cried into my chest. I rubbed her back, trying to comfort her. My poor children...

Liesle sat down and kissed the top of Nio's head. Nio watched with a smile on her face as Deep Sea's hand poured back into himself.

My wife panted as if she had just run a mile.

"Are you alright, Lisi?"

"I..." She clutched her belly. "Oh, Gods!" She set Nio down abruptly on the sand. Nio looked shocked that her mother would do such a thing. "I'm..."

"Is it the egg?" I asked. "Is it coming out?"

She nodded, grimacing in pain, and spread her legs apart. "That scare must have done it!"

"Su!" I yelled as loud as I could, though I wasn't sure if he heard me over the commotion of the other villagers. This being the sixth egg Liesle had delivered, I knew the procedure: Get out of the way. Su knew what he was doing, and his magic helped relax her.

Liesle roared louder than any noise Deep Sea had made. That got everyone's attention. In seconds, the villagers formed a circle around us. Su and our kids made a smaller circle around her.

Su helped Liesle remove her leafy skirt. Everyone was watching, but modesty be damned. He put two of his hands by her opening to grab the egg, and his other two hands on her knees. I went behind Liesle to prop her up. She grabbed one of my hands and clutched, tight. I could only imagine she squeezed my hand as powerfully as she squeezed the muscles in her cervix.

This was my sixth time and still I was nervous, anxious, terrified... and overjoyed. What joy would this child bring?

Gods, I hoped this baby had wings. I couldn't… I couldn't bear to have another Tawny.

Liesle groaned. Her forehead was slick with sweat.

"Mr. Lasteran, this is clean." Mr. Onoretti had gotten to my side without my noticing, and handed me a handkerchief. I wiped my wife's forehead.

"It's turquoise!" Su said with unparalleled joy. "A color close to your hair, Liesle. Maybe a little lighter thanks to Amiere's yellow. And with brown spots like Amiere, too. Well, if I hadn't watched you two create this egg, there'd be no doubt who the father was, even if we didn't have a Life church with a Mantodea."

I chuckled. Su was trying his best to lighten the mood. I was still rattled over Deep Sea's threat. So rattled, sadly, that I wondered if Liesle thought less of me. She clutched my hand with all her courage and power. What did I provide for her? I couldn't stop Deep Sea. I couldn't help deliver the egg.

I wondered if she was right about fear or panic triggering her body into releasing the egg. Could such emotions do that?

I helped Liesle put her skirt back on and stand. Su accepted a piece of cloth from another villager with which he cleaned the egg.

The egg was small enough to fit in one of Su's hands. That was normal. It would grow once the Life element imbued it with more nutrients. We were lucky to live on Aloutia, where the egg could bathe in the light of the Lime Moon, the Egg of the Sky, the Life Moon.

"Does blue mean the baby will have blue skin or blue hair?" Heliodor asked.

Su cleaned the egg with the cloth. "Probably skin, or fur if the baby is a quadruped like you. Fionn's egg was blue, though he has a golden mane."

Liesle leaned into me, her face nuzzling my shoulder. She was taller and stronger than me, but in that instant, she was more vulnerable than I'd ever seen her. I wrapped my arms around her.

"Good job, Lisi. I think that's the fastest you've ever pushed one out."

"I'm so tired."

"Let's get you home. Su, I'll be back in a moment to help clean up."

Mr. Onoretti spoke up before Su had a chance. "Oh, nonsense! Your wife needs you now. I'm sure your family would be able to make some plates of food for you and bring them to you."

"Yeah!" Eruwan said. "I know what you like, Papami. Stay with Mamali and I'll bring you two some food."

"We can handle clean-up afterward," Orienna said as she approached to help hold Liesle up. I was grateful for her assistance; Liesle was no small woman.

A strong breeze tousled my mane as I nodded my head in agreement. Liesle's mane tickled my nose. I helped her walk to the house.

Another child… Another opportunity for love, joy, contentment… and immeasurable sorrow.

Oboro Interlude

The Sasorin's nerves were frayed after all that had happened. Signore asking him to put a sacrifice into Deep Sea… Deep Sea! The Lord of Despair! An entity worshipped on the same level as the Gods by some Water elementals! And then to be almost squashed under the weight of his water…

And then a woman laid her egg. Gods, that might have been the most terrifying part of the day. A master creating a new life. *No, not a master.* Signore had told Oboro to stop thinking of women in those terms.

Women were to be respected and appreciated, but they were not 'masters.' He said Oboro should protect them when they are defenseless or if they ask for his protection. He should serve Mys Iola and Mys Beatrice when they ask for something, within reason, but he was not required to *obey* them. He was a slave no more. Oboro didn't know any other life, until a few months ago. Changing his entire worldview regarding the two sexes—no, there were *more* than two; that in itself was something he struggled to understand—had been a challenge.

But between the chaos caused by Deep Sea and the creation of life by that woman… Oboro thought the act of creation was more frightening. Even a stupid slave like himself could destroy. He would never create life.

No. He couldn't call himself a slave anymore. Signore said that was worse than calling a woman a master.

Signor Onoretti walked a few paces ahead of Oboro as they walked along a road lined by bamboo, with steena trees stretching their branches to reach overhead. A family of capybaras, hiding between the stalks, watched them carefully. Otherwise, they were alone. Mr. Onoretti had decided to leave the fire feast early since he was just a guest of the village. He didn't want to overstay his welcome, particularly at a funeral.

Signor Onoretti was so small and made such tiny steps on his trotting goat hooves that Oboro had to walk slowly to avoid getting ahead of him.

The Sasorin had never had much love for Yosoe until he'd met Signore. All the Yosoe he'd known in Ophidia were wretched field-slaves. Some had been yoked to their master's plows for lack of animals. He'd never known until he came to Aloutia that a Yosoe could be so amazing. So intelligent and caring and… and worthy of protection. Oboro swore he'd never let harm come to Signor Onoretti.

Never ever. He'd sooner take his own life than let anyone hurt him. If not for him, Oboro wouldn't have a life.

In a way, the Yosoe was like the masters who created life. No, something else. He *preserved* the lives that were already created.

Another Yosoe, one with brown fur and curved ram's horns, stumbled out from behind the bamboo thickets. He'd been so sudden, so unexpected, that Oboro's body assumed him to be an enemy. In one fluid motion, he drew his khopesh and lunged to stand in front of his mentor.

"W-whoa," the other Yosoe said. "What the fuck is this? I just want to talk to Mr. Onoretti."

Oboro kept his eyes on him, but awaited Signore's orders.

"Mr. Svelt, I trust you have a good reason for jumping out at me from behind a wall of bamboo, behind which is a jungle, and startling my bodyguard?"

"I just wanted to talk. Am I still gonna get the money?"

"We're *not* having this conversation in public," Signor Onoretti said. "Nor are we having it anywhere near Steena Village. You may schedule an appointment with me in my Chernagora office. Talk to the secretary at the merchants of light headquarters."

"Just answer the question! Yes or no?"

"Get out."

The brown-furred Yosoe scowled and bared his teeth. What did he think he was, a Wynnle? No Yosoe bared their teeth as a threat! Hadn't he learned to lower his horns if he wanted to fight? Oboro prepared to strike if Signore gave the command.

"Look, I know I wasn't the one who... did the deed. But I was there! I was ready! It's just a lucky coincidence the Wynnle was there, too!"

"If you say another word, I'll have my bodyguard toss you as far as he can throw you."

Oboro wasn't certain if he wanted to be tested in such a manner. Besides, it would not have solved the problem. The Yosoe could get back up and keep fighting.

"I need the money! Please! You're a wealthy man. I'm—"

Signor Onoretti snapped his fingers. "Oboro, get this man out of my path."

"Shall I toss him as far as I can throw him?"

He sighed. "That was hyperbole. Please don't actually do that."

Oboro wasn't sure how else to get the brown-furred Yosoe to leave short of killing him. He stepped closer, holding his khopesh at an angle so he could have swung and chopped off the man's legs. He begged Oboro to stop, to wait. He begged Signore to tell the boy to back off.

The pathetic Yosoe ran away with much greater speed than Oboro thought possible. Yosoe *could* run when they wanted to... He supposed Signore and his family never had a reason to rush.

Oboro looked back at Signore, hoping he'd look upon him with approval. Instead, he was frowning, eyebrows scrunched up, and his corkscrew horns sparking with electricity. Oboro didn't speak. He wanted to ask his mentor if he was okay, but he obviously wasn't... and Oboro didn't want to interrupt whatever important thoughts were going on inside his brilliant mind.

A mozzy landed on Signor Onoretti's arm, which earned it a blast of lightning shot from his horns. The thunder of his horns had once startled Oboro, but he had learned the signs. If they glowed or threw sparks, a bolt was likely incoming. Not that Oboro had ever been struck by it—Gods no, this man would never physically hurt him! Not like his previous master...

Nothing but smoke remained of the insect. As Signore's horns dimmed back down, he continued down the bamboo-lined road. "Thank you, Oboro. If that man approaches us in public, scare him away again. In private, I may speak to him, so await my orders."

"As you command, Signore."

Chapter Fourteen: Domovye

The next morning, after the older kids had left for school and Nio took a nap, my spouses and I sat outside under a tarpaulin stretching from our house to the short palm tree growing inside the foramen of our hip bone table. Rain poured hard, but we stayed dry under the tarpaulin. Su had protected the house's bones with snowbark resin. He applied it a few times throughout the year, but doing it before rainy season was a must. We *should* have gotten it applied sooner, but who could blame us for being lethargic in our depression?

We sat around a table made from a deformed longman's[1] pelvic bone. The deformation likely had not been helpful to the animal, but it made for a unique table. The surface was smooth on one side, then a trench—Su called it an acetabulum—in the center stored fruits, and a hole on the far end allowed a palm tree to grow through. Its fronds provided some shade when we didn't have the tarpaulin tied to its trunk.

Although the sky was covered by dark, grey rain clouds, Su knew where the Lime Moon was. He held the spotted turquoise egg in its general direction.

"Does it work on cloudy days?" I asked, referring to the way the light of the Lime Moon helped eggs grow.

"Probably not," he said. "But every little bit helps."

"We should get it to the Life church soon," Liesle said. "I've barely left the house since Tawny's death. I think I'd like to try and make the trip to Seabells. Which of you wants to go with me? We should probably remember our kamens this time."

"I should go with you," I said. "A Mantodea Life volkhv might want the biological father present."

"True. When the rain stops, let's go. Sugar, we might not be back before the kids are home. Can you handle dinner by yourself?"

"Absolutely. You can rely on me. If you're going to Seabells, though, could you place an order at the rendering plant for me? I want to special order a few bones."

---

1. A brachiosaurus

"Make a list," Liesle said. "I won't remember their names."

"Will do." Su set the egg in the acetabulum of the longman's pelvis, where it rested between a pitaya and a mango. He scurried into the house to get a pen and paper.

While he was gone, Liesle leaned closer. "I'm going to put my earring in once we're on the Daga."

She meant our earrings symbolizing that we were willing to have sex. Thoughts of my wife naked, wet, and moaning entered my skull and sent blood rushing to my baculum. I was stunned into silence, and by the time I found the right words, Su came back out.

He took his spot at the pelvis table again and wrote his list. "By the way, Ami-honey, will you tell us what you discussed with Mr. Onoretti? Is he going to sell you crystalights?"

"Yeah. He was excited about these ones, too. He said they had a longer lifespan than usual."

Liesle cocked her head. "Oh? How does he know that? And what is their lifespan?"

"They'll glow for one hundred eighty years. I'm not sure how he knows. I think the Domovye do something when they mine them. Maybe they can tell, somehow."

"I don't understand," she said. "How is it that previous crystalights have always had an eighty-year lifespan, but these ones are different? Why do they have a lifespan at all? The countdown starts the moment they're found, right? But haven't they all been under the ground since the creation of the world?"

"I think the Gods make them," Su said, tapping his pen on his chin. "Machenerate puts them in the ground for our benefit. Previously, she's always put them in Iuria. Why she put them under Steena Village, I have no idea."

"She's not your mother, is she?" I said in what I hoped he'd interpret as a joking tone. No one knew which God was Su's parent, but I liked to make jokes about each of them. There was an argument to be had for each Spirit being his parent, anyway.

Su grimaced uncomfortably. Perhaps now was not the best time to ask about his divine heritage. "Machenerate is known to be unskilled with magic. It's possible eighty-year crystalights were her limit until now. Perhaps she's been practicing and improving her magical skills. Though... honestly, I wish she'd have put these in Iuria."

"Mr. Onoretti also said this was a smaller deposit than usual," I said. "I'm not sure how he knows, since some of them are still underground."

"A small deposit..." Liesle stared at the egg, resting in the socket of the pelvis bone. "Are crystalights powered by Lightning elementrons? I hate to think of it, but what if... what if Tawny somehow... When she fell, maybe her tail..."

She couldn't complete her sentences without saying words too painful to speak.

"If that worked, wouldn't Mind Godbloods have already learned about it?" Su asked. "And gotten Lightning elementals to shoot lightning into crystals?"

Liesle half-closed her eyes, suspicious. "What if the merchants of light keep that knowledge secret because they don't want a bunch of one hundred and eighty-year-old crystalights? As long as they're in control of the supply, they can set the price. If crystalights lasted longer, demand would go down."

It sounded like the kind of scummy practices nobles did before the Greed Wars. Artificially limiting supplies to inflate prices had gotten more than one king killed and eaten. If I recalled my history lessons correctly, the destruction of the nobles' quarter in Seabells had occurred after the last king ordered eighty percent of all fruit trees burned down.

"Mr. Onoretti *did* say he could be picky with his customers because he planned to sell these at a higher price."

"Proof he's a businessman," Liesle growled. "He's earned his bright colors."

A group of Domovye came slithering down Bamboo Lane toward our house. They wore nothing, in fact two appeared to be mating, traveling together with stalks along their bodies entwined. One carried a container. It didn't surprise me to learn Domovye liked rain—they were slug-like, even if not evolved from slugs, and we had idioms about slugs loving rain.

But though I knew they were staying in the village, I wasn't used to seeing Domovye, so their presence startled me. Why were they coming toward my house? If they had a message from Mr. Onoretti, one Domovoi should have been enough.

"Wonder what they're here for," I said.

"We don't have anything to offer them to eat," Liesle said. "Other than what's growing on the trees, free for anyone to eat. Do Domovye eat regular food?"

"As far as I know, they only eat rocks and dirt. Different soil lets them create different colored glass." I stood and walked around the table, staying underneath the tarpaulin. I didn't want to walk out in the rain.

The Domovoi in front, holding the container, adjusted their speaking-pipe as they approached.

"Hail, drooks," I announced.

"Hail, Mr. Lasteran," they responded once they were close enough to be heard over the downpour. "We come bearing a gift from Signor Onoretti. He asks for your forgiveness, and wishes the best of luck for your new egg."

"I suppose I'll forgive him," Su said under his breath. "Though I still don't understand what he gained from interrupting my ritual."

"He didn't prevent you from talking to Deep Sea," Liesle said. "If he was hiding something, I think he'd have tried to stop you much sooner."

It was a weird situation all around. "He didn't have to give us a gift," I said. "Besides, if he really wanted to make amends, he'd have bought a new goat for the village to eat to make up for the one he sacrificed."

"That has been taken care of already," one of the breeding Domovye said. "He spoke to some others in the village about having another fire feast on the Domovoi Day of Sapience. Although it's only holy for us Domovye, we see no reason why other species can't celebrate with us."

"We would like to ask for permission to use this beach for our celebration," the other mating Domovoi said. "A proper celebration must take place in the light of a Godlight. Food and supplies will be paid for by Signor Onoretti. Everyone in the village is welcome to partake."

"That would be lovely," Su said. "We'd be honored to host your celebration. May God's light shine brilliantly upon you." He put his hands over his chest and bowed his head. The Domovye imitated the motion, hands in front of the mouths on their chest, and lowering their head-stalks.

"May your path glitter with starlight," the Domovye said in unison.

"Your gift," the one up front said as they passed the container to me.

It was an egg container, and not just any egg container, but a damn fine one. The outside was turquoise Domovoi glass, translucent so one could see inside. The inside was lined with byssus threads. Most such containers were lined with cloth or wool, and the Life volkhv would have to take the egg out to bathe it in amni water, but since byssus was the thread of pen and fan mollusks living in Deep Sea, they were not damaged by liquids. A hole in the top of the container allowed amni water to be poured in so the egg could soak while inside.

"This is outstanding!" Su said with a gasp. "Byssus threads, too? Mr. Onoretti must have paid dearly for that. The aquatic species don't sell byssus to land-dwellers for cheap!"

Liesle took the container and examined it, turning it in all directions. She gave it a solid smack with her hand. Not a dent or crack.

"It's real Domovoi glass," the Domovoi said. "I made it myself last night. Signor Onoretti provided me with the byssus—I couldn't guess how expensive it was—and told me to make it turquoise."

Liesle undid the latch and placed the egg gently inside. It was small now, though the byssus threads kept it cushioned against the glass. As it grew, it would fit more snugly. As it approached hatching time, it would have to be taken out. Babies wouldn't attempt to hatch if they didn't have space outside the egg. How they knew, I had no idea.

"Ah, who's the little one?" one of the Domovye asked.

The commotion must have woken Nio, standing in the door, balancing on the femur-threshold. She looked wide-eyed at our guests. Her hair was an endearing mess of blue. This might have been her first time seeing Domovye.

"Nio, look what we got from our Domovye friends." Liesle crouched beside her and showed her the egg container. "It'll keep the egg safe."

Nio held her hands out; it was her way of saying she wanted to hold something.

"Don't give it to her," I said. "I know she's clever enough to figure out the latch, and she might not know this is an egg we have to keep safe."

Nio gave me a dirty look and puffed up her cheeks.

"I agree with your father," Liesle said. "We're taking it to the Life church soon so you won't be tempted to break the egg."

Nio opened her mouth wide, showing off her sharp little teeth.

"You want to bite the container?" I asked, deliberately trying to get her mind off the egg. "You'll regret it. Domovoi glass is indestructible."

I had meant for it to be a warning, but Nio smirked, taking it as a challenge. She bit down hard on the container.

The crack of her tooth was audible even from a few feet away.

"Damn, girl," Su said breathily. "Either learn some restraint or we need to get you ready for military service."

Nio never cried. She didn't make any sounds out of her mouth. But she was hurt—she hopped up and down, flicking her electric tail, and held her paws over her mouth.

"Nio, baby, did you crack a tooth?" Liesle held her wrists apart so she could look at our daughter's mouth. "Yes, you did. Sugar, I think this is a job for a merchant of bone. Will you help her?"

"I'm on it. Come on, Nio. Let Mapa Su take care of you." He rose from the table, swooped Nio into his arms, and retreated into the house.

"An unspeaking child?" A Domovye asked. "May her path glitter with starlight."

"We're not sure why she doesn't speak," Liesle said. "We've taken her to professionals and they say there's nothing wrong with her."

"It happens often among our species," one of the breeding pair said. "We think nothing of it. Some simply prefer not to speak. They may be wise in other ways, or they may not. It's just who they are."

"We are doing our best with Nio," I said. "She is intelligent in other ways, so we aren't worried about her."

The leader lowered the stalks atop their head, similarly to how they did when they imitated Su's bow. "She is sapient. She has the Light of Sapience's blessing, and for that, we pray she walks along a path of starlight. Which, if you'll allow us to change the subject, was the next thing we wished to discuss..."

"We're not religious," Liesle said. "Please don't preach at us. We're Lightning elementals."

"Oh, may the Light turn me back into an animal if I tried such a thing!" they exclaimed. "I heard you were a merchant of faces, Mys Denwall. Are you taking jobs right now?"

Liesle considered it. She hadn't been in a mood to paint since Tawny's passing, but maybe she was ready.

"Yes, I will take a commission. Do you want something for the Day of Sapience?"

"You are truly wise," they replied. "A respectable image of the Light of Sapience. The God you call Lucognidus. We require an image of him for our act of worship. Can you provide this? We have money to pay you right now."

"Thank you. Yes, I can paint Lucognidus. I've done so plenty of times."

Religious art was always in demand, usually by churches, but sometimes citizens wanted images of the Gods for their own homes. I'd always found it ironic how often Liesle painted Lucognidus, despite her own hatred of the Gods.

I had no interest in listening to their business dealings, and I wanted to check on Su and Nio. I leaned closer to Liesle and whispered, "I'll leave you to it. I'm going to see how Nio's doing."

I found Su and Nio in our bedroom. Su had pulled out the box where we kept our kids' teeth, each one inside their own seashell. Wynnles frequently lost their teeth around the time they were Nio's age so bigger ones could grow in their place. Her recent obsession with biting was likely her body's way of encouraging her to take actions that might remove her teeth. Cohaku and Heliodor had been biters, too. Su had given them bones to chew on like they were dogs. Heli had even played tug with Maika over bones.

"See? All your big brothers and sisters have lost teeth, too."

Nio pointed at one.

"That was Eruwan's. She lost it when I gave her a rib."

She pointed to another.

"That's Tawny's. It got loose during a kiwi-batte game, then she asked Fionn to pull it out."

Tawny's teeth...

Fuck, I hadn't even thought of *that* until now! Did teeth store memories? Did they need to be sawdusted? If a demon took them, could they recreate a demonic-Tawny out of them?

Su looked at me. His face paled, expression turning grim. "Are you okay, Ami-honey?"

"Uh, should we be saving their teeth? Do we need to take Tawny's teeth to the Death church?"

"No, they're fine," he said. "The only parts that need to be sawdusted are parts that were attached to a person at death. There are no memories in teeth lost long ago."

My heart raced. "Are you sure? Do you know that for a fact? Is that something all merchants of bone are taught or are you just guessing?"

Su closed his eyes and sighed. "Yes, it's a known fact. King Susan herself taught me, and she would not lie about what can or cannot be used to turn a person into a demon. For bones to carry memories, they had to be attached to the same body as the deceased's brain at the moment of death."

"So Tawny is safe? For sure?"

"For sure," he repeated. "Amiere, I would *never* have suggested keeping our children's teeth if I knew there was the slightest chance they could be used in demonification rituals."

Even with his comforting words, I felt dizzy. I sat down next to him and Nio.

My daughter rubbed her paw through my mane and opened her mouth to show me her missing fang.

"Yes, I see it's gone. Are you in pain?"

She shook her head. I had no doubt she was pain-free, though I felt it was good to ask. Su had magical methods of killing pain in other people. It was his specialty as a dentist. He could toy around inside a person's mouth and they'd never feel his fingers or tools. If he had to remove a tooth, apply filling, or set a crown, he could do so, pain-free to the patient, without anesthesia.

"I should get a bone for her to chew on," Su said quietly. "Ah, I'll add that to the list."

Going through yet another trauma—this one of my own making—my body felt numb. My skull was cursed with a headache.

Su's eyes read every emotion on my face. "Do you need me to rub the misery out of you?"

"I'll be alright. Just scared myself with that thought."

Briefly, the only sounds were the wind, waves, and seagulls. My pounding head pretended to be a drum, louder than Orienna's timpani. Su clicked the box shut. "I've hesitated to ask this because it didn't feel right, but... I can... help erase your pain. The pain in your skull and sternum. The pain caused by Tawny. You won't forget about her, but... the ache will hurt less. Would you like that?"

I blinked, unsure how to respond. It didn't seem right to Tawny. Like my love was something that could be wiped away with a single magic spell. "No. The pain is meaningful. I don't think I could honor my daughter properly if I didn't grieve over her."

Su put his hand on my leg. "I understand. I just wanted to offer, so you knew what I was capable of."

I put my hand on his. "Perhaps another time, if the pain becomes unbearable. But *this*... this I can handle. This reminds me that she was here."

Su rested his chin on my shoulder. "You'll never swim alone in the sea of despair."

Codex Dominex: The Gods' Blessings

Soon after conquering the dominion, the Gods came together to think of ways to encourage people to worship and obey them. The Blessing System was one such idea.

All ten Gods contribute some of their energy into upkeeping the All-Elemental Blessing System. ALL souls, whether belonging to a sapient person or a near-sapient animal, are imbued with the blessings at the moment of the SOUL'S (not the body's) conception. All ten had the option of imparting a blessing, but some chose not to, while others were unable to assist even if they had the desire to do so.

The All-Elemental Blessing System is a 'package' of four blessings, one from four capable Gods:

- Flamboil's Blessing: protects the blessed from intense heat such as from fire, lava, extreme temperature, boiling water, and even spiciness (an aftereffect of combining with Cherribell's Blessing)
- Lucognidus's Blessing: protects the blessed from nightmares. This only work for 'natural' nightmares. It prevents a person's mind from conjuring disturbing thoughts while asleep. A person can still experience nightmares if they are brought on by an outside force e.g. mind-altering magic or a Demon Lord's curse.
- Windesoar's Blessing: protects the blessed from inhaling toxic air. This does not create air where none exists, so people should still take care not to suffocate.
- Cherribell's Blessing: allows the blessed to experience more tasteful and enjoyable food and drink.

In exchange for contributing their energy to upkeep, all Gods are allowed to put conditions on the blessings. However, their conditions only apply to people of that God's element. For instance, a Lightning elemental who breaks the conditions of Sparkato, the Lightning God, will lose all four blessings. If a Mind elemental were to disobey Sparkato's commandments, there would be no change, because they are only beholden to Lucognidus. People born to an element without a God (Light, Darkness, Force, Sound) can never lose their blessings.

On his own, Sawyer also keeps a blessing. His is not tied to the All-Elemental System, though he does contribute some energy and power to that one, too.

Sawyer's Blessing: Also called the Contract of Souls, this prevents anyone, sapient or animal, who has a soul, from having their soul destroyed or consumed by demons. This ensures that all souled people and animals go to the afterlife. There are no conditions for this blessing, and it is impossible to lose it (except by personally asking Sawyer to break their contract)

Sawyer does contribute to the All-Elemental Blessing system, as well, with a condition to all Death elementals. He now regrets the condition, and wishes he had never made it, but changing the system now would break all blessings and all people would lose them. His separate blessing does not have this condition. E.g. a Death elemental who breaks his condition will lose their package blessing, but not the Contract of Souls.

All ten Gods contribute energy Four Gods contribute their magical power	Sawyer alone contributes energy and power
All souls receive the four package blessings	All souls receive Sawyer's Blessing
A person will lose all four blessings by becoming a heretic of the God of their element	Sawyer put no conditions on this blessing. It can never be lost unless a person petitions him to remove it

Chapter Fifteen: Seabells

One moment to the next, my soul reached a state of tranquility during my trip to Seabells with Liesle. The last few weeks had been so rough, so stained by sorrow and pain, I feared her coldness would leave a permanent scar. Liesle had recovered, though, and her joy brought me joy.

Since we were going into the big city, we dressed as required there—pants instead of grass skirts, and our tails were wrapped tightly with leaves. When we got on the Daga, Liesle put her earring in and a kamen over her face. Kamens were masks of varying levels of concealment, worn in public, but especially in areas of larger populations so no one would learn your face. As with public names, many people kept their face hidden because some Demon Lords could be summoned if an enemy knew a person's face. My kamen was a yellow and brown sequined piece, covering only around my eyes and the left side of my face. It wrapped around my head with a strap much like the visor I wore in the ateli. People like me and Liesle with our ears atop our heads could not easily use the same facial wear—glasses, masks, kamens—used by people who had ears on the sides of their head, like Su. Liesle's mask covered even less; it was naught but a purple fabric that covered the area around her eyes. But as a merchant of faces, she would know if that was sufficient to hide her face from those who'd paint her.

Liesle leaned on my shoulder, wrapping a wing around my back like an arm. She clutched the egg in the Domovoi glass container close.

"I'm happy to see you feeling better," I said.

"I'm sorry for the pain I caused. I was jealous of the attention you were giving Su, but... I wouldn't have made for good company. I can't blame you for avoiding me."

"We wanted to be with you, but you had to heal in your own time."

Shifting water and a strong breeze were our only sounds for a moment of peace.

"I'll never heal," Liesle finally said. "It has broken me for life."

"We'll never permanently recover, but the pain has become less. Just look at us, traveling to Seabells! A week ago, I don't think anything would have convinced you to leave the house. I forced myself to go to the Death church only out of a sense of obligation."

"Perhaps that's how it was for you, but it's not the same for me."

I rested a hand on her leg. Her thick, strong legs. Gods, she was powerful. She hadn't done anything to cultivate her raw fitness, other than taking care of occasionally-rowdy children. It came naturally from her Wynnle genes. I could have looked like that too, if not for the Nilian genes my father gave me.

I never knew my father. My mother had fucked him once, to produce me, and that was it. All I knew was that he was a Nilian. I also knew my mother had fully consented to have sex with him, but couldn't tell that story to the community she'd lived in.

Many of the Wynnle groups living on the Wynndalic Plains were... troubling. By and large, they were Lightning elementals and had to obey Sparkato's disgusting rules regarding sex if they wished to keep their blessings. However, their approach to ensuring the rules were followed was equally revolting. Among those Wynnles, a person was not considered an adult—and therefore, could not legally have sex—until they performed a ritual. Among the rites, they had to kill a reza[1] with just their bodies and a few companions. Then they had to eat the reza's heart, brain, and sexual organs. At the end, a female Wynnle would have to penetrate her own vagina with her clawed fingers, and a male Wynnle would have to circumcise himself. Since it was easier for women, most such communities had only a few 'adult' male Wynnles who alone were allowed to breed with many women. Any man who hadn't gone through the ritual and was caught having sex with a woman would be killed or banished, depending on how the 'adult' men judged. Women who had sex without performing the ritual were usually given more lenient treatment, though they could expect banishment. My mother would have been executed if she'd admitted to having consensual sex. Instead, she had to lie and claim it was rape, claim that she feared losing Sparkato's blessing. That earned her mercy, and the judges instead decided to only banish her. More mercifully, they would let her choose whether she wanted to go to Ophidia or Aloutia after the egg hatched. Had I been born a girl, my mother would have gone to Ophidia. Sometimes, I was glad for that awful debacle, otherwise she wouldn't have moved to Aloutia, and I never would have met Liesle.

I'd known Liesle since before I could remember. We grew up in Steena Village together. My earliest memories were playing on the beach together. I would collect seashells and lalafinas[2] for her to put in her hair and clothes. When I got a bit older, I would carve dolls and figurines for her out of wood. From that experience, I learned how to carve, and those skills allowed me to graduate from art school as quickly as I did. I had taught myself the fundamentals of sculpting

---

1. A tyrannosaurus rex, which in the Pentagonal Dominion is a large, flightless scavenger bird.

2. Bright, multicolored flower

back when I was a teenager trying to impress the girl I liked.

Liesle had also gone to art school with me, though her medium was painting, particularly with acrylics. She'd wanted to be a merchant of faces ever since she was a kid. Her parents had bought her an art set when she was eight or nine. I still remembered fondly the day I gave her the name 'Liesle' by combining 'Lisi' with 'easel.' When she'd first heard that name, it was like a new awakening. She'd gasped, her blue hair had bounced, and her ears had perked. Gods, she had been so cute. She was still cute.

Her parents had made her follow all the rules adult merchants of faces had to follow. She could only paint in public, with witnesses to ensure she wasn't painting the beloved of Demon Lord Vinoc.

The Lord of Terror was summoned by creating an image of his lover, a demigoddess with the same name and title he had. He was, by and large, the primary reason anyone wore kamens out in public. Technically, any art medium worked to summon him. I could have sculpted Demigoddess Vinoc to summon Demon Lord Vinoc. But merchants of faces were given unequal suspicion due to the fact that if they painted a person in the same picture as woman-Vinoc, then man-Vinoc would torture that person without question. With any other medium, the artist would have to get a mirror for demon-Vinoc to materialize in and speak with him about what they wanted. Bargains would have to be made, with the summoner usually getting screwed over in some way. But a painting? According to Liesle, Vinoc allowed two 'free' summons. A merchant of faces could paint woman-Vinoc with their most despised enemy, then go to bed, and by the time they woke up, their enemy would have been tortured to death, all without the merchant ever speaking to the Demon Lord, or without him asking for payment. The third time, however... the price of summoning Vinoc thrice was for him to torture the person the summoner loved most.

It was a known fact that such paintings were cursed. The images would move. If the merchant painted the Demigoddess Vinoc standing still with the victim, then turned away, when the merchant looked at the painting again, the demigoddess might then be depicted with her butcher's knife slicing the victim's throat.

Paintings could have the curse removed by including an image of Lucognidus in them, though. His holy visage drove evil out of the paintings. Some claimed burning paintings was sufficient, as Flamboil's holy power would drive it out instead, and destroy any evidence in the meantime.

Summoning Lord Vinoc was strictly prohibited in Aloutia. If a merchant of faces was ever caught with paintings of Demigoddess Vinoc, they'd be in serious trouble.

Liesle was a good woman. She'd never summon the Demon Lord of Terror. Though she *did* have a secret ateli—a safe place she could paint in private—I would never accuse her of summoning Lord Vinoc. On the other hand, it wouldn't surprise me if she painted risqué art that the public had no business viewing.

Well, Su had just summoned the Demon Lord of Despair, the very ocean we traveled across. Maybe Vinoc wasn't any worse than Deep Sea. They were both part of the Trifecta, the three most powerful and feared Demon Lords. Hollow Void was the third, though I knew nothing about him except for his name, sphere of influence, and the fact that he was somehow tied to outer space and spiders.

I supposed there was a time and place for all things. A time and place to summon Deep Sea. A time and place to summon Vinoc. If my wife ever brought up a desire to summon Vinoc… to torment Miltico, in particular… I would support her.

That didn't make *me* evil, did it? It would be her choice, and we weren't directly causing his misery. And we'd get Usana a safe place to live. It might actually be a *good* deed.

Seabells was lively, yet calming. The gentle chimes of the bells along the shore put my mind at ease. The pleasant, melodic song reminded me of Tawny, running with her bell on her tail, but I no longer cried. Thinking about her, I felt longing and nostalgia, but my sternum felt light and airy, not heavy. My hyoid didn't suffer the lump it once had.

Although Seabells and Steena Village were located in Aloutia's Gigantification Zone, we rarely got the sort of enormous plants seen in northern cities like Aromavaria or Seed. Buildings here were made of painted wood and bamboo with mud brick foundations, not flowers or gourds as those cities had.

Several churches sat in a semicircle around the great statue of Cherribell. The Plant Goddess's monument was sculpted to be observed from the front. In one hand, she carried a bough of cherry blossoms, made from translucent pink Domovoi glass. In her other hand, raised above her head, she held a bellflower stem upward, as if to swing it down and ring the flowers as if they were real bells. When viewed head-on, Aloutia's planetary rings appeared to shoot out from the topmost bellflower. It was an awe-inspiring sight.

The Plant church of Seabells may have been the largest church in the area, but we were here for the Life church next door.

Citizens milled about, some working diligently, others relaxing and enjoying their idyllic tropical life. All wore kamens, at least while outdoors. The majority of the population of Seabells was Flora, a species of herbivorous Plant elemental people who took on traits of the plants they consumed. Most cultivated their appearance for beauty or cultural significance. The Life volkhv who greeted us at the entrance was a Floral man with green skin and rose petals growing around his head. As volkhvs of Entomothy went bare-chested in good weather, his petal-tipped nipples were also fully visible. His chest may have been bare, but he wore a rose-themed kamen.

Flowers signified one's sexual preference. I would call myself a tulip, for instance, meaning I was attracted to two sexes: women—Liesle—and those of an unknown or neutral sex—Su. Roses were men who were attracted to other men. I suspected this man's choice to appear as a rose was also a signal to others regarding his sexual inclination.

"What an adorable egg!" he said, clasping his thorny hands over his chest. "Have you registered with our church already?"

"We have," Liesle replied. "My husband and I have lived in Steena Village our whole lives. Our records are here. We've had six other children whose records are here. Well..."

Since she could not finish the sentence, I did. "We lost a daughter recently. The Death volkhvs may have taken her records from you and put them in their archives."

The rose man bowed his head, petals drooping. "My condolences. Would you consent to a Mantodea taking your genetics? Our keeper would do the honors."

"Please," Liesle said. "If it's the same one who's been here for twenty years, she should already have our genetics."

"This way, drook and drooka."

We were led into the keeper's room, where the same Mantodea who'd recorded all our children's hatchings sat behind a desk. Tall, light-green, and with an appearance like a praying mantis, some found the Mantodea to be a frightening species. I had only ever known them to be Life volkhvs—kindly, professional, and nurturing.

"Mys Denwall and Mr. Lasteran," she said. "My, what a beautiful egg container!"

Liesle set it on the desk. "It was a gift from the Domovye working the mines underneath Steena Village."

"There are mines under the village?" she asked. "I thought Steena Village was zoned for sugar production."

"We just had a crystalight mine appear," I said. "I thought it would be big news."

The Mantodea blinked her big mantis eyes and shook her head. "I've heard nothing about it, and I try to keep on top of the news. I thought all crystalights came from Iuria."

"So did we, until this happened."

It seemed the merchants of light guild was trying to keep the mines a secret. Perhaps that was for the best, though if they *really* wanted it kept secret, they should have told me so I wouldn't talk about it.

"Strange," the keeper mused. "Well, would you like me to taste your genetics again? I still have it from last time." She opened a drawer with her delicate green hand and pinched a piece of paper between two thin fingers. Mantodea forearms were abnormally thick compared to their upper arms and the hands themselves.

"We would," I replied. "What do you need? A drop of blood?"

"As long as I get some healer blood cells, yes, that will suffice. Carrier blood cells don't have genetic data in them. Oh, but you're Wynnles. Will the scent of each other's blood...?"

My wife and I glanced at each other. I looked with concern, but she shot me a seductive look, biting her bottom lip and flicking her earring.

She wanted to have sex.

"Um, Mys Keeper, I don't think it'll be a problem if you have any, err, breeding rooms here."

Not all Life churches had rooms where amorous couples could fuck, but it wasn't rare, and I would expect it for the church in a city as big as Seabells. With interspecies couples, sometimes the assistance of objects, lust-inducing foods, or incense was necessary for procreation. The Life church offered these services for a small fee.

The Mantodea stared with big, sideways eyes. "I suppose it's a long way to Steena Village. If you go berserk from this, I don't want you to be forced to wait until the journey back. Shall we fill out an egg registry first, then?"

The egg registry was purely a formality. We had to tell her when the egg was laid, who the parents were, and the likely elements the baby could be. Since Liesle's father had been a pure Wind elemental, technically Liesle carried a Wind elemental gene within her. Our children had a small chance of being Wind elementals. It would have been nice if that had happened. While Windesoar was far from a merciful God, he was easier to obey than Sparkato. Wind elementals didn't have to follow perverted rules for sex.

When the paperwork was finished, we handed over our egg in the blue glass box. The Mantodea took out two syringes, put fresh needles on each, wiped our fingers clean with an alcoholic solution, and stuck us. She opened her mandibles wide, even though the objects going into her mouth were quite small.

Liesle's drawn blood was too minuscule for its scent to even meet my maxilla. I hadn't expected to go berserk. It took a *lot* of blood to trick my skull into thinking there was prey nearby.

Afterward, we went to one of the church's breeding rooms. We took one with a large bed. We *were* members of a large species, after all. The room was supplied with all the things other people might find romantic or necessary for breeding: candles, incense, chocolate, and dildos.

"I've been playing coy this whole time, but let me make it clear," Liesle said as she removed her thin purple kamen. "I want to fuck you until your dick is as prickly as a cactus, Mo Ami, Amiere. You can ask me, and I will consent."

Her dirty language served to get my penis into a slightly-more cactus-like state.

"And I want to fuck you raw, Lisi, my strong Liesle. Will you have sex with me?"

Her feline face turned feral. She licked her lips, her pupils became thin slits, and her nostrils flared. She picked me up in her arms—Gods, she was strong—and dropped me onto the bed.

She climbed atop me, straddling my torso with her legs. She reached for her tail, covered in a leaf-sheaf while we were in public so no one would be hurt by her electricity. She released the sheath and swung her tail back and forth. It cast intriguing shadows on the wall beside us.

Liesle leaned down onto me, running her fingers through my mane. Strong, powerful fingers. She lacked the delicacy of Su, instead preferring to be dominant and vigorous. She pulled my kamen off, a bit roughly, but I would never complain—I loved when Liesle was rough. I didn't mind at all that the kamen's strap tugged at my mane. She kissed my cheek, nudging her nose underneath a braid so she could reach the spot underneath where my mustache connected to my mane.

It had been so long since I fucked Liesle. She was never in the mood for it when she was pregnant, and she sure as hell wasn't in the mood when she was depressed.

But as much as I craved her, loved her, wanted to make love to her... even after we'd stripped all our clothes off and feasted our eyes on each bodies—older every day, but still sexy. Despite my best efforts, I couldn't maintain an erection. My penis got somewhat hard, but the spines wouldn't stand up straight. Liesle brushed her fingers over it, trying to coax it, but it wouldn't work.

I didn't want to say it... after how jealous she'd been of him...

She said it anyway. At least she saved me the embarrassment of admitting it. "You can't get your dick up without Su."

I sighed. "I'm sorry. It's... it's not something I can control. Su's mouth is the only thing—"

"I know. You don't have to explain yourself. It's lucky we met him, or else we probably wouldn't have any kids. No, we'd have Fionn. We managed to have him, just the two of us."

Although we failed in our initial pursuits this time, we kissed and fondled each other just like we had since we were teenagers, exploring each other's bodies.

Gods, we were Eruwan's age when we'd started kissing. I couldn't imagine Eruwan with a lover! How had our parents allowed us to run around the way we had?

When we finished, we washed up with the sink and towels provided, dressed ourselves, and headed back outside. I wasn't used to sinks. Living right next to Deep Sea, we never saw the need to implement one. Only big cities had running water anyway.

We had more business to do in Seabells before heading home. Liesle had the list of bones Su wanted from the rendering facility. Outside, as I looked up at the statue of Cherribell, I felt compelled to do one more thing here. The Plant church next to the Life church might have some advice regarding Usana's condition...

"Lisi, would you let me take care of some other business while I'm here?"

"Hmm? What other business do you have?"

"It's about Milti's daughter, Usana. I think he's abusing her. I want to ask the Plant church if there's anything they can do for her."

"Oh Gods, I didn't realize that was going on. I haven't seen his daughter. Why don't you do that and I'll go to the rendering plant alone? I know how much you detest the stench."

Anyone with a nose would detest the stench. Rendering plants were places where the meatless carcasses of animals were turned into other products. They sold all their bones to the merchants of bone, and I assumed they used parts of other animals, though I didn't know how else those parts could be used. Such facilities were typically next to the ocean, so unused parts could be sacrificed to Deep Sea. He always found a use for every crumb of once-living matter.

"I'll stay near here, so come find me when you're done."

She nodded, and we parted ways for now.

I had no idea what the hell I was doing. Would a Plant church even be able to help her? Who was I supposed to ask for help if I suspected a child was being abused? Plant churches were hospitals and apothecaries. Would they have services to rescue her? If nobody inside had answers, surely they'd at least know where I could go next.

Chapter Sixteen: Abuse

I spoke with a Plant volkhv—an herbalist, tending to his garden of medicinal herbs in the greenhouse. An overhead trellis held glowlight lotus vines shedding their light throughout the room. I had only been inside a Plant church a few times in the past, and every time, my maxilla was overwhelmed by the aroma of so many flowers and herbs. They were mostly herbs used for alchemy or medicine, and as such, I did not recognize them. A bowl of cinnadyme incense burned at the entrance and I wondered if cinnadyme trees were grown here, too.

"You said this girl is starving?" the Flora asked as he snipped leaves from a plant with red-veined leaves.

"I know it's absurd," I said. "We grow excess food in Steena Village. Anything she wants to eat is right there. And she's a Lagodore-Yosoe hybrid, so it's not like she has strict requirements on what she can eat. Her father forbids her from eating, though."

"Plant churches can send food—if there wasn't already plenty—but the problem is with the father. We could send crates of food, and it would never reach her if her father forbids it. I'd recommend speaking with the Wind church. They handle cases of abandoned children. Perhaps they also know what you can do for abused children."

The volkhv moved on to the next herb. I got the impression he didn't want to get involved. He only wanted to get his hands dirty with soil and fertilizer, not the drama of a starving, abused eight-year-old girl.

The Wind church was also part of the semi-circle of churches, so it was not a long walk. I had *never* been inside a Wind church. Before we met Su, Liesle and I had discussed possibly adopting a child if we couldn't conceive, but we weren't certain we could provide a better life for an orphan than the Wind church could. The church provided plenty of social benefits and prepared the children well for adulthood. Besides, it would have been a bureaucratic disaster for two Wynnles to adopt a non-Wynnle. Even if we had no record of going berserk, the fear would always be there. Would the child accept us as parents, knowing that if they got cut and bled, the scent of their blood could drive us into a mad killing frenzy?

The orphans inside fled when they laid eyes upon me. I wondered if I was the first Wynnle they'd ever seen. Perhaps they thought I'd go berserk and kill the whole lot of them. My presence got the attention of the church's keeper, a Winyan man who quickly put on his kamen once he realized he had company. It was a lot like Liesle's in that it covered very little of his face. I wondered if wearing a kamen was more of a social obligation to him than one of functionality. He invited me to talk with him in front of the great statue of Lord Windesoar. The Wind God had a look of benevolence on his face as he held a Flora child in one arm and a feather in the other. His wings spread from one whitewashed wall to the other.

I briefly explained the situation to the volkhv.

"A Lagodore, you said?"

"Lagodore and Yosoe hybrid."

"Does she have siblings?"

"No, it's just her and her father. Her mother is there, too, but I rarely see her. I wonder if Miltico is abusing her, as well."

"You said the mother is the Lagodore?"

"That's correct. Excuse me, but does it matter? Can't you take in Lagodore children?"

"Oh, that's not the problem. We'd be happy to take a Lagodore in. However, it's very rare for a Lagodorian woman to have a single child from one pregnancy. Their species is meant to produce around four children per egg."

I stood in silence. What was I supposed to guess from this? That Miltico's other kids starved to death on Cosmo? And maybe that's what prompted him to return to Aloutia?

If they were boys... Gods, what if he sold them to Ophidian merchants of flesh? I wasn't sure if that was better or worse than dying. At least if they were dead, they would now be happy and full in Spiritua.

"Would the father being a Yosoe counteract that?" I offered. "Maybe hybrid Lagodores..."

"All that matters is the species of the mother. If the mother is pure Lagodore, she'll have many children per egg. If she's a hybrid, then perhaps."

"I haven't seen her much. She doesn't get out of the house often. But... anyway, is there anything you can do for Usana?"

"The Wind church cannot directly do anything, especially for an immigrant child. We take in children who are brought to us by lawkeepers or government services. We cannot step into a family's affairs. Before you go to the Lightning church or a government office, however, I have some advice."

"What's that?"

"They won't take an immigrant girl away from her father unless there's physical proof of abuse. Scratch marks, bruises, patches of missing hair, things of that nature. If the girl confesses to being abused in non-physical ways, they *can* still intervene, but it's harder. They'd be more likely to intervene if she were a citizen; Aloutia takes pride in protecting its citizens, but apparently, lawkeepers can let immigrants die without anything weighing down their conscience." The volkhv balked and rolled his eyes. "Sorry. I've had issues in the past with lawkeepers treating two children differently all because one was born in Aloutia while the other was not. It makes me sick."

It made me sick, too... "I didn't realize that was a problem in this country."

"It is. But *if* they listen to you and *if* they investigate, they're still going to question her on things she might not be able to answer. There's always doubt that a child is being truthful. If a child has been told to repeat a lie, they will. If an adult goads a child into speaking a lie, then rewards that lie and praises the child for being 'brave for telling us the horrors of what happened', you end up with children who describe more horrifying histories than what really happened. During the Greed Wars, people asked every orphan if they'd been kidnapped and put into demonic rituals or the demented games the nobility played. Although realistically only about a dozen children were involved, there are reports of thousands of children saying they had been tortured, all because the adults praised them for 'revealing the truth.' If we separate a child from their parents due to a wild fantasy, the lawkeepers could get in trouble. They won't risk it, especially not in Steena Village, which is even more opposed to lawkeepers than Seabells, and we practically live in anarchy compared to the rest of Aloutia."

"She's starving so badly you can see her ribs," I replied in a desperate voice. "Wouldn't that be enough proof?"

"But you also said they recently came to Aloutia. The lawkeepers will tell you to wait a while and see if her condition improves once she's had a chance to eat more filling meals."

"I had the same thought, and it's been a week! She hasn't improved. How long does a child have to starve before someone interferes? She'll be fucking dead if this continues!"

The volkhv's eyes shut tight. A twitch at his mouth made me think he was about to scold me for swearing.

"I'm sorry," I said under my breath. "I'm usually good about watching my language."

"It's quite alright. I instinctively tell the children not to swear, and I almost said the same to you. I would have been embarrassed to have said that to an adult. I understand why you'd have an emotional outburst. I'll file a report at the Lightning church to investigate, but there's nothing beyond that I can do."

That was that. What else could I do? I couldn't just grab Usana and drag her here. Would I even recognize signs of abuse on a Lagodore, with her body covered in thick brown fur? How would I see a bruise when I couldn't see her skin?

I left and waited for Liesle at the statue of Cherribell. I considered going to the Lightning church myself, but it was not among the semi-circle of churches here. It was normal for Lightning churches to be on the outskirts of cities, where soldiers could practice shooting arrows toward the wilderness. Seabells's Lightning church had been constructed on the rubble of the old nobles' quarter.

Well, part of it, anyway. The rest was a field of wildflowers. Rumors were, one or two burnt-out mansions had been left standing for soldiers to use as obstacle courses in training.

If I wandered too far, I might not be here when Liesle got back, and then we might end up walking around in circles, looking for each other.

I'd been to the Seabells Lightning church a few times in my life to pay due tribute. Not to Sparkato, the vile monster, but to the soldiers who protected our country. Aloutians were expected to pay a yearly tribute to the church of their God, or to their patron God if they were Sound, Force, Light, or Darkness[1] elementals. When I paid my dues to the Lightning church, I did so out of obligation rather than patriotism.

I shouldn't be so hard on Aloutia when the alternatives included Ophidia and the Makai. I was *glad* my mother was exiled to Aloutia, because I would not want to be on Cosmo, living in the Wynnle societies where men were expected to circumcise themselves. I was safely a citizen of Aloutia, and I dared not risk being exiled back to Cosmo. If I did anything out of line... if I hurt Usana or Miltico... I was sure the lawkeepers wouldn't waste a minute investigating Steena Village for a berserk Wynnle. I'd be lucky if they didn't kill me.

I knew in the deepest pit of my soul that the lawkeepers would not do the right thing until I was their enemy. They were content to wait until it was too late to save this child, but I knew they'd arrest me if I so much as looked at them wrong. They weren't bad people. Just busy. They couldn't be bothered to go out to a small village when there were so many bigger cases here. Who would even notice if a single Lagodorian girl went missing? Especially one who wasn't a legal citizen...

Come to think of it, why didn't Milti apply for citizenship? He would have lost it a few years ago since Aloutia requires its citizens to check in with authorities. Typically, paying taxes or the yearly church tribute was enough. If Milti hadn't come back to update his civilian status, they'd assume he was gone. He could have applied again, though, and started receiving benefits. It would certainly help him get into a regular house and get income apart from whatever his father gave him.

Maybe... maybe I just needed to talk to Miltico about getting help.

I could still see, in my mind's eye, the Milti I remembered from my childhood. A scrawny Yosoe who'd cry if he got lost in the jungle. His older brother Tico would laugh at how pathetic Milti was. But Tico knew the jungle. He alone knew where to get a certain leaf. Ingredients for crazy sugar, he claimed—the same substance that killed him.

---

1. The four elements listed are commonly seen in sapienti people, but no God of those elements has apotheosized yet. Certain Gods of the Decatheon serve as temporary patrons for those without a God.

Gods, maybe Miltico was still struggling with his brother's death. How could I blame him? I ought to just talk to him. Calmly. Rationally. Without choking him within an inch of his life for the mud and sludge that had already passed his lips.

As much as I hated the runty bastard, I knew it would be better to mend my relationship with Miltico than to continue aggravating him. If I could encourage him to seek help, it would help Usana as well. Liesle was skeptical, stating it would be better if I severed all ties to him. Su was a bit more optimistic. With his help, I packed a basket of leftover food from dinner and took it to the guest house where he had been staying until a proper house could be built for him.

If a proper house *was* being built. Usually, those were projects Su and I worked on... but we hadn't been asked to even plan a building yet. Perhaps it was because Miltico was no longer an official citizen of Aloutia, so he was not considered eligible for assigned housing, or perhaps it was because the people of Steena Village were giving us space to grieve over Tawny. If the other villagers had discussed housing in the last few weeks, I was oblivious to it.

We were in the process of building Eruwan's house, so maybe we would be asked to do a new project once it was completed.

His abode was in the jungle, a bit away from the village, in a grove of trees brimming with lush leaves, twisting lianas, knobby bark, and thick fruits. A carambola tree stood next to the house, its taller branches reaching over and dangling star-shaped fruit over the roof.

How could anyone starve when they had fruit growing right on top of their roof? Lychees, snakescales[2], and steenas grew nearby, too. Out of the corner of my eye, a capybara shuffled through the greenery. Deeper in the dark jungle, two toucans snapped their beaks at each other. Life was plentiful here. Animals thrived... why couldn't people?

The steps up his porch were rotting wood and I questioned if it would hold my weight. I knocked on the similarly-rotting door, thinking it might fall apart if I knocked too strongly... Thinking it might be a *good* thing if I barged in and took Usana away from him.

Miltico's voice said something indistinguishable, probably orders to his wife and daughter. Louder, he asked, "Who's there?"

"Amiere," I replied, only afterward remembering that although it was my legal name, it did technically mean 'my lover' and it might have been better if I'd

2. Salak, snake fruit

referred to myself as Ami.

"What do you want?" he asked from behind the door.

"I'm here to make peace. I brought food. I just want to talk."

He opened the door, but rather than let me in, he came out and closed the door behind him.

The stench of alcohol was unmistakable. His one good eye was glassy, and his horizontal pupil didn't dilate in the light of my tail. The eye with the scratch marks was the same as always—dead and milky white.

"Why'd you come here?" Miltico snarled.

I offered the basket of food to him. "You were my friend once, Milti. A long time ago. I wonder if that friend of mine is still within you, somewhere."

"You killed Milti when you made me leave Aloutia. I'm Miltico now. You have no fucking clue how cruel Cosmo is. I couldn't get in with any community. They'd see my scratch mark and assumed I got it because I deserved it."

"You *did* deserve it," I said. "But that was then, and this is now. If you seek forgiveness, I will forgive you. We can start over. Be neighborly again. Maybe not friends, but we can at least stop hating each other."

"Such wishful thinking, *Amiere*. Exactly what I'd expect from someone with such a romantic name. But I'm not your lover. Or Liesle's."

My sternum raised in anticipation of him calling Su a man-wife, and I would have pounded him... but he didn't say it.

"If you want to keep hating me, fine. At least take this food. Let your girl eat it."

He glanced downward, frowning, in a moment of what I thought might be genuine consideration. "Do you think I'm a bad father?"

I wanted to answer honestly, that I thought he was awful, but I kept my cool. "I think you need help. You need to become an Aloutian citizen."

"I can't. They'll do a welfare check and... they'll deny me based on what Lavina and Usana look like."

"Like they're starving? Then fucking let them eat. Why are they starving? There's food everywhere!" I waved my hand, motioning to all the fruit trees. "They're Lagodores! They could eat the fucking grass!"

Milti scowled. "It's not that simple."

"Explain it to me then."

"No. We're different people now. You'd never understand. You have never had to survive in the wilds of Cosmo. You've never had to watch out for predators while you ate, which is much harder with only one functioning eye."

He was right; I couldn't understand. Maybe there was a reason his wife and daughter looked starved. Something beyond my ability to comprehend. Or maybe he was a lying pond of mud and sludge and these were all excuses to hide the fact he was abusing them.

"Whatever your reason, I expect to see improvement in Usana's health soon. I'd also like to see her eat that food." I pointed to the basket in Milti's hands.

"We just ate dinner. She's full now."

"Great! Bring her out here so she can tell me herself."

Miltico set one arm akimbo. "She's scared of Wynnles. She'll panic if she sees you. Yet another thing you don't fucking understand. When you're a Lagodore-Yosoe, the natural prey of lions, and you're eating in a place where lions are actively hunting, you learn to fear things that look like lions."

"Then now would be a good time for her to learn the difference between animals and sapienti. Bring her out here, so I can teach her that I am a person, not a lion."

"I refuse."

I slammed my hand into his door, high above his head. The wood splintered and the Yosoe startled. "I'm trying to play nice, Miltico, but you're making it difficult. I want to see Usana right now."

Milti's eye shrunk in terror. His scrawny goat-legs shivered. "A-alright, Ami! I'll be right out with her!"

He scurried back inside. I listened for his voice and footsteps. If I suspected he would not come back, I would tear the door into rotten wooden planks and enter by force.

A minute later, he returned with Usana, dressed in a long-sleeved shirt and skirt. She hid behind her father's legs, trembling, unable to make eye contact with me.

"I told you," Miltico said. "Are you happy now, Amiere? For scaring this poor girl?"

I crouched down, though I was still much taller and bigger than her. Milti held the basket of food, but it was within range of my fingers. I reached in and pulled out the first thing I grabbed—in this case, a rambutan. I held the bright red, hairy fruit toward Usana.

"Would you like to eat this?" I asked.

Her eyes clenched shut, tears forming along the edges.

"Does she need your permission first?" I asked, glaring threateningly at Miltico.

"It's okay, Usana. You can eat it."

Even with her father's permission, she refused to budge away, hiding her face behind Milti's knees.

"Why is she wearing a long-sleeved shirt?" I asked. "It's far too hot." The heat itself wasn't intolerable, but the humidity triggered Flamboil's Blessing and made my mane slick with moisture.

"She's blessed, idiot. She doesn't feel the heat."

"She's still uncomfortable, especially with her fur."

"She likes it. Don't shame her for what she chooses to wear."

"Have her take it off."

"What? Why? You some kind of child molester?"

Molest. That word again. "Do you say that word often?"

"Huh? No, why would I? I'm not a fucking pervert like you."

"I want to see her arms."

Miltico's frown said everything I needed to know. He yanked Usana away by her horns and pulled up her sleeves.

I couldn't tell what I was looking for. Brown fur, nothing discolored. Some of it was raised up like it was growing over a welt, but maybe that was a normal part of Lagodorian bodies.

Miltico huffed. "You happy now, Ami? Have you gotten your sick, perverse pleasure looking at my daughter? Your own daughters don't do it for you, I suppose."

"Don't say that filth in front of her," I demanded.

"I've said worse. Hell, I've fucked her mother in front of her."

"And you accuse *me* of being a pervert? How old is Lavina, anyway?"

"I've never fucked a child. Lavina's age is none of your business, but I promise she's an adult. I'm attracted to adults. I've fucked plenty of adults. I've even fucked *your* wife, Amiere."

I hadn't laughed so hard since the idyllic era of my life before Tawny's passing. It was such a ridiculous statement. "Sure you have."

"Don't believe me? Ask her yourself. Ask her how I got these scratch marks." He pointed to his ruined left eye.

"I thought Orienna gave those to you."

"Orienna wouldn't dare risk going berserk. No, it was your wicked wife. I always wanted to be with her. Then you stole her from me. I was fine with her choice at first, but then she also picked that... fucking fish-woman-man. If polyamory had been available from the start, I'd have asked her for that."

"None of us wanted you, Milti. You were corrupted by your brother. High on crazy sugar all the Gods damned time."

"I know. It's why I made her fuck me. Either that or she would lose her blessing. I wanted a taste of her no matter what, so I could gloat about it to you later. I didn't think she'd claw my fucking eye."

"I don't believe this," I said dispassionately. No, more like I couldn't believe it *until* Liesle confirmed it. Miltico was just trying to make me angry, like he always was. For whatever reason, he liked goading me to the brink of violence. Did he want me to go berserk? For that matter, if Liesle had done what he suggested, *she* should have gone berserk.

Unless Miltico had managed to give her an orgasm... Ugh, I didn't want to picture that. An image like that is enough to make a man vomit.

"Ask her yourself," he said with a shrug. "Though if she hasn't told you yet, she'll probably lie about it. Great wife, huh? Someone who lies to you. If I find out Lavina has lied to me, I'll put her in her place."

I clenched my jaw, teeth grinding. "Why do you go out of your way to annoy me so much? Do you want me to hurt you?"

He laughed a quiet, pathetic laugh. "You wouldn't dare. Go berserk and kill me, Amiere. What would I care? I'll just go to Spiritua and be with Tico once we're both awake. Meanwhile, you'll be a murderer and exiled to Cosmo. I hope they banish *just* you, so you're separated from your family. I hope you learn what it means to suffer on another plane, forbidden from seeing your kids or man-wife ever again."

I grabbed the basket out of his hands and threw it on the floor. Fruit fell to the ground. The bowls of rice spilled out and a thousand grains scattered across the dirt.

"You're a sick fucker," I growled. "But you won't win this. I'll make your life hell. I'll save your daughter. Usana!"

My loud voice scared her. She cowered behind Miltico's legs.

"You won't starve much longer, Usana. Or have to fear your father's punishments. Help is coming. Soon. Soon, you'll be with a good family."

She did not look me in the eyes. She didn't dare, knowing that one wrong move might have provoked her father's ire.

"Go home, Amiere," Miltico said. "And leave us the hell alone."

Chapter Seventeen: Spouses

After the kids went to sleep, when the moons and pink stars shone brightly above, I asked my spouses to come with me to the beach. I wished to speak someplace where the kids wouldn't overhear if they happened to wake up, where the crashing of Deep Sea's fingers would drown out our words to small ears attempting to eavesdrop. We went to the fallen palm tree which we'd used as a bench since it fell two years ago. I wondered how long it would last before it succumbed to wind and rain. I had begun to wonder if Su had put snowbark resin on it—if snowbark resin could preserve the wood and bark of other trees.

"Your attempt at civility with Miltico didn't work," Su said as he balanced atop the palm tree. He held his arms out for stability.

"If anything, it got worse," I said. Liesle and I remained standing. I had thought to sit on the log, but, knowing what I was about to say, something about sitting felt flippant. I was about to ask Liesle something so terrible, so painful.

"I wish you wouldn't even talk to him," Liesle said. "Nothing good can come of it."

"Lisi..." I stopped. Did I really want to ask her whether Miltico had raped her? Maybe this was something she'd rather forget about forever. It had to have happened over ten years ago, at least. Had she healed? Did she ever think about it? I couldn't recall her mentioning being traumatized, nor had I seen any signs of it. Maybe she had hidden it. Or maybe I'd been an oblivious idiot.

Liesle and Su both looked at me, waiting for me to spit the words out.

"Liesle, I'm sorry. Miltico said some... things. I find them hard to believe."

If looks could kill, her eyes would have torn me asunder. Her pupils went thin, thinner than usual, especially for nighttime. Her tail flickered with lively electricity. "What kind of things?"

"He said you gave him the scratch marks over his eye."

"I did," she replied in a cold, dead voice. Her tone dared me to ask the next question.

"He told me why you did it. Look, I'm not angry that you did it. I just... wonder why you never told me. Told us. We would have understood. Supported you. Helped you. Why did you keep it a secret?"

"Why do you keep the secret about your mother?" she asked. "Why does Su keep the secret about his original sex or his parents? Am I not allowed to have secrets?"

I held my hands up, palms forward, hoping to calm her down. "Of course you are! If you don't want to tell us, you don't have to. But... I hope you didn't keep it a secret because you were afraid we'd react poorly. We're partners for eternity, Lisi. Anything that happens to you, you can tell me. It will never tear me away, and I know Su feels the same way."

He nodded. "Of course. Nothing will tear us apart. Can you tell us what happened? What did Milti do to you, Liesle? He didn't... force you...?"

Her tail flared. An arc of lightning ran toward her back. "He asked me for sex." Her voice was devoid of emotion. She spoke as if reciting lines from a book. "I didn't want to lose my blessings, so I agreed. I fucked him. Afterward, I scratched his eye. Told him I'd take out his other eye if he tried it again."

"Did you go berserk from it?" Su asked.

"I did. But I had enough control over myself that I didn't kill him, obviously."

"I suppose you went to Orienna then?" Orienna would have been her only living blood relative, depending on when the event took place. If Eruwan was born, she would have been far too young and small for Liesle to bite down on. Liesle might have done it if it were an emergency, but Wynnle parents only used their own children to calm a berserker rage as a last resort.

She shook her head. "No. I didn't want her to know what had happened. She was still trying to make it work between herself and Milti."

"But, surely she'd have asked Milti about his eye."

"We're not always logical in our berserker state, Mo Ami. I didn't think about that at the time. She found out later and agreed to keep my secret."

"How did you calm yourself down, then?" I asked. "Did you orgasm?" Once again the image of her climaxing to Miltico bore a hole in my skull and I nearly vomited.

Finally, she showed a hint of emotion. She cracked a smile. Her eyes lit up in the glow of the green moon. Ringslight[1] reflected in her slitted eyes. "You don't remember, Amiere? I fucked you hard. I had three orgasms that session. Su wasn't there that time. I don't recall where... I think he was performing dentistry in a town far away. You must have been craving it, because you managed to get your cock up and *keep* it up. Even in my berserker state, I remembered the story about how Wynnle men have spiny penises so they can scrape out the sperm of rivals. I... I wanted you to scrape out the sperm he'd left inside me. I thought for sure you'd feel it or see it or smell it or... something. I thought you would find out. But you didn't. You scraped it all out, Mo Ami, and left your own seed inside me."

I blushed, despite how disgusting it was. I had no recollection of that moment.

---

1. Light from Aloutia's planetary rings

We'd had a lot of sex, especially when we were younger, and I *had* managed to pleasure Liesle a few times without the assistance of Su's mouth.

"That was the moment we conceived Fionn," she said with a smile. "My precious boy. When I was pregnant with him, I kept thinking 'what if it's Milti's child?' I didn't know what I would do..."

"W-we would have raised him!" I said with no uncertainty. "It wouldn't have mattered whose sperm produced him. If he came from you, he's our child."

"Exactly right," Su said, nodding his head resolutely. "None of these kids came from my sperm or egg, but they're still my kids."

Liesle looked downward at the sand, her face flushed silver with shame. "You're both better parents than I will ever be. I don't... I'm not sure I could love a child that came from a man I hated."

"Don't say that," I said. "You're a wonderful mother. We all have had to learn along the way. You may think that now, but I guarantee if you'd had a child with Milti, you would love that child as much as your others."

She sighed. "Well, now you know. Honestly, I thought that conversation would be a lot more painful. I've dreaded this moment for twelve years, now. I knew I'd have to say it eventually. I thought you two would be angrier."

I walked closer to her and hugged her in a tight embrace. "We love you, Liesle. I could never be angry at you."

Su hopped off the log and stood between us, wrapping two arms around each of us. "Let us not be afraid to share with each other. It's fine to keep secrets, of course, but there's no judgment here. Whatever happened in our past, we can talk about it."

Liesle hiccupped. "You two are making me cry, now! I still have some secrets, but if the time comes I need to share, I'll do so freely."

I buried my face in her mane, inhaling the scent of her. She still wore perfume in addition to her bone jewelry. She was in the mood. Su, too, wore all the tusks, jawbones, and furculae he could fit on his body.

"Would this be a good time to..." I hesitated. If I worded it incorrectly, I could put her in a position where she would have to have sex or lose her blessings. "Would you like to go to the cave and relax a bit? See where it goes from there? I understand that conversation was... difficult?" I wasn't certain if that was the word I wanted to use. "But I want to show you how much I adore you, Liesle, no matter what you've done in the past. I will always be attracted to you, no matter who you've had to endure to retain your blessings."

She sniffed her runny nose. "Yes. Tonight is good. Let me lead, Mo Ami. If... if you are okay with that."

"Always. Tell me what you're comfortable with. I won't ask for anything or make any demands. You won't lose your blessings because of me."

She carried me in her arms while Su swam to the cave, where we enjoyed a passionate night rekindling our love for each other.

Liesle Interlude

The next day, while Amiere went to work in his ateli, and Su went fishing, Liesle took Nio and her art supplies into the village. Orienna and Piotr sat at a table behind her where they could see the canvas, as was legally required, though they took the law in stride. Neither wife nor husband paid attention to Liesle's work, instead opting for a casual conversation with her.

Liesle started on the art commission the Domovye had requested for their Day of Sapience celebration. First came a sketch of Lucognidus. Long ago, Liesle had been terrified of painting Gods. She feared if she drew them in a less-than-flattering way, she'd be a heretic or blasphemer. Now, after being a licensed merchant of faces for almost twenty years, she had drawn him so many times, she could have probably done so blindfolded.

"I'm proud of you for finally telling Ami about Miltico's scar," Orienna said, sipping her kumquat mimosa. "I've pretended to be the one who scarred him for so long I was starting to believe my own lie."

"It wasn't as though I brought it up myself," Liesle said. "Ami found out from Milti, so I confirmed it. I would have carried my secret to Spiritua if I could have."

Piotr cracked his knuckles—a much louder affair than most, given his stony skin. "Now, if only Scrimmy Su would tell us 'is secret. What God d'ye suppose is 'is?"

"Well, go down the list of the Decatheon," Orienna said. "Come up with a reason Su could be that God's child, and why Su would keep it a secret."

"Sawyer. Su doesn't look a fockin' thing like 'im, but Death Godbloods got genetic finaglin' and can look like damn near anything. Keepin' it a secret because Sawyer doesn't knob anyone but Laynie, and maybe Su's mama in't Laynie. 'E doesn't want tha scandal getting out."

The idea of Su being a Death Godblood made Liesle sick. If he were one, he would have likely had recourse to bring Tawny back to life, if not with his own elemental powers, but by entreaty with his father, Lord Sawyer.

"Windesoar," Piotr said. The next God in the Decatheon, in elemental order. "No livin' mortals know what 'e looks like. We're told he's an Orochijin-lookin' fella with white skin and silver hair, but he was also a duke of Yetrius, and the Yetrian are all dark-skinned, so who the fock knows the truth? Could be Su got his brown skin from either o' those. He kinda looks Yetrian, if ya ask me. Maybe 'is mother is Rubaiyan-Muinite. 'T would be a scandal because Windesoar supposedly refuses ta 'ave children. What would 'ave made him change 'is mind?"

Su being a Wind Godblood was unlikely, Liesle thought.

"Cherribell," Orienna said, then took a sip of her mimosa. "I suppose if Cherribell had a child through a Rubaiyan-Muinite, or a Rubaiyan with four arms through some other hybridization... That's convoluted, though. He has so little of Cherribell in his appearance. It would be a scandal because Cherribell declared after the death of Cherish the Monster that she'd leave all her future children in Aloutia, but Su was born in Ophidia."

Liesle could envision him as a Plant Godblood. The few times he'd used magic seemed to involve healing, or at least preventing pain from reaching a person's consciousness. She tried to remember if he'd ever used anything resembling Plant magic, but Steena Village was already on such blessed, fertile land. Any extraordinary growth of plants could be attributed to living in the Gigantification Zone or to the Green Moon's luminance.

"Entomothy," Liesle said, moving on to the fourth God. "As with Death Godbloods, Life Godbloods have genetic manipulation abilities and take on any appearance they wish. Life powers might also have helped me become pregnant, or helped with Amiere's... situation."

Piotr rubbed his chin. "Why'd it be a scandal, though? Life Godbloods are born all tha fockin' time, aye?"

"Entomothy is always portrayed as being a kind, gentle God," Orienna said. "But maybe Su was produced through forceful means. Not like we'd ever know."

"Life Godbloods have their own drama," Liesle said as she outlined what would be the Mind God's eyebrows. "He might be trying to avoid siblings, rather than parents."

"Flamboil," Piotr said. "I think tha's Ami's top choice. We don't know tha Fire God's gender. Could be a Fire Goddess. We're also told she—or he—is Rubaiyan. Tha'd explain Su's Rubaiyan tail. Could'a gotten tha lighter skin an' four arms from 'is other parent."

"Like Entomothy, it wouldn't be much of a scandal," Orienna replied. "There are Fire Godbloods everywhere, and they aren't involved in interpersonal drama."

Piotr wagged his finger at Orienna. "Wasn't Su's story in both his girl an' boy versions a tale o' how he was found in a burnin' village? What're the odds 'e burned it down?"

"Could be true," Liesle said. She wasn't sold on the theory if only because none of the magic he'd ever done around her involved fire. Unless he *had* lost his blessings and his fire dances were made possible by magic rather than Flamboil's Blessing. It still wouldn't explain his healing methods. The bigger issue there was, if he'd lost Flamboil's Blessing... how? Flamboil's laws were prohibitions again murder and child abuse. How and when would Su have ever done those things in his adult life? Unless the Demon King Susan had made him perform atrocities after age fifteen that he dared not speak of...

"Sparkato," Orienna said. "He has four arms and light skin. If Sparkato fucked—or raped—a Rubaiyan woman, you would have Su."

"An' there's your scandal," Piotr said in a humming voice. "Though there're also many Lightning Godbloods. I wouldn't be surprised if many o' them were made... that way."

"That one is my personal opinion on Su's parent," Liesle said. "Su does all the stuff we Lightning elementals do. Wears the jewelry, asks for consent to even *ask* for sex. He was practiced at it before we met him, like he'd been living as a Lightning elemental before he had to act like one around us. Also... we try to be careful with our tails around him, but I'm sure we've bumped into him before, yet it's never hurt him. I think he's immune to electricity."

"Perhaps..." Piotr mused. "Though next is Machenerate, an' they say Stone Godbloods would also be immune ta electricity if they existed."

"We've been told the Stone Goddess can't have children, so it would be a scandal if she had managed it somehow," Orienna said.

"I can't bear to think of Su as a Stone Godblood," Liesle replied. "What if he... caused Tawny's death?"

That silenced them, if only temporarily. After an awkward minute, they moved on to the next God in the Decatheon, Lucognidus—the subject of Liesle's painting.

"Mind Godbloods have illusionism powers," Piotr said. "Maybe Scrimmy looks like one, but is trickin' us into thinkin' he looks like somethin' else entirely!"

"That would be one hell of a trick," Orienna said. "But if anyone could pull off a trick like that, it's a highly-skilled Mind Godblood. What would the scandal be, though? Perhaps another rape? Volkhvs say Lucognidus would never force anyone to have sex with him, but at the same time, he's the highest God and authority in all the dominion. If any sexual encounter involving a person with authority over another is 'rape', then every act of sex he does is rape."

Liesle stared deep into the eyes she'd drawn on the canvas. Phoenian eyes, a completely different shape and color than Su's. She'd studied Lucognidus's face from a hundred other paintings and statues of him. He looked nothing like Su. If Su was an illusionist, his illusions affected him at all times, even when he was asleep or emotional, which rumors of Godbloods claimed was impossible. According to stories, Godbloods had to rest their powers occasionally or else they'd have seizures.

"Liqua," Piotr said. "She's my choice. Four arms an' can use 'er Water 'bilities to turn into an aquatic being. Exactly what Scrimmy does, aye. She could 'ave focked any darker-skinned man and gotten our Scrimmy Su."

"Maybe with Water powers, he's making healing ointments whenever he heals you," Orienna suggested.

"But why would he hide it?" Liesle asked. "Liqua is the most shameless of the Decatheon. She'd readily admit to raping men."

"Maybe one o' the male Gods raped 'er?" Piotr said with a shrug. "I can't think o' any other men who'd be powerful enough ta manage that. D'ya suppose *both* Scrimmy's parents might be Gods?"

"Could be," Liesle replied, releasing a sigh. If both his parents were Gods, it would make a lot of sense how, between his appearance and his powers, there was such variation compared to other Godbloods. Not that they *knew* any other Godbloods. Everything they had was speculation.

"Might be the father's Sparkato, too. Scrimmy'd wanna hide if 'e was an incest baby."

Liesle dreaded that possibility, but it would explain why Su didn't want biological kids of his own. Sure, *he* didn't show any signs of incest, but his children might.

"For the sake of completing the list, the tenth is Icsnow," Orienna said. "Who we're told has a body eternally like that of a child. Her statues display her as a white-skinned, white-haired being, though that might just be for snow symbolism, and not what she really looks like. If she were Su's mother, the scandal would be that her body is supposedly childlike. It would imply she's either not a child or... someone, probably a male God, got to her."

As Liesle's sketch of Lucognidus looked judgmentally upon her, so too, did she judge him. "I don't think the Mind Spirit would allow that. Everything we know about him suggests he wouldn't allow harm to come to a child. That includes the Ice Spirit."

Orienna crossed her legs and leaned on her arm. "You don't believe that, do you? If he doesn't allow harm to come to children, where was he when Tawny died?"

Liesle knew her sister was about to bring that up. As much as she abhorred religion and hated the Gods, Liesle didn't want Lucognidus being blamed for something out of his control. She never thought she'd defend a God, but his visage, drawn by her, demanded it. "Lucognidus sees the world through his Twenty Thousand Eyes. At any given moment, more than ten thousand children might be in danger, and he is with them, saving them. Occasionally, ten thousand and one children are in danger, and the last one slips through his grasp."

It was the mud and sludge the volkhvs had preached, back when they were kids going to the Mind church school, forced to kneel at Lucognidus's feet for daily worship. The previous Mys Volkhv preached things like that in hopes it would inspire the children to stay safe. She didn't want them wandering into the jungle or flying over Deep Sea.

Liesle wondered if any of that preaching was true. How had Lucognidus *not* watched over Tawny that day? Liesle wasn't so presumptuous as to assume her girl was more important than someone else's child, but... he should have known.

He knew the crystalights would be there. Hell, he probably had a *role* in putting them there, especially if he intended to bless them as Godlights one day.

He had to have known Tawny would die that day. He had to have seen her fall. Therefore, he must have allowed the catastrophe to happen.

Liesle gazed into the eyes she had sketched and hoped he was not Su's father.

Chapter Eighteen: A Walk Along the Shore

I sat in my ateli, working on a new piece... A personal piece. The Lagodore girl was complete. I had no current commission, but I was encouraged by the merchants of light administrators to work on anything of a general appeal. Sometimes, people didn't know exactly what they wanted, so they would shop around or buy something that caught their eye. Or, if we'd sold enough to meet the maxima, there was no reason we couldn't make something for ourselves.

Tawny. Well, it looked nothing like her, yet. I had carved only the most basic shape of her. It had been... difficult, at first. Even as a mere chunk of glowing crystal, I saw what it would look like, in my mind's eye. I saw Tawny, her spots, her thick, golden mane, and bright yellow eyes. How she looked like me! I had to stop every few minutes to let my mind wander, to think about those good old days, that golden past, my idyllic life, sparkling and fragrant, forever out of reach.

A knock came at the door which I recognized as Cohaku's. She had joined me in here a few more times since that first time. I wasn't sure if she *liked* watching me, or if she just wanted to get away from everyone else. I never pestered her with questions or demands like her mother or siblings would do. I think she appreciated having a safe, quiet place, now that her tree house had lost its appeal.

"Come on in," I said. "Visor's in your spot."

I had moved one of the bone pegs down, closer to where she could reach without having to fly up. She had taken to hanging the visor there.

"Daddy, you have visitors," Cohaku said as she opened the door just a crack. "Um, they're Yosoe, but not Mr. Svelt or his stupid son."

I chuckled at her descriptor for Miltico. I assumed the visitors were Mr. Onoretti and his family. He had said he'd come by one of these days.

I grabbed the Lagodore crystalight sitting on the shelf. I wasn't sure if this was a business or personal meeting, so I couldn't be certain if I'd sell the crystal back to him now. At the very least, I could get his opinion on it.

I hung up my visor and stepped outside, where a brisk sea breeze whipped my mane into a wild, unpresentable state. Ugh, I didn't want Mr. Onoretti to see me like this... Oh well, what could be done?

Cohaku followed close behind me. Mr. Onoretti stood with his family by the hip bone table where Liesle sat, playing with Nio. Su was in his ateli still, working on building Tawny's memorial. He'd had to pause while the bones he custom-ordered in Seabells shipped, but they had finally arrived this morning, packed carefully aboard a Daga's shell.

Mr. Onoretti dressed in casual attire, including some tropical leaves he must have had made here in the last few days. I'd never seen him in such informal dress; it was a bit humorous to me. I felt significantly less embarrassed about my mussed-up mane, now. His wife and daughter—both named Beatrice—were similarly dressed in outfits of grass, reeds, and flower petals. Oboro wore leather armor akin to what he'd worn the previous times I'd seen him. I wondered if he wanted to wear it, or if Mr. Onoretti had not given him a choice. Was he here on vacation, too? Or did he think of this as work? He was only fourteen years old...

"Daddy, they have a girl," Cohaku whispered. "Do you think she's my age?"

Little Beatrice rode on Mr. Onoretti's shoulders, holding on by his horns. While Mr. Onoretti had markhor-goat horns, his wife had horns curving around her ears. The daughter's horns were a perfect mixture of the two: curving around her ears, and twisted like a corkscrew.

"She's around Fionn's age," I said, remembering that Liesle had been pregnant with him at the same time the elder Beatrice had been pregnant with her only child. "But she's very good at troika. Maybe you could invite her to play with you and Nio."

Cohaku gasped. "Oh! She sounds fun. Um, maybe I'll ask later. I don't want to annoy her..."

I walked up to the group. "A pleasure to see you, Mo Senya. Are you here for that dinner I offered?"

Mr. Onoretti gave me an amicable smile. "Oh yes, absolutely! I hope you don't mind that I brought my family."

"I wouldn't have it any other way." I held out the crystalight Lagodore. "I finished this if you're here to trade."

"Yes, I will need to speak with you in private, anyway. Beatie, I need to speak with Mr. Lasteran for a while. I'm setting you down." Mr. Onoretti crouched down so the girl on his back could slide off. "Why don't you play with this girl?" He waved toward Cohaku. Having attention on her, she shyly slid behind my legs. It reminded me too much of when Usana hid behind Miltico's legs.

"Go on, Cohaku," I said, though I didn't nudge her away. I knew how much she hated that. "You're not annoying. She'll like you."

The Yosoe girl grinned with a smile reminiscent of how her father smiled when scheming. "Cohaku? That means 'amber' in Orochigo, doesn't it?"

"Y-yeah." Cohaku stepped out from behind me, all of her own volition. "Eruwan wanted to call me Amber because of my yellow mane, but Daddy's name already started with an 'A' and we wanted to make sure everyone on the chore board had a different initial. Mapa Su knows Orochigo and said Cohaku meant 'amber.'"

Beatrice scratched the short furs under her chin. "Ahh, but doesn't it start with a 'K'? Are you breaking the rules?"

"The Orochigo word starts with a 'K', but I write my name with a 'C.'"

The Yosoe girl nodded approvingly. "Clever. My name is Beatrice, but you can call me Beatie."

"Okay. Uh, do you live by the beach?"

"Nope. I've never seen Deep Sea. Can you show him to me?"

Cohaku's eyes popped open like it was inconceivable that anyone could live so far inland. "Really? Yes, let's go! Um, Deep Sea probably won't talk to you or anything. You have to make a pretty big sacrifice. And, uh, he's scary. The other day, he swept above Mapa Su and I thought he was going to kill him! Or all of us!"

Beatie startled back and blinked. "Really? We won't summon him on accident, will we?"

"You'll be fine," Liesle said from the table. "Su paid him another sacrifice to ensure his protection over the village."

Mr. Onoretti scowled, not seeming convinced by my wife's assurance. "Beatie, don't swim in Deep Sea. The sacrifice might only apply to people who live in the village."

I expected Beatrice to pout or protest, but she smiled and nodded. "Of course, Papa. I don't want to get crushed by him, either. Can Oboro come along, too?"

"Yes, that's a good idea. Oboro, keep my daughter safe."

The intimidating Sasorin boy clutched his lower hands over his two sidearm swords "As you command, Signore."

"Uh, you can relax a bit now, Oboro. Feel free to play with them, if you'd like."

"Yes, Signore." His hands did not unclench.

Mr. Onoretti scratched his forehead, between his horns. "I suppose that's the best I can get out of you at this point. Alright kids, go have fun." He shooed them away, waving his hands toward the beach.

The elder Beatrice had taken a seat next to Liesle. She chuckled. "That poor boy still thinks he's a slave, though our daughter isn't helping much. She's quite bossy."

"I wonder where she got it from," Mr. Onoretti quipped playfully.

"Oho, I wonder indeed! From you, Signore? Always bossing around your employees?" She said the word 'Signore' with a hint of sarcasm, possibly imitating Oboro.

"Or from you, Mys, always bossing around *me*?"

Beatrice laughed in a loud manner, not what one would expect from a refined woman. "We women know how to keep our men under control. Isn't that right, Liesle?"

"That's right," she said, staring me down with lascivious jade eyes. "My man and my Su."

Memories of our recent nights together came rushing to my skull. Liesle straddling me, sopping wet, her breasts so perfect... She liked to be on top. My baculum dared try to rise, but now was *not* the time and I willed it to relax.

Mr. Onoretti tapped my elbow. "We ought to flee before these women declare their allegiance to Ophidia and sell us to the highest bidder."

As we walked away, Beatrice laughed at our mock-cowardice. "What Ophidian would want an old goat like you, Gio? You're too literate for them!"

He chuckled to himself until we were out of earshot. I put the crystalight Lagodore in my antelope-skull pouch as we walked. We traveled along the beach, up The Corridor, away from where the kids played. Rain had fallen earlier and the sand crunched under our feet. The strong wind hinted at more rain coming, but according to the weather calendar, it wouldn't happen until nightfall. "I hope my wife's antics don't alarm you, Mr. Lasteran. She has a crude sense of humor at times."

"When Liesle is in a better mood, she's much the same. She lost her sense of humor after Tawny's death, but I think she's starting to recover it. The way she looked at me just then... Honestly, I think having her talk with Mys Iola will help. Maybe Liesle will get that sarcastic tinge back in her tone."

"You can call my wife Beatrice," he said.

"Are you sure that's appropriate, Mo Senya? Shouldn't she be the one to give me that right?"

"She called your wife by her given name, so it's only fair. And if I may be honest, I'm getting too old for this mud and sludge with calling people by their surnames. We're not children anymore, and it's hardly the sign of respect it once was. I can just as easily respect a person I call by their public name as I can disrespect someone I call by their surname. If you don't mind, Amiere, I'd prefer if you called me Giorvi from now on."

My breath caught in my throat. I'd become so accustomed to thinking of him as Mr. Onoretti that I'd stopped thinking of it as a difference in authority between us. To me, it was just his name.

When I didn't respond, he cleared his throat. "Ah, if you're not comfortable with that, I can go back to calling you Mr. Lasteran."

"No! It's fine. Though call me Ami. I know you're not fluent in our dialect, but the name 'Amiere' was... a poor choice. Fifteen-year-old me hadn't considered the future implications."

"And the registrar signing your adulthood documentation didn't talk you out of it?"

"I don't think she knew the meaning of my name. She likely didn't speak the North Corridorean patois."

"Ah. I'm lucky I didn't have that issue. 'Giorvi' is such a common name in Chernagora, you can't walk half a mile without bumping into one."

"It might take me a while to get used to saying it," I said.

He mused that over for a moment. "We have the rest of our lives, and then the eternity of Spiritua. You'll get used to it, eventually."

"You think we'll know each other in Spiritua?"

"I don't see why not. It's everlasting existence. We'll have time to be with everyone we've ever known and loved. We'll meet and make friends with people who died long ago. Maybe we'll become friends with people who lived during the Conquering or the Greed Wars. And thousands of years from now, we might be friends with people who haven't been born yet. Our descendants, perhaps."

That thought put things into perspective. If I were a two thousand-year-old man in Spiritua and met a relatively young two hundred-year-old man, would I know if he was my descendant? That far down the family line, I wondered if a Mantodea could tell by reading our genetics. And if he was my descendant, could I be his friend? Could we chat like two regular men together, drinking beer and watching kiwi-batte? I struggled to picture myself as a friend to Fionn or Heliodor. They were my sons; I had to be a father to them, not their buddy. How long down the line of hereditary would such feelings last for me?

"Well, I have no doubt you'll have descendants," Giorvi said. "Beatrice and I wanted to have more children, but it was difficult. We tried for so long. She became pregnant just before reaching the age where Yosoe women can no longer bear children."

I recalled those days. Giorvi was sixteen years older than me and had been trying to have children with his wife since they'd met in their early twenties. I'd gotten vibes of jealousy from him when Liesle became pregnant with Eruwan. I had apparently shared with him my difficulties with maintaining an erection—I must have been high on crazy sugar; I would not have revealed such information to my boss while sober. Regardless, he knew about my condition, so the knowledge that I had impregnated my wife so soon despite having problems with my male equipment while he hadn't managed it in sixteen years must have rubbed him wrong. Giorvi had been gracious toward me. If he was envious, it did not show in his business dealings.

He had impregnated his wife around the same time I had impregnated Liesle with Fionn—a story with much darker undertones, now that I knew her half of the event. I distinctly recalled our wives chatting together, both with bulging bellies. Giorvi had been getting older by then—young Beatie had hatched on his fortieth hatching-day.

"I am not sure if my daughter will have children of her own," Giorvi said. "I know she's only twelve, but so far she hasn't shown any interest in boys."

"You feel safe with that Sasorin boy around her?"

He laughed, genuinely at first, but then sadly. "Oboro was mentally and emotionally broken by his Ophidian mother-master. He wouldn't touch Beatie without permission, and he would probably run to me if she tried to touch him. He had a sister on Ophidia, and his mother had ingrained in him the importance of not touching girls. I know it's a different context than we have in Aloutia, but the result is the same. Oboro won't touch any girl or woman without permission. You know, his mother once made him stand in a freezing cold river until the count of two thousand because his sister tripped him and when he fell, he landed on her."

"That's sick." Ophidians should all go to Hell. If only it still existed... But Lucognidus in all His Infinite Wisdom had decided against the institution of realms of eternal punishment. He had long ago transformed the old Hell into the current-day Spiritua.

"Part of me is glad Beatie hatched female," Giorvi said. "If she had been a boy, I'd fret every minute that she could be captured by Ophidians and sold into slavery."

"Funny how we have those thoughts about our children, but we never thought about it ourselves when we were boys. Or, well, I never did."

He laughed. "Oh yes, when I ran away from my home, I never once thought Ophidians would find me. I thought as long as I stayed in Aloutia, I would be safe. And I was. I've never had to deal with those snakes. But still, I don't know where Beatie's path of life will take her. I can only hope it glitters with starlight, preferably the pink or dusty kind."

It was a poetic way of saying he hoped she would stay on Aloutia—where the stars were pink—or Cosmo—with its space dust clouding the night sky.

"Are you disappointed you don't have a son to carry on the Onoretti name?" I asked.

"Bah, I never cared for that sort of nonsense. My own father had enough sons, I'm sure there are a hundred worthless Onorettis in the Sunset Kingdom."

Come to think of it... what was Oboro's situation? "Does Oboro have a surname?"

"No. Ophidian slaves don't get surnames. He doesn't have one officially, yet. When he turns fifteen, he'll need to get one. I plan to write his certificate of adulthood myself—I am licensed to do so. I would not reject him if he asked to take my surname."

"Perhaps he's too shy to ask. If he needs permission to touch a woman, he probably feels it's an even greater violation to touch the *honored* name of the man who rescued him." My use of the word 'honor' was a pun. Giorvi had told me once that the name Onoretti was a diminutive of the word 'honor' and had roughly translated it as 'small honor,' though that wasn't quite accurate.

"You have a point," he mused. "I'll have to have a deeper conversation with him about that when the time comes."

"Eruwan's fifteenth hatching-day is coming soon." I scratched behind my ear. Fuck, I'd hoped to have her house completed before then, but I might not manage it.

"If you need someone to write her certificate, I can do so. Might save you a trip to Seabells, if no one in Steena Village is licensed. Though if she had an officiant in mind, I won't press it."

"I'll mention it to her. I don't think Eruwan cares or has anyone in mind."

If she *did* have anyone in mind, I'd have been shocked. No one in Steena Village had the authority to officiate an adulthood certificate, and as far as I knew, she didn't know anyone outside the village.

Giorvi stopped by a coconut tree. A few of the fruits had fallen to the ground. One had been claimed by a coconut crab. "Does this belong to anyone?" he asked as he rolled one with his foot—one free from crustaceans.

"No. All fruit trees in Steena Village are for communal use."

He set it under his hoof and crushed it. The liquid spread in a small puddle. "Let's sit down a moment, Ami. We're far enough away from eavesdroppers now, I think." He picked up the pieces of his coconut, sat on the sand despite it being wet, and bit into the fruit with a satisfying crunch. He ate the stringy shell along with the white innards. Well, there *was* the stereotype of Yosoe being able to eat anything...

"Did you want to talk about something in private?" I asked, taking a seat on the sand next to him. Far enough away from the puddle of coconut water, but still crunchy from the recent rain.

"Oh! No. I'm sorry for alarming you. I'm used to being paranoid about who's eavesdropping. My daughter is too smart for her own good and likes to meddle in my business. I suppose I have only myself to blame for that."

"I feel the same way about mine. Eruwan, Cohaku, and Nio... feels strange not putting Tawny's name in there. But those three are all so smart, in their own ways."

Giorvi took another bite of the coconut. "Oh, this is good. We don't get these in Chernagora. I'll have to import them. I wonder how it tastes in coffee. I hope Beatie plays nicely with your kids, Ami. She can be...a bit of a domineering presence. She likes to think she's in charge."

"Cohaku can be difficult to get along with," I said. "I have no idea if they'll become friends. Cohaku might say something rude without realizing it."

Giorvi rubbed his beard. "We do the best we can as parents, but some things are out of our control."

Yes, *we* did the best we could as parents. My skull flashed to the image of Miltico lifting Usana's sleeves, showing me the welts on her arms.

"Ami?" His horizontal pupils had thinned. Was that fear? Or aggression? I was used to thinning pupils in Wynnles representing fury, but it had always been different for Milti.

I had been staring off into Deep Sea, watching his fingers crash against the sands, as my mind repeatedly played scenes of Usana's abuse. I turned to Giorvi to allay his fears. "Sorry, something you said reminded me of... something else."

"You looked like you were about to go berserk."

I shook my head. "Even if I did, Wynnles never fully lose control. We're sapient. We always retain enough of ourselves to make conscious decisions."

"I hadn't meant to bring up negative stereotypes. I was merely commenting on your appearance. It was truly frightening. Are you okay? I hope what I said wasn't as bad as your expression makes it out to be."

Never before had I wished so much for a mirror. What did I look like that had scared him so cruelly?

"Apologies. I've had trouble with another person in this village. A Yosoe, but nothing like you."

"Mr. Svelt?"

I blinked, blindsided. I had never expected him to know anyone else in the village. "You know him? Or do you mean the shopkeeper?"

"I know about the Mr. Svelt who recently came back from Cosmo. I understand he was banished."

"Unofficially, but yes. I scared him off after he..." Originally, it was because he hit Eruwan, though if I'd known then that he'd raped Liesle, I might have done worse to him. I might have really killed him.

"He's a problem for me, too," Giorvi said. "He asked me if he could become a citizen of Chernagora, but I told him I'd have to look into the matter of his banishment first. We have, ah, rules and rituals one must perform if one wishes to rejoin society after a period of exile. A Yosoe must show they are penitent. I won't go into detail; it's not a clean story. Mr. Svelt refused to do it the *proper way*, but he had some ideas for another way. He's... in my way." Those words were spoken in a voice of pure dispassion and rationality. Not a hint of anger or sorrow. Milti might as well have been a twig on the road. In his way, but an inconvenience that he could easily step over... or crush under his hoof, just as the coconut had been. I imagined Milti's blood in lieu of the spilled coconut water, and the disturbing image brought me a surprising amount of delight.

"He has a daughter," I said. "He abuses her." Why was I bringing that up? I shouldn't bring Giorvi into my little village's trauma.

"I feel sorry for her, being raised by worthless scum like him. At least she's on Aloutia now. The authorities will get involved."

"They haven't, yet," I said. "Steena Village has a reputation. Ever since the Greed Wars, we've been too hostile toward lawkeepers for them to do regular patrols. We're too small and distant for anyone in Seabells to care about. If Usana was an official citizen, they might care."

"Nonsense. I'll talk to them myself. I'll go to Seabells first thing in the morning and demand she gets put into protective care right away."

"Good luck," I said. "She's half-Lagodore. I kept thinking about her as I worked on this." It was a clumsy attempt to change the subject to the crystalight I was still carrying, but I was desperate to get off topics that only served to make me angry.

"Very good work," Giorvi said, taking it into his free hand while the other held the chunk of coconut. He examined it from every angle. "You captured the essence in the eyes. Lagodore eyes ought to sparkle. Too much dye, and they look dead... soulless. The tiny pinpricks of light coming out from them is masterful work."

I was all too aware of the difficulty in leporine eyes. One of the projects we had to do in art school was a longfur monoceros, also known as an almiraj, or a one-horned rabbit. While I'd gotten a good grade on the fur, my instructor had said I hadn't given the eyes the care they'd deserved. Since then, I'd been meticulous when it came to eyes, especially rabbits and Lagodores.

"Did you want to buy it now, or later?" I asked.

"I don't have my checkbook on me at this moment." He handed the crystalight back to me. "Let me offer you another deal: This one in exchange for three similarly-sized crystalights, lifespan of one hundred and eighty years."

"Do you have a plan for them?" I asked as I tucked the crystalight back into my antelope-skull pouch.

"One of the crystalights is for myself, one is for the city of Chernagora, the other is for you to sculpt as you wish. I'll pay you out of pocket for mine. One hundred thousand coins, split into four payments. I'll write a check for twenty-five thousand tomorrow. The other two crystals will go through the usual methods."

That was too good to pass up. Splitting payment over time was a common practice, especially for more expensive items. It wasn't because the purchaser didn't have the money; in fact, Giorvi would likely put it in an escrow, just as he had with the whole mine. But rather because the Aloutian government was liable to impose the maxima on my income. The maxima ensured nobody acquired such an extreme amount of wealth that the Greed Wars could ever occur again. If Giorvi wrote me a check for one hundred thousand coins now, I'd be forced to stop working for the rest of the year or donate the money to one of the churches.

I wondered if the churches could save Usana if they had more members or were better funded. Perhaps I *should* consider donating my excess money to them...

I scratched my beard. I was a simple merchant of light. What did I know about economics?

"I started a personal project today, but only the rough shape. I might change that one and use the new one to make it."

Giorvi's teeth crunched loudly into the coconut. "Your daughter?" he asked.

I glanced at him. "How did you know?"

"It's what I would have done," he said. Tapping his forehead, he added, "We think very similarly."

"Because we're both fathers?"

"Fathers who *care*. Don't lump us in with Mr. Svelt."

I clenched my fists, wrists resting on my knees. My tail's light flickered and a shiver of electricity ran up my spine. "Of course. We care... We care too much, I think."

"What does it mean to care too much, Ami?"

A cormorant dove into Deep Sea while I thought about my answer. As it finagled with the fish in its beak, the fish flopped free and landed back in the water.

"I can't stop thinking about Usana," I said on the verge of tears. "I know I should mind my own business, but I *know* Miltico is abusing her. Starving her. How can I sit here and let it go on?"

"What are you willing to do, Ami? How far would you go to avenge your child? Or a child who's not your own? What if you didn't even know the child?"

"It doesn't matter that she's not my own. I'd kill to save any abused child."

Giorvi wiped his hands clean of coconut remnants and leaned on his knees. "Well, that answers that question, doesn't it? You're *willing* to kill. Lawkeepers don't come to Steena Village. Miltico is an immigrant and doesn't have the same rights as citizens."

My eyes widened. I had no doubt my pupils thinned. "I couldn't actually..."

"Oh, I'm not saying you *should*. But if you did? And if you got caught and tried for murder? I'd defend you in court, Ami, and you should know that as the legal liaison for the Aloutian government for the merchants of light, I know my way around a courtroom."

I turned to face him again. His eyes were as devoid of emotion as always, but he wore a clever grin, and the pentagram shape of his features sent a chill down my spine.

I would... keep what he said in mind.

Chapter Nineteen: The Two Beatrices

The next morning, I woke up wrapped around Liesle's strong, thick arms, but Su was missing. I was usually the first one to wake up, so seeing Su gone made me wonder what had roused him away. Did one of the kids need him?

Tawny... The pain never went away. For all of Liesle's strength, her arms could not compare to the sense that I had a jeweled elephant sitting on my chest.

I untangled myself from Liesle who groaned in half-awake protest, but released me and turned around. Her tail swatted me. Her electric sheath had come undone in the night and would have hurt like hell if I hadn't been a Lightning elemental.

I rose and stumbled out to look for Su. He wasn't in the living room. Sometimes he'd hum while working, or his bones would clatter together as he walked. Nothing. It was silent outside other than the usual sounds of Deep Sea thrumming the beach, wind in the palm fronds, and cawing gulls.

I checked the chore board to see if he'd planned to work today. Sure enough, he'd written 'bone project' next to his name, which had also changed. Or rather, he had two new Orochigo muji representing his name. One which he'd told me meant 'a door hinge' but which he used to indicate he was doing construction. Next to it was the character for 'sand.' Ahh, my sweet Sugar. When he used the 'sand' character, it meant he wished for me to hold him down on the sand and make love to him. My chest stirred with desire. I returned to the bedroom to get my bone earrings and placed them in my ears. Although he was at his ateli and would likely be away for most of the day, I would be prepared for his return.

The kids didn't have school today, so I had the luxury of making breakfast at my leisure. The fish in the ground oven was huge. Su had claimed it was an apology from Deep Sea for scaring us, though I thought it was more likely an apology to us *from* Su for provoking Deep Sea. I could not imagine a Demon Lord caring for the feelings of insignificant mortals like us.

As I set to work slicing the fish with my claws, I wondered if Giorvi had kept his promise to go to Seabells and talk to the lawkeepers about helping Usana. If they couldn't do anything, though, what was my next step? What could I do? Murder was out of the question, despite what Giorvi hinted about defending me in court. The lawkeepers might not give a damn about Steena Village, but they would throw out a dangerous Wynnle. I had no doubt about that in the depths of my soul. To many Aloutians, Wynnles were hardly better than the lions we evolved from.

Would they care if I kidnapped her? If the lawkeepers couldn't bother to take her away from her abusive father, would they bother to take her away from *me*? I would fill her up with delicious fruit, let her wear whatever she's most comfortable in, and let her play with my kids. She'd be happy. The lawkeepers wouldn't take away a happy child, would they?

I decided to wait. I'd wait until I heard from Giorvi, in case he had good news.

Soon after breakfast, the rain poured down as if Liqua had upended a bucket on top of us. In this part of the world, the rain was so predictable, you could arrange a schedule around it, but we weren't always told how much rain we'd get.

I brought out the troika board and played against Cohaku and Nio, both masters of the game despite their young age. Nio, especially, was better at it than she had any right to be. Sometimes I wondered if the part of her brain governing speech had vacated itself to allow room for troika strategy.

Eruwan laid back against the pillow pile, working on a new scrimshaw project. Of the several bones Su had special ordered, one of them was a pristine nue[1] scapula—perfect for scrimshaw.

He'd also ordered a thick, juicy cotza[2] femur for Maika to chew on. She gnawed on it, content, wagging her morel-tail to and fro. Fionn laid against Maika's side, tossing oko vertebrae toward Heliodor, who'd made a game of catching them around his tail.

Liesle had gone to Orienna's house with her painting supplies. By law, the merchants of faces were supposed to paint outdoors, though if she were to paint inside Orienna's house while it rained, I doubted anyone would report her. If lawkeepers wouldn't come to help Usana, why would they come to stop a harmless artist?

Su was in his ateli, working on the memorial.

My mind had long ago wandered out into the rain as I mentally imagined the new crystalight I'd work on. I designed Tawny's statue in my head, deciding on her pose and clothing.

Cohaku and Nio had teamed up to take me out in troika. Even if they hadn't, they would have defeated me easily with my current lack of focus. Despite their

1. A large, bipedal, predatory mammal found only in the Mu jungle.

2. Desert-dwelling bovines, farmed for their meat and milk.

age, these two girls were skilled at troika and no one else in the family could match their abilities. Certainly not me.

Maika's ears perked up and she raised her head, looking toward the entrance. She gave a low bark; her signal to us that someone was nearby. She would have stood up to investigate if Fionn hadn't been laying against her.

"Is anyone home?" a woman's voice called from beyond the leaf door. The elder Beatrice.

"Come on in, Mys Iola," I called.

Both mother and daughter Beatrice entered, followed by the Sasorin bodyguard, Oboro, holding an umbrella. He set it down by the femur threshold.

Cohaku's tail waved when she saw the younger Beatrice enter.

"It's just us today," I said. "Liesle is at her sister's and Su is working in his ateli. Sorry if you were hoping to chat with my wife again, today. Beatie, would you like to play troika with my daughters?"

The little Yosoe girl's face beamed with joy. It was the first time I'd seen the sparkle in a Yosoe eye that I was trained to see in Lagodore eyes. Perhaps their eyes weren't as empty as I'd once perceived...

"May I really?" she asked. "I love troika! I play with Mama and Papa all the time!"

I rose from my pillow and offered it to the young guest. "I'm no match for these two. Maybe they'll have more fun with you."

She giggled demurely as she took my spot. Cohaku purred in satisfaction. "I-I'm glad we get to play together."

The room had no shortage of pillows; a necessity considering how big my family was. I offered two spots to Beatrice the Mother and Oboro. "Apologies if you were hoping for actual chairs. Wynnles don't use chairs much."

Beatrice held up her grass skirt and plopped down. "Quite alright. I didn't come here to get the same experience as home. Gio said he had business in Seabells today that would have been boring for little Beatie, but I didn't want her to sit around in our rental house all day, either. Beatie mentioned making friends here, so I brought her here hoping she'd get to play with them."

"Of course. What about you, Oboro? Maybe you could play with Fionn and Heliodor?"

My sons stopped what they were doing to stare. A vertebra, tossed by Fionn, hit Heliodor on the forehead.

"I am working right now," Oboro said resolutely. "Signore's orders."

"Working how?" I asked. "Wouldn't you be with him in Seabells if you were working?"

"He asked me to protect his wife and daughter."

"They're perfectly safe here," I said. "Go play with my sons for a little while. We're not going anywhere."

"It's fine, Oboro," Beatrice the Mother said. "I won't leave this house until the rain goes away. Or until Mr. Lasteran has decided I'm too much of a nuisance to keep around his kids." She laughed like a raunchy old crone, certainly not the elegant lady she usually presented herself as. It seemed both Giorvi and his wife had lost interest in etiquette in their old age.

Oboro approached Fionn like he was approaching an actual lion.

"Um, hi."

"Are you a Sasorin?" Heli asked.

"Y-yeah."

"What happened to your tail? I thought Sasorin had stingers."

Fionn flicked another vertebra at Heli; he intended on hitting his forehead that time. "Hey, don't ask rude questions."

"Oh, was it rude? Sorry, I didn't know."

"It'd be like if he asked you why you're a quadruped. Don't ask about someone's body not being what you expect."

"I said I'm sorry!" Heli yelled.

"It's okay," Oboro said. "I used to have a stinger. My master would extract poison from it. But one day she messed up and my poison never grew back. She decided it would be safer to just cut the entire tip off. But I was useless at that point, so she sold me to the arenas."

My sons looked at each other curiously.

"What's an arena?" Heli asked.

The boys continued their conversation. Once Heli realized Oboro was from Ophidia, he had a million more questions about that wretched plane of female supremacists. The troika-playing girls were quiet, with the only sounds being the clicking and sliding of pieces across the six-pointed-star board.

I brought my attention back to Beatrice the Mother, reclining on the pillows as if it were her natural state of being. Legs crossed, an arm supporting her temple, a wicked grin... She was my guest, though, and I ought to treat her like one. I wasn't used to being the only adult home when a guest came by, so I'd forgotten my manners. "Would you like something to eat or drink, Mys? We have all the tropical fruit you can imagine, and we turn some into juice."

"I'm fine, thank you," she said. "Unless it's rude to turn food down in your culture. I apologize, I studied languages most thoroughly, and sometimes I pick up on cultural quirks, but I don't know the rules of conduct here."

"You're fine. We're a family of Wynnles anyway, and our idea of proper manners is nothing like the Flora or Winyans who live in these parts."

"True. You eat a lot of meat, don't you?"

"Not just that, but we don't use utensils. Su does, but most Wynnles would rather eat with their hands."

She lifted her head, eyes wide with shock. "What? Even the rice?"

"Especially the rice! We raise the bowl to our face and shove it in with our claws." I mimicked the motion with my hands. "I can't imagine eating a tiny spoonful at a time."

"Well, get a bigger spoon!" She laughed again, though I didn't see what was so funny. Perhaps it was just her personality; some people found humor in peculiar places. "I apologize again, Mr. Lasteran. It surprises me to hear you don't use utensils, but I suppose it would surprise you if you heard Yosoe don't use utensils *or* hands. We just bury our face into our plates and chow down!"

I blinked, flummoxed. I'd seen Milti and Tico both eat with forks and spoons. Or was that also a part of North Corridorean culture not present in Chernagora? The previous times I'd been to Chernagora, I hadn't paid attention to how the civilians ate. No, this must have been a lie. I'd been to some of Giorvi's fancy dinners where they ate with delicate tableware made of crystal, glass, and something akin to silver. But... those were meant to be fancy events, attended by dignitaries and high-ranked merchants. Did regular Yosoe eat the way she described?

Beatrice guffawed so hard she stomped the floor. "Oh, your face! You believe me, don't you? Oh, I am the worst. Gio didn't warn you about me, did he? Don't believe anything more I say. I love to get reactions out of people, such as what I got out of you. I'm a rotten woman."

Eruwan looked up from her scrimshaw to give me a piteous look. Beatrice noticed her glance.

"Oh, don't think too poorly of me, dear," the Yosoe said to Eruwan. "It's just my character. I have nothing but respect for your father. He's a truly good man. Oh, what is that? Did Master Scrimshander teach you how to scrimshaw?"

Eruwan pulled her bone close to her chest protectively. She closed her eyes, likely to stop herself from glaring scornfully at the woman who would intrude on her art. Or was she embarrassed?

"Sorry," Beatrice said, sounding genuinely apologetic. "I forgot, not every child wants to show off their art. Where is Master Scrimshander? At work?"

"Yeah," I replied, appreciating her quick diversion to a new topic. Eruwan appreciated it, too, if I had to guess. She resumed her work. "He'll probably be away for most of the day."

"I wanted to ask him about a job. Little Beatie's got a bad tooth. Girl loves her sweets too much and Gio can't say no to her."

I wished Su were here now. Not just because I was so in love with him that I wanted nothing more than to gaze lovingly at his perfect body. No, I wished he were here so he could be a better host. I swallowed, not knowing what I should say to Beatrice. She was so different from me. Her personality was capricious, unpredictable, and her humor was incomprehensible. I couldn't tell when she was joking and when she was serious.

Come to think of it, that was how Cohaku and Nio were to other people. Maybe they were more like me than I realized...

Gods, I was half tempted to go to Su's ateli and drag him here. He'd have been a better diplomat than me.

Nio Interlude

Nio moved her left archer two spaces toward Beatrice's army. Cohaku would see that she wished to ally with her to defeat Beatrice. Until they learned how their enemy strategizes, the wiser move would be to fight together.

Cohaku moved her Winyan into the sky-space. Why the neutral move?

Beatrice moved her right halberdier toward Nio's.

No! They were planning to team up to defeat her? Nio smirked. *Don't expect me to lower my defenses toward you, Sister. Now that I see your true intentions...*

Nio moved the same archer a space toward the sky-space, just barely in range to attack the Winyan. Because he only moved one space, she could have him attack this turn as well. She shot Cohaku's Winyan.

"Why'd you do that, Nio?" Cohaku whined. She moved her right double agent—the one which could only attack Beatrice—closer to the Yosoe's side.

Beatrice nibbled her lip as she decided what the best move would be. She was clever; a worthy opponent, in Nio's estimation. A stupider adversary would have brought the halberdier closer to take the archer, but she knew Nio's right Domovoi would trap her if she tried it.

"What are we going to do, Cohaku?" Beatrice asked.

"We? Are we teaming up?"

"Of course we are. How can you team up with someone who won't talk?"

Cohaku bristled, her mane sticking up like a circle of spikes. Her tail flared with angry electricity. "Nio doesn't need to talk. I know what she wants."

"How? Can you read her mind?"

"No, but... I just know. You don't have any siblings, do you?"

She shook her head. "No. We just got Oboro a few months ago, but he's not like a brother to me. He's more like... a friend?"

"You'd understand if you had a sister. A *good* sister, I should say. I always know what Nio wants. Sometimes I know what Eruwan wants. I never knew what Tawny wanted."

"Tawny was a bad sister?"

Nio reminisced on Tawny. She had been so bad at troika. And she was always loud and clumsy. Nio hadn't played with her much and was now wondering if she should have.

"I didn't mean it that way," Cohaku grumbled, looking guilty. Nio thought she might run to her tree house. "Sorry. I'm bad with words. Maybe I should become like Nio and stop speaking."

"Is it possible to be bad with words if you two understand each other so well?" Beatrice asked. "Maybe you're bad at speaking with most people, but I think if you've developed a way to communicate with someone else so well that you know what the other is thinking, you must be doing *something* right."

Cohaku shrugged. Nio kept her eyes on the board while they talked. She didn't like to look at people. But the troika board... She had to plan for the moves they were both most likely to make.

Beatrice moved her Winyan closer to Cohaku's side.

They both wanted to ally with Nio. *Perfect. This game is as good as over. I will certainly be the victor.*

Fionn Interlude

"I can't believe she beat us!" Beatie said as she tossed a seashell into Deep Sea.

"Nio is unnaturally good at troika," Fionn replied.

The rain had let up, and the mother-Beatrice allowed her daughter and bodyguard to take a walk outside. Fionn's father asked him to take them only as far as Su's ateli; not that they'd *want* to get any closer to it, given its stench. The kids had taken to calling it the 'smelly ateli' for good reason.

Deep Sea had deposited a dominion shell along their path. Beatrice picked it up curiously and asked Fionn what it was.

"It's the shell of a dead urchin," he replied. "We call them dominion shells because of the star pattern on their back. See, it's shaped like the Pentagonal Dominion." He tapped the five-pointed star.

"Wow! I didn't know something like this existed!" Beatrice's face beamed with delight. "Oboro! Have you ever seen anything like this?"

The Sasorin boy jittered uncomfortably at having attention on himself. He spoke with a thick accent that Fionn could hardly parse. "Uhh, no, sorry. Deep Sea isn't... in? On? Forgive, Mys. I do not know the word... Deep Sea isn't *on* Ophidia. Or, well, not where the Ophidia people... uh, like me... can see."

She rubbed her chin, stroking her fur the way her father stroked his beard. "Ahh, because he's underground. You're doing so well with our language. Keep it up!"

Beatrice looked earnestly into Fionn's eyes. "Can you show me more things that I can only see here? Are there other seashells I've never seen? Maybe fruits or animals? I want to see it all! Oh! What about fish? We don't eat fish very often in Chernagora."

"I can show you how to make seared ahi!" Fionn said most exuberantly.

"Can you?" Beatrice asked in equal interest. "Please! Oboro, what about you? Don't you like to cook?"

"Um... if you require it of me..."

"Never mind, then. I don't want to force you."

Oboro inhaled a quick, sharp breath as if he'd been taken by surprise. "I didn't mean it! I *do* want to learn, Mys Beatrice."

"Don't 'Mys Beatrice' me!" she said in a snide voice. "I'm just Beatie when we're alone. 'Mys Beatrice' is and always will be my mother. Also, I'm not the one who'll be teaching you. Fionn is! So perhaps you should 'Mr. Lasteran' him."

Fionn gulped. "Oh no, don't do that to me, either! 'Mr. Lasteran' is my dad! Just call me Fionn, please. Uh, but yeah, Oboro, if you want to learn how to cook and clean fish, I can show you."

Oboro... blushed? Fionn was not certain if the Sasorin's shivering mandibles and his golden skin turning a shade lighter meant he was blushing, but he chose to believe it. "I would like that very much, Fionn."

Codex Dominex: Aloutian Economics

Aloutia entered an era of anti-capitalist policy following the Greed Wars (300-310) when royals, nobles, landlords, and elite business owners were killed by the poor, starving, overworked, oppressed masses. In the year 561, most of Aloutia follows the Imperial Economic Standard (IES), in which vassal-level governments set limits to income on its people and collect taxes, with Imperial-level supervision ensuring money is not hoarded or misused. Eight communes of Aloutia have done away with money entirely and are self-sufficient, but trade with outsiders for luxury goods. The Church of the Mind God requires companies to trade with the communes under threat of annihilation. His Holiness, Lucognidus, does not suffer greed in Aloutia.

Under the IES, all citizens of Aloutia are entitled to a job that pays enough money to afford enough food and supplies to support three members of the individual's species (the Aloutian 'minimum wage', thus is meant to be enough for a single working parent to support themself, one partner, and one child). All Aloutians are entitled to free housing. Because housing is controlled on the vassal level, some people may be entitled to 'better' houses if there are class hierarchies, but the Imperial government ensures all people have a sufficiently warm and spacious house.

Aloutia also implements a concept called the 'maxima', a practice like a 'maximum wage' for individuals and companies. The maxima is calculated by Imperial officials for each individual based on their species' needs, local cost of living, and how many spouses and dependents the individual cares for. They may be capped monthly or annually, depending on company policies and vassal-level laws.

Companies are also capped to a maxima which is supervised by a board of Mind elementals who have passed rigorous ethics tests and sworn to eschew money in their personal lives. After all individuals working within a company have been paid, excess money is put in a 'project fund' which can only be used for board-approved improvements or construction projects. When companies do not have an ongoing project, or if they acquire more money than their project fund can hold, the remainder is put toward charity projects. Such 'forced charity' may include projects to improve cities, infrastructure, churches, or to rescue enslaved men on Ophidia.

Mind elementals are forbidden by the God Lucognidus from using money personally, but they are permitted to manage it on behalf of others. Most assessors are Mind elementals since they are often trusted to act within their religion's ethics.

While loopholes and tricks certainly exist for people to keep more money than allowed, fraud is easily discovered by Mind Godbloods. Some are tasked to perform regular rituals to find people who have hoarded significant money in secret. Punishment for the crime of hoarding money usually involves time on Hydra Island, Aloutia's prison island.

Inheritance is managed by assessors, usually Mind elementals. All of a person's money and belongings go to the state when they pass away. They may leave a will requesting certain things, such as sentimental objects, go to their loved ones. The assessors will agree as long as it is reasonable. Investigations may be ordered by the court if there is suspicion that a deceased person tried to circumvent the inheritance tax by gifting their money/belongings prior to death.

Aloutian schools teach children to be altruistic and do what is good for society. They are not raised to think of money as a reward or goal. The idea of a person becoming a doctor to make money is obscene to Aloutians. Even in businesses, guildmasters and executive administrators are selected based on their desire and ability to better their community and get goods and services where they need to be. Greedy people have no chance of ascending a corporate hierarchy.

Chapter Twenty: Fruit

Evening approached, the moons traversed the sky, a coconut crab finally reached the insides of its treasure, and everyone came back from their various tasks. Liesle returned with her painting of the Mind God getting ever-closer to finished. Su took a quick bath in Deep Sea to wipe off the stench of bone boiling, then came back with a fresh, sexy glow. The way he looked at me, brown eyes glimmering with lust, his hair wild and free... Gods I wanted to hold him down on the sand right then and there.

Giorvi came back from Seabells, too. His news hadn't been hopeful. He claimed to have spoken with lawkeepers at the Lightning church who said they couldn't arrest a non-citizen of Aloutia until he committed a crime against a citizen.

"I argued they had an obligation to protect that child," he said, leaning on a whale rib support as I scooped rice onto my patella plate. "They seemed sympathetic, but said they had too much to deal with right now. Too many cases in Seabells, not enough people who could take another child's case."

"That's what I feared." I put slices of seared ahi on the bed of rice. "It means nothing if they *seem* sympathetic. If no one saves Usana, it won't matter how many people feel sorry for her. She's still going to end up abused. Action is all that matters."

As I added handfuls of chopped mango, sliced spinehair, and coconut shavings, a sense of guilt and dread consumed my sternum. I was a fucking hypocrite. In the same moment I said we needed to act to save a starving girl, I stuffed my own plate full of food. I was about to have a pleasant dinner with my loving family and an honorable guest family. Usana would only eat if Miltico let her.

What could I do? A knot tied in my hyoid. It was the same unbearable feeling I'd had every waking moment for the week after Tawny's death. Now I got it for Usana. What could I do? Tawny was beyond my grasp, but Usana... I could save her. There was time.

"You're right," Giorvi said. I stepped out of the way so he could prepare his plate. "We have to be calm and collected, though. If a Wynnle marches up to Mr. Svelt's house and makes demands, it will go poorly. Let's talk to him after dinner, but allow me to come with you. Perhaps Master Scrimshander would like to come along, too?"

"Milti hates Su."

"He hates all three of us, but together we can put pressure on him to relinquish his daughter."

"You think he'd just give her up?" I asked. "What then? We give her to the Wind church? I'm sure Milti's father could take care of her, but I don't know if he has enough of a backbone to stand up to Milti. Usana might wind up back in his clutches."

"I wouldn't give her to any relatives. I know how to get children into the Wind church. I have connections to the keeper of the church in Chernagora. I gave Oboro the option of joining them, but he preferred the option of working for me."

"Very well. After dinner, let's do what we must do."

With both our plates full, we went outside to join the others at the hip bone table. Beatrice the Daughter took a seat under the shade of the short palm tree growing through the hip bone's foramen. She sat with Cohaku to one side and Fionn to the other. Huh... I would have thought she'd be next to Oboro, her mother, or left a spot for her father. She must have become quite close to her new friends in the hours they spent together today. Oboro was on Fionn's other side, engaged in a lively conversation with him and Beatie.

Su moved the rotary of fruit to the outdoor table so we could all easily reach it. It was filled to the brim with all colors of fruits—rambutans, lychees, and pitayas in red; papayas and kumquats in orange; mangos and spinehair in yellow; kiwis, limes, and carambola in green; bright açaí in blue; steenas and purples in purple. The centerpiece, a pure, bleached-white skull, held pieces of breadfruit, coconut, snakescale, and tamarinds.

"*Bone* appétit," Su said as he set it down. He intentionally pronounced 'bon' as 'bone.'

Dinner was wonderful, or it would have been if not for the tumult of wild thoughts and emotions plaguing my mind. Su sat next to me with a cup of ponzu sauce. With a bright smile on his face, he poured some on my ahi. I wondered if Su could tell I was troubled. Others extended their plates toward him so he could pour a little bit of sauce on their food as well.

I wanted to talk to him about the plan I'd just concocted with Giorvi, but I didn't want the kids involved. After dinner, I'd pull him aside. For now, I would enjoy my meal.

The kids enjoyed themselves. Oboro was shy and struggled with our language, but Heliodor prompted him into sharing a bit about himself. Beatrice the Daughter commiserated with Cohaku over their loss to Nio in a game of troika. It was truly frightening how good my youngest daughter was at the game. She was only five years old. How had she gotten so good? Fionn was happier than I'd seen him since before Tawny's passing. The joy in his tone as he spoke to Oboro and Beatie was a new sparkle in his life.

The kids were so happy and innocent. Playing, chatting, learning skills that would assist them into adulthood... Their paths glittered with starlight. Usana's path... was as dark and devoid of starlight as the caves of the Makai. As lonely as Solitude. As painful as Hell.

The kids went to play on the beach as the sun approached Deep Sea's horizon. It was a good opportunity for us to discuss our plan without being overheard.

Beatrice the Mother shot dangerous looks at Giorvi as he explained he would join me and Su going to Miltico's house. She grabbed his beard and pulled him close. "You paid Miltico, right? I don't want any problems with him."

"Yes, yes, he shouldn't have any complaints," Giorvi said, struggling against his wife's aggression.

She let go of his beard. "This was supposed to be a relaxing vacation, Gio."

"I'm sorry," he said, rubbing his hands through his beard to get it back to normal. "I'll make it up to you later. I'll take you to that cave Ami told me about."

Su elbowed me. "You told them about the cave of St. Alice's Lights?"

"I don't see the harm in it," I said. "They're just here for a short time. It's not like we're competing with them for space."

Liesle's eyes measured me. She had an expression, eyes half-closed, like she wanted to express her frustration with me. But she didn't. Why were they upset at me? It wasn't like the caves were a secret, and the Yosoe couple would be gone in a few days, anyway.

"Shall we go?" Giorvi asked. "I'll follow you since I'm not sure where Miltico lives. If he threatens us, let me do the talking."

I collected my wits and nodded. As we headed out, Liesle called out to me.

"Mo Ami, if... if anything happens and you need me, I'll be here."

Su's eyes widened in surprise. "I won't let him reach that point, but if he does, I'll handle him, too."

Liesle thought I was going to get violent. Did she think I was a violent person? Or did she hope I would finish the job she'd started twelve years ago? On the night we conceived Fionn...

Liesle's words weren't a warning against going berserk. Quite the opposite—it was permission. I had her blessing. If I hurt Miltico, she would support me.

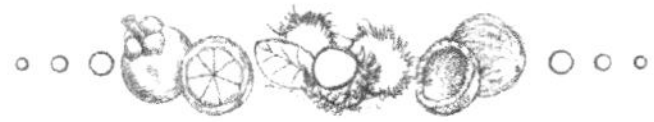

Giorvi knocked on the rotting wood door to the Svelt-Dem house. He stepped over a recently-fallen carambola. When there was no answer, nor could we hear movement from inside, he knocked again. "Mr. Svelt, it's me, Giorvi Onoretti. We have business to discuss."

Still nothing. The oppressive silence made my mane perk up. Even the songbirds and pink gulls were silent.

"Someone's inside," Su said under his breath. "I can sense them with my Godblood powers. Can you smell a Lagodore, Amiere?"

I wrinkled my nose. Wynnles who'd lived their whole lives on Cosmo, training to hunt for their dinners, had an excellent sense of smell, particularly for rabbits and Lagodores. I had not cultivated my olfactory organs to that degree, but I could sense *something*. The smell of Lagodore pervaded the air, but did that mean Lavina or Usana were currently here or had their scent lingered from merely living here?

"I'm not turning around just because Milti refuses to answer the door," I said. "I'll break it down if I must."

Giorvi opened his mouth to protest, or perhaps to offer a better idea... but when he stepped away from the door, I interpreted that as a sign of agreement.

"Mys Demiu!" I shouted. I made sure to raise my voice loud enough so anyone could hear me, no matter where in the house they were. "Open the door or I'll break it down!"

Tiny footsteps scurried close, unlatched the door, and opened it.

Lavina Demiu stood at the threshold, wearing nothing but a threadbare blanket to cover herself. Her massive brown rabbit ears helped, draping over her shoulders and covering her breasts. She was a small woman, a brown-furred bipedal Lagodore with large, pleading eyes.

She shook in terror, wide eyes staring at me, breathing heavily. If she wished to say something, the words were not forthcoming.

Giorvi edged closer to her. "Mys Demiu, we're sorry for bothering you, but this is important. Is Mr. Svelt here?"

She continued to stare at me. She shook her head 'no' in response to Giorvi's question, though she never let her eyes drift from me once.

"Is Usana here?" he asked.

Lavina shook her head 'no' again.

"It's vitally important we speak to them. We will wait here until they return."

"They won't," she said. "If they see a lion here, they'll hide in the jungle until it's safe."

Su huffed. "Don't you dare call Amiere a lion. Didn't anyone teach you not to call people by their ancestral animal names? You wouldn't appreciate being called a rabbit, would you?"

"Milti calls me a fuck-bunny all the time. What's so bad about that?"

I couldn't tell if she was serious or making some horribly inappropriate joke. Though if she was as young as I suspected—not that I could tell by looking at her; once a Lagodore was an adult, they looked ageless to me—then she might have started traveling around Starsine with him when she was still of an age where their relationship would have been illegal on Aloutia. Quite possibly, she wasn't old enough to realize how inappropriate her words were.

"Never mind that," Giorvi said. "Can I ask how you're doing, Mys? Are you eating well?"

Finally, Lavina pried her eyes off me, just long enough to size up the Yosoe man. Her eyes came back to me in a flash. "There's a lot of food here."

Giorvi spread his arms out, indicating the trees. "Indeed, Aloutia's Green Moon ensures a bountiful harvest, and fruit trees grow all year long here in the tropics. But that wasn't what I asked." He brought his hands forward, palms up, pointed at the woman. "Are *you* eating well?"

She did not look healthy to me, but I was no expert. She looked barely better fed than her daughter, with gaunt cheeks and patches of brown fur missing or discolored, lighter.

"We're fine," she said. Her voice was... tired? Uncertain? Aware of the lies she told?

Su grabbed her by the wrist. Lavina tried to pull away, but Su wouldn't let go.

"You're nothing but fur and bones," he said. "If Miltico is hurting you, tell me. You may think he has power over you, but he doesn't. We can protect you. I'm a Godblood. Whatever you think Miltico can do to you, I promise I can do ten times worse to him."

"God... blood?" She said the word as if it were a question. Surely she knew what a Godblood was. It would be like not knowing what the sky or grass was.

"Has Miltico hurt you?" I asked.

She hesitated. As I was about to ask if he'd hurt Usana, she spoke up. "Miltico is everything to me. He's the only one who's ever loved me. He saved me. I would do anything for him."

She'd probably deflect the same answer for Usana. I had one more question for her, related to what I'd learned from the volkhv at the Plant church. It hurt to even consider this question. "Is Usana your only child?"

"Yes, why?" She glanced aside, suddenly unable to make eye contact with me.

"I heard Lagodore women usually have four children per egg. Where did your others go? And you haven't become pregnant any other time, despite how much you fuck him?"

She scratched her lip. "It's just Usana. We can't take care of any more, so we don't... we make sure not to have any others. Um, are you finished now? I need to get back to, um, what I was doing..."

I put my hand over the door frame so she'd have to crush my fingers if she wanted to close the door. It would hurt, sure, but she was too small and weak to do much damage.

"As I said, I'm not leaving until Miltico gets here. If he wants to hide from me by running into the jungle, he's welcome to. I'm staying right here." My tail's light flickered; I only noticed because I saw my shadow dance on the dilapidated wall deep inside the dark house.

Lavina sighed and looked down, resigned. At least she wasn't trembling at the sight of me anymore. "I won't answer any more questions. Miltico can answer them."

"Fine by me, but I'm not leaving." I sat down, propping my back against the door frame. I pushed the door further open with my foot as I got comfortable. My tail's electric light illuminated the inside of their murky abode...

Usana's form flashed across the far wall, amidst vertical cage bars.

Lavina must have seen the horror on my face. She tried closing the door. I shoved her aside as I stood back up.

"What the fuck? Su, Giorvi, come inside!"

"What's wrong, Ami-honey?" Su rushed inside, right behind me.

"Dear Gods..." Giorvi whispered as he stepped through the threshold.

I held my tail in front for illumination. Usana shrunk back to the back of her cage, shivering in fright, hiding her eyes behind her long bunny ears.

Giorvi turned on his horn's lights, which were a more stable source of illumination than my flickering tail, and possibly less frightening to the poor girl. I swung my tail back, in case it bothered her.

As though being in a fucking cage didn't bother her already!

I turned to find Lavina, struggling to get up after I'd shoved her down. I picked her up by the neck and slammed her against the nearest wall.

"What the fuck are you doing to your daughter?"

"She's safe in there! Safe from lions!" Tears rolled down her cheeks, matting her fur. She quivered and shook with fright and kicked her legs uselessly. She grabbed my wrist in both her hands, but she could not budge me. Even if she hadn't been weak from starvation, she was so much smaller than me...

"There are no fucking lions in Aloutia!" I roared.

Lavina tried scratching my wrists, but her fingernails were dull. Even Nio's quick bite had hurt worse.

"Let her out of this cage immediately," Su demanded.

"I can't. I don't have the key. Only Miltico has it."

I dropped Lavina. She fell onto her rear and crawled back into a corner, cowering, shivering. I felt no pride in making a woman tremble in terror, but I would not let Usana's suffering continue... or go unpunished.

Usana must have been hungry. Miltico must have kept her in a cage while he was away to make sure she didn't eat anything without his permission. I stomped out of the house, to get fruit from the nearest fruit trees.

"Where are you going, Ami-honey?" Su asked.

I didn't answer him. He would see if he watched. I was too enraged to speak. Too emotional. I knew if I opened my mouth to talk, I might cry. Then Lavina would know how soft I was. She'd take it for weakness.

I took a fresh, ripe carambola from the tree whose branches extended above their house. The fruit could have literally fallen on their roof, and this girl is starving. What kind of absolute evil allows that to happen? What happened to Miltico to make him so fucked up? He used to be my friend. It couldn't have all been the fault of the crazy sugar his brother got him addicted to. There was something evil in him. As blessed as this land was, some demon must have infiltrated it, dug its claws into the marrow of his bones, enthroned itself inside his mind, and worn his fur like clothes. The Milti I'd once known couldn't be this wicked.

Su and Giorvi watched wordlessly as I came back in with a carambola. I sliced it with my claws and extended a star-shaped piece through the bars of Usana's cage.

"Please, take this," I said. "Eat it."

Small, pathetic sobs escaped her frail body. She did not move, except to shake in the corner. I held the fruit out a while longer but had to give up eventually. I laid the piece down, then sliced a few more pieces for her.

"You can eat it, Usana," Su said. "It's safe. Daddy gives you permission."

"He does?" She pulled her ears down and looked over them. My tail was close to Su's face, illuminating him so Usana could get a closer look at who was speaking to her.

"I'm a Daddy," he said. "Also a Mommy. I give you permission to eat."

That wasn't going to work.

Usana picked up the carambola and ate it. Her little jaws worked left and right to chew it. Gods, she was cute. She ate the next piece, and then the next.

"I'll get more," I said and headed back outside.

I stopped cold in my steps at the entrance. Miltico was coming up the path, laden with a huge bag across his back.

He also stopped dead in his tracks, face paling. He dropped the sack.

"Ami, what the fuck are you doing in my house?" he asked, a fearful quaver in his voice.

How was I supposed to reply? Viciously? Diplomatically? Should I threaten him? Should I placate him? I wanted to kill him, but... Gods, if I did that, I'd be tried for murder! I'd be separated from my family and banished to Cosmo! I could choke him until he passed out. It might make him angrier at Usana, but... I couldn't let this continue!

Yes, I would choke him. My claws extended on their own. *No, don't do that.* I retracted them again as I strode toward him.

"Ami-honey!" Su called. "No!"

Miltico bolted away. I was faster. I lunged after him, jumped, and tackled him face-down onto the dirt path strewn with leaves from a steena tree. I scraped my knees and the thrill of physical activity only excited me.

Reflexively, he turned on the electricity in his horns. To prove I wasn't afraid, I grabbed them and shoved his face in the dirt. If there was a demon inside him, I would drive it out...

When I let up, he coughed. "Ami! Please! Have mercy!"

I put my hands around his neck. In a low, growling voice, I replied, "I'll give you the same mercy you give to your daughter."

I tightened my grip. He choked, gagged...

And the world went black as I passed out.

Chapter Twenty-One: Eruwan

I awoke to the sound of Deep Sea's fingers crashing closer than usual. Spray from his fingertips misted my mane. Pink gulls called amidst a gentle breeze and a coal-black cormorant dove into the ocean. Warm sand below, darkening twilight skies above, with glittering pink stars along a galactic pathway.

Su's warm body lay next to mine, between my right arm and torso. His face snuggled close, his nose and lips brushing my skin, his two right arms swung over my ribs. He was in his aquatic form, wearing a lovely blue tang fishtail. His ears wore all the bones signifying a desire for sex.

He stirred when he realized I was awake. As thrilled as I was to wake up next to his beautiful, inviting body, the last thing I remembered was choking the life out of Miltico.

"What happened?" I asked. "Where am I? What...?" I sat upright.

Su crawled onto my lap, thrusting himself onto my torso and pushing me back onto the sand.

"Mr. Onoretti and I took care of Miltico," Su said. "He won't be abusing Usana anymore."

That sounded threatening. The expression of horror I gave Su made him laugh. "Not like *that*."

"How can you be sure? Are you going to visit him every day to make sure of that?"

Su nodded. "Yes. We're going to bring food to her, as well. And I'm going to talk to her. If she tells me she's been locked in that cage... well, Miltico knows I'm a Godblood."

"Where was I during this discussion?" I asked. "Was I passed out?"

He rubbed his hands over my arms and kissed my chest. "I told them you've been experiencing that lately. Every time it's happened has been when Miltico was around, so it's not new to him."

I wondered why it happened around him. Was he triggering it somehow? Was it my anger? Did my body shut down to avoid going berserk? It always happened when Su was around, too... and Su's exact magic was a mystery. He must have been doing it to me, to stop me before I went too far and committed a crime I could never take back. Was that why he'd asked me whether I believed my love was real or caused by his magic?

"How did I get back here? Did you carry me?"

"No, you walked." Su scooted up and kissed my lips.

I had so many more questions, but I couldn't ask while his tongue explored the inside of my mouth.

My heart thumped hard, pumping blood straight to my penis. I put my arms around Su's back as my dick went erect. My hands went down, grabbing scales where his tail met his torso.

He put his upper hands on my ears and rubbed while his tongue kept tasting my mouth. His lower hands massaged my shoulders.

He transformed his tail into legs while my hands held him. My palms and fingertips felt the magical change from scale to skin. As his ass cheeks formed, they cupped themselves in my hands as if they belonged to me. I brought my fingers lower to touch the sacred spot—the crease where buttock met leg. My cock met the bone between his legs.

Su broke away from the kiss and propped himself up on my chest. "Everything will be fine, Ami-honey. Let me take care of everything bothering you. Your anxiety, depression, worries, anger... let me soothe it all away."

"Su... soothe."

"You're trying to make a pun, aren't you?"

"I was, but I'm not in much of a humorous mood."

He flexed his grip over my upper arms. "I've got your two humerus moods right here."

I forced myself to laugh. I couldn't relax until I knew more about Usana's situation, though. I'd missed so much by falling unconscious.

"What else did I miss?" I asked. "Did you threaten him? Did Giorvi say anything I should know about?"

Su shook his head. His brown hair fell in waves over his shoulders. "Giorvi talked business with Miltico. Apparently, they knew each other and Giorvi had given Miltico a lot of money. They were both shady about it, though. Like they didn't want to discuss it around me. That's normal behavior around a Godblood, though. I'm used to it."

"But Usana will be alright?"

"I hope so. I'll check on her every day if I must. Papa Su won't let anyone hurt Usana." He thumped his chest with a fist and put on a mock stern expression, imitating a soldier. "It would be easier if I had her all to myself. I wonder if I could convince Miltico to let us raise her."

"I don't think Usana is comfortable around Wynnles. You might have to keep her in your ateli."

"The smelly ateli?"

That *would* be a problem.

With a playful smile, Su described how he'd raise Usana. "I'll give her kumquats to stick her nose in so she doesn't have to smell it. I'll be her only parent and I'll spoil her rotten. I'll give her tons of food, make toys for her, bring friends she can play with..."

"Change her last name to Scrimshander," I added.

"Ooh, good idea." Su pinched my cheeks. "I have always wanted a Scrimshander child."

"How are our kids doing? Did they wonder what was going on when we came back? I don't do or say anything strange when I'm... not in my right mind, do I?"

Su opened his mouth, only to lick his lips and sigh, turning his eyes away from me with a forlorn expression. The glow of Aloutia's rings reflected in his brown eyes as he gazed toward the horizon. "No, you don't say or do anything strange."

"Good. At least I haven't done anything I'd regret. Um, but the kids? Did they think something was wrong?"

Su's hands tensed. "Eruwan and Fionn, as well as Mr. Onoretti's daughter and bodyguard, followed us to Miltico's house. They saw what you did."

"What? I thought you could sense when people were around. Couldn't you tell they were following us?"

He grimaced. "Eruwan knows me too well. She knows my powers only work up to around forty feet. She instructed them to keep their distance."

I sighed. So the two oldest kids saw me beat the hell out of Miltico... or choke him, or whatever I did while I was unconscious. "They must be terrified of me now."

"I doubt it," Su said. "Though it wouldn't hurt to talk to them, I suppose. Actually, it was Onoretti's bodyguard who insisted on following us. He didn't want *Signore* getting hurt."

"That Oboro is a good kid. Wish Giorvi would let him live like a normal kid."

"I get the feeling it's not—did you call him Giorvi? I didn't know you were on a first-name basis."

"We are. You can call him that, too. He doesn't care for titles, anymore."

"Good enough for me. Anyway, it seems to me that Giorvi wants Oboro to live like a normal teenage boy, but Oboro was so abused in Ophidia that he can't. Oboro thinks he needs a master to function. I think Giorvi is providing that role in as gentle a manner as he can, and slowly trying to pull Oboro out of that slavish mindset."

"Maybe that's why he told Oboro to play with our kids. He wants him to socialize with kids his own age."

"Maybe so," Su replied, sounding tired.

I closed my eyes, wishing all my problems would just go away. If only Miltico weren't here, I could have grieved over Tawny in peace and moved on with my life.

"I've gotta talk to Eruwan and Fionn," I said after collecting my nerves. "Explain to them what happened. They need to know that what I did isn't okay."

"Eruwan... isn't in a good mood. She didn't like something she heard Miltico say."

It must have been something he said after I went unconscious. "More reason why I should talk to her. What about Fionn?"

"He walked the Iolono family home. He's taken a liking to little Beatie and Oboro."

"That's good. He needs friends. Tawny was his only friend. Heli's trying, but Heli just wants everyone to be happy. Anyway, I'll go talk to Eruwan."

I went back inside the house. Eruwan sat on the pillows, scrimshawing, with a focused expression—eyebrows scrunched, mouth frowning. She chipped at the bone with quick, sharp jabs of her claws. It was a technique Su had explicitly told her *not* to use under normal circumstances. It was less 'controlled art' and more 'expression of anger.' I knew it all too well in sculpting. Sometimes you just wanted to stab something repeatedly, but it was unlikely to become beautiful artwork.

Cohaku, Nio, and Heliodor played troika at the small scapula table. Due to his lack of hands, Heli had to tell them which pieces he wanted to move, and they would move the pieces for him. They were good about doing what he asked, but he wasn't skillful as a player. He was almost always one of the allied players, so he won often enough with his partner's help. It warmed my soul knowing the two sisters helped him unconditionally.

Liesle lay on the pillows with her eyes closed. I wasn't sure if she was asleep or just wished she was.

"Eruwan, can we talk?" I asked as I walked indoors. Su snuck behind me, sliding between the two leaves over our entryway.

Eruwan looked at me, opened her mouth to speak, but closed it when she saw Su behind me.

"Let's go outside," Su suggested.

"I don't need to talk," she said sternly. The three kids playing troika stopped to stare.

"Perhaps you don't, but *I* do," I said. "Please, Eruwan."

She put her bone down forcefully. Had the surface been anything other than a feather-stuffed pillow, she might have cracked it. "I heard what that bastard Miltico said about Papa Su. He deserved every fucking thing you did to him."

"Watch your language," Liesle said. Guess she was awake after all...

Eruwan rolled her eyes. "Fuck that. I can't even be angry?"

"You can be angry, but don't swear. Especially not in front of your younger siblings."

Eruwan gripped the bone. If she'd been a girl of a different temperament, I would have been afraid of her throwing it at Liesle, but Eruwan was nice. She had always been a good child. The best child new parents could have asked for. Some people believed Lucognidus toyed with the personalities of children and would occasionally make sure a family's first child was mild. It was all mud and sludge, of course, but I couldn't help but think of that superstition every time Eruwan proved what a darling, sweet girl she was.

"Race you to the lighthouse?" Su asked. It had been a while since they raced. Prior to Tawny's passing, they would run to the lighthouse almost every day. They both loved to run.

Eruwan buried her face in her hands. Oh Gods, was she going to cry? I... I hadn't realized it was that bad.

"I don't want to!" she yelled, sobbing. She pushed past in her flight to escape, jumped into the air, and flew down to the beach.

Liesle propped herself up on the pillows. "I can't deal with this right now, and clearly she doesn't want me, anyway. I'll watch these three if you two want to handle her."

Su put his hand on my back, just above my tail. "Actually, Ami-honey, would you talk to Eruwan alone? I think some things will be easier for her to talk about if I'm not around. I'll take care of Lisi-honey."

Whatever I'd missed due to blacking out, I had to trust Su regarding the best course of action. I kissed the top of his wavy brown hair and went back outside.

Eruwan landed on the top of a palm tree close to the lighthouse. Her house would be attached to the lighthouse when we were finished, but for now, it was a skeleton, literally and figuratively. She saw me coming, but she didn't flee a second time. Deep down, she must have wanted to talk. Perhaps the attitude had been in hopes Liesle would leave her alone.

Her blue skin gave an ethereal, almost magical glow in the light of the moons. She wasn't truly magical, not in the way Su or other Godbloods were. It was a sort of beauty only a father could see. Or, perhaps a lover could, too... She reminded me so much of Liesle. My nighttime walks on the beach with my wife, back when we were Eruwan's age, happened around the time we fell in love. Gods, in my mind, my daughter was still so young! I couldn't imagine her being in a relationship now.

It pained me to see her sad. She sniffed and wiped her tears as I leaned against her palm tree.

"I heard what Miltico said... About how Papa Su is in the way. About how we'd have been better off without him."

"I don't know what he said after I lost consciousness," I said. "But if he said that, it's a load of mud and sludge. And I don't care if you swear, Eruwan. Say whatever you need, however you need to."

Another sniff. "Thanks. That Miltico is a fucker. There, I said it. I hate him. You were right to hurt him. I wish you'd done worse."

"I don't think I've ever been so angry... at least not in your lifetime. I didn't want you to be afraid of me."

She choked a laugh out between crying sobs. "I'd never be afraid of you,

Papami. You're too gentle and kind. Actually, when I saw you... I thought you were cool. I'd seen Mamali and Papa Su get fired up, but never you. I didn't know you had it in you."

I blushed and covered my mouth with my hand. "I... I don't want you learning that kind of behavior from me, Eruwan. Violence isn't acceptable."

"Yeah, yeah, I know. I'm fourteen, Papami, not four. I know I can't let myself go berserk."

"But if you ever *do* go berserk—"

"I should run to you so I can bite you. I *know*. You didn't ask me to come out here just to lecture me, did you?"

A tight, painful feeling erupted in my sternum. "I'm sorry. I just wanted to comfort you. Whatever Miltico said, you can forget about it. Papa Su's not going anywhere. He's one of us."

"And you can't spell 'us' without 'Su.'" She made a squeal, a weak noise between a laugh and a cry. What she'd said was something Su had said repeatedly in the time we'd known him, the first time being when we decided to be a three-person partnership. "I know that, but it still hurt to hear. Papa Su is amazing. Wonderful. It doesn't matter if he's not our biological mother or father. He's still our family."

"You're damn right he is, and he's not going anywhere. He'll be your Papa Su forever, no matter what anyone thinks he should be."

She sighed a heavy breath and flitted down from the tree to stand next to me. "I feel a bit better now. Was there something else you wanted to say?"

There are moments in a parent's life that they look back on and think: *'That. That moment was one where I shaped my child's life.'* I held my breath, wondering if this was one such formative moment.

"I wanted to make sure you knew my actions today weren't *good*. I'm not proud of what I did."

"Why not? You made Mr. Svelt stop abusing his daughter, didn't you?"

I scratched behind my ear. "I guess I did. I think Su and Giorvi helped more in that regard."

"So you're saying I should learn from Papa Su?" she asked in a playful tone. Her adoration of him went beyond filial love. No matter how much she tried to keep it hidden, I saw how much she wanted to be like him. Her interest in scrimshaw, how she wanted to fish and cook with him, the way she wanted to play the drum at his bone dance...

I couldn't blame her, though my angle was different. I loved Su as my lover: eros and pragma swam like entwined okoes in the currents of my soul-blood. She loved him not just as a child to a parent—storge—but something *more*. No, nothing romantic or sexual; there was none of that depravity happening in our family.

Was her love agape[1] ? A worshipper to a God? She idolized him.

"You can learn a lot from him," I said. "You're the closest to him, out of all the kids, and he feels a special connection to you."

Her face beamed with joy. "I hope to make Papa Su proud. You too, of course!"

"You already have." I recalled what Su had told me about wanting to raise Usana, including changing her surname. I didn't care one whit about who had my last name, but for some reason, it was important to Su. And as Eruwan was closest to him, I wondered if she would prefer taking his surname. "I think you should become a Scrimshander."

"I'm getting better at scrimshaw. If this is about the time I didn't want Mys Iola looking, it wasn't because I was ashamed of my work. I just—"

"No, you misunderstood. I think—if you want to—you should change your surname to Scrimshander when you turn fifteen. It would mean a lot to Su. Unless you're attached to Denwall."

She gasped. Her eyes widened, and the way the ringslight and moonslight shone in her bright eyes reminded me too much of Liesle's eyes. "Do you mean it? Oh Gods, I... I really want that." She wiped her eyes. Wait, was she crying? Did it really mean that much to her?

"Uh, yeah. If it's important to you, do it. I don't think Liesle cares about her surname. Besides, she has Cohaku and Nio to carry it on, if it matters to her."

Eruwan clutched her hands to her chest. "I'd thought about this already, actually, but I thought Mamali would get upset. I... I don't know if Cohaku or Nio will ever have kids. I thought Tawny might. I was going to ask Mamali for permission to change my name on my hatching-day, but then Tawny died and I felt guilty. I thought I might be the only girl who'll pass on the Denwall name."

"How can you be so sure about Cohaku and Nio? They're young. Just because they have communication issues doesn't mean they'll never find a partner. Perhaps there are other kids their age in similar situations. Maybe there's a little boy somewhere who also doesn't like to talk, and is as good at troika as Nio is. Maybe they'll will make a fantastic team one day."

Eruwan grinned. "Maybe you're right. I guess I assumed..."

"But even if you *are* right—even if Cohaku and Nio grow up and never meet a partner, never adopt a kid, never want to have kids—that shouldn't stop *you* from changing your name if you want it. Your name is yours. It's not mine, Liesle's, or Su's. Your identity is something only you can determine. If Mamali is upset because you changed your name—and I don't think she would be—it shouldn't stop you. It's a minor thing that shouldn't matter to her, but it's *everything* to you. The name you pick at your fifteenth hatching-day will become your legal

---

1. Eros, pragma, storge, and agape are four of the eight forms of love in Spiritist philosophy

name, and it's hard to change that once it becomes tied to your professional life. Hell, I wish I could easily change 'Amiere', but it wouldn't be worth the effort, anymore."

Eruwan took deep, hard breaths. "I… I will. Thank you, Papami. Thank you for encouraging me." She plodded toward me and hugged me with all the strength in her skinny arms. She was growing, but still short enough that her head only came to my abdomen. I put my hands on her head and shoulders.

"Just to be clear, I'm not saying you should go out of your way to disappoint Liesle… but, in this one situation, I think your happiness takes precedence."

"Oh, absolutely! I wouldn't go against Mamali's wishes for no good reason. But you're right. This is something I want for myself. I want to be Eruwan Scrimshander, and after I turn fifteen, there's no reason why I can't be. If Mamali dislikes it, she'll just have to get over it. I'll still be her daughter. I'll still love her and take care of her the best I can. It's just a name. A sound. She'll never even have to hear it if she dislikes it."

I patted her head. "On the other hand, I know Su will be ecstatic. He's always wanted a Scrimshander child. You'll make him the happiest papa in the dominion."

"I'll talk to him about it, too, before I talk to Mamali." Eruwan stepped back from the hug. "I… have been thinking about some other things related to my fifteenth hatching-day."

"What sort of things?" I asked, worried she would express her disappointment that her house wasn't completed. "Look—I'm sorry, but I don't think construction will be done by then. With Tawny's passing, Su and I—"

"Oh, that's not what I'm worried about!" She waved her hands as if to brush away my concerns. "I don't plan to move out the day I turn fifteen, Papami. I'll move out when the house is ready, at your pace. No, what I'm worried about is keeping the Gods' Blessings."

I hesitated to speak. For Lightning elementals, because our blessings were based on our willingness to have sex, it was a private matter. Hardly something appropriate for a father and daughter to discuss, unless there was no mother in the family. I winced, hoping this wouldn't turn awkward, but I had to listen to her concerns, especially if she didn't feel comfortable asking Liesle.

"I don't want to live in fear of losing my blessings," she said. "So I think when I turn fifteen, I'll just… become a heretic right away."

"Please don't," I begged. "At least, let it happen naturally. If you live in this small village for your whole life, with considerate people, it's possible to live your whole life without losing your blessings. I can't… I don't want to imagine you suffering because you lost your immunity to fire. Even the smaller blessings make life a little more pleasant. If you lost Cherribell's Blessing, you wouldn't enjoy the same foods you eat now."

"I know." She wiped a tear from her eye. "But I don't want to wake up every day wondering if I'll lose them."

"Eruwan." I crouched down and put my hands on her shoulders again. "Are you aware that Flamboil's Blessing is the only reason we can even live here comfortably? With our thick manes and electric tails, we would overheat easily in tropical temperatures. If you lose your blessings, you wouldn't even *want* to live in that house we're building. You'd have to leave for someplace cooler."

She blinked back her tears. "I... suppose you have a point. Heh. Maybe I'm just scared about nothing. You and Mamali are still blessed, aren't you? Have you ever... no, I shouldn't ask that. Not to you."

"If you were about to ask if I've ever had sex without wanting it, but agreed for the sake of keeping my blessings... the answer is no. We're careful to ask only when we're sure the answer will be 'yes', and we communicate that intent in other ways." For the sake of Liesle's privacy, I avoided the topic of her encounter with Miltico twelve years ago.

"What would you do if a stranger asked?"

I explained to her that most species wouldn't dare as a male Wynnle for sex uninitiated, given the spikiness of our equipment.

"Female Wynnles don't have that luxury."

I pictured Liesle scratching out Miltico's eye. No... she didn't have that luxury. She went berserk to exact her revenge, and only calmed down because she had me. If something similar happened to Eruwan...

"If you are in a situation where you're about to lose your blessings, do what you feel is right. No one has a right to you. If you believe you are not ready for sex, lose your blessings. Papa Su and I will build you a house someplace else. Maybe in Chernagora, so we can visit quickly through the nearby portal. But if you choose to have sex when you don't want to... well, if you ever bite or scratch someone out of revenge, just make sure you don't kill them. Run back to me so you can quell your berserker rage. I won't ask questions, I promise. You can always bite me to return to normal."

"I know. You've said that since I was little."

"You're still little, and I need to keep saying it. It's a parent's duty to remind their children of important things like that. You'll always have my arm to bite if you need it... at least until I pass away. Hopefully, that won't be for a long, long time."

She hugged me again. "Please don't talk about it. I know it's an inevitability. I know Lord Death comes for us all. But I can't bear to think of it. It was hard enough with Tawny. I... I can't imagine you, or Papa Su, or Mamali dying!" She buried her face in my abdomen and wailed.

Eruwan... my precious daughter... she'd been so strong. She hadn't cried much after Tawny's death. I thought she was trying to stay strong for her younger siblings. She always seemed collected, like she knew what she was doing with her life. The younger kids thought she was mature. But she was just a child. My child.

It wasn't her responsibility to be a role model to the younger kids, it was mine. She was weak, tired, and vulnerable.

I held her close and let her cry into me as much as she needed.

A week went by without incident. The Iolono family met with us for dinner, business, and—for the kids—playtime on several days before they returned home to Chernagora.

Little Beatie proved herself competent in troika when she finally defeated Nio, though it was a one-time incident that Nio was unlikely to forget. Despite her silence, I could tell from the determined look on her face that Nio wouldn't forgive this humiliating defeat.

Oboro had become friends with Fionn, since they were close in age. Both were athletic boys, though Oboro had not had any opportunities to play sports when he was a slave. Fionn and Heliodor taught him kiwi-batte, and they played for hours. When Beatie wasn't playing troika, she played with Fionn and Oboro. At one point, I glanced over to them and Fionn had Beatie on his shoulders. She squealed something about not having horns to hold onto like she was used to doing when she was on her father's shoulders, but Fionn said she could grab his mane as hard as she wanted.

Giorvi discussed business with me and sold me numerous more crystalights while also purchasing his private commission. He didn't want to sour what was supposed to be a vacation with business, so most days, he came by with his family to eat, play troika, and relax on the beach. Unfortunately, dirty business was unavoidable—he'd agreed to help keep Miltico in line. Giorvi accompanied us as we went to Milti's house to check on him, Lavina, and Usana. Milti wasn't happy about what we forced him to do, but at least Lavina and Usana were eating... and I hadn't seen any new welts or bruises on either of them. After Giorvi and his family returned to Chernagora, Su and I took up sole responsibility of checking on the Svelt-Dem family.

Liesle wanted nothing to do with Milti, and I couldn't blame her now that I knew the truth.

One day, as the kids were getting ready to fly to school, Eruwan turned in midair, floating with the magic in her wings. She carried her lunch bag demurely in both her hands. "Papami, shall we walk Usana home today? We can check on Mr. Svelt and Mys Demiu for you. That way you can work on your new commission without interruption."

"No, don't involve yourself in the adults' matters," I said. "This is something we need to handle. You kids should just enjoy life. In fact, I'm not going to work on my commission at all after you get home. Let's play kiwi-batte after school."

Eruwan frowned. She wasn't fifteen yet, but was already thinking of herself as an adult. Even if she were thirty, I wouldn't want her getting involved with Miltico.

"Alright. If you say so..." she said with a dejected sigh. She tried to perk herself up before she left with a very forced smile. "I'll see you later!"

"Later! Bring home Nell and Demitris for kiwi-batte. We'll make a big dinner."

The four school-aged kids each said their goodbyes as they soared off toward the village.

Nell threw a fastball. She was a good pitcher, though not good at much else in kiwi-batte. She was definitely more of a musician than an athlete. Well, her mother could attest to her musical ability while I could attest to her athletic inability. I swung the batte—a hefty wooden paddle with an ivory handle—with a significant degree of weakness. If I put all my strength into it, I'd have hit the ball into the jungle or Deep Sea.

We weren't playing a real game. It was just me, Fionn, Heliodor, Nell, and Demitris. Not even enough players for one team. We were just hitting and catching the ball for fun, without concern for the rules or score. My spouses were both at work—Su in his ateli, Liesle preparing dinner. The kids said Eruwan stayed behind at school to finish a project, but there was no news about Cohaku. She didn't always enjoy playing with us, though, so she might have been in her tree house or some other secret place. Perhaps a place I did not know about.

Fionn, far out along the beach, flew up to catch the ball. He landed and threw it back to Nell.

"Papami! Help me!"

Eruwan's voice. My ears perked up as my sternum sunk in dread anticipation. Hearing one's child screaming for help was one of many things I wouldn't wish on any parent. That absolute horror was just a prelude to the tragedy about to occur.

Eruwan flew as fast as her wings allowed. She held Cohaku in her arms despite Cohaku thrashing about. Eruwan had also stuck a thick branch in her sister's mouth, which she gnawed upon wildly. Her pupils were thin slits—the thinnest I'd ever seen them on her. She snarled and her fangs tried to bite through the branch.

She'd gone berserk! I ran toward them. Eruwan descended, holding the branch to the side of Cohaku's head so she couldn't spit it out. I took it from her.

"I've got this," I said. "Step back."

She did, trembling with fear… and maybe a little guilt. Eruwan put her hands on her cheeks.

I held one of Cohaku's arms with my other hand so she wouldn't fly away. Deftly, carefully so as not to hurt her or pull her teeth, I plucked the branch out of her mouth, threw it, and put that arm inside her mouth instead. My daughter reverted to normal instantly.

The bite was just a slight sting to me. Better I serve this purpose than Eruwan, who could have had her arm bitten off. She did the right thing, using that branch and carrying Cohaku to me.

When she was back in control of herself, Cohaku sniffled, suppressing tears, and jumped into my arms for a hug.

Cohaku Interlude

Cohaku knew Eruwan would disobey their father.

After school let out, the boys headed home right away to play kiwi-batte. The Chak-Den siblings went with them, Demitris riding on Heliodor's back and Nell letting Fionn carry her in his arms. Cohaku hoped stupid Fionn remembered to fly slow and close to the ground in case he dropped her.

Cohaku told Eruwan she was headed home, but she secretly sneaked around the back of the school-church and went into the library where Usana liked to hide. She hid between two bookshelves a few rows down from the Lagodore, further from the door so Eruwan wouldn't pass by her.

Cohaku turned off her tail's electricity, in case the sparks made noise, though only Nio had ever told her—through signing—that she could hear Wynnle tails. But given Usana's huge ears, Cohaku wondered if she could hear subtle electric sounds, too. Ears that big could hear colors, so an old joke went.

After a few minutes, Cohaku's suspicions came true—Eruwan went to Usana's hiding spot. She couldn't see them, but she overheard their conversation.

"Can I walk you home today?" Eruwan asked.

"If Daddy says it's okay."

"I gotta make sure your Daddy is being good. Did he let you eat dinner yesterday?"

Cohaku didn't hear Usana's response. Maybe she nodded her head.

"Did he hit you?"

No words, but maybe gestures.

"Did he put you in a cage?"

Cohaku held her breath, scared that the slightest sound might give away her location.

"Let's go, Usana." Her voice was stern. It reminded Cohaku of her mother's voice. She hoped Eruwan wouldn't become a Mommy like their Mommy. She'd rather she become a Mommy like Mapa Su.

Usana's hooves clopping on the hard floor provided sound cover for Cohaku to crawl to the edge of the bookshelf and peer around the corner. Eruwan and Usana walked out, holding hands. The young Wynnle sneaked after them.

She stalked them as quietly as she could through the village. Eruwan didn't risk flying with Usana; she was much smarter than Fionn. Cohaku stayed hidden behind buildings, bushes, and trees, in case Eruwan turned around.

When they got to Mr. Svelt's house, Cohaku hid behind a steena tree. Mr. Svelt sat on a rocking chair on his porch, drinking something brownish from a glass bottle. It had the same strange scent she'd smelled on him last time.

"Usana!" he yelled. "What the fuck are you doing with that lion? Haven't I told you she could eat you? Get over here!"

Usana shrank back, making herself smaller. Eruwan didn't put up a fight to keep Usana by her side.

"I'm sorry, Daddy," Usana said. "I thought... she said you gave her permission." When she got closer to Mr. Svelt, he grabbed her by a horn in one hand and raised his other hand to slap her.

"You said you'd stop hitting her!" Eruwan yelled.

Afraid of being seen, Cohaku slid back behind the tree. She could picture in her imagination the sort of furious glare Mr. Svelt must have given her sister.

"You don't know garbage," he spat. "You're just a kid. You have no fucking right to talk to adults that way."

"Mud and sludge," Eruwan said. "I'm almost fifteen, but it doesn't even matter how old I am. When you're a fucker like you, I'll call you out on it whether I'm fourteen or forty!"

Cohaku's heart jumped. When did Eruwan get so courageous?

"Get in the house," Mr. Svelt ordered Usana. Cohaku winced at the sound of Usana tumbling over her hooves and falling on her knees.

"Are you gonna be nice to her?" Eruwan asked. "If not, I'll tell Papami and Papa Su."

"Get the fuck out of here!" he yelled.

"Answer my—what is that?" Her tone changed with that question. She'd been aggressive, but *that* was fear. Cohaku peered around the tree, terrified of what she might watch.

Mr. Svelt held a long, wispy tamarind branch. He swung it toward Eruwan, who backed away in time to avoid getting struck.

"Fuck off!" he yelled. "I'll hit you if you ever get close to my daughter or my house again!"

"I'm telling my parents!" Eruwan cried back.

Mr. Svelt raised the switch again and struck Eruwan across the nose. "Go! See if I care!"

That was more than Cohaku could stand. Nobody hit her family and got away with it! She ran out from behind the tree, snarling, and charged at him with claws drawn and tail flaring.

Mr. Svelt swung wildly at the little Wynnle, surprised by her sudden appearance more than anything. He hit her arm, but Cohaku was too enraged to care.

Eruwan called out to her sister, but her voice was background noise amidst the rage in her skull. "Cohaku, stop! You'll go berserk!"

She reached for Mr. Svelt, but he grabbed her by the wrists. He may have been a small Yosoe, but he was still bigger than a petite cub of a Wynnle. He lifted Cohaku, restraining her arms underneath one of his, and carried her back to his porch.

"What are you doing?" Eruwan shouted. "Let her go!"

"I'm gonna do what Amiere should have done a long time ago! If he won't teach this brat a lesson, I will." Mr. Svelt set Cohaku over his lap, holding both her arms down with one of his and grabbing her tail with the same arm's hand. With his other hand, he lifted her grass skirt and spanked her butt.

The weak, pathetic Yosoe hurt nothing but her pride, but that was enough. Her pupils thinned with fury. He may have held her hands down, but his thigh was right by Cohaku's mouth. She growled and bit his leg like he was nothing more than a yummy piece of roast goat.

Blood got in her mouth.

Blood.

Kill.

Kill.

Eat.

Kill!

KILL!

EAT!

EAT THIS FUCKING GOAT!

Chapter Twenty-Two: Berserk

I held Cohaku protectively, with fear coursing through my veins and screaming thoughts into my skull that made no sense. I imagined Cohaku dying in a pit the same way Tawny had, which was ridiculous since Cohaku had wings. I wouldn't let her die. Gods, not another one. Whatever had happened to make her go berserk, I'd fix it. I'd solve whatever problem needed to be solved. That's what fathers are meant to do...

"Daddy! Daddy! Mr. Svelt was mean! He hit Eruwan! He hit me!"

All I could see in my mind's eye was Miltico. That smirking, evil bastard. He hit my daughters? Last time he did that, I made him leave for Cosmo for ten years. What the hell did he think I'd do this time? Just let it pass? Right after we told him we would be watching him for bad behavior...

It *had* to be intentional. Miltico couldn't be so stupid as to think we'd keep letting him get away with abuse, not just to Usana, but now to my own kids? Was he goading me into killing him? Did he *want* to fucking die?

I gazed forward, hardly focusing on the other kids who had gathered around, asking for details of what had transpired to lead to Cohaku going berserk.

Eruwan told us everything. She had been hit, too, and pointed out a small scratch on her nose. Even though I'd told her to let the adults handle Miltico, I couldn't be angry at her right now. All my anger, all my fury, this indignant rage... could only have one target.

I petted Cohaku's mane as she cried into my chest. "It'll be alright, dear. I'm sorry you had to go through that, but you were very brave, standing up for your sister. I won't let anyone ever lay a hand on you. And I'll make Mr. Svelt wish he never had."

She sniffed. "I'm sorry, Daddy. I know I should have come and gotten you, but... I... I was so angry!"

I couldn't blame her. I was reaching that state, too. Half-dazed by rage, I barely remembered gently setting Cohaku aside, standing up with my mane hairs bristling and my pupils thin, and walking over to my discarded batte.

I grabbed the ivory handle, specially made by Su who had coated it with resin that made it easier to grip. I assumed it also strengthened it, because it had yet to break in the three years I'd had it. The wood was powerful... it had hit many balls so far they'd gone into the jungle and we had never found them. Once in a while, one of the kids would find an old ball and bring it back. I remembered a time Tawny came back with four after deciding she'd spend the day looking for them. If they went into Deep Sea, he'd always spit them back out eventually. They would wash up on our shore near the palm tree bench.

I shook my head and brought my thoughts back to the here and now. I couldn't let myself reminisce about Tawny when I had other daughters whose honors were at stake. My whole family's honor was at stake. If I let a random man spank my child, what sort of weak man would everyone think I was?

"Dadda?" Heliodor asked. "What are you doing, Dadda?"

I clutched the batte with all the strength I could muster. It was... a significant amount. Wynnles were naturally powerful, and I'd kept somewhat in shape by playing sports with my kids. I *was* powerful. Strong. One swing of this batte would...

"Just keep playing without me," I said. "I'll be right back."

I had to get Su. He always knew what was best. He knew the best course of action.

No.

I couldn't tell Su. I blacked out every time I was with him and Miltico in the same place. I couldn't help but wonder if he was causing it to happen. Was he using magic to stop me from... going too far?

Both my house and Miltico's house were outside the village proper, and I could get to his house through a path in the jungle. I went down Bamboo Lane a good ways, then slipped between bamboo stalks into the dense, fruit-thick wilderness inhabited only by capybaras, colorful songbirds, and a million different kinds of insects. Cohaku had loved this place, back when she had her obsession with insects...

I briefly wondered why she hadn't been here recently. Perhaps she'd just found other interests. Well, she *had* been spending a lot more time with me in my ateli... Perhaps the next time she came in, I'd ask if she still liked insects.

Cohaku... Gods, how could that man *do* that? And he hadn't *just* hit her, but he'd flipped her skirt! Was he... *that* kind of predator?

In my ateli, right now, there was a statue of Tawny I had just started. It wasn't the one I had begun working on before, but a second one. I would repurpose the first one into another shape. The second one was made from the one hundred eighty-year crystalights—the crystalights in the abyss that killed her. I swore to all the Gods who had supposedly 'blessed' this land that Tawny would be the only real child I'd make a statue of. If something were to happen to Cohaku or Usana, I would no longer be here to make statues of them. If that happened, the lawkeepers would *have* to come to Steena Village to stop my rampage. Rainyday flowers would open their petals for the fountains of blood I'd wash this fucking jungle with.

In this thick, liana-strewn, vine-crossed section of the jungle, nobody would witness me, enraged, carrying a batte to the bastard's house. Nobody went into this part of the jungle, overgrown with leaves larger than my head and curled ferns like tentacles as thick as my arms. Delicate lalafinas were crushed under my feet.

My mind clouded. I had no concept of how much time had passed. I walked onward without thought as to where I stepped or what I'd do when I reached my destination. Any vine or liana in my way, I sliced apart with my claws. An iridescent black spider dared to build a nest in my path, but my tail flicked it away, frying the spider and tearing the web.

The mozzies were as thick as tar today, but they, too, fell when my tail zapped them.

Die. Die. Die. Die you fucking insects. You small, insignificant pests.

I imagined Eruwan being hit with a tamarind switch. I saw, in my mind's eye, her crying face, a small contusion on her nose.

I imagined Cohaku being forced across Miltico's lap as he spanked her. I saw, in my mind's eye, her intense fury, her tail sparking, and her teeth digging into his thigh.

A toucan turned its head to better observe me. As long as that was only animal who saw me... I couldn't let any sapient person see what I was about to do.

When I had arrived Miltico's door, I paused only briefly to wonder where everything in my life had gone wrong. What had I done to permanently antagonize Milti that he now delighted in tormenting me? Had I ruined our relationship long ago? Or was this yet another facet of my life that I had no power over, yet which held power over my soul and filled me with sickening emotions?

I smashed his door open with the batte. I had no patience for knocking; I wouldn't give him the opportunity to know I was coming. He knew I was coming for him the moment he struck either of my daughters. The crunching of wood was the only noise around. Even the songbirds had gone silent.

I stood on the threshold, gazing into the dark abode. Light from outside—and my tail—illuminated the path down a short hall. All that stood in the sun's eye were splinters from the broken door. I stepped through. Wooden floorboards creaked beneath my feet. My tail provided more light, brightening up the living room. This place was filthy, littered with alcohol bottles and fruit rinds everywhere, and with no furniture of worth.

"Milti! I know you're in here! Show yourself!"

I didn't think the coward would actually appear, but his head peeked out from a room down the hallway. The whole house was a mere four rooms big: this living room, two bedrooms to the right of the hall, and a larger room to the left of the hall. Miltico had been in the bedroom on the right side, further down.

"What do you want, Ami?" he asked, emerging from the bedroom. He stood at the end of the hall, just out of reach of the light beam. "Are you here to scare me? Why don't you teach *your* daughters not to talk to *my* daughter? Oh, and tell them not to get anywhere near my house."

I dragged the batte along the floor as I neared him.

"Why are you carrying that?" he asked. Finally, his voice quavered with fear. As it should.

"Why did you hit my daughters?"

"The small one attacked *me*! Violent, fucking lion-girl..."

"You spanked her. You subdued her, restrained her, put her over your knee, pulled up her skirt like a sick pervert, and hit her butt."

"Is that the story she came up with? Did she tell you about biting me?" Miltico stepped forward on the leg that had been bitten. I saw the wound only after I waved my tail forward, allowing light onto it. He hadn't bandaged the injury. Clear, sticky blood matted the brown fur on his left leg.

"You deserved it for what you've done," I snarled. "Not just to her, but to everyone. To your wife. To your daughter. Oh, where are they? Lavina and Usana?"

"Lavina's gone. I won't tell you another fucking word about where she went. Usana is here, safe from lions like you."

I put a hand around Miltico's throat and pinned him to the back wall. Even still, the fucker just smiled. He put his hands on my wrist but made no attempt to pry me away. He *knew*.

"If you hurt your wife or child, I'll hurt you."

"What are you going to do? Kill me? You know you'll get caught. The lawkeepers will find you. You're not clever enough to get away with murder. Then what will happen? The best you could hope for is being sent to Hydra Island. Maybe they'll let you see your kids once a month. At worst, *you'll* be exiled to Cosmo. Hope you have the pain tolerance to circumcise yourself, because those wild lions won't let you fuck until you do."

"How many times have I told you not to call us lions?" I asked, growing. "What the fuck is wrong with you? I don't call you a goat."

"Ah, of course you're not a lion!" He had the audacity to laugh, or at least a sad attempt at laughter while my hand constricted his throat. "Lions and other cats land on their feet when they fall from a great height, but Tawny landed on her tail."

I...

I...

I lost control.

My claws extended, as if by reflex, and dug into Miltico's neck.

I drew his blood.

I smelled his blood.

I...

Must...

Kill.

KILL!
KILL!
EAT!
I WILL KILL THIS FUCKING GOAT!
I WILL EAT THIS FUCKING GOAT!

It tasted like the goat we'd had at the fire feast.

Well, not really. It was raw, unseasoned meat, but the essence was the same. Mouthwatering, juicy, goat meat. I could not stop eating until the rage burning inside my sternum and the electricity crackling through my skull were satisfied. Not until I'd eaten everything I could. I licked blood off my claws between bites.

Everything I could eat was eaten. Consumed. Devoured. Ingested. Engorged. Wynnles could store a large meal in their bellies and not eat for a few days. I could eat a goat this size easily.

The left arm that had held the whip that had hit Eruwan.

The right arm that had spanked Cohaku.

The legs that had walked throughout Cosmo the last ten years in exile.

The stomach that had ingested crazy sugar until Tico's death.

The liver that had already been close to dying.

The neck that had suffered my impaling claws.

The penis that had fucked my wife.

The eye that had been scratched blind by my wife in revenge.

The brain that must have sought its death, for why else would he have taunted me into doing this?

It was a fine meal. Juicy, delectable blood dripped down my claws. A piece of grey matter fell out from the foramen in the skull and got tangled up in my beard when I stuck my tongue inside to lick out that sweet, soft, moist tissue. The eyes squished like rambutans between my teeth.

The oh-so-satisfying taste satiated my appetite and relieved my berserker state. My mind cleared, and I was once again myself.

I couldn't eat bones. Wynnles hadn't evolved or been transformed by Life Spirits in any of our ancestral timelines to eat bones. The evidence of my crime—white, sticky with blood, and as solid as the reality that I had committed murder and cannibalism—lay on the ground for anyone to witness, if they only cared to come and look.

Usana Interlude

Lions! Just outside the bedroom!

She was safe in her cage. Safe. Secure. Daddy had promised. Usana scooted to the back, near the corner, away from the bars. Strong, metal bars that the lion couldn't break.

The lion brought light with him, carried on his tail. Wherever he walked, his shadow went with him. The light reflected in Usana's eyes.

He yelled at Daddy. Daddy screamed in pain, in panic.

Daddy! Mommy! Somebody! Help Daddy!

The lion's shadow was cast upon the wall by the light of his tail. His mane flared like fire. He lifted something that looked like an oar and brought it down on Daddy's head. A splattering noise filled Usana's ears.

Squish

Gloop

She held her ears tight to her body, hoping she wouldn't have to hear it again.

Daddy cried out. She'd never heard him in such pain. *Please, somebody, save my Daddy!*

The lion hit him again. *Plop*. And again. *Gloop*. And again. *Squish*. No matter how tight Usana held her ears, she heard the splattering every time. With each swing, the oar broke pieces of Daddy away. A trail of his blood reached the door to her bedroom.

When Daddy stopped screaming, the lion bent down, grabbed an arm, and bit into him.

She stayed quiet, hoping the lion wouldn't see her. She was safe in the cage. Safe. Secure. Daddy had put her in here for her own safety.

Chapter Twenty-Three: Viscera

Fuck. Fuck. Oh fuck.

I had to get out of here. I had to hide these bones. If I buried them, a clairvoyant or the lawkeepers or shinigami or...or someone... would find them. They'd know I was a killer. I would be banished from Aloutia! I would be separated from my family!

I had kids to raise and care for! I couldn't let this happen... Oh, Gods—Usana! Where was Usana?

I ran into Miltico's bedroom, tail swung forward to shed light in this disgusting, filthy room. More alcohol, some boxes and crates, a few scattered and unwashed clothes, their stench worse than a durian. A vase of dead glowlight lotuses sat in the corner of the room.

No Usana.

I went into the next room, where she was locked in a cage near the far wall. Gods, Miltico was a sick, twisted fuck. Who puts their child in a fucking cage?

I grabbed the cage and lifted it so I could see inside with my tail's light. Usana sat shivering inside, ears over her eyes.

"Are you okay?" I asked. "You're not hurt, are you? I, uh..." Fuck, did she know what I did to her father? Could she see it? Or could she tell based on the noise? "I've gotta get you out of here. Your Daddy's going to hurt you, Usana. I'll save you."

I pulled at the bars, but they were metal. I could have broken wood, but this was beyond even my immense Wynnle strength. What could I do?

Usana squealed and cried. Was I scaring her?

And where was Lavina? Oh Gods, what if she was on her way back right now?

The bones! I had to do something about the bones!

Su. Su would have an answer to everything. He could get Usana out. He could stop Lavina. He knew how to dispose of bones. I clutched Usana's cage close to my chest and fled into the jungle. I couldn't let anyone from Steena Village see me. I had to approach Su's ateli from the jungle side. I couldn't let my kids see me, either. What would I say to them? How would I explain why I had Usana?

Yet another thing I needed Su for. He and Liesle were the only ones I could trust with this knowledge. I couldn't let anyone else know about this.

As I ran through the jungle, leaping over logs, weaving through lianas, and cutting away vines as they tangled around me, my thoughts went to potential excuses. I could tell them I made Miltico go back to Cosmo. I could tell them I scared him off into the jungle. Would anyone believe those stories? They sounded like weak excuses. If any of my kids tried those on me, I'd know immediately they were lies. As if to mock my thoughts, a distant parrot laughed.

I smelled the atrocious odor of Su's ateli long before I reached it. I didn't know how he could stand to work in that place. The odor was caused by his work; boiling bones released biological material that smelled similar to the stench of bodies that hadn't been found by shinigami and were instead left to rot.

"Cover your nose, Usana," I said. "I know it smells bad, but I gotta get you there."

She hadn't said a word to me yet. She hadn't even squealed after that initial sound when I first picked up her cage. She hadn't moved save for the uncontrollable tremors that overpowered her small body. Poor girl. She must have been so terrified. Well, she'd never have to be scared again. Her father would never hit her again!

I held my breath to keep out as much of the foul odor as I could, ran to the door facing Deep Sea, and knocked repeatedly.

"Su! Su, it's an emergency! Open up!"

He flung the door wide open and stepped out, closing the door behind him. He didn't like anyone seeing inside. Presumably, he had magical artifacts inside that would hint at what element of Godblood he was.

Su's eyes went as big as our patella plates and his mouth gaped open at the sight of what—who—was in my hands.

"Amiere! Did you kidnap her?"

"Su, please, I need your help. I... I..." I licked my lips. How on all the planes could I confess to what I did?

"What did you do?" he asked as the color drained from his face.

I couldn't answer. How could I?

"Where's Miltico?" he asked, tangling his arms together in a worried gesture.

"Umm... I need to show you some bones."

I couldn't say it in front of Usana. I didn't know how much she had seen from her dark room.

Su's arms fell to his sides. "You didn't..."

"I did."

"Why did you go off speaking to him without me!?" he yelled. "Oh Gods, what are we going to do? We need to get Usana someplace... someplace that doesn't stink. Can you put her in your ateli?"

"Too close to the house and the kids. I don't want them to see her in a cage."

Su pursed his lips and tapped his foot on the soft sand. "That's another thing. We need to get her out. Where's the key?"

Lavina had once said Miltico kept the key on him, but...

In the midst of my madness, I vaguely recalled consuming small things that weren't Miltico's body. Bits and pieces of his clothes. And... perhaps a small piece of bronze or brass? It must have been a key, so small it went down my throat without difficulty. It would surely be destroyed by my gastrobacter in due time.

"The lighthouse," Su suggested. "I have some safe spots in the lighthouse where nobody will go. I'll... find a way to get her out of the cage. "I can make a skeleton key."

"I didn't know merchants of bone could make keys from skeletons."

Su looked like he wanted to roll his eyes, but the situation was too dire for such flippancy. "Normally I'd appreciate your unintended bone pun. That's not what a 'skeleton key' means, but I'll explain later. I *am* going to make it from bone, so you're not entirely wrong. Here, let me carry her."

He took the cage in his arms. "We need to approach the lighthouse from an angle so the kids don't see us. Follow me."

The anxiety of committing murder was compounded by the fear that my kids would find out. Su was careful, but I couldn't help but imagine Fionn hitting the ball toward the lighthouse, then any of the flying kids going inside to look for it.

"Pick up some fruits," Su said. "Ones you can either slide between the bars or slice easily. We might need to leave her for a few minutes and I don't know if she's eaten today."

Steenas frequently ended up on the beach. Although their trees were further away, they were wont to get blown off by strong winds. We'd had a few storms recently, so a few had found their way to the sand. I did as he asked, peeling away the shell so we could slip the smaller pieces through the cage bars.

At the lighthouse, I put my hand on a vertebra to steady myself, to calm my racing heart. Each coatl vertebra of Scrimshander Lighthouse was close to my height, and that was while laying on their flat ends. The diameter of each one would have been the length of seven or eight of me. And yet Su had somehow carried them from the Cosmo Plane. He'd claimed that he'd had help from King Susan's demonic troops, but I had never seen them. Perhaps that was the truth; perhaps he'd used his magic.

"Amiere, I need you to close your eyes," Su said. "I have to do something with magic, but I couldn't bear it if you saw me."

Closing my eyes sounded like a good idea. Gods, I just wanted to sleep. I wanted this day to be over. I wanted... I wanted to go back, back before I was a cannibal and a murderer. Fuck, what had I done? Life would never be the same again. I'll have to live with constantly hiding this fact from my children, forever.

Tawny's death was a trauma that made my sternum sink into my stomach. Committing murder was a trauma that made my sternum want to jettison out of my mouth.

"Keep your eyes closed," Su said. "Grab my hand and follow me."

He put one of his hands in mine and pulled me around the lighthouse, toward the entrance. The door faced Deep Sea, meaning we would have briefly been in view of the kids, had they chanced to look this way. Whatever magic Su conjured likely kept us hidden from their sight.

Although my eyes were closed, I knew this place well enough to know I had to step across the door's threshold carefully. I didn't have to duck, at least—Su had carved the entryway tall enough for Liesle to walk through.

"Open your eyes now."

My trail provided the bulk of illumination, but some light from the sun came through the door, much like it had illuminated the way into Miltico's house.

Oh, fuck. I shivered, unable to contain my anxiety. Had I closed the front door to Miltico's house? Could a passerby think something was amiss, and then peek inside? Were his bones far enough inside to be hidden in shadows? We had to hurry!

A series of clavicles wound around the vertebral walls, acting as steps to the second floor. The lighthouse had three levels, each tall enough for a Wynnle like Liesle to stand in comfortably. The third floor was crowned with the coatl's skull, jaws open with the crystalight shining toward Deep Sea.

Su went up the clavicle steps. I followed, testing my weight on the first step. They'd never failed to bear my weight, but they *looked* so frail.

The second floor was dim. A bit of light from upstairs crystalight seeped through, though once I left with my tail's light, it would be darker.

Su set the cage under the shadows of the clavicles leading up to the third floor. He crouched down and pushed it against the wall.

Usana hid her eyes behind her massive, floppy ears. She continued to tremble.

"You'll be safe here," Su said. "I'll come back soon. Ami-honey, give me those fruits."

I handed him what I had collected, and he slid them between the bars. Usana didn't move, but they would be there for her if she wanted to eat after we left.

"Usana, you have permission to eat them," Su said. "I'm a Daddy, alright? And a Mommy. You can eat as many as you like."

He stood, gave me a stressful look, and went back down the stairs.

We had to do the same… trick, or whatever it was… exiting the lighthouse. I closed my eyes, took Su's hand, and let him lead me to the side away from the kids' line of sight.

"Let's hurry," Su said as he broke out into a sprint. I had no problems keeping up with him. I may have been getting older, but Wynnles were made to run well into old age.

"I can't remember if I closed Milti's door," I said with so much anxiety that the words felt like they were caught up in bile on their way up my throat.

Su never stopped running. "We'll deal with problems as they arrive."

Near his ateli, Su took one of the unnamed paths used by fruit collectors. Hardly more than a trail we kept clear for people and their small hand-drawn wagons, it was dotted with durian, steena, papaya, mango, rambutan, and kumquat trees. There would surely be people on the road... They would see us. See me. See the blood on my hands.

My hands! I looked at my hands, but if there was any blood, it was so small and clear as to be unnoticeable. I sniffed, but... was that my imagination? Could I still smell Miltico's blood? Could everyone else smell it?

"Su! Take the jungle!"

"No! I'll have to slow down."

"We might run into someone."

"They won't see us."

"How?"

"They just fucking won't, Amiere!" he shouted, sounding more sad than angry. "I can't explain."

I guessed it was his magic. Whatever he'd done to keep our children from seeing us, I supposed he could make fruit-gatherers similarly blind to us.

Sure enough, we passed one of the village's fruit gatherers. She was a Flora with a steena appearance, gathering fruit into a small wagon. I knew her well enough; she'd lived in Steena Village as long as I had, though she was fifteen years my senior. She paid us no heed. Usually, she at least said hello when we passed by. Perhaps we were invisible to her.

We reached Miltico's house, where the door... Oh right, I'd smashed it open. That answered that question.

Su stepped inside, then aside to let me in and shed light with my tail. I held it in my hand like a torch and led him to the bones.

Gods, what a mess.

What remained of Miltico scattered across the hall and dripped into the floor. I'd eaten the meat and edible organs. His skull had been difficult to clean out and stared up at me in bloody, eyeless horror. I had broken one of his horns clean off in my rage, but the other was fairly intact, albeit chipped in a few spots. I recalled a piece of his brain had fallen on my beard. My hand shot to that spot reflexively, in fear it was still there. It wasn't. My beard was matted with blood, but no gore. If anyone saw me, I'd have to claim it was a hunting accident. That wasn't quite a lie...

"Well, you solved our old problem," Su said. "Now, we have a new one."

"Am I going to get caught by the lawkeepers?"

"The lawkeepers won't give a damn about Miltico. Who's going to report that he went missing? We'll tell his father and Lavina that he went back to Cosmo. They'll never know the truth. No, the problem we need to consider is the forces we don't see. Shinigami."

The ghostly servants of Lord Sawyer who patrolled the mortal planes in search of dead bodies and turned them into sawdust. Miltico's soul would be floating around nearby, too. I wondered if he'd fallen into centennial sleep already. According to the volkhvs who educated me when I was a child, dead souls went to sleep almost immediately after death, though there were exceptions.

"What if Miltico's awake?" I asked. "And he tells a shinigami what happened?"

"It's unlikely, but... I suppose it *could* happen. And I suppose if Sawyer cared enough to avenge him, he might send a shinigami to punish you. I just can't see it happening, though. Not since you killed him to save Usana. The merchants of dance do similar things, and they're Sawyer's own descendants. Or maybe the shinigami will see a rambling drunk and put him to sleep just to shut him up."

I cracked a smile, which I'd begun to think would never happen again for as long as I lived. Thank the Gods for Su.

"Is there anything you can do to make sure a shinigami never finds these bones? If you give them to Deep Sea, he'll pulverize them, right?"

"He will, but he might realize they're sapienti bones. While I don't think he'd go out of his way to alert authorities or the Gods, he could be summoned by lawkeepers and compelled to tell whatever he knows. Best to not get him involved. No, leave them to me. I can make sure no shinigami ever finds these bones."

I put my hand on Su's shoulder. The anxiety made me dizzy, but Su... my gorgeous, amazing Su... he knew how to solve all my problems. He would make Miltico's body disappear.

"Is there a bag or anything nearby we can use?" he asked. "Something to carry them in."

Miltico had often used burlap sacks to haul fruits or other goods to his father's shop. A few lay on the ground. One was full of empty alcohol bottles. I upended it, dumping all the bottles on the ground with a loud clatter. I winced as the sound echoed, and hoped no one was anywhere nearby.

"Amiere!" Su hissed.

"Sorry, I wasn't thinking."

He sighed. "I can tell. Thinking's not your strong suit."

"I've always left it to you and Liesle."

"Anyway, bring that here. Let's get the bones inside."

As he lifted the skull, a piece of Miltico's brain fell out. There was only so much I could have done to clean the bones...

"Close your eyes again."

I did, and when he told me to open them, the fallen piece of brain was gone. Su's arms were too full to have picked it up. Yet another magic trick, I was certain.

"Can you use that magic to make all the bones disappear, too?"

He looked at me with sad eyes. "It's a different process for bones. This is why I chose to become a merchant of bone. Well, one reason, anyway. They're the one body part I can't... no, I can't say any more."

"You can't... make them disappear with magic?"

His sad eyes turned into a warning glare. A warning not to pry into his magical background. “Let’s go back. This time, we go through the jungle.”

“Because we’re not in such a hurry to get to his body before anyone else… and just in case anything leaks out of the bag?”

“I wouldn’t want some ooze dripping on the path used by every merchant of fruit in the village. If they followed it to my ateli, I’d have some uncomfortable questions to answer.”

I couldn’t thank the Gods enough for bringing Su into my life. He was my everything. My love, my passion, my partner in crime, and my best friend. A lover will kiss and fuck you, but a true friend helps you hide your victims’ bodies.

Chapter Twenty-Four: Sickness

After stuffing the bag of bones in his ateli and locking the door, Su guided me down to the beach.

"Be calm," he said. "Although I was startled when you first told me about what you'd done, I think we'll get away with it. Logically speaking, no one has any reason to search for Miltico. For them to find what happened to his body, they'd need a clairvoyant Godblood, but there aren't many of those around, and I'm sure they're kept busy with more important matters. Moreover, if a clairvoyant sought us out, I have no doubt they'd send Lungidus Pavo to arrest us."

The name was vaguely familiar. He was a Mind Godblood living in Monoceros, serving as a lawkeeper. He was a year or two younger than me. I recalled when I went to Monoceros to go to art school with Liesle, Lungidus had just become the city's primary protector. I also remembered Su mentioning that he'd danced romantically with him, back before he met me and Liesle. That was no statement about Su's sex, gender, or sexuality—he'd danced with Lungidus's wife, too.

"You really think I can get away with murder?"

"With my help, yes. And with Liesle's. This isn't something we should hide from her."

I would take his advice. I doubted I could have hidden it from her for long. My anxiety would make me nauseous every time she mentioned Milti's name otherwise. Even if I never confessed to the crime, she would surely figure it out. She would see the guilt painted on my face as clearly as my spots.

"What are we going to do about Usana?"

"It will take me a few hours to get her out of the cage. She'll be fine. We'll take care of her. We'll... adopt her."

"I don't know what she saw," I replied. "She might know I killed her father. What if she tells everyone?"

Su licked his lips and took a deep breath, staring listlessly into the distance. The sun sat atop the horizon, the planet's rings appearing to shoot forth from it.

"I'll talk to her while I'm getting her out. Figure out what she knows and... and what she's willing to talk about."

"You wouldn't hurt her, would you? To hide our secret?"

"Never. I'd never hurt a child."

"What if she saw everything and she tells everyone?"

Su had no answer.

"Does any of your magic let you manipulate memories or behavior?" I asked. "Because that would be handy right about now."

"I'll make my decision after I've spoken with her," he replied simply and sternly.

I found myself staring at that faraway sky with Su, watching pink stars twinkle to life in the coming twilight. My mind felt entirely vacant, like a single thought would be too much weight on my skull.

Our blessed land would forever be stained with blood. Or had it been already? The day Tawny's life gushed out from her wingless back, painting those crystalights in her clear, thick blood, this land became cursed. That had been a Goddess's fault—Machenerate, Goddess of Stone, murderer of my child, though perhaps on accident.

"Can you go back home without making the kids suspicious?"

"I... I don't know. I ate so much, I don't think I can eat dinner for a few days."

Su rubbed his face. The frustration in his expression hurt my soul. I wished there had been any other way to solve the problem.

"We're going to tell them you got sick. Then go into the bedroom and stay there until Liesle and I can speak with you."

"They know I went to Miltico's house. The whole reason I went there in the first place was because he hit Eruwan and Cohaku. I went to... to..." To talk to him? Gods, they saw me leave with a batte. My kids wouldn't be naive enough to believe that lie, so why would I try it on Su? "To get revenge."

Su glanced downward as if the seashell at his feet was the most interesting thing in the world. "Fuck, what are we going to say? I'll come with you. Let me do all the talking. Don't say a word. Try to look ill."

"Make me black out again," I suggested.

He held his breath, but dared not look up at me, lest he give away that I knew he was responsible.

"You think I'm the one doing that?"

"It always—and only—happens when you're around. It's magic, isn't it? I don't know why you're doing it, but since it always happened around Miltico, I wondered if you were... maybe trying to prevent what just happened."

His throat bobbed as he swallowed. "That's right, Ami-honey. I did it. If you want me to do it again, I will."

"It's happened enough times, it won't seem strange to them. Use whatever excuse you've been using whenever you guide me away."

Su's mouth squirmed, and his eyes watered. He leapt onto me, hugging me with his smooth arms. "I didn't want to lose you, Ami-honey! I thought... I thought if you committed an act of violence and went berserk, I'd lose everything." He let his tears flow, crying as he professed his fears. "Our whole family would have to leave Steena Village, maybe even Aloutia! And me being a Godblood, I'd probably get sent to Mortebai Prison. I can't live that way! I'd rather die than live without you all. I... I would do it! I'd kill myself before I let them take me!"

I clutched him close, like he would vanish if I didn't hold on tight enough. He broke out into an uncontrollable sobbing mess, sounds muffled in my chest. "Please don't say things like that, Su. We all need you here, in the living world."

"I know. I would only do it if I knew there was no hope of ever being with you or the rest of the family again. If I were sent to Mortebai, I would never be released. Godbloods who are sent there are sentenced for life."

"You could escape. Surely you have some magic—"

"Mortebai was *made* to imprison Godbloods!" Su explained. "A Godblood's magic blood is drained out of them and replaced with donated clear blood, all while we're under hypnosis from a Mind Godblood. By the time I realize where I'm at, it'll be too late. All my blood will be clear and devoid of magic."

I ran my hand through his hair. "We won't be caught. Let this be the last time you make me black out. Now that I know it's your magic, I can stop wondering about it. And now that Milti isn't a problem, you shouldn't have any reason to try it on me. We should tell Liesle, too. Then..." I hesitated, inhaled the crisp twilight air, and released my tension in the same breath as my next words. "...we just forget about it."

Su took a deep breath comparable to mine for his smaller stature. His exhalation was hot on my chest. "Here's the story. *You* have to believe it's true, Amiere. It will only become our truth if you believe it to be true. You went to Miltico's house just now and saw he was taking out his anger on Usana. He was forcing her to eat something as punishment. You swung the batte at him to scare him, and he ran into the jungle. As far as we know, he's still out there. You took a bite out of what Usana was eating to make sure it was edible, then brought her here. Since she's scared of lions, I have her in my ateli, trying to calm her down. Don't mention that she's in a cage or the lighthouse."

"I can tell that story, but what story will Usana tell once she's free?"

"I'll convince her to go with that story," Su said with complete confidence.

"*Are* you a Mind Godblood?" I asked. "Are you making me black out with hypnosis? Is that how you're going to force her to believe it?"

"I'm..." he pulled away, staring to the side to avoid making eye contact with me. "I'm not a Mind Godblood."

That was more information about his ancestry than he'd shared in the entire sixteen years I'd known him. "I see. Well, it would be a betrayal of your trust to keep prodding, so I won't. Alright, make me black out, Su. Guide me to the bedroom..."

In some manner, the story that I was 'sick' wasn't a lie. I was sick. Sick to my stomach. Sick of myself. Sick of the lies I'd have to tell my kids. I thought I would vomit.

I laid on the reed-mat bed, eyes closed. My family ate dinner at the dining room vertebra table as rain pounded outside. The smell of rice, fish, oko, and fruits mingling with the pattering of rain soothed my soul. It wasn't the food itself—I wouldn't eat for a week after having such a big meal—but rather the smell of a dish that I'd eaten so often with my family. My skull associated that smell with love, companionship... a safe routine.

Perhaps it was the loss of my usual routine that had my sternum feeling tight and my ribs feeling like they'd tied themselves in knots. Before Tawny passed away, every day was practically the same as the one before, but I had liked it that way. Stability was comforting. I would gladly embrace a new status quo if it would only arrive. I couldn't navigate the stormy seas of my mind. Not alone.

Thank the Gods for Su. Where would I be without him?

I wondered if he'd gone back to his ateli by now. He told me to stay in the bedroom so the kids wouldn't ask me any questions during dinner, and I didn't dare go out to see if he was still there.

He'd told me that after he had dinner, he would check on Usana, feed her, and get to work on a skeleton key to get her out of the cage. If Su had Godblood powers, perhaps he could use some other method to get her out...

After a while, Liesle came into the bedroom, her tail's light brightening up the room. I scooted over to make room for her on the mat. She sat beside me and put her hand over my head, testing if I had a fever.

"I'd be surprised if I had a temperature," I told her. "I have a lot to tell you, but I can't do it with the kids around."

She purred, grinning. My wife wore all the bone earrings she owned. Damn, she must have been horny as hell, and here I couldn't provide relief to her. I wasn't in the mood. I'd removed my earrings just before playing with the kids earlier since I didn't want any of those earrings getting damaged during the kiwi-batte game.

"I'll take you to the cave if you'd like," she said.

"Yes, let's go. But... just to talk. I'm sorry, Liesle. I can see the mood you're in, but I can't provide you with that, tonight."

"That's fine. I will make love to Su later, if he's willing. And if not, he cleaned up a pufferfish skeleton for me."

After being properly cleaned and strengthened with chemicals, a pufferfish skeleton made for a decent dildo for Wynnle women. They would not last long, however; even with snowbark resin applied to seal the pores, they were difficult to clean.

As we left, the kids didn't question where we were headed. The girls played troika inside, and the boys played catch with Maika outside while there was still a hint of daylight left. The rain had finally let up, leaving a lingering wet smell. My feet sunk into soft, crunchy sand as we went closer to the rocks on the southeast side of the beach.

One rock had been flattened smooth after centuries of Deep Sea's fingers brushing over it. It had been our take-off spot since we'd first discovered the cave as teenagers. It hadn't taken long before the cave became our make-out spot. No one else in the village could reach the cave, as it was only accessible to flying or swimming folk. Liesle's father had been the only winged man in the village, and he'd been too lazy to go searching for his daughters if they didn't come home at a certain time. No, not lazy—complacent. Steena Village had been peaceful in those days. He must have never expected drama to come to our quiet village. He never would have comprehended the ground swallowing his children.

Liesle, being taller and more muscular than me, carried me in her arms and flew us into the cave of St. Alice's Lights. A blue haze greeted us near Su's femur pier. We held our tails in front of us as we worked our way into the larger chambers. The insects, taking us for predators, extinguished their lights as we intruded deeper into their space.

We sat on a smooth slab of rock where we'd done everything from kissing and holding hands to outright fucking—the same spot where we'd conceived the twins, with Su's help. We wrapped our tails together and turned off our lights. Soon, the insects would turn theirs back on.

"I need to tell you what really happened," I said.

"Go on. I can take a guess, but I'd rather give you the chance to put it in your own words."

"First off, did Eruwan or Cohaku tell you what Milti did to them?"

"Eruwan told me. Cohaku doesn't like me—she doesn't tell me anything." A tone of regret tinged her voice. Liesle tried to hide how much it bothered her that Cohaku didn't trust her.

"I was so furious when I heard about it, I stormed over to Milti's house to teach him a lesson. Then he... he said something that..." I shook my head as if the action would shake the words out of my skull. "I can't repeat it. It's too painful; too fucked up."

If Wynnles were cats or lions, they would have landed on their feet, but Tawny landed on her tail.

As the first of St. Alice's Lights flickered on, I continued. "I lost control of myself, and... I killed him. I killed Milti."

Liesle's tigrine eyes could have bored holes in my skull. Well, holes other than the foramina already in it. Let them. Maybe then the intrusive thoughts would spill out.

"You went into a berserker rage?" she asked.

"Yes. I let it win. I let the rage consume me, and in turn, I consumed... him."

She closed her eyes and sighed. "Su mentioned he would be at his ateli for a while tonight. He hinted it had something to do with Usana, so I assume you got her out safely."

"Yes, and to my knowledge, no one else knows she's here. I... I'm not sure what we should do about her. Should we give her to Phoebus Svelt to raise? He is her grandfather, after all."

"No. He raised two sons who grew up to be pure scum. I don't know how that poor old man fucked up so badly. I know *he's* not bad, but he failed at raising his children. I wouldn't trust him with children, anymore."

"I suggested the Wind church to Su, but... Lisi, I think Su wants to raise her. He wants to give her the last name Scrimshander and raise her like she's his own daughter."

"That would be fine," she said. "We still have Tawny's bed mat, so it wouldn't be difficult to provide for her. Speaking of Mr. Svelt, though... poor man. To have both his sons killed. He's going to be devastated."

"Killed? Tico died of a drug overdose. It was just an unfortunate accident."

Liesle bit her lip. "Of course. Just a turn of phrase. Anyway, keep an eye out for Milti's wife. Lavina, was it? Gods only know where she is, but if she comes back, she might try to get Usana."

I didn't have the faintest clue what might have happened to her. Milti hadn't explained, and she'd been at the back of my mind when I'd confronted him.

Yet another mystery to stress me with endless anxiety.

Liesle dug her fingers into my mane, claws brushing through thick strands. The cave's lights illuminated her bright green eyes, flashing like fire. Her passion was palpable.

"Amiere, Mo Ami, my love... We have another thing in common now, and it's burning me up from inside. I know you're not wearing your earrings, and I won't ask for sex, but I want you to know that I have never been more attracted to you than I am right now."

I blinked, confused. "What? Why? I'm a murderer! You... you're sexually aroused by that?"

"I'm sexually aroused by strong men. By men who assert their power and dominance over enemies, even to the point of murder. Oh, I wouldn't tolerate you being mean to me. I'm not going to fuck a man who tries to control me. But Gods, I would have loved to have seen you kill Milti."

Damn... I knew Liesle liked strong men. It was partially why I'd tried to stay fit and healthy, playing sports to keep up my physique. Su liked strong men *and* women. He would probably have liked strong people of all sexes, though I was unsure if he knew anyone other than himself who was neither male nor female.

But she liked murderers, too? I had no idea, and I'd known Liesle forever!

"Am I sick for saying that?" she asked. "Is it a mental illness that I want to fuck you more than ever, knowing you've killed and consumed the man who raped me?"

"Are you okay talking so casually about it?" I asked. "If you're traumatized, maybe we should... I don't know, talk to someone who's better at that sort of thing?"

She put her elbows on her knees, chin on her hands. "I feel nothing about... that. It was rape, yes, but I held power in the end. Milti was as powerless as a worm to me. I think that alone saved me from mental anguish and unbearable trauma. If I had been a smaller, weaker woman... well, perhaps I would have mentioned it to you and Su much sooner. I may have needed your help."

"I would have done my best to help you," I replied. "Though looking back on the kind of mess I was back then, you'd probably have been better off asking only Su."

She grinned. "I love you for so many reasons, Mo Ami, so don't take this the wrong way... but I'm glad you see why we need Su. He provides mental and emotional stability that we can't provide each other."

"You think we wouldn't be together if it weren't for him?"

She raised herself up and shrugged. "I think we'd still fuck now and again. Well, we'd try on days you can keep your dick up."

Ouch. I knew she didn't mean to hurt me, but it was a sore spot...

Liesle continued without pause. "When we were younger, we were both wild, carefree souls. Lightning that strikes wherever it wishes. I just wanted to fuck you and paint pictures that would shock people. You just wanted to fuck me and snort crazy sugar. Can you imagine us raising kids, just the two of us? Su brought steadiness to our lives. He is the foundation of our house, the bones that keep this body together."

She was right. Where would I be without Su? Would I have become the same kind of man Miltico had been? Addicted to crazy sugar and... doing things I wouldn't be alive to regret?

No, Su wasn't the one who had gotten me off crazy sugar. Hell, he'd done it with me, to test what it felt like. Merchants of bone used it to numb their patients' mouths before dentistry, and Su wanted to know first-hand what it felt like.

"Liesle, give yourself credit, too. You were the one who convinced me and Su to stop snorting crazy sugar."

She stared at me like she wanted to call me an idiot. "Are you saying that because I talked you out of searching for a new dealer or... do you actually know what I did?"

I cocked my head, confused. What she did? "I don't understand."

"Never mind, then. It's best left in the past. Now, for the present... you gorged yourself on Milti, didn't you?"

I rubbed my belly. "Yes, I did." I couldn't help but conjure a mental image of Milti inside me. Ugh, that made me *actually* feel sick. The man had been my friend once... and no matter what else, he had been a sapient entity.

"I'll keep telling the kids the story you said about eating something bad. It'll give you an excuse to not eat for a few days."

"Thank you so much, Lisi." I breathed a sigh of relief.

"Su might be able to help with his magic, too," she added. "Remember how he's sometimes helped the kids digest food when they have upset stomachs?"

"You're right! There was a time Tawny gorged herself on fish and kiwis and we thought she wouldn't eat for a few days, but Su did something magical to speed up her digestion."

How lucky I was for both my spouses to support me! How fortunate for me they would both help me get away with murder!

Su did not return until quite late at night after the children had gone to bed. That was for the best, anyway, considering the topic. We three sat in the pillow area of our living room. The crystalights, covered by blues drapes, effused a gentle, cerulean glow. Along with that, the fresh cinnadyme in the censers almost made for a romantic scene.

Su told us he had managed to free Usana, but she was too scared to exit the cage. He decided to leave her alone overnight and see how she was doing in the morning.

"Liesle and I spoke while you were in your ateli," I said. "We wondered if you could do anything to quicken my digestion."

Su's mouth hung open, scandalized, but closed it again with a look of determination. "Hmm, yes, I could do that. I'm sorry I didn't offer earlier. I... wasn't sure if I could do it correctly."

"Is it difficult magic?" Liesle asked. "You've used it on the kids, so it must not be dangerous, otherwise you'd have *never* done it."

"It's not dangerous; I just don't do it on people Amiere's size often."

"Or ever?" I wagered.

He shook his head as he stood to come sit next to me. "No, I did it a few times when I lived with King Susan, but it was mostly for training purposes. She wanted me to be the best Godblood I could be, and made me use my powers frequently and in various ways."

Once he was seated beside me, Su put his two right arms on my torso while propping himself up with his lefts.

"Are you... working your magic?" I asked.

"Yes. Just stay still, if you can. You might be full of energy tomorrow, so perhaps we should play sports with the kids to work it off. You will be able to eat now, though."

"Good. I don't want the kids wondering what I ate to gorge myself."

Su patted my belly after he was done and laid his head on my chest. "Keep them distracted tomorrow, okay? I still need to think of the story we'll tell them about Usana."

More lies... Who knew doing the right thing would be such a headache?

Su Interlude

Su had used magic to remove the nasty odors from his ateli before bringing Usana inside. He swung down all five bones acting as bars to lock the door, suspecting Usana would flee given half a chance. As short as she was, she would not be able to reach the uppermost bones. Su hated the idea of trapping a child, but if she bolted into the jungle in a fit of terror, she might truly get hurt. Poor Usana was not well by any metric.

He rarely performed demigod rituals in front of his family, since he felt it would be awkward answering questions regarding whether certain demigods were his siblings or cousins. But in the privacy of his ateli, he frequently performed rituals to Garnet Skull, Demigod of Bones, a long-dead Death Godblood. His powers allowed summoners like Su to strengthen bones, make them more flexible, or preserve them for longer than what applying snowbark resin alone would allow.

Su had crafted a skeleton key made from the bones of a gamayun, a small, slender songbird. The key would have been much too fragile without Garnet Skull's divine assistance, but no other bone would have sufficed. The lock on Usana's cage was *so* tiny. Its original key must have been miniscule... Well, Amiere *had* most likely eaten it without noticing.

Su swung Usana's cage door open and stepped aside, allowing the girl to run free—within the confines of his ateli—if she'd been inclined to do so.

She huddled in the far corner, shivering, not daring to move an inch closer to the door.

That would be alright. Su could wait there with her. He'd wait here all night if he had to. Next to him, a pot of rice cooked on an enchanted fire ring, a neat tool he'd received from a traveling merchant of magic not long ago. She had said it would only stay enchanted for four months, but that was good enough for Su. It was nearing the end of its life. Soon, it would lose its enchantments and be as dead as a darkened crystalight.

Su went to work cleaning out a monkey skull which he would set beside Usana, full of rice, when it was done.

Her father's bones were safely hidden in the cauldron deeper into the ateli, behind a black shroud. Slowly dissolving.

Hours later, and Usana had not moved or eaten.

Su had to sleep eventually, but he couldn't risk her running away... or finding her father's remains. Sadly, he had to lock her cage door again before leaving and returning to the megawhale house. Inside the cage, he left a bowl full of rice and more fruit than even Amiere could have eaten in one night.

"Usana... you have Daddy's permission to eat," he said before leaving.

Chapter Twenty-Five: Skeleton Key

Soon after waking up, Su went to his ateli, only to come back a short time later. Something was wrong, but the kids were awake and asking about breakfast when he returned, so we didn't discuss it. A forced, almost rictus, smile graced his face whenever one of the kids asked him for anything. Although he softened his demeanor by patting them on their manes and assuring them he was here to help, I saw his discomfort.

When the kids flew away to school, Su joined us in moving dishes to Deep Sea for washing. He let out a heavy sigh and explained the situation.

"She won't come out of the cage," he said. "I think she associates it with safety. When she's in there, nobody can hurt her. She *did* eat, thankfully. A little bit, anyway."

Liesle leaned on one of the whale ribs supporting the house and crossed her arms. "What do we do? Force her out? Wouldn't that make things worse?"

"I'm sure it would," Su replied. "But what other choice do we have? She might stay in there for weeks. Plus I'll need to boil bones *eventually*, and that's what makes the ateli stink so much. I don't want to move her every time I boil bones. But if I don't, the smell will be brutal to her."

I didn't know how Su could stand being in his ateli when that rancid stench wafted from it. If he didn't have some magic that could block his olfactory organs, he must have had some sort of mask to protect the nose the same way my visors protected eyes.

"She's afraid of me because I'm a Wynnle," I said. "But she likes you, Su. Everyone likes you. Whatever you do, I'm sure it'll be fine because you have a way with children of all species."

He blushed, and to hide the color of his cheeks which would have given away his element, he hurriedly set down dishes so he could cover his face with his hands. "Oh, Ami-honey, you're too sweet to me. I will try to get her out gently first."

Liesle's face scrunched into a scowl as she stared with intense focus at the wall. "The kids think Miltico ran into the jungle, but they'll learn the truth eventually when he never comes back to reclaim Usana."

"And we don't know what happened," Su said in a low, conspiratorial tone. "Maybe he got lost, or got stuck somewhere and starved, or got eaten by a wild animal. Maybe he was killed by something venomous or poisonous. It doesn't matter. We don't know, so we don't need to provide details."

My stomach churned, thinking of all the lies I would have to tell my children. It was worth it, I told myself. It saved Usana. She would live, happy, free, and never go hungry again.

Su lay on his back in the ocean, wearing a stunning blue tail that shimmered in the sunlight. He stared skyward with two arms behind his head and two on his chest.

I sat in the koa-wood boat, ready to yank the nets when any fish came near. It wasn't a matter of *if*, but *when*. We had made deals with Deep Sea—in exchange for our uneaten food, he guaranteed we would catch fish any time we needed some. Typically, when Su was with me, it was not a long wait. He could coax fish into the nets. Long ago, when I'd asked why other Rubaiyans didn't do that, he had winked at me and hinted that he was using one of his magic powers. I had no clue what elemental power could control the actions of fish. I'd once thought it was Mind elemental magic, but Su confirmed he was not a Mind elemental, and I believed he was being honest. Was it Water magic? Fish were within the domain of the Water Goddess's authority, even if she could not command Deep Sea.

Neither could we, though he would bring a fish to us eventually, if Su didn't find one sooner.

"I had no luck getting Usana to come out today, either. I spoke with her at length, but she's... she's not mentally well, Ami-honey. I don't know if I can get through to her."

"Can you force her mind to change? The way you guide fish, for instance. Can you make her trust us?"

Su frowned, his eyes widened, and he let the arms under his head spread out gently with the sea's rocking motions. "I could. But is it right? Is it the moral thing to do?"

"Under normal circumstances, I'd say 'no.' But this is dangerous. Her life is in danger if she's not eating as much as she needs to. Plus we need to get her accustomed to our family. What if Lavina comes back? We still don't know what happened to her."

Su remained silent, a look of terror staining his otherwise perfect face.

"What's the state of..." I hesitated, not wanting to give a voice to my crime. "Milti's bones?"

"I have to boil them."

"Do you think shinigami are looking for them?"

"I doubt it. They would not have seen anything in that house, so they wouldn't know for certain where he was killed."

"He might have been awake to tell them."

Su splashed upright and threw his torso onto the boat. "Amiere, there are a million 'mights' that are beyond our control. Yes, a shinigami *might* have found his ghost, he *might* have been awake, he *might* have told them all about what happened, the shinigami *might* report it to Lord Sawyer, and he *might* care enough to punish you. Or Lord Lucognidus *might* have known you were going to do it a week before you committed the deed and all this fretting is pointless. He most certainly knows now, as he is The Infinite Wisdom, who sees all with his Twenty Thousand Eyes. So what's the worst that could happen?"

I wasn't religious in the least, but it was true the God Lucognidus knew everything ahead of time and could have stopped me...

Lucognidus, the Conqueror God, who had slain countless demons and expelled the rest from Aloutia and Hell. Sometimes a merciful God, sometimes vengeful. Who's to say he even intended to punish me? Maybe he was as disgusted with Miltico as I had been and intended for me to do his dirty work.

Maybe I wouldn't be punished, but rather rewarded. Or maybe he would let me have this one sin for free since he had let my daughter be taken from me.

No, that was dangerous thinking. I recalled a lesson from my days as a child when my teacher made us kneel before the Mind church's statue of Lucognidus. One must never try to solve the inner workings of the Mind God's schemes. His brain worked on a higher level than ours.

"Is there a point in hiding my crime if God already knows about it?" I asked. "I will be punished in the afterlife regardless of what happens to me here."

"Not necessarily," Su said. "We simply don't know what each of the realms are like, so it's pointless to ponder, but at worst, it's unlikely Lucognidus has absolute power over the Lightning Realm. It's probably ruled by regents who keep Sparkato under control. Those regents might be subservient to Lucognidus, or they might not be. It's all speculation."

"What have the Hierophants said the Lightning Realm is like? What do you think Tawny is doing right now?"

Su fell back into Deep Sea. Sunlight dappled the ocean in puddles of light. "It's a great place, supposedly. The Hierophants of the past have claimed the realm is ruled by a Demigoddess of Magnetism who manages the Lightning God while a Demigod of Circuitry rules the day-to-day affairs. Tawny is probably going to school, meeting new friends, playing kiwi-batte, all the things she used to do."

I laid back in the boat, staring upward at the Hollow Void just as Su was. The silver and blue moons were overhead, on opposite sides of the planetary ring. I lost myself reminiscing about Tawny.

Su's voice came like a melody, so soft and sad. "Will you give me your honest thoughts, Amiere? If I were to magically manipulate Usana's mind and memories, would you hate me? Would I be a monster?"

"I would not think that for a second, but other people would. It would have to be yet another thing you hide from the world, along with your sex and element."

A slight chuckle, his masculine laugh. "I'm quite good at hiding my secrets. Very well, I'll bring Usana home tomorrow, but she won't be the same person she was before. I won't completely change her mind, but... I'll make it so she doesn't run away. I hope... I hope the Gods forgive *that* sin."

It hadn't even occurred to me that mind control could be a sin. What other magic did Su stop himself from using out of fear it would taint his soul?

"Oh! There's a big ol' fish nearby. Get your net ready!" Su dove inside Deep Sea while I stretched out the net. Moments later, a purplefin swam straight into my net, making no attempt to escape or divert its movements even after it saw where it was heading. I wrangled it into the boat and bore a hole into its head with my claws. I'd always been told that was the most merciful way to slaughter a fish.

Su breached the surface and examined our handiwork. The fish was big enough to feed our whole family for tomorrow's breakfast.

Was it wrong for Su to manipulate Usana if it meant healing her from trauma? Was it wrong for him to manipulate a fish to its death to feed our family?

Yet another lesson from my volkhv-teacher came to mind. On the topic of good and evil... an action is good if it bears good fruit. An action is evil if it bears bad fruit.

Killing Miltico, kidnapping Usana, then wiping the trauma out of her mind... had borne nothing but good fruit.

I wasn't an evil killer. I was a hero.

Well, I couldn't go announcing that in public. No one would see it that way, since they didn't know what Miltico had done. I would have to keep my actions—good or evil—secret forever.

"Usana is an herbivore, isn't she?" I asked.

"I'm not sure. Lagodores are, but Yosoe can eat damn near anything. Her head and body are Lagodorian, but that doesn't guarantee the inside of her mouth or stomach are. Perhaps to be safe, we should give her a Lagodorian diet until we're sure. I'll gather enough fruits for her. Don't worry about slicing up any of this fish for her."

"It's a large fish. I'll cut her a slice, in case she wants it. If she doesn't, I suppose one of the kids can take an extra piece. Or I could. Now that my appetite has returned, I think I could eat this fish by myself."

Su gave me a pitiful glance.

"What are those sad eyes for?" I asked.

"Just wondering what you would have done if you weren't a Wynnle. You couldn't have hidden the body so well, otherwise."

I scratched the back of my neck. "I wouldn't have been able to hide the bones without you."

"We're in this together. If you get caught, I get caught. If you get punished, we all get punished. Don't fuck it up for all of us, Ami-honey. Please. Our kids deserve to have all their parents in their lives."

"Who would I tell, anyway? I rarely leave Steena Village, and I'm not going to blab to Phoebus Svelt about what I did. Come on, we got our fish. Let's head back to shore."

Usana Interlude

Master Scrimshander knew there were lions out there. Usana thought he was part of their group since he had been with the same lion who ate her daddy. Lions would eat her, too, if they thought she looked delicious. But if she stayed small and looked starved, maybe the lion would lose interest. She wouldn't make for a good meal. No, in fact, whatever energy the lion gained from eating her wouldn't be worth the effort to chase her down and hunt her. She had to stay like this. Being small was being safe. Daddy had told her that.

She was hungry, but she was alive. She was safe. Lions didn't eat hungry bunny-goats. Master Scrimshander gave her a lot of food, but she ate just enough to stay alive.

He opened Usana's cage with a funny-looking key made from bones. She wondered if it was a trap. Would he catch her and feed her to the lion if she left? Usana vowed she would not leave. Mommy was still out there, somewhere. She'd come rescue her. Usana wanted to live, more than anything else in the world. Live to breathe and eat another day.

Su Interlude

Su wanted to try one other method before resorting to manipulating Usana's brain. Despite Amiere's trust in him and the words of encouragement they had shared, he had misgivings about the morality of brain-control.

Su took the tool known as a 'bone-saw.' A strange, wicked tool that he could have never described to Amiere. Not because it was utterly incomprehensible, but because it was powered by Su's magic. It was a saw powerful enough to cut through bones and metal. It was symbolic to the Demigod of Bones, Garnet Skull, who had taught Su how to make it long ago when Su first became a merchant of bone and sought to summon the demigod in a ritual.

The bone saw cut through the bars of Usana's cage. The noise, heat, smell, and flying sparks as metal slashed apart metal would have scared her, but Su had put her to sleep—the kind of sleep she would not wake up from until he was ready. Technically it used the same principles as brain manipulation, but he didn't feel quite so bad about using it just to make someone sleep. He'd done it to Amiere and Liesle a few times when the kids wanted their attention in the middle of the night and sleep had eluded them afterward. He had used it on the kids more times than he could count...

The bars sliced clean off. One by one, Su cut them all. He had to make Usana move to the other side of the cage at one point, lest he risk cutting her, but that was the most egregious act of manipulation he'd done... up until then.

He lifted the top of the cage off and set it aside. Before he woke her up, he double-checked everything in the ateli was safe. She might panic and knock stuff down in her attempt to escape. Su had cleaned up so no random bones were laying around. Various apparatuses, mechanical and magical, were present, though secured. The cauldron in the other room holding her father's bones had the lid locked on...

Su experienced something like a flashback to his childhood. His first mother, Sumire the Ophidian, stood in front of a door. The only way out. He was trapped. Something in his mind broke that day.

A memory from his teenage years came to mind. His second mother, Susan the Demon King, stood aside and told him he could run out the door any time he needed.

Never trap a child in a room unless you want to traumatize them. Sumire's skull ended up as a crown upon his head, while Susan still lived.

Su knew what he was doing was wrong, traumatizing, and harmful in every way...

He sat in front of the only exit to his ateli, the door barred with femurs, and made Usana wake up.

She stirred, wiggling her Lagodorian nose, perking her ears, then sat up. Their eyes met.

Su smiled as sweetly as he could, as sweet as the Sugar his spouses called him. "Usana, how are you today?"

She stayed seated and silent.

"Would you like something to eat?" he asked. "We have plenty of fruit. Steenas, spinehair, kiwis, pitayas... Or if you'd like rice—"

"Where's Daddy?"

He licked his lips. "He's not coming back. He realized he couldn't be a good Daddy, so he left you with us and left. He knew we'd take good care of you."

"Did the lions scare him off?"

Su shook his head. If she continued to fear lions, she'd never warm up to the Wynnles. "No. He left because he wanted to start a new life, but he didn't think he could take care of you."

Usana was eight... Su had been eight when he'd killed Sumire. He'd had the presence of mind to know the truth of what he'd observed. No one trying to sugarcoat the experience could make him forget what had happened. Usana probably knew he was lying.

"How will I know when I can eat if Daddy's not here?"

"You'll eat whenever you're hungry. Are you hungry now?"

She stared, wide bunny-eyed. "I don't know."

How could she not know? Was she hungry so often that she didn't know what satiety felt like? Was hunger her default state? "Can you tell me more? When was the last time you ate so much that you couldn't eat another bite?"

Usana studied him as if he'd asked a trick question. "Um, when we lived in the field where the sun never set, there was one time I ate, but I couldn't eat another bite because Daddy said lions were coming and we had to run."

That was just sad. "When was the last time you made the *choice* to stop eating? No lions, no Daddy telling you to stop. Have you ever eaten and eaten, and gotten to a point where you didn't want to eat any more?"

She shook her head. "No."

"Do you feel safe with me?" he asked.

"You're Master Scrimshander," she said. "A Godblood. Daddy said you would hurt me if I disobeyed you."

"But your Daddy hurt you too, didn't he?"

"Only when I disobeyed him. It was my fault."

Yet another thing he'd have to deal with, one way or another. He could try talking her out of believing Miltico's anger had been her fault, but that could take years. Or he could just... touch her brain with magic.

Which was correct? Which was the morally superior choice? Or did he even have the luxury of a choice? If she remembered Amiere killing her father, Su could not risk her telling what she saw to lawkeepers or volkhvs.

"Do you remember seeing my husband, Amiere, recently?"

"The lion? He tried to get me out of the cage. He wanted to eat me."

"Oh no, honey, he was trying to stop your Daddy from hitting you. Would it be okay if you lived with me and Amiere and our family for a while?"

She withered down like a leaf in autumn. She covered her hands over her long ears, which she pushed in front of her eyes. "Please, no... no lions..."

Usana's eyes watered, her nose wiggled. She could not stand on her weak Yosoe legs, trembling as pathetically as they were.

This girl could not be cured of her trauma—not in any reasonable time frame. It would take years, or she might never completely heal. Seeing her cry strained his sternum and brought tears to his own eyes.

Su was not happy with this decision. He wished there had been another way. A better way. A way that didn't make his skin shiver with revulsion at his own actions.

He approached her slowly, crawling on hands and knees so he wouldn't tower high above her. He put a hand on the brown fur of her hand, softer than any fur he'd ever touched, even that of a vicuña or fungermine[1].

And he changed her. Forcefully, magically, cruelly but with kindness in his soul, he manipulated Usana's personality, her thoughts, her fears, her dreams for the future. More tears came to his eyes. Was it out of sympathy for her suffering or guilt about what he had done to her?

"Come on, honey. Let's go meet your new family."

Usana blinked a few times and smiled at him. "I can't wait to meet my new Daddy!"

Su shivered at the horror he had committed and hoped that one day he would forgive himself.

---

1. Two animals renowned for their luxurious, soft fur coats.

Chapter Twenty-Six: Lies

When Su carried Usana into the house, I was not sure what state I expected her to be in. I was concerned Usana would panic when she saw me and Liesle, and scream about us being 'lions.'

But whatever she was feeling now... unnerved me. Her eyes stared blankly ahead, her body barely moving. It was like the descriptions I'd heard of Living Doll Syndrome, an ancient disease that no longer occurred thanks to the mercy of Lucognidus, in which a person was born without a mind.

What did Su do to her?

He could apparently tell my worries based on my expression. "She'll be alright in a few days," he said. "Her brain needs to figure some things out."

He set Usana down. Her legs were stable enough to stand, though her skeletal body looked like it would shrivel away to nothing from starvation. He placed her right beside the vertebra table where the dolphin-skull rotary sat full of luscious fruits. If she'd lunged at them in that instant, I would not have stopped her. I would not have even scolded her.

"Hello, Usana," I said as I sat down in front of her. Maybe if I got down closer to her level, I wouldn't be as scary. She didn't flinch away. I half expected her to hide in Su's legs the way she had once done with Miltico. Or flee out the door.

"Um, I know this is sudden, but I'm going to be your Daddy now," I said. She'd called Miltico 'Daddy.' That word might not be good. "Or if you'd rather call me something else, you can. Eruwan calls me Papami. Fionn calls me Dad. Heli calls me Dadda. If you prefer any of those..."

Was she listening? Her big round eyes met mine. A sparkle from a crystalight behind me reflected in those massive pupils, blinking as if she had just woken up. She was aware, but I couldn't tell if she understood the words coming out of my mouth.

Her nose twitched and she gazed up at the cinnadyme censer dangling from the whale's vertebra in the ceiling. It had been recently relit and churning out a thick stream of whitish smoke.

"Do you like the smell of that?" Su asked, pointing at the hanging bowl. "Did you have cinnadyme at your house?"

"Grandpa's shop smells like that. It's nice. Tastes like food."

"Well, don't eat cinnadyme incense," I told her. "If you want to eat something that smells like it, we'll get some cinnamon for you. Maybe Su could make cinnamon rolls."

He grinned. "I would love to."

Liesle came in from Nio's room with our youngest daughter trailing close behind. She had been replacing all our old reed mats with fresh, new ones.

"Welcome home, Usana," she said as casually as if Usana had been with us her whole life. "Would you like to see your bedroom?"

We'd discussed the details last night. Usana might as well take Tawny's old bed. Well, *new* bed now that there was a new reed mat in its spot, but it was the same space Tawny had once slept in. Nio had given no indication of being either bothered or grateful to have a room to herself. She hadn't touched any of Tawny's old toys or clothes or even gone to her side of the bedroom. If Nio complained later, we'd find another solution, but until then, we assumed she would be okay with this arrangement.

Nio tugged on one of the palm leaves of Liesle's skirt, then pointed at Usana.

"That's Usana. She's going to live with us from now on."

Nio made a 'U' with her hand.

"That's right. She's going to sleep where Tawny used to sleep. Will you be nice to her?"

She pointed to herself, then made a 'C', then a 'U', then tapped three fingers against her other paw.

"I don't think Usana knows how to play troika, but maybe you and Cohaku could teach her."

Nio smirked and took a step forward. Liesle grabbed her by a wing. "Oh, not today. She'll need time to get used to being around us."

She cocked her head, but when Liesle was not forthcoming with an answer, Nio turned to me instead.

"Nio, you know how you don't like to talk? Even though you can, and it's not a sign that you're stupid, it's just something you've chosen not to do? Usana is going through the same thing. She has chosen not to learn anything new for a while. Give her a week or so, then she'll be open to learning troika." I hoped. It wasn't a very good metaphor. Hell, it might have been a terrible one, for all I knew. Try as I might to understand any of my children, or to make them feel better, I was an awful father.

Usana squealed, drawing our attention to her.

She looked straight at me, and this time she was *here*. Her mind, her consciousness, her attention, whatever it was... was on me.

"Pa..."

A spark of hope wakened in my sternum.

"Papami."

"You want to call him Papami?" Su asked, joyously, putting both pairs of hands together. "That's the same name Eruwan uses. Oh, do you want to call me Papa Su, as well?"

"Daddy said your name was Master Scrimshander."

Su crouched down and fretted with Usana's fur. "You don't have to call me that. I have lots of names with the kids. There's Papa Su, Mama Su, Mapa Su, Pama Su..."

"Mapa?"

"That's the name Cohaku gave me. She decided that since I was both a Mama and a Papa, she should combine them."

"Mapa."

Su nodded. "Do you... want to call me that?"

Usana wiggled her nose. "If it's okay."

"It's okay," he said, embracing her in a gentle hug. She squirmed away, squeaking, and tumbled on her side.

Su hurried to help her up. "I'm so sorry! Do you not like hugs?"

Usana curled into a bundle of fur and cried. "It hurt. I'm sorry, Mapa. It hurt."

Su stood and put a hand on his chin. "I wonder if she has any broken bones. Bruises and abrasions will heal, but if Miltico broke her bones, I'll have to treat them."

A flash of anger burned in my sternum. "If Miltico broke her bones... what I did was too good for him."

"Sugar, can you take Usana and Nio into their bedroom?" Liesle asked. "Maybe she just needs to lay down for a while. I have something to discuss with Mo Ami. I'll tell you later."

Su did as she asked. He helped Usana up and, crouching down while holding both her arms—unlike her father who'd hold her horns—guided her into the bedroom.

Liesle made a few hand signs to Nio, which I knew was one of her ways of communicating, and those signs, in particular, meant to give Mommy some space. I had a few hand signs of my own that I used with Nio, but she understood speech just fine, so I tended to just talk if I needed to ask her something.

There were benefits to hand signs, though. Nio was one of the few kids I could 'talk' to without making a noise. Useful when she needed something in the middle of the night and I feared sound could wake up Liesle or Su. With our tails, we always had enough light to see by, too.

Nio followed Su and Usana. Liesle took my hand and beckoned me outside.

We sat down together at the table made from a longman's pelvis. Liesle rested her head on her knuckles. "We need to tell Phoebus Svelt about Usana. Soon. Nothing about Milti, though. Have you thought of the lie you're going to tell?"

I gulped. "I'm going to claim I went to check on him and Usana that day, and then Milti ran into the jungle—"

"No. He'll see right through that. He'll think you threatened Milti and that scared him away. Tell him you never saw him that day. You have no idea where he went or why he disappeared. Tell him Usana came stumbling out of the jungle and Su found her near his ateli. If he asks you why Milti and Usana were in the jungle, suggest they were looking for the leaf that makes crazy sugar. Tell him Milti hinted that he was going to try to create crazy sugar just like Tico used to do."

I didn't know if Liesle was evil or genius. Maybe both. Would Phoebus Svelt believe all that? It seemed plausible to me, and the shopkeeper wasn't the most suspecting man.

"And if he asks if he can take Usana, refuse. Say that whatever she saw in the jungle traumatized her and she needs to be with parents who can watch over her, and she needs to be with kids her own age."

"That would work. And when she found Su, she bonded with him. I think... it's not obvious now, but I think she will grow more attached to him than to the rest of us. Su has a calming effect on her."

"Great. That's our story, then. Don't forget it. We have to believe it so strongly that we forget the truth. This must *become* our truth."

If you believed a lie strongly enough, and you were the only one who knew it was a lie, would it become the truth? That was the kind of question Mind volkhvs, merchants of knowledge, and the God Lucognidus would answer 'no' to, but they weren't here right now. It was just me and my family. There was nobody to dispute our truth.

Phoebus Svelt sat at his cashier desk with a pen and paper, going over accounts, when I entered. He looked up upon hearing the door creak open.

He hurriedly closed his ledger and shoved it aside. "Hello, Mr. Lasteran. What can I get you today?"

I ran my hand through my mane, stressed beyond my own comprehension. I had practiced what I would say to him the entire way into the village, but coming face-to-face with him, the words flew out of my mind.

"I... We... need to talk. About Milti." Gods, I was a mess.

"Oh, do you know where he's been? He said he would help out at the store, but he's been slacking off again! How can I tell an inheritance assessor in good will that he'd be a good successor? They would never agree. Nell will probably end up having to run this place when I'm gone, and then she'll have to deal with Milti's nonsense."

I licked my lips. "I don't know where he is. Usana ran out of the jungle, traumatized. We think she may have seen something that scared her—maybe a jaguar or elephant. She... she can't tell us what happened, or why she was in the jungle with Milti."

Phoebus held his breath, mouth agape. "You haven't seen my son?"

I shook my head. "I'm sorry, but we haven't. His wife is missing, too."

He threw the pen aside, tossed in the direction of his ledger. "Damn him! Why would he go so far out into the jungle? For food? We have enough here! Anything he needs, I could have gotten it for him."

"Liesle suspects he may have been looking for the leaves to make crazy sugar."

The shopkeeper slammed a fist on the desk. "What the hell is wrong with him?! I didn't raise him to be that way!" He got to his scrawny legs and came around the desk. "I've got to check on his house. Where's Usana?"

"She's with us now," I said as he walked past me. I followed him out.

There was nothing to see at Milti's house; Su and I cleaned that mess up. I did not stop Mr. Svelt from heading that way, though. Let him judge the scene for himself. Let him believe I had nothing to hide.

"What are we going to do with her?" he asked in a ragged voice. "I... I failed at raising two children, despite my best efforts. I thought I was doing well as a father, yet both my sons..."

He stopped at the banyan tree at the crossroads. I thought he paused to catch his breath, but when I leaned closer, a sob escaped his mouth.

"Mr. Svelt, it's not your fault. Children are their own people. Sometimes good parents raise bad kids and bad parents raise good kids."

"I can't raise Usana," he said between sniffs and sobs, keeping his head down, one hand against one of the banyan's aerial roots. "I don't trust myself. I'll fuck up somehow, I know it. Maybe she'll end up making crazy sugar, too. She'll have to go to the Wind church. Gods, how can I say that? How can I *think* that about my own granddaughter?"

I put my hand on his shoulder, hoping he'd find comfort in it. He didn't swipe my hand away, at least. "After Su rescued her, she... bonded to him, I suppose is the best way to say it. She's become close to him. She wants to be around him. I think... I think we should adopt her."

Phoebus swallowed and stood straight. "That's for the best, then. Sorry, I... had to take a moment to gather myself there. I dread what I'm about to see."

It wasn't going to be pretty...

I walked beside Phoebus all the way to Milti's house. Carambolas had fallen around his door and all across his deck. If anyone was living there, they would have swept the fruit away, if not taken them inside to eat. I half-expected Lavina to be back. I wondered what she would think about all this. Would she try to get Usana back? Would she only care about Milti being missing? Would she know I had something to do with it?

Phoebus was right to dread going in, but I also dreaded him finding something that would incriminate me. What if I missed something? A bone, a scrap of flesh, a drop of blood...

He stood at the entrance, the house open to the elements ever since I broke down the door. Its splinters were still scattered across the floor. His hands shook as they clutched the door frame.

"What happened?" he asked.

"I don't know," I replied. I hoped I sounded convincing.

Whether he believed me or not, I could not tell. He only stood there, silent and awed, continuing to hold the door frame for balance.

"Is there anything worth seeing in there, Ami?"

I had to choose my words carefully. What would I have said, had I been ignorant of what had happened here? "I doubt it. Do you want me to look? See if anyone is inside?"

"If you don't mind. Well, you have light, anyway. I would just stumble in the darkness. My horns are for quick discharges, not long-lasting light."

I went inside, holding my tail in front of me for light. My search was cursory and quick; it was only for Phoebus's sake. I knew I wouldn't find anything. Hell, if I *had* found something, I would have done my best to ignore it.

The house hadn't been touched since the last time Su and I came to clean it. Well, clean up Milti's body. The rest of the house was the same disaster it had always been.

Milti hadn't owned any crystalights, which didn't surprise me, given how expensive they were. I thought he'd use candles or glowlight lotuses instead, but the house was completely dark. How did he light it up? His horns had always been the same as his father's, better for quick shocks. Milti had always been bad at using the Lightning elementrons in his horns for *any* purpose.

I remembered a time when we were kids. He was angry at me because I had found out that tamarind branches were flexible, and hurt when you hit someone with them. I had hit him with it, just being playful, but he'd hated it. He'd tried to zap me with his electricity, but the pitiful sparks that flew out of his horns wouldn't have hurt a pili-pala, let alone an actual Lightning elemental.

Wait... was *that* where he learned to whip people with tamarind branches? Phoebus hadn't abused his sons, but Milti had learned abuse somewhere.

From me.

I held back from choking as I stood in the hallway, looking into the dark room Usana had once been caged in. Completely dark, no windows, no decoration. A bedroll and a pile of dirty clothes. The humidity would have suffocated me if my emotions weren't doing it well enough on their own.

Fuck, was I responsible for Milti becoming an abusive father? No... no, it was his own choice. He was a sapient person. Just like I had told Phoebus, sometimes good people raise bad children. It wasn't my fault any more than it was Phoebus's fault. Milti had chosen to become the kind of man he had become.

But it was my fault for teaching him one way to abuse his daughter.

I went back to Phoebus, on his knees, leaning on the door frame. He rubbed his forehead.

"Where did it all go wrong, Ami?" he asked. From the tone of his voice, he was on the verge of tears.

"Probably when Tico learned how to make crazy sugar."

Phoebus cried, quiet sobs and tears glistening in my tail light. "Please take care of Usana."

"We will."

"It's... best for her if Milti never comes back. I... I didn't know what to do for her, Ami. I didn't know who to talk to. All my contacts are merchants. I don't know any... any volkhvs or social services who could have... I knew what was going on. I couldn't stop it. I... I failed her, just as I failed my sons."

I crouched down beside him. "Please don't think of yourself as a failure. Being a parent isn't everything. And besides, there's still Nell! She's learning how to run the shop, isn't she?"

He wiped the tears from his eyes. "Ah, that Nell. Just wants to play music. But she's a damn fine shopkeeper. Music might have to be her hobby, rather than a career. I don't think she has the talent Orienna has for piano or song."

"She can take care of the shop after you're gone, Mr. Svelt. Come on, let's take you back home." I helped him to his feet.

"I can get home on my own," he said. "Go back to your family, Ami. To Usana. Give her the life I couldn't. Oh, come on down to the store tomorrow for supplies. Take something home for Usana. She... she needs things. Clothes, food, toys. She can have it all."

I nodded, grateful for his assistance. "Thank you, Mr. Svelt. The kids don't have school tomorrow, so I'll come by later in the day."

"Oh! If it's not a school day, then Nell will come by early to help out. Could you come by early in the morning, Ami? I want to give you some things without Nell knowing. I, err, don't want her to get jealous."

"Jealous? I think she'd be okay with Usana getting the supplies she needs to live."

"Please, Ami. Please come first thing in the morning."

I blinked, confused, and swallowed. "Sure. I'll be there as early as I can."

Nell Interlude

Nell had told Grandpa Svelt she'd help out in the store on some of her days off. He was getting old and clumsy; the old man needed all the help he could get. He'd taught her bookkeeping, ordering stock, and introduced her to many of the regular merchants who came through, most going down The Corridor, but some traveling up the North Corridor Road to Seabells. She knew he wanted her to take over the shop when she was older. Her biological father thought the store would be his, but Nell would fight him for it if need be. And after she became an adult, an inheritance assessor would probably give it to her instead of him, due to how pitiful his current life was. One look at his crummy house, and they would know he couldn't be trusted to keep an establishment orderly.

When Nell entered, her grandfather wasn't at his desk. He was probably in the back room, checking on stock. She hollered so he could hear her, "I'm here now!"

Usually, he came out to greet her, but this time she was greeted by nothing but silence.

Was the old man losing his hearing now?

She went into the backroom...

His body swung from a rope tied around his neck, hanging from the rafters.

Chapter Twenty-Seven: Suicide

I was always the first one in the family to wake up, so I had no doubt I would get to Phoebus's shop early, perhaps even earlier than he wanted me there.

In the middle of the night, Nio shook my arm until I woke up. She probably would have gone for Liesle normally, but it was her turn to be in the middle of the bed, and I took the spot closest to the door.

Nio rubbed her eyes drowsily, frowning. An unfamiliar cry echoed from across the hall, coming from her bedroom. Usana.

I shuffled to my feet, patting Nio's head in affirmation. When I stepped beyond the leaf-door, I unwrapped my tail and let my light shine. In Nio and Usana's room, Usana sat crouched in a corner, her head down and between her knees. Her horns flickered with electricity, but she was unskilled at keeping them lit for long. I wondered if Milti had ever let her practice. Probably not. I couldn't imagine him being okay with his daughter having better control over her electricity than he'd had.

I crouched beside her, tail in my hand for light to make sure I didn't step on any toys as I crossed the room.

My presence startled her. She lifted her head, perhaps sensing my light or footsteps, and shoved her foot into the floor, pushing herself back into the corner.

"What's wrong, Usana? Do you need something?"

"Daddy?" she asked.

"I thought you wanted to call me Papami," I replied. "What's the matter? Can't sleep?"

Her eyes locked onto my tail. I lowered its intensity.

"Papami," she whispered.

"Right. I'm Papami."

She held her paw up as if to touch my light and... oh fuck, she was a Plant elemental. Could she be hurt by electricity? In my sleepiness, I'd almost hurt her! I brought my tail behind me, out of reach, just in case she wasn't immune. Sure, she had Yosoe horns, but I'd never seen them activated, and I was unsure how elemental immunities worked with hybrid children.

I could still see her, dim though it was. My pupils grew wide to soak in as much light as they could. Usana put her hands on her chest and breathed deep.

"Darkness," she said. "Monsters. Lions."

Oh no, not this 'lions' mud and sludge again. I thought Su got her to stop thinking of us as lions!

"There are no monsters or lions," I said, perhaps a bit more curtly than I should have used on a child.

"Daddy said monsters and lions will eat me in the darkness. Stay in the light. Stay on the Eversun Hills[1] . Daddy said that."

"Did you live on the Eversun Hills when you were on Cosmo?" I asked.

She nodded. "Daddy said we'd be safe there. Then he said we had to move to Aloutia. It gets dark here." Usana sniffed. "I hate the darkness! Monsters will get me! Lions will eat me! Daddy said so!"

She was afraid of the dark, and no wonder, when she'd gone her whole life without knowing what night was.

"Do you want to sleep in the living room?" I asked. "We have lights out there." Crystalights, carved by my own hand. They would glow for several decades still.

Usana put her paw on my leg. "I want to sleep where there's light."

I held out my arms for her to climb into. "Alright, let's go to the living room. I'll relight the cinnadyme and you can enjoy the smell of that, too."

She hesitated, looking at my arms, then my face, then my arms again. She lowered her head so her horns rested in my hands. I stepped away, lifting my hands. "Not like that. I won't grab you by your horns."

Gods, the fact that she thought it was the natural way a father carried his daughter... yet another trauma we'd have to work out.

"Do you want me to carry you?" I asked.

"I can walk."

I wondered if Usana only replied that way because she had been punished in the past for needing to be carried. Maybe it would be a good idea if I showed her it was okay.

I picked her up, which elicited a squeal and trembling paws. I brought her small body close to my chest, cradling her like a fragile doll. Her fur was softer than anything I'd ever touched, and she shook like a... like a rabbit staring down a lion.

I took her into the living room where crystalights shone through blue coverings, giving the room an appearance of being underwater. We put covers on them at night, otherwise they'd be too bright, but it was enough to see. And, hopefully, enough to pacify Usana's terror.

Near the pillow pile was a long crystalight shaped like the fingers of Deep Sea, blue with undyed tips for the whitecaps. I uncovered it, thinking its gentle, blue luminance would not be too distracting of a contrast while adding a touch more

---

1. The top of the hand of Cosmo's Starsine planet. A sun hovers above it, never setting.

brilliance and clarity to Usana's surroundings.

"Is this bright enough for you?" I asked.

Usana's eyes were tinged blue by the light. No, her whole body was a faint blue. Soft, soothing. As Deep Sea's fingers crashed along the beach just outside, it truly felt like we were underwater.

As I promised, I lit a cinnadyme stick with my tail and set it inside the censer. Soon, the room carried the scent of sweet cinnamon pastries. Had any mozzies been in here, they would have quickly fled to safer skies.

I laid on the pillows, placing one over my tail after extinguishing it. Usana wiggled off my chest but stayed between my torso and arm.

Nio had followed us out and looked upon us curiously. She put a paw up to her mouth.

I raised my other arm for her. "Come on, Nio. You can join us if you want."

A smile brightened her face and she quite literally jumped into my arm—using her small yellow wings to help carry her a few feet through the air.

"May Somniel give you a peaceful sleep," I whispered to them.

Usana must have not known the response. Nio wrote a 'Y' for Yume on my chest.

With the two girls snuggling beside me, nudging their faces—and Usana's horns—into my side on occasion, sleep did not come easily. Just as I was about to drift off, another jab would poke my side.

I had to wake up early to get to Mr. Svelt's shop first thing in the morning. For whatever reason, he insisted I get there before Nell.

Finally, sleep came, and no amount of prodding woke me up.

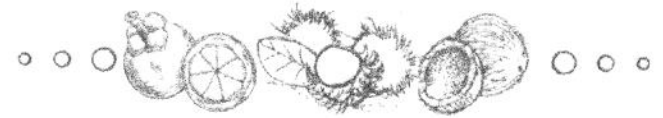

By the time I roused awake, the whole family was up and finishing breakfast. The smell of cooked fish, fresh mangoes, and papayas made my stomach growl. Liesle and Su, carrying dirty dishes in crates to be taken out for washing, stopped to talk to me.

"Spirits bless this day," Su said. "Hope you got enough rest."

I rubbed my side, sore from the prodding it had gotten from Usana's horns throughout the night. How on all the planes did Yosoe sleep together? Did they ever cuddle? I was half-tempted to ask Giorvi if his wife ever poked him in her sleep.

I could ask Phoebus Svelt, too, since I would see him soon, though bringing up memories of his wife while he struggled with his son's 'disappearance' hardly felt diplomatic.

"Damn, I didn't think I'd sleep in! Mr. Svelt asked me to come in early."

"Oh, don't be in such a rush," Liesle said dismissively. "At least eat breakfast first. You can take care of business later."

She was right. Whatever Phoebus wanted from me, it couldn't possibly be *that* urgent.

Usana sat at the table with a partially-eaten bowl of rice, half a pitaya, some rambutans, and mango cubes—diced by Liesle's precise fingers if I had to guess. The other kids had left the table already; I heard their shouts outside as they called to get a kiwi-batte.

"How was breakfast?" I asked Usana as I sat across the table from her. I piled fish and fruit on my patella-plate as I waited for her response.

She stared at her patella, sad and forlorn, tears budding in the corners of her Lagodorian eyes. "I'm sorry."

"About what?" I asked. I swear, if she told me that Miltico beat her for not cleaning her plate, I'd... I'd wish I could kill him twice. As my teeth tore into fish meat, I remembered tearing into *his* meat. Yosoe flesh and muscle, so similar to goat.

"Wasting food."

Yeah, I had no doubt my fears had happened. On Cosmo, food was not as plentiful as it was on Aloutia. Though if Lagodores could eat any vegetation as I'd been told, there should have been no shortage of grasses, ferns, and leaves on the Eversun Hills.

"We'll give the rest to Deep Sea, and he'll feed it to the fish. Nothing will be wasted."

Usana's floppy ears twitched and she glanced up at me. "Really? We can give Deep Sea everything we don't want?"

"Well, he'll take food. I suppose if you wanted to get rid of something that wasn't food, he would still take it, but he might not be excited about it."

"What does he do with things that aren't food?"

I scratched behind my ear. We had stories about it, but I didn't know if it was the truth. "He pulverizes them just like he does with food, but instead of giving it to his fish, he decorates beaches with it. That's what sand is."

Usana shook. "Pulverize?"

Was that a word she didn't know? "Sorry. It means he grinds it up into... well, into sand."

"Daddy said if I didn't obey him, lions and longmen would pulverize me. I didn't know what it meant, but longmen are big. I thought it meant they would step on me."

My blood boiled, but I had to keep a calm countenance. I didn't want to scare Usana. Gods, after all Su went through to make her trust us...

I focused on eating for a few minutes, but eventually, the silence grew too heavy. "You never have to fear lions or longmen ever again. As long as you stay here on Aloutia, anyway."

She lowered her head and played with a mango cube. I thought she would eat it eventually, but I finished my fish and she hadn't taken a single bite since I'd sat down. Was she waiting for permission? No, she'd eaten *some*. Maybe she was full and was waiting for permission to leave the table.

"You don't have to eat if you don't want to," I said. "If you're ready to go play outside, you can."

Usana rose and looked toward the leaf door over our entrance. "Do I have to?"

"You don't have to do anything," I said with a mouth full of rambutan. "Are you scared they'll hurt you?"

It was a fair fear, to be honest. Though if one of the kids scratched her by accident and went berserk, I was right here. They knew to come find me or Liesle. Regardless, Usana didn't answer, and I suspected it was because she feared getting an angry response from me.

"You can stay inside and play," I said, finishing up the last of my breakfast. "There are plenty of toys here you can play with. Su is almost done cleaning the dishes, too, so maybe he'll play with you."

Usana nodded. "I want to do whatever Mapa Su is doing today."

I pointed up at the chore board, in case she hadn't known what it was. "According to that, he's just doing housework today. Perhaps you could help with dishes or making clothes?"

"I'll do whatever I have to do. I just want to be with Mapa Su."

"I don't think he'd object to that. Anyway, I'll be back soon. I have business in the village." I put on my sandals and left for Phoebus Svelt's shop.

Dozens of villagers had gathered around Phoebus's shop and it didn't take long to find out why. One of the apiarists who worked with Piotr broke the news to me.

Phoebus Svelt had committed suicide in the night by hanging himself from a rope. Nell had been the one to find his body.

I stood still, dumbstruck.

Fuck.

That was why he wanted me to come so early. He was trying to save Nell from the trauma of finding him.

I put my hand over my face and cried. Not for Phoebus so much as for Nell. She didn't deserve this. She lost her cousin, now her grandfather… The image of him swinging from the rafters would never get out of her head. Just as I could never forget Tawny's final moments, so too would Nell never forget *that*. We would relive our traumas in our heads for all eternity.

The villagers shuffled me into the store where Orienna and Piotr held their crying children. Nell had to be held in Orienna's powerful arms or else her trembling Yosoe legs would have given out.

"Amiere, good timing. We were about to go fetch you," Orienna said as she rubbed a hand through her daughter's hair. "You and Liesle are strong. Would you be willing to carry Mr. Svelt's body to the Death church in Seabells? I know you've seen your share of that dreaded place recently, but... I need to stay here with Nell, and you two are the strongest people in the village."

"I'll do it," I said absentmindedly.

I went through the motions for the remainder of the day, all while my mind replayed the warning signs in my head. I should have known he would do this. I should have... what? Stopped him? How could I have stopped him, short of moving in and living with him, staying awake every minute of the night? Usana already took away most of my sleep. I wasn't responsible for the mental wellbeing of a man old enough to be my father.

Still, it was tragic that it had come to this. Poor Phoebus Svelt... he didn't have anyone to talk to. No close friends or family, other than his granddaughters, and he wouldn't have wanted to burden them with his problems. Especially when his problem was their dad. Gods, if only there had been someone he could have talked to. Why couldn't there be a church service where the volkhvs listen to people who are going through tough times and maybe try to find solutions? Or maybe just listen, if that's what the person needs? Maybe the Lightning volkhvs could take up that job, instead of being quartermasters preparing for war in a land that had been at peace for the last century.

After I delivered his body to the Death church, I would have to focus on the here and now. Focus on those who were still alive—his granddaughters. Usana needed support, but Usana barely knew him. Nell, though... Oh Gods, would the inheritance assessors let Nell take the shop? And if not her, then who? His shop was one of the only sources of imported supplies in the village. Nobody wanted to take the hours-long trip to Seabells just to pick up a clove of garlic and some kyamo herbs.

Was Nell ready for that? She was only fourteen, almost fifteen. The assessors were wary about giving businesses to children, but they were known to make exceptions if the child was competent and eager. Perhaps Nell would need help from professional businesspeople.

I may have had the title of 'merchant', but the merchants of light were hardly merchants at all. Still, I was her uncle, and I would do what I could to help, even if that meant asking someone better at business than me for advice. Giorvi would know what to do. I knew he'd visit again on business soon, and when he did, I would ask him if he could give any advice to my niece.

That was assuming she took over the shop. She was just a child. How cruel to ask her to grow up so fast.

Over the next several days, Steena Village sorted itself out. Running the village shop had become a group effort, though it was understood it would go to Nell when she came of age. It was projects like this that made me appreciate our little village. One of the teacher-volkhvs at the Mind church took over operation of the shop, invoking Mind elemental economic law while we awaited Nell's ascendance to adulthood. This ensured everyone would get what they needed, but they would not pay with money. While this wasn't the same volkhv I had once donated a crystalight to, she had accepted that donation as sufficient for the whole Steena Village Mind church, and exempted me from paying forever. I had brought light into her life for the rest of her life, and she intended to see that I would get whatever supplies I needed. Traders bringing things into Steena Village would also be required to accept non-monetary goods in exchange or sign an agreement that we'd pay later.

In actual Mind elemental societies, there was no option to pay later. Traders had to accept bartering, or else they would not do business with Mind elementals at all... and refusal to work with Mind elementals was a sin. The greediest merchants in Aloutia would not tempt Lucognidus's wrath by refusing food to his followers. Some would say the God was a cruel dictator, making people work and donate to people they'd never met. Others would say it was the only way to keep our perfect society where nobody starved or went homeless. Well, nobody starved so long as they weren't kept in a cage and beaten for touching food...

I wondered if Miltico would have faced the wrath of God eventually. When I had been a child, forced to kneel before Lucognidus's statue in school, the Mind volkhv filled my brain with stories of people who'd been cruel, abusive, or greedy, who had suffered divine justice when one of Lucognidus's Twenty Thousand Eyes fell upon them.

I went to the shop a few days after Phoebus's death to get a few goods. The volkhv was clad in their standard uniform—a purple dress with a black undercoat and lacy black trim, a high black collar, and a cylindrical hat, all adorned with artificial pavo feathers. She traced her pen through the accounting book. She had insisted on taking over this job for the time being, not only because the money situation would be more manageable with a Mind elemental in charge, but also because Mind elementals were generally better at certain mental tasks. She could keep track of each trade and exchange far better than most people could. But moreover, she had the sense of justice and morality to not hurt anyone or seek profit for herself.

This same volkhv had said Cohaku and Nio would likely develop similar mentality. They called it 'living in one's own plane and timeline.' It was normal for Mind elementals but rare in others. For two of my daughters to have it suggested a genetic link, though no one else in Liesle's family had it, and on my side, I only knew my mother. The volkhv was unsure if it was genetic or chance, but had told us not to worry about genetics too much. That kind of thinking could lead to thoughts of eugenics—whatever that was. Apparently, it was something Cherish the Monster had dabbled in, but I didn't understand the first thing about it. How Cohaku and Nio's mentality could lead to a third person committing genocide was beyond my understanding, but perhaps I, too, was living in my own plane and timeline.

"What do you need, Mr. Lasteran?" the volkhv asked, not taking her eyes off the ledger as she scanned a page with rapt attention. "Or are you here for your mail? Two letters from Mr. Onoretti. Likely the same thing."

"Probably. He has no faith in the merchants of mail."

She set the two letters on the counter. "He's smart."

The merchants of mail had their own internal gangs and turf wars. It was said if you wanted to send a letter, you had better send five copies on five different days, to make sure each one went with a different merchant. One of them might reach the recipient. It was exaggerated, of course, though I couldn't say how far the truth had been stretched. There had been times when I'd sent three letters and only two arrived at their destination.

I had come to the store for some salt and butter. Unlike the merchants of mail, the merchants of salt could be counted on to supply their wares. While there was no such thing as a 'merchant of butter,' I knew this butter had come from the jeweled elephant breeders in the north of the village. Elephants also provided milk, cream, and physical labor. Aloutian elephants were gentle, majestic creatures, jeweled along their foreheads, ears, and down their trunks. They eagerly helped however they could in the sugar cane and rice plantations. They produced milk for over two years after giving birth, and one elephant's milk could feed her own baby and twenty families here in the village. Our family did not eat much dairy, though because Liesle struggled to breastfeed, we were reliant on elephant milk after each child's hatching. In addition, every spring, the elephants shed their tusks, which would be bought by merchants of bone. Su had laid claim to every tusk produced by Steena Village's elephants.

I left with the supplies and letters. I went into my ateli to read Giorvi's letters, just in case they said anything that was meant to be confidential merchant of light business. As I suspected, the letters were identical copies of each other. Duplicated in case one was lost forever in some stupid duel between rival merchants of mail.

Giorvi planned to come to Steena Village again on business. Complications with the crystalight mine required his direct supervision for a few days. He wouldn't say what the complication was, exactly, but he may have been keeping it a secret from nosy merchants of mail more so than from me.

He also wrote more details about the commission he wanted for himself: a crystalight in the shape and color of the moon Aurora, with its vibrant tail serving as a base to hold it upright.

I was in a mood to work today. Or rather, I was in a mood to hide myself away from the chaos outside. Liesle and Eruwan were arranging things for Phoebus's fire feast. Su, Fionn, and Heliodor were trying to get Usana comfortable with Maika.

I had finished Tawny's crystalight yesterday. It was... done as well as I could remember her. My memory of her had faded. I could not picture her face as clearly as I once had. Perhaps some of the spots weren't exact. Perhaps the mane was a bit fluffier than she'd ever had it. Perhaps her mouth didn't quite have that tilt when she smiled. But at least she was smiling, just as she was in my memories. A smiling, happy child, eager to conquer the world when she grew up.

I would present the crystalight to the rest of the family when Su finished the memorial. He would have had it finished a week or more ago, but kept having to pause for other projects... such as covering up murder.

A knock came at my door. Cohaku wanted an escape from the loudness as well. In silence, wearing her visor as I'd instructed, she watched me begin the creation of Giorvi's commission of Aurora.

I started with a box-shaped crystal, which was how many were brought to me by the Domovye. Crystals grew in large chunks or veins, but it was unfeasible to transport them as such, especially the ones that grew monstrously long. Miners removed pieces gradually as they uncovered more of the vein.

I had always wondered why crystalights grew in veins like that. How did they know to clump together? Well, I was no geologist—I was just a merchant of light, carving away, making money to support my family.

My claws were useful for precision work, but that would come later. When I had a solid chunk, I needed tools to take off larger pieces. I would save some of those chunks for my own projects. One idea I had was to make rings for Usana's horns. That way she could wear light wherever she went. She could go to sleep wearing them if she wanted. I hoped that would help ease her fear at night. But Nio couldn't sleep if there was any light in her room... Maybe if I dyed it dark enough, it would be bright enough for Usana, and dim enough for Nio.

"Cohaku, are you sleeping well?" I asked.

"Yeah." That was it. No expanded answer.

"Is it ever too dark or too bright?"

"No. Eruwan keeps her tail off. If it's ever too bright, it's because my tail cover came off."

"You like it dark, then?"

She nodded. "Yeah. Even when my eyes are closed, I can still see light through my eyelids. I hate when that happens. Err, when I'm trying to sleep, that is. I like light when I'm awake."

I had a feeling she added that extra bit only because she didn't want me to question why she was here, watching me carve crystalights, if she claimed to hate light. Poor Cohaku was always worried about people misunderstanding her. If her answer wasn't a simple one-word answer, it was overly complex so no one would misinterpret her.

As far as I knew, Eruwan had no preference regarding the levels of light in her bedroom. We might have to swap some of the kids' sleeping arrangements, but if we finished Eruwan's house soon, that would be irrelevant. She'd move out, and Cohaku would have the room to herself. If Nio wanted darkness, she could move into that room, thus letting Usana have a brighter room.

It only made sense, as a parent, to listen to my children and see what I could do to make their lives more comfortable.

Chapter Twenty-Eight: Savior

The memorial was completed. Su brought it into the house and set it in a special spot near some shelves where we displayed some crystalights and the kids' various art projects.

The upright posts were made of femurs grafted to vertebrae for stabilization, a shelf beneath the main table was made from two scapulae, and the top piece—a flat table—was made from hip bones. Crisscrossing ribs connected pieces and added to the overall structural support.

With a heavy sternum and tears forming in my eyes, I placed Tawny's bright crystalight on the top. Su put the bell she'd always worn on her tail next to it. Liesle placed a miniature painting she'd made depicting a sunset over Kiwi Island. She had never mentioned that she was creating a painting, but it was no surprise to any of us. We wanted her to continue to paint as much as she needed to express herself, whether for therapy or any reason she needed.

"I'm working on another piece," she said in a raspy voice. "I'll bring it here when it's ready."

The whole family stood in silence for a moment that felt like eternity, but for all I knew, was probably less than a minute. The same length of time it took Tawny to fall to her death. Humidity was nothing compared to the clamp of emotion that wrapped its vicious claws around my throat and strangled me until tears came out.

I thought... I thought I had finished crying. I thought I had gotten all these treacherous, salty tears out of my body.

Su stood behind me as I fell to my knees, racked with sorrow as fresh as the day she'd died. Liesle and the kids gathered around me, putting their hands on me, some crying with me. Usana, too, put a paw on my arm.

"As you swim in the ocean of despair," Su said, "know that you will never swim alone."

My family was my strength, my anchor to reality, the force that allowed me to keep going every day. Tawny was gone, but the ones still alive needed me... and I needed them.

As the week came to an end, the family gathered around the chore board to schedule the upcoming week. Su had changed his name on the board to a muji I did not recognize, and he wouldn't tell me what it meant. But when he looked at Usana and his bright brown eyes shone and a smile spread across his face, I knew it was something to do with his feelings toward her.

The chore board still had Tawny's name on it. Instead of chores in the daily boxes, though, the kids had written things like 'sleep well, Sis.' Eruwan had drawn a picture of Tawny's bell. Fionn had drawn two simple figures of himself and Tawny eating kiwis.

I dreaded the day I would have to erase them. I hoped to convince Eruwan and Fionn to redraw those pictures on something permanent we could put on the memorial. Perhaps Eruwan could scrimshaw the bell's picture into a bone.

Eventually, we'd have to put Usana's name on the board, but I didn't think now was a good time. She was still adjusting to living with us. Asking her to do chores so soon didn't feel right. She didn't even know *how* to do some things. Su had mentioned earlier that he wanted to teach Usana how to weave grass clothes and prepare rice. First, she'd have to become comfortable even handling rice. Her abusive father had taught her never to touch food without permission. Su believed that if Usana could get comfortable handling food, some of her eating issues might be alleviated. Perhaps she would not fear starvation if she knew how to cook rice.

"Let's put her initial on the board for now," Liesle suggested. "So she can look at it and see she's part of the family."

I stared at the board, looking at Tawny's name. Usana would have gone in that spot, age-wise. She was younger than Cohaku and Heliodor, but older than Nio. But I... I couldn't erase Tawny's 'T.' I didn't have the strength to erase the messages and art the kids had drawn.

"You can put her at the bottom," Su said as if he had the same conundrum I had. "There's no rule stating we have to go in age order."

That would have to do. I drew a new row for Usana, extending the lines another level down. Then, where her initial would go, I wrote a 'U.'

"What is that?" she asked.

I pointed at the 'U.' "This? It's a 'U' for Usana. For your name. Do you know how to read?"

Her eyes widened, fearful.

"I don't think she knows how to read," Cohaku said, leaning casually on the vertebra table. "She's in our class at school, but Mys Volkhv takes her into a private room when it's time to read."

Su sat down at the table, eye-to-eye with Usana. "Can you tell me what you do at school? Have they been teaching you how to read?"

Usana opened her mouth, then closed it again.

Nio left the table, but no one stopped her, as we knew she was getting paper and pens.

"Can you read?" Su asked again. "Do you know the other letters on the board?" He stood and pointed to the 'A' for my name. "Do you know this letter? 'A.' Ahh. Ahh. Ahh-miere. This is Amiere's name."

Nio came back and put her paper and pens between her and Usana. She wrote out Usana's name, pointed at her, then back at the name.

Su scurried around the table to join them. He put his finger on the 'U' and pronounced each letter slowly. "Uuu... saaa... naaa. Usana. Do you like your name?"

She wiggled her nose. "It's the name Daddy yells when he's angry. When I did something bad."

A heavy silence fell over us. I hadn't considered the implications of calling someone by the name their abuser had used.

"Would you like a different name?" I asked. "We can call you something else."

She lowered her head. "I like... Su."

Su patted her head. "Oh darling, you're precious. It would be confusing if two people in the same household had the same name, though."

Nio wrote an 'S' in front of the 'Usana' written on her paper.

Susana.

Su's mouth hung open as the answer dawned on him. "What about that?" he asked. "Susana?"

She mouthed the word over and over, tasting it like a new food. Like food she had previously been denied.

"Can we call you 'Susana'?" Liesle asked. "Or is it too similar to 'Usana'?"

She tugged her ears. "I like that name. You can call me that."

And thus Susana was reborn. She likely didn't even have an official name, having been born on Cosmo and not yet made into an Aloutian citizen, but that would happen soon enough, and public names didn't matter. In our household, we called people whatever they wanted to be called.

After assigning chores for the week, there was one last matter of business to attend to—sleeping arrangements. I brought up my idea to switch Cohaku and Susana. All the girls were delighted with the idea. Even Eruwan seemed weirdly happy about it, and she had never mentioned having issues with Cohaku before.

I wanted to ask Eruwan about that in private, to find out if there were any problems between her and Cohaku I was oblivious to. It took until nightfall, but I finally had a moment alone with her when I asked if she wanted to check on her house. We hadn't worked on it much as we'd dealt with life, and the adults had our respective merchant work to do. As all our current projects would come to a finish soon, we'd be able to resume work on her house.

"We're hoping to finish sometime during the summer," I said as the two of us stood in what would become her living room. There was no roof yet, just whale ribs stretching up to the starry firmament. To my left, the lighthouse rose high, its brilliant light blasting toward the ocean. Although the crystalight's window faced away from the house, it was so powerful that the light emanated back and illuminated us in a soft glow notwithstanding the nighttime hour. Ringslight and moonslight high above certainly contributed.

"I'm excited for it to be done, Papami," she said. "What will become of my old room in the house? If Cohaku moves into Nio's room, will the new baby go into my room with Usana?" She shook her head, flicking her mane. "I mean Susana?"

"Probably," I replied. "Though, I'm concerned about the baby crying. We won't know until we bring them home and see how they do, but..."

"Usana—Susana—can come sleep in my house if she wants. I'll have plenty of light. I don't know if she trusts me yet, but... well, the option is there if she wants it."

I walked to the wall of the lighthouse, serving as one of the walls to Eruwan's house. "That's very kind of you. You seem happy to have her in your room now. Were things not going well with Cohaku?"

She fiddled with a long strand of mane-hair. "It's not her fault. She talks in her sleep, that's all. She'll get irritated if there's even the slightest noise or light. I think she'll be happier with Nio. And besides, I... I like Susana. I want to teach her things. Scrimshaw. Piano. Cooking." Eruwan blushed. "Is that weird?"

"Not at all!" I waved my hands. "Do you want to be a mother one day?"

She shrugged. "I'm not sure. I don't want to have sex, but Papa Su keeps saying I might be too young still to know if I'm a lotus or not yet sexually awake. I think I'm a lotus, though, so I don't think I'll have biological children. But I like the idea of raising kids. Maybe I'll adopt. If... if I take the Scrimshander name, I hope I can get my adopted kids to take it, too. Maybe there really will be a Scrimshander lineage one day. Papa Su would be so happy."

"I wonder if we should change Susana's surname, too."

"Probably," Eruwan said. "If 'Usana' reminded her too much of her father, obviously 'Demiu' is gonna remind her too much of her mother. Why not make her a Scrimshander as well? She's already so close to Su."

I grinned. "Your room is gonna become the Scrimshander Room then. And this house, if she does choose to live with you, will become the Scrimshander House."

Eruwan's mouth curled in a grin to match my own. "How appropriate, given it's attached to Scrimshander Lighthouse."

"Knowing Su, he's probably already plotting to get Susana to take his name. You saw how his face brightened when he saw her new name."

"You should go check on him, Papami. I'm going to stay out here a bit longer and enjoy the night sky."

Eruwan had always liked walks along the beach at night, particularly while alone. We had no concerns for her safety; Wynnles were more than a match for anyone living nearby, sapienti or animal. She reminded me of Liesle in that way. When we were teenagers, we'd often walked along the beach together, collecting seashells, kissing, building sandcastles... We had delighted in the sight and scent of each other in the ringslight many nights.

I went back into the house, looking for Su. He stood in front of the chore board while everyone else went about their usual activities. Liesle was demonstrating to Usana how to weave a reed-and-grass skirt. Cohaku, Heliodor, and Nio played troika. Fionn sat in front of Tawny's memorial... carving a toy out of wood? I had never seen my son carving with his claws before. Maybe he'd be a merchant of light one day.

The others were far enough away I could have a private conversation with Su if we spoke softly.

I stepped behind him and put my hand on his lower back. "What are you looking at, Sugar?"

"Oh, wondering if my ego is too big for my skeleton. The muji I wrote my name with..." He put his arms on his hips. "I ought to erase it. But no one else here knows what it means, and it... makes me happy."

"What does it mean?" I asked. "Or are you not going to tell me?"

His lips parted in a slight, almost imperceptible smile. "It's pronounced 'sukui.' It means to rescue or aid. It means 'savior.'"

"Well, you did help rescue Usana," I said.

"Susana," he corrected. "It honestly is a better name. You might not realize it, but 'Usana' is a pathetic pun in Orochigo. It's a combination of 'usagi' meaning 'rabbit' and 'yanagi' meaning 'willow,' which is Ophidian slang for a goat—or a slur for Yosoe—derived from the word for goat 'yagi' and the stereotype that Yosoe are thin and weak like a willow branch."

"So her name was a combination of rabbit and an offensive term for a Yosoe? I knew Milti had no naming sense, but that seems cruel..."

Su hummed in agreement. "Her magic name is Usanagi, by the way. I found that out when I performed some demigod rituals to try and help her."

"Then let us never speak it again for her own safety. What about her surname? Will she be Susana Scrimshander?"

The name made him jolt, but he relaxed back into my arms. "If she would accept that... I... I would be the proudest parent. That's what I want to be. A parent, not a savior."

I grimaced. "We both rescued her. We're both saviors."

He sighed, his shoulders slouching. "The word is, perhaps, a bit more powerful than I like."

I kissed the top of his head as I moved my hands up to his shoulders. "In the past, you have pushed around your power when it suited you, *Your Luminance*."

He reached around my torso. Had the kids not been in the same room, I imagined he'd have put his hand under my skirt and pinched my ass. He liked to do that. I liked it when he did it.

"I don't want any more attention on myself than necessary," he whispered. "When I came to Aloutia for the first time, I was sought out for my Godblood abilities. Chancellor Mira wanted me to assist the merchants of magic. General Economos wanted me as a merchant of dance. Hell, I even went to a Godblood matchmaking ball once—the one where I danced with Lungidus Pavo and Loyenie Rathmusen. I almost let them talk me into the Emperor's schemes. I... I just wanted to live here, in peace and quiet. I wanted to forget I had magic abilities."

"Your magic comes in handy all the time," I replied. I scratched behind my ear, realizing what I said was stupid since I didn't even know what magic he had. "Well, I think you're using it in helpful ways."

He chuckled in his feminine manner. "Perhaps it would be more accurate to say I wish everyone else forgot I had magic. I don't want to be drafted into the merchants of dance, Ami-honey. But with the way things are going..."

I cocked my head. "What do you mean? How are things going? Is a war about to start?"

He hesitated before answering, his breathing slower under the weight of my hands on his shoulders, his sideways glance suggesting knowledge of things I could not bear to hear.

"It might. And so many of Aloutia's Godlights are dying. You know, it's a miracle this crystalight mine appeared when it did. Many cities needed fresh Godlights. Without this mine, the next war against the Makai might have seen hundreds of cities razed. Millions might have died. *Hundreds* of millions."

"How do you know all that?" I asked. "Was it in the newspaper?"

Phoebus Svelt had occasionally purchased newspapers from the press in Seabells, but by the time they got here, they were a few days old. I wondered if Nell or the Mind volkhvs helping her run the shop ordered them more often. It seemed like the sort of thing a Mind volkhv would keep in stock. Regardless, I had no interest in news outside of the village.

He lowered his head. "No. Letters from other Godbloods. I have a... a relative who keeps me updated."

"A brother or sister of your same element?"

A small nod. "I won't say who. I don't want to say who I'm related to."

"I know, Sugar. Don't divulge your secrets. Anything else in the report about the mine?"

"They've told me how the merchants of light are one of Aloutia's greatest assets," Su said, forcing cheeriness into his voice. "Get a crystalight in every city, and hope one of the Gods blesses it. Then demons cannot enter that city for eighty years. Or one hundred and eighty, in the case of the crystals under our village."

I rested my chin on his head, looking askance. "Why *is* the mine so different?" I asked.

Su stood motionless, quiet.

I listed the ways this mine was peculiar. "It's not in Iuria. It's smaller than usual. The crystals will glow for twice as long. Why? If the Goddess Machenerate made it, why did she choose those traits? Why not put it in Iuria? Why not make a large deposit?"

"Ami-honey, please, don't worry yourself about it. The more you try to find out 'why', the more miserable you will become when those answers don't explain the biggest why of all: 'Why was Tawny right there when the crevice opened?' You're doing your job. Just get crystals to every city. Then the one who should be called a 'savior' will be you. Think of all the millions of lives you'll save."

Tawny's face appeared in my mind's eye. She smiled at me, but... the image was hazy. A distant memory. What had her body looked like? Where had her spots been? I had never been more grateful to have finished her crystalight as quickly as I had. If I'd put it off much longer, I might never have a solid image of her in my mind again.

I did not want to be called a 'savior' when I could not even save my daughter. My precious Tawny. My adorable, tender child. Gods, I was already forgetting what she looked like. I let go of Su's shoulders and went to my girl's memorial.

Fionn moved aside, but didn't say a word, just kept whittling away at the wood block in his hands. He was making it into the shape of a kiwi-batte—a nice, simple shape; a good choice for his first carving.

I said nothing to him, worried that he'd be embarrassed.

Staring at Tawny's smiling face in the crystalight, I lost myself in memories.

Susana Interlude

She may have lost her fear of lions, but that did not make Susana any more sociable than she'd ever been. All her life, her Daddy had stopped her from making any friends. If they had ever stopped in a settlement, it would only be long enough to get the supplies he needed. Her mother didn't go out in public—the monsters of the city were thirstier for blood than the monsters of the wild, she would always say. At least the monsters of the wild only hurt you because they were hungry and saw you as a snack, or you'd scared them and they attacked out of surprise. The monsters of the city would attack you simply to revel in the cruelty.

The lion family wanted to befriend her, and though part of Susana feared it was a trick, another part desperately needed their friendship to be true. The strange feeling Mapa Su had put in her brain encouraged her to trust them. That feeling, like a slippery worm wiggling through her brain, was warm and comforting, but Susana feared it, too, was a trickster. Mapa Su's worm-minion who he sent to lull her into a false sense of security. If everything about her new life turned out to be a trick, it would be the cruelest one of all.

They invited her to the beach to play. She enjoyed making sculptures in the sand. Cohaku showed her how to make towers with wet sand packed in buckets. The lion girl liked to crown each one with a dominion shell.

"What if we accidentally hurt her?" Heliodor asked. "Won't we go berserk since she's not related to us?"

"Have you ever gone berserk?" Fionn asked.

"Once, when I was really young. I don't remember it."

"At the age you are now, you should have enough control over yourself that you won't hurt her. You might *want* to, but you won't."

Eruwan's mane fluttered in the ocean breeze. "I'm sure Papami will tell us to rely on him and bring whoever went berserk to him, but you can bite me, too. If it's an emergency, we shouldn't take chances waiting."

Cohaku looked up from the sand tower she was working on. "But you didn't want me to bite you when I bit Mr. Svelt. Oops." She covered her mouth and looked at Susana with wide eyes. Her tail light flickered, too, but Susana couldn't have guessed what that meant.

Susana knew that 'Mr. Svelt' was her Daddy, and yet... the funny worm in her brain made her not care that Cohaku bit him.

Eruwan patted the tower with her paws, smoothing the sides. "Yeah, and it was a pain in the neck trying to wrangle you and get that branch in your mouth so you wouldn't bite him again! And flying you back home was *awful*. I've been thinking ever since then that I should have just let you bite me. I'm big enough now I could have dealt with it."

"Okay, but what if Susana got hurt *really* bad," Heliodor asked. "Enough blood we all smell it and go berserk. Then what?"

Fionn and Eruwan looked at each other with determined eyes. Nodding in unison, they knew their duties as the oldest siblings.

"Fionn will bite me," Eruwan said. "And I will bite him. Then we'll make you all bite us. Hopefully you can keep your bodies under control long enough, or Susana can get away."

"Do you have a cage I could hide in?" Susana asked.

The kids all stared like she'd suggested something inconceivable. Even Nio, minding her own business as she built her own sand tower, stopped to gawk. In the following moment of silence, Deep Sea's crashing fingers were deafening.

"What did I do?" Susana put her hands over her chest nervously.

Eruwan took the girl's hands in her own. "You didn't do anything wrong, sweet Susana. We just... don't put people in cages. It's not nice."

"Really? But I'm safe there."

Cohaku gasped. "Oh! Maybe you need a place like my tree house. You're small, so maybe we could make a shelter for you that's too small for the rest of us to get to."

Heli tapped the ground with his feet, a little quirk Susana noticed he did sometimes when he was excited. "Nio is smaller than Susana now, but she'll grow. I could help dig a hidey hole!"

"Good idea!" Eruwan grinned. "We could construct something into my house easily, too!"

The kids discussed their plans in greater detail. For Susana, just knowing they were willing to help build a place for her to hide from them made her not want to hide from them.

These lions weren't so scary. Dare she believe they might even be friends?

Chapter Twenty-Nine: The Domovoi Day of Sapience

We had been productive with our respective jobs. A few days before the Domovoi Day of Sapience arrived, Liesle and I had completed our projects.

She'd finished a fantastic portrait of His Holiness, the Mind God Lucognidus, in all his glory. The God was clad in a peacock-themed crown, a pearl usekh[1] , and emerald robes. He stood against a starry sky, one hand raised so his tentacles eclipsed a violet moon. She would hand the painting to the Domovye today.

I had finished Susana's crystalight hornrings. They slid down about halfway from the tip to her head. I dyed them blue to help dim them sufficiently if she wished to sleep with them, and because she'd told me that she loved the color blue now. She associated it with Deep Sea and the sky, which she in turn associated with her new life—a life of love and safety, here with us. I had been surprised to hear she did not see the sky much when she lived on Cosmo, but apparently, those who lived on the Wynndalic Plains and Eversun Hills did not look up much for fear of being blinded by the Eversun. Most of Susana's life, she had looked down, seeing only dirt, rocks, and plants.

Now Susana brought light with her, carried on her horns. Wherever she went, the soothing blue aura of the sea and sky went with her.

We agreed to let the Domovye use the beach near our house for their celebration. They did not normally partake in fire feasts, given they were accustomed to living underground, far from Deep Sea. But they were not opposed to it, either. In fact, they were quite charmed to learn our traditions and rituals.

Domovye consumed minerals—gems, stones, ore—but they encouraged us to bring whatever food we would deem appropriate. It wouldn't be a fire feast without a bonfire, and it wouldn't be a bonfire without a goat roasting above it. The Domovye carried bowls of gold, rubies, sapphires, and iron ingots, which they stuffed inside the mouths on their torsos.

They put the painting of Lucognidus on display facing the fire. As the miners

---

1. A broad collar and necklace, intricately made. In the Pentagonal Dominion, they are associated with Lucognidus.

arrived, they would bow down before the painting and recite a prayer. Although they were Stone elementals, they worshipped only Lucognidus due to what he did for them—the event they were here to honor and celebrate: the day he made them sapienti.

My family joined the fire feast and Su performed a bone dance. He had been carrying Susana around, but while he danced, I had her in my arms instead. She claimed to have discomfort when she walked. I wondered if perhaps she just wasn't used to walking if Miltico had kept her in a cage when she was at home. Though I also thought they'd done a lot of running when they lived on Cosmo. No matter, that was the past, and I didn't want to ask her about it. Better for her to forget Milti ever existed.

It was a more joyous dance than the one he'd done at Tawny's funeral, and not as formal. As he danced in and around the flames, juggling his bones, some stopped to watch while others kept eating and chatting. As more Domovye arrived, they performed their obeisance to the portrait. The mating pair arrived and lowered their bodies together.

One Domovoi began the prayer. "Great God Lucognidus, Light of Sapience, Lord and Master of our dominion, conqueror of those who had enslaved us, you who elevated us to the exalted rank of sapienti. May you be enthroned in glory for all eternity."

The attached Domovoi continued. "May your enemies tremble at your feet. May your supplicants be beautiful in your Twenty Thousand Eyes. May the Domovoi species please you and serve you until time is undone."

In unison, they spoke the final part. "We thank you for the gift you have granted our species. We delight in the love and joy we bring to one another and to other sapienti. We shall forever strive to ensure our sapience is not wasted, that we will live, love, and learn as passionately as our ascended minds may allow. Let us not waste our minds, but forevermore seek enlightenment."

I sat on the fallen trunk of a palm tree, close enough to listen, though my focus was on Su. He dressed in nothing but bones, and a scant amount at that. Now there's a God I would worship... My heart raced just watching him gyrate his hips as flames licked his flesh.

"What does that mean?" Susana asked as she sat on my lap.

I snapped out of my fantasy. "What does what mean?" I asked.

"What the Domovye are saying. Why do they lower their heads and say those things?"

"They're sending a prayer of gratitude to Lucognidus for making them sapient."

Susana tugged at her ears. "Should I do that, too?"

"No need. He didn't make you sapient. Lagodores and Yosoe come from another before-world. Yosoe were made sapient by Hestar, I think. I don't know about Lagodores." I only barely remembered that tidbit from history classes because of the theory that the word 'star' came from her name. Ever since I'd learned that, I thought about it frequently when I looked at stars.

"Should we paint a picture of Hestar so I can thank her?"

I chuckled. "Hestar is from another dominion. She can't hear your prayers from here. Oh, and when Lucognidus conquered the world, he forbade the worship of before-world Gods. All the old religions were wiped away and we were to start anew with Spiritism."

She shivered. "Would I get spanked if I prayed to her, then?"

"No! Absolutely not! The volkhvs wouldn't hurt a child. As your guardian, they'd ask me why I allowed it. *I* would get in trouble."

"They'd... spank you?"

I imagined a five-foot-tall volkhv telling me to get over her knees. The image made me snort, which in turn made me feel guilty for treating Susana's legitimate concerns so flippantly.

"No, they'd probably have me perform penance by doing community service. Cleaning up the village or helping on the plantations."

"With the elephants?"

"Yeah, I'd probably have to help pack the elephants' loads."

"What if you say 'no' to the volkhvs? They can't force you. You're bigger than them."

"If a situation escalates, they can call the lawkeepers to restore order." For all that I believed lawkeepers would stay out of Steena Village, I had no doubt they'd come to capture a rogue Wynnle. "They could force me into prison. They wouldn't hurt me unless I threatened them. Though since I'm a Wynnle, they would likely be threatened by my very existence."

Susana touched her hornrings. "I don't want that to happen."

"Hopefully it never will." As long as no one found out I had killed Miltico...

The mating Domovye approached. "Excuse us for eavesdropping," one said. "But we heard the Lagodore-Yosoe child ask about her before-world. We are lorekeepers among the Domovye, learning about all sapienti history and sharing it in our collective thoughts."

"If you have any questions, we will answer," the other Domovoi finished.

That was useful. "Was it Hestar who made the Yosoe sapient?" I asked.

"Indeed. She herself was Yosoe. Or rather, a goat who consumed the Mind core and died when her body could not digest it. She became sapient as she became a Goddess. It's said that her first words were 'Yosoe sapiente' which meant 'I am sapienti.' The word for 'I am' later changed into 'Io sono' in Caprise. They took the old word 'Yosoe' to refer to the goats Hestar elevated."

"Hestar did elevate some of the big cats into what we now call Wynnles," the other Domovoi said. "Specifically, she made tigers sapient. Lions were made sapient by the Mind God Nureshishal. When the Time Goddess brought tigrine Wynnles and leonine Wynnles together in this timeline, they interbred with such frequency that they soon had no 'pure' members. The word 'Wynnle' came from Hestar's dominion. In Nureshishal's dominion, they had been called 'Llewon.'"

"There's speculation that the original inhabitants of the Nureshian Dominion were actually from the Hestarian Dominion, based on language. Anem and Draeg had enough similarities to the Slevan languages, including Caprise, that some connection seems likely."

It was starting to go over Susana's head. Or maybe just mine.

"And what about Lagodores?" she asked.

The two Domovye lowered their tentacles as if in shame. "Unfortunately, almost all Lagodorian history has been lost. Even the name of their home dominion is unknown to us, though the great God Lucognidus knows. The story of how the Lagodores lost their cultural knowledge is a... a grisly tale. I am not sure you should hear it at such a young age."

"Is it related to the Starry Sepulcher?" I asked. That was the phrase used to describe an ancient situation. It was a euphemism. I hoped Susana hadn't heard it, and judging by her lack of reaction, I assumed she had not. Miltico had likely taught her about it, but had not told her its name.

"Indeed, drook. It is what you are thinking."

In the distant past, before the Gods conquered the world, when Demon Lords claimed ownership of our souls, Wynnles used to hunt Lagodores. Perhaps the last Lagodore to know the name of their home dominion had their body consumed by a Wynnle while a demon took their soul. The concept of the Starry Sepulcher went further—Lagodores who had been hunted and consumed in life were kept in cages in the afterlife, where they were eaten every day by deceased Wynnles. Their heads were left so their bodies could grow back overnight. It's said those Wynnles would lock those Lagodore's heads in place, staring up at the starry night sky. A horrific tale, unsuitable for Susana's young ears.

"Yes, let's not," I said. "Susana has had enough trauma, and I don't want her being scared of Wynnles."

The Domovye both bowed their clusters of tentacles. As they were conjoined at the mantle, one had little choice but to bow if the other chose to do so. "A gift for the young Lagodore. May we bestow a glass treasure upon her?"

"We wouldn't refuse," I said. Domovoi glass was nearly indestructible. It was valuable, but moreover, it was rude to reject a gift from one. In ancient times, when Domovye were still animals, it was said they would leave glass pieces in the houses of people who took care of them kindly. When they were animals, the Domovye hadn't always made their glass smooth. Sometimes they'd left sharp shards. One who sought to collect their glass for future projects would have to watch their step. After they became sapienti, they were careful. They had learned *art*.

"Do you like the color blue?" the other Domovoi asked.

Susana nodded shyly. In addition to her blue hornrings, her skirt was dyed blue seaweed and she wore a belt of blue seashells.

"I ate cobalt prior to coming here," one said. "In hopes I would get to create beautiful blue glass works. I would be honored to give it to you, young mys."

Susana hid behind her ears. I laughed. "She's just shy. She might not be able to show her appreciation now, but I am sure she will love it later."

"Appreciation is not needed. We serve God, the Light of Sapience, for the good of sapientkind." The Domovoi who'd eaten cobalt curled their tail partially around so their rear-pipe faced to the side. They turned their torso closer, with the cooperation of their attached mate who had to slither closer to the other's tail.

The cobalt-eater put their hands in front of their rear-pipe. I nudged Susana, encouraging her to watch. She might not get a chance to watch Domovye in action for a long time.

Blue, malleable, semi-liquid substance poured out of the tube. The Domovoi's adroit hands shaped the substance into a bivalve shell. Heat rose from the substance with a slight glow. I wondered if it was dangerously hot and if Domovye were naturally immune or if they relied on Flamboil's Blessing to create glass. Although they worshipped Lucognidus, they were biologically Stone elementals and had to obey Machenerate's rules to retain their blessings. Her rules were common sense things, though: no killing, no child abuse. She also forbade the hurting of animals, which made life difficult for carnivores. I had heard of a Stone elemental Wynnle long ago who required all his meals be prepared by someone else. But Domovye ate rocks and minerals, not animals. They had no reason to break that rule.

They occasionally blew on it, not from their mouth, but from the other pipes on their back. As I understood, their mouth was only for food. The pipes led to the lungs, so any act requiring air occurred through the pipes.

I didn't think Domovye used their mouths in glass-making at all other than to consume the correct materials, but I was proven wrong. Near the end, they stuck the blue shell inside their mouth, where it hissed like when red-hot iron is quenched in cold water. When they brought it out, the glow and steam had vanished. They held it out for Susana to take.

"Umm..."

I took it for her, thinking she was scared it might hurt. She couldn't have been afraid of being burned—she was a child, and nobody could lose Flamboil's Blessing until they had become an adult. Perhaps she feared retribution for taking such a beautiful object without my permission.

"Isn't it pretty, Susana?" I asked, holding it out in front of her. "I could add it to your clothes later. Maybe something to wear on your belt?"

"Is... is it okay?"

"Of course, it's okay. It's yours. Go on."

She took it, holding it as carefully as if it were a newly-hatched baby. "It's pretty."

I nodded to the Domovye. "I think that's all she can manage to say right now. Thank you for the gift."

They bowed and joined their friends around a table covered in bowls of gemstones and colored minerals.

I had nothing better to do than sit here and hold Susana, and so that's what I did. Domovye milled about, only occasionally speaking aloud. Many of them were mates who could speak directly into each other's mind, so there was no reason to use the wind in their pipes for a private conversation.

"—the easternmost buried crystalight," a Domovoi said. "It's a small fang. Can't be larger than—"

"A wedge-piece," their companion said. Then in such a quiet voice that only one with sensitive hearing such as mine could have picked up, they added, "Never, *ever* call it what you just did in public."

A shiver ran through my whole body. Why the secrecy? I'd never heard a Domovoi whisper, if that was indeed a whisper. Briefly, I wondered if it came out of one of the smaller pipes. What was wrong with calling it a fang? That explained its shape just as well as wedge-piece. Perhaps even more accurately, if it tapered to a single point.

"Sorry. I'm not used to this, yet."

"Surface-dwellers only know about crystalights. They don't know Aye-too terminology."

Aye-too. Another name for crystalights. I'd heard that name only twice in the past. Once by Giorvi, who had called it that when I had been standing outside his office and he didn't think I could hear. The other was by the former Guildmaster of the merchants of light, a Domovoi who'd used the word aloud when they thought they were speaking via telepathy. I had no idea how 'Aye-too' was meant to be spelled. Perhaps it was I-too or Ay-two, or some other combination. Neither did I know if those sounds were words. Was the 'too' part the number 'two'? Or was it simply the word for crystalights in another language?

The Domovye moved on and spoke in quiet, hushed pipes. Too low for my ears to pick up, even as strong as they were.

"Well, Susana, what say you we mingle around with some people? Try to be a bit more social?"

She made a wordless noise that seemed approving. I held her to my chest and stood.

I wandered about, making small talk here and there. Su stepped out of the bonfire to eat and chat with some Domovye regaling him with tales of buried bones they had found. Liesle, carrying Nio, spoke to a group of Domovye about the finer points to her painting.

Eruwan and Nell were together by the boundary of the sea. Nell sat with her head between her knees, and Eruwan rubbed her shoulders. Poor Nell... she'd suffer from the trauma of finding her grandfather's hanging body for the rest of her life. We would have another fire feast soon, as a funeral for Phoebus Svelt.

Fionn sat under a coconut tree with Maika's head on his lap. The dog's morel tail wagged languidly. My son had a miserable frown on his face. I went closer and sat beside him.

"Tired of the feast already?" I asked. Usually he was the most eager of the family to eat as much as he could.

"I hate it," he replied.

"What for? The roasted goat is amazing. Su didn't skimp on kyamo leaves."

"We can eat goat any time we want," Fionn said in a sharp tone. "We don't need an excuse. If those damn crystalights hadn't appeared, everything would be better. The Domovye wouldn't have come to mine them, they wouldn't be here to take over the beach on their holiday, and... and Tawny would still be here. I'd be playing kiwi-batte with her right now."

I didn't know how to respond. I sighed and rubbed a thumb over Susana's ear while she put the blue glass seashell up to her face.

"I'm sorry you're still so down," I told Fionn. "I... I have some tough days, too."

"Is she going to replace Tawny?" he asked, motioning toward Susana.

"She's not a replacement, Fionn. Nobody can replace Tawny. Susana would have joined our family even if Tawny were still with us."

He lowered his head. "I know you're right, but... I can't help what I'm feeling."

"I know, son. Emotions are difficult. I wish I could say they get easier to understand as you get older, but they don't."

Fionn wiped a tear at the corner of his eye. "I'm sorry I'm such a mess. Everyone else has moved on, but I can't. Maybe there's something wrong with me."

"None of us have moved on," I said. "Tawny is still on our minds, every day. If you ever want to talk about her, we can."

He sniffed. "It's alright. I don't want to bring the mood down any more than I already have."

I put my hand over his, resting on Maika's head. "Don't bottle anything inside. Whatever you're feeling, let us know. Or at least let me and your other parents know."

"I'll be okay. I just... don't feel like doing anything right now. I'm gonna stay here with Maika."

"Would it be okay if I stayed with you, then? I don't have much to do either."

He closed his eyes. "Yeah, it's okay. Thanks, Dad."

Susana rubbed the glass seashell as she looked at us with big, bright eyes. "What was she like? Tawny, I mean. Do you think she would have played with me?"

Those questions were all it took for Fionn to light up like the break of dawn. Enthusiastically, he went on about how amazing his little sister was—no, *is*—because she was surely up in Spiritua at this very instant, laughing at us silly mortals for crying over her.

Chapter Thirty: Difficult Conversations

We had fire feasts every few weeks for a few months. Soon after the Domovoi Day of Sapience, we held a funeral for Phoebus Svelt. Nell broke down in tears, adding her mournful wails to the song her mother played on an ivory flute during the farewell dance. Demitris cried just as much. He wasn't related to the Svelts, but had known Phoebus as our village shopkeeper all his life. Perhaps he'd even thought of the old man as a grandfather, like Nell did. I wondered if Phoebus had considered Demitris his grandson, or if he had always been a painful reminder of Miltico's failure.

Egg Day came and went. We visited Seabells to watch the Life volkhvs place the eggs outside so they could bathe in the light of the Lime Moon. Our turquoise egg had grown bigger, but was still a few weeks away from hatching.

Every year, Life elementrons radiating upon Aloutia on Egg Day enhanced the growth of eggs and caused a higher-than-average number of babies to hatch that day. Tawny would have turned eight. No, she *did* turn eight, albeit in Spiritua. Demitris, also an Egg Day baby, was accustomed to celebrating his hatching-days with Tawny. He held up better than I had expected. We all did.

Eruwan's hatching-day was next and fast approaching. We would have a fire feast for this one. Not all hatching-days warranted a fire feast, or else we *really* would have them every day, given there was probably someone in the village with a hatching-day on any given day. But this was Eruwan's fifteenth—her mark of entry into adulthood. She would have to sign a certificate of adulthood proclaiming her public name.

Giorvi arrived in the village two days before Eruwan's hatching-day. As his letter had explained, he came to oversee some matter with the crystalight mine. His bodyguard, Oboro, accompanied him everywhere he went. I had gone to the mine to invite them both to dinner.

A Domovoi escorted me down into the crevice and through the tunnels. The crystalights that had been in this area before were gone, shipped away to a storage facility. Many had been stored in my ateli, as well. It was dark enough here I didn't need to wear a visor, but still bright enough to forgo the use of a lantern, which I would have had to use with my tail covered up for safety. The only crystalights that remained in this wall were specks. Walking down the passageway was like walking among the stars in the Hollow Void. Yet this place brought me no joy or hope, as the old saying 'may your path glitter with starlight' was meant to impart. Although this passage had undoubtedly been scoured by Domovye over the last few weeks, I could not help but look around... just in case so much as a hair from Tawny's mane remained.

We turned a corner, and the next shaft was held up by wooden support beams. Giorvi, Oboro, and a Domovoi stood at the end of the tunnel. A portion of crystalight peeked out of the wall. It shone brightly, but it was such a small window that Giorvi had turned on his horns for additional illumination.

"—her claw extended outward and upward—" the Domovoi said, then promptly went quiet as he saw me turn the corner.

"Mr. Onoretti, you have a visitor," my escort announced.

Giorvi grinned, his eyes closing briefly. He was dressed in a fine emerald-green coat with white vicuña fur trim. Oboro was dressed in sturdy leather, two hands on his side-swords. His scorpion-clawed hands were down at his side, but I knew it would take him only three seconds to draw his giant khopesh and slice every sapienti in this tunnel in half, if he wanted.

"Ah, Mr. Lasteran. I mean, Ami. I was not expecting you." From the tone of his voice, I was not entirely sure he was pleased about seeing me, either. It put me off-balance, mentally.

"Um, I just wanted to invite you to dinner at our house, if you had no place else to eat tonight."

Giorvi nodded. "Yes, I'd appreciate that. Oh, my apologies for my rough tone. This mine has been giving me a headache with all the problems it causes, but I promise everything will be resolved soon. I'm sorry for alarming you."

"No offense taken," I said. "I'll leave you to it, then. I hope to see you at dinner, too, Oboro."

The Sasorin boy blinked, surprised I had addressed him. He didn't speak up. I couldn't imagine Giorvi ordering him to remain silent while on bodyguard duty, however. Most likely, his silence was a holdover from his training as a slave.

"Yes, we'll both be there," Giorvi replied. "Thank you for your hospitality."

Feeling awkward, like I'd walked in on a private conversation, I blushed and shuffled out.

Susana's gait had gotten worse, and she preferred to not walk at all. Su had examined her bones and found nothing wrong with them. He had taken to carrying her around everywhere, except when he had to work in his ateli. On those days, Susana would stay in the house while Cohaku and Nio attempted to teach her troika. Their efforts were not going well. Perhaps Susana was in too much pain, or perhaps she just wasn't suited to troika, but she was not picking up on it. It didn't help that Cohaku and Nio were poor teachers. Cohaku stumbled on her words and sometimes forgot the words she was trying to say. Nio, of course, didn't use words at all, and seemed to expect Susana to learn by watching her move pieces across the board.

Su was on his way to his ateli, carrying a recent shipment of bones in bags, when he saw me returning home. He called my name and jogged across the sand, closer to me.

"I'm getting more concerned about Susana," he said, biting his lip and glancing downward. "I wonder if we should take her to the Plant church in Seabells."

"We need to take her there eventually," I said. "She's a Plant elemental. I don't know how to worship Cherribell, and I don't know if Plant elementals have any religious obligations. If Susana needs to be raised a certain way..."

"I don't think they do. Cherribell's heresy laws are sensible. Far more than Sparkato's, in any case. No murder or torture. Easy enough, right?"

I was a murderer.

Su blinked and frowned, realizing what he had just suggested.

"I don't think Susana will ever be in the kind of position you were in, Ami-honey. Don't worry about it. I may be wrong, actually. Cherribell might be okay with murder and torture. Stories claim Cherish the Monster was blessed, and she committed more murder and torture in two years than most Demon Lords manage in a century."

The Decatheon were such a strange bunch. Some of them had absolutely fucked-up ideas regarding what should be heretical.

"I'll take her tomorrow," I said, stepping toward the house.

Su touched my arm with the only hand of his he had free. "Actually, I had a concern, and I'm scared of what might happen if we let a professional look at her. Can we discuss it? It's a very... private matter."

I glanced around, searching for eavesdroppers. Su could sense people with his magic. I suspected he was doing so now, else he would never have brought it up.

"What's wrong?" I asked.

"Do you wonder if Susana was sexually abused?"

My stomach dropped. It felt like a weight went from my sternum to my pelvis, and pili-palas danced in my throat.

I fumbled for my words. "Su, I... How? I can't, you know... ask her about that."

"I know," he said, eyes closed. He still had his hand on my arm, and I couldn't help but wonder if he kept me calm with his magic. "I will. She trusts me, perhaps too much. I can also give her an exam. She did well when I tested her bones."

"Su, you're a merchant of bone, not a physician!"

"I am Doctor Scrimshander!" he protested.

"A dentist, not a... a sexual health specialist."

"I don't need to be a specialist to see... well, *some* things. And I would rather see for myself and consider our next option, rather than ignorantly go to the Plant church and be accused of being her assaulter."

My arms shook, and I hadn't noticed until Su gripped me tighter.

"Are you okay, Ami-honey?"

"If... if I find out Miltico... did *that* to her..."

"You've already killed and eaten the man. You can't do that twice. This isn't the Starry Sepulcher."

"I'll find him in Spiritua once I'm dead and woken up. I'll pummel him into goat meat."

"Lucognidus will wipe your memories of him if you really mean that."

"Well, he better get his mind-wiping magic ready, because I *do* mean that."

Su sighed. "I understand your anger, but it'll just scare Susana now. Let me take a look at her. Hell, I'll do it right now. My work at the ateli can wait." He dropped his bag of bones right there at his feet. They sunk into the sand, wet from a recent rainfall. "I think Cohaku and Nio are with her right now. Could you keep them occupied? I think I'll take Susana someplace where no kids will accidentally walk in on us."

Su took my silence as acceptance. Which was fine, because I would keep my daughters distracted if needed, but I hoped he didn't misinterpret my silence for derision. I was still shocked at the very notion that a father could... could do what Miltico might have done.

Perhaps my greatest sin was not killing him sooner.

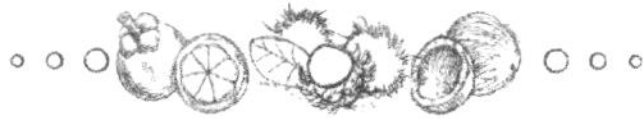

An hour later, Su returned, carrying Susana in his arms. I had played a few games of troika with Cohaku and Nio. I'd lost every time, but as long as they were distracted, I considered it a success of my fatherly duty.

Su set Susana down on the pile of pillows near the troika board, then walked by me, beckoning me to walk with him outside.

The wind had picked up. Palm fronds billowed. The calendar said we'd have a storm tomorrow, but Windesoar often practiced a day or two before his big shows.

"Well?" I asked Su as we walked side-by-side along the beach.

"I don't think she was sexually abused," he said.

While it was a relief to hear, and Su was a professional I could trust, the question remained regarding why she had pain while walking.

"I examined her... in places you would not want me to talk about," Su went on. "She was intact and clean. There was no indication she had ever suffered from

Female Familial Rot[1] . I asked her some questions about her father. I asked if he had ever touched her in... those places. She said he had not, nor had her mother. I'm not an expert on child abuse, Ami-honey. I was abused until I was adopted by King Susan, yes, but I can only speak from my own experience. I have heard that some children behave in particular ways or say certain things. So far, Susana has not said or done any of those things."

"Milti may have been a monster, but I suppose even he had his limits," I said, kicking away a dominion shell.

"It's still possible I was wrong, or he just didn't leave any lasting damage, or that Susana doesn't remember it. However, I think it would be best to assume that she was not sexually assaulted. When adults refuse to believe children and keep prodding them for answers, it can lead to children saying what they think the adults want to hear. In some cases, they can even develop false memories. If a child tells an adult 'I was abused' enough times, they might believe it to be true. And if a person comes to earnestly believe their story to be true, it can be hidden even during a ritual to Neri, the Demigoddess of Truth."

"You mentioned before that you thought it would be best if I convinced myself so strongly that Miltico died in the woods from a wild animal. Was that your fear? That I would be caught and forced to undergo Neri's Ritual?"

He stopped at the edge of Deep Sea's fingers. The incoming wave washed over our feet. "Yes. I am still afraid of our crime being found out. Our advantage is that Miltico was nobody of importance, and not even a citizen of Aloutia. To be honest—and oh Gods, this is a terrible thing to say—I can't help but feel that Phoebus Svelt's death was a blessing in disguise. He is the only one who would have reported his son's disappearance and gotten the authorities involved. If Lavina were to return, they would have no interest in her story. She's an undocumented immigrant, so the powers-that-be see her as a liability more than as someone who needs to be protected."

"I feel the same way," I replied. A cold gale swept across the beach. I could not be certain if the shiver down my whole body was from the chill wind or the old man's ghost haunting me. "We'll keep that between ourselves. If we told anyone we were happy about our dear shopkeeper's death or Lavina's disappearance, *we'd* be the monsters."

"Of course. And Ami-honey... my offer still stands. I can manipulate your feelings and thoughts, to a degree. I can help you convince yourself that you were innocent, if you want."

That didn't sit right with me. I felt like I owed it to Susana to one day tell her the truth. One day when she becomes an adult. "Only do it if I'm ever arrested,"

---

1. A disease that may occur in women and girls after incestuous vaginal intercourse involving semen.

I said instead.

"If I can. I have to touch a person to do it. If they take you from me..."

"They won't," I said, gripping his hand tighter in mine. "You're a Godblood. You could command them."

"If anyone ever comes to arrest you, they will bring a Godblood officer to stop me. A hypnotist, most likely, to ensure my cooperation. I might lose control of my own thoughts and actions a day before they arrive. They'll probably send Lungidus."

That was too risky. "It would be better if you erased my memory of the truth, wouldn't it?"

Su shrugged. "I don't think anyone will ever ask the lawkeepers to search for him. I believe we're safe living our lives as we are. Plenty of murders occur in Aloutia every year and the victims are never found. There are only a few dozen Godbloods who are of any use to the lawkeepers and court system, so they are saved for only the highest-profile cases."

"Did they try to recruit you into that?" I asked.

"It was one of the recommendations Chancellor Mira gave me, in addition to helping the merchants of magic."

"I'll trust your judgment, Sugar. I would like to keep my memories intact, painful and awful as they may be, but if it means saving my family, I would gladly let you do whatever needs to be done."

He graced me with a gentle smile and a feminine chuckle. "Your trust might be your downfall one day. Until that day comes, though, let's carry on with our lives. I can sense Mr. Onoretti and his bodyguard coming."

I turned toward Bamboo Lane. Giorvi walked closer at a leisurely pace while Oboro maintained an ever vigilant watch for enemies. Although the most he'd find behind those bamboo stalks were capybaras, I couldn't blame him for fearing the unseen.

Su and I went to greet them. Giorvi whispered something in Caprise to Oboro which caused the boy to relax. He even *smiled.*

"Welcome to our house," Su said. "Dinner is still an hour away, but please, feel free to go inside and relax if you'd like."

"Thank you, as always, my friends," Giorvi said. "I look forward to the meals you've prepared. Truly, they are most excellent. I shall have to return the favor one day and invite you to Chernagora."

Su tickled my back. "Ami-honey, I can handle dinner alone, if you'd like to talk with him."

I kissed the top of Su's head. "Thank you. Where did Liesle go? I haven't seen her in a few hours. Is she painting in the village? If she were here, she could help with dinner."

"I'm not sure. I haven't seen her, either. She doesn't have any work, but she might be painting for her own pleasure." Our sneaky way of saying she was in her secret ateli. "I can manage dinner on my own. I'll have Eruwan help. She wanted me to show her my fish deboning technique." He twisted his wrist and fingers in an elaborate manner, far more detailed than what he actually had to do when deboning fish. He was, perhaps, making a sexual innuendo, trying to excite me about the things he could do with his fingers. Gods, he didn't have to go through so much work to arouse me; his existence was enough.

I led Giorvi and Oboro into the house, where the three youngest girls had given up on troika for the time being. Nio and Cohaku sat at the table, writing on paper. Nio was getting better at writing, and she didn't have the same aversion to it that she did with speaking.

Susana sat on the pillows with nothing to do but watch the other two.

"Do you want me to move you someplace?" I asked her. "You seem bored here. I could take you into your bedroom and you can play with toys in there."

She held her breath upon seeing the two visitors. "Scorpion..." she said so quietly I barely heard.

"Oboro is a Sasorin," I said. "We don't call sapient Sasorin 'scorpions.'"

Oboro opened his mouth to speak, but decided against it.

"I didn't know Usana was here," Giorvi said, sounding genuinely surprised by her presence. "Are you raising her now?"

I admired the man's tact at not mentioning Miltico's name. "I am. Her name is Susana now. She's having trouble walking, so if you'll pardon me, I'll carry her to her room."

I lifted Susana, cradling her legs so they didn't swing about.

"Do you know why her legs hurt?" Giorvi asked.

"We aren't sure yet. Su did some tests to rule out a few ideas. We're going to take her to the Plant church tomorrow."

He intercepted me on the way to Eruwan and Susana's bedroom. "May I look at her foot?"

Susana wasn't of a mind to agree or disagree. Giorvi exuded confidence; I had no reason to refuse him. As a Yosoe, he might have knowledge I didn't regarding her Yosoe legs.

"See this discoloration on her hoof?" he asked.

I hadn't noticed it until he pointed it out. Or rather, I never would have expected it to be something worth noticing. Her body had recovered after eating properly and getting frequent baths, so something changing color could have been mistaken for a healthy change.

"This is a bacterial infection," Giorvi said.

Cohaku and Nio both ceased what they were doing to overhear.

"Yosoe aren't evolved to live and play on beaches. Our hooves are prone to picking up bacteria living in sand, and then our bodies don't know how to fight them. *Do* go to the Plant church tomorrow, as you intend, and ask for an antibiotic. Also buy her shoes for Yosoe feet, and make sure she wears those at all times when she's on the beach."

I was grateful to have him here to notice that. It made sense that a Yosoe would know what ails another Yosoe. I had only ever raised my own Wynnle-Nilian-Winyan children with knowledge of what I knew as a Wynnle-Nilian myself, with Liesle helping fill in the blanks of what I didn't know about Winyans. I had failed to recognize the unique issues a Lagodore-Yosoe would face. When I went to the Plant church, I would ask how I could better raise this girl.

"Sandals," Cohaku said.

Giorvi nodded. "Yes, sandals would work as well, though shoes offer better coverage."

"She means 'shoes,'" I said. "She refuses to say that word. When she says it, it sounds like 'Su' and she doesn't want to be misunderstood."

He shrugged. "Very well then, get her 'sandals' that cover her whole feet."

"We will," I said. "Thank you for the advice. Let me get her settled, and then I'd like to show you my current project."

Chapter Thirty-One: Plans

I asked Giorvi to come into my ateli to see the crystalight statues I'd made since he was last here. Some smaller jewelry pieces—scraps from the larger Aurora piece—were ready for purchase. He had anticipated making a purchase, clearly, as he'd brought a thick pouch of high-value coins.

I had only two visors: the one I always wore, and the one I'd gotten for my kids. It was small for a Wynnle, but the perfect size for Giorvi. Unfortunately, I had no extras in Oboro's size, so the boy had to stay outside. When Giorvi gave him the order, I had the feeling he was more distraught at being torn from his guardian's side than at not being allowed inside to see the crystals.

Over the last week, many raw crystalights had been brought to my ateli for safekeeping. Their ardent white light would have blinded most species if they hadn't worn a visor. As they were raw pieces, chunks removed by the Domovye, they were nothing more than boring cubes at the moment. I kept lemontine incense burning constantly so they would remain as fresh as possible until I could apply snowbark resin to them. That had to go last, though. If I applied the resin before it was dyed, the color would not seep inside.

Aurora was coming along nicely. The shape was set; I just needed to carve out a few details, and then I could dye it. It sat on my work desk, next to some of the tools I'd used to smooth out the small jewelry.

"This is the one you asked me for," I said, standing next to my desk and nudging Aurora forward. "You said it was a personal commission? If there's any changes you'd like me to make, tell me before I move on to the coloring stage."

I usually referred to it as the 'dyeing' stage, but the other day Cohaku had been in here watching me, as she had done often recently. I had told her about the different stages and she had thought I called it 'dying,' as in ceasing to live, and it upset her so badly she'd cried. I'd had to stop to hug and comfort her.

Now I felt silly calling it the coloring stage to my commissioner. He didn't comment on it, and I could not judge his facial expression from behind the visor. Not like I was good at judging Yosoe facial expressions anyway.

Giorvi took the statue and examined it from all angles. "Now I'm glad we left Oboro outside, because this is going to be his gift on his next hatching-day."

"Is it coming up soon? I can be sure it's done by a certain day."

"Far enough away. Nothing you need to rush. Speaking of hatching-days, though, your Eruwan's is very soon, isn't it?"

"Day after tomorrow. We'll be having another fire feast that day, if you're still here and care to join."

"I would love to. I owe Steena Village a fire feast for how I interrupted the ceremony with Deep Sea during Tawny's funeral. Would you allow me to pay for Eruwan's feast?"

"I thought you paid for the feast during the Domovoi Day of Sapience?"

"I tried, but because we have so many Domovye in the merchants of light, Guildmaster Thousand-Diamonds used his post-maxima money to pay for celebrations for all Domovye in the guild."

"I see. Well, I don't think Eruwan would mind, and if she doesn't, I don't, either. I'll ask her, just in case. But are you sure about doing this? She would probably be polite if the feast were small, but the rest of the village might not be."

"Oh, Ami, are you saying I'm going to skimp on food or something? I'm as wealthy as an Aloutian can legally be. Nobody, and certainly not Eruwan, will be disappointed. Also, do you have anyone who can certify her documents?"

"Not here in the village. We planned to take her to Seabells later to get it done officially."

Giorvi set the crystalight back down. "I can do it. You're going to Seabells tomorrow for Susana's antibiotic, right? Go to the Life church's office and ask for a blank certificate of adulthood. They will give you one."

"They won't ask why an unlicensed person such as myself is asking?"

"Not at all. It's worthless while blank, and for all they know, Steena Village is full of licensed officiants. They frequently give a hundred blank certificates to merchants of mail in hopes that one makes it undamaged to its designated location."

I chuckled. "You really hate the merchants of mail."

Giorvi shook his head. "I could eat a letter, take it to the recipient, and puke it back out, and it's more likely to arrive legibly than if one of those fucks got their hands on it."

"Anyway, if Eruwan is okay with you signing her certificate of adulthood, it's okay with me. It would save her a trip to Seabells, and I don't think she cares to travel far from the village."

"Wow, nothing like my little Beatrice. That girl wants to see the whole dominion."

"She's ambitious like both her parents."

Giorvi bent down to evaluate my dyes. "I hope she imparts some of that ambitious attitude on Oboro. Boy has no fire in him at all." He pointed at one of the yellow dyes. "This one for the main body of Aurora."

"Understood," I replied. "Oboro will be overjoyed to receive this gift from you. Now that I know it's for him and not just your own personal collection, I feel motivated to make it extra special."

"My personal collection? Ami, you wound me. Other than a few select pieces which I use to illuminate my house, my collection is made mostly of dimming pieces. Old pieces, often sold to me by somebody whose grandmother or grandfather owned the piece since childhood, but have since passed away. All the crystalights in my study barely produce enough light for me to see by."

"My apologies. I thought you had more."

"Bright ones? No. But dim ones, yes. Sometimes I even keep pieces that have gone entirely dark because they are nice sculptures. A skilled merchant of light can create a work of art with value that lasts long after the light goes out."

"This crystal will shine for one hundred eighty years. It'll shine long enough Oboro can pass it on to his grandchildren, and they can keep it for their entire lives."

"If that nervous wreck of a boy can ever summon the courage to speak to a woman. I suppose he could always adopt. Oh, you needed adoption papers for Susana too, didn't you? I'd be happy to sign those, as well."

"You're legally certified for that, too?"

"There was a point in my life where I had an opportunity to become licensed in many legal matters. My wife encouraged me to do everything I had time for. She said we never knew when a situation would arise where I'd need to officiate an Olivian wedding, or sign adoption paperwork, or hire a merchant of dance."

"You can legally hire a killer?"

"I could. I've never done it. Having a wide range of legal options was key to my promotion in the merchants of light. Dia—sorry, I mean the Guildmaster Thousand-Diamonds—finds it helpful to have someone around whose name on a piece of paper can pull a thousand strings."

I hadn't realized what a dangerous man he was. To think he could hire a merchant of dance! I thought only Godbloods and vassal kings had that type of influence.

"Would you kill to protect the trade secrets of the merchants of light?" I asked, and regretted it as soon as the words were out of my mouth.

"I doubt it. Those secrets aren't so big that they're worth taking a life."

I had already asked one dangerous question. "Why do the Domovye have different names for crystalight pieces? They call them fangs and claws."

Giorvi waved his hand brusquely. "They use names like fangs and claws because it's a rough 'translation,' so-to-speak, of their telepathy-language. When they were animals, they didn't speak in words, but in pure thoughts and images. We asked them to use softer words when speaking around others. Since you're a Wynnle, perhaps hearing 'fang' and 'claw' doesn't frighten you, but it does scare other species. It's a euphemism; nothing more."

"So what is aye-too, then?"

He did not answer. I thought he was, perhaps, trying to remember what it was. I couldn't see his expression behind the visor. I wondered if he was angry or suspicious of me, or just trying to remember an obscure name.

"Where did you hear that word?"

"A Domovoi said it. It was in the same context as the 'fang', but I don't know what scary thing an aye-too is. Is that a monster or demon or something? Also a euphemism?"

"I don't know what it is, Ami. Perhaps you're right."

"But you've heard the word?" I was testing him. He was one of the few I'd heard speak it.

"I have, yes," he answered. If he claimed to have never heard it, I would have called him on a lie. "But I do not know what it means, other than that it is the Domovoi word for crystalights."

Nothing I could do with that information. "Ah. One of them said it aloud and was promptly scolded by another. I thought it was strange."

"Domovye have customs and language quirks I don't fully understand. To be honest with you, it took me a while to get used to they/them pronouns. It simply wasn't done in the Sunset Kingdom. I didn't learn them until I went to Chernagora, joined the merchants of light, and met a Domovoi for the first time."

"We have a few people in the village who use they/them," I replied. "It never felt strange to me."

"I'm surprised Master Scrimshander doesn't use they/them with how secretive he is about his gender."

"It's a taunt to the Ophidians. It's his way of giving them the V-sign[1] and challenging them to enslave him. Since he's become neutral from eating shubin marrow, he thinks they would consider him the so-called 'slave sex' anyway."

Giorvi shook his head. "Ophidians are disgusting. I'm sorry I got us on this topic. Let's get back to business. You have a few completed pieces? I'm ready to pay for them, if you're ready to sell them."

I wrapped the completed pieces in palm leaves and put them in a box he could carry home. He gave me enough money for a single man to live off of for a year. In our household, it would last about four months. We saved a lot of money by making our own clothes, doing our own repairs, and fishing and gathering our own food, for the most part. A good portion of this money would go toward buying supplies for Eruwan's house.

We removed our visors and exited the ateli. I locked the door while Oboro stood nearby, diligently awaiting his mentor.

---

1. A hand gesture in which a V is made with the fingers. Meant to symbolize Demon Lord Vinoc. The gesture is rude, meant to imply one hopes the other person is tortured by Lord Vinoc, the Lord of Terror.

Liesle came home, flying from the direction of Steena Village. Perhaps she had been painting at her sister's house, after all... Or possibly just visiting. She didn't have any of her art supplies. She landed gracefully on the sand, waved to us, and went to help Su with dinner. With the wind picking up speed for tomorrow's storm, we would have to eat indoors unless we wanted bright açaí berries rolling in our laps.

I approached Liesle as she carried two patella plates to the table. "Were you visiting your sister?"

"Huh? Oh, yeah."

"How is she?" I asked. "Is Nell okay, too?"

Liesle frowned and brushed past me to set the plates on the table. Her actions were rougher than I had expected, and it startled me. Was she in a bad mood? She didn't answer the question, either.

"Um, Giorvi and his bodyguard Oboro will be joining us for dinner, as we discussed earlier." I wondered if she was upset that we had guests, but I had talked about it with her and Su already. I would not have invited them unless both my spouses agreed to it, and they had. Hospitality was important in a small village like this.

"I know," she said. "They're welcome here anytime."

I didn't want to make the conversation awkward by pressing her on the issue of what she had done in the village. Maybe she had spoken to Orienna about what Miltico had done to her all those years ago, and she didn't want to discuss it in front of the guests. I gave her some space, intending to ask about it later.

Ignoring Liesle's intense quietness, we had a decent dinner. Susana had been playing with toys in her room. Su carried her out so she wouldn't have to walk.

Fionn sat next to Oboro, even though it put Cohaku on his other side. They usually avoided being so close. Cohaku didn't seem to care, just eating in her peculiar way. Fish first, then rice, then fruit, and no bite of anything else in between.

"Do you like steena?" Fionn asked, putting one on Oboro's plate.

"It's a nice village," he replied.

"Not our village. The fruit. This." Fionn poked it with an extended claw. "Can you eat steena?"

Oboro pinched it between one of his scorpion-pincers. "Signore, can I eat steena?"

"I believe so," Giorvi answered. "Sasorin don't typically eat fruit, but I don't think it would hurt you."

"I mean, may I eat it?"

"Of course you can! Oboro, I've said before, you don't need my permission to eat. We're guests of the Last-Scrim-Den family, and if they've said you may eat, you may eat your fill."

Susana tilted her head. "Um..." Whatever she was about to say died on her lips.

"What is it, dear?" Su asked. "Did you have a question?"

"If everyone can eat however much they want... what do we do if we run out?"

My sternum sank with sorrow. Was that related to some punishment Miltico had used to control her? Or was it their reality on Cosmo?

"Aloutia produces so much food that there aren't enough people living here to eat it all," Su said. "We owe that blessing to the Goddess Cherribell, your Goddess. When we go to the Plant Church tomorrow, perhaps we should thank her for the bounty she has provided us."

"But it's not that way on Cosmo or Ophidia?" Oboro asked. "Cherribell doesn't want Ophidians to eat?"

Su shook his head. "It's not as simple as that. She *wants* everyone to eat, but the Gods need help from their moons to cast some of their larger spells. Aloutia produces so much food because the Green Moon nurtures the planet, and Cherribell nurtures the Green Moon. She doesn't have anything quite like that on Ophidia or the planets of Cosmo, other than Munil. She can nurture the lands of Munil through the Plant elementrons produced by the life trees. But Susana, you were on Starsine, which is difficult for Cherribell to nurture. It would take her so much time and energy to keep the Starsine healthy. She *does* help it as much as she can, but what you saw is the best she can do."

"Everybody should just move to Aloutia," Cohaku said.

"That's a nice dream," Giorvi said wistfully. "We would have to convince the Ophidians to free their slaves."

"You freed me, Signore," Oboro said between bites of steena. He ate the husk, as well.

"Yes. The Ophidians let me have you because I gave them money. As Aloutia transitions into a moneyless society, eventually we will have no way of bargaining with them. Eventually, the only way to save men will be through force. A war is coming. It might be next year; it might be in one hundred years."

Fionn clenched his fists. "I won't let those snakes take me or Heliodor. We can fight them."

Heliodor looked up at his older brother while keeping his head down. It was both an adorable and harrowing expression. Gods, I hoped my sons wouldn't go to war. Ophidians did unspeakable things to their male captives. Female prisoners of war were usually mercy-killed, but the men...

"It's not the Ophidians you need to fear," Giorvi went on. "It's the Makai. If Ophidia allies with the Makai, then Aloutia's entire military and all the merchants of dance couldn't stop the demonic horde or the assault of every available Demon Lord."

"It's troika," Liesle said. "Troika was developed to symbolize Aloutia, Ophidia, and the Makai. All three have reasons to fight the other two. Whoever allies with another will almost certainly destroy the one they've teamed up against. Ophidia and the Makai could ally to destroy Aloutia. Or Aloutia and the Makai could ally to destroy Ophidia."

"Could Aloutia and Ophidia team up against the Makai?" Heliodor asked. "I don't want to fight alongside man-hating slavers, but..."

"If the demons were a big enough threat, we would," Giorvi answered. "Ophidia has occasionally requested help from Aloutia with things outside their control. Rogue Godbloods, namely. Our diplomacy isn't so terrible that we can *only* fight the snakes. It's also why I was allowed to simply purchase your freedom, Oboro. If Aloutia and Ophidia were truly such vicious enemies, they wouldn't have accepted our money."

"Are we really going to become a moneyless society?" Eruwan asked. She sounded hopeful. So many people feared it, but for her to be enthusiastic about it? Perhaps that was for the best, if that's the direction society was headed.

"I believe so," Giorvi said, prodding the fish pieces in his rice bowl with a fork. Wynnles never used utensils, but we kept them in our house for Su and guests. "It's the will of Lucognidus for the world to function without money, but he knows it cannot happen overnight. The Greed Wars forced Mind elementals to discard the concept of money over the course of twenty years, and that came at the cost of many deaths and people beaten for blasphemy. Slowly, one vassal nation at a time, Aloutia has obeyed the will of God. The Commune of Morn became a moneyless society within ten years of the Greed Wars, and the Commune of Silk took thirty years to do the same. Neither of them were predominantly populated by Mind elementals, and yet they submitted to the will of Lucognidus."

"As long as he is the God of Aloutia, such changes are inevitable," Su said.

Cohaku stopped chewing with a big piece of fish in her mouth. "Um, there's no way for him to stop being a God, is there?"

"Surely not," I said, scoffing. "He singlehandedly conquered Aloutia. What could stand up to him?"

"Whatever convinced him to *cease* conquering the rest of the dominion," Su said with a tone of dread. He stared blankly at the fruit rotary, though his mind was probably elsewhere. "If Lucognidus had been unstoppable, he would have conquered Ophidia and the Makai, too. But he didn't, and nobody knows why. Some believe there's a force more powerful than him. Perhaps a Demon Lord, or another God, or something beyond our understanding."

"If... If Aloutia goes to war against Ophidia and the Makai, would Lucognidus protect us?" Fionn asked. "I don't mean he would conquer them. But... would he stop their armies if they invaded?"

None of us could answer.

"Keep in mind, the Ophidians worship him, too," Giorvi said. "Even though they think 'he' is a 'she' with all the equipment expected of what they call a woman. And many Demon Lords are allied with him. Aloutia might be Lucognidus's favorite of the three nations, but we cannot predict his actions when the other two also have his favor. Besides, whatever is stopping him from conquering

Ophidia and the Makai could very well prevent him from defending Aloutia. If war comes, we may be on our own, without the help of any Gods."

"The crystalights will save us from the hordes of the Makai, though," I said. "If they're turned into Godlights and distributed across Aloutia, we could stop the Makai from sending their armies."

Giorvi grinned at me. "Yes! That's entirely true. Millions of lives will be saved thanks to the crystalights here."

Millions saved... all at the cost of Tawny's life. Nobody but our family would ever care. Giorvi must have known what I was thinking because he did not bring it up; he didn't want to sour the mood. He changed the subject to avoid the conversation heading in that direction.

"By the way, could I ask a favor of you, Ami and Master Scrimshander?"

Su's eyebrows rose. He hadn't expected to be addressed. "Just call me Su, if you're calling my husband by his name now."

"Very well. Su, could I hire you for some dentistry work in a few months' time? My little Beatrice loves her sweets too damn much, but I will need a merchant of bone for some other small jobs by then."

"Certainly. I'll have more free time after summer, once we've finished Eruwan's house."

"Excellent. I'd like Ami to come, too. There's an event in Chernagora for guild members. I would like one of my master merchants of light to accompany me. Having a master... merchant of bone there would be a pleasure, as well."

I thought he was about to say a 'Master Godblood' and I wasn't convinced he meant otherwise. Su tried to hide his Godblood status as much as possible, but everyone knew. Just because we didn't talk about it didn't mean we were ignorant of what he was.

"I'll be there," I replied. "By then, I'll have a few more crystalight pieces finished, so I'll bring them to you."

"I'll come, too," Su said.

Giorvi breathed a sigh of relief. I couldn't imagine what gave him such anxiety. Perhaps something or someone at this future event threatened him enough he felt he needed the security of a Godblood. "Thank you, both of you. I will make arrangements for you to stay at my house."

Chernagora was a cold city and would be even colder in a few months. I'd have to prepare warm clothes. Though, it would also give me a great reason to ask Su to snuggle with me... His warm body on mine would be a delight.

Codex Dominex: The Merchants of Light Guild

Guilds in Aloutia provide job security for people who share a trade or who provide similar goods and services. The merchants of light deal primarily in four kinds of light:

- crystalights
- glowlight lotuses
- candles
- oil laps

A 'merchant of light' is anyone who works in the guild, regardless of what their job entails. Whether they are an actual merchant dealing with sales, a sculptor of crystalights, a chandler, a lamp-maker, or an administrator, they all have have the title 'merchant of light.'

The guildmaster during the year 561 was a Domovoi named Thousand-Diamonds. Beneath them are thirty 'upper administrators' who perform various executive tasks. Below them are about two hundred 'lower administrators' who deal with day-to-day paperwork, finances, and management. Then there are about one hundred Domovoi miners who extract crystalights and a few thousand manufacturers who produce or craft the various sources of light.

Laborers and artisans are commissioned by the upper administrators who purchase the materials and sell it to their merchants, then buy it back for an increased price, and sell it to the customer for the final price. To use an example, take a business administrator (B) and a crystalight sculptor (C):

B purchased a crystalight deposit for the price of five years of the guild's maximum project fund allowance. This is the equivalent of about 500,000,000 lime coins, but came out of the guild's allowed profits within the Aloutian Imperial

Economic Standard.

- B sold a five-square-inch block of crystalight to C for 10,000 lime coins.
- C sculpted and dyed the crystal the desired shape and color.
- C sold the crystal back to B for 50,000 lime coins
- B sold the crystal to the intended customer for 100,000 lime coins.

In the above example, C made a profit of 40,000. If his maxima is capped at 200,000 in a year, he can only make five crystalights of the same value before he might as well stop (which is encouraged so people can go on vacations and spend time with their families). B made 60,000, but only keeps 20,000 for his own personal use per crystalight sold. The remaining 40,000 goes into the project fund or, if that has reached its cap, into the guild's charity service fund.

Chapter Thirty-Two: Scrimshanders

A Wynnle carrying a Lagodore would have raised eyebrows in Seabells. Su held Susana in his upper two arms while he carried bags in his lower two arms, for any shopping we did while here. We'd already bought new Yosoe shoes for Susana, but we did not put them on her. Pressure on her hooves put her in unbearable pain. She had been delighted by her kamen, though; the dark blue mask covered her upper face and the top of her head, the straps going around her ears. I'd set the tiniest of crystalight sequins in a few spots that wouldn't shed light into her eyes. Overall, the mask looked like white stars against a night sky and Susana adored it.

Su's kamen was a work of art that he'd designed himself, made from various animal bones and scrimshawed with images of flowers, vines, seashells, and fish. It covered more of his face than mine or Liesle's, including his mouth, though Su's voice had the benefit of coming from a Rubaiyan larynx. Since Rubaiyans had to be able to speak underwater, their larynxes contained Sound elementrons that helped convey sound through obstructions.

We spoke to the same volkhv at the Plant church who had been tending his herbs the last time I came here. He remembered me; not surprising since Wynnles were rare in these parts. Even more rare was a Wynnle asking questions about Lagodore-Yosoe hybrids. I couldn't help but wonder if the man suspected I wanted to eat Susana. Were these people bigoted toward Wynnles?

Su pointed out the discoloration on Susana's hoof, and the Plant volkhv went into his medicine cabinet to retrieve the appropriate antibiotic.

"Beach-hoof," the volkhv said, returning with two jars: one of white ointment and one with small brown pills. "We see it often here in Seabells. Yosoe, Equaras, Centaurs, and Dromedaries are prone to it. Species with skin for feet or padded paws are immune. Rub this cream on the girl's hoof. Be *very* gentle. If she can do it on her own, that would be best. The slightest pressure may hurt her, so just put on what she can manage. Apply it three times per day. At first, you might only be able to dab it on, but after a few days, you can rub it in if she can tolerate the pressure. The pills should be taken twice daily. Swallow them, if possible. They're small and can be put in cheese or other foods if that helps."

"Thank you," Su said, accepting the two jars and putting them in his bags.

"Would you accept this as payment?" I asked, holding out a crystalight ring.

I had finished it a few nights ago. Even though this church accepted money—it wasn't a Mind church—this ring was more valuable than the usual cost of an antibiotic pill and ointment.

The volkhv's eyes widened. "Is that a real crystalight?"

"It is. It will shine for one hundred and eighty years. If a God blesses it, it can even become a Godlight."

Su winked; a motion almost missed behind his kamen. "It may already be one."

I wasn't sure what he meant. I had never heard of Godbloods being able to enchant Godlights. Perhaps he asked his Godly parent to bless the light. Su had told me once, long ago, that a Godlight could technically be blessed by any Spirit, although the vast majority were blessed by Lucognidus, with a handful blessed by Sawyer or Flamboil.

"Thank you, kind drook," the volkhv said breathlessly as he took the ring. "I cannot possibly hope to match this in gifts."

"Not necessary," I said. "Could you instead share your knowledge? My husband and I are raising this child, and it's the first time we've had a Plant elemental in our house. What should we do to care for her? We were told she needed shoes for playing on the beach, but is there anything else we should know about Lagodores or Yosoe? And Cherribell... Well, our family are Lightning elementals and we've never been religious. We don't know the first thing about teaching her about the Gods. What are Cherribell's heresies?"

The volkhv had taken a few steps back, overwhelmed by my barrage of questions. "Goodness, you are a curious one! Would you like to take a seat? I will teach you all I can." He motioned toward a bench on the side of the greenhouse, flanked by thick, leafy plants. Without a doubt, he had more time for us now that I'd paid for his time with a priceless artifact.

I sat down eagerly, my covered tail drooping over the side of the bench. "Please, tell me everything. I want to be a good father to this girl."

The volkhv sat beside me and started telling me everything I'd need to know, and some things I didn't. He was not frugal with details.

Su sat on another bench nearby and applied the first dose of the ointment to Susana's foot. He used his magic to make sure she did not feel any pain. The volkhv wouldn't have known Su was a Godblood or had any such pain-eliminating powers. It only worked while Su was around, hence why he had not been able to heal Susana of her pain entirely. Besides, he had told me last night it would be best if we got the pills and ointment so we would know in the future what Susana would need if it ever happened again. One day, perhaps when Susana was an adult, Su might not be here to eliminate her pain, but she would still need to know what to ask for.

The volkhv's instructions were more than thorough. He told me about Lagodore and Yosoe digestive systems, which informed me on what I should be preparing for her meals. Kyamo wasn't good in large quantities unless the consumer was a Lightning elemental, which Susana was not. I'd have to be careful when seasoning our food not to overdo her portions.

Cherribell was an easy Goddess to please, but Plant elementals were strongly encouraged to participate in certain festivals. The Floras in Seabells would surely include her in those festivals if we asked. One of Cherribell's requirements to remain blessed was the belief that she was truly a Goddess. If one started to doubt, or started to believe the Decatheon were just bullies with magical powers, they could lose their blessings. To a questioning mind, it was easy to fall into heresy, but it would be easy for her to remain blessed if she participated in worship rituals. If she got into a habit of worshipping Cherribell now, it would be easier when she's of an age where she could lose her blessing.

Perhaps the strangest idea I had to wrap my head around was whether I wanted to encourage her to worship her Goddess. I was a Lightning elemental, and all my children until now had been Lightning elementals. We had always lived with the knowledge that we could and *should* become heretics if we were ever put in a situation where someone asked us to have sex against our will.

Cherribell was nothing like Sparkato. While Sparkato forced people to agree to have sex or else be punished, Cherribell's only demand was that her people acknowledge her as a Goddess. There was no harm in that, was there? Susana could live her whole life safely, never at risk of burning or having nightmares, just by being true and honorable to the Plant Goddess. The Goddess who ensured she would never go hungry again. Hell, if I were a Plant elemental, I would happily bow down to her statues.

We finished our business in the Plant church. Su and I took Susana to the great statue of Cherribell in the center of the ring of churches. We took her to the proper viewing angle, facing the Goddess so that Aloutia's rings in the background appeared to erupt from her upraised bell. A strong zephyr whipped by, tousling my mane, and ringing every bell in the city. A chorus of chimes echoed around us.

"She is your Goddess," I said. "She's the one who will make sure you never go hungry again."

"You and Mapa Su aren't doing that?" she asked. "I thought you were the ones feeding me."

"We are only able to feed you because Cherribell grows the food you eat," Su said. "Without her, we would all starve."

We performed a few other errands in Seabells since we were here, but we didn't want to stick around too long. A storm was brewing, and we wanted to be back in Steena Village before the wind grew to such strength that Deep Sea would have to fight to keep his water in place.

The Life church was part of the ring of churches surrounding Cherribell's statue, so we paid a visit to our upcoming child. The turquoise egg had grown, safely secure in its Domovoi glass container. The volkhvs had just poured amni water[1] into the holes and the egg swam in the mixture. Amni water was not strictly necessary for an egg's development, but it didn't hurt. Usually, eggs grew thanks to the ambient Life elementrons in the environment, but we were more than animals—we were sapienti. While the eggs of animals might not grow without assistance, we had the knowledge and tools to ensure nearly all eggs hatched with strong and healthy babies.

"Look at that bright color!" Su exclaimed. "The child will have skin the color of a mixture of yours and Liesle's."

"Like Nio's?"

"I believe so."

Susana's big eyes blinked in wonder at the egg. "I've never seen one that color. When will it hatch?"

"Soon," the volkhv answered. "It could be in a week or two. We'll take the egg out of the container in a few days to see if the baby tries poking out."

"Ahh. Will the baby be my sibling?"

"Yes, they will be," I said. "Speaking of that, Mr. Volkhv, we came to get adoption papers. This girl is joining our family."

I thought the Life volkhv would put up an argument, but he did not. He did not even question why a Wynnle would adopt a Lagodore. He was happy to hand over the forms for Eruwan's adulthood certificate, as well.

That was easier than I'd thought. I confided as much to Su, once we had left and headed toward the rendering facility.

"Why did you think it would be difficult, Ami-honey? Yes, you are a Wynnle, but we are a civilized society. Polite people aren't going to ask about... The Starry Sepulcher."

The name of that book and philosophy had become a euphemism for Wynnles eating Lagodores. As long as Susana did not recognize what the book was about, we could furtively discuss matters that would otherwise traumatize her.

"Perhaps Aloutia is a greater country than I gave it credit for," I mumbled as the wind blew my mane back.

"It's certainly the best of the three. I've lived in all three major countries, so I ought to know. Oh, the rendering facility will smell terrible. Perhaps you should carry Susana and stay out here while I do business inside."

I took the little girl in my arms. She eagerly clung to me, just as she had done with Su. Whatever fear she'd once had of me was gone. Perhaps I had won her

---

1. a nutrient-rich soup that can be absorbed by eggs. Ingredients vary based on the needs of the species of the baby in the egg, but most Aloutian mixtures include some kind of milk.

over with the hornrings and kamen. She still wore the rings, shining a bluish light on my chest.

Nearby, an ube jam vendor sold a jar of his dessert to a young customer. The Plant volkhv had mentioned ube as being particularly good for Lagodores. Our family rarely ate it, as it was a plant we could not simply pluck off one of our nearby trees. The purple yams grew plentiful in these parts, but unless you were a farmer or growing them for your own use, you had to buy them. Su liked them, however, so they were occasionally on our dinner table.

"I'll be over here," I told Su. "I wonder if Susana likes ube."

"Ooh, buy one for me, too!" he asked. "I'll eat some on the ride back to Steena Village."

Wynnles generally didn't eat yams. One of my earliest memories of Liesle was both of us at four or five years old eating one at the same time. Her face of disgust had been burned into my memory. Her mane hairs stood on end, so powerfully had she hated ube. I wondered if I'd had a similar reaction. I could not remember, though I knew I still disliked it.

I bought two jars of the thick, purple jam from the vendor and sat down on a bench.

"Do you know if you like ube?" I asked Susana.

"What is that?" she asked.

"Hopefully, a food you like." With her stable on my lap, my hands were free to open the lid. "Here, dip a finger inside and taste it."

She did. Her ears quivered when the flavor hit her tongue.

"Was that a good shiver or a bad shiver?" I asked.

Susana squeaked. "It's... is it okay to eat?"

"If you want to eat it, you may," I said, careful with how I phrased things. Su had taught me to be careful with my words around her. If I made it sound like I was ordering her to eat, she would eat things she did not like. "If you do not like it, Su will eat it."

She swiped her paw in again and licked it. "I like it. I've never had anything like this before."

The burden on my sternum lifted. She was not only eating; she *enjoyed* it.

"Eat as much as you want, Susana." I remembered Su telling me yesterday that it was unwise to tell a child with an eating disorder to eat as much as they could because it would lead to overeating. If they were used to food insecurity, they'd eat until they got sick. Quickly, I corrected myself. "If you want to save some for later, I'll keep it safe. No one can take it away from me, and I don't want to eat it." Su had mentioned food hoarding as well. He had done it as a child. His Ophidian mother had restricted what he could eat, so he'd hidden cookies in secret places. It wasn't until he was under the care of King Susan that he broke that habit.

After Susana had eaten half the jar, I wondered if that was enough. I didn't want to force her to stop, especially not after I'd told her she could eat all she wanted. But I was worried that my words were useless against her ingrained fear of not having food any time soon.

"Oh, I have an idea, Susana. Mapa Su wanted to eat some, too, remember? Why don't you save the other half in your jar until we get home? Then you can eat yours with him. He might have some ideas for things to eat it with. Maybe you can spread it over bread or something."

Susana took one last swipe with her paw and licked it clean. "Okay. If you want me to eat with Mapa Su, I will."

I only wanted her to regulate herself, but she didn't know how, yet. I put the lid back on the jar and talked with Susana until Su came back. She had never been to a big city like Seabells before, so all the sights and sounds were new to her. She wasn't scared, at least. If anything, being around other people calmed her down. Perhaps her father had behaved well when he took her into towns so he wouldn't get ostracized as a child abuser. Lagodores usually lived in cities, anyway. There was power in population, and for small, weak species like the Lagodores, they needed any kind of power they could muster. The Warrens was one of the most populous cities in the dominion. Maybe when Susana grew up, she would prefer to live in a city like that. Until then, all I could do was keep her safe and happy in our rural little Steena Village.

Another day, another fire feast. I should have been more excited, but I felt only dread.

My child was an adult now... I was the father of an adult child and I frankly didn't know how to handle it.

Losing Tawny was a unique kind of pain. A greater pain. A pain that no parent should ever have to suffer through. But watching Eruwan grow up made me realize the inevitability of my own death. I was one day closer to seeing Tawny again.

Eruwan was legally grown up, and that made me feel older by comparison. One day, all my children would be adults. Perhaps they'd have kids of their own. Imagine that! Me, a grandfather! But Tawny would always be a child, at least in my memories. Her crystalight would always be in the shape of a seven-year-old child. And though I could no longer picture her face unless I was looking at that crystal, I still remembered *her*.

Tawny would be young forever. No, I supposed I would meet her again in Spiritua after I died and slept for one hundred years. Only then, after I met her as an adult, would I be able to imagine her as an adult.

I could vividly recall the first time I'd ever held Eruwan. My first child, the one who had turned me into a father. I had been such a wild young man in those days. I'd caused so much trouble with Su, always sparring with him or trying new 'substances' with him. Back when Tico was alive and provided us with whatever we asked for. I'd once got a huge supply of crazy sugar from him in exchange for a crystalight hookah. It hadn't worked well. At the time, I didn't realize the implications of crystalights being porous, and I had not applied resin to make it waterproof.

But I'd quit all that nonsense the first time I'd held Eruwan. Her tiny, perfect body in my arms. She'd always looked more like Liesle than me, but she had my spots. She had been undoubtedly mine from the start, even without a Mantodea testing her genetics. Not that I had any doubt, or that it would have mattered if she'd been Su's or Miltico's child instead. Holding Eruwan was my wake-up call. I had to grow up. I had to be a dad. Now my firstborn baby was an adult and... what was I waking up to this time? Nothing but the dread of being one step closer to becoming sawdust.

We'd set out one of our smaller scapula tables on the beach. Eruwan sat on one side, facing Giorvi as he went over the official certification of adulthood documents. The whole family stood around, watching. For the kids, this was the first time they'd seen someone enter adulthood.

"As an adult citizen of Aloutia, you will be required to contribute to the welfare of the nation. You will be required to pay taxes if you make an income greater than ten thousand coins annually. If you convert to Mind elemental Spiritism or join a commune, you are legally required to inform the local keeper of the church within two months so they can determine how you will pay your dues to society. You are also required to make annual donations to the church of your hatching date. This date being Vayura, the day belonging to His Holiness, the Wind God Windesoar, you are henceforth expected to donate to a local Wind church orphanage, wherever you live. As an adult, you may be required to perform civic duties, although these are not guaranteed to happen in your lifetime. Such duties include but are not limited to jury duty, military service, support of Mind elementals, and participation in large-scale rituals, either demonic or divine."

Eruwan diligently sat straight, meeting Giorvi's eyes without fear. Gods, I was fairly certain when I had my adulthood ceremony, I had stopped paying attention after the first sentence. I couldn't even remember who my officiant was. Probably somebody employed by the city of Seabells who did this sort of thing daily.

"As you have come of age according to your species, you are henceforth eligible to lose the Gods' blessings. As a Lightning elemental, you will have the full support of the state and church if you choose to become a heretic. Please be careful with who you associate with from now on, if you wish to avoid becoming a heretic."

I did not think that last line was part of the official speech. Giorvi grimaced slightly as he delivered it. Since he was a Lightning elemental, too, I wondered if he'd added that line based on a personal memory.

"By the power vested in me by the Holy Empire of Aloutia, I, Giorvi Onoretti, sign this sapienti into adulthood. Please state here and now the public name, first and last, you would like to be known as in all official documents and correspondence. Remember that your public name can be changed at any time at an official registry, but it is strongly encouraged that you stick to a name for life. If you change your name later, it may become difficult to access records from before your name change."

That was why I had never changed my public name, despite the problems with 'Amiere.'

"Eruwan..." she hesitated to say her last name. She looked at each of us in turn.

Liesle nodded. "We talked about it. You have to do what makes you happy."

Eruwan bit her lip and turned back to Giorvi. "Scrimshander."

It was not a surprise to Su, who had also given her his opinion on changing her name. It was, nevertheless, a moment of intense pride and joy. He wiped tears from his eyes.

"Please write your full public name on the line here." Giorvi handed her the pen.

Her handwriting had always been beautiful, all lovely curves, each letter spaced perfectly apart. The ease and quickness with which she wrote her new surname suggested practice.

Eruwan's mouth turned into a wide grin as she looked at her new name. It meant so much to her. I couldn't understand why—a surname was just a surname to me. But if it made her and Su happy, I was happy for them.

A few hours later, after the party had quieted down and Eruwan had settled from her time in the starlight, Giorvi performed a similar ceremony for Susana as she sat on Su's lap. Liesle and I stood to either side, listening.

"With this contract, you will become the legal parents of this child," he said. "Please write her public name on the line here."

Su wrote the girl's name. I had not noticed until then that Eruwan's handwriting was so similar to Su's. I wondered if it was a coincidence or if she had meant to imitate him.

Su wrote the name 'Susana Scrimshander' on the line. When Giorvi added his name to the line below as an officiant, the adoption was complete.

The number of Scrimshanders in our household tripled today.

Chapter Thirty-Three: Turquoise

Rainy season came and went. Hatching-day celebrations came and went, including my own. I turned thirty-seven years old with minimal fanfare. At my age, hatching-days were barely worth noticing. One day at a time, our emotional wounds healed. The pain of Tawny's passing lessened until she felt like a distant memory.

Then came a new pain: the fear that I was a wretched father for letting my pain heal. Su and Liesle had talked me through that misery, too.

Susana healed from her various miseries. Well, not entirely. I doubted she would ever mentally heal from the abuse she had suffered, but at least she was doing better. She no longer asked permission to eat. Her legs recovered from the infection and she made sure to wear shoes every time she left the house. She had improved in all aspects of her life—her body was full and healthy, her fur no longer falling out or her skin bruised. Even her horns were thicker and stronger. She still wore the blue hornrings, but closer to the tips, where the horns were thinner, as they'd gotten too thick near where she'd first worn them.

During the dry season, when it was summer in other parts of Aloutia, we finished construction on Eruwan's house. One door led directly into the lighthouse, allowing her entry into the massive coatl skeleton without needing to go outside. At her request, we'd also built a room for Susana with a small door only she could fit through. We'd started with a Wynnle-sized door while we needed access to the inside for construction, then at the end, we filled the gap with plaster until it made a Susana-sized hole.

Su had been planning on making a special present for her fifteenth hatching-day—a large, precious gift to go inside her house—but due to all the trauma that had happened earlier in the year, he had not been able to finish it in time.

A piano with ivory keys, with scrimshawed scrollwork on the upper parts, near the black keys. Eruwan had been moved to tears when she walked in and saw the instrument awaiting her in the room she'd been claiming for months would be her art room. As soon as the roof was up and she could store things without fear of them being damaged by the rain, she had moved her favorite pieces of scrimshaw there.

Many nights, the family gathered at Eruwan's house to hear her play piano while we listened to Su's stories or read from books. Nio and Susana were learning to read well, but they still asked me to read to them. All my kids said I had the best reading voice. Huh... I'd never thought about my own voice before. I could not 'hear' myself the way others heard me. In private, Liesle and Su had used other words to describe my voice: 'sexy' and 'seductive.'

The months passed, our lives went back to a semblance of normalcy, and we embraced the prospects of serenity.

The kids were all at school, including Nio, who had just started taking classes at the Mind church. We took the opportunity to have some intimate fun, now that we had hours alone.

Su's mouth did things to my cock that sent my mind to heaven. His teeth bristled my spines, his tongue wet the tip... At the same time, one of his hands explored Liesle's cunt. She broke away from our kiss to roar when a wave of orgasmic pleasure pulsed through her. Her verdant eyes rolled back in her head.

Liesle regained her focus and stared at me, sweating and panting as I lay on our reed-mat bed. She did not stare long. She plunged her mouth on mine, our tongues twisting together. Her fingers, claws extended, clutched my mane. I had one hand on one of her plump breasts while my other hand dug into Su's hair.

Sex with Wynnles when there was a non-Wynnle in the mix could be dangerous to the untrained, but we'd done this for years. For me personally, it felt more natural to fuck both my spouses simultaneously than just one. Our bodies melting together was perfection. Sure, it was great with just Liesle, or just Su. Likewise, Liesle and Su could have great sex without me. But when we were together, we were like fire: hot, passionate, excited. And just as fire needed three components—air, heat, and fuel—so too did our strongest fire require the three of us.

My baculum had risen and extended to its fullest potential. I clutched Su's scalp as a warning I was about to release.

He removed his mouth only to say, "I'm ready, Ami-honey." One of his hands massaged my balls. They shriveled as I unloaded into Su's mouth.

Previously, we might have adjusted and let Liesle take me instead, but we had firmly decided we would have no more children. Even though Liesle was in her post-egg laying phase and could not become pregnant for another few months, we had decided to practice risk-free sex from now on. We also could have imported silphium[1] or sheep intestine condoms, but the idea of that order arriving while my niece was tending to the store made me sweat with anxiety.

Liesle climbed on top of me as I laid on my back and continued to wage war on my tongue long after I surrendered. Energy fled my body along with my semen, but she was not finished. Su turned his full attention to Liesle's needs, burying his face in her lower regions.

Her hands explored down to my ass and tail, the latter which she grabbed and pulled between us. Her own tail's electricity flickered in intensity as Su's tongue brought her ever closer to an orgasm.

I took my tail from her, holding it at the base of the electric puff. Gently, I touched it to her sternum and traced around one breast, then the other, like I was writing a sideways '8' made of electric pulses.

She craned her neck and moaned the way Wynnles do, which to those unfamiliar with our vocalizations, might have sounded like she was in pain. Her mane bristled and her eyes rolled back as her body shivered with pleasure. Her moans and physical reactions were a gift of normalcy. It had been so long since I could feel intimate with my spouses without feeling guilty. Finally... finally, I felt like a good husband doing the right thing for my spouses.

I drew a spiral on her breast with my tail, gradually coming inward to her pointed nipple. Her legs tensed, toes curled. She brought her mouth down to my shoulder. Her neck, so close to my maxillae, smelled of feminine sex and sweat.

"I shouldn't," she growled.

"Go ahead," I said. "If you think you're close..."

She panted while a bead of sweat slicked down her forehead. I brought my tail's spark to her other breast, to give my wife's body symmetrical treatment.

She scraped her tongue over my shoulder. It was a sensation like sandpaper brushing over my skin, which to my Wynnle mind was what a tongue *should* feel like. The texture aroused me, though I was past the point of getting hard any time soon. Liesle nicked my shoulder as gently as she could while still drawing blood. She licked the droplet of blood that trickled out, her nostrils flaring in delight. Her pupils thinned, green irises sparkling in the light of my tail's spark, as the berserker signals coursed through her body. Her mouth quivered, teeth bared, but she did not clamp down.

Su's efforts at her clitoris sufficed. I continued my work on her breast with my tail, and between the two of us and Liesle's berserker state enhancing her experience, she climaxed. She rose away from me, arching her back, and stretching her neck so she looked up as she let out a wild feline noise between a hiss and a roar.

Then it was over, and we cuddled and rubbed each other while engaging in light

---

1. A contraceptive

but uneventful conversation. Su curled up between us and massaged our legs and abdomens. I brushed one of Liesle's furry ears and stroked her mane. She purred in contentment while giving Su's scalp a similar rub.

After some time just enjoying their presence, I closed my eyes, not *intending* to fall asleep, but doing so anyway. When I awoke, Liesle and Su were both gone. Pink light came through the semi-closed bamboo window, glinting off a brass incense holder, indicating it was nearly sunset.

The kids were probably home by now, so I put on cotton underclothes and a grass skirt before leaving the bedroom. I could not hear them, but they could have been outside playing.

A plate of food had been left for me on the dinner table, covered so the mozzies wouldn't get to it first and if I didn't wake up before the cinnadyme incense stick burned out. I wandered out into the warm, inviting light of the tropical sunset. Su was collecting seashells with the kids. I couldn't find Liesle. Recently, she had flown off to be alone more often, claiming she was going to visit her sister.

I never asked Liesle what she did or where she went when she left so mysteriously. I suspected she was painting. I understood why the rules for the merchants of faces were in place, but I also felt sorry for her, being prohibited from enjoying her own hobby in private. Su and I had promised her we would never ask her where she went, if only for plausible deniability. If she were caught, we wouldn't be charged with participating in illegal activities.

My stomach growled and I gave in to my body's demands to eat. A thick fillet of purplefin, grilled to perfection. Su claimed I was the best at grilling fish, but he was just as good as I was. A bowl of rice, papaya, rambutans, mango, and slices of a spinehair nestled to the side of the fish. I chowed down, digging in with my claws extended.

Tawny's memorial had a fresh kiwi on it. I supposed Fionn flew to Kiwi Island before he came home from school. The crystalight-specked bell Su and I had made hung from an antler, now. It would stay there forever if I had anything to do with it. Nobody would take it down while I still had breath.

My ears twitched, hearing the slightest hint of commotion outside. I couldn't make out what was happening, but it didn't sound like panic or anger, so I kept eating. Su could handle whatever was going on.

The sound of Liesle's wings flapping as she descended to the femur door frames was unmistakable. While the younger kids still flapped their wings as if it helped them fly, Liesle had learned to use her Wind elementrons to keep her aloft and only flap her wings for better aerodynamics.

She pushed the leaf door open vigorously, hurriedly.

"Mo Ami! You're awake. Good. We just got a messenger from the Life church. Our egg is hatching."

From the moment an egg started hatching, it could take upwards of a day for the baby to get out completely. Although we wasted no time getting dressed and putting on our kamens and tail coverings, we were not so rushed that Liesle felt the need to fly us there. She could carry me or Su, but both of us together would have been too much for her. We prepared to get a ride on one of the Dagas who regularly ferried people to and from the outlying villages of Seabells.

Eruwan asked if she and the other kids could come along, but we knew from experience that the Life volkhvs preferred only adults in the hatching rooms.

"It may be a long wait, anyway," Su said. "You would all get bored. Actually, Eruwan, you'd be doing us a big favor if you made sure everyone here went to bed on time."

"We don't have school tomorrow. Maybe everyone can come to my house and we can play music together."

"That would be lovely," Su said and kissed her forehead. "I think Susana wants to learn piano, but she's been too shy to ask you about it. I know her fingers are short and not well suited for it, but maybe you can teach her something easy? Or you can play together?"

Eruwan rocked back and forth on her toes. "I'll do what I can, Papa Su."

We left, headed toward the Daga pier a mile up the North Corridor Road from our house. Even if we had to wait a few minutes, a Daga would soon land. They regularly moved from one village to the next. One was waiting at the dock, passing time by listening to a Flora read to them. Su paid them a fair amount of money for passage to Seabells, and soon we were off. I got comfortable on the Daga's golden shell with my spouses sitting to either side of me.

My sternum fluttered with pili-palas. A new child always brought along such feelings, but this time... there was something different. Fear. Dread.

Utter terror that I would outlive this child, too. Parents weren't supposed to outlive their children. It was a perversion of what was *meant to be.*

Liesle grabbed my hand and clutched tight as the Daga set off. When I turned to look at her, she kept her gaze on the setting sun. She frowned, and I wondered if she had the same thoughts I had. I looked at Su next, but his expression was hidden behind his face-concealing bone kamen.

With all my previous children, I had thought about their future in a positive light. I had imagined them having various jobs, growing up and finding love, having families of their own. I imagined playing kiwi batte and troika with them.

With this child... I pictured a blue-skinned, wingless child falling to their death as a chasm opened beneath them. I imagined them, a Lightning elemental, turning fifteen years old, and being asked to have sex. I imagined them saying 'no', and fighting the one who assaulted them. Killing them, going berserk, eating the body, and then being arrested and sent to Hydra Island, or exiled to Cosmo where they had to hunt for their own food. I imagined them saying 'yes' to sex, if only to avoid losing their blessing, and... being raped.

Gods, what the fuck was wrong with me? I wiped the tears from my eyes with my free hand, shifting my kamen up in the meantime. Liesle's grip on my other hand was so strong I thought she might break my carpals.

Su cradled the hand I was using to wipe my tears in two of his arms and cleaned my face with a third hand. His fourth held my kamen in place.

"Don't be sad, Ami-honey. This child will live a beautiful life. What happened to Tawny was a weird, freak accident. Nothing like that will ever happen again in our lifetime."

"How can you be so sure?" I asked. "And it's not just that. There are a million things that can go wrong. How did you know what I was thinking, anyway?"

"We're all thinking it, Mo Ami," Liesle said in a low, melancholic voice.

Su placed my kamen back over my face and ran his upper hands up my spine. A chill of calm enraptured me. A wave of peace and serenity clouded my mind. All my sad thoughts vanished, and in my mind's eye, I saw the blue-skinned child with big, healthy wings. They smiled at me and thanked me for letting them be born into this world. They wanted to live. They wanted to feel love and have a family of their own. They wanted to meet their siblings, play kiwi batte with Fionn, and troika with Cohaku and Nio. They wanted to play music with Eruwan and Susana. They wanted to wrestle in the sand with Heliodor and Maika.

Maybe the child would have a nice life... I could only do everything in my power as a father to help them along.

I sat beside Su and Liesle in one of the Life church's hatching rooms, chest aflutter, trying to be patient, but filled with so much excitement for my child's arrival. Now that we were in a more private location, we could take off our kamens.

The baby's egg had a massive crack from top to bottom by the time we arrived. Two Life volkhvs, one of them a Mantodea, the other a Coleopteran[2], stood on either side of a basin. A layer of amni water coated the bottom of the basin. The

2. One of the 88 species of sapienti people. They are usually bipedal and resemble various types of beetles, usually ladybugs.

two volkhvs had pails of the brownish milk to pour as needed. I did not think adding more amni water would help the baby at this point, but the volkhvs had rituals. In the past, they had always poured a little bit of it over our babies as they emerged.

Life volkhvs would give a baby a whole day to hatch on their own before intervening. Long ago, some societies believed that only strong babies should be allowed to hatch, so if the baby could not hatch on their own, they would have been left to die. Another component of eugenics. Even thinking about that left me unbearably sad, and I was grateful not to live in such a cruel world.

The Mantodea was the female keeper of the church, the same one who had attended my other kids' hatchings. This very room had been the same one Eruwan had been born in. Now she was an adult.

The room had barely changed at all since then. They had the same statue of the Demigoddess of Hatching that had been here since Eruwan came into this world. The rainbow ribbons and bunting holding up vines of glowlight lotuses provided color and light. Murals depicting babies from various species decorated the walls. There were no Wynnles painted, but we were not a commonly seen species in these parts.

Slow as a hatching was, we had plenty of time for small talk. We discussed potential names for the child—magic and public.

"We should let the siblings decide the public name," Liesle said. "That's how it always goes, and is what will end up happening no matter what we try. Older kids give nicknames to younger kids as a rite of passage. Do you remember when we gave each other our public names, Mo Ami?"

"How could I forget? You had been 'Lisi' at the time. Your parents bought you an easel and art supplies. I thought I was just being silly by making a pun from Lisi and easel, but the look on your face when I said it..." I grinned, memories sparkling in the nostalgia. "It's a moment I'll treasure forever."

Around midnight, the baby's hatching horn poked out. A solid, spiraling blue horn, prodding at the eggshell. All babies had horns to assist with hatching, but they typically fell off soon after. Only a few species like Yosoe and Equara kept theirs. In species where the horn would fall off eventually, an attending Mantodea would bite it off to read the baby's genetics.

An hour later, a piece of eggshell fell away, revealing the left side of their face.

Fur, not skin—indicative of a quadruped like Heliodor. I had difficult feelings about quadrupeds. Of course, I loved my son, my precious Heli, and I had done so much to accommodate him. But his life would be more difficult without the use of hands. Cohaku was a good twin sister, always helping him with tasks that required dexterous hands, but it was unfair to her to be her brother's caretaker. And yet quadrupeds had a right to live, too. Although I was ignorant on many aspects of eugenics, I recalled learning the history of discrimination against quadrupeds, specifically those who were born without hands. Cherish the Monster had tried to kill or sterilize them all in her attempts to make a society of only 'perfect' people.

Oddly, it felt nice having another quadruped child if it meant all the changes we made to the house for Heli would serve a second child, too. Did those thoughts make me a bad father? Or a bad person? I didn't dare ask aloud for fear of being judged.

Slowly, my child made their way into the world. At an hour until dawn, they rested and gathered energy. Half an hour later, they burst out all at once, spreading their wings as the egg fell apart. Fluid and sticky matter from inside their egg went flying. The baby collapsed in the milk puddle, letting out a single cry like a mewling cat.

My child—my son—was indeed a quadruped, with bright blue fur dotted with brown spots, massive blue wings, and a surprisingly plain tail with no spark on the end.

"He has no electricity?" I asked.

The Mantodea keeper swooped my son into her long, wide arms and opened her mandibles. Had I not known what was going on, I would have sprung upon her, claws and fangs flying in defense of my son. When a Mantodea opened their mouth wide and put a baby's head so close, it looked like they would bite off the head. Such was not the case. She bit off only the horn, then handed the baby to the volkhv.

The Coleopteran held the baby in the crook of one arm and poured amni water over his back and wings. "Three-seven-thirty. Half an hour till dawn. Jalama, Razum Seventeen, Year 561 since Lord Lucognidus's conquest. I declare that this baby was born in the Seabells Life church."

"Confirmed son of Liesle Denwall and Amiere Lasteran," the Mantodea said, voice stern and commanding. "Sixteen of eighteen male-associated genes active. Likely to develop masculine biology. Strong heart, lung, and bone genes. Allergic to fungi, peanuts, lalafinas, and coriander. Approximately sixty-four percent Wynnle-associated genes, twenty-two percent Winyan-associated genes, fourteen percent Nilian-associated genes. Wind elemental, with Wind elementrons in the wings."

I blinked and leaned back. "Wind elemental... I knew there was always a chance, but I didn't think it would happen."

"Liesle is a carrier of the Wind elemental gene," the Mantodea explained. "Since you are half Winyan, I assume one of your parents was a Wind elemental Winyan."

"My father, yes," she said. "We've never raised a Wind elemental baby."

"We're going to have to look into their rules and heresies now, too," I said. I did not know much about the Wind God, Windesoar, but I had never heard of heretical Wind elementals. It must have been easy to keep his blessing.

The Wind God was typically portrayed as being cruel, but not in the same way Sparkato was. For one, Windesoar would not punish someone for refusing sex. This child, at least, would be able to say 'no' without fear of divine reprisal. For another, Windesoar's cruelty was always directed at adults. He had a renowned fondness for children, as evidenced by the fact that he had ordered his churches to be orphanages.

The Coleopteran placed the wiggling baby in a basin of fresh water placed before a statue of the Demigoddess of Hatching, and washed the milk off him. While he began the prayer, the Mantodea prepared for the following procedure.

At the altar, the Coleopteran held the baby while invoking divine providence. "Demigoddess Pheala-She, blessed of our God, Lord Entomothy, Great God of Life, bless this child's hatching. Watch over him from first dawn till first dusk, or until he is taken to his home, or until his soul departs his body and he is returned to your bosom in the Life church, whichever comes first."

The volkhv's words were a recitation, but I'd never before felt such sorrow at the mention of the possibility of the child dying before his first day had passed.

"I give this child's magic name to you, O Demigoddess Pheala-She, and to the Demigod of Names, They-Who-Have-No-Name." The Coleopteran whispered the name we'd chosen. "As a boy-child, the son of his father Amiere Lasteran, we give him the surname Lasteran. May his path glitter with starlight."

The Coleopteran took him out of the water and dried him with a pink towel while the Mantodea approached with the next step: the vaccine kit. The syringe was small in the Mantodea's large hands.

"O God Lucognidus, God of the Mind, Lord Conqueror of Aloutia, by your order, we inoculate this baby against the many diseases that have been conquered by you and the Goddess Cherribell. Demigod of Vaccines, Seion, blessed of Cherribell, Great Goddess of Plants, imbue this child with immunity. May he live long and happy, free from the fear of disease. May his path glitter with starlight."

The Mantodea gently took my son's arm in one hand and jabbed the needle in with the other. A tiny squeal came from his mouth, but he was so unbothered, he hadn't even opened his eyes.

"The father is present," the Coleopteran said. "I give this boy to his father, to love and behold." He held my precious blue baby toward me, and I happily took him into my arms. Tradition was to first hand a baby off to the same-sex parent, if they were at the hatching.

He was an active, wiggling baby, nuzzling my arms as I cradled him. Liesle and Su crowded around me to stroke his soft fur. I handed him to Liesle, who kissed the top of his head, then she gave him to Su, who held him in two arms while primping his feathers with the other two.

My darling son, so perfect, so healthy... I would break the world asunder to protect him.

"He's a quadruped!" Heliodor jumped with joy upon seeing his younger brother. "This is the best day ever! I have a little brother like me! When he's older, I can wrestle with him and show him how to fly through the jungle."

"Aww, his fur is so blue!" Cohaku said, petting between his ears.

"What's his name gonna be?" Fionn asked. "Something about how blue he is? We already have Nio. Maybe Cobalt?"

"We can't have Cobalt," Cohaku said. "We can only have one of each letter on the chore board, and I already have 'C.'"

"I thought you were gonna change your name to Amber when you turned fifteen," Fionn replied. "We can put his name up then."

"He still needs to go on the board so we remember doctor appointments and stuff. And I might *not* change my name when I turn fifteen. I don't know. It depends on if I can move out or not, since I don't want to be Amber while Daddy has the 'A.'"

"We can have two 'A's,'" I said. "Maybe I could do like Su does and write mine in Orochigo."

"Don't be silly, Daddy. It would be weird if your name was in Orochigo while you only know five Orochigo words."

Blunt, but accurate.

"Aqua?" Heliodor said. "Oh wait, that starts with an 'A', too."

"Turquoise," Eruwan announced in a determined voice.

"But 'Tawny' starts with a 'T,'" Cohaku noted.

A period of silence fell upon the kids. I had a feeling they were all thinking the same thing, and perhaps it was time...

"Maybe we should erase Tawny's name now," I said. "It doesn't mean we're forgetting about her. We'll have the memorial here forever. But the chore board is for the living."

"It's time to move on," Liesle said, though by her tone, I doubted she had convinced herself.

Su sat, fidgeting with a bone-and-pearl necklace he'd been working on, not wanting to voice his opinion on the matter. I took the cloth and wiped away Tawny's 'T.' Then, hands trembling, I erased the drawings the other kids had done in the adjacent cells. I erased where Fionn had written 'Sleep well, Sis.' I struggled to be strong, but tears betrayed my expression. I wiped that traitorous water from my eyes as I fixed the rest of the board. Since Susana was between Heliodor and Nio age-wise, I put her 'S' where Tawny had been. Then I erased the old 'S' at the bottom and put a new 'T.'

Turquoise.

Well, that settled it.

I adjusted the rest of the schedule so Susana's chores were in their new spots, then erased the old ones. Turquoise wouldn't be gathering fruits with Eruwan tomorrow, after all.

"Turquoise," Heliodor said. "Turq. Aww, I love it! Just like how my name gets shortened to Heli, we can shorten his name to Turq!"

I worried Heli was getting his hopes too high. It seemed like he wanted Turquoise to grow into his best friend, but there was no guarantee such a thing would happen. Children became their own people. Parents and siblings could try to influence them, but they could never demand from them.

Maika came in, tail wagging, and dropped a bone at Su's feet. He grabbed it and tugged once Maika grabbed ahold of it again.

Turquoise sneezed, surprising every kid in the room. Heli, Cohaku, and Susana gathered around him, making adorable children-noises, as if the sneeze was the cutest thing they'd ever heard.

Fionn crossed his arms. Although he'd been surprised by the sneeze, he was not amused by it. He glanced at the chore board, then stared at Tawny's memorial.

"I'll talk with Fionn later," Liesle whispered in my ear.

The baby sneezed again.

"Goodness!" Su said as he won the tugging battle against Maika.

Turquoise let out a third sneeze and had finally had enough. He started crying. Cohaku pulled her ears down and fled outside.

"I've got him," I said. "Everyone go play outside." I took the baby in my arms and carried him into our bedroom.

Poor boy... I wondered what caused him to start sneezing so much. I laid back against the wall and rocked him gently.

Now that the baby was born, I felt like my life had a chance of returning to normal. Ever since Tawny's death, it had been one thing after the other. One trauma to deal with, followed by another. But now? I think things were alright. I could relax, enjoy the family I had without fear of losing or gaining anyone else, and make crystalights at my leisure. The world was at peace, and so was my mind and soul.

Fionn Interlude

For a few days, Turquoise would sneeze uncontrollably, usually in the evenings. Sometimes it got bad and he'd break out in hives. Luckily, the family had a cream to rub into his fur that helped.

Su figured out why. The Mantodea had said Turquoise was allergic to fungi. He was reacting to Maika, the family's shroomhound with fungi all over her body, and Fionn's best friend. Every time she wagged her morel-tail, she released tiny particles that would trigger allergic reactions in his new baby brother.

They were gonna take Maika away.

First they took Tawny away, now they're gonna take Maika.

Susana was supposed to be a replacement sister, but Fionn found her to be boring. Now they wanted to replace Maika with a boring baby brother.

I don't want Susana and Turquoise. I want Tawny and Maika!

Chapter Thirty-Four: Journey to Chernagora

Eruwan agreed to let Maika stay at her house. It took a few nights for the dog to understand, but once we moved her pillow-bed to Eruwan's house and Su left some bones in a designated area for her, she figured it out.

Fionn spent more and more time there, too. He wasn't happy in the same house as the younger girls whom he had no interest in playing with. My eldest son was becoming broodier as he entered his teenage years. Su insisted it was normal for teenage boys to go through a phase like that, but I could not remember ever being that way. When I was his age, I was starting to fall in love with Liesle. Everything I remembered doing was to impress her. Fionn didn't have any romantic or sexual inclinations that I could see. He had a few male friends in the village who occasionally came over to play kiwi-batte, but they were mostly Florae, thus Fionn couldn't play to his full ability with them. They could not run, fly, or hit the ball as well as he could.

Nell was also spending more time at Eruwan's house, especially after working at the store. She was getting better at being a shopkeeper, but didn't like the extra work put upon her young shoulders. Susana had said she wanted to be a shopkeeper when she was older—and she promised to always keep lots of food in stock—but she was only eight years old. Nine, soon. Much too young to help her older sister in any professional capacity. Of course, my opinion was that Nell was also too young, but there was nothing to be done about it. Nobody else wanted the job. Orienna and Piotr helped out on occasion, but they had their own jobs to commit to. Orienna was a merchant of song and helped take care of the village's elephants. Piotr was a full-time apiarist and no one else in the village could do his job without protective gear, since the gwenyn couldn't pierce his rocky skin. If not for the Mind volkhvs helping Nell with the store, we would be out of luck.

Often, if Nell and Eruwan were busy practicing music together, Fionn would stay away from their house. He used those days to instead fly to Kiwi Island, bringing back a fresh kiwi to put on Tawny's memorial. Sometimes he went into the jungle to gather fruits.

I had a feeling my son was lonely, but I didn't know how to broach the subject.

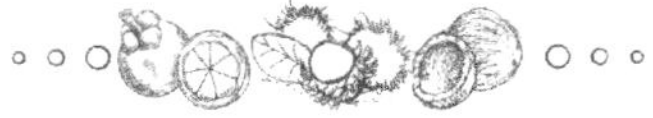

I had received a few letters from Giorvi over the summer months regarding business, both our own merchant of light business and to remind us that he would like to hire Su for dentistry services, soon. The day of our journey to Chernagora approached.

It was autumn in the temperate lands. Cooler weather, though no snow, thank the Gods. I could not abide snow. Any weather that made me wish my whole body was covered in fur or that my mane went down to my knees was no weather I could live in.

We prepared for the journey by packing plenty of warm clothes. We ordered wool clothes, including formal business attire, from Nell's store. The clothes we made from grasses and leaves here would not keep us warm where we were going.

As Su and I folded the clothes carefully into packs, Fionn came in.

"How long will you be gone?" he asked.

"I'm not sure," Su answered. "I do not think it will be longer than a week, but the business is extensive enough to be longer than five days."

Fionn lowered his head. "Um, can I go with you?"

I glanced at him, trying to measure what he was thinking. "We're not going on a fun vacation," I said. "You'll be bored the entire time, and probably cold, too. We didn't get clothes that would fit you."

"Can't we get clothes once we get there?" he asked. "I-I can stay warm at least long enough to get to a store."

"There's no guarantee any random store we enter will have clothes for you, Fionn," Su said. "You have wings and a tail. Chernagora mostly serves Yosoe who don't have wings and consider it proper to hide one's tail in their pants."

Fionn deflated, his face falling into a miserable frown. "Oh. I didn't think of that."

"Why don't we plan for a vacation next summer?" I suggested. "We can all go as a family when it's warmer." I grinned, pleased with my own idea.

"That would be lovely," Su said and giggled in his feminine manner. "That will give us time to prepare, too."

Fionn's wings quivered. "That sounds great, Dad, Mama Su." His voice lacked any enthusiasm at all, and he fled out of the room as if he were embarrassed to even be around us.

"I guess he didn't like that idea," Su said with a shrug.

I stared where Fionn had been standing. "I'll mention it again in a few months and see if he still wants to do it. Maybe he's just moody today."

"He really ought to see more of the world. Chernagora may not be the ideal tourist destination, but it's something different than what he's used to."

"I think it would be good for Susana, too. She should meet other Yosoe. Perhaps learn about their culture and traditions."

Su hunched over the pack of clothes and closed it with a grin. "I suppose next you'll want to take her to The Warrens to meet other Lagodores."

"Yes! That would be exciting for her."

He slid toward me, almost seductively, and put his upper hands on my sides. "Oh, Ami-honey, you don't know, do you? They wouldn't allow a Wynnle family into The Warrens. They're not Aloutian, so they aren't required to allow all people in regardless of species. I would be happy to take Susana there one day when she's older."

I blushed, ashamed that I didn't know that about The Warrens. "Do they think Wynnles will eat them?"

"Yes. There's a long history of violence between the Wynnles of the Starsine Plains and the Lagodores of The Warrens. They don't allow Orochijin or Dragons, either."

"It's up to Susana," I said. "When she's older, perhaps she'll decide on her own that she would like to travel there by herself."

Su nodded. "The world is a scary place for a Lagodore-Yosoe to travel alone. I must advise her to stay close to those she trusts."

"Do you suppose Lavina went back to The Warrens?" We had not seen her since before Miltico's 'disappearance.' I had almost convinced myself that he really had disappeared...

"It's possible. She may be dead, too; she relied on Miltico for her survival. Or maybe she integrated somewhere here in Aloutia and wants to make a clean start. That would be for the best."

All I could do was hope that the path she'd taken glittered with starlight. I shook my head and went back to packing supplies.

Long-distance travel in the Pentagonal Dominion required portals. Going from Steena Village to Chernagora without portals was physically possible since both locations were on the Aloutian Plane, but the journey would have taken months by foot. Such a journey would have involved crossing The Corridor on a Daga's back, then traversing the treacherous Jukalyan Rainforest, the toxic Summershade Shroomery, the deadly Yetrian Wasteland, the hostile Olivian Desert, and finally the imposing Slevango Mountains where Chernagora circled Black Mountain.

It would have made for a long, perilous journey.

Instead, Su and I traveled an hour north-east to the Stee-Nil Portal House. Portals were named after the two locations they connected, usually shortened to one or two syllables, and always with the Aloutian name first, no matter how small and humble the Aloutian location was in comparison to the Cosmonite location. Stee-Nil connected Steena Village with a population of about five hundred, to Nilia, a city-state of millions.

The Stee-Nil Portal House was technically on Bamboo Lane. We continued down the road, passing through the village. On this side of Steena Village, most of the bamboo had been cut to make houses and mats. The road was lined with paper lanterns filled with glowlight lotuses. Rice terraces gracefully sloped over the land like giant green steps. Small streams poured over them in repeating waterfalls. Occasionally we passed jeweled elephant tamers riding their animals. The path was usually wide enough for us to pass without problem, but a few times, we stepped aside for the massive, tusked creatures. Aloutian jeweled elephants were gentle by nature, but sometimes didn't know their own size.

Su held my hand and pulled me to the side as an elephant pulling a cart of rice stomped down the path. Even after she and her tamer had passed, Su kept holding my hand. He did not let go until we reached the portal house. My other hand gripped the strap of a pack over my back wherein I kept my spare clothes, miswak sticks, and the crystalights ready for purchase. One of them was Giorvi's personal commission, the moon Aurora, a gift for Oboro. Another depicted the numerous types of Yosoe horns and would serve as the city's Godlight once it was blessed.

The portal had been discovered about two hundred years ago on the side of a rock outcropping. Rice farmers had been trying to cultivate the spot into terraces, but the value of a portal was far more enticing. A bamboo house had been built around it and it was now patrolled and regulated by the Aloutian military. A soldier in an Aloutian red uniform guarded the entrance. In some places, they exacted a toll for portal use, but this one was free. When the portal had been discovered all those years ago, the Greed Wars had been fresh in the peoples' minds. Nobody dared restrict passage through this portal to Aloutian citizens. Even most Cosmonites could get in without trouble. The guard was likely stationed there only to arrest fugitives or keep Ophidians out. The inside was even something of a tavern or rest stop for travelers.

Some portals, mostly on the Cosmo side, required identifying papers to use. Traveling merchants often had these on hand, but we did not. If Su had an identification card, I had never heard of it or seen it. Such cards usually had one's sex and element listed, so it made sense Su wouldn't want one. Or wouldn't want anyone seeing it.

The guard—a Neuropteran with pink and purple fractal-patterned wings—allowed us in without argument or asking to see identification. His only advice was for us to put on our kamens before going through the portal since the Nilian side was quite populous.

Inside the bamboo house, glowlight lotus vines had conquered the walls and ceiling, leaving the room awash in gentle light and tones of pink and green. The vines crawled into the portal itself: a slab of grey stone shimmering with light. Had the lotuses not been here and the house blocked all sunlight, the glittering wall would have still shone in the darkness.

Su and I stopped inside just long enough to put our kamens on. A few people sat around, playing cards at a table or writing letters. A Takyufon merchant of mail leaned over the bar with a heavy mug of rice beer, chatting away to the Kraken bartender. I did not want to judge, but the Takyufon looked to be doing little to improve their organization's reputation. The bag of mail on the ground by his stool had spilled a few letters out already.

"Ready to step through to Nilia?" Su said. I could not see his mouth behind his full-face bone kamen, but I could *hear* the grin in his voice.

"I am." I took his hand once more, having found it comforting to hold during the walk here.

Stepping through a portal was unintuitive. As I stood before it, it looked like a rock. One could not see what lay on the other side of a portal until they put their head through. I always worried there would be another person on the other side and I would stumble into them. My tail was covered, so I wouldn't have any electric accidents, but if a small Nilian woman bumped into a Wynnle man? Some would panic.

I had intended to step through first to show I was not afraid, but Su was quicker. He never let go of my hand, but he leapt into the portal, stretching his arm back and gripping my fingers so tight I feared he'd coax the claws out. From my perspective, it looked like his arm jutted out of solid rock.

For some reason, I always held my breath and closed my eyes as I stepped through a portal. It was instinctive, like a part of my brain thought I was stepping into water rather than stone, though I never felt the stone anyway. A person could be throttled at high speeds through a portal and the structure wouldn't so much as slow them down.

A person walking through a portal never felt anything. All the times I'd stepped through a stone portal, it was like taking a step through air. I'd never been through a water portal, but I'd heard you didn't even get wet from them. The first hint that I was on another plane was when I felt so light in Munil's gravity, it seemed as though my mane would float. My tail—covered with leaves for other peoples' safety—wanted to rise. Every step I took in the Nilian Grand Portal House felt like I was about to jump, as my legs felt twenty pounds lighter.

If Wynnles were big cats—lions, tigers, jaguars—made sapient, then Nilians were house cats made sapient. While we shared similar feline features, Nilians were small and lithe. They had also kept their whiskers while most Wynnles had lost theirs somewhere, generations ago. My biological father was a Nilian, but seemingly the only trait I had acquired from him was bipedalism and shortness that made me either large for a Nilian or small for a Wynnle.

"Ami-honey, let me do the talking, especially if anyone demands a toll," Su said sweetly, suggestively. Like he had a clever plan and *wanted* someone to demand money from us.

Nilia was not part of Aloutia, and was not bound by Aloutian laws. Some of the popular portals—the ones leading to Monoceros, Vela, Labyrinthis, Takyu City, and Olivia—were not only blocked by toll-collectors, but stationed with guards. Even Mind elementals had to pay *something,* which would have been illegal in Aloutia, though most got through by handing over things as simple as clothes or food.

I carried a purse of Aloutian coins, and no small amount, either. I figured since we were going to a wealthy part of Chernagora for a few days, I ought to be prepared. Su had a pouch of money, too, and some bones he'd been working on the last few days. He also had his dentistry equipment, of course, since that was his entire reason for coming along.

The Chernagora portal was also popular. So much so, there was a line waiting to pay the toll-collector. We got in line behind a merchant of mail.

My ears twitched at the incessant and senseless noise. Oh, it made sense to whoever was speaking it, sure, but it didn't make sense to me. The merchant of mail turned around and said something to us, but it was a language I did not understand. Su replied back in the strange tongue and they shared a laugh.

"What language was that?" I asked.

"It's still English, but with a very Takyu accent."

"Really? I couldn't understand a word of it."

"The language we speak in Steena Village has so much Fleur influence that it's hardly English anymore."

I did not travel much, but doing so made me wonder how few people spoke the same language as me. How many languages were there in Aloutia, anyway? Or accents or dialects? If I were to go on that treacherous journey by foot to Chernagora, how far could I travel before I could not comprehend the local language? Every Daga I'd ever ridden on could speak my Fleur-English, but what about the people on the other side of The Corridor? Perhaps as soon as I stepped on Slevango soil, the locals would only speak Sleva.

"Chernagora is a fascinating place, linguistically," Su said. "I am not surprised Giorvi's wife, Beatrice, loves it there. She's a polyglot, you know, and a linguist and etymologist by hobby."

"She mentioned that to me," I replied. "Giorvi also said he only learned Fleur-English to speak to me, and he learned it from her. What makes Chernagora so interesting? They speak Caprise, don't they?"

"They do, but even the name 'Chernagora' is Sleva. Caprise and Sleva have been mixing in interesting ways over the generations, and the people of Chernagora will be speaking a completely new language in a century."

Su may have been impressed with Beatrice's mastery of multiple languages, but it seemed to me he could speak to anyone anywhere. "You're a polyglot too, Sugar. You're amazing."

He instinctively put his hands over his cheeks to cover his blushing even though his mask covered his cheeks thoroughly. "A-Ami-honey, I'm not nearly as impressive as you think I am!"

"But you can speak, what? All English? Orochigo? Sleva?"

"That's only three languages! Well, I know many dialects of English... And specifically the Chernagora dialect of Sleva, which I only learned so I could help you talk to Giorvi while he was learning Fleur-English."

"*Only* three? How many do you have to know before you're considered a polyglot? 'Poly' means three, right? We're in a polyamorous relationship, and with Liesle we're three people."

"'Poly' just means 'many' and..." Su huffed. "Well, when it comes to languages, I am not sure when one can technically call themself a polyglot."

When our turn with the Nilian toll-collector came, Su communicated with him in the local Nilian-English language. After a few words that sounded friendly, Su held out a small, lacquered box. The Nilian's eyes lit up like he'd just seen the love of his life. He could not resist flexing his tail upward in joy. What in the dominion could be in that box to make one person so excited? I peeked over Su's shoulder.

Bones.

Just regular bones, as far as I could tell. Was this Nilian also a merchant of bone? Was this a signal? Were these bones worth more to him than all the coins in my pouch?

The Nilian took the entire box from Su, purring and waving his tail, ears pinned to his head, as he beckoned us through.

We stepped into the door leading into a small chamber where the portal—a piece of brick wall—was anchored in place. "What was that all about?" I asked. "Why was that Nilian so ecstatic?"

"That bone came from a coatl," Su said. "The same one I built the lighthouse from. That piece had to come out when I was connecting Eruwan's house to the lighthouse. Nilians really love coatl parts. Feathers mostly, but the bones are sought by collectors, too."

I scratched my ears. "I am half Nilian and I can't say I've ever felt anything special toward coatls."

"It's not a genetic love, Ami-honey." Su pinched the cheek exposed by my half-face kamen, much to my chagrin. "It's a cultural thing here in Nilia. I suppose anyone who grows up here, regardless of their species, might be raised to admire them."

"Well, I'm just glad we got through. We could have paid him coins."

"We could have, yes," Su said. "But coins are cold and soulless. I wanted to give away something with energy. Something which would be valued by the recipient for what it *is*, not what it represents."

"Even though you don't know that Nilian? Even though we'll probably never meet him again?"

"Especially because of that. Those bones were wasted with me. I couldn't make anything with them, now that they were just in the way of Eruwan's house. Now they will be treasured. I am happy they're with someone who appreciates them."

I didn't quite understand his feelings, but if he was happy, I was happy.

Holding hands, we stepped through the portal. Our feet landed on the pitch-black cavern floor of the appropriately-named Black Mountain of Chernagora.

Chapter Thirty-Five: The Iolono House

The moment I stepped into Chernagora's portal house, the essence of autumn enveloped me. Crisp, cold air carried scents of pumpkins and dead leaves from outside. The chill made my hairs prickle and my mane fluff out, until the warmth of a nearby hearth danced up my arms. Atop a roaring black stone fireplace mantle was an obsidian statuette of Lord Ashen Soul, Demigod of the Hearth and Home, son of Lord Flamboil. Throughout Aloutia's colder regions, many families had an image of him near their hearth. Our family did not, mostly because Su was hesitant about worshipping demigods. I did not see the demigod's face often, but something about this one struck me as bearing a strong resemblance to Su.

"I feel like we're being welcomed into somebody's home," I said, nodding toward the demigod's statue. "We're only in the portal house, and already I can feel the love people have put into Chernagora."

Su gripped my hand, head down, and pulled me toward the door. "This place isn't as cozy as they want you to believe it is. Keep your guard up."

"Why? What's going on?"

"Giorvi asked a Wynnle and a Godblood to accompany him to an event attended by people wealthy enough to hire a merchant of dance. He didn't invite us to be escorts, no matter how pretty we both are. We're here to intimidate."

All I could think of was Su dressed as a *sexual* escort, clad in a silky, shimmering red dress clinging to his body.

"He said he invited me because I've been working on his commission, and he's hiring you to work on his daughter's teeth. We would have been invited if we'd been clearblood Lagodores."

"Invited to his house to perform our jobs, yes, but we wouldn't be at the fancy party tomorrow night."

His letter had said the party was for executives from the various guilds. He went as a representative of the merchants of light, but it was normal for such parties to allow guests to bring two or three others. Usually, it was family, but I could imagine him wanting to bring another merchant of light.

"Doesn't he have that Sasorin boy to intimidate others?" I asked. "Hell, he intimidates *me*."

"I have no doubt Oboro will come along, too. Perhaps Giorvi's thinking is that three frightening bodyguards are better than one."

Outside the room, and into the main hall of the portal house, we found Giorvi right away. He wore a full-face, cream-colored kamen with elaborate carved geometric shapes, but I recognized him right away by his corkscrew horns and businessman attire. He'd been waiting for us. Oboro stood behind him with stern eyes visible through a black kamen shaped specifically for Sasorin heads. The boy had a way of keeping his eyes downcast, yet I had no doubt he knew where every other person in the hallway was, and how long it would take for him to cut them down with that massive khopesh across his back.

"I'm glad to see you made it," Giorvi said most munificently, hands spread in welcome. "I'll lead you to my house. You didn't have any issues along the way, did you?"

"Not at all," I replied. "The Nilian gatekeeper was oddly excited about a coatl bone."

He laughed. "What might be trash to you could be a treasure to another. Our job as merchants is to bring treasures to people. Sometimes we make them, sometimes we find them, but we always sell them. Nilians don't use crystalights, so your toll-collector might have been more impressed with the coatl bone than with any crystalight you could have offered."

"Good thing I wasn't offering. All I have on me are the ones you've agreed to buy."

He nodded. "I'll be happy to finalize the transaction once we get back to my house. Come, we shouldn't keep my wife waiting much longer or else she might decide to feed you Yosoe food."

I grinned at his joke.

"Speaking of that, how is Susana eating?" he asked. "Does she eat Lagodorian food?"

"She does," I answered. "Fruits, vegetables, and rice mostly. She has quite an appetite for ube, which we previously never bought, so we've had to keep some in the house for her."

"Ube?" Giorvi asked. "I have never even heard of that."

"It's a purple yam," Su explained. "Grown only around the Seabells region. You would have to import it."

"Ah, we have plenty of yams here, though our family doesn't eat them. Oboro, have you ever had a yam?"

"No, Signore. In Ophidia, only women were allowed to eat them. Men had potatoes instead."

Giorvi reached under his kamen to scratch his beard. "Hmm. Honestly, I prefer potatoes, but that's still a shame. I'll get us some yams for later. You ought to know what they taste like."

"Th-thank you. I had always been curious. My mother and sister ate yams, but when I asked to try them, my mother whipped me."

"Oh, Oboro... If there's anything you want to try now that you're in Aloutia, just ask me. Any food that I can get at the store or order for import, I will get for you."

The boy swallowed. "I will think about it, Signore."

The Iolono family lived in the wealthy Black Mountain district, which was quite literally built inside the mountain. The portal house stood at the base of the mountain and had been carved from that location when a large portal was discovered there. Over the centuries, portals that *could* be moved had been brought to this centralized location to make it into a proper portal house.

The mountain was poked through with thousands of vents and pathways leading to the outside, hence how the scents of autumn had been able to waft into my nose, though a significant portion of the pumpkins I had smelled were artificial. Along the tunnel corridors, candles scented like pumpkins lit the way and provided pleasant aromas. They shone with little light, but it was not a necessity here—crystalights were held in cages amidst chandeliers. Though, to be honest, they were dimming and would need replacing soon.

"Last time I was here, those crystalights were brighter," I said.

"Indeed," Giorvi said as we passed underneath one. "All the crystalights down this hall came from the same deposit—the one from eighty years ago—so they will all die around the same time. Many Godlights, including the ones in thirty major Aloutian cities, were also created from that deposit. We have about a year to get the new ones sent out and blessed before the demonic hordes of the Makai have a chance to invade. Some of those Godlights might already be dead, but I doubt the Demon Lords will strike until they can take most of Aloutia in one fell swoop."

He said those dreadful words with such calm and calculation, it sounded more like he was discussing troika strategy rather than reality.

"You don't sound concerned," I said, unnerved.

"I'm not. If we have to send raw crystalight blocks to those cities and have merchants of light carve them into art later, we will. Having them in place and blessed comes first, and it *is* happening. I signed paperwork yesterday to ship five crystalights to Slevango. Ever since we secured the ground at the wedge-piece underneath Steena Village, the mining has gone smoothly."

"Wedge-piece?" I asked.

"Ami, there's nothing to be concerned about. We took every safety precaution, and nothing bad happened. You would have never known about it if I hadn't told you."

"But what could have happened?" Su asked. "Would it have caused a cave-in?"

Giorvi guided us to a vertical shaft with two spiral staircases. One was for people going up, and the other was for people going down. The railing was tall enough that even a person of my height would not fall if I stumbled. Even still, there were nets placed periodically across the gap. The steps were carved out of the mountain itself, black as ebonwood and sanded to a smooth finish. Specks of pink quartz had been scattered on the steps and embedded in imitation of the stars in Aloutia's sky. It was a path glittering with starlight.

Giorvi put his hand on one of the rails at his height. "A cave-in, yes. If the miners had removed the wedge without securing the ground, it would have collapsed. That piece was underneath part of Steena Village... the Mind church, in fact. If it had collapsed while your children were at school..." He sighed and started up the staircase.

While our kids were at school... Fuck, was it too dangerous to live in Steena Village anymore? One wrong move by a miner and the village would be destroyed as it sunk into the ground. I swallowed, terrified. If the school had sunk while my kids were there... I would have killed myself. I could not live with that sorrow.

Oboro jerked his head, indicating to us that we should go up next and he would follow behind us. His angry eyes behind that black kamen and the way his arms were solidly crossed over his chest gave him a grim appearance. He would brook no nonsense and would happily put any challengers in their place. To think he was only fourteen. Or was he fifteen now?

"Should we move to another town?" I asked as I took the first step on the starlight staircase. The steps were small—made for Yosoe feet. I took every other step.

I'd directed the question at Su, but Giorvi answered instead. "The top layer has been secured, so there is no chance of anything like what happened again."

"I suppose the only danger now is if Machenerate decides to put more crystalights under our village," I said.

Giorvi nearly stumbled and Oboro knocked me and Su into the wall on his way to make sure he was alright.

"Shall I walk beside you, Signore?"

"Oh, don't be worried about that, Oboro. I can't fall over the edge with that stupidly tall rail. Moreover, look, you pushed our guests aside rather roughly."

The boy hesitated. What expression lay beneath his mask? Was he embarrassed? Blushing?

"A-ah... I'm sorry, Signor Lasteran, Master Scrimshander."

I had already regained my balance, but Su had two hands on the ground and a third on the rail. Oboro helped him up.

"My deepest apologies, Master Godblood." Oboro fell to his knees, at least as best as he could on the staircase. One knee was on one stair while the other was on the one below it. He bowed his head. "My body moved on its own. I promise I did not intend to hurt you, but I am ready to accept any punishment you or Signore feel is right."

Giorvi grabbed Oboro's thick claw arm and pushed upward, though the Yosoe man was so small in comparison it reminded me of one of my children trying to nudge me. "None of that Ophidian slave nonsense now, Oboro. We don't bow in Aloutia, and no one is going to punish you for being a little clumsy. You apologized, and that is enough. Well, it's enough for me, anyway. Is it enough for you, Master Scrimshander?"

Su nodded. "Yes. Please, Oboro, you are in Aloutia now. I used to live in Ophidia, so I know about all the bowing and punishments they do there, but you're safe here. I would never bring Ophidian customs into this free land."

"But try not to be so rough in the future," Giorvi continued. "Perhaps you should have gone up the steps immediately after me."

"Yes, Signore. I will do so from now on. I—I thought it was best to keep them in front of me, in case..." He trailed off, perhaps too afraid of the implication he was about to make. "Apologies. I will make no excuses."

Giorvi tapped the boy's arm until he stood back up. "I'm sorry I even stumbled. Ami, something you said surprised me, and though I do not wish to blame you, I think that's why I nearly fell. Did you say Machenerate put the crystalights in the ground?"

"That is our working theory, since we have no other explanation. How else would crystalights appear anywhere but in Iuria? How do they appear at all?"

Giorvi ran his fingers through his beard. "That's a good theory. Well, let's continue."

The Iolono house had been carved out of the Black Mountain tunnel system. They had a window and door to the outside and to the inner tunnels. The cave-houses had been designed for Yosoe residents, so their ceilings were only high enough so those with long horns wouldn't scratch their chandeliers. I had to duck to enter the house, and then pay attention to the chandeliers as I navigated each room. I learned my lesson the first time I got my mane caught on a spiraling silver arm.

Yosoe houses were tight and cozy. Far too small for me, and almost too small for Oboro. It was a two-floor residence, walls decorated with scenic tapestries and paintings, and the floor a plush wine-red carpet.

When we first entered, the aroma of venison hit my nostrils. My neck shivered in anticipation as if I had killed the deer myself.

"We're home!" Giorvi announced as he removed his kamen and set it on a display where his wife and daughter had similar kamens. Aloutian customs dictated that guests should remove their kamens and shoes once inside a person's home, so we followed Giorvi and Oboro's lead.

The two Beatrices stepped into the foyer from a room on the second floor. The mother, dressed in a fancy black dress with gold lace, leaned on the balustrade. "Welcome to our home, friends. We've prepared a dinner that we hope you'll find appetizing. Please, come up this way."

Su squeezed my hand and grinned. "Smells like red meat. Seems they didn't make us Yosoe food after all."

Giorvi chuckled and started toward the stairs. "You can thank my partner for knowing what to cook. If it had been left to me, I'd have assumed all species enjoyed pine cones, bark, and worms!"

The mention of worms almost made me vomit... Thankfully, the wafting venison scent subdued that urge and made me hungry again.

We walked up the steps together. Like the ones leading up the Black Mountain, they were small steps made for Yosoe legs. I took them two at a time again.

"The table might be a bit crowded," Beatrice the Mother said as she moved plates into position. "We aren't used to having so many guests here. I hope this chair is your size, Mr. Lasteran. We got some bigger chairs for Oboro—Gods bless that poor boy, when we first got him, he thought we were gonna make him eat on the floor! And he said he'd be happy just being allowed to eat in the same room and at the same time as us!" Oboro walked into the room as she said that last line, prompting her to pinch his cheek affectionately. I doubted he felt anything on his chitinous skin. "Go on now, take your sword off and have a seat."

"Can I help you with anything, Mys Iola?"

"You can help us all eat this food! I wasn't sure how much a Wynnle could eat, so I may have gone overboard."

The table was loaded with food, some for me and Su, and some I wouldn't eat even if Giorvi offered me enough money to retire on the spot. Paid over the course of my lifetime so we wouldn't violate maxima laws, of course. Venison steaks, baked potatoes, asparagus, fried rice with eggs, carrots, onions, shallots, peas, and other such temperate vegetables which I didn't eat often. Plus a plethora of sauces, toppings, and garnishes to add wherever I desired.

In the center of the table was a croquembouche of pine cones and whole shallots. As neither Su nor I could eat pine cones, only the Yosoe would eat it, though I was aware they'd made it as a symbol for us. In places that grew shallots, they were a symbol to houseguests that they were not expected to pay for their food or lodgings. It was a tradition started after the Greed Wars when many people stopped using money. Why shallots, though, I had no idea.

The Yosoe each had large bowls of thick green leaves with chunks of potato, carrots, and pine cones. A bowl of curled cinnamon bark sticks sat close to the chair claimed by Beatrice the Daughter. She took one as she watched us choose our seats.

I only had two choices, as only two of the chairs would support me. Whichever one I did not take, Oboro would. I took the one across from young Beatrice. To my left were Giorvi and Oboro. To my right, Su and older Beatrice.

"This is wonderful," I said before I'd even taken a bite. The smells and sights were enough of a feast for my senses. "Thank you very much, Mys Iola."

"Oh don't just thank me," she said. "I would not have gotten this deer cooked on time if Giorvi hadn't told me how long they take!"

"I thought Wynnles ate raw food," the younger Beatrice said.

Her mother waved a hand. "It's still polite to cook food for guests. And besides, Master Scrimshander might want some, too."

Su licked his lips and brought a piece of steak to his plate. "Very much so! Thank you, Iolono family."

I took a venison steak as well and bit into it. Su had a particular philosophy about food, and he would usually not eat meat until someone else at the table had. He did not like the idea of eating meat if the animal had died *only* for him. He would likely have been a vegetarian if he didn't live with a family who required meaty diets. As long as the animal's meat went to sustain another person, he was okay eating his share.

Gods, I loved venison. All red meat, honestly. We mostly ate fish and okoes in Steena Village. Venison, goat, cotza, and susi were monthly meals at most.

"Easy on the cinnamon and sugar sticks," Giorvi said to his daughter as she gnawed on one. "Although you're probably giving Master Scrimshander a good idea of why we asked him to come here."

Su chuckled in his masculine manner while little Beatrice's ears perked up. If she was embarrassed, I could not tell. Her furry face did not flush with clear blood as skin-based faces did.

"I can't blame her for liking sweets," Su said. "I like them, too, Beatie."

She finished eating the cinnamon stick, staring intently at Su the whole time.

"Why are you called 'Master' Scrimshander?" she asked. "I thought 'Master' was only used for evil Ophidian slave owners."

Giorvi coughed, and I worried for a second he would choke on his food. The girl's mother let out a peal of raucous laughter. Oboro, stern-faced, kept his eyes on his plate.

Su smiled politely. "It serves two purposes for me. 'Master' is the proper title for a Godblood, which I am. It's also gender-neutral, which I am. I could go by either Mister or Mys if I were so inclined, but I don't like either of them. Not for myself, at least. Amiere goes by 'mister' and Liesle goes by 'mys' and I think they're quite fitting for those two. But I do not fit either word."

The concept must have been new to young Beatrice. "When I played with Fionn, he called you 'Mama Su', but he also used 'he' and 'him.'"

"That's right," Su said. "All our kids use different names for me, but Fionn has always called me Mama."

As a young child, Fionn had been closer to Liesle and Su than he was to me. I wasn't sure why... Some failing on my part. As he grew older and I could roughhouse with him, we started playing sports and he grew to like me more than before. Still, I think my inattentiveness to him at that young age might have been why he leaned toward a preference for maternal parents.

Little Beatie's eyes were practically aglow with interest. "What does a Godblood call their parent? Would you call yours Mama or Papa? Or something more respectful?"

"The parent who is a God?" Su asked. "Or the one who raised us?"

She shrugged as she shoved a forkful of potatoes into her mouth.

"We all have complicated relationships with our Godly parent," Su said. "Since they are in the afterlife and we are here on the mortal planes, few of us have any means to speak with them. Some Mind Godbloods speak telepathically to their father, Lord Lucognidus, but... well, we aren't all Mind Godbloods. Most of us refer to our divine parent as Lord Father or Lord Mother. Liqua uses the archaic 'Lady' title, so some Water Godbloods call her Lady Mother instead, or Mother Goddess."

"What do you use?" she asked.

Su grinned. "I am not at liberty to say which God is my parent, but I would call them either Lord Father or Lord Mother, depending."

Beatie looked to both of her parents in turn. I wondered if she was imagining calling them Lord Father and Lord Mother. Well, knowing the elder Beatrice and her love of languages old and new, she might prefer Lady Mother, too.

"And here I thought it was weird when Oboro told me he called his mother 'Master,'" the girl said.

Oboro kept eating, not wishing to defend or explain himself further.

"Oboro didn't know his master was his mother," Giorvi added. "Slaves in Ophidia aren't taught anything except what the master thinks is valuable to her. The only way they'd learn about where babies come from is if they observe it. Oboro has a younger sister, but she was already hatched by the time he could form memories."

Beatie turned back to Su. "Okay, and what about the parents who raised you? What did you call them? Didn't they worship *you* for being a Godblood?"

Su shook his head sadly, holding a piece of venison up to his mouth. He set it down before answering. "No, she did not worship me. My egg hatched in Ophidia, and I was raised by a slavemaster named Sumire. I... well, let's play a game. The same game I play with my children. I will tell you two stories, and you can decide for yourself which one is true. If I was born a girl, I called her 'Mother' and if I was born a boy, I called her 'Master.'"

"Either way, it doesn't sound like she respected you," the mother Beatrice said. "That is no way to treat a Godblood."

"She abused me. If I was a boy, she treated me like her slave and made me use my magic to coerce the others in her village. If I was a girl, she propped me up as her puppet and still made me coerce the others, then abused me in private."

Oboro raised his head and gave Su a calculating look. "But *you* were the Godblood in that situation. If you wished to snap her neck, you could have done so."

"Why did you not do the same to your master, Oboro?" Su asked.

He frowned. "I had no power over her. She was a Sasorin like me. Bigger, heavier, faster, and with a proper tail. If I had tried to fight back, I would have lost, and she would have punished me."

Su set his utensils down and crossed both sets of his fingers together. "Oboro, I'm sorry, but I don't believe you."

The boy stopped mid-chew. He managed to swallow only after everyone turned their attention to Su.

"What do you mean? How would you know what my mother looked like?"

"Oh, I believe that part," Su said. "But I do not believe you ever once thought to overpower her. You were born and raised as a slave. It never occurred to you that your life could be anything different. Serving your mother was simply the way things were. You lived in a rural cottage, didn't you? Far from any cities? You could have run away, but you didn't."

"I-I tried once, but a Shinkou Sueba[1] officer found me. Master made me sleep chained to my bed for a year afterward."

"Did you 'run away', though?" Su asked. "Or were you curious about the world and went exploring? Perhaps got lost in the woods? Did you think to escape from slavery?"

Oboro winced. "No, I suppose I didn't. I thought boys everywhere were enslaved."

"Exactly. You know why I endured the abuse that I did? Because children grow up thinking that the way their parents treat them is simply the way things are. Oh, we eventually learn the truth. Usually. You learned the truth when you came to Aloutia. I learned the truth when I was eight years old."

"How did you learn?" the Sasorin boy asked. "Did someone in the village teach you?"

Su licked his lips. "No, I learned by accident. I don't remember what caused me to snap. Sumire must have done something I did not like, and instead of accepting it, I threw a tantrum. The next thing I remembered, the village was in flames. I sat next to Sumire's corpse and... Never mind. The rest is not suitable for the dinner table or children."

I knew the rest of the story, though. Somehow, though he didn't remember it, Su had cleaned the flesh, muscle, and everything but the bone itself from Sumire's skull, and he put it on his head like a crown. The Ophidian government, not wanting to send clearbloods to deal with a Godblood, summoned the Demon King Susan to check on the village. She found Su amongst the ash and rubble, and took him with her to The Boneyard, her castle in the Makai.

---

1. Ophidian military police, rangers, and slave drivers

Little Beatrice scratched her chin. "I think you were a girl."

Su laughed. "Oh? And why is that?"

"I think an enslaved Godblood would have had a temper tantrum and destroyed his village a lot sooner than at eight years old, even by accident."

Su merely shrugged. "Perhaps you are correct."

"I think you were a boy," Oboro argued. "Because I don't think your mother would have done those things to you if you were a girl. She had to have known the consequences."

"You think an Ophidian mother has never abused her daughter?" Su prodded.

Oboro hunched over in his seat. "It's not that. What would she have to gain from abusing a Godblood? You said you live in a village, right? So there were other people around who knew her. And you, I assume. If she was abusing a girl, it would have looked suspicious. At least if you were a boy, she could have claimed she was imposing her mastery over her slave. The villagers would have never questioned it."

"But maybe the villagers were afraid of her," little Beatie said. "Or maybe they didn't know she was abusing him. Or maybe they were all evil in that village."

The two went silent.

"So which of us is right?" Beatie asked.

Su giggled. "I will never say. It wouldn't be very fun for me if anyone knew my original sex. I love hearing debates such as what you two just had."

Liesle and I used to have similar debates, though we flipped on which sex we thought he was. That had been so long ago, though. Somewhere along the road of life, we stopped trying to uncover the mystery he didn't want to be solved, and we accepted him for who and what he was now.

Man. Woman. A gender in-between. A gender out of the binary. A gender incomprehensible to anyone but himself. Su.

Chapter Thirty-Six: Merchant of Bone Business

"Hold my hands," Su told the young Beatrice, who sat cringing, almost on the verge of tears, on one of the kitchen chairs.

She wiped her eyes first, then wiped her hands on her wool pants.

"This is why I couldn't take her to any other merchant of bone," Giorvi said fretfully. He tugged at his seven-color-cloth belt, which I'd never seen him do, but it struck me as being an anxiety tic. He seemed as worried about his daughter as she was about Su. We all stood at the far end of the kitchen, near the stove and cupboards where they kept their pots and pans.

Beatrice took Su's lower hands. The tools of his trade lay on the counter to his left. His upper hands prepared a metal pick-like instrument.

"I want you to have absolute trust in me," Su said. "If you feel the slightest discomfort, squeeze my hands, and I will immediately back away. Alright?"

She nodded. Her horns lit up for a split second. Giorvi took a step closer to calm her, but his wife grabbed his shoulder and pulled him back.

"She'll be alright, Gio. I know what Master Scrimshander can do."

"I do, too, but..."

Little Beatie closed her eyes and opened her mouth. Su went to work. I stood behind Beatie, as I did not have much of a stomach for Su's dentistry work. It was one thing when I explored his mouth with my tongue, but a whole other thing when he explored other peoples' mouths with metal probes and pliers.

Su used his magic when performing dentistry. I did not know what element he was, nor could anyone see anything different happening to his body. It was said that Godbloods shifted portions of their magical blood into certain body parts when they used magic, and if that location was in a blood vessel close to the skin, you could see the discoloration of their skin. That also only worked for light-skinned Godbloods, of which there were few. Liqua and Sparkato were the only white-skinned Gods who frequently had kids and who weren't covered by an exoskeleton. Entomothy appeared light-skinned, but his 'skin' was really a layer of chitin that hid his blood vessels. Of course, the color of a God's skin said nothing about their children. Sparkato could produce a child with a woman whose skin was as black as ebony and their resulting child could have skin darker than Su's.

Su's skin, a rich brown color, made it impossible to guess which God was his parent based on that alone.

Whatever magic Su used, his patients never felt a thing. Beatrice held his hands as gently as when the procedure started. With her eyes closed, it was possible she didn't know he'd even started.

I wondered if she was conscious. The times Su worked on my teeth, I remembered nothing of the event afterward. Liesle and the kids had similar tales. They trusted Su to be their dentist, not just because he was family, but because his magic made the experience tolerable.

Oboro sat at the kitchen table, a look of horror on his usually-stoic face. But for all the fear it inspired, he could not look away.

"You can close your eyes," I said under my breath, hoping only he would hear. Giorvi and elder Beatrice were too distracted by the scene to notice us anyway.

"I must watch over Mys Beatrice," he said in a tough, determined voice. "If any harm befalls her, I must... Err, excuse me." He hadn't realized until the words were out of his mouth that he was threatening my husband. Oboro was just a kid, though. I couldn't blame him for speaking before thinking. Gods only know I didn't stop that habit until I was well into adulthood. Maybe I'd never stopped.

"Do you like Beatie?" I asked. "Or are you just following your boss's orders?"

Oboro turned his attention to Giorvi. The man stood by his wife with one hand clenched on his belt and the other tight in her hand. His ears were low, pointed downward. I could not recall ever seeing his ears in such a position and wondered if it was akin to canines who pin their ears down when in pain or as a sign of submission. Was Giorvi... scared?

"I guess I shouldn't ask when he's within hearing range," I said with a wry chuckle.

Before my laughter abated, Oboro said with utmost confidence, "I do like Mys Beatrice. And... I hope she likes me. I want to protect her forever. I'd gladly be her bodyguard after Signor Onoretti and Mys Iola are gone. Well, even if she doesn't like me... even if she falls in love with Fionn instead... I'll happily be her bodyguard. Even if she hates me..."

Fionn!? When did my son enter the picture?

"She likes Fionn? *My* son Fionn?" I had to be sure, on the off-chance he was referring to someone else with the same name.

"Of course she does! He's so cool, and funny, and talented. Gods, I'd love it if he taught me how to make seared ahi one day. Or if we could play kiwi-batte again."

I'd taught Fionn how to cook about a year ago, but he'd barely helped out since then. He likely would have kept helping if not for the depression that overflowed within after Tawny's death. Maybe I should invite him to cook with me again one day.

"I didn't know you liked him so much."

"Me? Oh... yeah, I guess I do. Mys Beatrice likes him, though, so I won't get in their way."

"Does Fionn like both of you?" I asked. He had never so much as spoken their names after they'd left, but Fionn had become much more secretive in the last few months. There was also the fact he wanted to come with us to Chernagora. Had he wanted to visit his friends?

"I wouldn't dare guess his opinion," Oboro said. "I'm just a servant. A bodyguard."

"When you three are older, if you all still like each other, there's no reason you couldn't form a polyamorous triad."

Oboro clenched his fist. "I… I would never dream of such a relationship with Mys Beatrice. Signore would…" He trailed off, intently staring at the table in front of him to avoid looking at Giorvi.

We were surely close enough for him to hear us, even if we did speak in low voices. On the other hand, Su was in the middle of a procedure with metal picks in Beatie's mouth. Perhaps Giorvi really was distracted.

"I wouldn't worry about it now," I said. "You're still young. Only fourteen, right? Much too young to worry about romance."

"Signore says I will be fifteen tomorrow."

"Oh, is that right?" That must have been why Giorvi asked us to bring the finished crystalight of Aurora. He intended to give it to him as a hatching-day present. "You didn't know your age when you were a slave, did you? I assume you learned after you came to Aloutia and had a Mantodea read your genetics."

"Yes, Signor Lasteran. I didn't even know Mantodea could do such things as tell the exact day a person hatched from their egg."

Beatrice the Mother tugged at Giorvi's shoulders and pulled him closer to us. "I swear, this man would fret over Beatie chipping a hoof."

"I can't help it!" he said. "She is everything to me."

"He's *fixing* her teeth, not sucking her soul from her body, you silly man. And maybe he wouldn't have to fix her teeth if you didn't give her so much candy!"

"She buys her own candy," Giorvi grumbled.

"Oh? And who taught her how to forge his signature on checks, go to the bank, and get as much money as she wants to go *buy* that candy? Who orders Oboro to watch over her when she goes shopping?"

Giorvi gave his wife a sly look, which she returned along with the most wicked grin I'd ever seen a Yosoe make.

"Do you feel no shame, Gio?" Beatrice asked. "Acting like such a foolish man in front of your bodyguard and your merchant of light?"

"I'm sure Ami can relate to being concerned about the welfare of his children!"

"And Oboro should learn how to be a father from a good man," I said. "If he wants to have children in the future, anyway. No pressure, if you're not interested. I imagine you didn't have a father figure in Ophidia."

I had not had a father figure, growing up in Aloutia, but somehow I'd managed.

Oboro gave no outward indication regarding his opinion.

"We'll work on that as he gets older," Giorvi said, patting Oboro on one of his thick scorpion claws. "You might become a legal adult tomorrow, but you're still far too young to think about starting a family. At least wait until you're twenty."

"Yes, Signore," Oboro said meekly.

"And your partner should be around that age, too. If you're twenty, they should be at least eighteen. Understood?"

"Yes, Signore. Um, but 'they'? As in... more than one?"

"If that's what you arrange, sure. I meant 'they' as in whether you choose a man, a woman, or something else. Not all neutral people are like Master Scrimshander who uses masculine pronouns. Some use 'they.'"

"It's also standard to use 'they' if we don't know the gender of your future spouse," Beatrice said. "And since you haven't given us the slightest inclination as to what kind of flower you are[1], we couldn't guess."

Oboro stiffened. "Um, well, it doesn't seem appropriate, but... if you'd like to know, I don't have a preference."

"So are you a tulip?" the woman asked. "Or a lalafina? Tulips like two genders. That usually means men and women, but there are exceptions. Ami is one such exception, isn't that right?"

"Indeed," I said. "I call myself a tulip because I'm attracted to women and neutrals. To be honest, I am only attracted to Liesle and Su."

Beatrice nodded. "And lalafinas are people who are attracted to every gender. Or many of them, at least."

"Oh. I... I don't think I've met many neutrals, or... or anything other than men or women."

"They aren't common in Chernagora," Giorvi said.

"And Ophidians don't believe in the concept," Beatrice added. "Anyone who's not completely female—by their standards—would get labeled as 'the slave sex' and would get called men no matter what."

My mother had chosen to come to Aloutia because of me. She claimed that if I had been born a girl, she would have chosen to be exiled to Ophidia instead. How different would my life have been? I could not imagine it.

"Would it be okay if I had multiple partners?" Oboro asked.

"I can't make that decision for you," Giorvi said. "Beatrice and I are monogamous by choice, and because we never fell in love with anyone else. There's no reason you have to follow what we do."

"Did you two always know you'd be monogamous?" I asked. "Or had you kept your options open when you were younger?"

Beatrice put a thick hand on Giorvi's shoulder. Perhaps I read too much into

---

1. Aloutian way of saying 'sexual orientation.'

it, but she seemed possessive of him. "It would have taken one hell of a woman to get me to share Gio. Another man, though? I would have considered it, but I have high standards. If I hadn't had faith in your ambition to become chief liaison of the merchants of light, I might have passed you over."

Her husband laughed. "When I was younger, I thought I was too low-class for you. I wanted to have a partner—a woman. Boring as it is, I am strictly a gladiolus [2]. But I thought you were out of my reach. If not for old Gionella—Giorvi Campanella—assigning us to the same jobs, making sure we slept at the same inn—"

Beatrice interrupted, "That Gionella once made sure the inn was so crowded, there was only one room left! And that room had only one bed!"

"I *distinctly* recall telling the innkeeper I'd sleep in the stable's hayloft."

"And I distinctly recall *tying* you to that bed because of some fool notion you had about how men should sleep in the hayloft while women get the nice bed, even though you were *clearly* weaker and more prone to catching a cold than I was."

"You did not tie me to the bed," Giorvi said, wagging his finger. "You only threatened it. And I convinced you to sleep on the floor of our inn room, and to take enough pillows and blankets to stay warm."

"That you did," she conceded. "And the next time Gionella got us assigned to a one-bed inn, we... well, I was the one to suggest *you* could sleep in *my* bed."

"And I offered to let you tie my hands to the bedposts if you wanted."

Beatrice let out a raucous laugh. "I was a novice at tying ropes back then. I think we're both masters of the craft now."

I hadn't realized the two were into such fun and games. Beatrice being involved in rope play did not surprise me, but I had only known Giorvi as a rich and respectable man. Hearing what he did in his bedroom...

Giorvi shook his head. "You'll say anything in front of Oboro and Ami to embarrass me. I don't have to act like a fool when you so enthusiastically talk about every foolish thing we do in private."

Beatrice swatted his arm playfully. "Oboro needs to learn how to be a good man, and how else will he learn unless he hears how well you treated me when you were a young man? And Ami? Oh please, Gio. Take one look at Liesle and Su and tell me Ami hasn't been tied up."

I snorted, and would have choked on something if I'd been drinking. "Um, it's actually not something any of us are into..."

---

2. A straight man

Beatrice shrugged. "Surprising. Liesle struck me as a lirist[3] , and every God-blood I've known has been domineering."

"If anything, Su is..." I coughed. "Well, it's a private matter, and nothing appropriate to talk about in front of Oboro... or without Su's permission. But he doesn't 'dominate' me."

Beatrice's low chuckle was the noise an Ophidian slave master would make as she plotted to whip her men. Or at least, that was how they were portrayed in theater and traveling performances.

"Well, if you choose to get adventurous," she started and leaned closer to my ear, "our guest bedroom has plenty of exciting things under the bed. Oh, don't worry about propriety with us! We'll clean the sheets."

My cheeks burned with embarrassment. This woman had no shame whatsoever!

"And you worry about *me* making a fool of myself," Giorvi rasped. "Ami, we're a wealthy family and we hire people to do certain chores for us, including laundry. My wife is correct—feel free to do what you want in the guest bedroom—but don't be embarrassed. None of us will be cleaning the sheets, if that's what you're worried about."

"Aww, you're ruining my fun, Gio!" Beatrice said in a cute, sing-song voice. "Well, perhaps I was ruining Ami's fun." She turned to me. "Gio is right. I was teasing you."

Su finished with his work, just in time for that awkward conversation to end. He guided little Beatie to a basin, turned on the running water, and had her rinse her mouth out.

"How was it?" Giorvi asked once his daughter could speak again.

"I don't remember a thing, Papa. How much time passed?"

"Perhaps an hour," he replied.

"It was ten minutes," the mother replied curtly. "Your silly papa only thinks it was an hour because he was so needlessly concerned."

The Iolono family went about bantering with each other, but I turned my attention to Su. He had gotten elder Beatrice's permission to use some of her alcohol solution to sterilize his tools, which he labored over now, rinsing them under the faucet. Many of the larger cities in Aloutia had running water systems, but the infrastructure hadn't been developed in Steena Village yet. We were close enough to the ocean not to need it, though.

"Well, your job is done," I said. "You could probably go back to Steena Village if you wanted. It's warmer there."

Su gave me a warm grin and scratched around my neck, ruffling up my mane. "And leave you here in the cold? I'll warm your bed, Ami-honey. Besides, I am *not*

---

3. A sadist, named after Lira, sadistic daughter of the founder of Ophidia.

done. I told Mr. Onoretti I would attend tomorrow's party, remember? I have work to do for him."

"Just to be his bodyguard?" I glanced over at the family. Giorvi had a hand under his daughter's chin as he looked at her teeth. "He has me and Oboro."

"No, I have... something else to do. I can't talk about it. It's merchant of bone business."

"What, are you going to debone whatever animal they plan to serve as the main course?"

Su giggled. "Perhaps I am. It's best if you don't worry yourself over it. I don't meddle in your merchant of light business, and I must ask you don't meddle in merchant of bone business."

He said it as sweetly and gently as he could, but I was still off-put. I held my tongue. We all kept secrets from each other. We had decided long ago that we wouldn't pry knowledge or hold it against one another if we chose to keep something a secret. In this matter, I had to respect his wishes.

"Just stay safe, Sugar."

"I will. Nothing in this city can harm a Godblood, Ami-honey. You needn't be concerned."

Chapter Thirty-Seven: Aurora

Giorvi had asked to speak with me privately in his study that evening. His bookshelves held a hundred tomes, including the complete collection of the Codex Dominex, Year 557 edition. Interspersed between books stood statues of dying and dead crystalights. The two red rabbits—one hopping over the other—had nearly lost their luster, a blue octopus had perhaps a year of light left, and a vine thick with leaves was nothing more than a viridian-painted statue. A crystalight of geometric shapes shone the brightest, and it sat on his desk, serving as a lamp.

A lapidary globe of Aloutia loomed beside me as I sat in a plush chair across from his desk. The room had not a speck of dust; if the books went unread, they were at least brushed off on occasion to construct the illusion that they were loved. But knowing what I knew of Giorvi, I would not be surprised if he did earnestly consult them.

One of the books on his desk was an Orochigo-Caprise dictionary. I supposed for teaching Oboro.

"You have Aurora?" he asked as he poured wine into two glasses for us both.

I unraveled the cloth around the completed crystalight. The Yellow Moon, Aurora, with its magnetic rainbow tail trailing down and swirling out to become the statue's base.

The light reflected in his horizontal pupils as a wide grin spread across his face.

"Ahh, it's so beautiful. I will give it to Oboro tomorrow for his hatching-day. If he keeps it around, it will last his lifetime and the lifetime of his kids and grandkids! If it gets turned into a Godlight, they'll be safe for at *least* that long." He picked up his wine glass and took a drink.

"You see the crystalights underneath Steena Village as a blessing, don't you?" I asked in a low voice. Tawny's fall flashed through my mind. Fuck, it had been weeks since the last time I had that intrusive thought.

Giorvi set his wine glass down. "Amiere..." He sighed. "I understand what you lost. I cannot begin to imagine your pain. Frankly, if I lost my little Beatrice, I'd..." He shook his head. "I shouldn't say that."

"Parents should not outlive their children," I said. I took the glass, but only stared at it, sloshing the red liquid in swirls.

"If only such a law was divinely written into fate. Well, Lucognidus *does* hate fate."

I took a drink. It was the first alcoholic beverage I'd had on my tongue in years. Perhaps since before Eruwan was born. No... I'd had a few drinks after that. Around Fionn's hatching was when I stopped.

When had I started judging time based on the births of my children?

"Can I ask you a question?" Giorvi asked. "Just a philosophical question. Theoretical." Sitting in his dark wood chair against a backdrop of books and crystalights, he looked like a philosopher already.

"Go ahead, but I'm not much of a thinker."

He took a drink before asking the question. "If you *knew* that your children were likely to die in ten years... No, not just *your* children. Every child in Aloutia. And perhaps the odds aren't one hundred percent. Let's say each child has a fifty percent chance of living. If you knew for a fact this lottery would occur, but you could stop it by killing a single child—a stranger's child, not your own—would you do it?"

I had no answer. I drank the entire glass of wine as I tried to conceive of such a scenario.

"I would want to protect my children, of course," I replied. "But... I don't have it in me to kill someone else's child, either. I'd tell Su or Liesle. They have the strength to make that choice."

Giorvi's hand shook and he had to put the glass down. His eyes stared into Aurora, but he wore a blank expression. He might as well have been looking at the real Aurora up in the night sky. "Right. No reason to stress ourselves out over these theoretical scenarios. I'm sorry I even brought it up."

"What would you do?" I asked.

"I would... I would do anything for Beatrice. In the scenario I described, I would not be happy about it, of course. I would beg Lucognidus for forgiveness. I would weep at his feet until I shed my weight in tears. I would make any sacrifice needed to pay even a coin of my debt to the parents, knowing that all the money, jewels, blood, and tears in the world could never repay that debt... Knowing that such a debt cannot be paid." He sighed. "Gods, wine makes me philosophical. Look at me rambling, Ami. Amiere. Hmm, I like the name Amiere. You don't object to me calling you that, do you?"

It would have been awkward in North Corridorean Fleur dialect, which he spoke now only for my sake. The nuance of my name was not internalized for him. Perhaps he heard it and only heard a normal name.

"I don't care. If I was dumb enough to make that my public name and then lazy enough to never change it, I ought to live with the consequences. In any case, it seems you've thought about that particular scenario a lot."

He cracked a smile. "I did a lot of thinking when I was a younger man. Anyway, here, let me write the check for the crystalights you finished. I'll let you get back to your room. I'm sure Master Scrimshander has grown bored waiting for you."

When I entered the guest bedroom, Su was laid on the bed with his bare back—and ass—to me. He was nearly naked, dressed only in a fur-lined covering over his breasts and a thong so tight it looked uncomfortable. The sight of his beautiful butt cheeks made my heart skip a beat. I licked my lips. He wore all the earrings to indicate he was eager and willing to fuck.

He raised himself up and turned his head to see me, while also keeping his back to me, very clearly wanting to display his rear. "Ami-honey? If you're in the mood, come warm me up. It's *cold* here in Chernagora."

My penis was erect before he finished. "I am in the mood, Sugar. But... perhaps just cuddling tonight. Despite what the Iolonos said about hiring people to wash their sheets, I would be embarrassed if they got *too* dirty."

He beckoned me over with a seductive roll of his head. He gyrated his hips, enticing me with that perfect ass.

I removed my clothes, letting them fall unceremoniously to the floor, and crawled into bed. I pressed my body against Su's back and slid my cock along the string of his thong, enjoying the feeling of his cheeks against my barbs. I laid my head on my arm over the pillow and wrapped my other around him, between one of his upper and lower arms.

He'd claimed to be cold, but his body was far warmer than mine. The sensation was like touching rocks that had been in the ground oven, but left to cool long enough that Flamboil's Blessing wasn't triggered.

"It's nice not having to worry about kids barging in on us," Su said. "We should do this more often."

"Wish Liesle were here," I replied, imagining her warming up my backside. Out of us three, I was the middle in size, so I was usually in between them. It was a nice spot to be in. "We can leave the kids with Orienna and Piotr some time and go to one of our secret caves."

"Mm. Maybe Liesle could take us to her secret cave some time."

"Is that innuendo?" I asked. "I think we've both been to her 'secret cave.'"

Su giggled in his masculine way. "I hadn't intended that to be innuendo, but now that you say it... No, actually, I found the cave where she goes to paint in private. It was an accident on my part. I chased a pufferfish into the lagoon nearby. Ironically, it was so I could make a dildo for her. Who would have guessed that fish would find her 'secret cave' before it was ready?"

"Did you explore any deeper?" I asked.

"No. For one, although I could see it, I could not reach it—it's high up, where one must fly. Secondly, we all keep our secrets. If I had gone inside, I would have violated her privacy the same as if she tore my clothes off to see what my genitals look like. Or cut me to see the color of my blood."

I was all too aware of the fact that my barbed penis was close to doing both those things. "Should I stay on my half of the bed?"

"Oh, nonsense. Your dick isn't going to tear this thong, I promise. Nor will it prick my skin. And that's not an insult about your penis. I've enhanced both with my magic. You couldn't cut me with your claws or teeth, either."

What element was that power? Something in the Stone element, maybe?

I rubbed my hand down Su's side and down to his ass, giving it a strong grab. He wiggled delightfully.

"Ami-honey! I'm ticklish there!

I moved his hair aside so I could kiss the back of his neck. "And you wanted me to grab it, or else you wouldn't have seduced me with it."

His fingers scratched inside my mane. "I wanted you close to me."

Despite my arousal, my cock was losing its erection. I was fine with that. Even if he wore all his earrings, I was not in the mood to do anything more than what we were doing.

I fell asleep with Su in my arms. The last thing I remembered was him whispering something to me, but I was too far gone to respond.

When I woke up, Su was already awake and dressed, clad in one of the thick woolen shirts we'd had to order from a clothier who specialized in making garments for quadrubrachial people.

"Spirits bless this day," he said in a chipper tone. What had him so happy?

"Sounds like they already have," I replied. "What time is it? Did I sleep in?"

Su sat beside me as I sat up. He rubbed my back with both right hands. "Compared to usual, yes, but it doesn't matter here. We're just going to relax for today. Giorvi's big party is tomorrow. He hasn't explicitly said that our role is to be intimidating, but I can read subtext. He could have invited any merchant of light, but he invited you, a Wynnle. And he invited me, who's not a merchant of light at all. But I *am* a Godblood, worthy of being feared, I suppose."

"To anyone who doesn't know you."

Su brought one of his hands down to my knee and patted it. "You think too highly of me. Or perhaps you have known the peaceful Su for too long. You've never seen my wrathful side."

"I hope I never do." I wanted to kiss him, so lovely was his gentle smile, and so powerful was my yearning, but he wasn't wearing any of his bone jewelry.

I got dressed in warm clothes, similar to Su's in style, but I put my bone earrings in. If he changed his mind later, he would know that I was in the mood.

My perception of Oboro changed each day. I'd first thought the boy was a stern, dangerous adult man. Then I'd learned he was only a child. Yesterday, he confessed to wishing to become friends with my son. Today, the boy broke down in grateful tears after receiving his gift from Giorvi.

He wiped his tears away with his claws while holding the statue of Aurora in his lower hands.

"I... I don't deserve this, Signore." He sniffed. "It's too expensive and... and pretty."

"Don't think for a minute you don't deserve nice things," Beatrice the Mother said. "I didn't rescue you from Ophidia just so you could keep acting like a slave. Now, when you receive a gift, you should say 'thank you.'"

Oboro bit his lip, but managed a weak "Thank you."

"You should keep it in your bedroom," Giorvi said. "You can use any of the coverings here in the house, if there's one you like, or we can go shopping for a new one later."

Oboro opened his mouth, but no words came out. His face streamed with tears.

And if I thought the crystalight statue brought out the boy's most emotional state, I was not ready for the topic of his official public name.

Giorvi set the paperwork on the table and read the Aloutian rights and responsibilities. Since Oboro was a Darkness elemental, he didn't need the same warnings that Eruwan had gotten about becoming a heretic. The Pentagonal Dominion had no God of Darkness, so Oboro could not commit heresy no matter what he did. He was under no threat of ever losing his blessings.

"Now, I'll need to write your official public name on this line here, then sign it on this one," Giorvi pointed to each line with tip of his pen. "Per Aloutian law, you need a first name—the name you intend to be called in public. It *can* be your magic name, but preferably it's something else. Then you'll need a surname, a name to be passed down to your male children and to be combined into your future family-name."

Oboro gulped. "I... I really don't have any name other than 'Oboro.' Can that be my public name?"

Beatrice the Mother nodded. "A magic name isn't only a sound, it's also a spelling. Orochigo names often have two spellings for the same pronunciation. While you can summon demons or demis with just the sound, other people would need to know how to write your magic name in order to hurt you. We don't know how your mother wrote your magic name—probably with the muji for 'misty moonlight'—but in all likelihood, you are perfectly safe using the name

Oboro and writing it in Caprise letters.

"Then please let me do that. Even if it *is* my slave name... even if it is what my master called me, it's what I'm used to. I don't think I could change my name."

"You don't have to," Giorvi said. "Has someone pressured you into changing your name just because it was given to you by an Ophidian?"

He bumped his claws together. "Well, no, but... some people at headquarters said my name was 'too Ophidian.' They said it made me sound like a slave."

Giorvi brushed his hand like he was swatting a mozzy away. "Bah, I know the people you're talking about. They just like to gossip. Don't pay them any heed. Now, have you thought about what surname you'll have?"

"I, umm..." Oboro's face went pale and he could not hide his shaking hands no matter how hard he tried to hold himself steady. "I would accept any surname you give me, Signore. I don't... I don't think I can give myself a name. Anything I choose would just disappoint me, but if you give me a name you like, then I'll like it because you chose it for me."

Perhaps some people would call it a slavish mindset, but I understood where the boy was coming from. He wanted to please the people around him. There was, of course, one surname in particular I knew he wanted, but to say it would be to assume too much of Giorvi's intentions.

"As you wish, Oboro. I have intended to officially adopt you into our family for a few months now. If you wish to become my son, I'd happily sign off that paperwork, too. I have it in my office. If you agree to that, I'd like you to take my surname."

The Sasorin boy's mouth struggled to keep a sob inside. He sniffled. "S-Signore, are you sure? I'm... I'm nothing special. I'm not smart or clever like Mys Beatrice. I—"

"Cleverness isn't a requirement for adoption," Giorvi said gravelly. "I won't argue with you about whether or not you're clever, because you'll deny that for years still, I think. Maybe one day you'll break that self-doubt the Ophidians hammered into you. But regardless, I want to adopt you. You've become a member of our family already, all that's left is to put it on paper. I must confess, there's nothing special about the Onoretti name. All my male relatives in the Sunset Kingdom are poor peasants and miners. Even if the name *does* mean 'small honor,' you truly won't get any honor out of it at all."

"No! It would be the greatest of all honors! One I'm not worthy of! Is it really okay? You're not going to take it back? This isn't just some joke, is it?"

Beatrice the Mother clapped her hand on Oboro's shoulder. "If it were a joke, I'd be laughing, wouldn't I? A crude woman like me would be grinning and cackling at you, a poor fool of a kid, if this were a prank."

Giorvi set his pen on the line where he would write Oboro's name. "I cannot do it until you agree to it. Would you like to become Oboro Onoretti?"

He took a deep breath. "If you think I'm worthy..."

The little Beatrice rolled her eyes and stomped toward her father's chair. "He'll never agree to it! No matter how much he wants it, he will never say he's worthy. Can I have the pen, Papa?"

I raised an eyebrow. Surely the little girl didn't intend to write on official documentation. The Life church would check the handwriting and know immediately if a child wrote it.

"I think you're right," Giorvi said, handing the pen to her. "Just his name, please."

The younger Beatrice wrote the name 'Oboro Onoretti' in a perfect imitation of her father's handwriting. I had read countless letters from Giorvi; I knew his handwriting well. I was no handwriting analyst, nor did I have to check signatures for forgeries, but my amateur eyes could detect no difference between her handwriting and her father's.

"Are you sure you're willing to sign *your* name now, Papa? I can do that, too!"

"I would prefer for Oboro to give me confirmation first."

"I... Yes! Yes, please, Signore. If this isn't a cruel joke, if you truly mean to adopt me, then please let me become Oboro Onoretti."

"Can I sign now?" Beatrice asked.

"Just my first name," he said. "I think it would be more meaningful to Oboro if he saw me sign the paperwork."

The girl wrote Giorvi's first name precisely the way he did. Every letter was an impeccable imitation of his signature.

She handed the pen back to him so he could sign his own surname, though judging by how she'd written it in Oboro's surname, she could mimic that just as perfectly.

Beatrice could forge her own father's signature. Surely that wasn't *good*. She could have signed his checks! In fact, hadn't the elder Beatrice joked about it when we first came to their house? I couldn't help but feel this was something that would get her in deep trouble later, but... Well, Giorvi knew best for his child. Perhaps it was useful in a city like Chernagora.

"There," Giorvi said. "It's done. We'll take it to the Life church later and it'll all be official."

Oboro rubbed his eyes with his upper hands, though he could not hide his tears. "I... I have never been this happy in my life, Signore."

"Shouldn't you call him 'Papa' now?" Little Beatie asked.

"I could not!" Oboro dropped his hands, showing his cheeks as they paled, blushing.

Giorvi brushed his fingers through his beard. "It would probably be best to call me 'Signore' while we're at work, anyway."

"Yes, Signore!" Oboro clenched his hands into fists. "I won't disappoint you! Um, when are we going to the Life church?"

"Tomorrow would be best. We can drop off this paperwork on our way to the party." Giorvi glanced up at me and Su. "I hope that won't be an issue. I would like you two to accompany me the entire time, but if taking a detour to the Life church is an inconvenience, you could go on ahead of me."

Su shook his head. "Not an inconvenience at all."

It wasn't like I had other business elsewhere. "We will accompany you wherever you go."

He smiled. "I knew I could count on you."

Besides, I was curious if the Life volkhv would even *look* at the signature. Or, even if the volkhv knew the signature was a fraud, would they say anything? Would they question a man of elite status? Chernagora was not like Steena Village in regard to social equality. This was a city of finite resources; there was only so much space in the Black Mountain for people to live, so only the 'best' of society were given homes here. This was a society of hierarchies.

Giorvi had climbed his way up that hierarchy by reaching the highest levels in the merchants of light guild. Beatrice had acquired status as a polyglot and operatic singer, too. As I had no experience living in a hierarchical society—well, not one as structured as this anyway—I could not begin to imagine the perks the couple enjoyed here. If Giorvi had the clout to hire a merchant of dance, could he commit murder himself? If a humble Life volkhv dared to speak out against a fraudulent signature, what then? Would Giorvi have the volkhv removed? Killed?

Sometimes the traitorous brain inside my thick skull truly manifested the worst, most heinous thoughts. Of course he would not commit murder; that was not the person he was. Giorvi was just an aging man, doing his best to raise his family and save Aloutia by getting Godlights to every city that needed one.

Chapter Thirty-Eight: A Grand Party

The elder Beatrice had ensured Su and I were dressed in sufficiently fancy garments for the event. It was a high-class soirée for the merchants of light and some of the other guilds in this city. A certain degree of dignity was expected of all guests. Giorvi and Oboro were dressed in the fanciest suits I'd ever seen them in, colored bright, and their faces only partially hidden by filigree masquerade kamens.

I asked Giorvi if he was sure he wanted me to be there. I had no social graces. I had spent the last fifteen years chiseling crystals, cooking fish, and cleaning up baby vomit while most of the attendees had spent that same time sipping expensive wines.

My garments resembled the formal attire I had at home that I reserved solely for meetings with Giorvi or trips to Seabells, except this one was a bright, nio-blue with a scarlet mantle and matching kamen. The mixture of blue, red, and my yellow mane made for a hideous look, but it was meant to imitate poisonous animals with such coloration. It was high-class fashion to elite businesspeople.

Su's clothes and kamen were similarly garish and, in my opinion, the ugliest things he'd ever worn. I already wanted him out of them, and not just because I preferred seeing him naked. I supposed from the clothes' perspective, they had the honor of being worn by the sexiest person in the dominion.

The party took place inside the Black Mountain caverns, near the summit. The Life church was on the way, so we did not have to step outside into the cold, thank the Gods. As in Seabells, the Black Mountain had a circular chamber where churches of several elements sat in a circle. In this city's case, the churches were carved out of the cavern walls. I only recognized the Life church by the egg-shaped relief above the door.

Giorvi's encounter with the Life church volkhv went exactly as I had envisioned. We went in as a group, the church keeper accepted his paperwork without even looking at the signature, and wished us all a good time at our party. That was that. Oboro was now an Onoretti in the eyes of the Holy Aloutian Empire.

The event was so exclusive that a Yosoe doorman stopped us at the entrance. Giorvi showed him his invitation and announced us three as his bodyguards. I would have thought three bodyguards was excessive, but he was not the only one bringing along that number. In the ballroom, hired muscle outnumbered the executives.

The ballroom was the most beautiful and extravagant room I'd ever set foot in. Crystalight chandeliers, carved by a master merchant of light, shone from high arched ceilings adorned with murals. Marble pillars stood tall with vines of morning glories spiraling to the top. In any other building, the vines might have been glowlight lotuses. Yet here, because the light of the crystalights was so overbearing, perhaps the interior designer felt a more subdued flower was in order, so as not to blind the guests.

The tables were made of clearest glass, with legs shaped into gold foil curls in imitation of leaves. The tablecloths were a shimmering, gossamer fabric that looked too brittle to be used more than once, and knowing the wealth on display here, it probably *would* only be used once. The chairs were colored Domovoi glass featuring similarly elaborate curls on the arms and legs.

The attendees were mostly Yosoe, Domovye, and Stone Gluckans, all dressed in finery and filigree masks similar to what I'd been stuffed in, though every person in this room had more elegance in their small fingers than I had in my entire body. I was the only Wynnle, and Oboro was the only Sasorin. We stood out like a raging fire against the darkness of the Hollow Void.

Domovye, with their bunches of eyestalks instead of faces, wore silky coverings that blocked the stems from view while exposing the bulbous tips. I supposed those veils were their equivalent of kamens.

"Giono!" a voice boomed as we entered. A Domovoi from across the room raised their arm high and beckoned us over. Guildmaster Thousand-Diamonds. They had been the Guildmaster for several years, but I had only met them three times. I only recognized them as the Guildmaster because they wore the ceremonial chain of office. While most species wore it like a necklace, Domovye wore it around their pipes. The many chains connecting Thousand-Diamond's pipes resembled a spider's web, and the dozens of tiny crystalights dangling from each link were like dew drops... or prey caught in the web.

"Dia!" Giorvi shouted back cheerfully and made his way to the Guildmaster's table, where a feast of gemstones and precious minerals was laid out for them. I hesitated, unsure if I was allowed in their space, but Oboro followed, ever the diligent henchman. Su grabbed my arm and forced me along.

Giorvi and the Guildmaster embraced each other and made small talk in Caprise.

"Ah, you remember Mr. Lasteran, don't you, Dia?" Giorvi asked. "He's one of our best! I can't remember when he was last here, though."

"Yes, we've met!" Thousand-Diamonds spoke English for my benefit, but with a heavy accent, and loud enough I was sure everyone in the room could hear. They only spoke through one pipe... Gods save the ears of anyone who listens to them speak through all their pipes. "You made that magnificent sculpture of an oak tree, didn't you?"

"Yes, Guildmaster. That was my work." That had only been a few years ago, when Nio had just hatched and Tawny had been in her mischievous toddler years. Fionn had been in the midst of his bullying of Cohaku. I had been so stressed in those days, I had used the oak tree sculpture as an escape—an excuse to get away from my chaotic family life for a while.

"Excellent," they said, rubbing their hands together. "You're the merchant who lives near the recent aye-too deposit, yes? Quite fortu—"

"Excuse me, Guildmaster," Giorvi cut in with a dire tone. "I think Mr. Lasteran knows them as 'crystalights.'"

Thousand-Diamonds stroked one of their facial stalks. "Ahh, yes, crystalights. We're lucky to have a merchant close to the deposit. Saves on transport fees."

Giorvi grimaced. I wondered if he was embarrassed on my behalf. For my sanity, I had to assume the Guildmaster knew nothing of Tawny's death, or else they would not have called the whole situation 'lucky.'

"Indeed," I said. I didn't want Thousand-Diamonds to pity me, so I chose to remain silent about my daughter's death. "I've made a few sculptures already from the fine crystalights under my village. I've heard they will shine for twice as long as usual."

"That they will! They will make good Godlights, if the Gods deign to bless them."

I nodded, not knowing what else to say. I had nothing to do with the blessing of Godlights, and the idea of discussing the Gods' intentions scared me. For some reason, it felt like I was intruding in Su's business. Whatever God blesses the Godlight might be the one who parented Su, and... well, somehow, trying to get inside their mind and understand them felt wrong. It was a betrayal of Su's trust in some manner that I knew in my soul but could not logically explain.

"Why, just look!" Thousand-Diamonds pointed up toward one of the chandeliers. I hadn't noticed when I first walked in, thinking it was just an elaborate decoration, but on careful examination...

Hanging from the chandelier was a cage imprisoning a *demon*. It couldn't have been larger than my head, mane excluded. It had been stripped of any clothing and handcuffed to the bars. Grey skin, a deformed smile, and gemstones on its chest which were too far removed from any of the sapienti species for it to be anything but a demon. It sat with thin legs dangling out between the bars.

"What's it doing here?" Su asked.

"Harvesting negative emotions for a Demon Lord," the Guildmaster replied. "We captured it and decided to use it to gauge when the Godlight was blessed. When it melts or turns to ash, we'll know one of the Gods has infused a crystalight with divinity."

"You'll know which crystalight was blessed?" I asked.

"The Gods who bless us do not play tricks," Giorvi said. "All crystalights are blessed by either Lord Lucognidus, Lord Sawyer, or Lord Flamboil, and we are certain they will choose the one in our designated spot at the top of the mountain."

Thousand-Diamonds took a piece of sapphire from their tray, popped it into their mouth, then returned their attention to Giorvi. "Mr. Onoretti, you were going to speak with the, uh, spione, right?"

What was a spione? Was that one of the eighty-four sapienti species? I'd had to learn the names of all of them in school, but I had forgotten some since becoming an adult.

"Yes, is he here?"

The Guildmaster subtly pointed with one of the stalks atop his head. "The sheep ram-Yosoe at the table with a Domovoi, an ibex-Yosoe, and a Plecopteran."

"Thank you." He turned to face us. "Mr. Lasteran, Master Scrimshander, Oboro, I have business with the man at that table, but I'd like you to accompany me. He only speaks Caprise, so you may not understand what I'm saying, but I promise you, your presence behind me will be much appreciated. And, ah... Oboro, you know what to do. Mr. Lasteran, Master Scrimshander, please don't interfere with Oboro's work unless this ram-Yosoe resists."

Su was right... Giorvi *did* want us as bodyguards. A Yosoe, especially a ram, would likely be intimidated by a Wynnle and a Sasorin. If he knew Su was a Godblood, well... anyone would be intimidated by *that.*

Giorvi sat across from the ram-horned Yosoe without being invited to the table. I may not have known what passed for good manners in Chernagora, but surely that was not proper. Giorvi steepled his fingers underneath his chin as he spoke to the man in Caprise. I didn't know the words, but his tone was disconcerting. Dangerous. Threatening.

The other people at the table tried to keep their eyes on Giorvi, but I caught them stealing glances at me from behind their fancy silver and gold filigree kamens. Fearful glimpses, so short that they turned back to Giorvi by the time my eyes found theirs. They looked at me the way rabbits looked at lions. They knew I could have killed them in three seconds.

They didn't know I had neither the willpower nor the courage to do it. It had taken me weeks of watching Miltico abuse Usana before I'd found the resolve to kill him, and I still hated myself for taking so long.

"Oboro!" Giorvi shouted an order to his adopted son, but before another word could be uttered, the Sasorin boy leapt over the table and restrained the ram-Yosoe. I blinked in surprise, and when my eyes opened again, everyone in the room had jumped to their feet—or in the case of the Domovye, had slithered around to face the commotion. The three people who'd been with the ram-Yosoe stood ready to pounce. The Plecopteran stared at me. They had a shaking hand on a dagger at their belt and their membranous wings vibrated in anticipation. Were they shaking because of me?

I gaped, heart pounding, terrified I was about to be involved in a fight. Plecopterans were insanely quick. One who was trained to fight could have easily stabbed me with their knife a dozen times and jumped out of my range in the time it took me to swipe my claws. Were they truly afraid of *me*? Why? They had the advantage.

Giorvi stood, turning toward his audience. "Merchants of light!" he announced. "We have a traitor in our midst!" He thrust an accusatory finger at the Yosoe writhing in Oboro's grip. "This spione has been selling information to Iuria! Now, what do we do to traitors here in Chernagora?"

"Tagliare il corno!" several people shouted in unison.

"Exile the fucker!"

"Cut off his middle horn, too!" a woman spat.

"Cut off his finger!"

The demon locked in the cage rattled and swung his prison beneath the lights. I could not tell if it was scared, excited, or aroused.

Ultimately, of the options presented, 'tagliare il corno' won out, and the whole room chanted it. I didn't know what it meant, though I assumed corno was related to 'horn,' since the Fleur word was similar. Were they going to cut off a horn? Possibly both?

As if to answer my question, a large Domovoi approached the Guildmaster's table with a fucking *saw*. Giorvi instructed Oboro to take the ram-Yosoe to that table and restrain him. The Guildmaster themself had no qualms, in fact, they were chanting along with the crowd and pushed aside their plate of rubies and sapphires to make room for the 'spione.'

What the fuck was going on? I thought these were civilized people. I expected better from the upper administration of the guild, the high class of Chernagora. They were behaving little better than the animals they'd evolved from. I shuddered, unsure of what I should do. Giorvi didn't expect me to participate in this madness, did he?

Su touched my lower back, right above my tail. His soothing presence was all I needed. I stole a glance at his face—his warm, smiling face; his gentle eyes. Whatever was happening, Su was okay with it, and therefore I was okay with it.

"You! You bodyguards who were hired by this spione!" Giorvi waved his hands toward the door. "We excuse you, understanding that you were hired by him. Leave now, and you will be compensated. Fight, and we'll throw you in prison."

The three who'd been with him—the ibex-Yosoe, a Domovoi, and the Plecopteran—nodded to each other and left without saying a word.

The traitor bellowed and begged as Oboro held him down on the table.

"How dare you! This cannot be legal! I demand to speak with a lawkeeper!"

"Oh, this is perfectly legal," Giorvi said. "Or have you forgotten that I am the Chief Liaison to the Aloutian Empire? You want the lawkeepers? I know Commander Freya Rubaiya and Captain Lungidus Pavo personally. They have authorized us to perform castigo on spiones like you. Now, cut off this fucker's horn!"

The crowd continued to chant. The heat of the room intensified. My blood rushed throughout my body, only to calm down again when Su's finger danced up my spine.

"Just watch, Ami-honey," he said in such a quiet whisper that I was honestly not sure how I heard it over the incessant chants of 'tagliare il corno.'

The Domovoi with the saw brought it down on the Yosoe's horn and went to work cutting it off. The party-goers, all dressed in their fine sheer gowns and silk or fur suits, holding delicate flutes of wine or rafa[1], bellowed as if they were at war. Their shouting drowned out the noise of the saw as it chiseled back and forth in the Domovoi's powerful arms. As the horn came off, a cheer erupted that echoed through the ballroom and shook the chandeliers.

The cutter held the horn up high, displaying it for the roaring crowd. Even the caged demon danced in joy at the violence.

"Now, now, let's settle down," Giorvi said, motioning with his hands for the room to mellow. "I have to ask him if he's a coward or not, and *I* can't even hear what I'm saying."

As the crowd quieted, I found myself inadvertently inching closer to Su. I put my arm over his shoulders, seeking his warmth and comfort.

I kept my eyes on Giorvi the whole time, and something raw and visceral awoke inside me. I'd never known him to be such a monster before, to be capable of such brutality. His horizontal eyes had once unnerved me, but I had attributed that to a subconscious bias. A speciesist bigotry best left unspoken. But now... was there something demonic within him? Something cruel and perverse?

"What'll it be, spione? Azione cordado? Or do you seek repentance?"

The ram-Yosoe babbled incoherently, shivering under Oboro's body as it pressed him hard into the table.

"I-I can't leave Aloutia! My family is here! My house! My son needs medicine!"

"Then you have only one choice," Giorvi said. He twisted his head to find me and Su, and beckoned us with his hand. What on all the planes? Was I supposed to *do* something?

"Stay here," Su whispered, stepping away. As he approached Giorvi, he withdrew a sharp, ivory-hilted knife. Su had made that knife himself, not too long ago. He'd scrimshawed paisley patterns into the handle. It was a work of art.

Su handed the knife to Giorvi, who in turn set it in front of the ram-Yosoe.

"*You* must show us that you want forgiveness. Oboro, let his hands go."

The Sasorin obeyed, releasing the Yosoe's hands, but retaining his grip on the man's waist.

---

1. Champagne.

"You know what to do, spione," Giorvi said in a crackling voice. "Your small finger or exile. If you intend to seek forgiveness, I suggest you do it quickly. The blade is sharp and can make a clean cut."

What the fuck? Had this disgusting behavior always been part of the merchants of light's upper administration? Nobody had ever warned me that they'd make me cut off my finger if I... well, I didn't know what this man had done. What was a spione? What did it mean to sell information to Iuria? Like a merchant of knowledge? They weren't illegal! I had hosted a merchant of knowledge in my house a while ago to help teach my children! I had better keep that a secret if this is what happens to people who speak with them.

The ram-Yosoe bawled like a baby. Gods, I couldn't stand to watch. I was embarrassed for him, cringing for the pain and humiliation he had to endure. How I wished to run away.

Giorvi faced me and my stomach lurched. Pili-palas danced on my hyoid as his eyes met mine. "Mr. Lasteran, thank you for your assistance, but please leave the room if you think his blood will trigger your berserker rage."

My throat felt tight and dry, but a wave of relief washed over me. He hadn't spoken to accuse me, but to give me an excuse to leave. Thank the Gods. I would have thanked *him*, but I suddenly felt as though I could not speak. Fuck, was this what it felt like to be Nio?

I left the room, not just to avoid going berserk at the smell of blood, but to avoid having a mental breakdown. How could they do something that cruel? How was this ritual allowed? I had thought Aloutia to be a civilized country, but to hear the Commander of the Godblood Brigade had authorized this sick practice... what was the world really like? Some places had not advanced beyond the petty cruelty common during the Greed Wars.

Outside the ballroom was a hall with similar decoration, lined by flawless marble pillars. I leaned against one as my head spun. Dizziness, nausea... Gods, don't let me vomit on the sparkling, crystalline floor.

I took off my kamen so I could rub my face.

The three bodyguards who'd been with the ram-Yosoe stood a safe distance away from me, watching warily. I had no interest in them and if they wanted to paint my face, well... at that moment, I didn't care what they did. The sooner this strange night was over, the better.

I sat on the floor with my back against the column and put my hands over my face. I did nothing but sit there, waiting for Su... waiting for the madness to end. How much time passed, I had no idea.

A cheer erupted from the ballroom, and I could only imagine it was because the ram-Yosoe had succeeded in slicing off his own finger. Why was Su still in there? How did he have the stomach for that?

I put my head between my knees and thought about happier things. I imagined being back at home, the sea lapping at the shore, wind billowing through the palm fronds, my kids playing on the beach, songbirds, Tawny's bell...

The ballroom door swung open, but while my ears heard the sliding hinges and the momentary swell of the cheering crowd, my skull barely processed it.

Su's hands caressed my head and bristled the small hairs behind my ears.

"Ami-honey, let's go. Our work here is done."

I did not think I could get to my feet on my own. My body felt like it had shut down. Something similar had happened when Tawny had died, but somehow I persevered. Su gave me the strength to stand.

Together, with Su's hand behind my back, we walked back to the Iolono house. If I spoke a single word on the way back, I could not recall them.

Chapter Thirty-Nine: The Nightmare

Much of the rest of that evening passed in a daze. I returned to the Iolono house with Su, where the elder Beatrice prepared a mixture of tea and alcohol to help calm my nerves. I rarely drank tea or alcohol, but her concern was welcome and I drank the beverage in a single gulp.

Hours later, Giorvi returned home with Oboro, ever-vigilant. As shaken as I was, he asked me to speak with him in his study so he could explain what had happened.

"What was that?" I asked. "Did he… cut his finger off?"

"He did," Giorvi said, taking a drink of wine in a fancy Domovoi glass flute. "It's what we do in Chernagora—no, all of Capra—and a few other Yosoe-dominated countries. It's even more prevalent in the Sunset Kingdom. We, at least, have the courtesy to do it behind closed doors."

I stared blankly at his desk. I could not manage to make eye contact with him. "Why did you bring me? Weren't Su and Oboro enough?"

"I didn't think you'd be so panicky about it, Amiere. I brought you because I did not know what sort of bodyguards that spione would have, and I felt that bringing a Wynnle along would help my odds that they would not dare start a fight. And look, I was right. No fight broke out, and the spione surrendered as soon as he realized his bodyguards wouldn't fight you."

I gulped. "What is a spione? What did he do?"

"Didn't I say he sold information to Iuria? Oh, you must have blacked out before then. You know how Seabells and Iuria are arguing over legal rights to the crystalight mine beneath Steena Village? That bastard sold top-secret information that might give Iuria the edge in the legal case. I don't want to bother you with it, Amiere. Already you look like you can't handle what I'm saying. I wouldn't want to—"

"Tell me," I said. "It's about my village, and I'm a member of the merchants of light, too. I deserve to know."

Giorvi furrowed his brows and set his wine glass down. "It would do nothing to ease your soul."

"I deserve to know!"

"It's something that did not even come to pass! It's irrelevant."

"Giorvi... what are you hiding from me?"

"I'll tell you if you tell me about your little secret."

What was he referring to? I clenched the arms of the chair. My claws extended, spearing tiny holes into the wood.

"What happened to Miltico?" he asked in a dangerously low, knowing voice.

"I... I don't know. He disappeared into the jungle."

"Don't feed me mud and sludge. I told you a while ago if you ever killed the fucker, I'd defend you in court. Tell me the truth."

I had to say it. I had to confess my sin. "I... killed the fucker." There was something poetic about using the same terminology Giorvi used.

He laughed, whether because he enjoyed my mimicry or because the death of Miltico genuinely amused him, I could not guess. "You did me a big favor," he said. "Care to listen to me ramble about Yosoe castigo? The 'punishment' system we've set up to deal with traitors?"

"S-sure."

"When a Yosoe commits a serious crime against their superior—a king, a guildmaster, what-have-you—we cut off one of their horns. It's painless, but humiliating. Anywhere they go in public, people will see them and know they are a traitor. Some cities prohibit merchants from selling to one-horned Yosoe. Some will not sell them a house. Nobody will fuck or live with a traitor. It becomes impossible for them to live here, so they are given a choice. They may lose their Aloutian citizenship and be exiled to Cosmo, or they may apologize by taking off one of their fingers. Out of mercy, we typically allow them to remove the small finger—nothing that would interfere with their daily lives. A one-horned Yosoe can still buy groceries or own a house if they show the merchant that they have performed penance."

"I see... Sounds like something Miltico should have done. Well, according to your rules, anyway. As much as I hated him, I'd have never... demanded he cut off his finger. I wanted him gone."

"You are correct. He knew me through you, and contacted me. He wished to move to Chernagora so he could be among other Yosoe. I could not simply welcome him back, however, since he had been exiled. I spoke to the elites of Chernagora, a group I am part of. It was a peculiar situation, being that Miltico was exiled by *you*, a non-Yosoe, and had never had his horn cut off, or been given the option to cut off his finger. We came up with a solution that would satisfy both him and us. I gave him a task to perform, and when it was finished, he could come live in Chernagora without having to cut off any horns or fingers. I had even looked into putting his daughter into the same school Beatrice goes to."

I blinked, trying to figure out what this task even was. "And he didn't do it?"

Giorvi shook his head, disappointed. "He didn't. I grew increasingly worried about his daughter, too. I had hoped to get her out of his clutches, but... well, that doesn't matter anymore. You solved our problem."

"What was Miltico's task?" I asked.

"I cannot share that. It's a solemn secret between him and me. Well, that spione found out and sold it to Iuria. At least Miltico cannot reveal the secret."

"It must have something to do with the merchants of light," I said, thinking. "Or Steena Village. The crystalights underneath our village. Did you ask him to *steal* them?"

Giorvi's shoulders and hands stiffened, but relaxed quickly after I asked my question. "Yes. I asked him to steal crystalights. And since he's dead, he can no longer squeal. Hence, you did me a favor."

I rubbed my forehead. "Why stealing, though? Evading the tax assessors?"

"Technically, yes, but not for greed. I don't give an ulega's ass[1] about money. The merchants of light are only allowed to sell a certain amount of lights every year. Once we go over a certain monetary threshold, we cannot make money. When all our guild members make the maxima, any excess money has to go to charity projects, such as the one that rescued Oboro, but even *those* are capped. The government reasons that if we sold all our crystalights at once for a year, we'd have no way of making money until the next deposit is found—which could be decades from now. The law states we have to spread out crystalight commissions over the years so there's a constant flow of income."

"Wouldn't that make it so I don't get any money until the next deposit is found?" I asked.

"Under the current system, yes, but we're working to make a new system. We want to offer cities the option of paying in increments throughout the crystalight's lifespan or until the final price is fulfilled. The system could be implemented in a year or two. I've drafted all the documents and sent them to be approved by the powers that be, but even after it's approved, it would be up to each city to decide how they wish to pay. If cities choose to pay incrementally over the course of several decades, that money would get funneled to you and the other merchants of light."

"I don't have a problem with it, then. But why go through the trouble, anyway? Are you worried about cities not getting crystalights until their lifespan is partially up?"

"Not exactly. I wanted to have a few sold in secret so they wouldn't be documented with the government. Not so I could sell them for a profit, but so I could sell them at *all*. Amiere..." Giorvi sat up, leaning over his desk, clutching at the edges. "So many Godlights are about to lose their light and the Makai is poised

---

1. An ulega is an ice-based shrew-like animal. The idiomatic phrase "ulega's ass" is the Pentagonal Dominionist equivalent of a "rat's ass" i.e. "I don't give an ulega's ass" = "I don't give a rat's ass/I don't care."

to attack us any year. The Demon Lords are waiting for our Godlights to die. We need these lights in as many cities as possible, as *soon* as possible! If we don't act now, *our* children will be drafted into a war against the Makai, who would likely ally with Ophidia against us."

His hircine eyes shone with determination and ferocity. This was not a man who'd let silly, intangible concepts like 'laws' stop him from saving the world… or his daughter.

"But you said the Godblood Brigade authorized your actions? So they're legal?"

A sly smirk. "Yes. What I've done is legal. I had a long conversation with His Luminance, Captain Lungidus Pavo, before giving Miltico his orders. I will not be charged with any crimes."

His stealing wasn't any of my concern, honestly. His posture felt oddly defensive over something I could not have cared less about. I told him bluntly, "Steal all the crystalights you want. As long as I have material to carve and I'm getting money every year, I'm satisfied."

He relaxed, sitting back in his chair and taking a drink of wine. "I apologize. You seemed anxious. I thought you disagreed with my actions."

"My anxiety was due to that scene at the gathering. I was not expecting to watch a man cut off his own finger."

"Ah. Well, I won't ask you to do that again, then."

A knock came at his door. Su. I recognized the way he knocked; it was the same way he did it on my ateli door.

"Come in," Giorvi shouted.

Su walked in carrying a decorative box with ivory inlay in curls around the corners. It reminded me of some boxes he'd made intended to store ceremonial daggers.

"Part three is finished," Su said. He put one hand on my shoulder and set the box on Giorvi's desk.

"Good work," Giorvi said, dragging the box closer. He swiftly placed it into a drawer underneath his desk. "Thank you, Master Scrimshander."

"Part three?" I asked.

Su winked, and though he usually did it to be seductive, I couldn't help but get an uneasy feeling from him this time. "Mr. Onoretti asked me to do four things for him. Looking at little Beatie's teeth was one, and acting as his bodyguard at the party was another. I can't share what the other two are, though." He patted his hand on my shoulder and I felt like he was patronizing me. It was like the way we parents patted our kids' shoulders when telling them 'you'll understand when you're older.'

I opened my mouth to speak, but whatever I was going to say died on my lips when Su kissed them. It was a far more sensual kiss than I expected him to do in front of my boss, but, well, maybe that was his way of showing him who my real boss was. Thinking about it that way, I felt a slight stirring in my loins.

"Don't worry about me, Ami-honey." He stroked my mane with two lower hands while bristling the short hairs on my ears with his upper hands. Into my ears, shivering at the feel of his hands, he whispered, "Mr. Onoretti is paying me a *lot* for this, and it's not official. We won't be taxed on it."

Was he also skirting the law? I doubted Su had the permission of the Godblood Brigade, but he was a Godblood himself. For all I knew, he was Captain Pavo's or Commander Rubaiya's sibling and could ask them for leniency if he got in trouble.

"I'm going to finish my last task," Su said. "I'll be leaving for a bit, but I'll be back before bed. If you're in the mood, we could—you know." He mumbled nonsense words, spoken seductively so my mind could decide on its own what he'd said. "If you want, of course."

"I will be in the mood."

With a soft smile, he patted my head and walked out.

I stared, lost in thought, forcing my mind away from Su and back to the topic of crystalights. I thought about everything that had happened ever since that accursed mine appeared beneath the village. Everyone else may have seen it as an omen of good, but it had taken away my daughter. Giorvi may have had plans to save every child in Aloutia, but it was too late for Tawny.

I glared at Giorvi after Su left. "If you're asking my husband to do anything that would get him in trouble..."

He met my eyes and did not back down. It was like staring at a wild animal establishing dominance. But although I was a lion and he was a goat... we weren't animals. We were sapient people. And he *was* my boss, no matter what Su said or did to make me think otherwise. "What, Amiere? What would you do to me?"

I realized only then that I had just threatened him. Oh Gods, what was wrong with me? I was irrational... drunk, tired, and emotional. I pushed the wine glass away.

"Sorry. I shouldn't have said that. I must be drunk. I'm going back to my room."

He did not stop me, nor did he say another word as I stood and left, my cheeks flushed with shame.

I waited in the bedroom, dimly lit by nothing except my tail, silently repeating in my skull every stupid thing I'd ever done in my life. It started with me repeating the idiotic thing I'd just said to Giorvi, but while I wallowed in my shame, I started remembering embarrassing things from years long past. The time I kissed Liesle without her permission. One of the times I hit Miltico with a tamarind branch.

One of the times I snorted crazy sugar with Su...

I would never be able to fall asleep with my mind like this. I wouldn't enjoy my time with Su, either, if I were preoccupied with revisiting past mistakes. I had to go right back out there, find Giorvi, and apologize. I'd beg on my hands and knees if I had to.

Gathering my courage and humility—two things which should not have gone hand-in-hand, and yet now they did—I stepped back out of the guest bedroom. He might have gone back to his bedroom, for all I knew. Gods, his wife would have probably tied him to their bed and kept him there, if she could. I'd heard Yosoe loved sex, but I'd assumed it was some speciesist mud and sludge. Even if it was, by the sounds I'd heard coming from their bedroom on the previous nights, they at least fit the stereotype.

I walked around the corner and encountered Giorvi and Su sitting in the living room. They both looked at me with embarrassed faces, as if I wasn't supposed to come out of the bedroom. Like they hadn't planned on my presence.

"Ah, Ami-honey!" Even Su's voice sounded apprehensive. "I thought you were asleep."

Something new sat upon the coffee table between them. Giorvi took a cloth draped over a crystalight, meant to dim the brightness, and draped it over the object on the table.

He'd done it too late. I'd seen it. It was the cage that had been dangling from the chandelier. The demon—or what remained of it—was still inside. It was a charred, blackened husk. Legless, motionless, dead. Some of it had melted into the bottom of the cage.

Had Su brought it back with him? For what purpose?

"What is that?" I asked.

"Nothing to concern yourself with," Giorvi said in an aggressive tone. I had already made him angry, and I'd come out here to apologize. What the hell was I doing making things worse?

I grimaced, scratching my beard. "I'm sorry. I don't know what's come over me lately. I apologize for my awful words earlier, and for intruding on this meeting. I... I didn't think I'd be able to rest well tonight if I didn't apologize."

"Apology accepted." Giorvi stared me down like before. "You were drunk, Amiere. That's all there is to it. Tomorrow, you'll wake up and probably forget you ever said it. Now, I have some more business with Master Scrimshander. You can have him soon. Perhaps he'll help you forget those bad memories."

Gods, I couldn't even apologize right. Su could make me black out and forget some things I'd done... maybe he could make me forget about this, too. Blushing furiously, I stammered out another pathetic apology for interrupting and went back to the bedroom.

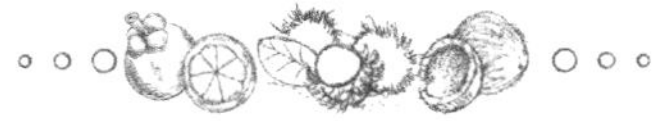

When Su joined me in bed, he helped ease my mind. I could have believed he was a Mind Godblood, with how gently he soothed my anxiety. He lay on top of me, naked except for his bone thong and the thick binding across his chest. While I clutched his ass, he smothered me in kisses; on my lips, my cheeks, and a few attempts at my neck, though he could not penetrate my mane.

I achieved an erection, which Su took into his mouth, taking me all the way to climax.

After that, sleep came all too quickly and easily.

My eyelids felt the heavy touch of Somniel's fingers pressing upon them. Darkness overtook me.

"Amiere..."

What was that voice?

"Mo Ami... Ami-honey..." The voice was Su's and Liesle's, both in one. A dream.

I was dreaming.

"Amiere... watch our children, won't you?"

I stood in the park where I used to take my children to play. Used to, because it was now the site of the fissure. It was... the last place Tawny had ever stood.

"Daddy! Catch!"

I turned around, more from shock at the voice than from any desire to catch whatever was thrown at me.

A kiwi had been chucked at my head, but I caught it easily. As I brought my arm down, I looked at the figure in front of me.

Tawny. Or... what I remembered of her. I had forgotten some of her facial features, so it was... blurry. Her golden mane, magnificent for a child-Wynnle, framed her face like a God's aureole. Tears poured from my eyes. Oh Gods, my precious Tawny! I reached out my shaking arms and took a step forward, praying for this dream to be *just* real enough to touch her.

The ground opened up beneath her. She screamed, a flash of light shone from the crevice and... blood. A fucking fountain of blood erupted. No... no, that hadn't happened. This was just a dream. A nightmare. Still, my body reacted to what it saw, no matter how rational my thoughts. I fell to my knees, shaking, crying, and vomited over the grass.

The world turned dark. The sky black, the sun and moons all deep red and violet. The ocean waves were as black as pitch and roiled with Deep Sea's demonic rage.

This was just a dream.

A skeletal hand with bones made of crystalights reached out of the crevice, eclipsed the black sun with its palm, and came down upon me. I had neither the time nor energy to scream.

When I opened my eyes, I was seated on the pillows in our living room, Tawny asleep on my chest. I rubbed my hand over her back, over her shoulder blades where my other children had wings.

Was this a dream? It felt so *real.* Moreover, I was fully conscious and *aware* of being here, alive. Every sense worked perfectly. Every detail of my house was correct, the ocean scent wafted in, the sounds of Deep Sea's fingers were unmistakable, and the soft fluff of Tawny's hair was embedded into my memories forever.

Had I been living in a nightmare until now? Tawny's death, all the sludge with Miltico, Susana, the trip to Chernagora... was that in my imagination?

Tawny's hair turned to ash and slid between my fingers. She didn't so much as cry out when her body crumpled, skin sloughing off, then melted into slime. I pulled my shaking hand away, watching in horror as the yellow slime clung to my claws and dragged strands of her hair along.

I *did* scream that time. I bolted up and tried wiping the slime off my body. Part of my fucked-up brain still thought of that slime as Tawny. Part of me wanted to be careful, to be gentle getting it off, as if some possibility existed where I could bring her back to life if I just gathered up all that sludge and kept her safe.

Realizing how ridiculous that was, I ran to the ocean, crying, snot running out my nose, to wipe the ooze off. Outside, the scenery was the same unnatural colors as before. A black sun spun like a circular saw halfway down the ocean's horizon.

I washed my hands in Deep Sea. "Did you do this, you demon?"

No, it couldn't have been Deep Sea's fault. Su had made deals with him and he was contractually bound to leave our family alone while we were out of his body, and to help us out if we were in danger while inside. I couldn't blame him for not saving Tawny, considering we'd been in a park far from his reach.

"Wrong Trifecta Lord," a man's self-assured voice said.

My heart held still in my sternum; my breath caught in my hyoid. As I looked down at my hands and reflection on the water's surface, my form changed. It did not reflect me; it showed someone else.

Shifting within the water was the image of a white-skinned man with short, scruffy blond hair, his long bangs covering his eyes. Skull pauldrons decorated his shoulders from whence came black raven wings. His wicked smile spread unnaturally, disturbingly far across his face.

"Lucky you, Amiere," he said in a voice full of glee. "Liesle loves you the most!"

Chapter Forty: The Demon Lord Vinoc

I woke with a start, jolting upright and nearly toppling over Su, who had been on top of me... and not in any sexual manner. He was fully dressed, an expression of concern painted on his face. Giorvi and his wife stood in the door frame, watching with wide eyes.

I labored for breath, but when I had the energy to speak, I asked, "What's happening?"

"I should ask you!" Su said, jamming his finger into my sternum. "You've been kicking and thrashing about so violently in your sleep that I could not sleep next to you! I... I used some of my magic on you just now. I thought it would help wake you up."

The nightmares were already fading from my memories. As my heart calmed, my pain subsided. "I had a nightmare. Did I become a heretic?"

My eyes widened. I stood, grabbing a blanket on my way up so I would not expose myself to the Iolonos. Su may have gotten dressed to go out so he could inform them of my situation, but I was nude except for the covering over my tail. I had to test if I was a heretic.

"Amiere?" Giorvi said. "What are you doing?"

"Please move," I said as I strode toward the door, holding the blanket up with one hand.

He and Beatrice got out of my way.

I went to their blazing hearth in the living room, where Oboro was preparing two kettles of hot water and leaving a prayer to the Demigod Ashen Soul.

"—may you be blessed by your holy parent, the God or Goddess Flamboil. Please grant us—Hey, what are you doing?"

Oboro sidestepped as I intruded into his territory. The kettles had been underneath the flame long enough they were boiling. I held my free hand close, hesitating. I'd heard that if a heretic touched a boiling kettle, it would *hurt*. How badly was I willing to test it?

I had to. Lucognidus's Blessing protected against nightmares, but all the Gods' Blessings save for Sawyer's were part of the same package. If you became a heretic, you lost them all. If I lost Lucognidus's Blessing, I would have lost Flamboil's, as well.

I clenched my jawbone, gathered my courage, and put my hand on one of the kettles.

Flamboil's Blessing activated. The kettle was hot, without a doubt, but I felt no pain from it.

The other adults gathered around me. Su seemed like he wanted to touch me, but waited, as if unsure I wanted to be touched.

"How do you feel, Ami-honey?"

I sighed. "I'm still blessed."

"How did you have a nightmare, then?" Su asked.

Beatrice the Mother waved me back to my room. "Get dressed, Amiere. I know of only one way a blessed person can have a nightmare, but I shall not explain it while you're one slight movement away from accidentally exposing yourself to a child."

I closed my eyes, gathering my wits about me. Gods, I did not think before I acted sometimes. I apologized to everyone present and went back into my bedroom with Su.

My husband leaned against the closed door as I dressed myself. No bone earrings today for either of us—sexual activity was the last thing on my mind. He had a contemplative look. Both pairs of arms were crossed over his chest.

"Do you know something, Sugar?" I asked.

"I think I know what Beatrice is going to tell you. I'll let her say it, though. I... I don't want to think of the implications."

I pulled my trousers up. What else could cause a person to have a nightmare? Was there a demigod messing with me? A demon? Although my memories of the nightmares were fading, I vaguely recalled a winged man tormenting me.

When I went back out into the living room, Giorvi and Beatrice sat in their usual seats, each with their preferred beverage—coffee for him, tea for her.

"Would you like a drink, Signor Lasteran?" Oboro asked. "And you, Master Scrimshander?"

I sat down on a large chair across from the two adults. It had probably been purchased recently for Oboro, as it was the only chair large enough for me. They had let me sit in it since my first day here, so I did not feel like I was stealing it from the boy. Su sat beside me, in a much smaller chair that had probably served the Yosoe family for years.

As for Oboro's question, I didn't care either way for coffee or tea, and frankly I was too rattled to drink anything. I feared I would only vomit anything I tried to ingest.

"I'll take a coffee," I said, for politeness's sake.

"No, get him tea," Beatrice ordered. Leaning closer to me, she whispered, "It will help with your nerves."

"Tea for me, too," Su requested.

I took a hot cup from Oboro and took a sip, doubtful it would do a damn thing for my nerves. "What was it you wanted to tell me?"

"Ah," Giorvi interrupted. "Oboro, would you go play with Beatie for a while? I don't want her listening in on this conversation by accident."

"Of course, Signore."

Beatrice the Mother sipped her tea while Oboro crossed the living room. He had to duck as he went through the door.

When she was certain we were out of hearing range of the kids, Beatrice sighed, set her tea down, and looked me in my eyes. "Amiere, what I'm about to say might be painful. Are you sure you want me to tell you my theory?"

My stomach felt like it was doing rolls. If she didn't tell me, eventually Su would... maybe.

"I understand. Please tell me."

"You may know that there is no Demon Lord of Nightmares. A few ascending Demon Lords have attempted to gain that as their sphere of influence, but as of yet, none have succeeded in convincing King Ayuthiel that it's sufficiently different from 'Terror.' For the last five hundred years, Lord Vinoc, the Lord of Terror, has also been called the Lord of Nightmares, though it's an unofficial title. He gets called the Lord of Storms sometimes, too, which is equally unofficial."

"You think somebody summoned Lord Vinoc to torture me?"

"Not quite," Beatrice said, wagging a finger. "Vinoc would have left you dead at worst or a bumbling, incoherent, traumatized wreck at best. Well, I suppose whether that's best or worst depends on your perspective. You might *wish* to be dead after the terror he put you through."

Su fidgeted with his fingers, and now I understood why. I, too, saw where Beatrice was taking her theory...

"You were not the intended victim of a summoning; you were the payment. Your wife is a merchant of faces. The first two times a person summons Vinoc, he will kill or torture their victim for free. But the third time, he demands a payment: the summoner must let him torture the one they love most."

"This is ridiculous! Liesle would never summon Vinoc! And... certainly not *three* times! And why me? She surely loves our children more than me."

Beatrice shook her head. "Vinoc won't torture children, so they aren't valid forms of payment. He also likely considers Eruwan a child, regardless of what Aloutian law says. He has his own opinions on when people become adults."

"Still, why me? Why wouldn't Liesle pick Su? He's far more worthy of love than I am!"

"Amiere!" Su yelled with such animosity in his voice that I thought my heart stopped.

"Su?"

He clenched all four of his fists. "We don't know what went through Liesle's mind, and we shouldn't be focusing on that, anyway. What matters is that *something happened* to provoke her into summoning Vinoc for a third time. What could have set her off that she would do that? Who did she want dead or tortured so soon and so badly that she allowed you to be tortured—even if lightly?"

Oh, Gods, I hadn't thought that far ahead. Were the children in danger? I stood up. "Fuck, we have to leave right now!"

Su nodded. "Yes. If harm came to any of the kids, she'd—"

"She would kill for them. If somebody hurt our children, she'd tear them apart with her own fucking claws and teeth. Or fry them with her tail. She's vicious. She'll go berserk. She'll... Oh Gods, Liesle!"

I didn't wait another minute. I didn't return to the bedroom to collect whatever possessions I had. I didn't put on my kamen. I didn't say goodbye. I just fucking left. I overheard Su tell the Iolonos that he'd be back for our belongings later as he joined me on the painful walk back to Steena Village.

Dread bubbled in the pit of my stomach the whole way back to Steena Village. Whatever expression I wore on my face scared the Yosoe gatekeeper in Chernagora so badly that he allowed me to go through the portal without paying. Su, walking beside me, paid the man anyway.

I said nothing while we were in public, both in Chernagora and in the Nilian Portal House. Not until we were on the path through the jungle heading toward Steena Village, where the only ears within listening distance were the big, floppy ears of jeweled elephants, did I dare ask Su the question that had tormented me since I stormed out of the Iolonos' house.

"Did you know Liesle had painted Vinoc before?"

"I only knew of one instance. I thought she still had a 'free' summoning left."

I couldn't be too angry at her considering we'd all promised not to pry into each other's secrets. But now? What use was hiding it now?

"Who was her victim that time?"

"Tico Svelt."

That stopped me in my tracks. Su almost collided with me.

Fuck, it all made sense now. Of course he hadn't died of a crazy sugar overdose. He sold crazy sugar, but had never taken it. We'd all thought it was strange that he'd decided to consume his own product. No, he hadn't died from such mundane substances... He'd died from Vinoc's terror. He'd died screaming and thrashing until his heart exploded.

"She killed Tico." It was a statement, not a question.

Su held onto my arm, resting his soft cheek against my skin. "It was right after we experimented with crazy sugar and you... no, *we*, made mistakes we could not take back."

I shook my head. "I don't remember it, Sugar. It addled my mind. If I could remember, maybe I could make amends, but how am I supposed to regret a lost memory? How can I redeem myself when I don't know my sin?"

"It doesn't matter. It's in the past, and nobody holds you responsible for it anymore. All that matters is what Liesle thought at the time. She feared we would become addicts. She dreamed of an idyllic family life that was about to crumble before her eyes. She was pregnant with Eruwan at the time, and she needed us both to be there for her and the baby. You had to shape up and become a good husband and Papami. I had to shape up and become a good wife and Papa Su. So... she removed the one who was supplying us with crazy sugar. No one else in this tiny village was about to take up Tico's mantle."

With heavy emotions weighing in my chest, I carried on. Through the jungle, through the village, and down to the beach. The music of Deep Sea's lapping fingers usually quelled any tumultuous feelings, but today they did nothing but remind me that I was edging ever closer to a horrid truth.

Su stopped me as we stepped onto the road to Seabells. "*He's* here."

"Who?" I looked around.

"Me," a smooth male voice said from behind us. We spun to face him.

He was a Phoenian with black skin, tentacles for fingers, striking purple eyes, and black hair tied in a tail and stuffed under a brimmed hat. No kamen at all. Dressed in an Aloutian red military uniform with two rows of buttons and a chain linking his tie and left epaulet, he was obviously a lawkeeper. One of the badges on his left breast was a peacock feather, the symbol of Lucognidus. A Godblood.

"I am Captain Lungidus Pavo of the Godblood Brigade. Amiere Lasteran, Su Scrimshander, you two are under arrest."

Fionn Interlude

Fionn hadn't asked for a timid bunny of a sister. He hadn't asked for a pathetic baby brother with such a weak body that he couldn't be around Maika. He wanted his old life back. Tawny, Maika... he wished they still lived in the same house as him. Sure, Maika was just living with Eruwan now, and he could go play with her anytime, but it wasn't the same. Maika used to sleep in his bedroom, but now... it was lonely, just him and Heliodor. And one day, that stupid, weak brother Turquoise would take his bedroom, too.

Or maybe not. Fionn figured he would move out when he was fifteen, and he had just turned thirteen. When Turquoise was old enough to sleep in the boys' room, Fionn might have left to live somewhere else.

He wasn't completely against changes. Fionn remembered the absolute joy he'd had playing with Beatie and Oboro. They were his age, so fun and adventurous! They'd wanted to go into the jungle and to Kiwi Island, just like Tawny had wanted to do! The only reason they'd refrained from it was because they knew they'd get in trouble with Mr. Onoretti if they went anywhere dangerous.

Gods, he wanted to see Beatie and Oboro again. He'd asked his Dad and Mama Su if he could join them on the trip to Chernagora, but they wouldn't allow it. They'd promised to take him next time, though.

One day, after Dad and Mama Su went to Chernagora, his mother went into the village to paint. She'd told Fionn to watch the younger kids, but he didn't see what could possibly happen to them. The boring girls would just play troika, and Heli would play with Turquoise. Eruwan was helping Nell run the shop that day, or else she'd have babysat the infant instead.

That left Fionn alone. He stood on the beach, kicking a seashell, then a coconut, wondering what he could do by himself.

"Boy!"

His ears twitched and perked in the direction of the voice, one belonging to a young woman. It came from the thick, vibrant green bushes lining Coconut Crab Circle. Fionn approached to investigate, thinking that he must have misheard something. After all, who would be hiding in the shrubbery? And why?

A woman took a step outside the bushes, enough that Fionn could see who she was, but still partially inside so she could hide at a moment's notice. She was a Lagodore like Susana with dark brown fur, long rabbit-ears, and big, round, pleading eyes. But unlike Susana, she had Lagodorian legs—thick hips leading down to thin legs, then large digitigrade feet good for jumping. And no horns, of course. That was another feature Susana had gotten from her Yosoe side.

"Who are you?" Fionn asked.

"Please!" she cried, holding her hands to her chest. Tears welled in her bunny-eyes. "Please, I just want to see my daughter again."

"Are you Susana's mom?"

"Susana? Did she change her name? I called her Usana, but... yes, the little Lagodore I've seen playing on this beach. She's my daughter. Please, she misses me, and I miss her. I need to speak with her."

Fionn could not recall Susana ever mentioning her mother, but he had not particularly cared to listen to her stories, either.

"I've been away from her for so long... You lost your sister recently, didn't you? Wouldn't you want to see her one more time, if you could? Please understand. I want to see my daughter again."

Fionn held his breath. He would have done anything to have Tawny back. He may not have known this woman, but if she was in a similar situation...

Fionn wasn't mean, nor a bully. Not anymore. He may have thought his siblings were boring and annoying sometimes, but he didn't want them to get *hurt*. Mama Su had taught him about empathy, and right now, his chest swelled with empathy for this woman.

"I could bring her to you."

"Please do," the woman said. "But not here. I... My husband did bad things to her, so... So people in the village think I'm bad, too. But it's not true! He abused me, too! Look!" She showed Fionn her arms, scarred and bruised, or at least he thought so. It was hard to tell on a person with a fur coat. He'd learned to identify bruises on Heliodor who liked to play rough, but he wasn't sure if Lagodorian markings were comparable to a Wynnle's. Fionn thought they looked recent, too. He supposed that must have meant Miltico *was* still alive.

"Um, okay. Where should I bring her?"

She pointed deeper down Coconut Crab Circle, where it turned north and into the jungle. "That way. You know where the caves are? I'll be at the entrance to one of them, so you won't miss me."

"O-okay. I'm supposed to be watching my little brother, though."

"A brother?" Her voice carried a slight hint of pleasant surprise. "Oh, bring him along, too. Hurry! Before your mother comes back home. I don't want her to know I was here."

Susana Interlude

Susana wasn't very good at troika, so when Fionn offered to take her somewhere else to play, she was fine with it. It was a little strange, since Fionn had never wanted to play with her in the past, but she did not question it. Older people sometimes changed their minds about things for seemingly no reason, and Susana had been taught not to question it. Whenever she had asked 'why' to her previous Daddy, he would hit her.

She touched her pretty blue horn rings to make sure they were on tight before heading into the jungle. Sometimes, when she walked under the canopy of so many tall trees, it got too dark for her.

Fionn asked Susana to hold his hand as he took her into the jungle. Maybe he wanted to find rare fruits? Or maybe the game he wanted to play involved collecting vines or lianas or flowers. In his other hand, he carried baby Turquoise. Susana knew her new mother had asked Fionn to watch him, so the fact that he brought the baby along only proved he was a good big brother.

Susana did not go into the jungle often, since she'd been told it was full of lions, tigers, jaguars, snakes, nues, coatls, and animals who could eat her in a single gulp. Well, her old Daddy told her that. She wasn't sure if it was true now, since none of her new parents had mentioned them. She was safe with Fionn, though. He could fight back with his claws and tail.

Fionn helped her jump over thick lianas and roots, and a climb over fallen logs. An animal somewhere made a strange noise and Susana shrieked back in terror, but Fionn told her it was only a lagushka[1].

The caves came into view. Most of the tunnels were underground, and the entrances were little more than a small mound jutting from the ground, overgrown with climbing vines.

Susana's breath caught in her throat and her hooves planted themselves on the ground when she saw the woman at one of the cave entrances. Fionn tugged at

---

1. Pentagonal Dominionist name for frogs and toads, generally. A Slevan word that came to be used in English and other languages due to a religious story.

her to keep moving. "What's wrong? Let's go."

"I know her... I don't want to go back!"

"She just wants to talk to you for a few minutes. You're not getting kicked out of our family." He said the last line with a dry chuckle.

Susana did not want to talk to her previous mother, but she also knew not to disobey people older and bigger than her.

The woman had once been Mommy. Or perhaps Lavina? That was what Daddy had called her. Mommy was not as mean as Daddy, but she had hit Susana a few times, in those days back when she was called Usana. Susana reasoned that if Liesle was her Mommy now, then this woman was just 'Lavina.'

Lavina fell on her knees and wrapped her arms around Susana. "Oh, my precious daughter!" Tears flowed from her eyes and got Susana's fur wet. "I've been so scared for you! Have you been safe?"

"I've been okay," she said, not knowing how she was supposed to respond.

Lavina stood up and wiped her tears. "Come inside, let's have a talk. You too, Fionn. I made some drinks. You can have some, too."

"You made drinks? In the cave?"

"Oh, yes, I've been living in here. Come now."

Fionn didn't give Susana a choice. He held her hand tight and led her inside the cave. The Wynnle boy's tail-light provided illumination. Susana's horn rings gave off a gentle light that would have allowed her to see, but not very far. If not for those light sources, the cave would have been pitch black. How could Lavina live here without crystalights or lotuses?

Something glittered deeper into the cave. Sparkling like the way the sun shimmers on the ocean waves. Perhaps she *did* have some source of light.

Lavina held a glass of bright red juice to Fionn. "Here, as thanks for letting me speak with my daughter. You look thirsty."

Fionn smiled. "O-oh, no, thank you, Mys." With Turquoise in one hand and Susana's hand in his other, he had to let go of the older girl to take the glass. He looked at it with a ponderous expression. Susana did not recognize the contents, so maybe Fionn didn't, either. Regardless, he took a drink.

He fell unconscious as soon as the liquid touched his tongue. He fell to his knees first, and then crumpled to his side, away from Turquoise, who squirmed in Fionn's limp arm, but was unharmed. Lavina rushed over to her daughter and clutched her tight to her chest.

"He's ready!" she shouted. "Take him and that baby for all I care."

Susana's face was pressed to her mother's chest, but she could see a little from the corner of her eye. An Orochijin woman slithered into the light provided by Fionn's tail.

"A Wynnle?" the snake-woman asked. "Not much use in them. The gladiator arena *might* buy him."

"I don't care what you do with him. I have my daughter back, and that's all I care about. Come on, Usana. We're going home. I'm sorry you had to live with those scary lions for so long, but you're safe now. You're safe, darling."

The Orochijin woman beckoned to another woman deeper in the cave. The two locked Fionn in chains, snapped a collar around his neck, put a muzzle over his face so he couldn't bite, and iron mittens over his hands so his claws wouldn't come out.

"What about his tail?" the second woman asked. "Shall we cut it off?"

"No, just wrap it up. The arenas like Wynnles to have all their body parts intact."

"And the baby?"

"We'll sell him to an auction house."

The first woman hefted Fionn over her shoulder while the second handled Turquoise. Lavina held Susana tight, squeezing tighter when she tried to squirm away. They went to the edge of the cave where Susana realized what the shimmering lights were: portal sparkles. Lavina stepped through, into Cosmo, carrying her daughter with her.

Liesle Interlude

When Liesle returned home and realized two of her sons and her adopted daughter were missing, she suspected the worst. She flew back to Steena Village, where she'd just been painting, and stirred up everybody to search for them.

She *knew* Lavina had to have been involved. Any mother would have wanted her daughter back. Liesle had seen Lavina—or thought she had—a few times in the last week. Always a brownish blur in the jungle, darting into the foliage when Liesle's head turned toward it. She'd assumed they were wild capybaras at first, but this blur—whatever it was—was far too furtive. Even wild cappies were wont to enter civilized spaces and socialize with other animals and people. Specifically, she'd noticed the figure was often in the bushes whenever Susana was playing on the beach.

She didn't know where Lavina had taken her children. She doubted they would ever find them if she took them into the jungle. Liesle wasn't sure how she'd managed to subdue Fionn, but if she had help... it wasn't unthinkable.

She had seen Lavina in the past, even if she hadn't gotten a good look at her recently. She recalled what the woman looked like well enough to paint her.

Using the excuse that she was going to search the deepest, darkest parts of the jungle, Liesle looped around, flying far out to sea where nobody who recognized her would see her, and retreated to her secret art cave. She pushed aside the painting she'd been working on and set a blank canvas on the easel.

Using only her own tail for light, she collected the materials: her brushes, other tools, and the pigment itself—bone char, likely made from Miltico's bones. Su had told her in private that he'd turned most of his bones to fertilizer, then sold it on Cosmo where they did not have the Green Moon to rejuvenate their fields. Fertilizer could be sold for good money on the other planes. But Su had also given Liesle a block of black bone char for use in painting. He had been too nervous to say he'd made it from Miltico's bones, but... Liesle suspected that was the truth.

She painted a portrait of the Demigoddess of Terror, Lady Vinoc, an Umi woman with striking eyes and a gentle smile. Next to Vinoc, Liesle painted what she could remember of Lavina. How sickly perverse... using Miltico's bones to paint Miltico's wife.

Summoning Lord Vinoc was an art, quite literally, and no one quite knew how or when any given piece of art was considered worthy of his attention. It required a good deal of skill; somebody scribbling a stick-figure and labeling it 'Lady Vinoc' would not suffice. But when was it considered 'good enough'? Demonic magic had the peculiar capacity to work retroactively. It was 'good enough' if Lord Vinoc considered it good enough, but it summoned him prior to getting his opinion.

Liesle painted like she had no time to lose. It was a rushed piece, with a few sloppy details, but good enough for Vinoc's taste.

This was her third time summoning him... She would have to pay a price this time. Would it be one of her children? A spouse?

"I, Liesle Denwall, hereby summon Vinoc, Demon Lord of Terror. By my sacrifice of this image, you have found me worthy. Appear before me!"

She turned to her right, where a mirror shone by the light of her tail. A man emerged in the inky blackness, the skulls on his shoulders standing out against the background. A wicked smile crossed his face, eyes hidden in shadows and beneath his hair.

"Well, well, what have we here? It's been over ten years since you've summoned me. Did you think you'd never call upon me again?"

"I hoped I would never have to," she said, her tone heavy with regret. "But this is important. I need you to kill this woman." She pointed a clawed finger at Lavina. "She kidnapped my children. Please, do what you do. Oh, but if torturing her would hurt my children in any way, or leave them abandoned in a place they can't escape, can you wait until they're safe?"

"Dear summoner, I can do that and more," Vinoc said, grinning ear-to-ear. "We must discuss my compensation, however. The one you love the most. No children. Pick one of your spouses: Amiere or Su? Which one do you love more? Do not lie—I will know."

Liesle grimaced. There was no way she could pick one spouse over the other. Just as she could never pick one child over the others. But Vinoc could not actually read minds or know what her feelings entailed. He always knew more than he should have—such as Amiere and Su's names—but Liesle did not know what information Vinoc received upon being summoned.

If Amiere had a nightmare, the worst that could happen is he would thrash about during the night.

If Su had a nightmare—if one of his Godblood powers brought destruction—he could level a city and kill millions without trying.

"Amiere," Liesle said. "I am still crazy about him, all these years later. I love Su, but I don't get as excited about him as I do Amiere."

It wasn't... entirely a lie.

"Your choice has been made truthfully," Vinoc said. "Now he shall pay the consequences."

Chapter Forty-One: Captain Pavo and Tynan

Every hair on my mane stood on-end. I could not fight a Godblood, and fighting a lawkeeper would only end in disaster regardless—but my instinct told me to...

No, Captain Pavo wasn't a threat. He had no weapons. He wouldn't hurt me or my family. I knew this instinctively. That smile he gave me, his lips favoring the left side of his face, was the smile of an angel.

"Su Scrimshander," he said. "Remember me? We danced together, back during the Chancellor's ball."

"I remember. I danced with the woman who would later become your wife, too."

Captain Pavo rubbed his stubbly chin with a wiggling tentacle. "For me, that ball was one of the defining moments of my life. I met her there. But for you? Did it mean anything to you? You informed the Chancellor quite sternly that you had no intention of letting anyone know your sex or element."

"The ball was set up so Godbloods would mingle and fuck each other. She only wanted you and Loyenie as part of her disgusting eugenics program. How many child-soldiers have you made for her so far? Four? Five? I hope you're proud of yourself."

Captain Pavo nodded toward a palm tree behind us. "Tynan!" When we turned to see what he was motioning to, a shadowy figure dropped between the fronds. It was an amorphous, black blob.

"Make yourself look like you're my child," Lungidus said.

"Yes, Father." The shadowed entity spoke lucidly despite not having a visible mouth. It reshaped itself into a new form—a body that looked like what Lungidus probably looked like as a child, though this entity did not present as a girl or boy. Their androgynous body had been shaped with clothes on. Oddly, they were dressed in the supposed garments of a shinigami—black slacks, a white shirt under a black waistcoat, and a black tie with an imprint of a white circular saw.

"Meet my youngest child, Tynan Pavomusen."

Su crossed his upper arms and set his lower arms on his hips. "Tynan? 'Tyn' as in the traditional prefix given to the fifth-born in ancient Phoenia?"

Lungidus smirked. "Look, we weren't going to call them by their magic name, but they hatched fully aware and *wanting* trouble to find them. They chose to go by their magic name. But yes, Tynan is my fifth child. They're six months old now."

"Chancellor Mira must be proud of you!" Su said sarcastically. "Five children. Five toy soldiers for her future war and this one popped out of their egg ready to kill. Gonna get any more out for her? Gonna try for six children for the Godblood Brigade? Or are some of them joining the merchants of dance?"

"Your mockery doesn't hurt me," Lungidus said coldly. "There will be no more children between me and Loyenie, and I will not speak of the Chancellor's plans again. Shouldn't you be more concerned about your own wife? She's a demon summoner, you know."

If Su hadn't told me, the casual and flippant way Lungidus said it just now would have sent me into a rage.

"We know," Su said. "Amiere had a nightmare, despite being blessed. We know it was Liesle summoning Lord Vinoc. Do you know more? Why she did it? Also, are we *really* under arrest, or did you just want to scare us?"

Lungidus shrugged. "You two are truly under arrest, but I'd be willing to make a deal with you to hold off on taking you to Monoceros for a few days. Let me explain the situation with your wife, first. Mys Liesle Denwall summoned the Lord of Terror to kill a certain woman, Lavina Demiu, who was working with some merchant of flesh scum to sell boys in Ophidia. She took her daughter and your boys, Fionn and the newborn, to Ophidia."

My sternum sunk deeper than it ever had. Gods, I didn't think even Tawny's death scared me this way. At least Tawny was in a better place. Fionn and Turquoise... Fuck! My claws extended before I'd thought about what I was doing. A blanket of warmth wrapped around me. I tried moving my arms, but they were pinned down.

"I have you in telekinesis for your own safety," Lungidus said. "Just until I know you aren't a threat. Listen, we know where your children are. I have a deal to make with you, and if you agree to it, I'll tell you where they're at and how you can get there."

"What am *I* under arrest for? I understand Liesle summoned a Demon Lord, but I had nothing to do with it!" I struggled to keep my voice as neutral and calm as possible. I needed to know what he was here for—if he knew I killed Miltico, that was one thing. If he was only arresting me under suspicion of aiding and abetting Liesle, that would be easier to talk my way out of. But regardless of the crime, one did not speak aggressively with a Godblood *or* a lawkeeper, let alone a Godblood lawkeeper. And when one was a Wynnle? People were already prone to being suspicious of me. Some lawkeepers would attack me just for looking at them the wrong way. I supposed Lungidus was merciful—in his way—by merely holding me down with telekinesis. Perhaps he wanted to be gentle while his child watched on... or he was extra cautious for fear I would hurt Tynan in a fit of rage.

"For the kidnapping of Usana Demiu."

Oh no...

"Her name is Susana Scrimshander, Father," Tynan said with no emotion in their voice whatsoever.

Lungidus smirked, seemingly annoyed by the correction, but glad it came from his child instead of Su. "Right. I forgot. You are under arrest for the kidnapping of Susana Scrimshander. Feels ironic using that name, when she would not have that name if you *hadn't* kidnapped her."

"Your Luminance, with all due respect, if I hadn't kidnapped her, she might be dead right now. Her father—"

Lungidus held up a tentacled hand. "No need to defend yourself here and now, Mr. Lasteran. Frankly, you have bigger problems. Your wife is already in custody and your children have been allowed to stay with their aunt, Mys Orienna Denwall. If you want your missing children back, I'd suggest you take my deal. Do you want to hear it?"

Su growled, not unlike a dog. "We'll hear it, but if I don't like it, I'll dance with you."

The lawkeeper laughed in such an ominous manner it made my skin crawl. "Oh, I would *not* recommend that, Master Scrimshander."

"I could match your steps," Su said with a grin of his own.

"I'm sure you could. I'm not the one you should be afraid of. Behold my child."

We turned back to Tynan who had transformed into... not even a person. A machine, completely metallic, with rotating saw blades for hands, rings of knives spinning around their body, curved blades serving as a skirt, and prehensile barbed wire for hair. It had no face, until I had that thought, then it grew eight eyes circling a mouth full of lamprey teeth on its torso.

What the fuck *was* it?

"Tynan is a master dancer," Lungidus said. "You don't want to find out what they're capable of doing. Trust me; listen to my deal. If you take it, great. If not, I suggest you quietly accept going to jail. Tynan, make yourself look like a person."

"Yes, Father." They transformed back into a miniature androgynous Lungidus in a shinigami uniform.

"My deal is this: I will let you go and do... *whatever* you need to do in Ophidia to get your sons back. In exchange, you have to come back and tell us everything involved in Susana's kidnapping. When *you* kidnapped her, I mean, not this incident with her mother taking her back. Specifically the father. We need to know what happened to Miltico Svelt."

My stomach turned upside-down. There was no way... I couldn't...

"Mr. Lasteran, Tynan and I are both telepaths. We *know* what you did. But we would like to speak to you during a formal interview so we can understand the whole story. There's far more going on than you realize. However, there are legalities that must also be observed and obeyed."

"I understand," I said, lowering my eyes, if only as a show of obedience. I certainly did *not* understand.

"There's another clause I need you to agree to before I can make good on my offer. I need you to sign a statement that you will not bring charges against the Aloutian government or the merchants of light for any losses or damage sustained by the emergence of the crystalight mine."

I shrugged. "I hadn't planned on it. It was the work of the Gods, wasn't it?"

Lungidus gave me a sad frown. "True. Regardless, I will need a signed statement from you that you acknowledge that the death of your daughter was an unfortunate accident and that no one is at fault, legally."

I had never intended to make a fuss. Why even bring it up? "Sure. I'll sign that. I wouldn't want to get involved in a legal case against Gods anyway."

The Godblood put his hands in front of him and teleported a writing pad, paper, and pen in midair. He held them with telekinesis and pushed them toward me.

The fact that everything he'd just said was already written, including the clause about Tawny's death... Why? The form listed my daughter by her magic name, Shiara Denwall, as public names weren't official until the child became an adult.

The whole thing made me sick. Why would they want me to acknowledge that in the first place? Why was this document already written, prepared for me to sign? I looked up at Lungidus curiously, not intending to ask the question, but I supposed he read my mind.

"We simply want to cover our bases for all possible futures, Mr. Lasteran."

"Let me read it first, Ami-honey," Su said. He shot Lungidus a glare that would have stopped me dead in my tracks, but his fellow Godblood only smirked.

I was glad Su asked to read it, honestly. He was much better at understanding legal stuff than I was. I had gotten through life just floating by, never involving myself in politics. All this legal jargon was... difficult.

"We should agree to it," Su said after a careful reading. "I don't see anything meant to trick us, or which would screw us over."

"Master Scrimshander, you wound me," Lungidus said.

"You're a lawkeeper and a eugenicist," Su replied viciously. "You deserve *real* wounds worse than my words."

With surprising harshness of his own, the lawkeeper spat back, "I am doing everything I can to be kind to you! I could have treated Mys Denwall much rougher than I did. I could have let your children fend for themselves. I could have arrested you two on sight and not even *given* you this deal. It is overwhelmingly in your favor. You know why? Because I'm kind. Because I am also a father and I sympathize with what you're going through. Because I want you to *win*." He thrust a tentacle back, pointing at our house. "Don't you want to go back to your normal family life? If Liesle is sent to Hydra Island for her crime, your precious life will be gone. If you spit on my kindness again, I will rescind my offer."

Su seemed taken aback. His mouth hung open ever so slightly. "I don't know if you're using your telepathy to make me *want* to believe you or if I truly believe you. I know in the deepest recess of my mind that you cannot be trusted, Lungidus Pavo, but I will put on a facade for my children's sake. If the price of getting my sons back mean you put strings on me and make me dance like a puppet, I will."

"You're not the puppet dancing on strings," Tynan said in a tone of voice that displayed the first hint of emotion from them.

"My children are my highest priority right now," Su said. "We agree to your deal. Sign the paper, Amiere."

I did as he told me. I always trusted Su to know what was best. My signature turned out shaky, written in my fearful hand.

"Now tell me where my sons are. And Susana! She is our daughter, too!"

"Fionn and Turquoise are in Morigumo. They've been sold to a gladiator arena. Well, Fionn was. Turquoise is in the slave nursery for now."

"I have Susana," Tynan said, with no other explanation.

"What do you mean you have her?" Su asked.

Lungidus cut the explanation short. "It's complicated, but believe them. They will bring Susana back here."

"I agree to your deal," I said. "Now let us go so we can bring our sons back."

"Patience, Mr. Lasteran. I will remove your telekinetic bindings, but... if you would, please, wait a moment."

The magical force surrounding my body that had previously only allowed my hands to move vanished. I clenched my fists and gritted my teeth.

"Why the hell are we *waiting*?"

"You're about to lose yourself," Lungidus said. "I don't mean you're going to go berserk. No, there will be no bloodshed here, if I have my way. I mean you've had one difficult thing atop another in the last several hours. You had a nightmare, you learned how Tico Svelt died, you learned your wife was arrested, and three of your children were abducted. You're about to jump into Ophidia without a plan, with a head so full of complicated emotions that you haven't processed, that you will undoubtedly just get yourself enslaved. I know this for a fact, because I am in telepathic communication with my daughter, Steffa, who is a precognitioner. She's telling me right now that if you and Master Scrimshander go to Ophidia right now, there is a fifty percent chance you will be killed or enslaved, and a ninety-five percent chance that Fionn will die. If you wait until I give the order, your odds improve. Wait one hour here, and the chances that Fionn dies in Ophidia drop to thirty percent. Will you take those odds, Mr. Lasteran?"

I blinked. "What the hell am I supposed to do for an hour!?"

"Take in the view of the ocean, of your home, of your beautiful husband standing next to you, I don't care. Check up on the kids at Orienna's house. Ask them how they're doing. One hour, *then* I'll let you go to Ophidia."

If I hadn't known Lungidus was a father, his words would have proven it to me. As I looked into his eyes, I saw a gentle soul. A nostalgic yearning lay serenely on his visage. The wind tousled his hair in an almost whimsical way, and for a brief second, I saw this man, this Godblood, for who he was. Not His Luminance, Lungidus Pavo, son of the Mind God Lucognidus, but a regular sapienti man. Rather than a lawkeeper arresting a criminal, he was one father speaking to another.

I glanced toward the beach, to Deep Sea, to my house, and to Scrimshander Lighthouse. It was the same as ever. Did Lungidus want to give me one last opportunity to soak in the image because he intended to exile me to Hydra Island after this?

"I will do everything I can to free you," he replied. "But even I must obey the law. Let's go speak to your children, Mr. Lasteran."

"The villagers won't take kindly to a lawkeeper walking through," Su said. "Or do you plan to scare them away with Godblood powers?"

"They won't see me," he said. "I'll have an illusion on. Once we arrive at Mys Orienna's house, I will allow her to see me. She already has, when I instructed her to take your children."

An illusionist. I should have known a Godblood would have some sneaky solution already in mind.

The Chak-Den house sang with the music of Orienna's piano. Eruwan and Nell sat on the bench together, playing a piece made for quadrubrachs, though it could just as easily be played by two bibrachs. Despite requiring four hands, it was a slow, relaxing piece. Perfect for Cohaku's current mood, crouched against the wall, head in her knees.

When we'd first entered, Orienna shook her head in despair and informed us that Cohaku refused to budge. Heliodor leaned against her, offering his soft fur if she needed to pet him. Maika lay on her other side, her mushrooms occasionally twitching as she slept.

Nio read a book with Demitris, both silent as they let the music sweep over the room.

"Dadda!" Heliodor got up and flew into my arms. I nuzzled my son's soft fur, petting his neck with one hand as I held him by the haunches in my other arm.

Eruwan and Nell stopped playing and greeted us.

"Papami! Is everything gonna be alright?"

"Yes," I answered, not even thinking about whether it was true or not. The truth mattered less than the gift of hope.

"But Fionn..." Eruwan bit her lip. "What's going to happen to him?"

"We know where he is," Su said. He stood behind Eruwan on the piano bench and wrapped his arms around her in a tight embrace. "Captain Pavo knows and he's going to let us retrieve him. We'll be back soon with him, Turq, and Susana."

Cohaku's toes wiggled, and her wings fluttered, or tried to, though as she sat against the wall, they were mostly pinned in place by her own body.

"How are you doing, Cohaku?" I asked. I feared that she might actually *like* that Fionn was gone. Her despondency might have been caused by something else.

"I don't want to talk here," she said.

Probably because there were too many people. "Do you want to go to your tree house? Or to my ateli?"

"Yes." She raised her head up. Her eyes were puffy from having cried recently, though the tears were dry for now. "Can we? Will that Godblood let us?"

Captain Pavo had escorted us to the Chak-Den house, but had stayed outside to give us a little privacy. I wondered if he would permit me to take Cohaku someplace where she could talk freely. She had complicated feelings about Fionn, and letting her speak those feelings out loud might be therapeutic for her. It might also elucidate who she was becoming as a person. But the lawkeeper had already shown us plenty of kindness in allowing me *this* conversation. He might not be so excited at the idea of escorting me back to our house just for my daughter's comfort.

"I don't know, but I could ask him. Su, will you stay here?"

"I will. I'll comfort the children as long as I can."

"I'll be right back, Cohaku. Heli, will you stay here and keep your family cheered up?"

"Of course! That's my specialty!" He laughed and flew backwards, out of my hands.

I exited the room and, as I passed through the space between the hall and living room, crossed paths with Orienna bringing a tray to the kitchen.

"Gods, Ami, I don't know how to serve Godbloods. Do they expect drinks and food? I offered them a seat inside, but they declined. Should I bring a chair outside to them? Am I supposed to bow to them? I... I haven't been doing that. I got so used to Su."

I put my hand on her shoulder. "You're alright. I don't think they expect anything from you except for your cooperation."

She let out a heavy sigh. "Well, I just gave them some juice and steena slices."

"Relax. I'm sure they're appreciative, but you don't need to go out of your way to serve them. I'm sure they have *actual* servants to do their bidding when they're not working."

I stepped outside just as Tynan had taken some monstrous form around my size while their father poured his juice down a funnel extruding from their neck.

"Ah! Mr. Lasteran!" Awkwardly, Lungidus shuffled back to a normal standing position, as if he hadn't just poured his drink down his child's throat. "Steffa didn't tell me you'd be out so soon. Um, Tynan, transform back to a regular form."

"Yes, Father." The funnel sucked back into the monster's body, then the rest of their body changed back into a person who resembled a cross between Lungidus and a Death Godblood. Although I had never seen Loyenie Rathmusen in person, I knew she must be Olivian if she was the daughter of the Death God. Unlike the other Gods who would freely have children with people of any species, Lord Sawyer only had children with his beloved Laynie, Demigoddess of Mercy. And since both were Olivian, their children, the half-Spirit Death Godbloods, were also Olivian.

I pursed my lips, wondering if Su was a Death Godblood. If Sawyer had fucked another woman to produce him, it certainly would be a scandal worth hiding from other Godbloods. But didn't he also say he danced with Lungidus and Loyenie at the Chancellor's matchmaking ball? I couldn't imagine siblings would dance with each other there. Of course, it was odd that he danced with both a man and a woman. Su had not fully transitioned to a sex-neutral body at that time, if I had the timeline straight in my head, so he may have had either male or female reproductive organs, meaning he could have had children with one of them. Either way, one of his dances had just been for show. The Chancellor must have known Su's sex, but I wondered if she knew at the time that Su had no intention of playing her eugenics game.

"Please don't tell our host about what I did," Lungidus said, looking downward and—was he *blushing*? I could not tell easily against his ebony skin, but it acquired a purplish tint. "I didn't want to make her uncomfortable by refusing a drink, but I truly cannot stand the taste of fruit juice. The steenas were nice, though."

"I won't say a word. Your child likes them, though?"

"Tynan can change their taste buds instantaneously. They can make themself like anything."

"Convenient," I mumbled, thinking about how much easier it would be to make dinner if my children had similar powers. I was about to ask my question when Lungidus raised a hand to stop me. I thought he was about to wrap me in telekinesis again, but he did not.

"I can read your mind, Mr. Lasteran. It's my desire that you have no lingering regrets when you go to Ophidia. Steffa has not predicted a one hundred percent chance of success for you, after all. You may speak with your daughter at her tree house. I must stay here to watch over Master Scrimshander, but Tynan can take you there quickly."

"If I may be rude, Your Luminance... why go through so much trouble to let me rescue my own son when you could just as easily go to Ophidia and rescue him yourself?"

His smirk returned. "I am an Aloutian officer in the Godblood Brigade. If I went to Ophidia and did what I'd love to do to those snakes, I would start a war between our two countries. Tynan cannot enter the Ophidian Plane due to... well, it's between them and the Gods. All I can say is that they are under a magical obligation that prevents them from going to Ophidia."

"A magical obligation?"

"Yes. A geas, it's called, from Anemone mythology. When Tynan hatched, my Lord Father saw that they would be too powerful, so they placed this magical obligation upon them. Tynan must obey any order given to them by me, Loyenie, Lord Lucognidus, or Lord Sawyer."

"That sounds..." I was about to say it sounded terrible, both for the parents to be burdened with such responsibility and for the child to be at their mercy, but I did not want to offend His Luminance with my clearblood opinions.

"Mr. Lasteran, you are welcome to think anything you want. You may also ask me anything. I am a servant of the law, and I would not hurt you unless it were in defense of another person. Godbloods should *not* be above reproach, and we should be held accountable to the public. If you feel owed an explanation, I will answer to you."

"Thank you for your kindness," I said. "I have no questions." It was hard to trust him. It was hard to trust anyone wearing that Aloutian red uniform, but to compound that on top of his Godblood status? Even Su, as gentle and soft as he was, and as much as he sometimes acted submissive in my arms, had sometimes been possessed by a terrible fury and demanded other people call him 'Luminance.'

I returned to the room to retrieve Cohaku. She had put her head back on her knees, probably thinking that her request would be denied. When I told her we could go to her tree house, she raised her head, eyes wide open in surprise.

"Really? We can? You don't mind?"

"Captain Pavo wants me to speak with you, it seems. He won't let us leave for Ophidia if I have any lingering regrets."

"And you would regret it if you didn't speak to me?" she asked.

"I would. Come, let's talk."

She scurried to her feet and flew into my arms, much like Heliodor had the first time I walked in. She rested her head on my chest, our manes mingling. She was so small, so vulnerable, my precious daughter. I clutched her tight as I walked outside. My skull forced me to imagine more intrusive thoughts—what if Cohaku had died instead of Tawny? What if Su and I didn't come back from Ophidia? Cohaku could be a difficult child... If we didn't return, and Liesle were sent to jail, who would take care of her? Who *could* take care of her? She had temper tantrums if different foods touched each other, and she refused to wear anything uncomfortable. If she were forced to go to the Wind church, they wouldn't give her what she wanted. Hell, they might spank her for being so picky. My poor Cohaku... I couldn't let anyone else raise her! She'd grow up to be such an angry adult if she was forced onto parents who didn't understand her.

"Mr. Lasteran?" Lungidus said as I stepped outside. "Apologies, but I heard your thoughts. Please don't worry about that possibility. If... if that happens, I will make sure everything is taken care of."

Cohaku looked at him curiously, but she didn't ask any questions.

"Thank you," I said. It was all I could say. Oh, I could have ranted about how Godbloods should have been doing more to protect the citizens of Aloutia. Maybe Lungidus and Tynan couldn't personally rescue my sons, but they could have gotten someone *else* to do it.

I suppose they were, though... by getting Su to do it.

Regardless, ranting in front of my daughter was not something I wished to do. It was my job to comfort her, to relax her, and to let her say whatever was on her mind.

"Tynan will carry you back to your house," Lungidus said. "They can get you there quickly, so you don't have to walk there and back. Don't be alarmed by their body."

The child shifted into an animal unlike any I'd ever seen. They were enormous, large enough to hold me and Cohaku safely in their hands, with wings larger than a coatl's, but black as pitch. They held me in those giant, soft-pawed hands in much the same way I held Cohaku.

Despite being only a few months old and a merchant of dance, Tynan had learned to be careful and gentle. They held me close to their body, a form lined with soft fur which I found immensely comforting, and shot into the sky.

Codex Dominex: Those Who Use Magic

All magic in the Pentagonal Dominion comes from the cores, and those cores are under the control of their masters, the Gods. In addition to the Gods, there are a few ways other people can acquire magical powers over an element, though each case involves a God's blood.

- Godbloods: direct descendants of Gods (to a maximum of three generations), who acquired their magic through blood inheritance. Their magic is restricted to their element.
- Drinkers: people who acquired magical blood by drinking the blood of a God. Their magic is restricted to the element of the God who graced them with their blood.
- Demons: entities who may have acquired magic through the Evil element channeling other elements. Their magic is varied and unpredictable. Not all demons have magical powers. For those who do, it is bestowed upon them at creation. The Hierarchical powers given to demons who ascend to the rank of Demon Lord are channeled through the Evil element. Since any corpse, including that of a Godblood or drinker can be put in the Crucible, there can be Godblood or drinker demons who retain their powers from their mortal lives. However, the instances of Godbloods or drinkers becoming demons are quite rare.

Although the Gods are immortals dwelling in the afterlife plane, Spiritua, they must have their children on the mortal planes. Deceased people in the afterlife lose the ability to reproduce, but the Gods' ghostly forms were revitalized so they and their sexual partners are capable of reproduction. Even still, due to the nature of Spiritua, any baby whose egg is laid there will not survive. Godblood eggs are left in the care of mortal parents.

Since Godbloods are the offspring of Gods, their numbers depend on the proclivity of their respective God to reproduce. As of the year 561, only seven of the ten Gods have an interest/capability in having children: Sawyer, Cherribell, Entomothy, Flamboil, Sparkato, Lucognidus, and Liqua. Out of them, Cherribell is quite reserved and only has two living children. Sawyer has a child with his wife every ten years, and when they are unable to conceive, he will select a drinker from amongst the mortals instead. Lucognidus always has eight living children (not counting grandchildren or great-grandchildren Godbloods), so when one passes away, he will produce a new one. Entomothy is exceptionally virile and prone to impregnating the many women of his harem, thus it is common for the world to have hundreds of Life Godbloods at any given time.

Demigods (demis) are people, either Godbloods or drinkers, who have been selected by a God to serve them in a specific capacity. All demis have a title, job, and at least one ritual or prayer mortals can perform to request their services. Because the status of being a demigod is based on a job, they can retire or otherwise be forced to quit. It is not a permanent station, though as of the year 561, there are some demis who have served their God since the Conquering. In Aloutian-English, demi(god/dess) is traditionally uncapitalized unless referring to a specific one by title. Supposedly, this is to represent their subservience to the Gods (always capitalized).

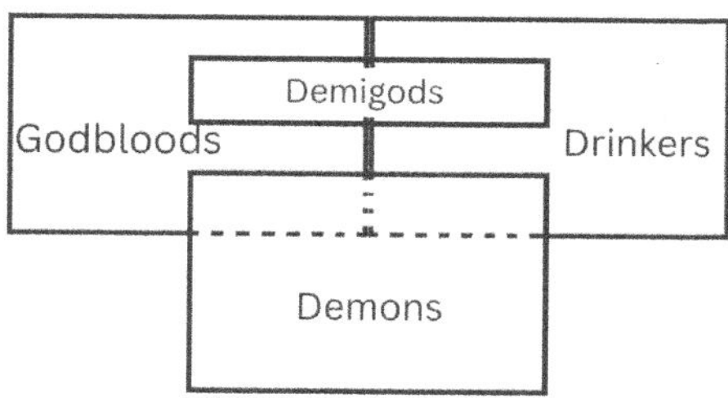

Chapter Forty-Two: Liesle's Secrets

Tynan landed on the beach near our house and set us down on the soft, white sand.

"I shall be nearby," they said in a deep, rumbling voice. "If you need me, I will be here. If you try to run, I will capture you. Per my father's orders, I cannot let you leave."

Per the geas, they couldn't disobey, either...

"I understand. We're just going to that tree house over there." I pointed to the tree across Coconut Crab Circle.

Tynan nodded and transformed into an azure alkonost. They flitted away to another tree nearby, out of earshot. Well, out of earshot for most people; I had no doubt Tynan could grow an ear that could hear colors, if they so wished.

Cohaku flew to her tree house. She laid down on her belly with her head at the entrance so she could look down upon me. I sat on the grass in the shade of the mighty tree, illuminated by the light of my daughter's tail waving above her head.

"Daddy, I've been wanting to talk to you alone for so long. I feel bad when I interrupt your work in the ateli, but when you're not in there, you're with everyone else. With Mommy and Mapa Su, or playing with Fionn and Heli, or teaching Nio and Susana to read, or building Eruwan's house. I didn't want to be a bother." She sniffled and rubbed her eyes. Tears erupted like the first downpour of rainy season.

"Are you okay?" I asked, startled by her sudden outburst. "You can come back down if you want. Do you need a hug?"

She cried wordlessly for a minute, her body shaking. When the emotions were all out, she sniffed one last time and dried her tears. "I'm alright. I just wish we had more time to play. And now, will we ever play again?"

"I'm not leaving forever, Cohaku. I'll be back as soon as I get your brothers and sister back. I promise we'll play more when I return."

"Will you?" she asked. "How can you spend time with me when everyone needs your attention? Fionn used to have Tawny to play with, but now he needs you. Susana used to have a different family, and now she needs you to teach her how to read. Turquoise is gonna need you all the time, too!"

"Your mother and Mapa Su are here to help me. Raising a family is like kiwi-batte; it's a team effort. If you need my attention, I can count on them to take care of things while I talk to you. Wouldn't you rather talk to Mapa Su, anyway? He can help you with whatever is on your mind much better than I can."

Su was all the kids' favorite parent, and I couldn't blame them. He was so amazing, so perfect in every way. It didn't surprise me when Eruwan took his surname; she had been enthralled by him ever since she was an infant. He just had a way with people that made them *want* to like him.

"No!" Cohaku yelled. "I want to play with *you*, Daddy! I like Mapa Su, but I don't want to talk to him. He doesn't understand me! He's never even tried. You are the only one who cares."

My entire perception shattered like a glass ball slammed against a wall. My perfect picture of Su, forever tarnished by the words of a nine-year-old girl. How could Su not understand her? He understood everyone! I certainly had not done anything different...

Oh sure, I had talked to Cohaku after her temper tantrums. I had let her into my ateli and showed her my work. I had done what any father would have done. Surely Su would have done the same thing if she'd only asked. Well, she wouldn't want to go into his ateli, with how bad it smelled.

"Everyone talks about Mapa Su like he's a saint," Cohaku said. "I... I like him, but not *that* much. He sometimes tells me I should forgive Fionn, but I don't want to. Mommy says the same thing, and I hate it. I will never forgive him. Even when we're old, I won't forgive him. You're the only one who doesn't tell me I have to change my mind about him. That's why you're my favorite, Daddy."

I'd never thought about how Cohaku viewed the family. I had thought this household was perfect, with happy, smiling children. All this time, Cohaku must have disliked half of us and couldn't wait to live on her own. I imagined her yearning for the day she would become Amber.

"Are you upset that I'm putting myself in danger to save Fionn?"

She shook her head. The furculae pinned in her mane sang as they clattered together. "No, I know you have to do it. I know parents love all their children equally, and I know you'd do anything to save any of us. I just... I also know Mommy and Mapa Su are gonna make me be all nice and mushy with Fionn when he comes back. They're gonna force me to hug him and tell him that he's safe now and all that mutton slugs[1] . I don't want to, Daddy. I'll live with him until he turns fifteen and moves out, but I don't want to play with him!"

"You won't have to," I said. "I promise. I'll talk to them. They won't bother you about Fionn, anymore."

Gods, Liesle might not come home if she was sent to Hydra Island, and if I told Su about what Cohaku just told me... he might be too scared to talk to her.

---

1. Euphemism of the swear phrase 'mud and sludge.'

"Please, Daddy… I'm so tired of pretending." She wiped away a few more tears, though she had won the battle with that tantrum before it began. "Every day, I have to pretend to like Fionn. I have to pretend I'm happy. I have to pretend to like Mommy and talk the way she wants me to talk. I'm tired of it."

If her mind was living in her own place and time, the experience of her body being trapped outside that space and time had exhausted her. She wanted to be alone more than anything. She bore the semblance of a well-adjusted Wynnle girl in front of others, but she craved the freedom to live, speak, and act the way her soul had been born to do.

"I know you're tired of it," I said. "I'll do everything I can so you don't have to keep pretending, but you might have to pretend a little longer. I'll build a house for you after we finish Fionn's house, and when you turn fifteen, you can move there. Where do you want it to be? Further up the beach, away from everyone else? If you want to move to another city, I can't build it, but I can commission somebody else to start."

"See? You're always so nice to me. You always think of solutions, instead of telling me that I should 'just try to get along with Fionn.' I don't know if I want to move far away or not. I'll wait and see what Fionn decides to do. If he leaves, I may stay here."

"That's a wise choice. Whichever you choose, I will support your decision."

She smiled, showing all her teeth. I had never seen her smile so wide and proud before. She didn't have the best teeth—Su was always making her use the miswak stick—so she usually smiled with her lips closed.

Ah, this was her true smile. The smile she would only show me because I was the parent she trusted. This was Cohaku in her most genuine state. Gods, she was cute.

"While I'm sharing my secrets with you, do you want to see Mommy's secret art cave? It's not a secret anymore—that Godblood lawkeeper made her show him where it is. I've known for a long time, though. I followed her once. I've seen the pictures she draws in there."

Part of me felt like it was a violation of Liesle's trust to intrude. We three had always agreed to treat each other's secrets as sacred. But another part of me knew it would all come to light soon anyway. She would be put on trial for summoning Lord Vinoc, and her private art gallery would be used as evidence against her. I could see it now, under my own terms, or under the judges' terms. Perhaps I was doing Liesle a favor by revealing her secrets to myself in private first. I wished I could have asked her for permission, but I doubted Captain Pavo would care to grant me that request.

There was the matter of Tynan. I glanced at the tree they'd perched in. A tiny blue alkonost, watching us from afar. My thoughts must have screamed too loudly, for the Godblood child glided to us and transformed into their standard shape.

"My father commanded me to not let you leave. However, I do not know where the boundary of 'leaving' is. He could have meant you aren't allowed to leave the village, or perhaps you're not allowed to leave Aloutia. Maybe you're simply not allowed to leave the Pentagonal Dominion. I do not know, therefore I can interpret his order as I wish. If you want me to take you to Mys Denwall's cave, I will."

"You will?" Cohaku hopped down, flapping her wings for balance as she touched the ground. "Can you carry my Daddy to the entrance?"

"I will do that," Tynan said stoically. "As well as carry him back down."

The merchant of dance transformed themself into another avian with large hands extruding from six great rainbow-colored wings. Tynan may have chosen a different form and colors this time, but the body served the same function. They held me and Cohaku safe and secure in their hands as they ascended to the skies.

Tynan took us to the stacks along the coast where the caves of St. Alice's Lights had made an underground labyrinth. Some of the entrances were impossible for me to reach, as they either required swimming under Deep Sea or flying along sheer cliff faces.

Liesle's cave faced the setting sun. I imagined her setting up her easel at just such an angle that the dying sun shone on her artwork.

It was not a deep cave, but the floor was so smooth, I assumed Liesle had sanded it down at some point. On one wall, her collection of paintbrushes, and a few pails for storing water hung from pegs. Against the other wall were tubes of acrylics, a case of gouache, an easel, palettes, and blank canvases.

On the far wall, directly in front of me... Liesle's secret paintings lay hidden behind cloth drapes. I approached, pili-palas dancing in my chest. Not for fear of what I'd find, but for fear that Liesle would despise me if she found out what I was doing. Gods... my dearest wife... please forgive me.

I grabbed the cloth off one canvas and pulled it away.

My eyes bulged open and I quickly put the sheet back on so the children wouldn't see.

It was a painting of *me*... naked, sexually evocative. She had put a high level of detail into every spine of my cock.

I turned to the children. "Um, could you two look away, please? These aren't things children should see."

Cohaku gulped and turned away. Tynan, confused, grew a pair of thick eyebrows just for the sake of raising one. They must have been so desensitized to sex and violence already that it didn't faze them.

"Please, Your Luminance," I begged. "I know it sounds silly, but please do it for me. I cannot have it on my conscience that I allowed a child to look at... at this sort of thing."

"I understand," Tynan said. "I shall remove my eyeballs."

They transformed their face, indeed removing their eyes, leaving empty sockets in their head. I wondered if they were aware of how unnerving that was. Perhaps that was the idea. A merchant of dance *should* intimidate.

I hadn't meant for them to do that, but... I supposed it worked.

I turned back to Liesle's artwork and uncovered the picture of me. I didn't know how to feel. On one hand, it was an explicit picture of *me*, drawn without my consent. On the other hand... it was made by Liesle, who I loved, and it showed how much she loved me. I looked stunning; my mane was thick and elegant, my muscles were in better shape than they had been in years, and my eyes had a seductive look which... well, I had certainly *tried* to make that look before, but wasn't sure if I had succeeded.

I thought of Liesle coming here and painting this. Perhaps it had been on a warm, summer day. I envisioned her standing in this cave, light shining in from the setting sun, a breeze playing with her mane as she added a splash of color to my image. Was it a recent painting? Was there any way to tell? Maybe she had painted it years ago when I really had looked this good. Before sorrow had sapped my energy and age had made my belly sag.

Gods, I was both flattered and a bit bothered at the same time. I put the sheet over it again, unable to look at myself for long. I had never contended with this emotion before. Happy that Liesle was so proud of me, but also a bit... violated? I wished she had told me what she was doing. But she'd had to keep her art cave a secret. If we knew... if we had told anyone... Well, what was happening now would have happened sooner.

I removed the cover from another painting. This one depicted two naked Sus, one with testicles and a penis, the other with a vagina. Their arms were hooked together, as if Su were indeed two people, interacting with himself. His features were exaggerated; the one with a penis looked far more masculine than the real Su, and the one with a vagina was far more feminine, even having noticeable breasts.

Both Sus had the sweetest facial expressions. The male Su had a twinkle in his eye like he had just told a dirty joke. The female Su laughed demurely at the joke.

I couldn't help but stare at both Sus and wonder... which would Su look like if he hadn't ingested so much shubin marrow that whatever parts he originally had were shriveled and gone now?

It was interesting to me to find out that Liesle also wondered. That she had sexual fantasies of Su both ways.

The third painting I uncovered was also of Su... a single Su equipped with both a penis and a vagina. He laid on his back on the beach, his hair a wild mess with seaweed and seashells in it. One hand's fingers wove through his hair. Two hands cupped his breasts. His fourth hand touched the shaft of his penis and the skin around his vagina.

Damn... I swallowed, unsure if I should be looking at these pictures, either. They were Liesle's treasures... her secrets. Should I tell Su about them? Maybe he *knew* about them already. He'd known about Tico Svelt, after all, so maybe Liesle shared more of her secrets with him.

The fourth painting was Tawny. Perfect, sweet, precious Tawny. Forever seven years old, with each freckle in the right place and every mane hair exactly as it had been when she was alive. To prevent our daughter from being cursed should any troublemaker find Liesle's cave and desecrate the art, my wife had first drawn Lucognidus, resplendent in his Godly attire and seated upon the Amethyst Throne. Tawny sat on his lap, her small hands around his tentacled fingers. She was dressed in the sort of grass-and-bone garments we made for her, even though I doubted her caretakers in Spiritua would clothe her in such a manner.

Seeing her face painted so flawlessly—Gods, Liesle's memory was better than mine—unlocked the dams in my lacrimals. A flood of stinging tears fell down my cheeks.

The painting was not complete. Specifically, Lucognidus had not been fully colored. Tawny was done other than for a bit of shading. I wondered if Liesle had made sure to finish her first for fear of forgetting her face, too.

My sternum sunk thinking about the pain my wife must have been in as she'd made this artwork. And yet, sculpting Tawny had been a work of love and nostalgic joy for me. Joy, but also sorrow. Gods, I couldn't make sense of it with words. There were no words for the contradictory nature of our feelings. I once again imagined Liesle here in the late afternoons, sun illuminating the painting as it passed by flower barrettes in her mane. I visualized her face, forlorn yet serene. Somewhere, right now, Liesle was alone and scared, and there was nothing I could do to help her without provoking the anger of my Godblood wardens.

With bittersweet pangs assaulting my body, I put the cover back over the painting. I hoped that one day, Liesle would finish it and share it with the rest of the family. We could put it above the memorial.

The fifth painting was undoubtedly the one that had summoned Lord Vinoc. Rather than being sexual, it was intensely violent. In charcoal, Liesle had drawn an Umi woman who I had to assume was Lady Vinoc, the Demigoddess of Terror. She stood over the corpse of a Lagodorian woman. In one hand, Lady Vinoc held her butcher's knife. In the other, the head of Lavina Demiu, held by her long ears. When I first uncovered the painting, Lady Vinoc had her head bowed, her visage hidden beneath swaths of long, charcoal-black hair. I stared just long enough to blink, and when my eyes opened up, Lady Vinoc stared back at me with huge, round, purple eyes and a wicked smile. Those eyes were the only color on the canvas. I screamed and threw the cover back over it.

"Daddy! Are you okay?" Cohaku cried. She did not turn to see for herself, the trusting little girl.

"Mr. Lasteran!" Tynan said. "The painting is still cursed, but it cannot hurt you."

I put my hand over my sternum, still hurting after the scare. "I'm alright, Cohaku. You can turn around now. Your Luminance, thank you for your wisdom."

I knew cursed paintings were harmless to viewers. Still, it seemed better to flatter the Godblood child when I had the opportunity. I might very well be at their mercy one day, and I'd rather they remember that I called them wise.

Cohaku looked up at me as if expecting me to say what I had seen.

"I've seen what I needed to see," I said. "Cohaku, you knew about this place? Did you know what Mommy was painting here?"

"Yeah, I've seen the naked pictures. I... I don't like them, Daddy. I didn't look long. Sometimes Mommy painted normal pictures. I think they're in the back. She kept the naked ones out front because she liked to look at them. I don't get it."

Internally, I groaned, not wanting to have these conversations with her while she was still so young. I had neither the time nor mental clarity to discuss it now.

"You might understand when you become an adult, but until that day comes, don't worry about figuring it out."

"I know about sex, Daddy," she said in an irritated voice. "I'm not interested in that. I want to know why you screamed just now."

I shook my head. "I... Well, I suppose you're old enough to know about Vinoc's curse if you're old enough to know what sex is. When did you learn that, anyway? Did Su teach you what that means?"

"Yup. Mapa Su said that if he never taught us what sex is, we'd never learn because you and Mommy are too anxious talking to children about it."

Well... Su was right. I didn't think I could ever talk to my daughters about sex, and my sons... well, Fionn might be old enough that I wouldn't get flustered at the attempt.

"Daddy? You're staring off into the Hollow Void again. Why did you scream? What's Vinoc's curse?"

I explained what little I knew of the Demon Lord of Terror and his summoning ritual. Paintings that had been used to summon him were cursed, and the image inside could move, usually in creepy ways. What I saw was standard; legends always claimed the image of Lady Vinoc would always act in freakish ways. She might kill other subjects in the painting, or change her facial expression to something far more sinister than what the artist had painted. Paintings could be uncursed by painting the God Lucognidus in the same picture. Destroying the painting was not recommended, as it was believed the terror and negative energies associated with the two Vinocs would haunt the artist forever, with no way to relieve it.

Cohaku looked at the covered painting. "Do we need to paint Lucognidus in there now? Or else Mommy will be haunted?"

I hadn't considered it... I didn't want Liesle to suffer any more than she had. But who among us could possibly paint the Mind God? No one else in the family was near the level of skill possessed by a merchant of faces.

"Those stories are untrue," Tynan said. "Believe me. I have spoken to my Lord

Grandfather about curses. I have also met Lord Vinoc and spoken at length about his ritual of summoning. Cursed paintings cannot do any more harm as they are, nor will they hurt the artist if they are destroyed. Lord Vinoc added the 'uncursing' option to his ritual as a sign of friendship between him and my Lord Grandfather."

I blinked in surprise. I had no idea this child, Godblood or not, had spoken to Gods and Demon Lords. Su had never spoken to any Gods, as far as I knew, and only knew the Demon Lords because of his chance adoption by the Demon King Susan. I wondered how this infant had gotten so experienced in such little time.

"So I have nothing to worry about if I just leave the painting here?" I asked.

"Correct," they replied.

"And nothing to worry about if I shred it into pieces?"

Tynan stood deathly still and hesitated before answering. "While that is also true, I think my father would prefer—"

"I'm not giving a lawkeeper any more evidence to use against my wife." I uncovered the painting, just to be sure I'd grabbed the right one, and ripped it in half. The canvas was strong, but I was no weak man. I was a Wynnle—strong, athletic, worthy of being feared. I tore each of the two halves into their own halves before Tynan transformed into a hideous tentacled creature and enveloped me in their limbs. Each of my arms and legs, my torso, and my neck, were entangled by thick tentacles with suction cups resembling the fingers of a Phoenian.

I did not struggle. Part of me knew Tynan would do it, and had expected it. At least I did what damage I could...

"Mr. Lasteran, please don't resort to violence. In a court of law involving Godbloods, there is no need for physical evidence. We can acquire all we need to know through my Lord Grandfather's magic. Hypnotists, clairvoyants, knowledgeables, and Neri's Ritual can all discover the truth far more effectively than a painting's existence."

I breathed heavily, straining against the child's tentacles around my neck.

"I'm sorry. I... I just want to save my wife."

"I know," Tynan said. "I have watched men lose themselves to save a woman they love."

I stared at the four pieces, wondering if I'd done any good at all. Maybe I only made things worse.

"I don't think it's either better or worse," the Godblood said. "You and Mys Denwall will be judged fairly. Now, if you're ready to return, I will take you back to my father."

I sighed. "There's nothing else I need to do. Not here. My business is in Ophidia now. Yes, take me back to Captain Pavo so I can get my son back."

Chapter Forty-Three: Disguises

Tynan swooped down toward the Chak-Den house and set me and Cohaku down beside their father.

Captain Pavo leaned against the side of the house, arms crossed. He gave us a knowing smirk. "I see you went to the crime scene. Tynan, we need to talk about intentionally twisting my words."

"I did not disobey you, Father. If I did something wrong, perhaps you should reflect on how you could have phrased the order so I could not interpret it in a way that displeases you."

Lungidus didn't seem to appreciate his kid's cheekiness, but neither would it have been appropriate to make a scene here, so he dropped it. They were both telepaths, though… Perhaps their argument continued through mental waves.

"Thank you for giving me the opportunity to talk to my daughter before I…" I let the words go unspoken on my tongue, but Lungidus could hear the rest in my thoughts. *Before I went and got myself killed or enslaved in Ophidia.*

"You need not thank me. I had my reasons for asking you to wait. In fact, here they come now." He nodded his head, motioning behind me.

Giorvi walked up to the house, Oboro right behind him. They were both dressed in leather clothes and sturdy boots, prepared for a hike. Oboro had his full accoutrement of swords; the two at his side, and the enormous khopesh behind him.

"Amiere!" Giorvi hunched over, hands on his knees, breathing hard. "I got here as fast as I could. I knew there'd be trouble, and you would need my help." He eyed the Godbloods. "Your Luminance, may we talk?"

"In a moment," Lungidus replied. "We have much to discuss and we will have time for it shortly. One matter needs to be dealt with immediately, however. Mr. Lasteran's son Fionn has been captured by Ophidians. We know where he's at—Morigumo."

Oboro's eyes widened at the name. His lower hands clenched tighter around the hilts of the swords on his belt.

Lungidus continued, "No Godblood associated with the Aloutian military can go there to assist him, else we'll start a war. Master Scrimshander can go, though, and he certainly will. However, my precognitioner daughter has foreseen that the greatest chance of success lay with the help of a third member in the rescue party. That Sasorin boy. Oboro Onoretti is your name?"

Oboro stiffened, standing tall and proud. "Y-yes, Your Luminance! My name is Oboro Onoretti. If I can serve you in any way, please tell me how." I wondered if he was beaming with pride at being part of a Godblood's plan or at being called by his new name. Perhaps a little of both had swelled the boy's ego. I was happy for him; after the hard life he'd suffered through, he needed the boost.

"What I'm about to say is not an order. Although I'm a Godblood and a lawkeeper, your choice is yours to make. I understand you are under a contract to serve your patron, Mr. Giorvi Onoretti. If you need to take a moment to discuss this with—"

"I must go!" Oboro interrupted. He blushed, realizing he'd cut off a Godblood mid-sentence. "Please, Signore. Fionn is important to me. I know it sounds silly. We only spent a few days together last spring. But... I like him. He's special to Mys Beatrice, too."

Giorvi looked back and forth between Oboro and Lungidus, mostly confused by everything going on so quickly. "Wait, what's happening? Fionn was sold to Ophidia? What about the Demon Lord who haunted Amiere's nightmares? I thought we were coming to rescue Mys Denwall. And... what's this about your daughter's prediction, Your Luminance?"

"I'll answer everything later," he said. "My daughter has predicted that the greatest chance of Fionn coming back alive is to send Mr. Lasteran, Master Scrimshander, and the young Mr. Onoretti on a rescue mission to Ophidia. Without the Sasorin boy, the chances of success are low. Mr. Lasteran, in particular, will likely die or be enslaved himself."

"Dear Gods..." Giorvi said breathlessly. "And Oboro? What are his chances of dying or being enslaved?"

Lungidus looked Oboro in the eyes. "Do you want to know? Would it even change your mind about going? Fionn will likely remain a slave for life if you do not join the mission."

"I don't want to know the odds," Oboro said. "It doesn't matter. Whether it's ten percent or one hundred percent, I am going to do everything in my ability to rescue Fionn. I will make ten percent turn into one hundred percent!"

I had to admire the boy's enthusiasm, even if it wasn't how math or probabilities worked.

Lungidus chuckled, his crooked smile more exaggerated than usual. "I like your attitude. I can't go to Ophidia with you, but I can at least give you some enchanted jewelry to help you out. Go on, take them. I would like them returned when this is over, but don't berate yourself if they're lost. My daughter knows there's a chance I won't get them back, and I'm okay with that." He teleported three rings into his hands. They were wide, thick, silver rings made for Lungidus's tentacles, but they would fit around a Sasorin's chitinous digits, too.

Oboro accepted them with widened eyes. "Your Luminance, I..."

"Take them," he insisted. "You might not even need them, as their primary purpose is to protect against Mind elemental magic, and you may not even encounter a Mind Godblood. But they'll be put to better use with you than me. That one has a telepathy enchantment. It doesn't quite read minds, but it will help you feel what someone else is feeling. The second one will prevent any Mind Godblood weaker than me from hypnotizing you, and the third will make you more persuasive. People will be more inclined to believe you or to do as you say. I wouldn't risk it too often, but you might be able to convince even Ophidian women to do things they normally wouldn't do for a man."

"Wow, these are amazing!" Oboro bit his lip to prevent getting overexcited. "I will keep them safe, Your Luminance." The boy put the rings on his fingers right away. They had to go over his lower hands, of course, given that his upper hands were shaped like scorpion claws.

Su and Orienna stepped out of the house. Su had gotten changed into trousers and a long-sleeved shirt with a high neckline, decorated with floral patterns. He appeared to have breasts comparable to Liesle's, which elicited a questioning look from me.

"Do they look real?" he asked, pushing them up. "Ami-honey, take a feel."

Well, since he asked... I grabbed the mounds on his chest. They felt nothing like breasts, though I supposed it wouldn't matter if someone was only *looking*. Close as I was, the scent of jasmine perfume was unmistakable.

"What is it?" I asked. "Did you get sacks of rice and grass and strap them to your chest?"

He stroked my mane underneath my chin. "Close enough. If we're infiltrating Ophidia, one of us will need to look like a woman, and I don't think you or Oboro could pull it off."

I couldn't argue with that. Besides, I wouldn't have had the skill to pretend to be an Ophidian. I didn't know the first thing about the culture, customs, language...

"You realize what that means, though, right?" Su asked, putting a finger on his lower lip. The gesture made me want to kiss him. Gods, was he wearing lipstick, too? I'd heard Ophidian women adored make-up, though they wore it to impress other women, not men as was often the stereotype Aloutians believed. In Aloutia, all genders wore make-up in roughly even amounts, though not so much in Steena Village where most of the population were the ever-changing Flora for whom make-up might not even be safe.

"I have to play your slave?" I asked.

Su grimaced. "Yes, I'm glad you understand. I promise I will be *so* gentle with you, Ami-honey." He ran his fingers through my mane along my cheek. "And we will be there for as little time as we can. We'll find Fionn and get out as quickly as possible. But, if for some reason I have to prove to them that I'm your master...

Well, just obey me, okay? I promise I'll make it up to you when we get back home."

His fluttering eyelashes and the twinkle in his eye suggested that when we returned home, he would get on his knees to serve *me* if I asked for it.

"I will do everything I must to save Fionn," I replied. "If you have to whip me or... anything else... I am ready. Do I need certain clothes or a kamen or anything?"

"Kamens are only worn by the elite of Ophidia," Su said. "And never by slaves. Fear of the Lord of Terror just isn't as prevalent there. Perhaps because the punishment for summoning him is far crueler, most women wouldn't dare it. And of course, no man would ever be given the opportunity. They aren't given supplies to make art or taught how to make sufficiently skillful depictions of people. I doubt many know how to summon Lord Vinoc, anyway."

"I see. That's fine by me if I don't have to wear a kamen. By the way, Orienna, are these your clothes and Piotr's make-up?"

"Oh hell, I could never fit in those!" she said with a wave of her hand. "The clothes are Nell's. I gave her a little bit of money to order new clothes and make-up from the store. Now that she's running it, she knows how to order exactly what she wants. But yes, the make-up is Piotr's, though Demitris has borrowed it at times."

"Tell them thanks for us, for letting us borrow them," I said. "I'm ready to go now. Your Luminance, how are we to get to Ophidia?"

"Follow me. I'll take you to the portal Mys Demiu had used. Giorvi, would you please wait here? I have business to discuss with you when I get back."

"Certainly," the old Yosoe said. "Oboro, you be careful now. If I find out you were enslaved again, I will do what I can to get you back, but I don't want to imagine what I'll say to Beatie about why her playmate is missing."

Oboro tensed. "I will return soon, Signore. I won't let Mys Beatrice worry about me."

Lungidus walked onward, taking the path that led to the jungle northwest of the village. The place we'd always told the kids not to play in, where my mother had told me not to play in... and yet I had played in it almost every day as a young teenager. My kids probably knew the jungle just as well as I had at their age.

The Godblood continued to explain the plan as he led us in toward the border of koa trees. "Tynan cannot go to Ophidia, but they will accompany you through Cosmo, at least. The portal will take you close to the city of Lemongraves, on Solsun. It's a Solue stronghold, and specifically, I mean Solue who are aligned with Ophidia. Since Lemongraves is close to the border of Sasorin lands, I believe your cover story should be thus: Su and Tynan, disguised as women, will pretend to be merchants of flesh. Oboro and Amiere will play newly-captured slaves. Having Oboro around will make the story believable, as they receive many captured Sasorin slaves every day."

"But they'll believe a fully-grown Wynnle went into slavery without a fight?" I asked.

Tynan transformed into a female leonine Wynnle, approximately my coloration, but also a foot taller than me. They looked about how I imagined Tawny would look if she had lived to become an adult.

No, she *will* become an adult. She'll grow and age in Spiritua. The next time I see her, she will look like Tynan does now, though perhaps a bit shorter. She had inherited many of my traits, so perhaps she had inherited my height—short for a Wynnle.

"Play submissive to me," Tynan said in a deep, husky voice. "Pretend that I have been your master for years."

Lungidus stood before the jungle, a veritable wall of lush greenery, thick lianas, and vines taut enough that one needed a machete to get through. I had often clawed my way through such entanglements. The Godblood waved a tentacle. Vines snapped, lianas crumbled into dust, leaves and shrubbery wilted. Even the ground smoothed itself into a path so His Luminance wouldn't be forced to suffer a difficult hike. A flock of birds-of-paradise scattered in the wake of his destruction.

My mind wandered—I couldn't help it. I knew he was a telepath, but I couldn't stop my brain from thinking its traitorous thoughts. I wondered if a Godblood like him ever struggled physically, or if he just used telekinesis to move things on a whim. Did he ever get sore feet, or would be move by floating himself in midair before such an inconvenience could afflict him? And if his feet ever *did* get sore... did he have a legion of servants to rub them? I shook my head, not wanting to think such private, salacious thoughts about a mind reader.

He chuckled. "Amiere... I won't embarrass you. I must say, though, that my lifestyle isn't as glamorous as you're envisioning. I live with my family, that's all. We have a professional chef and launderer, but they are in the Chancellor's employ and serve many Godbloods."

"I apologize for my stray thoughts," I said, blushing. He may not have wanted to embarrass me, but knowing my thoughts could be laid bare before him, against my will... Well, what right did *I* have to complain when my son had just been sold into slavery?

"Don't apologize for what you can't control," he said. "I've been a telepath all my life. I've heard much worse since I was a toddler." He stopped in front of a collection of rock formations. I had been to this spot countless times as a child. I remembered once I'd climbed atop one of those rocks and taunted Milti who was too short to reach the grip I had used. Liesle had just flown to the top, of course.

Had we ever been back here since? A marking had been clawed into the side of the stone. I wondered if one of my kids had made it... or maybe I had done so over twenty years ago and the memory of it was lost to time.

Lungidus flicked a tentacle and vaporized a blanket of leaves that had been draped over a stone formation. Even a quick glance would show the blanket was unnatural, like it grew directly out of the stone. Had Lungidus put it there to hide the cave beneath it?

"I did not put this here," he said. "And until now, I had no reason to destroy it."

The rock formation had been carved into a cave venturing down into the dirt. Deeper in, the tell-tale sparkles of a portal shimmered on the cave wall.

"You may want these," Lungidus said. When I turned to him, he held the outermost tentacles of his hand out, each one holding an iron collar.

My heart dropped. I knew it was just pretend, but...

"The Ophidians will require it," he said. "Remember, Amiere, they won't hesitate to strike down a man they view as a threat, and they are threatened by the very existence of male Wynnles."

Su took one of the collars. "Ami-honey, would you feel better if I put it on you? We can pretend that it's... part of our fun."

I blushed furiously. My tail flickered as I blustered. "A-ah, yes, that would be fine."

Lungidus grinned and went about helping Oboro with his collar.

Su whispered in my ear as he put the collar around my neck. He had to wrestle my mane out of the way—an effort in itself. "My sexy, sweet Ami-honey... I'll put this collar on you and yet still you'll be the master of my soul, and I your slave. When we get home, put a collar on me. Hold me by a collar while I suck your dick. Ooh, perhaps I'll make one out of bone."

If nothing else, his words helped get me in the mood to wear a collar. It had gone from being purely an object of oppression to being an object of sexuality. Damn, now I *wanted* to see Su in a bone collar...

When we were ready, Lungidus crossed his arms and stared intently at the portal. His lips quivered, mouthing inaudible words. Yet another mental conversation—perhaps with Tynan, perhaps with his precognitioner daughter. He turned to me and spoke aloud, "I'll have this portal guarded until you return. Or until I hear you won't *be* returning, if that's the future in store. The Cosmo side is too close to Lemongraves to be of any use to Aloutia; we will destroy it."

"As long as it's taken far from our village, I don't care what you do to it," Su said. "And don't you dare say we won't be returning. I *will* get my son back, even if I have to ravage Ophidia to do it."

The lawkeeper only gave him a sly smile. "I wish you luck, Master Scrimshander. Kill as many of those snakes as you want—as long as you don't kill an Aloutian citizen, I don't care how murderous you or your family are."

Su scowled as he went into the cave. As I did not want to anger Lungidus any further, I kept my head low and my eyes forward. With fear pounding my sternum and trembling in every bone in my body, I stepped into Cosmo.

Chapter Forty-Four: Lemongraves

The desert planet Solsun was always hot as hell to the extent that only Fire elementals or people with Flamboil's Blessing could feasibly live here. Having lived in the tropics my whole life, I found warmth comfortable, but I was accustomed to wet heat wherein droplets from Deep Sea dampened my mane, and Solsun's heat was excruciatingly dry. The double suns beat down with cruel rays, evaporating any remnant of water that had stubbornly held on to my body or clothes.

Solsun actually had three suns, if I recalled my school lessons correctly, and perhaps all three were in the sky today, but I could not look in their direction long to find out. I had heard that nights, when they came to Solsun, were short. At least one of the suns was enchanted as a Godlight, too, and thus demonic activity was almost nonexistent. The merchants of light rarely sold crystalights to this planet; our only customers were wealthy individuals who wanted to display them for their artistic merit.

The portal exited out of the side of an enormous butte with scaffolding set up for quick access. Two female Orochijin guards slithered up the planks, guns in their hands, prepared to accost us. I had heard of guns before, but this was my first time seeing them. Were they really so dangerous? They had such long barrels that the women carried them in both hands.

"Who the hell are you?" one of the women asked. "And who are these? Is that Wynnle collared?"

"Yes, he has a collar." Su pulled me down and reached his hand into my mane, shoving fistfuls of hair away to show them I had this wretched piece of metal around my neck.

"As for your other question, we are merchants of flesh," Tynan replied. They crossed their arms over a voluptuous female chest. Their disguise would have fooled me.

"When did you go through that portal?" the other asked. "I don't recall authorizing you."

Su sighed and walked closer. When he put his hands on their shoulders, their faces slackened. Their arms fell to their sides, each holding their gun in one hand.

"I'm sorry," he said quietly, speaking to the women. "I don't have time to come up with excuses." Su turned back to us. "Let's go. They'll be out for a few hours, and by then, I want to have passed through Lemongraves and gotten to Ophidia."

The city of Lemongraves was easily seen from our height. It was a walled city, mostly brown stone and brick both on the outside and inside. The wall appeared to be made from buttes much like this one that had been placed in a hexagon, then connected by thick crenellated walls. Each of the six buttes were topped with twin ballistae pointed in angles away from the city.

"A fortified city," Su said as he started down the ramp. "If this is a Solue city, they're on the lookout for raiding parties of Sounites and Sasorin. We get on the main road and act like normal travelers. Normal merchants of flesh, I should say."

"All their fortifications, and I could level the city in less than a minute," Tynan said. "An army of winged people could take it in a day."

"Cities like this one are old," Su said. "Made during the pre-Spiritism era. We don't build forts anymore—no point to it, when a Godblood could destroy it so easily. If anything, walling your people in only makes it harder for them to escape."

"I'd tear it down myself, if I could," I growled. I would have glared at the city, if not for the scaffold being awfully precipitous and the ramp skinny and wobbly.

If I fell from this height... I imagined how far Tawny must have fallen.

"Mr. Lasteran," Tynan interrupted before my thoughts could repeat the images again. "If you were to fall, I guarantee I would transform into a large body with Plecopteran wings quickly enough to catch you."

I knew they were only trying to be comforting, but... well, it made me wish they had been there when Tawny passed away.

"I'm sorry. I had not hatched yet. Had I existed earlier, I would have tried to save her."

"You don't have to do all of your grandfather's dirty work, Lord Tynan. Lucognidus could have saved her, and he didn't." I exhaled a long, resigned sigh. "Twenty Thousand Eyes, and not a single one to spare for my little girl."

Tynan had no response—verbal or emotional—for that. They merely continued on.

At the bottom of the scaffolding, Su instructed us to head for the road first, even though our path was perpendicular to the city. From this distance, nobody watching from the walls could see us, so if we got on the road first, the guards might not know where we'd come from. Su and Tynan knew the plan; I just had to nod and obey. I would keep my eyes down and act subservient; pretend I'd been a slave my whole life.

Gods, when I thought about what Fionn might be going through *right now*, my instinct was to do the exact opposite of acting subservient. I wanted to roar, scream, pummel, electrocute... tear some Ophidian throats and eat their fucking livers. My claws extended; a subconscious reaction to my emotions. I forced them back in with great mental effort.

The road to Lemongraves was paved with some black material I'd never seen or walked upon before. It was so smooth a wagon could travel across it without hitting a single bump. It reminded me of the roads used by merchants of mail, though their roads were grey.

The desert in our approximate vicinity didn't feature a single plant. Not so much as a tumbleweed or wilted blade of grass could be seen. Only when we got closer to the city did I see its namesake—lemon and lemontine trees lined the road to the gated entrance, their yellow fruits within reach for visitors to pluck without having to leave the road. They were short trees—even the shorter species could easily reach one. The difference between lemon and lemontine was miniscule from a distance. One had to look at the fruits or leaves carefully to distinguish them.

I knew what a lemon was, but not what 'graves' meant. I assumed it to be a Solsuni word.

More armed guards stood between the gates. One was Orochijin, the other Solue, a species of people who were all born with female reproductive organs. I did not know the details of their reproduction, or how they managed to bear offspring who were also fully Solue. What I *did* know was that Aloutians associated them with Ophidians more often than not. Solues had black skin, but usually not so dark that their tattoos wouldn't show up. They always tattooed themselves head-to-foot, so looking at one was more akin to looking at a piece of art. Tattoo culture was intrinsic to Solues. I was sure there were Solues somewhere who had not tattooed themselves, but they were the exception, the rebels, not the standard. The one who approached us with a hand on her gun bore Ophidian symbols on her face—a snake tattoo around her eyes, Orochigo writing on her temples, and on each cheek, the symbol of a serpent coiled around a winged staff. Just seeing those made me sick. No decent Aloutian would scrawl that trash on their body. I hadn't even known what they'd meant until I'd met Su and he had taught me—they were symbols of female supremacy.

Su spoke to the women in Orochigo. Without argument, they allowed us in. I glanced at the Solue, curious to see if I could find other symbols I might recognize, and she spat on me, then growled something in Orochigo. The spit hit my leg. I lowered my head and kept walking. Only after we'd passed through the gate did I dare wipe the wad of saliva off.

Lemongraves was as brown up close as it was from afar. Interconnected buildings of sandstone bricks made a labyrinth. Arches and bridges allowed for travel on the ground level and across the rooftops. Camels, cotza, and wagon beetles occupied the streets, pulling their burdens laden with bronze wares, spices, and cheap clothes made by Ophidian slave labor.

The city may have been under Ophidian influence, but it was not Ophidian. Although rare, a few men walked the streets freely. A Sounite man led an auction selling his glass products. Although not as durable as Domovoi glass, Sounite glass was still a desired commodity. Being more common, it was cheaper, but no less clear or beautiful. I'd had to incorporate Sounite and Domovoi glass in my commissions before. Since glass could not be carved, I had been asked to instead carve crystalights to fit inside glass containers.

Early in my career, I'd been asked to carve a crystalight that would go inside the head of a glass Lepidopteran. The statue's wings had been razor thin, and clearer than ice. So clear and thin as to almost be invisible, and I thought it was priceless. I had knocked that statue down while I was high on crazy sugar, shattered it into a million pieces on my ateli floor. Giorvi had just become my commissioner at that time, and he'd taken me aside, comforted me, and told me that breaking a Sounite glass container wasn't a big deal. It was easily replaced.

"We might have to search around for the portal house," Su said.

"No, I know where it is," Tynan replied. "Follow me."

They must have used some Mind elemental power to divine the knowledge.

Tynan's presence as a large Wynnle woman kept others from approaching us. We followed them through the lemon-scented streets of the town, eventually ascending a flight of stairs up a sandstone building that took us to the upper-level streets. With all the animals competing for space below, this was the preferred walkway for pedestrians.

The portal house reminded me of an ancient temple to before-world Gods. Constructed of grey stone and supported by magnificent pillars, it was large enough for a Daga to enter. Friezes above the entrance depicted Solue women commanding the elements—probably the Elemental Spirits from the Solue before-world. Short granite obelisks—about half my height—surrounded the building. Behind each one grew a lemon or lemontine tree. The obelisks bore vertical Solsuni script written in an elegant, cursive hand.

Tynan made a small, squeaking noise. I turned to them, curious.

"Oh, never mind," they said. "I know what those things are, but after careful consideration, I decided it would only upset you."

"Tell me later, then," I said. "I must focus on rescuing my son."

"Yes, indeed. I cannot go to Ophidia—my grandfathers forbade it—but I can at least get you to the portal without being interrogated along the way."

We went inside the temple complex. If I thought the portals connecting Aloutia and Cosmo were well-guarded, I was a fool. *These* were well-guarded portals. Those connecting Cosmo to Ophidia each had a Shinkou Sueba officer standing beside it, her gun and whip ready to be used.

Tynan strode up to one, swaggering on their digitigrade Wynnle feet, arms swaying wide back and forth. They exuded confidence as they approached the Ophidian officer standing guard at a huge Daga-sized door. It would have been too heavy for any of us to open, even if we all worked together, but a lever above the woman's head suggested it might be connected to gears inside the wall.

After a quick exchange in Orochigo, Tynan beckoned us forward.

They pointed to each of us in turn as they spoke to the woman. She eyed me suspiciously, but relaxed around Su and Oboro. At first, I thought it was odd that Oboro would not instill a similar fear or revulsion, but then I remembered he wore an enchanted ring that supposedly made him more 'charming.' I already liked the kid well enough, so perhaps the effect did not work on me.

The guard pulled the lever which opened the door, as I had speculated. Machinery in the walls slid the door inside. I doubted *that* had been present in the days when this building was first constructed. Clockwork was associated with the tyranny of the age cured by the Greed Wars, when rioters in Aloutia had destroyed their overlords' clockwork structures in rage. It didn't surprise me to see some unscathed in Cosmo, however.

As the door parted, the portal came into view. A water portal, contained inside a tub with similar designs as the pillars and obelisks outside. Su took the lead, per his disguise as our master.

Taking on a powerful, commanding tone, and using the most feminine voice he could muster, he barked, "You, Sasorin, go first. Fall into it so your whole body teleports. If I have to put your collar, rings, or clothes back on you, I'll give you a whipping you won't forget."

Oboro bowed his head. "Yes, Master. At once, Master."

I imagined Su had him go first so he could demonstrate to me how it was done. Even if Oboro had only gone through a water portal once in his life, it was once more than I had ever done. He stood atop the rim of the pool, stretched his arms to his sides, and fell horizontally so that his whole body hit the surface simultaneously.

Su winked at me, a subtle sign that he didn't want to say what he was about to say. "Now you, Wynnle! Do as he did, and don't mess it up!"

It was almost *cute* seeing Su act so domineering. I stepped up to the tub and fell in the way Oboro had.

The water was so shallow, if it didn't teleport me, I'd smack my face on the bottom. Come to think of it, how did water portals not teleport the containers holding them? The edges did not shimmer like the center did; perhaps that was part of it. I closed my eyes and grimaced as if preparing to hit the bottom of the tub.

I did not even get wet. The first notable sensation was a shift in gravity, as I went from falling horizontally to sitting upright with a much stronger gravitational pull than I was used to. The second sensation involved my mane being freed from that wretched collar. The metal contraption lay a few feet away from me, closer to Oboro, who had arranged himself in a kneeling position, bowing away from the tub. I dared a glance at where he looked.

The room we were in was more like a jail cell: hard, solid, concrete blocks surrounded us in a room large enough to fit a Daga. The barred door was also large enough for the turtle-people, assuming it was unlocked. The two Shinkou Sueba guards on the other side, watching us while fingering their guns, gave me reason to suspect the door was, in fact, locked.

I knelt the same way Oboro did. Ears pinned down, my tail flat against the floor, I tried to make myself look as meek as a kitten.

Su materialized beside me, standing up. Lucky him.

With my eyes downcast, I did not see what he did, but I heard his hands patting his body. It truly would have been a disaster if he'd teleported in front of all these women and lost any articles of clothing integral to his disguise.

"Master, the collar came off the Wynnle," Oboro said while remaining knelt.

"Ah, so it did," Su replied. He took the collar and leaned close to my ear as he put it back on. "I'm sorry I have to do this," he whispered. "They're watching. When I hit your back, scream and roar as if it hurt like hell." He stood up and the façade began. "You idiot Wynnle! I gave you one fucking order and you couldn't even manage that?" He made a show of slamming his hand against my back, though I barely felt it. The sound was much worse than the hit itself.

I let out a mighty yelp of pain, anyway. He 'hit' me two more times, if such gentle taps could be called hits, and I screamed after each one. Were the Ophidians fooled? Did they really think Su had hurt me?

My husband snorted derisively—somehow femininely, too, in my opinion—and approached the gate. He bowed to the Ophidian women and greeted them in Orochigo. After a brief exchange, they opened the door.

Worried that any proactive movement would alert the Ophidians, I waited for Su to order me up before I followed him out. I kept my gaze down and avoided looking at the Shinkou Sueba guards as I walked by, close behind Su.

I could not stop thinking about how heavy I felt here. Even my tail carried extra weight, to the point I wanted to let it drag on the ground. The iron slave collar would not have bothered me normally, other than for its significance as a tool of oppression, but on the Ophidian plane, it pulled down, yanking my mane with it.

The portal house's décor was much more welcoming—if such a word could ever apply to Ophidia—once we were out of the individual portal room. Ophidians may have been awful, but they still had standards for architectural beauty and aesthetics. The theme of Morigumo involved curves, swirls, and spirals. Murals along the hallway repeated patterns of spirals interlocked with each other. The columns supporting the tall roof ascended in a corkscrew fashion. There was little color to be seen. Spirals on the walls were grey, white, and silver with the exception of a green line painted across every vertical surface—every wall, pillar, and door—at around the nine-foot mark. Sconces for torches were set at the green line, placed between the pillars and on the pillars themselves.

We stepped out into the city. A thin mist hung in the air, though I could see my immediate vicinity clearly enough that it didn't bother me. My mane was moisturized within minutes; a comfortable contrast to the wretched lemontine-aided dryness of Solsun. The streets were lined with gas lamps. The deepest I could see into the mist were flickering flames, safely contained in the glass cages. Slaves went to each lamp, lighting them with wicks on long poles. It was midday, but perhaps the rulers of Morigumo had decided the lamps should be lit on misty days, too.

The merchants of light refused to sell crystalights to Ophidians, so all their sources of light were likely gas lamps and glowlight lotuses. It would not surprise me if a few noblewomen had crystalights in their private collections, but they would have been purchased from an intermediary. Giorvi would sooner toss a crystalight into Deep Sea and let him grind it into dust before he'd sign the paperwork for an Ophidian customer.

Su led us to a private seating area, a quaint table surrounded by benches with long seats designed for the serpentine Orochijin species. The swirls engraved in the seat gave it a sense that it was genuinely something of this city, although it made for uncomfortable sitting.

"I don't think anyone can hear us here," he said. "But call me 'Master' just in case. Oboro, you know this city?"

"Yes, Master. My previous master—my mother—lived on a farm on the outskirts of this city, but after my tail was cut, she sold me to the gladiator arena here in Morigumo. I don't know the city well, I'm afraid, as I was restricted to the arena. I only lived here for a few months before Signore bought me and took me to Aloutia."

Su bit his thumb. "Captain Pavo said Fionn was sold to the gladiator arena."

Oboro put his pincer-finger to his chin. "I can take you there. I could even sneak in, possibly. If I pretend that I was bought by another master who then sold me back to the arena, the guards might believe me."

It was a sound idea to me. "If you can infiltrate wherever they keep their fighting slaves and see if Fionn is there, we'll make a plan afterwards."

He clenched his jaw and nodded. "Let me scout ahead. If you want to purchase a seat at the arena, Master Scrimshander, perhaps he'll be brought out during a fight?"

The thought of my boy fighting... it turned my stomach and made me want to vomit. Even if he was a Wynnle, he'd never been in a fight. An adult from any of the larger species could easily slay him...

"You... you don't think he's dead, do you, Oboro?" I asked, voice shaking. "If you were there for a few months, they don't fight to the death, do they?"

"Accidents happen, but it's rare. Slaves are money, and if any man were to kill a fellow slave, it would be the same as burning his master's money. I saw only one death when I was here; a Sounite killed by a Fomata. The master of the arena had all the Fomata's limbs stretched out and flogged."

"Were there Wynnles?" Su asked. "If Fionn was forced to fight, and if he drew blood, he'd go berserk."

Oboro opened his mouth, but then closed it before answering.

There were three ways to calm a berserk Wynnle. They either ate their prey, bit a family member or... well, through sexual gratification. I put my hands over my face, dreading the worst. "Gods, don't let them use Fionn!"

"There were Wynnles," Oboro said. "They fought and went berserk. They... didn't die." He seemed on the cusp of saying more, but refrained. He knew the truth would be too painful for me to hear.

"We can't waste any time," I said, standing up as I slammed my hands on the table. "Su! I mean, Master! If I... if I find out what they did to our boy—"

Su's grin was malice and wickedness and a fiery inferno. "Amiere, if they did anything to our son, you'll be the least of their concerns."

His voice sent chills down my spine. That tone was neither feminine nor masculine. It was demonic evil and divine wrath.

"I don't know if I'll be able to hold myself back," he continued, his big brown eyes widening in rage and madness. "My dear Amiere, you might learn what element I am soon. I had hoped to keep it a secret forever, but... if anyone hurts my child, I will call forth the wrath of my Godly parents, and I don't care who bears witness to my divine glory."

I gulped. I sure as hell wasn't going to stop him.

Chapter Forty-Five: The Greatest Sin

Oboro led the way to the arena. We watched the structure gradually come into sight as we drew closer through the mist. At first, all we saw were the torches along the green stripe painted high above the walls and the braziers glowing atop the highest level of seats.

The dread I felt as I approached that gargantuan building was unlike any emotion I'd ever felt. It wasn't simply the dread of death or loss, but something more sinister. Something larger and scarier than I could face. I could accept Tawny's death because it had been an accident. At worst, it was the fault of a Goddess who had meant well, but messed up. If Fionn died here... it was entirely because of hatred... malice... and the negligence of us, his parents. Fuck! I should have let him come to Chernagora with us!

We came close enough to see the Shinkou Sueba guards and other staff who worked at the arena.

Oboro held his hand out to stop us. "Master Scrimshander, I know some of these women. If you allow it, I can pretend I was bought back, and get on the inside."

"Do it," Su said. "But don't put yourself in danger. I have to get you safely back to Mr. Onoretti."

"I'll be perfectly safe, Master. Well, I won't put myself into any situations I cannot get myself out of."

I put a hand on the boy's shoulder. "Please, if you see my son... save him."

Our eyes met and, despite our generational and species differences, for that moment, I believed Oboro and I were of one mind and drive. I had never known such a bond to a Sasorin.

"Signor Lasteran, I swear I'll do everything I can for him. Now, you two should try to get a seat. If he's fighting now, or is due to fight soon, I might not be able to find him."

Su pointed toward a nearby inn. "If we don't find him before tonight, we'll buy a room at that inn. We'll also need to look for Turquoise, so if we're not at the inn, wait until we come back. If you can get to us, do so."

"It's unlikely I'll get a chance," he said. "We were kept inside locked cells at night, and if we weren't in our cell at roll call, the guards would turn the city inside-out looking for us. I will reach you in the morning, if I can."

"Very well," Su replied. "Be safe. If I don't see you after a whole day has passed, I'll assume they intend to lock you inside forever. Then *I'll* turn this place inside-out looking for you."

Oboro blushed. "A-ah, thank you, Master. Alright, I'll get going!"

The boy faded into the mist, becoming a golden blur in silver, though never quite disappeared from our view. He approached one of the Shinkou Sueba guards at a side-entrance intended for slaves.

Su grabbed my elbow and nudged me away, taking me to the proper entrance of the arena.

"I hope they allow you in," he said. "I could see them refusing entry to a Wynnle, since you might smell blood and go berserk."

My sternum sunk at the idea. What would we do, then? "I suppose you could leave me at the inn while you wait for Fionn?"

"We'll see if it comes to that," Su said. "I might... try a few things. Do as I say, alright, Ami-honey? Not as my pretend-slave, but because I might do things that I can't explain."

"I'll always do anything you ask," I said. "As your husband, friend, and trusted confidant."

Su shivered almost imperceptibly as he walked ahead of me, brown hair bobbing as he picked up the pace. "There's the entrance. Don't say a word."

We had to wait in a line that included slaves accompanying their masters, so at the very least, *they* were allowed inside. Whether the gatekeeper would be okay with a Wynnle was still an unanswered question, and judging by the terrified and curious looks I received, I suspected the answer would be 'no.'

Su put all four hands on the ticket master's podium. "I'd like to purchase a seat for myself and my slave."

"Apologies, Mys, but no Wynnle slaves are allowed inside. They—" The woman trailed off, her eyes glazed, and her mouth hung open.

"We're allowed in, right?" Su asked in a prodding, demanding voice.

She nodded her head and handed him two green-striped tickets.

I spared a glance to some of the other women who'd gotten in line behind us. Arched brows, squinting eyes, one woman whispering to another while hiding her mouth behind a folded paper fan. Me being allowed in would cause quite a stir, and I wondered if Su had a plan for dealing with the consequences of whatever magical feat he'd just performed. Of course, if he could afflict everyone watching us with the same magic... But he didn't. He urged me onward, into the seating area.

A fight was already underway when we entered, and was close to ending when we took our seats. Su took a spot as far from any other attendees as he could find. Even still, a guard walked our way. My eyes remained glued ahead, at the two sparring men—a bipedal Orochijin and a Sounite. Best to let Su do whatever he planned to do to keep people from asking us questions.

The guard approached, hand on her gun. "Oy! You with the Wynnle!"

Su gripped the seat's arms tight, his fists clenched with such fury that his knuckles turned white.

Without saying another word, the guard turned and left us alone.

"Are you a Mind Godblood?" I asked in a near-whisper, though we were so far from anyone, I doubted they could have heard me even if I spoke at my usual volume.

Su stared down at the gladiators. The silence was enough of an answer.

"You're using hypnosis, aren't you? So, Captain Pavo is your brother? And Tynan would be your... uh, what *is* the gender-neutral word for a niece or nephew?"

"There are other powers that can make someone do what you want them to do," Su replied. "It's not only the Mind element. Some of the others have abilities that *resemble* hypnosis."

Whether he was telling the truth, or just saying that to hide his element... I let the conversation end. He was determined to hide his parentage until circumstances made such secrecy unsustainable.

The two gladiators wore flaming bracelets and anklets so their movements could be seen whenever the mist thickened up and hid their bodies. The Sounite's hair served as a strong enough fire to track him easily. The Orochijin was agile, weaving and ducking between the muscular Sounite's vicious attacks. Neither man had weapons, though I had no doubt either could kill with just their hands, if need be. Their skill with using their hands and feet was obvious even to an amateur like me. They were experts at their art. I wondered if they'd been gladiators for years. Hell, maybe they were good friends.

Not a single drop of blood was drawn. The mist had mostly faded by now, giving me a better view of their bodies, and they had taken very little damage. If this was what the fights were always like, I was at no risk of going berserk. Unless a Wynnle dealt the damaging blow, it took the scent of a *lot* of blood to awaken our rage. Droplets from a few cuts wouldn't even reach my maxillae. This fight couldn't be representative of what usually went on, if they refused to allow Wynnles inside.

A woman with a whip and katana on her belt stepped into the arena, blowing a whistle. The two men disengaged. She announced something in Orochigo, probably declaring one man the winner. The gladiators patted each other on the back, kissed each other on the lips, then exited on opposite sides of the arena. Good friends indeed...

The woman's next announcement was spoken in a vicious, almost seductive tone. I may not have known the words, but I could take a guess—whatever came next was meant to arouse in the worst ways possible.

Su grimaced. "She said that since the mist is clearing, she wants to give us a bloody fight next, so we can be enthralled by the sight of blood. Let me keep you calm, Amiere."

I startled back, thinking of the way he used to keep me calm after we sparred, back when we were younger. Healthier. More fit. Surely he wouldn't suck my dick here, in front of all these people. I couldn't imagine an Ophidian woman getting on her knees for her slave. For Su to blow me would also blow our cover. "Are you sure you should... here?"

"Not like that, unfortunately," he said with a gentle smile. "I will use my magic. I have no other option."

"Could you have used your magic all those times in the past?"

"Yes, I could have, but... I loved to make you happy. Giving you sexual gratification gives *me* sexual gratification. Whenever I calmed you from a berserker rage, it wasn't merely to get rid of an inconvenient state of being, Amiere. I wanted you to feel free to be who you were. To know it's okay to be a Wynnle. It's okay to go into a rage. I love you no matter what's going through your head, whether you're in your right mind or not. You don't stop being sapienti just because you're angry. You still deserve my love."

His words put a weight on my soul. My chest felt heavy, but also... glad? My sternum swelled with gratitude to have a person like him in my life.

I swallowed, flustered at the emotions swirling in my chest and head. Love for Su, fear for Fionn, hate at the Ophidians. Gods, I hadn't felt this emotionally fucked-up in a few months.

Two new gladiators entered the arena: a sapphire-haired Kroedan man with an elaborately-carved halberd that was nearly three times his height, and a Neuropteran equipped with a sword and a fractal-patterned, multicolored shield. The shield was designed to look like the mushroom *called* a Neuropteran shield. Perhaps the Ophidians thought such a pun was the pinnacle of humor, but I found it atrocious.

The Neuropteran had entered facing us, and with the mist gone, I saw the expression on his face clearly. Terror. Madness. His wings had been clipped to prevent him from flying. Were I a betting man, I would have guessed this match would not end with a kiss.

The judge sounded her whistle and, without missing a beat, the Neuropteran lunged toward the Kroedan, sword swinging wildly.

I couldn't watch. I closed my eyes before the Neuropteran made contact, fearing the Kroedan would slice him in half. The clang of metal-on-metal rang in my ears. Cautiously, I opened my eyes, peeking between my fingers. The gladiators had exchanged spots, and the Neuropteran held his shield up, blocking an incoming slash of the halberd.

The Kroedan may have been smaller, but the look of boredom on his face suggested this wasn't his first fight. The scar across his nose and his shattered sapphire beard suggested he hadn't always won those fights, either.

After a few more parries and ripostes, I let my own mental and emotional guard down. Just as I had relaxed, thinking this wouldn't be as bloody as I feared, the Kroedan jammed his halberd's spear into the Neuropteran's thigh.

My nostrils flared. The blood-scent, metallic and sweet, aroused me to salivation, but my rage remained subdued.

The Neuropteran's sword met the Kroedan's arm. Clear blood squirted out from a shallow wound. The Kroedan's face remained as stony and stoic as ever. He brought the halberd down, but when the Neuropteran raised his shield to block it, the Kroedan twisted the polearm and jammed the butt into the Neuropteran's chest instead. The winged man gasped and fell to his knees, choking.

The Kroedan held the halberd in preparation to continue the fight, but he glanced to the judge for permission.

She gestured. The Kroedan stepped forward and speared the Neuropteran through his shoulder next.

Gods, what the fuck was wrong with these women? What evil could infect a society and become such an insidious part of their culture that half the population saw nothing wrong with this brutality?

No, there were good Ophidians. Some women were born here, but had no power to change things. Su, whether he was born a boy or a girl, had been born in Ophidia, and he was not one of them.

The Kroedan landed a vicious slash with the axe-blade, cutting into the Neuropteran's side. Cheers from the women in the crowd drowned out the man's crying; his pleas for mercy worthless against an uncaring audience.

The blood... the blood... I closed my eyes and, in the darkness of my inner eyelids, swore I could see sparks and bursts of color. The scent... the absolutely delectable *aroma*! I clenched the arms of my chair, allowing my claws to extract. A force bubbled inside my chest. Gods, how I wanted to *taste* that blood!

Su put his hand over mine and, in a flash, that sinful desire fled my body. Just like that, my violent instinct was gone.

The judge blew her whistle and the Kroedan stepped back, planting his halberd in the turf. Two scrawny slaves ran onto the field, assessed the wounded Neuropteran, and carried him through the exit. Perhaps he'd live to be sliced up another day for the entertainment of these evil women.

We watched several more matches, some violent, some less so. Never with Fionn, though, and I wasn't sure if I was glad for that or not. If only he'd come out, Su could rescue him and we could get back home. And since he never came out, it made me wonder if he'd already been forced to fight... Gods, what if he was as injured as that Neuropteran? What if he was *dead*?

I couldn't bear to lose two children, especially not one in this way. Tawny's death had slain half my soul, but if Fionn were lost to senseless brutality, I'd lose more than the other half of me that remained. I would slaughter every fucking Ophidian I found until they riddled my body with bullets or cut off my limbs. Not even Su's calming magic could stop my vengeance.

Oboro Interlude

Oboro's pulse raced so fast he could hardly tolerate the pain of his surging emotions, but what choice did he have? He had to find Fionn. *Had to.* Oboro had never had a friend before. Not a boy his own age, who he could play with, laugh with, cry with...

He twisted the 'charming' ring around his finger. With its magic making him more persuasive, Oboro had convinced the Shinkou Sueba guard that he had been sold back to the arena. She'd allowed him in without question. Another ring on his finger, a 'telepathy' ring, had made Oboro feel that she was easy to convince. He had never made such assumptions before; he'd been taught to *never* make assumptions about what women were thinking. But the Godblood had told him to trust his instincts while wearing the ring; trust his assumptions about what people—even women—were thinking.

Oboro went into the barracks where gladiator-slaves of all ranks lived. He'd only lived here for a short time, but he'd quickly learned there were hierarchies among slaves, too. Some were nothing more than Morigumo's trash, to be tortured and slain. Of course, he could not have given that information to Mr. Lasteran, who needed hope for Fionn's survival. Above the trash were the slaves who had been sold to the arena for cheap because they'd outlived their usefulness, but hadn't necessarily done anything worthy of execution. Above them were the more experienced gladiators, often those who had initially been part of the lower rank, but proved their worth after winning enough matches. At the top were the Arena Master's favorite pets, the crowd favorites who'd been here for years. Oboro suspected the sapphire-haired Kroedan had actually been here for *decades*.

A Wynnle would automatically be put into the second-highest rank for their sheer ferocity. The fact that they had electric tails was a bonus—they could put on a show during the misty matches. Morigumo rested on the shores of a lake that misted over every morning and the mist wouldn't disappear until afternoon. During the misty hours and at night, the Morigumo arena played with fire and lightning. Sounites and Wynnles fought all their matches at those hours. Other species were put in manacles, bracelets, anklets, sometimes whole plates of armor doused in oil and lit on fire so the audience could see them, or at least the flames on their limbs, dancing in the fog and darkness.

Oboro had fought in plenty of matches while his wrists were bound in manacles set on fire. Quadrubrachs were popular for such matches, but the six-armed Foma were even more popular. Of course, a Fomata's popularity still wouldn't save him if he killed one of the Arena Master's favorites. The tale Oboro had told Signor Lasteran was no lie; a Fomata had indeed been brutally punished, but only because the slave he'd killed was a favorite who'd brought in large crowds.

He strode by slaves engaged in their usual activities, all while the musk of manly sweat and blood pervaded the air. Some ate their meals at the communal table, some sparred in the practice area, and some nursed their wounds. The sapphire-haired Kroedan sat around a dice table with the Arena Master's other favorites. Gambling. Oboro turned his gaze quickly. He had always assumed the favorites hated him. Wearing Lungidus's ring, Oboro knew that assumption was the correct one to have.

"Oboro!" the Kroedan hollered, his voice echoing throughout the dank, malodorous hall. He stopped in his tracks and turned to the fearsome fighter. "I thought they sold you to some brothel!"

Oboro tried to act natural, like he belonged here. He put one pincer on his hip, taking on a confident pose. "Eh, I was too big for those tiny women. They sold me back here."

The Kroedan guffawed and slapped his knee. The other favorites did the same, not because they thought it was funny, but because their leader did. Oboro had always thought the others were just following the Kroedan, but now Lungidus's ring confirmed it. The Kroedan pointed at the Sasorin boy. "That's mud and sludge, but I'll believe it."

He grimaced, not knowing how else to respond to such a strange assertion. "Was there a Wynnle boy brought here? Little younger than me?"

"Yeah, he's here. Clawed the fuck outta one of the trashies. He's in a cell for now. He's got a lot to learn if he's going to survive here."

Oboro flashed a smile that he tried to make menacing. "Perfect. I wanted to see him. Size him up. See if he's worth fighting."

The Kroedan was unmoved, but some of the other favorites gave him fearful glances. He twisted the telepathy ring, realizing how truly intimidating he was. He wasn't a kid anymore, and he wasn't the stinger-less slave of a much bigger, more powerful Sasorin. Fully grown, Oboro made for a striking, fearsome figure.

He headed for the cells. They weren't just for holding enraged slaves or men who were liable to flee; they were where the gladiators had to sleep. By Ophidian law, slaves could not sleep in any place where they could escape from their bondage or cause harm to a woman. When he'd lived with his Sasorin mother, Oboro had always slept with a manacle on one leg, chained to the wall.

A young boy—maybe nine or ten years old—stepped out of a cell and locked the door behind him. As he walked down the hall toward Oboro, he kept his eyes downcast. He dared a quick glance, but turned away in fear as his eyes met the large Sasorin's piercing gaze. A trickle of clear blood oozed from the corner of the boy's mouth.

Oboro had not meant to frighten him. He hadn't seen the boy before; he must have been a recent acquisition. What was his purpose here? He was too small and scrawny to be a gladiator. Perhaps the master intended for him to provide other services for the men...

He stopped at the cell the boy had just walked out of, and his breath caught in his throat.

Fionn.

Slouched on a bench up against the wall, breathing heavily, his eyes glazed over. Bandages had been wrapped around his torso and limbs. His legs were chained to opposite walls with chains so short it forced his legs apart. His arms dangled between his legs, as ragged and loose as a puppet with its strings cut. His tail had been locked into an iron ball chained to the wall behind him so his spark would not electrocute anyone.

Fionn lolled his head to the side. Sweat and blood matted his mane.

Oboro put his hands on the bars and withheld from screaming.

"Fionn? Are you awake?" the Sasorin whispered. "Can you see me? Hear me?"

The Wynnle boy's eyes stared at the ceiling senselessly.

"Fionn!" Oboro hissed a little louder.

He blinked a few times and turned his head toward Oboro's voice. "You... Oboro? What are you doing here?"

"What are *you* doing here, Fionn!?"

With a hiccup, the Wynnle cried. "I... I fucked up. She... That woman said she wanted to see her daughter again. I imagined myself in her situation, and what I wouldn't give to see Tawny again. So I got Susana and Turquoise... Fuck, Oboro. She... she was an Ophidian!"

Fionn's sorrow and disappointment in himself were so intense, Oboro almost took the ring off so he wouldn't feel the full brunt of emotions crashing into his mind.

"Did they make you fight in the arena?" Oboro asked.

Fionn sniffed and nodded his head in affirmation, his muzzle scrunched up in shame and self-loathing. Tears escaped his eyes, but he did not move his hands to wipe them. His hands... covering his genitals. He had no pants.

"Um, I could get clothes for you. Hold on."

"Who cares?" Fionn said, louder than Oboro would have liked. Too loud, and he might get a woman's attention. "Don't want to make it difficult for them to... to... *calm* me down."

Oboro knew in that instant what had been done. What the boy leaving Fionn's cell had done. Had been ordered to do, likely under threat of a lashing if he refused. When Wynnles went berserk, there were only a few ways to calm them back down...

Oboro closed his eyes, his claws clenching the metal bars so tight he thought he'd break them. Of course, any metal that could have been bent by a Sasorin's claws would have never been used to restrain slaves. The Ophidians were evil, not stupid.

But Gods, were they evil. And here, in this cell, they had committed the most evil, despicable sin imaginable. One that no moral soul could forgive. One that Oboro, certainly, would *never* forgive.

He fell to his knees, weeping for the crime that had been committed against his friend.

"Oboro... Why are you here?" Fionn asked. "How did you find me? Where are my parents?"

"They're here," he whispered. "Your Dad and Mama Su. I... I need to go tell them that I found you. Just stay here, okay? Do whatever the women tell you to do. We'll rescue you, Fionn. I swear to all the Gods, we will!" Oboro struggled to keep his voice down—and his eyes dry—to avoid suspicion if anyone overheard, but the nearest cells were all empty.

Fionn gave a grunt that Oboro chose to interpret as begrudging agreement. His head fell sideways, against the wall, his eyes glazing over again.

If there was any justice in this world, Oboro would make damn sure Fionn got back home to his family.

Chapter Forty-Six: The Nursery

Thankfully, matches did not go on all night, else I doubted Su or I would have ever left. If we'd left, only to find out later that Fionn came out afterward, we'd have never forgiven ourselves. We were already packing more guilt into our souls than we deserved for letting this mess happen in the first place.

We had to find Turquoise as well, but Su had an idea where he was being kept. We found the nursery in a building next to the arena, connected by a walkway of spiraling flagstones. They were clearly on the same property; perhaps owned by the same master.

Su was as distraught as I was, but he made a show of it for the sake of his charade. He barged into the nursery without a care as to who might stop him.

"Where is my slave?" he demanded. He marched up to a young woman—barely older than Eruwan, if I had to guess, and smaller—and pointed his finger at her chest. "Did you buy my stolen slave?"

The woman staggered back, almost bumping into a rack of cages where they kept quadruped babies. Bipedal babies lay in what amounted to a horse's manger with just enough fluff and blankets to keep them comfortable. They weren't the cleanest I'd ever seen, either...

"I-I only work for the Arena Master!" the woman pleaded with her hands up. "If she made an illegal purchase, please take it up with her!"

He was right there... My little boy, Turquoise. He was in the fourth cage up on the rack, mewling and trying to stretch his wings, but they could not extend to their full length while trapped between cold, metal bars. Su went to the cage and stuck his fingers through, brushing against our son's light-blue feathers.

"This is him!" Su said. "This is my slave! He was kidnapped by merchants of flesh."

The caretaker bowed her head low. "I'm so sorry. Please, discuss the issue with the master. I cannot just hand him over. I promise I'll take care of him until you get it resolved."

Su bit his lip as he scanned the room.

There were at least a dozen baby boys in the room, all of species who were often thought of as tough or frightening: Wynnles, Sasorin, even a Kraken and a Dragon. Babies who would grow up to be respectable gladiators, if they lived that long.

I couldn't imagine it being worthwhile to raise a baby from infancy just to have it fight when it became old enough. Then again, how old was 'old enough?' Maybe the Ophidians started them early... I had not seen any particularly young slaves in the matches, though I may not have been the best judge of age, especially for species other than Wynnles. But regardless, how old could a gladiator-slave possibly expect to live? Even if I allowed myself to be completely callous, to imagine myself in the shoes of this young woman, would I think it was worthwhile to raise a slave from infancy to, say, ten years old, only for them to die choking on their own blood after a botched match? Especially slaves like these, who could accidentally hurt their masters? That Dragon may have been a baby, but if the caretaker wasn't blessed by the Gods, a single sneeze could torch her to cinders.

Su stood before Turquoise's cage for so long, I almost asked him what he intended to do. I knew he must have been thinking, coming up with a plan. How were we going to get out of here with both our sons? Was Su patient enough to try and talk his way into getting them back? Or was he planning to just grab them and run? And... I looked at the other babies, in cages, in their shoddy cradles. Gods, if we were going to grab Turquoise and run... shouldn't I grab one or two babies, as well?

Or would we need to fight our way out? I couldn't hold a child if my hands were occupied with ripping out Ophidian throats.

"I will come back later," Su said. He brushed back a strand of brown hair. The flicking of his fingers, the subtle lifting of his chin... it was delicate, but they were feminine movements. Su couldn't afford to be seen as neutral or masculine. "Come, slave." He beckoned me with a single waving finger.

When we were out of earshot, he confided his plan. "We'll get Turquoise last, on our way out of here. There's little chance I can get our sons out by talking to the Arena Master. If I try to do this the peaceful way, it'll require legal nonsense I don't have the time or body parts for. The only way I could claim they belong to me is if I provide proof that I'm their master. Even with forged documents, they'd make me prove that I am worthy of mastership, if you catch my meaning."

"They'd look at your private parts," I replied.

"Yes. Now, don't go assuming that means I was a biological man. Even a biological woman would have... ah, shall we say, parts the Ophidians don't approve of... once they've eaten as much shubin marrow as I have. So, whether I was once a boy or a girl wouldn't matter; the Ophidians wouldn't accept me as the master sex."

"What's the plan, then? Are you going to go berserk with your Godblood powers?"

Su stopped in his tracks. "I... I wanted to keep it a secret forever."

I put my hands on his shoulders. Although no Ophidian women were near enough to hear, some might see us... I hoped this wouldn't be something so out of the ordinary that they'd investigate. Surely men would rub their master's shoulders if commanded, right?

"Sugar… If I could forget what element you are after as you reveal it, I would. I'm never going to talk about it. I won't even tell Liesle if you don't want me to. I know it's difficult for you, but please do what must be done for Fionn's sake." I pressed my face against his scalp. Salty, stinging tears escaped me and soaked his hair. "Please, Su… If I lose my son, I'll kill myself here. I swear I will."

"Don't say that, Amiere!"

"It's true! I'll die because the Ophidians will have to put me down like a rabid dog after I go on a murderous, berserker rampage."

"Don't *say* it," he repeated. "I know you'll *do* it, but don't *talk* about it. I will go on a rampage before you do. You don't need to fight anyone. You don't need to kill or go berserk. So don't tell me about how you're going to go off hurting yourself when there's no reason for it. I can't stand to hear you talk like that!"

My sternum was so full of pain, I thought it would break through my chest. Oh Gods, how I loved my Su! I clenched his shoulders even tighter, and he put his upper two hands on mine while his lower hands bent back and—ever so gently—touched my hips.

"Tomorrow, we try again," he said. "We'll go to that inn tonight, wait and see if Oboro comes back with any news. Failing that, we go to the arena again as soon as it opens. We'll stay all day and night if we must, until we see our son."

Su bought a room for us at the nearby inn. Since he had a slave—me—with him, he was forced to purchase a room with suitable equipment: manacles attached to the bed posts and to brackets on the far wall, as well as doors that could be locked from the outside by one with a key. The innkeeper informed him that although slaves were allowed to move unattended through the halls if they were going about their master's business, they were not permitted to leave without a specific sash around their arms which the inn would provide upon the master's request. She informed us of many more rules in Morigumo which were numerous, cruel, and arbitrary. I could not be bothered to memorize them, as I had every intention of leaving here soon—and violently, most likely. Why should I care about needing a sash on my arm to go out in public when I'd soon be leaving bloody sashes across the arms of any woman who dared get in my way?

Su sat cross-legged on the bed, lower hands on his knees, upper hands rubbing his temples.

"I'm at the limit of what I can handle, Ami-honey," he said, voice cracking. Away from any women eavesdropping, he allowed his voice to go back to its normal register.

"I am, too." I took a seat at the edge of the bed. I couldn't help looking at the manacles. Even knowing Su would never force me to use them, they inspired a sickening terror. Perhaps Fionn was forced to sleep in chains last night, and would be again tonight.

"I'm angry," Su said in a tone that was anything but. He sounded defeated, tired... like the world had already ended and he was just waiting for the ground to open up beneath him next.

"We'll get our sons back, go back home, and everything will go back to normal."

Su didn't reply to that. Whatever was on his mind was something deeper than I could perceive. I lay down on the bed, staring up at the ceiling. I had nothing else to do.

"Aloutia plays too nicely with Ophidia," he said. "We play along with Ophidia's rules. Aloutia has its charity services, such as the one that bought Oboro, where we go through Ophidia's legal means to save men. Doesn't it infuriate you, Ami-honey? That we had two Godbloods tell us almost everything we needed to know to return Fionn, but who refused to actually come to Ophidia themselves?"

I sighed. "I don't know the business of Godbloods. I suppose I'm just glad Captain Pavo and Tynan helped us at all. They came to arrest us. Letting us rescue our sons was a kindness they didn't owe us."

"The Godblood Brigade exists to protect Aloutian citizens. They absolutely *did* owe us. They should have gone after our kids, Ophidian rules be damned. Even if there's some reason Lungidus and Tynan couldn't personally get involved, they should have gotten *somebody*. There are hundreds of Godbloods in Aloutia. One of them could have helped out."

"Perhaps they think you should have helped them at some point," I replied, and regretted the words as soon as they escaped my mouth.

I sat up and faced him, expecting to see a cold expression, disappointed that I'd pointed out the reality of the situation.

Su had moved his upper hands from his temples to cover his eyes. My husband sobbed quietly in his palms.

"I just wanted to live a quiet, peaceful life," he cried. "I didn't want to get invested in their political schemes, their creepy breeding programs, or their demented magical experiments. I just wanted a family to love. Why? Why am I being punished for this? Why do my parents hate me so much?"

My nose tingled; I was about to cry, too. I reached around Su and pulled him into a tight embrace. "I'm sorry. I'm sorry you have had this life. I've tried to make it wonderful for... for all of us. Please, don't give up. There's still time. We can get our kids back and... and go back home. We can get Liesle back. We can be a normal family again."

Who was I kidding? Our agony would reforge the family forever. Tawny's death had left a permanent hole in our lives. Fionn's trauma would haunt him forever. Susana's pain would shape the adult she'd become. Liesle would always bear the stigma of being a demon-summoner.

"Amiere, I love you," Su said between sobs. "No matter what happens to our family, swear you won't abandon me."

"I swear." I clutched him tighter. He grabbed my wrists, two hands to each. "It would be easier for me to tear my soul into pieces and scatter them to the six planes than to abandon you."

He leaned into my chest, eyes closed. "If I continue on this path of destruction, I'll end up doing the same thing. Then at least our souls' shards can wander the dominion together."

Oboro Interlude

The Sasorin boy thought he might be allowed out, given he had a positive reputation with the women staffing the arena. If he could just leave for a few minutes, he could reach Signor Lasteran and Master Scrimshander and let them know he'd found Fionn.

Unfortunately, the Shinkou Sueba guards at the barracks entrance wouldn't let him through, even with the enchanted ring improving his charm and persuasion. If anything, it made the guards more attracted to him. One woman offered to take him to her private room to explore her 'masterly parts.' Oboro considered himself lucky that he was allowed to decline; few women allowed slaves to say 'no.' The woman only laughed at what she thought was his insecurity, and Oboro quickly fled back into the barracks where the stench of men kept most women out.

He paced around the training area, racking his brain to figure out what his next plan would be. On a table lay a clipboard with the schedule for tomorrow's matches. It was here for the guards' sake; slaves did not know how to read, and it was illegal to teach them.

But Oboro had learned to read a little bit in his time spent with the Iolono family. Most of it was learning English and Caprise, but Mys Iola had thought it important that he learn some Orochigo characters, too. She'd taught him how to write his name in all three scripts: the feminine Hira's script, masculine slave script, and muji.

He recognized the muji for several of the sapienti species. There, scheduled for an early morning match, was 'Wynnle boy.' Oboro could not read the name of his opponent. The names had all been written by the same person. There was a distinct style to the handwriting. Certain elements of muji that were not easily replicated. One small element which meant 'moon' had a higher-than-usual tail in this woman's handwriting.

He gulped, knowing that if he was caught changing the schedule, the masters would beat him as badly as they had that Fomata...

He took the pencil chained to the clipboard, erased the opponent's name, and wrote in his own name in muji. He took care to imitate the original author's handwriting. As Oboro's name included the 'moon' element, he gave it the same exaggerated tail.

He had to thank Mys Beatrice the Daughter for that lesson. She had taught him how to forge signatures. Although he was nowhere near as talented as she was, his forgeries were at least passable... he hoped.

Oboro set the clipboard back exactly where he'd found it, and resumed his activities of pretending to be a slave.

If all went well, he was scheduled to fight Fionn tomorrow morning. He could at least make sure Fionn wasn't seriously hurt, and if Signor Lasteran and Master Scrimshander were watching at that time... they could make their getaway.

Chapter Forty-Seven: Sparks

I woke the next morning with the same sense of dread, anxiety making knots in my hyoid and along my ulnae, the utter despair at losing a child yet again. The same horror I felt every morning since Tawny's death, only this one was... more pathetic. I could bear the pain of losing a child in an accident, but if I lost one to a senseless act of violence? I would have puked, but Su was already awake and used his magic to calm me down.

His magic also gave me my appetite back. Su insisted I eat so we'd have energy for whatever would be required. We ate a meal of millet, toast, and oko in our room so no woman would bark at us about how I was breaking some rule. The oko meat tasted nothing like the ocean okoes I was accustomed to on Aloutia, but it wasn't awful. With some peppers, kyamo, and onions, it could have even been *good* food.

Su intended to go to the arena as soon as it opened and stay there all day. Although slaves with trays laden with meat-stuffed brioches and tankards of beer served the audience, Su felt it would be best if we were satiated before entering. Whenever the slaves walked by, he had to use his magic on them to ensure they didn't see anything wrong with a Wynnle slave being among the crowd.

Early mornings in Morigumo were plagued by a problem I never had to deal with in Steena Village—the fog suffused across the city, spreading a white, ethereal blanket. It was thicker today than it had been yesterday. Or perhaps when we'd arrived yesterday, it was on the verge of clearing up. As it was now, this early in the morning, we could barely see the gladiators in the arena. The first match was another Sounite with his hair blazing bright—a beacon in the shroud—versus a Dragon with fiery cuffs on his wrists and ankles. He spit a ball of fire to the ground which sizzled away in the sand.

They threw fire at each other often, though it was clearly for the audience's benefit and excitement, being as both species were Fire elementals and couldn't be hurt by flames. Even if they had lost Flamboil's Blessing, most Fire elementals were immune to intense heat anyway.

Su put his two right hands on my knee. His tension was palpable; his hands shook, and for a moment, I thought... oddly warm.

Three matches went by while the fog refused to evaporate. Each gladiator came out with oil-soaked clothes or accessories, lit aflame for our viewing convenience.

Then finally… rather than flame, the arena was illuminated by a flickering, electric Wynnle tail. Fionn was forced a few steps out of the barred gate by a team of three slaves yanking on his chains. One of the slaves shoved a cloth soaked in blood up to his nose while the other two detached the chains.

As he smelled the blood and roared in a berserker frenzy, the slaves fled back to safety.

Oboro stepped out from the opposite end of the arena, rubbing at the bandages over his upper left arm where they'd cut him to get his blood.

Fionn lunged, claws out, teeth bared, and his tail throwing sparks.

Su rose once he was certain the boy was Fionn. My attention was transfixed on our son, so I only saw Su out of the corner of my eye. He jumped on top of the seat in front of us, turned to me, and beckoned me up.

"Come on, Amiere, get up and go! Fuck the rules. We're leaving a trail of chaos all the way back to Aloutia!"

I could not recall willing myself to stand; my legs did it on their own. Or perhaps Su had controlled me. I jumped onto the seats next to Su and we stormed the arena side-by-side.

"I'll make Fionn bite me," I said as my feet hit the sand.

All around us, Ophidians screamed. They sounded annoyed and angry, like we were pests for interrupting their entertainment. A gun went off, but my brain was so focused on only one thing that unless it hit me, it wouldn't have stopped me.

But Su…? What if it…?

I turned to check on my husband. A small wound had punctured his shoulder, oozing blood.

Blood. Bright orange blood, the color of the sun. A sunset, kumquats, a toucan's beak, the inside of a mango… Su's blood.

What God had orange blood? None in the Decatheon…

It was too little and too far away to trigger my bloodlust, thankfully. I turned my attention back to Fionn and ran as powerfully as my aging legs would allow.

Another gunshot. No… thunder. A bolt of lightning struck the seats.

Ophidian voices screamed out again—this time in fear. Forked lightning landed near the booth where the guards had been stationed, then danced around the arena. Fire, too, erupted in seconds; an infernal wall of flame as tall as I stood.

Fionn and Oboro wrestled in the sand. Oboro gained the upper hand on Fionn and pinned him down. The Sasorin boy bled from his neck but was utterly unfazed by his wound. For most species, a bite to the neck would be a death sentence, but a Sasorin's chitinous skin was naturally rough and armored. Fionn's fangs had made only superficial punctures. Enough to draw blood, but not from any of the major arteries.

I grabbed Fionn by the mane so I could control his head's motions. It was far rougher treatment than I liked seeing any parent do to their child, but when that child has gone berserk with bloodlust… I had no time for gentleness.

Fionn shrieked as he flailed his body, attempting to get free of Oboro's grasp. Carefully, I brought my forearm down to Fionn's bared teeth. With just the tiniest prick, a droplet of clear blood fell into his mouth and his mind cleared.

Amidst the chaos, thunder, screaming, inferno, and gunshots, I heard only my son. "Dad! Save me!"

Oboro rolled off Fionn and offered a hand to help him up. Fionn trembled so severely that he needed the help, and I was unsure if he could even walk well.

As if to mock my thoughts, a gun went off, its bullet lodging itself into Fionn's leg. He screamed in pain, collapsing to his knee as his hands covered the wound.

Su had all four hands fanned out, pointing around him. Lightning blasted from his fingers. At the boundary of the fog before everything turned white, I watched as a bolt fried an Ophidian woman holding a raised gun. Judging by her position, she may have been the one who shot Fionn.

"Fionn! I will make your pain go away, but be careful how you walk!" Su fired off three more strikes, each with a different hand, while he raised his fourth hand. Tiny sparks danced between his fingers, and with that, Fionn stopped screaming.

"It doesn't hurt," my son said. "Mama Su? What's happening?"

"We need to run!" Su ordered. He pointed a finger at a woman just as she fired her gun. His lightning bolt exploded her bullet in midair, then continued toward her.

Most of the audience was in total chaos, screaming as they fled from the flames. I could not see them through the heavy fog, but the sounds were unmistakable.

Fionn took a single step, hobbled on his leg, and would have fallen again if not for Oboro catching him.

"I'll carry you," Oboro said. He didn't wait for Fionn's consent or our permission. He swept my son into his lower arms while his upper arms—his pincers—were poised to snap at any Ophidian who got too close.

Su led the way out, blasting people away with fire and lightning, sometimes both together. He twirled both pairs of hands together like a clockwork taffy machine. He conjured fire from his lower hands and electricity from the uppers. When he thrust all four hands forward, a beam of fire shot forth with spiraling forks of lightning around its periphery. The fire turned the buildings it touched into a roaring inferno while the lightning sought out anyone standing too close, slave or woman. Unfortunate as it was, we did not have the time to destroy in an orderly fashion.

"We're getting Turquoise!" Su yelled.

The nursery was on fire. Fuck, had one of Su's lightning bolts struck it? The young caretaker we'd spoken to earlier scrambled out with two babies in her arms, running them to safety. She handed them off to a slave, then ran back into the nursery for more.

The babies would not burn to death—Flamboil's Blessing prevented that—but they might asphyxiate on the smoke or be crushed when the structure collapsed.

"Help me get them out!" the woman cried.

Inside, she grabbed two more infant boys whose cradles were engulfed in flames.

Embers flared as I glanced at the stack of cages the quadrupeds were in. Gods, how were we going to get them out of those cages?

Su didn't waste time trying to open them. He handed the topmost cage to me, then grabbed Turquoise's, as his was next.

The woman left with two babies, one in each hand.

The cages conveniently had handlebars, so we could carry one in each hand. Although it would make running awkward... I *could* carry another.

There were three more cages in the stack. Su looked at me, mouth hanging open, tears in his eyes. Wordlessly, we shared the same thought. He grabbed the remaining three, filling up all his hands.

There were still some boys in cradles, though. Fuck it. I had a free hand. I scooped one up.

"Dad!" Fionn said. "Give me one. I can't walk, but my hands work."

I handed him the one I'd just taken.

Oboro gulped. "Uh, I'd offer, but my upper hands aren't made to hold babies."

"You're doing fine, Oboro. Somebody needs to protect us. I'm counting on your claws." I grabbed one more, now that I had a free hand. The last boy in the nursery, as far as I could tell.

Su's hands were full of cages. Could he cast his magic with his hands occupied?

"Hurry!" he shouted. As I was closest to the exit, it was a command for me to get out of the way.

A support beam fell behind us as we fled. Embers hit my back, but for a blessed man like me, it was little more than a tickle.

Was Su a Lightning elemental? Or Fire? It seemed he could perform magic with both.

The caretaker ran up to us, panting. "Oh, thank you for saving them!" She held her hands out. "I can take two—"

Su glared at her with a look that could have killed a Demon Lord on the spot. "If you *try* to take these babies from me, I'll turn you to ash!"

The woman fell on her ass, surprised by Su's sudden outburst. We continued on our way, unimpeded as everyone around us was too busy saving themselves. Women and slaves alike shouted for water, help, or just screamed wordlessly. The chaos was unbearable. All I could do was focus on Su running ahead of us, toward the portal house. Oboro charged beside me, his claws raised as if to snap at someone, though nobody cared to accost us while they had bigger problems.

As we ran up the marble steps of the portal house, I realized how rough I was handling these babies. My running was jostling them around. But I *had* to hurry!

If I slowed down now, if they were caught by the Ophidians… I must save them!

Two guards pointed their guns at Su. I thought he might be helpless if he had to point his fingers at them to shoot electricity. His hands were full, each one holding a cage by its handle. But he didn't need to point, as the two guards fell, streaks of electricity dancing across their limbs and through their hair.

Another guard charged at us with her katana drawn. Coming from behind Su, he didn't see her in time. Oboro caught her katana in his scorpion claw and wrenched it away. As he stepped closer to snip her with his other claw, Fionn flicked his tail and zapped her. She fell to her knees as static electricity coursed through her body.

In this dark hallway, the flickering of sparks from our tail lit our path and guided us home.

Su ascended the steps to the room with the portal to Lemongraves. Oboro and I trailed close behind. The guards who had been here previously were gone.

"Wait," he said, pausing at the edge of the tub. "We can use a water portal to our advantage. If I put each cage in the water, it should teleport the cage away, but not the baby. That might be the easiest way of getting them out."

"Won't the baby fall through next?" I asked. "They won't have a hard landing, will they?"

Su grimaced. "I'm going to try to catch them before they hit the surface, but if I don't… they should land softly beside the pool on the Lemongraves side. I'll go through after the first one to make sure he's safe, though. I'll go through over and over for each one if I must." His determination was palpable in the timbre of his voice.

"We'll get all these boys back to our home safely," I said. "Go on, Su. Do what you need to do. I'll stand guard at the entrance here and keep any women out."

"Thanks. It seems my little act of arson is keeping most of them busy, but I need to focus on this now."

Oboro looked back and forth between me and Su. "Um, what should I do? I can help you, Signor Lasteran. But if you want me to keep Fionn back, I will."

"No! Let me zap them!" my son begged. "I can't walk, but my tail works just fine." He waved it back and forth. Oboro did not seem at all concerned about the ball of electricity so close to his own body—hell, it probably had struck him on accident a few times as he ran. Perhaps Sasorin were naturally immune to electric shock, though I'd never heard of that being the case.

"Alright, Fionn. You can stay here. Oboro, stand next to me. If any women come our way, lure them closer. We can zap them with our tails."

"Will do!" he said.

I feared an Ophidian woman with a gun would come around that corner and shoot at us from afar. If that happened, how would we fight back?

Judging by the shouts in the main hall, everyone had concern only for the fire. A woman did enter our portal room, seemingly to escape, but she was unarmed and fled when she saw three members of stereotypically 'warrior' species ready to fight her.

Su's experiment with the cages was going well, from what I could tell the few times I spared a glance back. He caught the first two babies and laid them on the ground beside him. Since they were quadrupeds, they could be laid on their bellies where their heads were in no danger of banging on the stony floor.

The third one fell into the portal, so Su informed us he was going through to check on him.

I hoped the women on the Lemongraves side wouldn't give him trouble. They weren't quite Ophidian, but they certainly weren't friendly toward men, either. However they perceived Su, they'd still question why he was smuggling babies out of Ophidia. He might have to throw lightning at the guards on that side, too...

"Dad?" Fionn said in a low, scared voice.

I kept my eyes on the hallway ahead, watching for women. "What is it, son?"

"Is... is Susana okay? I... I thought..." He could not finish his sentence.

"I've been told she's been found," I replied. "We learned your location from a Godblood lawkeeper, Captain Pavo. He told us that Susana had already been rescued and we'd see her by the time we got back home."

Fionn released a heavy sigh. "Thank the Gods. I... I'm so sorry. I keep fucking up. I thought I was doing the right thing."

"Don't blame yourself, son. You have a good soul, but you're still young and haven't yet tempered good wisdom to match your good soul."

"When will I do that? When did you temper good wisdom?"

"Me?" I chuckled. "I'm still working on it. No wise man would be running through Ophidia with his arms full of baby boys."

A slave entered our hallway, panting from running. He skidded to a stop when he saw us.

"Hey! Come here!" I yelled.

He shrieked and ran out. I suspected he was afraid of me for being a Wynnle. Unfortunate. I would have helped him escape to Aloutia.

Fionn sniffled. "I want to be a good big brother to *somebody*."

"You are," I said. "You're a good big brother to all your younger siblings. Don't mind Cohaku; she's stuck in her ways. But you *are* kind to her—now, at least—whether she acknowledges it or not. Heli, Nio, and Susana all love you. Turquoise, too, will love you."

"And all these ones?" He hefted up the baby laying on his chest. "Or... are we going to give them away?"

I hesitated, thinking about the implication. Gods, in addition to Turquoise, we'd picked up six baby boys. Could our family raise them all? *I* wouldn't be opposed to it, but I could not speak for my spouses. I could give them a better life than what they'd get at the Wind church. But damn, this was a lot of babies... I was in for endless tiring nights, stressful days, and needing more time to prepare much larger dinners.

"I'll have to talk to your Mom and Mama Su about it first."

Su came through the portal, landing gracefully on his feet.

"Captain Pavo and Tynan are on the other side, waiting for us. Lungidus's precognitioner daughter foresaw our success and told her father to come help us. At least, to the extent that he can. Tynan is in a form with multiple arms and can carry all these babies. Let's go!"

Even knowing the two Godbloods were on the other side of the portal, we took caution as we placed each baby in the pool. Once we were finished with them, I had Fionn and Oboro go through. Su insisted I go next. Just before I fell into the pool, a woman came down the hall, pointing her gun at us. Su threw fire and lightning at her, but I disappeared from the Ophidian plane before I could watch her die.

Chapter Forty-Eight: Safe and Sound

The rest of our escape was nothing extraordinary. Lungidus and Tynan intimidated the people of Lemongraves enough by their very presence that we were not confronted. Captain Pavo carried an elegant bardiche with one hand, shaft resting on his shoulder. His outfit today was not that of a lawkeeper. Perhaps he intended to enter Steena Village without arousing suspicion. Or perhaps the people of Lemongraves held similar convictions toward Aloutian lawkeepers. It was a fancy outfit, nevertheless, a long-tailed coat in greens and blues like a peacock over a purple vest and white shirt. His marriage-tie, an eternal symbol of his bond to his wife, tucked tight around his neck. Atop his head, he wore a silk hat with a wide brim. A good choice for keeping the sun out of his eyes.

Yet as frightening as he may have been to the onlookers, he was nothing compared to his child who had morphed their body into some enormous, complex monstrosity with dozens of hands. Or whatever those appendages were. They were arms with cages on the end, with fleshy bars and soft folds that wrapped around the babies and held them secure. Tynan alone carried all the boys back to Aloutia.

Oboro, still carrying Fionn, tried to return the enchanted rings Lungidus had given him, but found it difficult while his hands were full.

"Let's get out of this city first," the Godblood said. "Then I'll take the rings back and do what I can to help Fionn. There are too many uncomfortable eyes on us right now."

We left Lemongraves from the same entrance we'd come from yesterday. Well, yesterday according to the calendar. This part of Solsun likely had not seen nighttime in weeks. Lungidus pointed his bardiche to a tall orange-and-brown striated rock formation and ordered us to rest in its shade while we reorganized.

"Fionn, are you unable to walk on your own?" he asked once we were close enough to touch the structure.

"I don't think I can, but I could try," he groaned. "Oboro, let me down."

"No," Lungidus said sternly before the Sasorin could finish his motion. Being the obedient boy he was, Oboro had started to set Fionn down immediately, then stopped just as suddenly at the Godblood's command. "I can't do much with the powers at my disposal, but I can at least mend the wound with some medicinal help."

"Okay," Fionn said. "Thank you. It doesn't hurt. Mama Su is doing something to keep the pain away."

Lungidus pulled a vial of light green liquid from out of his jacket pocket and poured the contents on my son's leg, right over the bullet wound. Telekinesis corked the empty vial and brought it back to his pocket as he put his free hand over the spot, his tentacles not quite touching skin. Some types of magic were invisible. I saw nothing—no sparks, no clouds, no glowing lights. When he withdrew his hand, Fionn's leg was patched up.

"The Mind element doesn't have proper healing," he said. "But I can manage a decent mend with telekinesis and some of a Plant Godblood's medicine. Go on, see if you can walk now."

Oboro set Fionn down carefully, supporting him if his leg gave out. My son wobbled on his digitigrade feet, but found his strength and gave the Godblood a grateful smile.

"I feel fine now," he said. "Thank you, um... Your Luminance." The only Godblood Fionn was used to was Su who only ever made people—and never his family—call him Luminance when he was angry. For Fionn, using the traditional honorific must have felt like sand in his mouth.

"You're welcome. Oboro, the rings, please."

The Sasorin took the rings off with such urgency you'd think they were cursed.

"Let's get going," Lungidus said as he put the enchanted rings in his pocket. "If anyone needs to take a break or you feel something's wrong, stop us. We're not in a hurry anymore."

Fionn nodded and we continued on our short trek through the desert between Lemongraves and the portal.

"I thought you could teleport," Su chided the captain as we made our way across the hot desert sands to the Cosmo-Aloutia portal.

"It's not my strongest skill," he said. "I don't trust my magic to teleport living beings. If I'm in a hurry, I may teleport myself, but I won't teleport anyone else, and especially not children."

"You didn't train your abilities when you were younger?"

"You know nothing of the Mind element, do you? Teleportation is an advanced technique of telekinesis. The fact that I can do it at all should prove my proficiency."

Su smirked. "Apologies. I thought I could bond with you over our shared deficiencies. My magic is only good for destroying things, and part of that is because I had no teacher when I was growing up."

"As far as Mind magic goes, mine is as close to pure combat-oriented as it gets. But no, I'm sorry to say I did not neglect my training regimen when I was a child. The Hierophant raised me and made sure I practiced using my magic every day in a safe, controlled environment."

"I envy you. Your mother laid your egg in a safe place. She allowed you to be raised by a loving family."

Lungidus nodded considerately. "As I understand it, my Lord Father instructs his consorts to lay their egg where he foresees we can do the most good, but some have been laid in Ophidia. I have a sister in Ophidia who's as cruel a slaver as any you've had to deal with in the last few days. I wonder if my father places some of his daughters in Ophidia hoping they will grow up to be good people and change the system. Maybe hoping they can use their magic to force an end to slavery. Perhaps—and I'm just guessing here—your mother also hoped to put you into a position to end slavery, Master Scrimshander."

Su pressed his lips together, silent for a long minute before finally responding. "My mother... is one of the most misunderstood entities."

Amidst all the chaos that had occurred in Ophidia, I had not had a chance to think about who his mother was. He had Lightning powers... but also Fire. Or was the fire caused by the lightning? No, he had thrown fireballs.

A million memories flooded back. Times I thought the temperature had changed to be just perfect, always while Su was around. Times when I thought dinner hadn't cooked enough. Times during the rainy season when I had struggled to get a fire cooking. The time he told me he had to get his cauldron to an extremely high temperature in order to boil bones, but I was sure he didn't have the right materials to make such a fire... Su, dancing in the flames, the bones on his costume clacking in tune to a drum's rhythm. I had always assumed he had retained his blessings.

Flamboil, the God of Fire, had a biological sex. It was known that she'd produced Godbloods throughout history. In fact, the current Fire Hierophant was her grandson. But most mortals did not know what that sex was, and her gender was even more cryptic. Traditionally, people used a pronoun for Flamboil which was the opposite of one they used. Men like me and neutral people like Su who used he/him would typically refer to Flamboil as she/her. Similarly, people who used she/her would use he/him for the God. The topic of Gods had rarely come up when I spoke to people who used they/them or other pronouns, but I recalled at least one Domovoi who spoke of Flamboil with pronouns I had never heard before or since.

Su had to be a Lightning elemental too. And his blood was orange—a mix of red and yellow. Red for Fire. Yellow for Lightning.

Sparkato, the God of Lightning, was definitely a penis-bearing man. The stories of his reprehensible actions were not vague on that topic.

Therefore, if I assumed Su's parents were both the Gods themselves, rather than a Godblood of one who'd fucked the other God, then Flamboil was a uterus-bearing individual and the biological mother of Su.

Flamboil was always portrayed in art and stories as powerful, kind, and determined. She had been a figurative force of nature even before she became a literal force of nature. Having her as a mother would not be shameful. But having Sparkato as a father? Certainly, there were many Lightning Godbloods who proudly announced their existence, but I could see it being a point of contention for some.

And what did it mean for Flamboil and Sparkato to have a child together? The stories never depicted Sparkato's sexual encounters as anything less than rape. Had he… done that? To another Goddess? Did Su keep his parentage a secret for fear of revealing that his Goddess-mother had been raped?

Flamboil's stories depicted her as powerful in her love, domineering with kindness, an unstoppable, fiery force of good will. She was Godly and benevolent in the same breath. She had been the one to come up with the idea of the blessing system in the first place, all out of love for sapientkind. Had Su wished to preserve that image of an indomitable Fire Goddess?

My soul hurt for her. Of all people, I never thought I'd feel sorry for Flamboil. I wondered what went through her head in those moments after the encounter. Pain? Despair? Shame? Fury? I then wondered what she thought when she learned she had become pregnant. She'd made a choice to have Su. If she had wanted to abort him when he was nothing but a soulless blob of cells, she could have snapped her fingers and burned them away. Theologically speaking, abortions were fine until the soul entered the body. All the Gods agreed on that, so Flamboil wouldn't have had qualms about destroying a few cells. She must have wanted Su to exist or was perhaps opposed to giving herself an abortion. Had she put him on Ophidia as a punishment?

No, that didn't seem like the sort of thing Flamboil would do. Not the Flamboil I'd learned about in school, anyway. I supposed the stories could be wrong.

Lost in my own thoughts, I had ignored Su and Lungidus's conversation. My ears perked as I came back to reality. The two Godbloods were in an entirely different conversation now.

"It's difficult to explain, so I shan't even attempt," Lungidus said, "but Tynan is both here and in Aloutia. The other Tynan has Susana right now. Is that correct?"

"Yes, Father," Tynan replied.

If Susana was safely back at home, then I had gotten all my children back home… plus more. Gods, were we really going to adopt all these babies? They were all in Tynan's hands now, so if the Godbloods had their own plan, they might just fly away with them, and there would be nothing I could do to stop them. Perhaps that would be for the best.

"You're still going to let Susana live with us?" I asked. "Even though you said I was under arrest for kidnapping her?"

Lungidus graced me with the Pavo smirk. "Legalities, Mr. Lasteran. Once we've proven to the court that you helped her out of an abusive situation and that you've cared well for her, the words 'kidnapping' will disappear from the court record and the judges will believe you rescued her instead."

"And you're confident the court will look in favor of me?"

"Yes, I don't see why not. As long as certain other topics are kept secret." He must have meant the murder of Miltico.

We arrived at long last at the platforms leading up to the portal in the butte wall. The two guards who had tried to stop us yesterday were here again, but made no effort to stop us. On the contrary, they looked downright terrified. I'd be afraid of Tynan, too, in that monstrous form.

"Lord Lungidus!" one of them called. Cautiously, she slithered forward, head bowed. "W-we've watched the portal as you asked, Your Luminance. Nobody came through."

"Good. You two can go look for a new job, then. After I walk through it, I'm destroying it."

The other serpentine lady gulped. "At your command, Master Godblood." She bowed, too, and slithered away toward Lemongraves with her companion in tow.

Lungidus chuckled as he took the first step of many on the way up the zig-zagging stairs. "I love rankling Ophidian women. They can't stand to take orders from men, but they know better than to defy a Godblood."

Su matched his laugh. "I can agree with that, though when I came through here yesterday, they thought I was a woman."

"We have more in common than we initially thought, Su Scrimshander," Lungidus said. "Perhaps, in another timeline, we'd have become a fantastic pair."

"Only if I'm a biological woman," he said.

"I didn't mean to imply we had to have children together. I'm a tulip. Perhaps in that other timeline, I refused the Chancellor's call to make Godblood toy soldiers. Maybe we're relaxing on a beach right now, drinking coconut and spinehair rum, rubbing our toes in the sand, and listening to the sound of Deep Sea's crashing fingers and the cawing seagulls."

"Wow, you've imagined that quite thoroughly," Su stated. "You're more romantic than I thought."

"Hardly. I was just... remembering a day at the beach I had with my wife."

"A pleasant memory," I said. "Sounds like something I've done with my husband and wife. Something I hope to keep doing in the future."

Lungidus could read my mind, so there was no need to say my fears and anxieties about imprisonment out loud.

"I hope that future comes to pass as well, Mr. Lasteran."

I'd hoped for more comforting words, but perhaps I was asking too much from a Godblood who'd been sent to arrest me in the first place.

We exited to the Aloutian side. Outside the cave, another Tynan stood, holding Susana's hand. Or at least I assumed it was Tynan; they were in the form they'd first taken when I was introduced to them. Not the amorphous blob, but the form in which they looked like a smaller version of their father.

"Susana! You're safe!" Su fell on his knees before the girl and embraced her.

"I was so scared, Mapa Su!" she buried her face in his chest, careful with her horns. "I'm happy to be home."

Su petted a hand over one of her long, furry ears. "Are you okay? Have you eaten?"

"I'm fine. Wh-when Tynan found me, they checked my body for injuries. I was a little sore from my Mommy dragging me away, but I don't hurt anymore. Then when they brought me back here, Auntie Orienna made a big bowl of steena pudding for me. It was so much! Nio and Heli helped me eat it."

Su put his chin on Susana's head, eyes closed, brushing her ears. He looked so peaceful, so serene... so satisfied. "I'm glad they took care of you. I had to go to Ophidia to get Fionn back since he was in danger, else I would have gone searching for you, too."

I crouched down beside them and rubbed a finger across her long, floppy ears. Months ago, this would have sent her fleeing, but Susana had grown closer to me.

"I'm glad you're safe. Did you have steena pudding yesterday? If you're hungry again, let's go home and get something for you. What do you want?"

"Ube! Durian! Spinehair! Pitaya!"

Her excitement over food made me chuckle. To think that only a few months ago, she wouldn't even touch those foods until someone gave her permission. "Alright, let's go." I eyed Lungidus as I stood back up, expecting him to stop me. If he did... I'd have no choice but to comply. He wouldn't deny a little girl one last day to eat dinner with her family, would he?

He grimaced, undoubtedly reading my mind and struggling to find the right response. He tipped the brim of his hat, hiding his eyes. Was he ashamed of his actions? Did he not want to arrest me? Was I being overly naive and hopeful? "Mr. Lasteran, Master Scrimshander, I'll return tomorrow morning and take you to where we're keeping Liesle. I hope the process will not be long, and you may all be home again soon, but I can't make any promises. I will ensure your children are cared for, though I think Mys Orienna Denwall has that covered. Because you are under arrest right now, I cannot leave you unsupervised, and since one of you is a Godblood, you must be watched by a Godblood. Tynan will be nearby, ensuring you do not try to escape, though I will permit you privacy. Tynan will not watch the inside of your bedroom or your private cave, if you choose to do anything there."

Su picked up Susana as he turned to face Captain Pavo.

"Thank you. I know you don't have to do these things for us, but they are appreciated."

Lungidus smiled, still hiding his eyes under his brim, and for once, the crook of his mouth didn't feel like such a derisive smirk. "Just doing to others what I would have liked done to me. Enjoy this night with your husband, Master Scrimshander. I will try to get you into the same cell as your spouses when I take you to the jail house, but it's not my decision to make."

"What about all the babies we took from Ophidia?" I asked. "Are you going to take them away?"

Lungidus rubbed his chin, stroking the short beard barely growing there. "I would not take Turquoise from you. Go on and give him back, Tynan."

On their father's orders, Tynan deposited Turquoise into my outstretched hands.

"The others I will take to Monoceros. At the Life church, they'll receive official Aloutian citizenship records. If you are legally allowed to adopt them after the trial, you are free to do so. Now, I must ask you all to stand back as I destroy the portal. I don't think anything dangerous will happen, but better to be safe."

We gave the Godblood ample space, standing in a semicircle behind him.

Lungidus lifted the bardiche over his head and waited. I imagined him imbuing the polearm with magic somehow, although once again, there were no visual cues to hint he was doing anything other than standing there. He swung it down in the direction of the boulder and it shattered. First the rock broke into smaller rocks, then pebbles, then into dust, and finally even the dust became nothingness. Not even debris hit the soil. Where the rock formation had once been, now there was only a hole in the ground.

"There." Lungidus teleported his bardiche away and dusted off his hands—not like there was anything to dust off them. "Now those Ophidian snakes won't come to your village again. "He turned to face the rest of us. "I shall take my leave with this Tynan and the rescued babies. Oboro, feel free to walk Fionn home. I will spend a moment in Steena Village speaking with Mr. Onoretti, so I'll tell him you're safe and will be with us shortly. Mr. Lasteran, Master Scrimshander, I shall return tomorrow. Please, make the most of this day that you can."

Fionn Interlude

Fionn could bear neither the pain of his sins nor the sins that had been committed upon him. It was too much. Too powerful. And how could he ever discuss it with his parents? It wasn't that they didn't understand—they would. They would do their best to comfort him. But... he needed that part of his life to stay clean and pure from the taint of sin. He didn't want his memories of Mama Su or his Dad Amiere to be smeared with mud. Let his childhood remain sacred.

Once they'd gotten back to the house, Fionn asked his parents to let him speak to Oboro alone. He would have to go back soon, back to the man he called Signore, then to Chernagora. Maybe Fionn could visit him in Chernagora one day...

Fionn and Oboro sat beside each other on the fallen palm log.

"You went back into Hell to rescue me," Fionn said, looking down at his hands, leaning his elbows on his knees.

"It was just Ophidia," Oboro said. "I lived there for fourteen years. I was never afraid."

"Is your neck okay? They sliced you to get your blood... to make me go berserk."

Oboro touched the spot on his neck where they had drawn blood, but the scar was already imperceptible to his massive claw. Sasorin chitin was quick to repair. His tail would never repair, but he'd lost far more than chitin to that injury.

"I'm fine," he said. "I'd do it all again and endure far worse to save you, Fionn."

The Wynnle boy didn't know how to respond. No one had ever been this caring to him. Oh, his parents had, of course, but they had to remain in the light of his past. Oboro, perhaps, could become his companion in the darkness that would shroud his future.

"I wish we could spend more time together," Fionn said. At the last word, his voice cracked. He fought back the onslaught of tears attempting to break free from the dams of his eyes.

"We will, one day," Oboro said. "When we're adults, maybe you, me, and Beatie can..." He trailed off, perhaps too terrified to end that sentence.

"Can we live together?" Fionn asked, raising his head to look his friend in the eyes. Hope shone on his face like sunlight, his mane a perfect aureole. "Do you want to? Really? Or at least try to? I suppose we can't make a promise like that now while we're still young..."

"We can't guarantee it'll work out, but we can promise to try it out," Oboro said. "I know Beatie would be happy to be with us. Maybe one day, we could be a triad like your parents."

Fionn smiled for the first time in a long time. "I want that so, so much."

Oboro put one of his lower hands—the ones that weren't big scorpion claws—into Fionn's hand. Warmth. Comfort. Family. Fionn would make sure not to fuck this one up.

Oboro Interlude

With his work in Ophidia done—and a solemn promise to Fionn made—Oboro went back to Steena Village.

He assumed Signor Onoretti had stayed in Nell's future house for the night, as he had done whenever they came here. After the death of her grandfather, Nell had implied that she might not move into that house after all, and instead take up residence in her grandfather's store. The empty house would likely remain a guest house for a while yet, or until the next villager to come of age needed a home. Regardless, it was used by guests for now.

Oboro stopped before getting too close to the leafy door. Inside, the voices of Signor Onoretti and Captain Pavo were engaged in an emotional conversation. The Sasorin boy waited, not wanting to interrupt.

He sat down against the mud brick wall, right beside the door, and listened.

"Are Mr. Lasteran and Master Scrimshander being sent to jail tomorrow?"

"Yes," Lungidus replied in an equally low tone.

If he could read minds, he should have known that Oboro was listening in... Perhaps his telepathy only worked within a certain range or if he knew somebody was nearby.

"We can't afford to let either of them speak with Representative Boura."

"He's been trying to get an audience with Mys Denwall."

"Fuck." Giorvi stomped a hoof against the bamboo floorboard. "Can't you send them to any other jail?"

"All Godbloods under suspicion of a crime have to go to Monoceros, and if Amiere requests being in the same cell with his spouses, we must legally oblige."

"Can we block Boura from requesting an audience with any of them?"

"So far, we've been successful at blocking him from Liesle, but only because her crime was demon summoning, so we can claim it's for his own safety that we keep them separate. Since all we have on Amiere is kidnapping..."

"He's a murderer, too!" Giorvi hissed under his breath.

"Do you want me to add that to his charges?" Lungidus asked. "You were the one who wanted *that* kept under wraps."

A moment's hesitation. "Keep it secret. If Amiere finds out about Rini Laan..."

Lungidus forestalled his next words. "What would it matter? What's done is done. Our plan is in motion. My Lord Father has granted you clemency for your actions. It doesn't matter what Amiere learns."

Giorvi inhaled a heavy breath. "Yes. I would have liked to have continued being his friend. If he finds out, I fear... well, I'll have to remove him from the guild. There can be no reconciliation between us."

"You're a sentimental old man, Mr. Onoretti," Lungidus said in a soft voice, trying to appease him. "What happened to Tawny is unfortunate, but it was never your intention. You can't keep blaming yourself for that."

"If Boura talks to Amiere, he'll convince him that I'm to blame."

"I know. By then, it'll be too late. Too late for either of you. He will no longer be your friend, but he can no longer stop us. Let him go, Mr. Onoretti. You did it all for Aloutia. No, for Beatrice. You saved *her*."

Chapter Forty-Nine: Shame

I feared for my children's future. If all three of us were imprisoned for our respective crimes, they might all be put under Orienna's care. Which was not a slight on Orienna—the woman was a fine mother and caretaker—but I couldn't burden her with all my children. Oh, I'm sure she would have said they were not a burden. She would have done the job splendidly and raised them to be well-adapted adults. It did not make me feel any less guilty for shoving them onto her. Eruwan was an adult and could continue living on her own, at least. Or the kids would be put into the collective care of the village with each kid living with a different person, if only for a short time.

Since we had no leaders in the village, the decision would have to be made by everyone gathered together, but that meeting would not happen until a judgment regarding our imprisonment was made. I had faith in the people of Steena Village to treat my children right.

Su and I did everything we could to make our last certain day here a good one for the kids. We made their favorite meals. Su made chocolate cupcakes for Cohaku, ube cheesecake for Susana, and spinehair gelatin for Eruwan. I prepared purplefin for Nio, crabs for Fionn, and tuna for Heliodor. We invited Tynan to eat with us, which they accepted, albeit seemingly surprised. Did they think we wouldn't feed them? When I asked what their favorite food was, they had none. Since they could change their taste buds at will, they could change themself to enjoy anything.

Fionn flew to Kiwi Island and brought back a few of the fuzzy green fruits. He placed one on Tawny's memorial and handed the others out to his siblings. Tynan got one, too, and ate it in a single bite once they made their mouth large enough to fit it in.

After dinner, Nell and Demitris came for a visit, so we played modified kiwi-batte. I only knocked the balls into Deep Sea three times.

As the day drew to an end and the last rays of sunlight threw glitter across the ocean and painted the sky a tranquil pink, we retired to our rooms.

I wanted to discuss Su's magic, if he would let me. He had not put on any of his bone jewelry since we came home, so I knew he wasn't in the mood for sex. He was probably too morose for most topics.

We laid together on the bamboo mat, his head on my chest. The only light came from my tail, which I had always held away from him on the off-chance he wasn't a Lightning elemental.

His skin was so warm. So unnaturally warm. Of course it was; he was also a Fire elemental.

"If you want to make me forget what element you are... you can," I said. In my sleepy state, my voice was a low growl.

He rubbed his hand over my chest. "I won't. I thought about it, but... I don't know if it matters anymore. My mother is Flamboil. My father is Sparkato. Think what you will of them. I used to hide my powers in honor of them, but I don't see why I should honor them anymore."

"No reason to honor Sparkato. Fucking rapist."

Su scooted up so his head rested on my shoulder now. "Was he? What if it was the other way around?"

I arched an eyebrow. "How is that possible?"

"Women can rape men, Amiere. Even the Ophidians have their ways. You think Gods wouldn't have more elaborate methods?"

"I... I just... Sparkato has always been portrayed as a pervert and a rapist. Flamboil has always been portrayed as valorous, powerful, kind..."

"Flamboil is all those things, but she's also domineering. If there's something she wants, she'll take it. And she *is* a sexual being. She has produced many Godbloods, sometimes with one of the male Gods. She had a daughter with Lucognidus; that woman is the Commander of the Godblood Brigade, Freya Rubaiya. Also, what you've heard about Sparkato isn't the whole truth. He is... well, we don't know for certain. Lucognidus has only allowed some information to reach us mortals. But we know he's under the control of the other Gods, whatever that means. I take it to mean he's imprisoned or... maybe even hypnotized. I am not certain if he *can* consent to sex."

I hadn't thought of it from that angle... "So, what do you think happened?"

"I don't know, and I don't want to guess. I don't see any point in guessing which was the rapist and which was the victim. And hey, maybe I'm wrong. Maybe my parents have a deep connection and my conception was a moment of loving, meaningful, consensual sex. But if it wasn't, I don't want my hopes to invalidate the pain of whoever was the victim. So, I have no opinion on the matter, and I refuse to make one, and I do not want to put the thought into anyone else's head so they can form unnecessary opinions."

"I can't promise that I'll never wonder about it," I said. "My skull makes me think about things I don't *want* to think about."

"Nobody can control their thoughts. It's not worth panicking about."

"Can you answer some questions about your powers? Like, the stuff that looked like hypnosis. Making me black out. Manipulating Susana's brain. How did you do that with Lightning or Fire powers?"

"That's a branch of Lightning magic. Nerve control. The brain is made of cells sending electric signals to each other. A sufficiently skilled Lightning Godblood with that ability can… shut off neurons, or turn them on. Grow new ones. It looks like Mind magic, but it's all about changing the physical brain."

"Wow." It was all I could say.

We lay there in silence. Su's warmth and softness brought me joy—perhaps the last joy I would have for a long time. I relished these feelings while I could have them—while I had the universe's permission to be happy.

"You know, Ami-honey… sometimes I'm afraid to fall asleep. I'm a heretic, so I get nightmares. I… I had a lot after Tawny's death."

I tightened my grip around his shoulder. "I wondered that. You've twitched and said things in your sleep that made me suspect. But then you danced in fire and cooked without a seven-color cloth mitt."

He giggled. "I have lost my mother's blessing, but I still have her fire-resisting genes."

What did one have to do to lose Flamboil's favor? It was something that only a truly cruel person would do. Or would Su lose all the Gods' blessings for disobeying Sparkato, too?

"How did you lose your blessings?" I asked.

He hesitated for so long that I thought he'd fallen asleep. I had given up expecting an answer when he spoke. "It's… not a happy story. You were there when it happened, but you don't remember."

"Can you remind me?"

He sighed. "Godbloods of more than one element can lose their blessings by becoming a heretic to one of their Gods, so even though I had yet to betray Flamboil's laws, I lost her blessing and all the others for my act of disobedience against Sparkato."

"Someone asked you for sex and you declined."

"Yes."

"Who the hell was it? I'll teach them a lesson they won't soon forget."

Silence. Then, finally, the answer: "It was you, Amiere."

The realization struck me like a sack of stinky, spiky durians.

"It was so long ago… just before Eruwan was born. You were high on crazy sugar. It's why I can't blame you for it. You weren't in your right mind. You wanted to know what I looked like… down there. You wouldn't take 'no' for an answer. I had to knock you out before you tore my clothes off."

"Gods… I… I'm so sorry, Su."

"I forgive you. I forgave you long ago. You stopped taking crazy sugar, and you were always in control of yourself when you were sober. It was never a problem afterward."

A deep shame gnawed my soul. A shame that no bath could ever wash off and no amount of scrubbing could scrape off my skin, though perhaps if I rubbed myself raw and bloody, the punishment would be my catharsis. It didn't matter that it happened so long ago. No, if anything, I felt *more* shame for not remembering.

"Besides, I would have become a heretic anyway," Su said in a soft, faraway voice. "Flamboil prohibits murder, and I just murdered a *lot* of Ophidians."

The thought gave me little comfort.

A knock came at the side of our door. Since we had leaf-doors, that was the closest place to knock, but none of the kids ever knocked. They'd all speak up, or Nio would just walk in. My chest felt heavy at the idea of some intruder; my tail flickered involuntarily. An intruder wouldn't have knocked, but who...

"Tynan?" Su asked. "Is that you? You can come in."

The child slid past the door, turning into a nearly flat shape so as to not rustle it on their way inside. They transformed back into their usual form, a black-skinned androgynous child who looked to be wearing a shinigami uniform. Their eyes glowed ominously red.

"I think you two should check on Fionn. His thoughts are very distressing."

My chest was already in pain and fear from thinking Tynan was an intruder; now it sunk into the abyss of my soul like a rock in Deep Sea. I scrambled to my feet, grateful that Su hadn't been in the mood for sex, otherwise I'd have been naked, and I did not have the mental wherewithal to think about how to dress.

Tynan literally shrank and glided aside before I was on my feet. I bounded out the door, headed toward Fionn's room.

"He's at the ocean," Tynan said.

I hurried out the door. Su was right behind me.

Usually, quiet nights like this were romantic. Palm fronds wafted in the slight breeze, casting dancing shadows in the light of the rings and a half dozen moons. Deep Sea's fingers crashed rhythmically, soothingly, over the soft sand. Maika stood on the porch of Eruwan's house, her head tilted the way dogs do when they're confused.

Fionn stood where the oncoming waves reached his waist. I approached slowly, not wanting to scare him, but Su yelled his name and took off toward him at a sprint.

By the time I reached them, Su had two hands around Fionn's torso and the other two held his arms. Fionn writhed, struggling for freedom, but soon gave up.

"Stop! Stop it!" my son cried. "It's... it's not what it looks like!"

"Why, Fionn?" Su asked, his voice strained by a throat near to crying.

"It... it was Maika. I was playing with her, and... she was a little rough."

"Mud and sludge. Maika is all the way up at Eruwan's house, calm as she can be."

I swallowed hard, terrified of what I'd see if I stepped into the ocean to see what Su saw.

Deep Sea had turned tendrils of his water into a gelatinous ooze that clung to Fionn, absorbing the Demon Lord's attribute—Despair.

Fionn broke down into a mess of tears and mucus. He budged his arms to wipe his face, but Su stopped him, forcing his arms outward, instead. A drop of water fell from his wrists during the struggle. No, not water... blood.

His wrists bled from self-inflicted wounds. His claws were still wet with sticky blood.

"Let go of me!" Fionn screamed.

"No!" Su said sternly. "You want to scratch someone? Scratch me instead."

"I don't want to scratch you. I want... I want..." He could not finish saying what he wanted, as he launched into a wordless scream.

My chest was hollow, pained... Deep Sea leeched despair off *me*. Had I failed as a parent? My son... my beautiful, strong, kind son... Why was he doing this? I had stopped abusing myself for Tawny's death, knowing it was out of my hands, but this? Could I have stopped it? If I had only let him come with us to Chernagora. If I had only been a better father, maybe I could have... I didn't know what. Done something differently? How could I have raised Fionn differently? Was his pain caused by some personal trait I could have shaped, or was this also out of my control?

I wanted to hug him, to tell him everything was okay—that nothing was his fault and his future would shine with starlight. But I couldn't. The sight of his slashed wrists had nailed my feet where I stood, and not even Deep Sea's shifting waves moved me.

"Cut me if you must cut someone!" Su yelled. He held out one of his hands that had been around Fionn's torso, then forced the boy's claws closer.

Fionn sheathed his claws, but not before Su got a good swipe on his own wrist. Orange blood crept out, slid to both sides of his arm, and dripped into Deep Sea, mixing into the gelatinous ooze.

Fionn trembled as tears streamed down his face. "Why? Why? I don't want to hurt you, Mama Su."

"You already did the moment you decided to hurt yourself like this. Come out of Deep Sea, Fionn. Let's go sit on the palm log and talk."

Su let go of Fionn's hands and helped him out of the ocean. I followed in silence, hoping my presence was enough... or that it was welcome.

Su took him to the old fallen palm tree that we had never cleared away because it made for a decent bench. We sat on either side of Fionn.

I took a deep breath, the stress inside built up to intolerable levels. "Fionn, I... I love you, son. I don't know what you're going through. I can't imagine the trauma you went through when you were in Ophidia. But if you need... something. Anything. Please tell us."

"I want Tawny back. I want Mom back. I want... I wish I could go back in time and undo what I did to Susana. I shouldn't have taken her to her mother.

While I'm at it, I might as well go back in time and treat Cohaku right from the beginning. She'll never forgive me."

"I'm sorry you're feeling that way," I said. "We can't change the past, but is there anything we can do to make the future better?"

He sat there, numb, staring at the space between his feet.

"We're going to build your house next year," I went on. "Or, if you'd rather make a clean start somewhere else, we can look into that."

"I want..." He'd started energetically, but stopped. Weakly, he finished, "Gods, I'm pathetic. Never mind what I was about to say. I'll never be worth anything to anybody."

"Fionn, I want to tell you a story about myself," Su said. "I don't mean for it to invalidate or minimize your problems. I hope your takeaway from this is that I have gone through a similar pain as yours, but I still found a family who loves me."

"I know about your past, Mama Su. Your first mother abused you. Your village burned down and you were the only survivor. Demon King Susan found you and raised you."

"That's all true, but now I think you should know more details. The village wasn't burned in an accident. *I* burned it down. I killed everyone, including other children and blessed people. If I couldn't burn them with my fire, I killed them with my lightning. I burned my adoptive mother's skin, muscles, everything off her bones, until bone was all that remained. When King Susan took me back to the Boneyard, she didn't know what to do with me. She didn't exactly have a room for a mentally unstable Godblood. She had me put into a bedroom and brought toys, hoping it would calm me down so she could talk to me. Mind you, demons have fucked-up ideas about what 'toys' are. One was a doll carrying a knife."

Shivers ran down my spine. I'd never heard *this* story from Su...

"My evil mother had always said I was special because I was a Godblood, because my blood was orange. I thought that was why she abused me, too. And so... I thought if I got rid of all my blood, I could be loved. I cut myself severely. It hurt... It hurt so fucking bad, Fionn. But the pain of being unloved was worse, so I endured it. Well, I only got a few slashes in before King Susan stopped me. She had a precognitioner tell her I was going to do it, so she was on her way to my room before I'd even raised the knife."

Fionn held his breath, so tense was his body.

"It wasn't the last time I cut myself," Su said. "When I was about your age, I started to... hate my body. My sex. I didn't want to be what I was. My body said one thing and my mind said another. At first, I thought it was something like my blood. Something that I just had to live with. Something I would have to ignore in order to be happy. But while I could ignore my blood—I never saw it if I didn't cut myself—I couldn't ignore my body. Every time I looked in the mirror, or hell, just putting on pants made me all too aware of what was between my legs."

"Did you... try to cut something off?" Fionn asked.

Su nodded. "I'll let you guess whether it was a penis and testicles or a labia."

I shuddered. I could not imagine his pain. How powerful must his misery have been that he was more comfortable in a body with mutilated genitals?

"You didn't know about shubin marrow?" Fionn asked.

"I had kept my shame about my body a secret," Su said. "I didn't think there was any way to change. After I did that, King Susan told me about shubin marrow. Said she could get me as much as I needed. If it hadn't been for her, I'd have probably died a long time ago. Before I ever met Amiere and Liesle. All because I kept my shame bottled up inside. So, Fionn, if you're feeling ashamed about something, please tell us. Maybe there's a solution and you just don't know it yet."

"And even if there is no solution," I said. "I think you'll feel better after speaking it out loud."

Fionn clutched his knees. "I'm ashamed that... what I did got Mom in trouble. I'm so scared she's not gonna come home."

I lowered my head, staring at the sand between my feet. Summoning the Demon Lord of Terror was a serious crime in Aloutia. Liesle... would probably be exiled to Hydra Island.

The truth of it finally hit me and I covered my eyes, crying.

Fuck... Fuck! I was supposed to be the strong one in this situation. I was supposed to be the adult—the dad—and here I was crying my eyes out in front of my son.

Su came around to both of us and pulled me and Fionn into a hug.

"Shh, shh, we'll be alright," he said. "We'll be alright. Worst case scenario, if she's sent to Hydra Island, she could come back within five years. Now, I know that seems like a lot to you, Fionn, but..." Su was at a loss for words. "But it's not the end. You'll visit her, and she'll be back home soon."

"Soon? I'll be eighteen! I *hope* I've moved out by then."

Su backed away from us, breaking the hug. I had restrained my tears, too, regaining some of my composure.

"You will, son," I said. "We're gonna build your house next. Wherever you want it. In the village? Somewhere else? If you want to move far away, we'll need to look into the construction laws in other places."

Fionn fiddled with his fingers. "I... I want to live with... Ugh, it's so stupid! I'm so stupid."

"What are you talking about?" Su asked. "You know who you want to live with?"

"Yeah, little Beatie and Oboro. Well... I really like them as friends. Maybe... maybe when we're older, we can be a family?"

They could—and should—just be friends until they became adults. Familial matters could be dealt with later.

"If they want to start a family with you, I suppose we'll have to build a house somewhere designed for your bodies. Oboro is quite tall, though you might get taller in a few years."

"You mean, he won't be able to carry me as he did?" Fionn sounded oddly disappointed about that.

"He'll probably always be able to carry you since he's got such strong arms," Su said, "even if you grow as tall as Liesle."

Fionn released a sigh of relief. "So... you're all okay with me wanting to live with Beatrice and Oboro?"

"Why would we have a problem with it?" I asked.

"To be clear, you are too young to make that kind of decision *now*," Su said. "But we're talking about hopes and dreams for the future. It's okay to hope you're still friends with them once you're old enough to decide if you want to take that relationship further."

Fionn nodded. "Yeah. I... I really like them. Oboro... He's amazing, Mama Su. He talked to me while I was in... that place in Ophidia. I think he really cares about me. Gods, I didn't realize I liked boys! I thought I was a gladiolus, but maybe I'm a tulip like you two and Mom."

"That's fantastic, son," I said.

"Truly it is," Su said. "Though give yourself time to grow. You're only thirteen. You might discover new things about yourself as you become an adult."

Fionn nodded anxiously. "I understand. Umm, I think I'm alright now. Can I go back into the house?"

"Yeah, get some sleep," I said. "You have school tomorrow. You're gonna be the oldest one in the house, so make sure your siblings have lunches ready."

He smiled. "Of course! I'll show them I can be a good big brother!"

Chapter Fifty: Monoceros

The next morning, bright and early, I was the first to wake up. I listened to the cheerful tunes of the songbirds, the crashing of Deep Sea's fingers, and Su's slow, rhythmic breathing as he lay cuddling on my chest.

Would this be the last time I woke up in my bedroom? Perhaps not forever. Aloutia wasn't the sort of country to send people to prison for extended lengths of time, and executions were unheard of in the modern era. Still... many of my crimes were sufficient enough to see me sent to Hydra Island, where they might keep me for five years or more.

What awaited me today? After today? When I went to sleep that night, would I be in the same cell as Liesle and Su?

My time alone with my intrusive thoughts did not last long, thankfully. Su stirred awake, gave me a kiss, and offered one last act of oral pleasure in the safety of our own bedroom, since he, too, did not know when we'd next be here.

We couldn't delay the inevitable forever. With a heavy chest full of dread, I rose to my feet. We dressed in clothes that would be appropriate for a formal affair, donning appropriate kamens for the Imperial capital and eschewing our jewelry entirely. Our masks didn't hide much; they were hardly more concealing than the flimsy filigree ones we'd worn to the party in Chernagora.

On our way to the living room, we check in the kids' rooms. They were all still asleep. We uncovered the crystalights throughout the room, transforming the soft blue interior to one of a myriad of bright colors.

"Should we wake the children up?" I asked. "Say one last goodbye to them?"

"Let's let them sleep," Su said. "We shouldn't keep Lungidus waiting, and though I may have my problems with the man, he *did* help us, and I don't want our kids despising him. Which some of them will, as sure as slugs in rain, if they see him hauling us away. And if anyone's going to be back soon, it'll be you. The only crime they're charging you for is kidnapping, but once they find out Susana is better off with us, they'll probably drop it."

"Doesn't Lungidus know I killed Miltico?" I whispered, in case any of the kids *were* awake and listening in. "He's a telepath so... he *must* know, right?"

Su closed his eyes and held me tight. "If he knows, he hasn't mentioned it, and it wasn't one of the crimes you were charged for. Don't talk about it, Amiere. Stay quiet, don't offer any information you weren't asked about, and give the most bare-bones responses you can. Of course, don't lie to the lawkeepers, either."

I held him close for a long minute, extracting every ounce of joy I could before we were possibly torn apart.

We stepped over the femur threshold, greeted by a warm breeze carrying the scent of steenas and mangoes. Several paces across the beach, Captain Pavo sat next to their child, Tynan, on the fallen palm tree where Su and I had comforted Fionn last night. Tynan had transformed themself to resemble a child-aged version of their father. Despite how much I should dislike them, I felt stirrings of sympathy. I couldn't help but wonder if those two had ever had a father-child bonding moment like I'd had with Fionn. I wondered if Tynan had ever feared whether they'd see their mother again, or if Lungidus ever thought his last act of sex with his wife would truly be the *last*. Surely not. Godbloods like them were above the law, as I understood it.

Lungidus stood and approached us. He was dressed in civilian clothes again—a fancy, silken, colorful vest and jacket, along with a green silk hat with pavo feathers. It was no uniform, nor did carry any of the tools of a lawkeeper on his person. His bardiche was nowhere to be seen, and still he wore no kamen.

"I didn't want to come here as a lawkeeper," he said. "Not only because we have traditionally been unwelcome in these parts, but because I'm not here as your enemy. I'm here to take you safely to Monoceros. I won't put you in handcuffs or a collar unless you give me a reason to."

"If I did that, you'd outright kill me," I replied.

He conceded my point with an awkward grin. "I also know for a fact you will cooperate because my dear Steffa told me you would with a near-certain probability. Come, Mr. Lasteran, Master Scrimshander. We'll go to the Stee-Nil portal, and from there, to Monoceros."

It wasn't my first time in Monoceros. I had lived here for two years when I went to art school with Liesle. However, we'd rarely left the fashionable Art District, and we certainly had *never* gone to the Godblood District where Lungidus led us now.

Monoceros was on Aloutia's equator and close to the sea. In many ways, it was similar to Steena Village—same scents on the air, same birds singing and diving into Deep Sea, many of the same plants and pests, and the same intense heat that damn-near required one to be blessed to live comfortably.

The difference lay in the fact that Monoceros was *huge*. It was the capital city of Aloutia, with citizens of all living and common sapienti species residing within its boundaries, and I would not be surprised to learn that even rare species like the Iurion, Odonata, or Mabera had a representative living here.

The portal house alone took up several city blocks and, despite attempts over the years to widen the walkways for the immense traffic, we still had to push through the crowd. Lungidus held a tentacle out and lightly kept people from jostling him by pushing them aside with telekinesis while Tynan turned into a small creature and hid under their father's hat. With all the chaos around, nobody noticed they'd been shoved by a Godblood. One swearing Neuropteran man whose foul language I could hear long before he got anywhere near us even had the audacity to yell at His Luminance. Lungidus only smiled, offered a perfunctory apology, and continued onward.

The same man took one look at me and didn't dare. Through the holes of his kamen, I saw the fear in his eyes.

The halls were lined with vendors selling souvenirs. Plushes of the various animals called a 'monoceros'—scale, shortfur, longfur, roughhide, wooly, and aquatic monoceroses[1] —were quite popular. I had carved several such animals in my life for some of the more high-class souvenir shops here.

Being shuffled around by the crowd, I inadvertently allowed three people to get between me and Captain Pavo. He stopped and I felt a tug at my wrist pulling me closer to him. The three people went around, and I was once again right behind him. He may not have put handcuffs on me, but he nevertheless had the means to keep me close. Su grabbed onto my arm, probably to avoid the embarrassment of having Lungidus pull him with telekinesis.

I thought about the time Su said that he'd danced with both Lungidus and Loyenie. Su wasn't related to either of them. Maybe in another timeline, he joined them in a polyamorous triad. Gods, why did I think of that? Why did it hurt my sternum to think about alternate timelines without Su? It's not like I'd have known about him. Perhaps in those same timelines, I was extraordinarily happy with just Liesle. I probably *was* happier in those timelines. Without Su, I would be unable to have as many kids. Maybe I only had one or two... and had never felt the pain of watching one die or having one kidnapped and sold into slavery. Perhaps I wouldn't be hauled off to jail to answer for my wife's crime.

Once we were outside, the crowd fanned out. Lungidus led us to a plaza with only a few people loitering around, sitting on stonework benches and drinking lassi[2] . Most people in Monoceros wore a kamen, though it was not mandatory, so some bold souls showed their entire face. I couldn't help but wonder if Lungidus

---

1. Respectively, a centrosaur (one-horned dinosaur), unicorn, almiraj (rabbit), rhinoceros, xiezhi (sheep) and narwhal.

2. A yoghurt-based drink

went about with his face visible to the world because of some immense Godblood courage or if he was in some way immune to the Lord of Terror's torture.

The centerpiece of the plaza was an elaborate clockwork post with clock faces on each side and a crystalight encased in Domovoi glass on the top.

"We're going to the Godblood District," Lungidus said. "I might be recognized on the way. Do not speak unless I give you permission."

I had no intention of disobeying. I stayed silent; if he wanted my thoughts, he could read them.

Monoceros was a grand city, not only in its length and breadth, but its height. Impressive, soaring white towers marked the headquarters of numerous guilds. Crystalline walkways arching hundreds of feet above pedestrians connected near-by spires, providing a spider web-like appearance if one were to fly high above and look down. Some towers were more obvious with their clockwork, with gears and pistons visible behind Domovoi glass; others kept their innards hidden behind whitewashed walls. From the crystal bridges, colored banners blew in the breeze.

We were too far to see the greatest monument in the city, the Armillary Spire, decorated with silver, crystal, and precious gemstones, and topped with a massive lapidary globe of Aloutia, its rings, and the fourteen moons. They rotated in real time and served as an accurate model of where the moons were currently. The spire itself was a place for tourists and love-struck couples. The inside featured restaurants, indoor parks, music rooms, a ballroom, and of course, the planetar-ium at the top.

Liesle and I had gone on many dates there when we were in art school. A memory sprung in my head; one I had not thought about in at least a decade. She had wanted to fly me to the top, but I had been so terrified that she'd drop me, I made her put me down. She'd been sad, then. Disappointed, perhaps, that I hadn't trusted her strength to hold on to me.

I had gone on a date with another woman a few days later. Someone else I had met at art school. A Coleopteran lady who'd been in painting classes with Liesle. I had thought they were friends. She and I had climbed to the top of the Armillary Spire, had a nice dinner, chatted, and went on our separate ways. I couldn't even remember her name now. Gods, that was sixteen years ago! After our date, a week passed and I had not seen or heard from her again. I had asked Liesle if she knew her, but she'd told me the Coleopteran had left school and gone back home.

That was the same week rumors had gone throughout the school about an artist who'd been killed by Vinoc. We'd never learned the truth. The school tried to hide all instances of demon summoning for the sake of its reputation. Students were required to wear kamens in class, but the school could not enforce it when we were off campus.

Fuck, I hadn't put the pieces together until now. I had not once suspected Liesle. I had not once assumed the victim was that Coleopteran woman. Did Liesle kill her because I went on one date with her?

“Mr. Lasteran,” Lungidus said, snapping me out of reverie. He kept walking, but turned his head sideways, watching me through the corner of his eye. “Those are some interesting thoughts you have. I’d like to interview you personally when we get to the law offices.”

Did I have a choice? “As you wish, Your Luminance.”

The Godblood District was so different from the rest of Monoceros, it was like stepping into a whole other city. While much of the construction was the same—white marble, crystal, Domovoi glass—there were far few people. Not all were Godbloods; some were servants or teamsters making deliveries. A Takyufon merchant of mail skated by us and almost lost their balance when they saw Lungidus. They gave a military-style salute, hand to chest, and hurried on, spinning their feet-wheels for all they were worth.

Here, Captain Pavo was surely known and recognized by all. Feared, too.

The law offices were in a building no less grand and elaborate than its neighbors, with crystal pillars and painted frescoes depicting the Decatheon and various demis above its massive Daga-sized doors. Upon the door was an engraved image of Sione, Demigod of Justice, a nine-tailed Viemeno[3] . One tail stood up behind him, while the others splayed across the doors, four to each side.

A pair of Isopteran guards stood to either door, ready to open them upon request, but Lungidus made a gesture with his tentacle which put them at ease. He opened the double doors with telekinesis, splitting Sione’s image in two. I supposed the demigod didn’t mind.

Our footsteps were the only noise as we trod the marble lobby and a wing of the building lined with portraits of what I assumed to be Godbloods, given they were all of the Gods’ species. Their judgmental gazes did nothing to welcome or reassure me that I’d be treated fairly here.

We turned a corner and came face-to-face with two individuals. I did not have to be told they were Godbloods. One was a Phoenian girl of an age close to Fionn. She was a rotund girl, but had remarkably similar facial features and skin color to Lungidus. It was no surprise when she greeted him as ‘Papa.’

The other was an older woman, perhaps in her sixties with charcoal-black hair beginning to turn ashy. Black-skinned, with the white specks and crescents of a Rubaiyan that made them look like a Cosmonite night sky with stars and moons. A Fire Godblood, most likely, as Flamboil was the only Rubaiyan in the

3. One of the 88 sapienti species. They resemble foxes.

Decatheon. Su's sister. I supposed Su's brown skin came from a mixture of his parents. He was lighter than Flamboil and lacked her celestial marks, but darker than Sparkato.

"Su Scrimshander," the older woman said. "Remember me?"

"How could I forget?" he said in an acerbic voice. "Are you going to make me join the Godblood Brigade before you free my family?"

"What sort of monsters do you take us for?" she replied in an equally hostile tone. "We're here to see justice done, nothing more and nothing less. I came here so I could receive you for your interrogation."

"I see. I thought Lungidus would have the honor." Su gave Captain Pavo a sarcastic glance. "Well, take me away, Commander."

I expected her to turn on her heels and walk away with Su following behind, but she paused to look at me. "Amiere Lasteran, yes? I am Freya Rubaiya, Commander of the Godblood Brigade. I apologize for having to take your husband away. I will return him to you shortly. Interrogations involving spouses must be done separately."

I understood why. They didn't know we had a loving family. If I was in a situation like Miltico and Lavina had been, they would want us to confide in private if any abuse had occurred. I nodded my head to Commander Rubaiya, not knowing what else to say.

When she and Su had taken their leave, Lungidus put his hand on the young girl's shoulder.

"What are you doing here, Steffa? If you needed to tell me something, I would have preferred you tell me via telepathy. Or... are your legs...?"

The child wore a purple long-skirted dress with elaborate lace and frills. I could not see what was wrong with her legs to draw such concern.

"I had a scary prediction, Papa. But as long as I'm here..." She glanced at me, fear gleaming in her deep purple eyes.

Lungidus turned, his face in profile from my perspective. I could not see his eyebrows beneath his tousled hair and silky hat, but I had no doubt they were scrunched in anger. The man gave off an aura of murderous intent. I stepped back, unsure what I had ever done to provoke such ire. And although I stepped back, I knew he could drag me closer with telekinesis... or disintegrate me with a thought. What could I *possibly* do in the future, according to Steffa's precognition? Surely... surely I couldn't be punished for a crime I *might* commit?

"Papa, please!" Steffa tugged on his arm. "It's not what you're thinking! He would never harm a child. If... if something were to happen, I could stop him *because* he won't hurt me."

Lungidus's attitude changed so suddenly and completely that he was like a whole other person. His killing intent subsided, replaced instead with respect. How did I ever *feel* his intentions? Was that part of his hypnotic magic?

"You are, above all else, a father, Mr. Lasteran. As one father to another, I hope you'll take that as a compliment. Would you give me a moment to speak with my daughter?"

"Of course."

Lungidus crouched beside her and wrapped his tentacles around her shoulders, behind her neck, and woven through her hair. It looked odd to me, but perhaps this was how Phoenian parents comforted their children.

Steffa closed her eyes and mouthed words, but did not speak them aloud. She put her tentacle-fingers on Lungidus's cheeks and neck. Whatever they said through their shared mental space, it elicited a sigh from the father as he rose to his feet.

"Mr. Lasteran," Steffa said. "My father is about to ask you if you'd prefer to be interrogated by him or by a clearblood. It is a... a legal thing. I don't fully understand yet. I only know what my predictions tell me. You may choose either option, but if you agree to speak with my father, your trial will more likely go in your favor."

"I... see. Thank you, Your Luminance."

She smiled ever-so sweetly, only to wince in pain a moment later. She bent down to rub her right leg.

"That's enough magic today, Steffa," Lungidus said. "Tynan, carry your sister home, please." He removed his hat, revealing Tynan's hiding spot. The child had taken an insectoid form, clinging to their father's hair like a giant louse.

Tynan jumped off Lungidus's head and transformed mid-leap into a creature with massive, velvety arms. "As you command, Father. Steffa, let's go home. I'll make you some susi lomi[4] , just the way you showed me, then I'll give your legs a nice massage."

"Thanks, Tynan." She lifted her arms so they could gently pick her up. "Ooh, your arms are so soft! You're getting so good at transforming."

The monster-child giggled. "Yay, I'm so happy you think so!"

I had never seen Tynan so... cute. So genuinely childish. I hadn't realized they *could* be that way.

Lungidus once again stared at me with eyes that would have punctured holes in steel.

"Steffa already told you, but I am legally required to ask: Would you like a clearblood to interrogate you, or shall I? Whoever is chosen will be a licensed lawkeeper and barrister. They will not hurt you nor seek to use anything you say against you once you come before the judges."

"I'm fine with you," I replied. Mostly, I just wanted this done and over with. Getting someone new would have been a hassle.

---

4. A soup of a pork-like meat, noodles, and vegetables. Considered a comfort food by many in Monoceros.

"Very well. Please, enter my office. It's this one here."

He motioned to a nearby door, mahogany wood in a marble frame with fine crystal embellishments.

The idea of being interrogated by a Godblood made my stomach churl, but Steffa had said it would be for the best. Why I trusted Steffa, I could not say. She was the man's daughter, and for all I knew, he'd *told* her to say those things. But that was not the impression I had. Whether it was my intuition or Lungidus hypnotizing me into believing him and his daughter, I wanted to trust her prediction. I would do absolutely anything a precognitioner said if it meant improving my chances of returning to my normal life. What other hope did I have? What would resistance offer me? Even in a best-case scenario where the Godbloods didn't retaliate against me for going against them, I was still at the mercy of the clearblood judges. Obeying Lungidus and giving him the information he needed would at least keep him on my side.

Chapter Fifty-One: Smirk

Captain Pavo's office was as beautiful as I expected. Not extravagant or rich—Mind elementals weren't allowed such displays—but clean and respectable. His table was fine mahogany, and the ebonwood bookshelves were arranged neatly. The crystalight hanging above and slightly to his side was carved in the shape of a pavo-bird in flight. It was not one specific bird, in fact, its tail feathers had been painted in all three varieties. It was a fairly simple design, and didn't seem to have any masterful crafting to it, but it was larger than most pieces a merchant of light would ever be asked to do. Upon the Godblood's desk were papers, globes of the inhabited planets in the Pentagonal Dominion, and a small painting of himself with an Olivian woman who I presumed to be his wife.

"Have a seat, Mr. Lasteran." He motioned to one of three high-backed chairs. Elegant, with plush red cushions, he wanted his prisoners to feel a modicum of comfort. I took the chair with a piece cut out for my tail. The other two chairs were one with a thin back for winged folk and a full-back chair for people without wings or tails.

Lungidus crossed his tentacles on his desk and leaned forward. "I don't want to make this difficult. Please just answer my questions honestly and fully."

"Can't you read my mind?" I asked. "If it's not allowed, well, there's no one here to verify *how* you're getting information out of me."

"My telepathy isn't as strong as you think it is, unfortunately. I can only read the most surface-level thoughts—things you are consciously thinking about. I still have to ask you the right questions to summon forth the answers in your thoughts. Besides, there's value in seeing how *you* answer. The court doesn't only look for physical evidence—your personality and character will inform the judges' decision."

I gulped. To think my fate was in the hands of three strangers. May Sione have mercy.

"First, could you clarify a thought you had on the way here. Something about your wife possibly summoning Lord Vinoc to kill a woman you went on a date with once?"

"I barely remember the event. Seeing the Armillary Spire reminded me of her. That woman—Gods, I can't even remember her name—disappeared soon after.

I never assumed Liesle had anything to do with it."

Lungidus nodded. He crossed his fingers as his hands rested on his desk. "Thank you. I shall pursue that line of investigation with her later, in private. For now, tell me about the Lagodore-Yosoe girl you've been raising. Who are her biological parents?"

"Miltico Svelt and Lavina Demiu."

"Lavina was the woman Liesle Denwall killed?"

"I do not know that for truth, but that seems to be the case, Your Luminance."

"And Miltico? What happened to him?"

Memories of me bashing his head with the kiwi-batte came rushing into my skull. The reminiscence of his flesh left a phantom taste on my tongue. Was there any point in lying to Lungidus about that? The thoughts were right there on the surface for him to read.

"I... removed him." It wasn't a lie, but I couldn't bring myself to say 'kill.'

"Was Miltico Svelt a citizen of Aloutia?"

I shook my head. "He was born here, but after a decade in Cosmo, I believe he'd lost his citizenship status. He was trying to get it back, last I knew."

"So you 'removed' a person who was not an official Aloutian citizen?"

"I believe so, Your Luminance."

"What was your relationship with him like prior to his 'removal'?"

"Miltico was my friend a long, long time ago. But he started snorting crazy sugar and his personality flipped. After he hit my daughter, I..." I paused, thinking about the timeline of events. Miltico would have had sex with Liesle just before that instance. "I made him leave. When he came back with a daughter, and I saw that little girl was being abused, I had to do *something*."

He glanced at the picture of his wife for such a short instance of time, I believed he did not want me to notice.

"You like kids? In a fatherly sort of way, I mean. Not in a... well, I won't say it."

I opened my mouth to speak, but no words were adequate to express my love for my children. No, all children. The young, the innocent, the defenseless. I had killed to save Susana. My only sin was not killing Miltico sooner. I had grabbed as many baby boys in Ophidia as I could hold in my hands, and I was only distraught that I didn't have more hands.

"That answer will suffice," Lungidus said. "Sometimes being unable to speak is an answer all of its own. Perhaps that's why Steffa wanted me to ask you these questions, so I could hear your answers more eloquently than your tongue could provide."

"I'm not a smart man like you, Your Luminance. Or like any other Mind elementals. I don't know the fancy words you'd use to explain your emotions."

He turned his eyes again to the painting of himself with his wife, but this time—perhaps knowing I'd noticed and that he didn't have to hide his actions—he let his eyes stay upon it. Upon her. "It's not just you. Sometimes even

I don't have the right words." His eyes shot back to me with an intense glare studying my soul.

"How is Master Scrimshander with kids? I understand none of them are his, biologically."

"That's correct. He believed being a Godblood was a curse. He wanted to raise kids, to be around kids and play with them, but not to impart his curse upon them. I apologize if such words are offensive to Your Luminance. I'm only repeating what Su has said."

"No offense taken," he said. "It *is* a curse. He and I simply have different ways of dealing with it. He's good with kids, though? How did he fare at the hatching of the first child?"

Eruwan's hatching. I spoke the words as they came to mind. "Gods, I was a mess that day. I was still addicted to crazy sugar at the time, but holding Eruwan in my arms... I realized I had to clean myself up. I had made a promise to Liesle to be a good husband to her, and that meant being a good father to our children. Per custom, Liesle held Eruwan first. She handed her to me next and... Gods, I was afraid I was going to drop her. It felt like an eternity, but it was probably only a second or two before I handed her to Su. He was... so delighted. His face was sunshine for this baby girl who was his starlight. He held her in his two lower arms while petting her mane with his uppers."

Lungidus leaned on his fingers, elbow resting on his desk, grinning in his usual way. Though instead of seeing it as a manipulative smirk, I saw genuine joy—or maybe just sympathy—in his Pavo grin. His eyes opened wide and he sat up. "Oh! You just had a thought... when was Eruwan's hatching day?"

"Pozhar 23," I replied. "In the year 546."

His breath caught in his throat and for a moment, his fierce glare returned.

"Pozhar 23, 546?"

"Yes?" Dread bubbled up in my sternum.

"What a coincidence." His face went dour, marked by a stern frown. Lungidus looked at his wife's picture and made no effort to hide that he was thinking of her.

"What happened that day?" I asked.

"My first child *also* hatched that day."

"You do not seem happy about it."

A long, resigned sigh. "When I first held Longinus... my beautiful, smart, powerful daughter... I cried. I wept more tears than I thought my eyes could make. Isn't that ironic, Mr. Lasteran? I chided Master Scrimshander for his decision, yet while his face was sunshine as he looked upon his firstborn daughter, mine was a rainy, moonless night."

I studied his expression, trying to understand him. "What for? She was a healthy daughter, wasn't she?"

"Indeed she was, and now she's a trainee in the Godblood Brigade. My pride and joy. Which is why I cried for her. Mr. Lasteran, my children are all expected to join the brigade. They're expected to serve the Aloutian Empire, to kill Ophidians and demons if war comes. The day Longinus was born, her fate was sealed, and it was my fault. I brought her into this world to be a puppet, a child soldier, a toy for the Chancellor and Emperor."

"Yet you stayed in Monoceros and kept having kids?"

He closed his eyes and set his jaw. The determination on his face sent a chill down my spine. "I did, because I believed I could find a way to prevent a war from happening. I wanted to live a happy life with my wife and children. If I could just push the inevitable war a century away, my kids could live out their lives in peace. There'd be no need for them to become merchants of dance or soldiers."

"And... have you?" I expected the answer to be silence, if not a sorrowful 'no.'

"I *did*," he said. "But, look at us, going so far off topic! Perhaps you *should* have been interrogated by the clearblood. They would not have chatted you up and wasted so much time." He laughed cordially, but I was too perplexed to laugh with him. "Next question... Would you kill to save your own children?"

"What parent worth a damn wouldn't?"

"Would you *die* to save your children?"

"I'd die twenty thousand times if that was what it took! What about you? Have you ever even considered it? Or do you think your children are all so powerful that they'd never come into a situation that required you to sacrifice yourself to save them?"

"I *have* died to protect my children."

I sat back in the chair, eyes wide in shock. I couldn't imagine what he'd been through.

Lungidus steepled his tentacles and leaned into them. "I admit, I find it odd that you ask me questions, too. I'm supposed to be the interrogator here."

"If you didn't want to answer, you wouldn't."

"I'm accustomed to playing the Game of Eight Questions with merchants of knowledge. If I am asked a question, I feel obliged to answer."

"I won't ask any more if the mere act of asking offends Your Luminance."

"It's not offense, but I would like to finish soon. As you should, too, so I can return you to your spouses. Now, will you give me a detailed picture of what Susana's life with you has been like?" I did not miss the fact that he called her 'Susana.'

I told him everything I thought was relevant. Her name change. Her legal adoption, signed by Giorvi Onoretti. We took her to the Plant church when she was injured and got medicine for her. We found out how she can worship her Goddess. We encouraged her to eat more and become healthy. We encouraged our kids to play with her so she could socialize properly.

"So, here's my plan to get you the lightest sentence possible," Lungidus said. "You're only charged with kidnapping, not murder, so we gotta push *that*. We need to push the narrative that she's doing better with you. If the topic of murder *does* come up, our best argument will be that Miltico was not an Aloutian citizen. It's not illegal to kill someone if they aren't an Aloutian citizen. After all, Master Scrimshander killed a lot of snakes in Ophidia, didn't he? And we couldn't possibly care less about them. Of course, the fact that you committed murder at all—and admitted you would kill to protect your kids—is a trait that the judges will look at regardless of who the victim was. So although I think you'll be safe from accusations of illegal murder, it's not something you want to flaunt."

"I understand, Your Luminance." Did I, though? I couldn't help but fear he was trying to allude to something. Some political scheme in Monoceros that I was so far removed from that I could not being to guess what it was.

He must have read the uncertainty and dread in my thoughts. "There are people here who will try to push a murder charge onto you, Mr. Lasteran."

My sternum felt like a lead weight plummeting through pili-palas in my gut.

"One man in particular is out to ruin every soul in Steena Village, if he can." Lungidus's voice was a low, dangerous growl. He sounded more like a dog than a sapienti man. "Representative Hashma Boura."

I had never heard of him, and the name didn't fit any of the cultures or naming patterns of Aloutia I was familiar with. "Representative of where?"

"The Chthonic Family Estates of Iuria."

Iuria, home of the Iurion, a giant species of people who lived underground. Iurion never left their homeland, or so I'd heard. Even though all representatives lived in Monoceros, I had no doubt they allowed exceptions for certain species who were unable to make the trip or for whom accommodations would be too difficult.

"We make accommodations wherever necessary," Lungidus answered in response to my thoughts. "However, you are incorrect about Hashma Boura in particular. For about two hundred years, we have had the Iurion representative come to Monoceros for the duration of their term."

"Is he angry about the crystalights in our village?" I asked. Giorvi had said something about a legal battle between the merchants of light and Iuria.

"Yes," Lungidus replied, and did not elaborate. "Mr. Lasteran, please, if Representative Boura asks to speak with you, I highly recommend you *don't do it*."

Those last three words were punctuated with divine command. I almost believed he hypnotized me, but if he had, would I have been aware of it?

Lungidus cleared his throat. "Apologies for that. I have to ask this as a matter of course. Do you feel safe with your spouses? Please answer for both of them alone."

"Yes, I do. I am safe with Liesle. I am safe with Su."

"Has Master Scrimshander threatened you? Blackmailed you?"

"No, none of that."

Lungidus nodded. "When we interview the clearblood spouses of Godbloods, we must make sure there's nothing malign going on at home. I've read your mind and I see nothing to be alarmed about. Do you accept that?"

"Yes, Your Luminance."

"While we're holding you three for trial, we must keep you in jail. We can put you three together in a comfortable cell, if all three of you agree to it. Mys Liesle Denwall has already agreed to have you both. Would you like to be with them? Either one or both?"

"Both, please." I couldn't imagine a scenario where Su would decline. Not unless *he* was being blackmailed...

"Very well. Come with me. I'll take you to your cell."

The cell was a comfortable room ringed by a vine of glowlight lotuses that fed through tiny holes into the adjacent cells. An extra angel's lips[1] was placed with us when I joined Liesle. It was only Liesle here for now, sitting on the bed, leaning against the wall; I supposed Su's interrogation was still going on.

The bed was large enough for me and her, but it would be a tight fit to include Su. A bookshelf lined one wall, full of either harmless fiction, nonfiction, or religious texts. Nothing I had any interest in. Liesle had a book beside her on the bed, though she wasn't much of a reader. She was probably just so bored that it was better than doing nothing.

A table in the center of the room held the remnants of her meal—the bone from an aurochs steak, a few stray grains of rice, and a red sauce I didn't recognize. Quite a nice meal. Unlike the Ophidians and demons who felt prisoners deserved nothing but mud and sludge, Aloutian jails and prisons were nice. They weren't meant to make us uncomfortable or agonized. We weren't convicted criminals yet, anyway, so to make us suffer would go against the laws of Lucognidus.

After Lungidus left us alone, Liesle came up to me and gave me the biggest, tightest hug of my life. She was so strong and emotional, she lifted me off the ground.

"Gods, Amiere! I've needed you these last few days!"

I couldn't speak until she set me down again. "I'm here now, Lisi. Everything is alright. Everything will be alright."

"Really? Where are the kids?"

---

1. A flower that exchanges carbon dioxide with oxygen at the same rate as a person who breathes into it. Permits people to breathe in enclosed spaces or with poor ventilation.

"Home. Safe."

"All of them?" I'd never heard her voice tinted by so much fear.

"All of them."

She fell into me again, crying on my shoulder, her strong arms clutching around me so tight I couldn't move my own arms.

"Fionn had a... troubling moment," I said. "We're going to have to work with him. Talk to him. I don't know, Liesle. I'm scared for him. But he's *home*."

"We'll do whatever we need to do," she said. "He'll listen to me. He's always liked me the most out of us three. I can't say I understand why. Gods, Cohaku hates me. I wonder if the other kids also hate me."

"You've been an excellent mother!" I protested. "We did the best we could with the knowledge we had. It wasn't like anyone taught us how to be parents. My mother was all alone, and your parents weren't great either. We've had to learn on our own."

She wiped tears from her eyes. "I thought Fionn, Turquoise, and Susana were gone forever. I summoned Vinoc to kill Lavina and I would do it again. I have no regrets! I—" She stopped suddenly and stepped back. "No, you were tortured by Vinoc, weren't you? Gods, I... I had no choice."

I remembered those dreams so vividly. They would not leave my head any time soon, but they were hardly any worse than the intrusive thoughts I'd already given myself. They couldn't hurt me any more than I'd already hurt myself in my wild imaginings of Tawny suffering.

"I can't blame you for what you did," I replied. "I would torture myself a thousand times to rescue our children."

Liesle sniffed. "I knew you'd understand."

"I was just... surprised it was me. Surprised you'd summoned Vinoc twice already."

She stared downward, eyes blank, then went back to the bed and sat down. "I never planned to summon him again. I never thought I'd be pushed to the edge of what I'd tolerate from other people. I thought we'd live the rest of our lives in peace and tranquility there in Steena Village."

"I did, too." I sat beside her and put a hand on her leg. "I thought that on Vinoc's third summoning, he made the summoner choose their favorite person to be tortured as payment."

"That's true."

"Why was it me, then? I heard he won't accept child sacrifices, but why me over Su?"

Liesle chuckled. "Amiere... I love Su. I love him so much it *hurts* being away from him even now, but you will always be the one I yearn for most."

My cheeks burned hearing such words. I couldn't imagine loving me over Su. Su was... everything. Sexy, smart, dependable, capable, mentally stable. I was a mess, my mind was failing me with how much it made me think of things I didn't want to think of, and my body couldn't satisfy Liesle on its own. Why would she ever pick me over Su?

"Or did you pick me because you feared that if Su had a nightmare, he might use his elemental powers in his sleep? And that might have burnt down all of Chernagora?"

Liesle shook her head. "I thought about that, but... I don't know if it's possible to lie to Vinoc, anyway. He knows when summoners give him false payment. Had I told him I loved some random person from the village most, it's not like he would have taken my word for it. He can see into our souls and minds. Even though he *asked* me who I loved the most, it was a formality. He already knew. I had no choice but to speak truthfully."

My sternum felt heavy again. When Su was reunited with us, he might have similar questions for Liesle. If he knew how Vinoc chose his victim—and I had every reason to believe Su knew all the details, having lived with a Demon King for ten years—he might be aware that Liesle loved me more than him.

Gods, I didn't want to be part of that conversation. The trepidation tore my soul apart.

"Can I ask you about the first two times you summoned Vinoc? I know about Tico and why you chose to kill him. But who was the other one?"

Liesle exhaled, and with it, part of her soul left her body. She had no more secrets to hide from me. "You probably don't remember her. It was a girl we went to art school with. You went on a date with her one time."

"Were you jealous?"

I thought she would glare at me, accuse me of being clingy, of making assumptions. But she sat there, broken and dejected, accepting her new reality. "I suppose I was. She only went on a date with you because she wanted to annoy me. We had been rivals since the first week of school."

"You didn't kill her *just* because she went on a date with me, did you?"

"Mo Ami, if I killed people for that reason alone, I would have killed *Su* long ago. I'm not monogamous and never have been. If that woman had been decent from the beginning, I might have been open to dating her, too. But she was a snob who disliked me. She believed Wynnles were too crude and barbaric by nature to be artists. I doubt she liked you, either. She only dated you to try and tear you away from me. Su loved us both. And I'd be lying if I said his Godblood powers weren't also a contributing factor to why I initially gave him a chance. I knew if trouble ever came to our little village, he would protect us."

I grimaced, and yet part of me felt honored that Liesle had desired me with such passion that she summoned Vinoc to bring me back to her. Gods, what an amazing wife.

"I suppose you saw my other paintings," she said after a moment.

"I did." I wouldn't mention the naked art. If Liesle had any shame regarding it, I wanted to give her the chance to bring that topic up. I didn't not think she was ashamed of drawing us naked, but rather painting us without our consent.

I put my arm over her shoulder. "I saw the beautiful painting you had started of Tawny. I hope you can finish it."

She leaned into my embrace. "Thank you. I doubt I will be allowed to finish it soon, but at least Tawny is finished. I just need to finish coloring Lucognidus. Hell, you could probably get another merchant of faces to complete him. After this, they'll probably send me to Hydra Island. If you want to put that painting on display above the memorial, I would love it. I'll finish it when I come back home, if you don't get someone else to do it. The rest of the art in the cave... you can burn it. Or do whatever you think is best, if the lawkeepers even give you that choice; they might confiscate it."

I was conflicted. On one hand, the art she'd made of me was flattering. On the other hand, where could I store it to make sure none of the kids would stumble upon it? Perhaps destroying it would be for the best.

Hours passed, and Su was not brought to us.

A guard came by with a meal for me, but when I asked about Su, all she said was that she wasn't allowed to speak to the accused.

More time passed. Liesle and I talked about everything we could think to talk about. We had sex—or attempted it, in any case. Wynnles rarely used their tongues on one another's genitals due to the rough, sandpaper-like texture of our tongues. Su was a master of using his tongue, and we would have had a much better time if he'd been here. I used my fingers on her while I kissed her neck, digging my nose through her mane in search of skin.

Despite our difficulties and the awkwardness of our situation, Liesle smiled at me. She kissed my cheek, and all was better in the world.

Another hour passed with no sign of my husband. Why the hell hadn't Su been put with us? Surely he hadn't asked to be kept in a different cell...

Lying next to Liesle, I asked her what she thought. "Do you think the God-blood commander convinced him to sleep away from us?"

"I don't know," she said. "Maybe he isn't ready to face me for what I've done."

"I suppose he's had enough confrontation for one day."

A knock came at the door, a warning that the guard was about to come in. Lawkeepers and guards were polite; they knocked before entering a cell, in case the accused were engaging in private or amorous activities.

The guard permitted a messenger to enter: an Isopteran man. Big, strong, muscular, with a hard outer shell, and a solid three feet taller than me. This was not someone who'd be easily subdued by someone who disliked his message.

"Mr. Lasteran?" the Isopteran said. "A message for you, drook. A man is requesting to speak with you regarding a legal matter. If you agree, I can escort you to him."

Captain Pavo's warning repeated in my head. Representative Hashma Boura wanted to talk to me about... something. An issue related to the crystalights in

Steena Village. Nothing that had to do with murder of kidnapping. I had no reason to speak to him, and for some reason, Lungidus was quite insistent that I refuse.

The messenger continued. "The man is a Mr. Giorvi Onoretti. He says you know him well. Shall I escort you to him?"

I blinked, surprised. I had so prepared myself to refuse Hashma Boura that to hear it was Giorvi instead caught me off-guard. I had to recalibrate my mind to what I should expect.

Giorvi had told me before that he would defend me in court for Miltico's murder. Was he putting his promise into action? With any luck, the topic of Miltico's death would never even be brought up during the trial.

"Yes, take me to him, please."

The Isopteran motioned to the guard and beckoned me to follow him out.

Chapter Fifty-Two: Hashma Boura

I shouldn't have been surprised that Giorvi had his own office here in the Monoceros lawkeeper's hall. I already knew his job involved legal affairs. The contracts he drafted were made with full knowledge of Aloutia's laws and the merchants of light's resources. He was also available to all merchants of light who requested help with taxes. And yet I was surprised, because I had assumed all the offices here were solely for use by Godbloods or judges.

What surprised me even more was who he had with him. In addition to his bodyguard, Oboro, he had his daughter. Little Beatrice sat on a chair near a globe, spinning it and stopping it suddenly with her finger.

The room had many of the same objects as Captain Pavo's office had: thick legal tomes lining the walls, globes, stacks of paper and pens, and a few chairs for various species. But where the Godblood had a single pavo crystalight to illuminate His Luminance, Giorvi's was practically a storeroom for crystalights. Perhaps it *was* storage. I'd heard that crystalights were kept in odd places to prevent theft, and what better place than the middle of a well-guarded facility full of Godbloods? They were mostly raw, covered in drapes so as not to blind the inhabitants. One crystal was massive—long and thin, with a tapered point like a tooth. It was sharp on one side, though... almost like a rough, oversized sword.

"Take a seat, Mr. Lasteran," Giorvi said as he waved toward the chair with a slot for my tail.

"Thank you for being here," I said. "I owe you a lot right now. If not for you, Oboro would still be in Ophidia. And if not for Oboro..."

The Sasorin boy blushed.

"I'm glad he was there, too. Now, allow me to help you with this trial. Let me be your defender-barrister, Amiere."

I put my hands on his desk and breathed a heavy sigh of relief. "I was hoping you'd offer. I don't know my way around a courtroom. I don't know what to say to the judges."

"You aren't expected to. Defenders are hired to speak on behalf of their clients. In fact, it might be preferable if you let me speak, since you might..." He hesitated, scratching his beard. "You might say things that would bring other crimes to light. You don't want that to happen."

"Captain Pavo told me to stay quiet about Miltico."

"Yes, that's good advice. If you must say anything about him, only talk about his treatment of Susana. Don't even bring up that he disappeared. The judges know he disappeared—make no mistake about that—but they don't need to be reminded. It might lead to them asking questions we don't want to answer."

"Understood."

"And whatever you do, don't mention anything about the crystalight mine or your daughter's death. I know it's hard, Amiere. I know your emotions regarding Tawny were a contributing factor to why you felt the need to save Susana, but that's a separate issue. Again, you don't want the judges thinking about that or asking questions. You want them to think that you rescued Susana from an abusive household purely out of altruism—not because you're a grieving father, not because you had a grudge against Miltico, and not because anyone bribed you with crystalights."

I arched a brow. "That last thing never happened anyway."

"Indeed, but the judges might think it did. We don't want them to wonder about it."

"They could force me into doing Neri's Ritual, couldn't they?" I asked.

"They could... but Demigoddess Neri is a busy woman, and doesn't often agree to be present unless the ritual is scheduled well in advance."

In the ensuing silence, Beatrice's finger hit the globe with an audible *thunk*. It drew my attention to her.

"Why is she here, anyway?" I asked, curious about the girl's presence.

Giorvi steepled his fingers and leaned forward. "Ironic you should ask, given I just mentioned Neri's Ritual... I am scheduled to perform it tomorrow evening and my opponent requested her presence."

"Odd," I whispered. "Why would..."

"I'd rather not talk about it, Amiere." Giorvi's voice was sharp and absolute. "It has nothing to do with your trial. It is a personal matter, and one which has annoyed me for a long time."

I sunk back into the chair. "Sorry. I didn't mean to intrude."

Now it was his turn to sigh in relief. "No, I should be the one apologizing to you. You were just curious. You didn't do or say anything wrong. I've just been tense. If you still want me as your defender, I just need you to sign this document. I will submit the paperwork."

He slid the paper toward me.

"Yes, of course," I replied. Taking a fancy ballpoint pen—quite a luxurious item—I signed my name on the line next to Giorvi's name.

"Excellent!" he said. "Now, allow me to instruct you more on what to say—and what not to say."

His lecture was about standard court etiquette, more than anything. He told me when I would have to answer, and when I could leave the answers to him. He told me about the nine court roles, which I only knew a bit about from learning about civics back when I was a schoolboy.

By his estimation, Su and I would probably get off with minimal punishment, but Liesle...

Summoning Lord Vinoc was a serious crime, regardless of who was killed by it. He didn't have high hopes that she would be allowed back home soon. But, if she behaved well on Hydra Island, and didn't so much as pick up a paintbrush, she might be back in five or so years. If that were to happen, the entire Last-Scrim-Den family would still be allowed to visit her.

Already assuming the worst, I thought about what we'd need to prepare for her absence. As much as I hated the idea of asking her for help, I might need Eruwan to watch her siblings at times. Turquoise would need elephant milk, but that was normal for our family. Liesle had struggled with breastfeeding with all our children. She'd attempted it with Eruwan and Fionn, though still used elephant milk as a supplement. When the twins were born, she gave up on the idea of breastfeeding entirely. Perhaps I *could* raise the kids alone...

Beatrice's finger jabbing the globe snapped me out of my reverie.

"Amiere?" Giorvi asked.

"Oh, sorry. I don't think I heard the last thing you said."

He frowned. "You are under a lot of stress right now. I wish I didn't have to give you all this bad news."

"It has to come from someone, and I'm happy you're here to help us. I don't think any other defender-barrister would understand my feelings as well as you do."

"That's true. Other people might also try to sabotage our case. Did... did Lungidus Pavo warn you about anyone in particular?"

"He said the Representative of Iuria might try to speak with me."

Giorvi gritted his teeth, just for a second, then calmed himself down again. "That Hashma Boura is out to ruin the merchants of light! I must agree with and reiterate Captain Pavo's warning. Do not listen to Boura. He despises us merchants, and if he can think of a way to turn you against us, he will. It'd be best to not even give him the time of day."

The more I was told not to speak to Hashma Boura... the more I wanted to. My curiosity had reached the tipping point. Besides, what could he possibly tell me? They were just words. He could do far less harm to me than Lungidus, an actual hypnotist, or Giorvi, who kept me employed. What's the worst that Iur could do to me? Of course, whether I spoke to him or not depended on *if* he requested an audience with me. The odds he knew about my presence here and cared enough to speak to me seemed as likely as the odds that he could convince me to betray my guild.

After my conversation with Giorvi was finished, two guards escorted me back to the cell with Liesle. Still no Su...

I shared what I'd learned with Liesle. No more than half an hour later, another knock came at the door, and the Isopteran messenger walked in again.

"Mr. Lasteran? Another message for you. Another man would like to speak with you. If you agree to go, I will escort you to him. The man is Hashma Boura, Representative of the Chthonic Family Estates of Iuria."

My anxiety peaked at the first mention of his name and had not abated by the time his full title was spoken.

"You should go," Liesle said. I had told her about Boura, and how both Lungidus and Giorvi had suggested I *don't* speak with him. She, too, was curious what he had to say. What information could he have that two powerful men didn't want me to know about it?

The Isopteran guard led me to an indoor courtyard, a small grove featuring carefully-manicured flowers, topiary, and rock sculptures. A small trickle of a waterfall fell around three walls of the room, entered a thin divot, and fed into an elegant pond of lagushkas on lily pads. Save for me and my escort, there was not a soul to be seen.

The Isopteran pointed to a stone bench with swirls along the surfaces. It reminded me too much of the motifs of Morigumo. "You may sit there. Your guards will be waiting outside the doors."

I sat on the bench and looked forward. A patch of petunias, dahlias, and chrysanthemums formed a semicircle around a mound of dirt, and in the center of the mound was a hole. No, more than that... a tunnel.

A petite creature popped out of that hole—a puppet, I supposed. It looked to be made of stone, with metal plates mimicking clothes, and crystalights for hair.

"You're Amiere Lasteran, I presume?" the puppet asked in a voice far too deep and menacing for something of its size. That voice came from the pit of darkness itself, echoing from a source deep beneath the ground.

"I am," I said. "You're... Hashma Boura?"

"Indeed. Have you spoken to an Iur before?"

"No, drook, I have not. Am I looking at a part of you?"

"That is the truth, drook. Were I to present my entire body to you, I would destroy half of Monoceros. You need not worry about such a thing, however—were the thought to cross my mind, every precognitioner Godblood in Aloutia would have alerted Emperor Ivan and I would be dead before I could move one incorrect inch."

I gulped. To have such a carefully-supervised existence... I would have gone mad.

"What is it you wish to ask me, Representative?"

"Please, just call me Boura. Long names and titles do not suit Iurion." The puppet had no expressions, no movements. It unnerved me that I could not tell Hashma Boura's feelings by examining his visage. I had nothing but his words and tone. "I asked you to come here because I want to know what you got out of your crime."

Kidnapping. Focus only on the kidnapping. "I rescued a little girl."

A low, terrifying rumble. Laughter? "Did you? 'Rescue'? That's funny. You are a murderer, Amiere Lasteran. Tell me to my face that you are not, and let the Gods judge you."

"I cannot speak of it," I said.

"Are you afraid? Afraid the Gods will strike you down for saying the name? Speak! Say the name of the one you murdered! Do you even know it?"

"I refuse."

"But you did commit murder? You don't deny that?"

"I... did. Yes. I am a murderer."

"What did Giorvi Onoretti offer you, to make it worthwhile? Did you get a good deal on the 'crystalights'? Or did you do it for the pleasure of it?"

My breath caught in my throat. "He had nothing to do with it. All he did was offer to defend me in court if I got caught."

"Then why did you do it? What was your motivation?"

"To save Susana! The man I killed was abusing her. I... I couldn't bear to watch it any longer."

Hashma Boura waited in silence. "Man?"

"Yes, 'man'! You want me to say his name, I will. Miltico Svelt! I was his friend once, long ago. But he turned against everything he once was. He was scum. He was an abusive father and husband, and if the Gods are just, they will throw him in Solitude for a thousand years."

"I do not know this Miltico Svelt. Amiere... did you not kill Rini Laan?"

I shook my head, slowly, unable to comprehend what he was even referring to. "I've never heard that name in my life."

"I see. Did Giorvi not mention her to you? Did he mention Ciu Laan?"

"No. I don't know them. Are they Iurion?"

"Indeed. Ciu Laan is my wife, and Rini is our daughter."

"And Rini... died?"

"Don't make it sound like an accident. Giorvi Onoretti schemed to have her murdered. I am certain of it! I will pry the truth out of him tomorrow during Neri's Ritual. I would request your presence there, if you wish to know the truth."

I blinked, flabbergasted. "How... how could anyone kill an Iur? Even the children of your species must be *massive*."

"They are," Hashma Boura said. "But we are not immortal, and we have one particular weakness. Have you not heard of the Yosoe-Iurion Wars?"

"No. You're at war with Yosoe?"

He let out a condescending chuckle. "Not anymore. It's ancient history, centuries before The Conquering. Ever since Lord Lucognidus conquered Aloutia, the Yosoe and Iurion have not fought. I am sad to hear you did not learn of those wars."

"I may have, back in my school days," I said. "Forgive me, Boura, it has been nearly twenty years since I was last in a classroom as a pupil. I have forgotten most things that don't affect my daily life."

"I understand. Let me tell you the result of the Yosoe-Iurion Wars: We, the Iurion, lost. Badly."

"How is that possible?"

"It takes only a tiny spark of electricity to course through our bodies and kill us. Even a child-Wynnle could kill us with the electricity on their tail. In the war, Yosoe killed us with the lightning from their horns."

My tail was exposed; the jailers hadn't commanded me to keep it covered. I became intimately self-aware that I might have been putting Hashma Boura in danger, and held my tail up to my chest. I covered the spark in my hands.

"The puppet is insulated," he replied. "If you were to swipe your tail against it, I would be fine. But just a few feet down... and yes, you could kill me."

My heart pounded like a drum against my rib cage. "But why? Why would anyone want you dead?"

His laugh was so powerful it made the ground rumble.

"Why, indeed? I could answer that for you, but I'd rather let you hear it from the mouth of Giorvi Onoretti himself. Let him answer for his sin. I will request your presence at Neri's Ritual tomorrow. Come, if you want to know the truth."

"Wait, answer one more question. I just... I don't fully comprehend the Iurion. Your daughter, Rini Laan... she died in Steena Village?"

"So it seems," Boura said.

The usual nightmare played in my head: the ground opening up and Tawny falling in. It wasn't a God who did that, it was Rini Laan!

"Why? I thought Iurion didn't leave Iuria. How did she cross half the planet to Steena Village? Why would she do such a thing?"

"I, too, seek these answers. One thing I believe: she missed me. You are correct in saying that no Iur leaves the Estates unless there's a very good reason. In the last several centuries, only I and the representatives who preceded me have left Iuria. But Rini Laan was a child. Small, young, and even if she knew the rules, that didn't mean she'd follow them. If she was, perhaps, experiencing a bout of sadness at her father's absence... perhaps she left in search of me. Perhaps she met someone who pointed her in a direction and told her to go. Perhaps the journey underneath Deep Sea hurt her. You know we breathe air, right? In Iuria, we have many vents to allow air into the tunnels. But in unfamiliar territory, she'd have to breach the surface on occasion to find air. But as she crossed The Corridor... Deep Sea would have kept her down, prevented her from breaking the ground beneath him. Imagine, if you can, crawling through darkness, unable to turn around, unable to go up, where you know air is. Bit by bit, you use up the air in your tunnel. It gets hotter, and stuffier. Your brain, losing air, begins to think irrationally. You claw and claw your way forward, hoping that eventually you will reach a soft spot where your breathing apparatus can poke through. Just when you're about to give up, you reach that spot. You're *so* desperate for air—so thirsty for that primeval need—that you thrust an air intake valve up regardless of who might be in danger. No, even if you knew there were people in danger, you're just a kid who can't breathe. You don't think of them. You think of yourself. Your lungs are the most important thing in the world at that moment. So you poke the surface... and before the air can even reach your lungs, you're killed by a jolt of electricity."

No.

Fuck.

Oh Gods, it couldn't be...

I put my hands on my head, trembling, crying, visualizing Tawny's death again and again.

And then, I remembered the last words Miltico ever said before I bashed his brains out. The words that triggered an anger so fierce that no law or God would stop me from exacting my vengeance.

Lions and other cats land on their feet when they fall from a great distance, but Tawny landed on her tail.

Such a minor, stupid statement. A detail hardly worth paying attention to. But how had he guessed Tawny had landed on her tail? How did he know Tawny fell on top of an Iur?

"Why do you grieve, Amiere Lasteran? Do you feel remorse for killing my daughter at last?"

"I didn't kill her!" I yelled. Softer, more melancholic, I added, "But... I know who did."

If Hashma Boura was shocked by that, he could not express it.

"Tell me the murderer's name."

No... I must not. What would he do to Tawny's memory? Would he spread rumors that my daughter was a cold-blooded killer? Would my whole family be painted with a reputation for death and destruction? I had to protect Tawny's reputation. I couldn't save her life, but I could save her honor.

"I refuse," I said. "You can't take her from me."

"You defend a murderer? You want to protect a baby-killer? You truly are a sick man, Amiere Lasteran. You and Giorvi Onoretti can both rot in Solitude. Leave this place, child-murderer!"

The metal-and-crystalight puppet sunk beneath the soil, and I could do nothing but weep until the guards came in to escort me back to my cell.

I was still crying when I joined Liesle—still no Su. She rubbed my back and comforted me. I became so sick with sorrow that I vomited in a bucket—thank the Gods the jailers had had the foresight to put that there.

"What did he say?" Liesle asked after helping me get cleaned up. The jailers were amenable to my needs. They gave me plenty of water and towels to wash myself, and replaced the bucket with a clean one.

Of course, she'd been curious, too.

"I can't... I can't bear to talk about it right now," I said. "One day, Lisi, I promise. But not right now. It's too soon. Too painful."

She sat behind me, massaging my back and shoulders with her strong, muscular arms and hands made for kneading.

"Hashma Boura asked me to be present at Neri's Ritual tomorrow. He's going to ask questions to Giorvi. I... I need to go. He asked Giorvi's daughter to be present, too. I fear I know what Boura's setting up Giorvi to say, but to do so in front of his daughter is cruel."

"I don't understand it," Liesle said. "There's too much we don't know. Go to the ritual tomorrow if the guards allow you. They should. Neri's Ritual is a serious matter. I believe both parties can request up to three witnesses."

"I wonder if Giorvi requested anyone," I mused.

"Maybe Oboro and Captain Pavo."

"Perhaps..."

We stayed awake a while longer. I kept thinking Su would be brought into our cell, but he never was. As I lay in bed next to Liesle, I wondered if it was because Su didn't want to sleep with us or if the other Godbloods had convinced him to stay away tonight.

Did Su know something? Gods, what if it wasn't Tawny who killed Rini Laan, but Su? He had electric powers... On the day of Tawny's death—Rini Laan's death—Su was away from the village. He'd gone to Seabells to trade bones. But what if he hadn't?

Su often did jobs for Giorvi. What if that was one such job? Like whatever happened to that demon in the cage? What did Rini Laan's death accomplish? Or that demon's?

Had Giorvi used her to uncover the crystalight mine? But how had he known of it in the first place? And why couldn't he have just asked Domovye miners to explore the area? Crystalights only appeared in Iuria. Iurion never left Iuria. It couldn't be a coincidence—Rini Laan must have brought them with her. Perhaps she used them to navigate dark, underground tunnels.

I had too many questions, and was too scared to ask for answers. He was my defender-barrister now, and if I said anything to make him suspect that I was suspicious of him, he might step down from the role. Worse, he might actively try to get me imprisoned on Hydra Island. No... the worst he could do was fire me from the merchants of light forever so I'd have no chance of continuing my career even after returning home.

In the past, whenever I found it difficult to sleep, I could ask Su for help. He could put me to sleep in an instant. Must have been electric powers. Nerve-control. Without him, I was left staring upward at the ceiling. At night, the guards pulled a lever that made curtains drape down in front of the glowlight lotuses.

It was dark enough to sleep, but enough light peeked out to illuminate our surroundings.

It was far too quiet here. Normally, Deep Sea's crashing fingers lulled me to sleep. Here, we were too far from the ocean to hear him.

If I got any sleep that night, it was restless, and full of tossing and turning. The Demigoddess of Sleep, Somniel, had not graced me with her power. Liesle stayed asleep through the night, despite my inability to hold still.

Well, most of my chaos was inside my mind, anyway. The tossing and turning of my mind could not wake her up. Thank the Gods *she* wasn't a telepath...

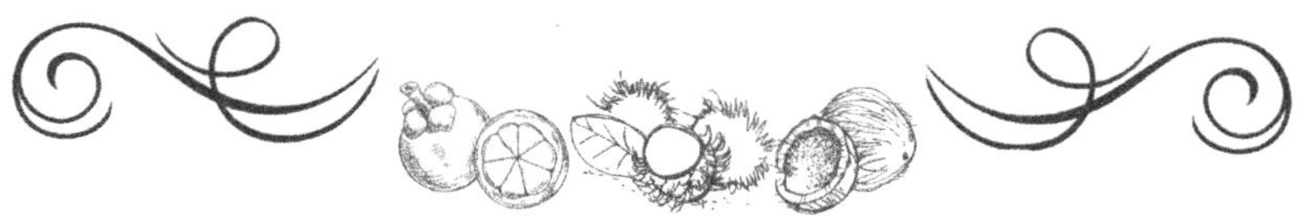

Codex Dominex: Aloutian Courts

The Aloutian legal and court systems are based on the philosophy of Sione, Demigod of Justice and Priest of the Purple Flame. Sione was a Viemeno who took control of the Cosmonite city of Nine Fires in the year 300. At the time, Nine Fires was plagued with crime, weak leaders, and corrupt lawkeepers. Sione reformed the city's legal code, removed people who were in the way, and established codes of ethics that were taught in mandatory classes to all Viemen children. In the year 312, St. L'tsok, the Hierophant of Lucognidus received detailed instructions from the God about how he was to invite Sione to Aloutia and implement his legal and court system into Aloutia. This reformation is called the Sionese Reformation. After Sione's death in 327 and the declaration that he was the Demigod of Justice, the Aloutian courts also implemented his iconography into courtroom aesthetics.

In a courtroom, there are nine 'souls' (other than the defendants, witnesses, and relevant experts) who must be present for a trial to occur. All nine traditionally wear a fox-tail ornament somewhere visible on their person. The ninth soul is Sione himself, symbolized by his statue being present in a courtroom, and his upright tail represents himself.

The other eight souls are:

- Mind judge dextra
- Mind judge sinistra
- Non-Mind judge centrum
- Court volkhv, always a volkhv of the God of the primary defendant (or a volkhv of a patron God)
- Bailiff, who in cases involving Godbloods is always a member of the Godblood Brigade
- Court stenographer, who may be accompanied by clerks, junior

clerks, and experts
• Advocate-barrister, who defends and argues on behalf of the defendant
• Prosecuting-barrister, who argues on behalf of the plaintiff or similar prosecuting entity

Aloutian courts do not use juries, though the concept exists from previous systems used before the Sionese Reformation. Two of the three judges must agree on a judgment for it to pass, and the non-Mind judge must be one of them. If the two Mind judges agree and the non-Mind judge disagrees, and no resolution can be made, they will take the trial to a higher court. For high-profile cases, if no judgment can be made, it will eventually be decided upon by Emperor Ivan.

In important cases where the truth must be ascertained, such as in murder, rape, or terrorism charges, it is common for either telepathic Godbloods or Neri's Ritual to be used. During the ritual, a person is asked eight questions. If they lie, the questioner will know it is a lie. A person cannot be forced to perform Neri's Ritual, however, and there are loopholes in answering which wise judges must consider. Neri's Ritual is a game of wordplay and trickery more often than not. Telepathic Godbloods will lend their services as they see fit, but because of their small number, they tend to reserve their powers for high-profile cases.

Aloutian courts are far more likely than any other court system in the Pentagonal Dominion to utilize character study in reaching judgments, though the flaws are well-known and attested. Some judges will refuse to hear character study-based testimony on principle, though this is rare. Community members who know the defendant will frequently be interviewed prior to any trial.

Aloutia is not fond of setting precedents quickly. Generally for a particular ruling to become precedent, it must happen hundreds of times. The Aloutians would rather take trials on a literal case-by-case basis than make policy based on the decision of one triad of judges.

Chapter Fifty-Three: Neri's Ritual

I had never expected to witness Neri's Ritual in my life. Sure, I'd heard about it in school and read accounts of the ritual in newspapers for famous cases, but never had I seen one in person. I never wanted to. The only time the Demigoddess of Truth was invoked was to pry the truth out of somebody.

The ritual took place in Hashma Boura's grove. A decently large statue of Lucognidus had been transferred to the spot by his tunnel. The God's amethyst eyes, set in an ebonwood face, stared forward impassively.

Giorvi stood to one side of the statue while Hashma Boura's puppet poked out of the hole on the other side. As Boura's requested witnesses, I sat next to Beatrice the Daughter on the stone bench near the Iur. We made for an odd pair—a little Yosoe girl and a big Wynnle man. Then again, did it look any stranger when I carried Susana in my arms?

Giorvi's witnesses were, as I had suspected, Oboro and Captain Pavo. They sat on a similar bench closer to him.

When I had first entered, Giorvi and Lungidus were both clearly disappointed to see me. I wouldn't have been invited had I not accepted Boura's request for an audience, which they'd both told me to decline. My mere presence was proof I'd disregarded their advice. Or disobeyed them. I wondered whether they'd considered their words a suggestion or an order.

A Mind volkhv in full pavo-feather regalia knelt before the statue of her God, reciting the words to summon the Demigoddess of Truth. Unlike demonic summonings, demis were not physically present when summoned. Their bodies would not materialize, though their souls were supposedly nearby.

There were a few other people present whom I did not recognize, nor did they deign to introduce themselves. Two in military uniforms, a few in formal attire. A Plecopteran stood near the wall with a tablet and pen—a stenographer.

"The two questioners will be this man, Buongiornovici Onoretti, and this man, Io-Hashma-na Boura-lis."

I had never heard the magic name of an Iur. Few societies included a magic surname. Usually, it only extended to the given name. Regardless, hearing a person's magic name always made me shiver. I *shouldn't* have that knowledge.

"Mr. Onoretti, Mr. Boura-lis, please display a pose of respect toward the God

Lucognidus, and touch the statue of His Infinite Wisdom."

Giorvi knelt, but kept his head up—Yosoe didn't bow their heads; to point their horns at someone was to challenge them—and put his hand on the statue's right foot. Boura lowered his puppet's head in a pose that vaguely resembled a bow, though it was almost comical to think of this gigantic man 'bowing' by slightly moving a body part that was smaller to him than my toenail was to me. He touched the statue's left foot with the crystalight portion of his puppet's head.

"We must ensure the demigoddess is present. You will each tell two truths and a single lie, in any order you wish to speak them. Tradition is to make the lie an obvious one, though the choice is yours. If the other person lies, you will feel a sensation in the part of your body touching the statue. Some have described it like an electric shock, but it will not hurt you, Mr. Boura-lis, nor will you be immune to it, Mr. Onoretti. If you've prepared your statements, will you begin, Mr. Onoretti?"

Giorvi clenched his hands into fists over Lucognidus's shoe. "My name is Buongiornovici Onoretti, I am fifty-three years old, and I am the Emperor of Aloutia."

I had heard tales that the lie about being the Emperor was one of the most common to use during Neri's Ritual, to the point of being a cliché.

"I felt the sensation," Hashma Boura said.

The volkhv nodded. "Your turn now, Mr. Boura-lis."

"My name is Io-Hashma-na Boura-lis, I am sixty-one years old, and I am a fungus farmer."

"I felt the sensation," Giorvi said.

"Very good. Mr. Onoretti, you have agreed to let Mr. Boura-lis ask a full eight questions without reciprocation. You *are* allowed eight questions of your own, if you choose to use them. Both of you, please word your questions carefully. If an answer is unsuitable, I will serve as adjudicator to decide if the answerer must provide additional details. Now, begin any time, Mr. Boura-lis. First question."

"Did you kill my daughter, Rini Laan?" he asked.

"I did not kill Rini Laan," Giorvi replied.

"Did you order Domovye to befriend her and instruct her to go toward Seabells?"

"I did not issue that order."

"Mud and sludge! Your name was on the paperwork!" Hashma Boura's rage shook the ground.

"I did not issue the order!" Giorvi said acerbically. "Am I lying? That question was rhetorical, Mys Volkhv. I did not mean for it to be one of my eight."

Boura waited for a moment, perhaps to consider what his next question would be.

"Did you sign paperwork authorizing a team of Domovye to speak to my daughter?"

"No, I did not."

A slight tremble from below... and a sob? Was the Iur crying? "Impossible... Impossible... I saw that paper! I compared the signature on it to other orders you've sent!"

Giorvi pressed his body against the statue of Lucognidus, if only for support as the ground shook. "I did not sign my name on the document you saw."

Fucking hell... it couldn't be...

I dared to look at the young girl sitting beside me. Beatrice's eyes were so wide, it was unreal. Her mouth hung open in shock. She knew as well as I did that she had signed her father's name. I wondered what the situation had been. Had Giorvi tricked her? Or had she signed the paper, knowing what was written on the document?

"Do you have a fourth question, Mr. Boura-lis?" the volkhv asked.

"Yes, one moment, I must collect my thoughts."

Beatrice's hands were clenched in fists on her knees, trembling. She turned her face down so I could not see her expression.

"The Guildmaster," Boura said in a tone that betrayed his desperation. "Was Thousand-Diamonds involved in the murder of my daughter?"

"He was not involved."

Not involved... but he might have *known* about it.

"You, Godblood. Did Captain Pavo... no, did *any* Godblood authorize the killing of my daughter?"

"No Godblood authorized the murder of your daughter," Giorvi answered, as only his response would be registered by the ritual.

"Then who? Who signed the order authorizing the Domovye to guide my daughter to her death?"

Giorvi hesitated, his lips shaking. "It wasn't me."

"Say 'I don't know'!" Boura shouted.

"I cannot."

"Then say their name. Volkhv, I must have a thorough answer."

"I did it," Lungidus said before the volkhv could intervene. "I'll take the blame for what happened."

"You were just cleared," Boura said. "I want the *truth*."

Lungidus crossed his arms. "Go on, Giorvi. Try it again. Say it was me."

"It was Captain Pavo," he said in a strained voice.

I wondered if it was a lie.

"I don't believe it," Boura said. "Is Neri still here? That doesn't count as one of my eight questions, I hope."

"No, it doesn't count," the volkhv said. "Mr. Onoretti, speak a lie so Mr. Boura-lis can be sure Neri is still here."

Giorvi looked straight into the Iur's puppet's eyes. "I am a Plant elemental."

The shiver of a lie must have flowed into the Iur. After a pause, he admitted he felt it.

"You have two more questions, Mr. Boura-lis," the volkhv said.

"Was Amiere Lasteran involved in the death of my daughter?" he asked.

Not expecting to be mentioned, my heart beat loud and hard.

"He was not involved."

"Mr. Boura-lis, be aware that your next question will be your eighth. This is all Neri has time for. Take care to ask a thoughtful and thorough question."

"I already know what I'm going to ask. *Who killed Rini Laan*?"

"You fool. You should have asked that first! The one who killed Rini Laan was killed by Rini Laan. There's no vengeance to be had. The murderer is dead. Since you've been scheming with Mr. Lasteran, you can ask *him* how Rini Laan died. Ask him about Tawny. He knows."

Giorvi stood up, took his hands off the statue, and stormed out. "I have nothing more to say."

I stared downward, unable to meet the eyes piercing into me. I didn't even know if anyone *was* watching me, but I felt the shame and terror of their eyes, nevertheless. Although Giorvi had told Hashma Boura to ask me what I knew, the Iur stayed quiet.

Lungidus came to stand over me. "Mr. Lasteran, you are not legally required to say anything. I would recommend you stay silent. I apologize for this treatment, but you are still accused of a crime, and we must return you to your cell now."

I stood up. Beatrice was still despondent, shaking on the bench.

"Did you sign the order?" I asked.

Beatrice sniffed. "I... remember. Most of the paper was covered with other papers. Papa said it was for practice."

Lungidus pushed me with telekinesis closer to the exit. "Mr. Lasteran, the thing you must understand about Neri's Ritual is that Neri determines what is true and what is not, but she is a demigoddess servant of my father, Lord Lucognidus. The ritual doesn't detect *the* truth. It detects Lucognidus's truth. A person can lie, if the Lord wishes that lie to be his truth. Lucognidus wants the truth to be that *I* signed the order, therefore, that is what the law will see as the truth."

"Why?" I asked. "Why does Lucognidus want the murder hidden?"

Lungidus cocked his head to the side. "Let's talk on the way to your cell. Our presence is only aggravating Representative Boura even more."

He must have read the Iur's mind, because I could see nothing in the puppet's unchanging expression. I followed the Godblood out of the grove.

"Will you please tell me what is going on?" I asked. "I understand that Tawny electrocuted Rini Laan when she fell into the abyss, which was created by Rini Laan breaching the surface for air. But what is all this about murder? About an order?"

"It's not my place to discuss the details of my father's plan," Lungidus said. "You know how Giorvi was able to say that no Godblood authorized him to kill Rini Laan? It's true because none of us Godbloods had any say in it; the authorization came from our God himself."

"It doesn't make sense! Why would he kill a little girl? Two! What the hell did he want Rini Laan's soul for? Why did Tawny have to suffer?"

"She didn't suffer," Lungidus said. "I don't know if this will comfort you, but Lord Lucognidus took Tawny's soul out of her body before she struck Rini Laan. Likewise, Rini Laan's soul was pulled away before she suffered a death of electrocution."

"You know that because... your father told you?"

"Correct. Well, I can't say that officially. I was raised to be the Hierophant, but when I declined the position, I also formally declared that I did not hear my father's voice anymore."

According to Spiritist dogma, each God had an Hierophant, and that individual was the only person who heard commands of their God. When the Hierophant spoke, it was with the voice of their God, and that voice was the embodiment of their authority. Anyone else who claimed to hear the 'voice of a God' was a fraud. At best, they were a harmless dreamer, at worst, a would-be cult leader. In the past, such crimes were heresy—or perhaps blasphemy, I didn't know the difference—and punishable by death. These days, we didn't jump to murder as punishment so quickly. Legally, Lungidus could not claim to hear his father's voice, since he was not the official Hierophant, but that didn't mean Lucognidus *didn't* speak to people.

"He seems to have told you a lot."

"I'm sensitive to the death of children, Amiere. You ought to know that—we're both fathers, trying to do what's best for our children. When he told me how two kids were killed as part of his plan, I was... distraught."

I took several steps in silence and contemplation. Not paying attention to where I was walking, I almost walked into Lungidus as he stopped dead in his tracks. With a shove of telekinesis, he pushed me into the marble wall. My arms were pinned to my sides.

My breath caught in my hyoid. Captain Pavo glowed with a violet aura, his disheveled hair swaying in a breeze that touched no one but him. His eyes were intense, sharper, and more purple than they had been before. He stretched a hand toward me. Tendrils of amethystine energy swirled around and emanated off the suction cups of his fingers.

"Amiere," he said in an ethereal, otherworldly voice. It sounded as though I were listening to him while my head was submerged underwater.

I blinked in surprise. "Wh-what is happening?"

"Come with me," he said in a tone that tried to be gentle.

He teleported us far away to a cold mountaintop. A layer of frost blanketed the rugged terrain. Below, in a valley that stretched out for miles, the jagged ground was strewn with chunks of upheaved rock and soil. A labyrinth of escarpments and cliffs marred the landscape far into the horizon. No greenery grew here—anything that took seed risked the dirt underneath erupting upward at any moment.

"Iuria," he said. "Where this tragedy started. Amiere, if I told you that the one speaking to you is not Lungidus, would you believe me?"

I shivered. "I... I have no choice, do I? Lungidus said he never teleported people other than himself. Unless he was lying about that, I have to assume you're..." I couldn't say it. I dared not. And if I believed it, was I committing heresy? That I was not speaking to Lungidus, but rather his father Lucognidus, was obvious yet morally wrong to believe.

"Look down there." Lungidus—or the God possessing Lungidus—pointed a tentacle toward a clearing in the escarpments. "Do you know who those are?"

They were so far away, I could barely make out the figures. One was an Iur puppet poking out of the ground, the other was a biped, though I could not determine their height. Probably someone from one of the many species who were Su-sized.

"Correct," he said before I'd said a word. True, Lungidus was a telepath, but that was a far stronger act of telepathy. My assessment had been subconscious. The Godblood could only read the most conscious thoughts; the God could probably have dug up memories I hadn't thought about in decades. "The Iur is Ciu Laan, wife of Hashma Boura and mother of Rini Laan. The smaller person is a Takyufon merchant of mail, come to deliver a letter from Hashma Boura. She knows, now, where Rini Laan was killed."

Ciu Laan... A grieving mother. I wondered how she had coped with her daughter's death. How did Iurion live? Did she have a bed? Had she curled away in the dark and cried, as Liesle had for a week after Tawny's death?

"I wanted you to know about her," the God said through his son's mouth. "She will be coming for you soon. Her sorrow is indomitable. Her rage can tear mountains asunder. I have come to offer you a trade, Amiere Lasteran. The only trade that can save you from her wrath."

My throat was so dry, I couldn't gulp no matter how hard I tried. "Yes, Lord?"

"You are a merchant of light, so I wish to trade light with you. The light of your fifth-born in exchange for the light of Lungidus's fifth-born."

"You... already took the light of my fifth-born." Tawny was at his mercy in Spiritua now.

"Not in the way I'd like to have her. Give her to me, and I will give you Tynan."

"How do you 'want' Tawny?" I wished I could have stopped my thoughts. I could only imagine 'wanting' someone in a sexual way, and I did not want to think of my daughter in that situation, nor did I want to think of Lucognidus doing that to her. I knew he would not—it wasn't his nature. Sparkato was the pervert-God, not him! But my mind could not be controlled.

"Be at peace, Amiere." With those words, a soothing calm set over my mind. Those troubling thoughts evaporated like the snow nearest my tail. "I have a plan for Tawny. I wish to make her shine like starlight. But I'd prefer to have her father's blessing before I begin."

The irony of a God asking *me* for a blessing. I had no idea what 'shining like starlight' meant, precisely, other than the obvious tie to the idiom. Did it mean she would be happy? *Yes, Lord, please do that.* "But what about Tynan? What do you mean you're giving them to me? Shouldn't Lungidus have a say in the matter?"

"It has been settled already. You may ask Lungidus about it later. There are complications in their relationship that you cannot grasp yet. You will soon, if you accept this proposal."

"I accept," I said. "If only for Tawny. Please, give her a good life. Or death. However you say it in Spiritua. Let her shine like starlight."

Lungidus nodded his head. "The exchange of light is done. Thank you, merchant. I will take you back to your wife now, and give Lungidus back his body."

The God made my vision blur, then go completely dark. I closed my eyes instinctively, and when I awoke again, I was sitting on the bed in jail.

Liesle sat at the table, eating a thick cotza steak. She licked the juices off her fingers. "Mmm. Oh, are you finally awake? Come eat."

I shuddered, regaining my composure. "What happened? How long have I been here?"

"An hour or so, perhaps?" she said. "Captain Pavo said he had to do something to your mind, but that you'd be fine. I'm glad to see he wasn't lying."

"Was that real? I just... the last several minutes to *me* have been bizarre."

Liesle shrugged. "You've just been sitting there for the last hour, Mo Ami."

I laid down on the bed and put my hand over my head. "I don't know what's happening in my life anymore."

"Neither do I, but I know this steak is delicious. Come share it with me."

I joined her at the table. She ripped her steak in half—it was already a much larger size than any Wynnle would have needed—and put one half closer to me. Although the aroma of juicy, well-peppered steak made me salivate, I couldn't bring myself to eat.

"Captain Pavo said Tynan would be living with you from now on, after the trial."

I gulped. That deal I made with Lucognidus made no sense to me, but who was I to deny a God whatever he wanted?

"That implies to me that you won't go to jail," she continued. "He must know for sure. Maybe he's already convinced the judges. It seems silly for him to hoist a Godblood onto you if you're going to be stuck on Hydra Island."

"I... Maybe you're right."

"Eat, Amiere!" she poked my half of the steak with her claw, nudging it closer to me. "This might be the last time we eat together for a long time. I'm sure they're going to send me to Hydra Island."

Hearing those cruel words—that this would be the last time we ate together—broke the last ounce of strength I'd had. I covered my face in my hands and cried.

"Oh, we'll be back together soon enough," Liesle said, so nonchalant that she spoke while chewing her steak. "What's five or ten or even twenty years compared to the eternal time we'll spend in Spiritua?"

Logically, I knew she was right, but *emotionally*... Gods, I wanted her *now*! I could not articulate a reply. The only sounds to escape my mouth were pathetic sobs.

Eyes closed, I only heard her chair scrape across the floor as she stood and came around to hug me.

"Mo Ami..." She held me close to her chest and petted my mane. "Please don't have any regrets about the choices we made. We saved our children. We would do it all over again."

"I don't regret it. I just wish we weren't punished for it."

Liesle kissed the top of my head and held me long, long after I stopped crying.

Chapter Fifty-Four: The Trial

My wife stood in the center of our trio, Su to her right and me to her left. Since she was the primary defendant amongst the accused, her part of the trial took precedence.

We three stood insignificant next to the trio behind the bench—the judges. In Aloutian courts, trials were presided over by three judges: two were always Mind elementals and the third was always any other elemental. A verdict could only be obtained if two out of the three judges agreed, and one of the agreeing judges had to be the non-Mind elemental. However, if the two Mind elementals thought their partner was corrupt, bribed, or otherwise incapable, they could move to have them replaced. Not that such a scenario was likely to happen here—the judge sitting in the middle was an elderly, bespectacled Neuropteran man who embodied calm and serenity. To his side, the Mind elemental judges were a Macadalian woman wearing a tall mitre over her stacked heads, and an Ulese woman with feather pins in her long eyebrows.

They sat in front of a marble statue of Sione, Demigod of Justice, whose nine tails spread out like a fan.

The court volkhv had recited a prayer to the demigod before the trial began. Aside from us accused, there were nine other people in the room, the appropriate number for an official Aloutian trial. Each of the nine carried a pendant of a fox tail, a symbol that they were in the service of Sione for the duration of the trial. Well, technically there were only eight other people; Sione himself was considered to be 'here' in essence, if not in body, and his upright tail on his statue symbolized his role.

The Neuropteran and Ulese judges wore theirs as a necklace while the Macadalian kept hers on her mitre. The volkhv—a Lightning volkhv, since we three accused were all of that element—wore his on a strand around his wrist between two spiked metal bracelets. The bailiff, Captain Pavo, wore his around his neck next to his marriage-tie. The court stenographer, a Plecopteran, wore hers on a headdress while her hands moved so fast as to be a blur. The defender-barrister, Giorvi, wore his as a horn ornament. The prosecuting-barrister, a Phoenian, wore theirs as a long earring.

During the prayer, the court volkhv asked Sione to bless the judges with guidance to come to a verdict that was 'morally and socially right.' In the pre-Conquering era, absolute law was more important than doing what was right. A person who committed a murder would be hanged no matter what, regardless of their reasoning. We lived in an ethical society now—any crime could be forgiven if the accused was found to have had a decent reason for committing it.

For the most part, we did not need to speak. Giorvi knew our case well enough and presented it to the court with our best interests in mind. The few times one of us had to speak for ourselves, it was usually Liesle explaining what went through her mind when she decided to paint the Demigoddess Vinoc.

Her fear sent chills down my spine, and yet it was all too familiar because it was what I had felt, too, upon hearing my children were missing.

"I knew Lavina was in the village. I had seen her hiding behind trees or bushes. I'd suspected she was sneaking around, trying to get her daughter back. So when Fionn vanished with Turquoise and Susana, I knew without a doubt that she was to blame."

The Neuropteran judge spoke in a slow, deliberate voice. "And did you, Mys Denwall, make any attempt to find your children before resorting to demon summoning?"

"Yes, Your Justice," she replied. "I searched the jungle for about an hour. I flew above the canopy, shouting Fionn's name and looking for the spark of his tail."

"Did you involve any of the other villagers in the search?" the Macadalian asked. Her accent was so thick I could barely understand her. That was *my* problem, though—her accent was proper Monocerotis English, which I hadn't heard since my days in art school. I was so accustomed to the rural Seabells dialect that formal language eluded me.

"I did not, Your Justice."

They waited for Liesle to explain her reasoning, so when she did not, the Macadalian prodded her further.

"I... I didn't want the other villagers finding Lavina or... her husband."

That was a very careful way of saying she didn't want them to find out Miltico was dead. Lucky for me the judges couldn't read minds—and for whatever reason, Lungidus wasn't offering any knowledge he may have pried out of our skulls.

"Why didn't you want anyone finding them?" the prosecuting-barrister asked.

"I was worried they would run further into the jungle—into danger—if they knew the whole village was searching for them."

"Understood." The Neuropteran pushed his spectacles up the bridge of his nose. "So after an hour of futile searching, you went to your cave where you hid painting supplies?"

"Yes, Your Justice."

"Knowing full well that this was your third summoning, and therefore that the Demon Lord Vinoc would torture an innocent?"

"Yes, I knew. I knew he would torture either Amiere or Su, but regardless of his choice, I knew my spouses would endure it. They would endure any torture to save their children."

The Ulese judge had a sharp, domineering voice. She rarely spoke compared to the other two, but when she did, it was a voice of authority and power. "Did it save your children, Mys Denwall? Or did you still need your spouses to go to Ophidia to rescue them?"

Liesle licked her lips. "Obviously, I could not have known where they were. I believed them to be traveling with Lavina and some merchants of flesh at the time. I asked Lord Vinoc to tell me if he saw my kids when he went to wherever Lavina was. He only found Susana, and he told me he kept her safe until... Well, he said another Demon Lord was coming to rescue her. I don't know what that was about."

The two Mind elemental judges tried to subtly glance at Lungidus, but I caught their wandering eyes. I didn't know what Liesle was referring to or who the other Demon Lord was.

"How did you know the boys were captured by merchants of flesh?" the prosecutor asked. "Or was that an assumption?"

"It was an assumption. I had reason to believe Lavina had worked with merchants of flesh in the past. No reason to doubt she had stopped."

My eyebrows twitched. *I* had never had that assumption. What made Liesle think that? I wanted to ask, but knew it was better to stay quiet and avoid accidentally incriminating her. Well, doing worse damage, in any case. Not that my silence mattered; the prosecutor asked my question next.

"What made you think she had worked with the merchants of flesh?"

"May I take this question?" Giorvi interrupted. "I have spoken to the clients at length and I believe I understand the situation. During the time Mys Denwall and Master Scrimshander cared for Susana, they asked her careful questions about her life with her biological parents. Susana recalled her mother being pregnant numerous times and even laying eggs. She had even mentioned a few times thinking she had siblings, but she would never see them again. In some cases, she would be fed meat a few days later. Considering the fecundity of Lagodores and the family's dire financial situation on Cosmo, we believe Lavina may have produced children constantly, selling her sons to Ophidia and cannibalizing her daughters."

"Isn't that just some speciesist garbage against Lagodores?" the Neuropteran judge asked. "I can't accept that as evidence."

The court stenographer—typically also a very well-educated individual who served to dispense information as needed—supplied an answer. "It is indeed a negative stereotype of Lagodores who live outside of society, but there *have* been historical cases of it happening. Last year, there were three cases in Aloutia involving a Lagodore cannibalizing their young while under extreme duress. In all three cases, the Lagodore committed the crime outside of Aloutia, but their cannibalism was used in a character study to examine a different crime committed in Aloutia."

"I see," he said. "Continue, Mr. Onoretti. So you believe Mys Lavina Demiu was a... a breeding factory, if I may be so crude?"

"Yes, Your Justice."

"Why would Susana be spared the same fate?"

"I can only speculate," Giorvi said as he paced in front of the judges' desk. The tapping of his hooves resonated through the chamber and mimicked my heartbeat. "As a parent, I suspect they wanted at least one offspring to care for. To put their hopes and dreams of the future on. Or perhaps to abuse. When things went poorly for the parents, they may have abused her to relieve their own frustrations."

The judges silently mulled over this theory.

The Neuropteran grimaced and turned his attention back to Liesle. "Mys Denwall, tell us what went through your mind—your soul—as you painted Lady Vinoc, knowing you were about to kill a woman and torture one of your spouses."

Gods, how could anyone answer a question like that? I felt for Liesle. My poor wife... She answered to the best of her ability.

"I felt... terror. Fear. Not from Vinoc, but the fear that I'd never see my children again. Like I said before, I had no doubts either of my spouses could handle the torture, and would have encouraged it if it meant rescuing our children. While the thought *did* cross my mind that I was about to submit them to torture, I never faltered."

The Macadalian asked, "Did you consider that a precognitioner would foresee the Demon Lord's summoning and that you would be arrested?"

Liesle nodded. "Yes, I believed that was a possibility. Even if it was a surety, I would have done what was needed to save my children."

"Valiant," the Ulese said. "Thank you, Mys Denwall. Now, Mr. Onoretti, tell us about what transpired on the day of..."

The trial went on, with Giorvi telling her what Su and I had shared with him regarding our journey to Ophidia to rescue Fionn and Turquoise.

I *should* have paid attention, but I couldn't. It was so long and drawn out, and it sounded like Giorvi was handling it well. Better than I could have. And so my mind wandered... to thoughts about the strange deal I had possibly made with a God. Part of me wondered if I had dreamed that whole scenario up. What had I done in trading Tawny for Tynan? Was I going to raise Tynan now? Or one of the two Tynans? I still didn't understand how the 'two bodies' thing worked. That was partially why I wasn't concerned that I was somehow taking Lungidus's child away from him. Perhaps one body would stay at home with their family while the other body was with me?

Lungidus glared at me with eyes daring me to keep that thought going.

The prosecuting-barrister brought the topic to the mystery of Lavina's missing husband. Giorvi handled the questions with grace—officially, Miltico had gone missing and we knew nothing else. Some Death Godbloods had queried shinigami—somehow, some could speak to ghosts—and asked if they had sawdusted Miltico's body, but they had reported nothing. Summoning Deep Sea to ask if he'd turned a sapient Yosoe into marine snow had also borne negative results.

"It's simply unbelievable that he's missing," the prosecutor said. "Our clairvoyants would have found him by now if he were on any of the mortal planes. Plus it's odd that you got Susana away from him without a fight. Also, how has Lavina been seen so many times, but not him?"

We stayed silent. We would not incriminate ourselves. Lungidus read our minds, knew the truth, and also kept his mouth shut.

"It's *possible* for a Wynnle to kill and eat a Yosoe, which would hide the body forever after it's sufficiently destroyed by gastrobacter." The Phoenian prosecutor rubbed their chin with a tentacle. "Unless Master Scrimshander confesses to killing Miltico, we may have to pursue the line of thought that one of you two Wynnles did it."

The underlying threat was clear. If either of us were killers and cannibals, we would be exiled from Aloutia forever. Exile to Hydra Island was acceptable—the island was still part of Aloutia, and prisoners could return home after a while. But when one was exiled out of the Empire, it was permanent and destructive. There would be no pre-built homes waiting for us. On Cosmo, we'd be on our own.

"I did it," Su said with barely a moment's hesitation. "I killed him. I incinerated his body with my Fire powers. I turned his ashes into fertilizer and spread him across the jungle."

I started to speak: "Su, what—"

"Mr. Lasteran, quiet!" Giorvi interrupted in a harsh voice he'd never used on me. "Let Master Scrimshander tell *his* truth."

Not *the* truth, but *his* truth. In an Aloutian courtroom, an individual's truth was gold—shining, heavy, beautiful. It could be worthless or it could hold invaluable magic.

"I can't let Su—"

"The punishment he'll take for the crime is significantly less than what you or Mys Denwall would get. Let him tell the story."

I swallowed my pride—and a wad of spit welling in my throat.

Thus, the official story told to the judges was that Su killed Miltico while I got Susana out of the house.

During the entire trial, we did not mention Tawny, crystalights, or the Iurion once. My mind certainly thought about it all, and wondered how everything connected, but my thoughts were safe from the judges' scrutiny.

The three stepped into a private chamber off to the side of the courtroom where they deliberated and discussed their final verdicts.

Giorvi let out a sigh and rubbed the spot between his horns. "I think it went well."

"You did the best for us that you could," Liesle said. "I do not have high hopes for myself, but... I can live with whatever they decide, as long as I can see my children."

The Yosoe put his hands on Liesle's as they rested on the desk. "I will advocate for you. I will make sure your children can see you as often as possible."

I stood still, my stomach roiling with pili-palas. I had no clue what they'd do to me. Did they believe the story that my only role was kidnapping Susana? Or did they *know*...? They had to have suspected, as soon as I, a Wynnle, walked into the courtroom, that murder and cannibalism were possibilities.

The judges reentered and took their positions behind the bench. The Neuropteran cleared his throat. "We have come to a unanimous decision. Mys Liesle Denwall, we find you guilty of the crime of summoning the Demon Lord of Terror. Because the murder was of a non-citizen and the torture was of a retroactively consenting partner, the standard punishment for a woman of your lifespan is reduced from ten years of exile to five. Because you acted in defense of your children, you may be granted parole after three years. You will be entitled to monthly supervised visits with your children and spouses."

Liesle quietly acquiesced.

"Your Luminance, Master Su Scrimshander, you are guilty of the murder and unlawful bodily destruction of a non-citizen. Because you did it in the interest of saving a child's life, and due to your Godblood status, you have the choice of a different punishment. We do not believe you would be suitable for Mortebai, though you may choose to serve five years there if you wish. There is another option available to you. Per a previous agreement we came to with His Luminance, Lord Captain Lungidus Pavo, you may choose instead an eight-year house arrest supervised by Their Luminance, Lord Tynan Pavomusen."

Su exchanged a glance with Lungidus. I wished I could read minds, because whatever passed between them in that look would have been fascinating to know. The captain graced him with the Pavo smirk, seeming not at all to mind that his child would be with us.

Odd that Lucognidus offered Tynan to *me*, and yet now they would be living with us as part of Su's punishment. Or were both of Tynan's bodies going to be with us? That might get confusing after a while...

Of course, that was assuming I would also be allowed back home. Perhaps I was hoping for too much... Maybe I'd be exiled to Hydra Island with Liesle.

"I accept the second offer," Su said. "And if Lord Tynan's father would be so gracious as to allow it, I'd be happy to welcome them into my family. I'll cook meals and prepare a bedroom for them."

Lungidus smiled a genuine smile for once. "That pleases me, but the kid doesn't need to eat or sleep."

"They might change their mind about eating once they have a taste of my delicious fruit gelatin."

The look that passed between them was one of mutual understanding and respect. Two fathers who may have parented in different ways, but would still trust their kids with the other.

"As for you, Mr. Amiere Lasteran." The Neuropteran judge pushed his spectacles up. "We find you guilty of being a wonderful father. Your actions have saved many children. Thank you for your service to Aloutia. You may return home. Have a good day."

The other two judges intoned that they were in agreement with the judgment, then they all shuffled out.

Guilty… of being a wonderful father? It was so absurd I wanted to laugh.

But, I supposed it was true, wasn't it? Maybe it wasn't *the* truth, but it was the judges' truth, and in the end, that was all that mattered in the court of law.

I could go home.

I had committed murder, cannibalism, and kidnapping… and gotten away with it. The ecstasy made my head spin, and for a second, I thought I was going to faint.

Giorvi put a hand over mine. "Amiere, you owe me. You would not be walking free today if it weren't for me. Remember that. There will be legal things to take care of first. I must work on some things for Liesle, but I want to speak to you in my office before you leave Monoceros."

He probably wanted some kind of payment. Although I thought his offer to defend me in court would be free—didn't he say something like that?—I was more than happy to compensate him for a job well done. Besides, Giorvi was my friend. I wanted to remain in his good graces. Even if he wasn't going to ask for a payment, I'd gladly give him something, perhaps a free crystalight, as a thank-you gift.

"I'll be there," I said. "Truly, I can't thank you enough. I'm just glad it's over."

As soon as the words were out of my mouth, I knew I was wrong. His expression darkened; he knew that 'it' wasn't over, either. Whatever 'it' was.

Lucognidus had told me that Ciu Laan was coming for revenge. She would want to kill Giorvi for his presumed murder, I supposed.

Oh Gods, did he want me to kill Ciu Laan? Zap her with my tail the way Tawny had killed Rini Laan?

Whatever look my face displayed, Giorvi must have known that I'd thought of something cruel. "I'm sorry, Amiere. This is important. I tried to hide it from you, for your own protection. But the truth must come out. I'd prefer to speak in the privacy of my office if you don't mind."

With a sad, wry smile, he lowered his face to avoid my gaze and left the room.

Chapter Fifty-Five: Blood

Oboro stood outside Giorvi's office, his recently-polished khopesh glistening with reflected light. A normal employer of a bodyguard likely would have wanted him standing guard, but Oboro was throwing a ball back and forth with young Beatrice from across the hall.

"You haven't gone back home yet?" I asked her. I'd assumed Beatie would go back home after Boura was done with her.

After catching the ball, she clutched it tight to her chest and looked down. "I... I was feeling sad after Neri's Ritual. Papa said he wanted to cheer me up with a day of fun here in Monoceros. We're gonna go to restaurants, then the beach, and to the Armillary Spire. Oboro is gonna come with us, too. We'll be going after all Papa's work is done, of course. He has a lot to do."

I smiled. "That sounds like fun. I'll try not to take up too much of his time."

I walked in. Giorvi wrote hurriedly on a paper, which he set aside as I came closer. The chair I'd used before was still in its spot. He motioned for me to sit. I would have been more appalled if he had insisted I stand.

"Amiere. This is important. I did not want to have this discussion with you, but the lives of you and your family could be at stake."

I blinked, my heart pounding, and put my hands on his desk, claws extending into the wood. "My *family!*? I don't care if I'm put in danger, but what do you mean my *family*?"

"It's Ciu Laan. Hashma Boura's wife. She's... not well. She's going to Steena Village. She wants, um, revenge."

"Why? You said yourself that the one who murdered Rini Laan was killed by Rini Laan. That there was no revenge to be had."

Giorvi shivered. "She's going to... retrieve something Rini Laan left in Steena Village. And like I said, she's not mentally well. Even if *I* say there's no revenge to be had, she very well might seek to destroy your village just to satisfy her own rage."

"Well, let her take whatever she's coming for and go! And evacuate everyone before it's too late!"

He closed his eyes. "It's still a 'maybe' that she'll try to destroy the village. We could convict her of a crime if she did, though, so we're going to see what she does. Tynan is on standby to stop her in a worst-case scenario. Your children are safe... we think."

I rubbed my forehead. What the hell could she want? "Is it the crystalights?" I asked. "Did Rini bring a bunch of fucking crystalights from Iuria and *that's* why they're under Steena Village?"

Giorvi breathed short, rapid breaths. Was he *panicking*? I must have been right.

Why did Rini Laan bring crystalights with her, though? A gift for her father, for some reason?

The crystalights in Steena Village made a small deposit compared to normal. Rini Laan was a small child.

The crystalights under our village will glow for one hundred and eighty years. Most crystalights only glow for eighty years. Rini was seven years old, and most Iurion live to be one hundred and ten or so.

When they thought nobody was listening, Domovye called some crystalight shapes 'claws' and 'fangs.'

It couldn't be...

"Giorvi, what does Ciu Laan want?"

"The crystalights, like you guessed. We merchants of light have been ordered by the court to return them to her. Unfortunately, we cannot sell any more of the ones found under Steena Village."

My hands clenched into fists, my claws scratched deep divots into the wood. I didn't care. He could replace his desk. "What are crystalights? No... what is *Aye-too*?"

That forbidden, secret name I'd heard only a few times, and each time, the speaker was quickly reminded to never use it where it might be overheard.

Giorvi took a blank piece of paper and his pen and wrote it out. As I had only ever heard the word, I could not have guessed its true spelling or meaning.

I2

"I2? Two of something that starts with an 'I'?"

"It's an acronym for 'Iurish ivory.'"

I stared, dumbfounded. My hands trembled. My tail flickered.

"Crystalights are the bones of the Iurion," he said in a voice suffering from intense emotional anguish. "The... the crystalights under Steena Village are..." He stopped, gulped, licked his lips. "Ciu Laan is coming to retrieve her daughter's bones."

I had ceased breathing. I stared at Giorvi, at this Yosoe who...

"I'm sorry, Amiere."

"I thought... bones were turned to sawdust."

He shook his head. "Not Iurion bones. Yosoe have used Iurish ivory since before the Conquering. During that era, we made a deal with Lord Sawyer, who had conquered Iuria while Lord Lucognidus conquered the Sunset Kingdom. He agreed that we could continue harvesting Iurish ivory as long as we stayed loyal to the Gods. And so we have. The Iurion resisted the Gods to the bitter end, and were thusly punished. Now, when an Iur dies, Sawyer himself performs the sawdusting. He destroys most of the body, but leaves the bones to be dug up. It used to be Yosoe who did the mining, but we've since hired Domovye to do it for us."

"You... conspired to murder Rini Laan to harvest her bones?"

"Yes, Amiere, I did. Those crystalights would have been turned into Godlights that would protect Aloutia for generations. Crystalights glow for one hundred and ninety years after the Iur is born. When they die of natural causes around age one hundred and ten, their bones last eighty more years. One who dies at age seven will have newer ivory that will shine for around one hundred and eighty years. All the current Godlights were burning out, and we would have gone to war with the Makai and Ophidia in the next five years. But now... Well, if we could still use them, our children would have grown up in a world of peace."

"*Your* children... Not Tawny or Rini Laan. You murdered them."

"I never wanted Tawny to be hurt!"

"But you were okay with Rini dying?"

"Sacrifices had to be made. I let one child die so *billions* would live. And it was no sin. I have the permission of the Godbloods. No, not just them, of Lucognidus hims—"

"You killed my *daughter*." The words came out as a weak squeal, for all that I wanted to roar them like the lion I was.

He put his hands on mine to steady them. "Amiere, I... What happened to Tawny was an *accident*. She wasn't supposed to be there! Miltico was going to electrify Rini Laan as she surfaced, which would have put him in the good graces of the merchants of light. We were then going to invite him to Chernagora. I was going to get him the help he needed. And his daughter! Gods, Amiere, I had already gotten paperwork ready to send Susana to the same school Beatrice goes to!"

"You killed Tawny." I lifted my hand, swatting his away. My claws, extended, swiped across the back of his hand, and drew blood.

Blood.

Giorvi's blood.

Sweet, delicious, Yosoe blood. Yosoe. Like goat. So delicious.

"YOU KILLED MY TAWNY!" I screamed in the voice of a starving lion.

Giorvi got up from his chair in the time I grabbed the nearby tusk-shaped crystalight. Oh, the hilarity! It probably was one of Rini Laan's tusks!

I swung it at him. Trapped between his desk and the chair, he couldn't run. He ducked, and the crystalight hit his horn with such ferocity it broke it off halfway.

"Amiere, stop!" he yelled.

KILL!

KILL!

I WILL KILL THIS FUCKING GOAT!

I grabbed the edge of his desk in my other hand and threw it up and to the side. His papers went flying.

I WILL EAT THIS FUCKING GOAT!

I raised the crystalight tusk high.

"Oboro!" he screamed.

KILL! KILL! KILL!

KILL THE FUCKER WHO KILLED TAWNY!

VENGEANCE FOR TAWNY!

KILL THE CHILD-KILLER!

EAT THE FUCKER WHO KILLED RINI LAAN AND TAWNY!

The crystalight hit him between the horns. His goat-eyes bulged out, and he let out a pathetic cry as he crumpled to the ground. I raised the crystalight up, the pointed part facing downward.

Gritting my teeth, I drove it hard into his leg. Blood spurted out, sprayed my face. I licked it, savored it, craved more of it.

"Signor Lasteran!" a boy's voice screamed in a panic. In my berserker phrase, he sounded like he was a thousand miles away, underwater, no concern of mine. "What are you doing!? Signore, are you—"

I snarled at the intruder. I would kill this murderous goat and eat him. My mouth salivated with anticipation. The blood staining my face trickled into my mouth, taunting me.

I raised the crystalight with both hands. It wasn't heavy, but it was unwieldy and difficult to—

Swish

The crystalight fell out of my hands.

A chunk of metal had sliced my right arm off. Clear blood gushed out from my shoulder like a geyser. It painted the bookcases. It splattered across the other crystalights. It fell across the face of a Sasorin, eyes wide with rage, as he lifted his bloody khopesh for a second strike.

I swung my tail at him, thinking to electrify him. He grabbed it in one of his scorpion pincers and snapped it right off. In the chaos, the electric part *did* hit him. He stiffened as my tail and his khopesh dropped from his hands. My tail floundered like a fish out of water, the electric tip sputtering.

As he was shocked in place, I grabbed the crystalight tusk in my one remaining hand, hefted it up, and struck the scorpion hard against his head. It was an awkward flail, as I only had one arm... Gods, I only had one arm! It didn't hurt... Wynnles didn't feel pain in their berserker phase.

His head was so hard, I doubted the tusk had done much to hurt him. I kicked him in the chest. He flew to the back wall, landing on a bookshelf. As he fell onto his rear, books and crystalight knickknacks cascaded upon his head. I thought he would get up, but he did not. Blood poured from gash on his head made by the crystalight.

KILL THE GOAT!

EAT THE GOAT!

I lifted the crystalight—no, Rini's tusk...

I lifted *Rini's tusk* onto my shoulder and turned back to Giorvi, unconscious or dead on the floor. I prepared to strike him one last time, to ensure he was dead, before I feasted.

REVENGE FOR TAWNY! REVENGE FOR RINI LAAN! YOU CHILD-MURDERER!

How could *anyone* ever hurt a child?

Even in my berserker phase... a phase that stopped me from feeling pain, from feeling remorse, from feeling that I could be executed for my actions... I knew I could never hurt a child. And yet *he* had, in his most conscious, sane mind.

I raised Rini's bone to land the killing blow. How appropriate that Rini's body should kill the one who killed her. He had spoken truly during Neri's Ritual—Rini Laan *would* kill the one who killed her.

"Don't kill my Papa!"

My arm swung in an arc. The force I put into this strike would bash the brains out of this goat. This murderer. This child-killer.

In a heartbeat, Beatrice stood before me, between me and the murderer. Her arms stretched to her side protectively, her eyes wide with absolute terror. Tears welled in the corners of those eyes, glittering in the light of Rini's bone, a half-second away from crushing her.

KILL THAT GOAT!

I stopped my arm mid-swing. The tusk shook in my grip, hovering an inch above her horns.

"Please, Mr. Lasteran! Don't kill my Papa!" Beatrice sniffed, trying to hold back any sign she was crying. Her body was so tiny, so frail, and shaking like a leaf in a storm. She was barely a rat in the shadow of a lion.

KILL THE GOAT WHO KILLED TAWNY!

My eyes twitched. I had to kill that goat... but this one was in my way. But I couldn't kill this one. I *couldn't*. Even enraged, even with my blood screaming for vengeance...

"I can't live without my Papa," she said, sobbing. "I can't imagine how painful it is for you to have lost your daughter. It must hurt so bad, not having Tawny here. So... please... if you must punish Papa, kill me instead."

KILL!

She tightened her arms, flexing her little muscles, arms that were barely thicker than my fingers... Beatrice wore a brave expression. Or at least, as brave as she could make herself in the face of a hungry, enraged lion.

EAT!

"If you kill Papa, I'll cry forever. He'll go to Spiritua, and he'll go to sleep, but he'll be happy and healthy when he wakes up. That's no punishment, is it? But if you kill *me*, you will make him feel the same pain you feel. So... go ahead. You have my permission. Kill me, Mr. Lasteran! Smash me until your soul is satisfied!"

Kill...

I breathed hard, unable to process what was happening. I had to kill the goat behind her... but I couldn't get her out of the way without hurting her. I couldn't hurt a child...

"Do to me what he did to you!" Beatrice screamed, tears flinging from her eyes as she shook her head. "It's only fair, right? He took your daughter, so take his!"

Even in my most insane berserker phase...

"Take your vengeance!"

...I could NOT kill a child!

My body lifted into the air by magic. I clutched the tusk in fear of dropping it on Beatrice's head.

"Your rampage is over now, Mr. Lasteran." My body spun on its own to face the speaker. Lungidus Pavo, holding his bardiche pointed at me, tight in his tentacled hands. "You'll thank me for this one day."

My vision went black. So much like Su whenever he knocked me out...

Chapter Fifty-Six: Ciu Laan

I woke to the familiar music of Deep Sea's fingers crashing on the beach, the various sea birds chirping and cawing, and the wind billowing through palm fronds.

Gods, what was real? What was a bad dream? I put my hand on my forehead to rub away the headache that not even sleep could cure. Intending to sit up, I tried pushing myself up with my other hand.

I… didn't have another hand. My right shoulder ended on a bandaged stump, wiggling uselessly as I tried to brace myself with a nonexistent limb.

I was halfway up just pulling myself up with my torso's muscles when the full extent of my life hit me, and I fell back onto the reed mat, crying.

All the damage I'd done, all the damaged I'd received, came piling onto my soul. Fuck, I had attacked Giorvi, my commissioner, my defender! The man who had gotten me and my family as lenient a sentence as possible. Surely he would… take it all away now… as revenge.

The man's actions had inadvertently killed Tawny, but even if I could forgive that, he was the one solely responsible for the murder of Rini Laan. He was evil, a villain, a child-killer by choice. I could *never* speak to him again, for if I ever laid eyes on him, I would have to kill him.

His son, too. Gods, did I kill Oboro? In my rage, I had not considered him a child. When he attacked me, I attacked back with all the ferocity I would have given to a properly grown man.

My screaming brought a crowd into the room. My family, except for Liesle… The lawkeepers must have taken her to Hydra Island already. The two Tynans were here, too.

Su knelt by my side and put his hands on my head. "Amiere… Ami-honey, it's alright. You're alive and free. We're here with you."

My kids gathered around and hugged me from all angles. Even Susana jumped on my lap and wrapped her small furry paws around my torso as far as her arms would stretch. She wore puffs on the ends of her horns to avoid poking me.

Tynan—or the Tynans? I wasn't sure if they were to be considered one person or two. Whatever the case was, the two bodies stayed by the leafy doorway, watching.

"Everything's okay, Daddy," Cohaku said, her face buried in my arm.

"We're all safe," Heliodor added.

"What happened?" I asked. "The last thing I remember is..." Gods, I couldn't say it in front of my children. I couldn't tell them how I might have killed Giorvi and Oboro.

Su petted my mane. "Lungidus said that as long as you stay in Steena Village, he won't pursue any more charges against you."

"I don't understand," I groaned, still sleepy, suffering from a head-ringing ache in my temples. "What happened to Giorvi and Oboro?"

"They're both alive," Su said. "You knocked them out, but they've been treated and are both awake and doing well."

That was a relief, like Deep Sea washed over me and carried my worries away and grinded them into marine snow. Fuck, how could I have let my berserker state rule me? "What about the trial? Do I need to go back to court after assaulting them?"

"My father kept your actions a secret from everyone outside of that room," Tynan said. Both bodies spoke simultaneously. As they continued their explanation, the more masculine-appearing Tynan, dressed in a shinigami uniform, spoke alone. "The Plant Godblood doctor who healed Giorvi and Oboro is involved in my father's schemes, so he has not told anyone, either. My father wants what is best for Aloutia, and he did not believe that bringing attention to your actions would help the national crystalight situation. He doesn't want to punish you for being upset over what is, truly, an upsetting experience. He believes that you can be a safe, happy, and productive member of society as long as you remain here. Although I am legally here to supervise Master Scrimshander, my father has ordered me to watch over you first and foremost. I am to accompany you if you leave Steena Village."

Su helped me to sit up. "Just relax, Amiere. Take it easy. We live in paradise, so let's delight in our days together. You don't have your job anymore—Thousand-Diamonds has dismissed you from the merchants of light permanently—but we don't need it. We have enough money saved up, and I'll keep—"

"A merchant of light and a merchant of bone," I said with wry laugh. "Ironic. Did you know crystalights were bones? I've actually been the merchant of bone this whole time."

"Yes, Amiere, I knew."

I had meant for it to be a stunning reveal, but... he already knew?

"The merchants of light hide the real meaning and name of 'crystalights' because they know people would never purchase them if they knew they were sapienti bones. But we need them to enchant into Godlights. Without them, we'd be conquered by demonkind again. No other source of light works as well as crystalights for holding a God's blessing. I ought to tell *you* the truth now, Amiere. It's true I make a decent amount of money as a merchant of bone, but I have been promised a lifetime pension as long as I keep enchanting Godlights. I... I am actually more of a merchant of light."

The irony was so painful I could have died. I laughed, and if I had died laughing, it would have been only too appropriate.

"I thought enchantment was done by Death Godbloods. You mean to tell me you're somehow a Death elemental, too?"

He smiled sadly. "No, just Fire and Lightning. The Demigod of Bones, Garnet Skull, is a Death elemental enchanter, though. I know his ritual. I learned to summon him back when I was training under King Susan. I can summon him to assist me in enchanting Godlights. When we were in Chernagora, Giorvi paid me a significant amount of money to perform the ritual and enchant the new crystalight you carved for them. Remember the demon in the cage who later melted? That was to prove the Godlight was active."

"Why did they need Rini Laan's bones?" I asked. "Why can't old ones be reenchanted? Isn't that how other enchantments work?"

"Yes, but light carries the enchantment. If you reenchant a dead crystalight, the demon-killing magic only works if you touch a demon with the bone. Enchantments into light-based structures use light to carry the magic. Moreover, as an Iur grows, their bones develop the structures to hold elementrons. As their bones deteriorate, these structures also deteriorate. When the light dies, any elementrons once enchanted into the bones vanish without the structures to hold them in place."

Although I asked the question, I had no interest in the answer. Just knowing there was an answer was enough. Of course, nobody would be killing children if they could just reenchant the same bones over and over...

"All this time, I've been a merchant of light who sold bones, and you were a merchant of bone who sold light."

"I know," he said in the same melancholy tone. "And I hoped you'd never find out."

All the children knew our sorrow and despair now, too. This drama would be scrimshawed into the bones of their soul and sewn into the tapestry of their lives. Clutching me supportively, they did not back away.

"So what happens now?" I asked. "Where are Rini Laan's bones? Did Ciu Laan come for them already?"

"She's on her way now," the more feminine-looking Tynan said. "Most of them are still underground, but the courts gave her the right to take them all, at her leisure. The merchants of light lost their rights to them. All the Domovye have left."

I thought about all my half-finished projects. I'd need to get the finances on them squared away. Even if I was fired from my job, they owed me for labor. Hell, maybe I'd give those half-finished projects to Ciu Laan as a peace offering. I wouldn't have desecrated her daughter's bones if I'd known what they were.

The only personal project I'd made with Rini Laan's bones was... the statue of Tawny. I had carved the image of my daughter from the bone of someone else's daughter. The idea of someone doing that to my children's bones made me sick.

"Ciu Laan is almost here," Tynan said. "My sister, Steffa, has been predicting her movements. Ciu Laan will surface in ten minutes."

"I need to talk to her," I said. "Su, can you help me get up and get dressed?"

The kids left us alone so I could put my clothes in private.

"My arm... doesn't hurt," I said as Su put a formal business gown over my shoulders.

"Lungidus took you to the best Plant Godblood healer in Monoceros after... after he knocked you out. I cauterized the wound, though. If you feel any pain, tell me. I can make it go away."

"The only pain I feel now is in my sternum and my skull. My soul hurts. I want to cry."

Su tied the long sleeve of the right arm into a knot, then kissed my chest. "We can begin that healing after Ciu Laan is dealt with."

I finished getting dressed. No jewelry today... I wasn't in the mood to do anything but die, but I couldn't even do that for as long as all these children depended on me.

The kids were bustling with activity in the living room.

"I want to see an Iur," Cohaku said.

"She's angry at us," Eruwan said. "We need to leave her alone."

"She wouldn't hurt us, would she?" Susana asked. "I've heard the Iurs are so big."

"Iurion," Fionn corrected. "Yeah, they're big, but I'll protect you, Sis."

One of the Tynans transformed into a winged ermine and flew onto my shoulder. "I will stay with you. Ciu Laan will be here in five minutes."

On shaking legs, I walked over to Tawny's memorial. Liesle's incomplete painting had been brought here and put on display next to her painting of Kiwi Island. I wondered who had found it and brought it here.

"That would be me," ermine-Tynan replied. "It was your wife's request, and my father wished to honor it. The other paintings and supplies in her cave, unfortunately, had to be confiscated or destroyed per law."

I sighed, saddened, but also grateful I didn't have to make that difficult choice.

Tawny's statue shone with a brilliant light. A light that should have been guiding Rini Laan through her home tunnels in Iuria. I touched the top of Tawny's head and wondered if this came from Rini's skull. Maybe it was just a tooth or nail. Maybe it was something deep, like a sternum or rib. It didn't matter, I supposed. It was Rini Laan's body, and now it was Ciu Laan's right to have her daughter's remains, regardless of how I had desecrated them.

"I need to go to my ateli," I told Tynan. "There are more raw crystalights in there. They're bright. Do whatever you need to your eyes so you don't get blinded."

"Understood. Thank you for the warning."

I didn't bother to put the visor on when I entered. My body was fucked up already, what would it matter if I lost some of my vision? Besides, I only had one arm. I would have had to set Tawny's statue down in order to put it on. As long as I could see my children and Su, and Liesle when next I could visit her... I didn't care if my vision was less than perfect. I scooped up a few more crystalights that I knew came from Rini Laan, carrying them as best I could in the crook of my single appendage.

I wondered who some of my older crystalights were from. Who was the last Iur to die, before Rini? Whose bones had I carved for the last sixteen years? There was the mismanaged 'mine' that had been 'found' ten years ago. Perhaps an elderly Iur. Before that was the one eighty years ago. The vast majority of Godlights used throughout Aloutia had been created from that individual's bones which were now fading.

"Those two Iurion were quite old," Tynan said, having read my mind. "Their deaths were natural. The eldest living Iur is not predicted to die for a long time. My father and Mr. Onoretti were concerned that no Iur would die before the Makai waged war on Aloutia."

"They killed one child to save billions," I said. "Well, they killed two. Tawny was collateral damage. Still, even one child is unforgivable."

Tynan had no response.

I exited my ateli with my arm full of crystalights. Standing beside the door, I looked out to sea. Soon. Deep Sea was far too peaceful for what was about to happen.

"She'll be here in a minute," Tynan said. "Her puppet will pop up over here." They flew to a nondescript spot on the beach, a few steps away from the fallen palm log we often used as a bench. A dominion shell had washed ashore there. Tynan grew longer arms for the sole purpose of picking it up and throwing it farther along the beach.

Su approached us, carrying Turquoise in his lower arms and a baby bottle in one of his upper arms. "Amiere, what are you planning? I should probably be the one to speak to Ciu Laan."

"I was the one who dug my claws into her daughter's bones, Su. Not you. I have to apologize. I have to give back what belongs to her." I let the crystalights on my arm fall to the sand, except for the statue of Tawny clutched in my hand. Gods, I had spent so much time—so many tears—carving this.

I was eternally grateful that Liesle had painted Tawny. Grateful, too, that Lungidus had allowed us to keep it. At least I would not lose my last image of her. I would not forget her face.

Tynan tapped my shoulder with their arms, now returned to regular ermine arms. "Steffa is telling me there's an eighty percent chance that Ciu Laan will be too enraged to see reason."

"What does that mean?" I asked. "I don't plan to reason with her. I just want to give her the bones back and let her go on her way."

"Eight-five percent now. It means she's going to destroy this village. She'll tear down every house looking for Rini's bones. She wants to kill those who killed her daughter for money."

Su grabbed my only arm with the only one of his that wasn't preoccupied. "We should run. Let her destroy to her soul's content. We'll rebuild our house when she's satisfied. We need to get everyone out!"

I yanked my arm away. "I can't, Su! I have to apologize to her. It might not be enough, but... she needs to hear something. She needs to know that *somebody cares about Rini Laan*!"

Su gritted his teeth. I felt a tingle in my spine, a spark... and then he stopped. "No. I won't force you. Amiere, Ciu Laan might kill you. You need to fucking run!"

"I will protect him," Tynan said. "But perhaps *you* should run, Master Scrimshander. Ciu Laan will be here in thirty seconds. I will do everything I can to protect your children, too, but there are so many of them and I only have two bodies."

Su's eyes popped open, wide, and he ran back to the house. "Kids! Kids! We have to go!"

The ground rumbled. A shake. Just like last time.

A year ago, I didn't know what it was. I had stood in place, stupidly, wondering what was the quake meant. This time, I stood my ground bravely, treasure in hand. The sand shifted beneath my feet.

"A brief explanation of our relationship," Tynan said. "While you were unconscious, my geas was transferred to you. I must obey your every command. Whatever you tell me to do—or not do—I shall obey without question."

"What?" I asked, incredulous. "Why...?"

"You traded Tawny for me. My Lord Grandfather Lucognidus has plans for her. And for me. He's very happy you agreed to the trade. But for my sake, please be careful what you command me to do."

I had no time to contemplate the situation—the absurdity—of thinking I could command a Godblood. I turned my attention to the ocean.

Deep Sea's waves parted. I wondered if Cui Laan's tunneling beneath him was an annoyance.

A strand of water rose ten feet up and slammed back down unto himself. I hadn't been near Deep Sea when Rini rose up. Had he done that back then, too?

"Is Deep Sea trying to push her down?" I asked.

"Yes," Tynan replied. "I could try to talk to him... to let her surface through him."

"That sounds safer than erupting through the ground."

Tynan leapt from my shoulder and went to the edge of the ocean. They transformed into a fish and went inside him. A moment later, the puppet of Ciu Laan poked her head out of sand before me. Like Hashma Boura, the puppet had a dress of metal and stone... and hair made of crystalights. How had I not questioned that? The puppet was a natural part of an Iur's body, and the crystalights were just their naturally-growing ivory. Fuck, I was stupid...

"Who are you?" she asked. "You know of my coming?"

"My name is Amiere Lasteran," I said. "I did hear you were coming, Mys Ciu Laan. I heard about what happened to your daughter... to Rini Laan."

"Do not speak her name!" she screamed, and the world shattered.

The ground opened up like last time, starting at the puppet and fracturing into Deep Sea. Fish-Tynan jumped out, turned into a cormorant, and rushed back to my shoulder. "Deep Sea agreed to let her surface."

They didn't have to explain, as Ciu Laan emerged, massive, grand... terrifying.

Out of the corner of my eye, I saw Su rush out the front door. In his four hands, he carried Turquoise, Nio, Susana, and Heliodor. Cohaku clung to his back the way Eruwan used to do. Fionn and Eruwan stood close behind him.

"Amiere!" he screamed. "Run!"

He wasted no more time. He took off into a sprint with the older two kids on his heels.

I ignored him as I kept my focus on Ciu Laan. My eyes drifted from her puppet to the rest of her body as she erupted from Deep Sea. The ocean's fingers sluiced off her in waterfalls.

Chunks of metal, rock, flesh, and muscle, some larger than my house, drew upward. And upward. And upward. A hundred feet. Five hundred feet. A thousand. Ten thousand... So tall that a halo-shaped piece of metal surrounding a brown, vaguely face-shaped structure touched the clouds. Crystalight limbs and formations decorated this mountain of a woman.

"Amiere Lasteran," a voice echoed out of a metal protrusion some five thousand feet up. The voice was no less deep than Hashma Boura's. "I know you. You are a merchant of light. You have profited off Rini's body parts. And you, a Wynnle, were probably the one who killed her."

"It wasn't me," I said, trembling in awe of this gigantic person. "I swear to you, it was not me. I lost my daughter, too, when she fell into the fissure opened by Rini Laan when she surfaced for air. Our daughters died together, *by* each other."

"You are a despicable man!" Her voice could have probably been heard for miles. "How much money have you earned selling Rini's body!?"

I held Tawny's statue out to her. My little girl's smiling face looked upon this giant woman with the eternal innocence I had carved there. I would not answer her question; that discourse would only lead to destruction. "Take what is Rini's," I said. "I didn't know the truth. I'm sorry, Ciu Laan. We who live on the surface don't know about Iurish ivory. We even call them 'crystalights' as a way of hiding what they are. But… take it back. Take Rini's bones. I hope you are able to grieve properly, knowing her body is safe."

"Idiot man!" A tentacle unwrapped from around her massive form and slammed into a nearby mountain. I had spent many hours getting lost on that mountain, in the thick jungle. I had always been worried about my kids getting lost, but they had always been able to fly up and find their way back once they found the ocean. Only Tawny hadn't had wings, but she'd always stayed with Fionn when they went out playing in the jungle. Now nobody would ever play on that mountain again.

"I am sorry about what happened to Rini!" I screamed. "I care about her! I care about you! Please take her bones and return home! Go home and cry and grieve and *cope*. Destroying this village will only cause more sorrow!"

"She will not listen to you," Tynan said. "She will kill you."

I couldn't find it in myself to be scared. After all I'd been through, it might have been what I deserved. I only wished I could remain alive to raise my children.

"I could kill her if you give me permission."

"No," I said sternly. "We don't need any more death. Don't give Hashma Boura another family member to grieve over."

"But what about *your* family?" Tynan asked. "They shouldn't have to grieve over you!"

Ciu Laan raised her tentacle behind her, holding it much like I had once held Rini's tusk above Beatrice's head. Ahh… this must have been what it felt like for that little girl, in that one terrifying, dreadful moment. It was almost blissful, knowing I would be dead in a second. I would be with Tawny the next time I woke up…

Another tentacle made of muscle, metal, and ivory unraveled from seven thousand feet up and shot behind me… down Bamboo Lane, where Su had run with the kids.

Ciu Laan opened a vertical mouth to scream. Her teeth, rows upon rows of them like a lamprey, shone with the light of twenty thousand suns.

Su Interlude

Su had seven kids, but only four arms. He cursed his evil, rapist father for, among a million other things, not granting Su enough arms to carry all his children. But then again, maybe it was Flamboil who had been the rapist.

He was lucky that Eruwan and Fionn were fast runners. How many times had he raced Eruwan to the lighthouse? All those days spent running with her, he had only wanted to bond with his child, and now it had come in handy as she ran for her life.

Fionn had always been athletic. Always playing with Su, Amiere, and the other kids. He'd run with Tawny all over the place. Into the village, into the jungle, along the beach. Tawny would have been a fast runner. If she had been any slower, perhaps Demitris would have fallen into that fissure instead.

If Demitris had fallen instead of Tawny, Su realized, then it would have fallen to Miltico to kill Rini Laan, per the original plan.

Cohaku cried loud as she clung to Su's back. She hated riding on his back like this, but she couldn't run or fly fast enough.

Heliodor begged to be let go; he claimed he could fly fast enough. Su knew it wasn't true. He was a fast flier, true, but he would still lag behind. The poor boy just didn't want to be a nuisance.

Susana cried, sobbing that she didn't want to die. She didn't want to go to Spiritua, where her parents might be waiting for her. Su didn't have time to explain that they would be asleep.

Tynan took the form of a falcon, flying at the same speed Su ran. "Ciu Laan will kill you, too," they said. "I do not have permission to kill her to protect you."

"Fuck, fuck, fuck," Su screamed, crying, running as fast as his legs would take him. As fast as he could go with five children weighing him down.

"Mapa Su!" Cohaku screamed. "It's coming! It's coming toward us!"

Su slid to a stop and spun.

Ciu Laan's tentacle shot at him at such terrifying speed that even if she wanted to stop, she could not. The inertia alone would crash into him, driving him and all his kids into the ground. There would be no bodies to sawdust; they would be pulp in an instant.

As that ten thousand-foot-long chunk of metal and glowing ivory came closer,

Su knew he had no choice.

Inches away from his face, he incinerated it. Ashes and sparks blew past harmlessly. Fire and lightning spread down her tentacle, vaporizing every part of her, save the bones.

Epilogue I: Light and Bone

I watched in astonishment as Ciu Laan's body erupted into flames. She screamed in pain, in agony. Black tears of a grieving mother erupted from exhaust pipes which soon melted into nothingness.

Ashes carried on the wind darkened the sky and blocked the sun, but it did not affect the lighting of the beach, illuminated by crystalights—no, by Iurish ivory. Ciu Laan's skin, muscle, and stone burned away, but her brilliant bones remained.

A ten thousand-foot-tall crystalight skeleton crashed into Deep Sea with a sickening, sudden finality. The Demon Lord of Despair did not grant her the dignity of splashing away in her honor. The waves embraced her remains like a parent embracing a long-dead child, now reunited in Spiritua.

I hoped he would grind those bones into marine snow and feed them to his pets in the abyss. The merchants of light didn't deserve them. Let the traitors who created this tragedy go to Hell. Let Giorvi and Thousand-Diamonds and whoever the hell else was involved walk in Solitude forever. I was no merchant of light, but I refused to be a merchant of bone selling the body parts of dead children. I might as well call myself a merchant of calamity for all that I had created had brought misery and suffering.

Screaming, I threw Rini Laan's bone—the one I'd carved into the shape of my own daughter—into the ocean to be with her mother.

Epilogue II: Letters

Eruwan landed on the sand beside me as I sat on the palm tree log. She carried a basket of herbs, spices, medicine, and bandages on her arm. Nestled between a jar of cinnamon and a jar of garlic cloves was a stack of envelopes.

"The merchant of mail came today. Here are your letters, Papami."

"Thanks, Eruwan," I said as I took them from her.

"Do you need help opening them?"

I wrestled with one, holding it down with the heel of my hand while trying to open it gently with my claw. A breeze came by at the most inopportune time and blew the others off my knee. Eruwan dropped her basket in retrieving them again.

"I'll open them for you," she said and did exactly that.

Being stubborn, I didn't want to ask her for help. Upon reflection of her life, it seemed we parents had always been asking Eruwan to do things to help out. We had practically treated her like she was the fourth parent. It hadn't been fair to her. She deserved to enjoy her childhood.

But I didn't have to ask; Eruwan helped out without needing to be asked. She set the jar of cinnamon on the letters as a weight.

"I'll come back for that later. I don't need it now. I'll be at my house. Just holler if you need me!"

"Thank you," I said. Her face lit up and she jumped into the sky, leaping toward Scrimshander Lighthouse. Her home. I would not be surprised if she lived there until she died. Susana stood in the doorway with a sack of ube in her hands. I wondered what they were going to make with it... Susana sure did love ube. I was happy that she had discovered it. If she lived with Miltico still, he wouldn't have allowed her to have any. And if she had moved to Chernagora, she probably never would have *seen* an ube.

I turned my attention to the letters. One from Lungidus Pavo. He could have sent a message to Tynan through Steffa, which meant whatever was in this letter was something he didn't want Tynan to know. I had forbidden Tynan from reading my mind, and that, surprisingly, had done the trick. One letter was from Liesle. Likely an update on how her sentence was going. *Two* were from Giorvi. Gods, I didn't want to read them... I hoped one was just a copy of the other. He always wrote multiple copies of any letter, anticipating that the merchants of mail would lose some. Well, they might be about my final payment, so I had to read them.

First, the one from Lungidus.

Mr. Amiere Lasteran,

> *The boys you rescued from Ophidia are doing well and you have been cleared to adopt them if you wish. They are currently in the care of the Wind church of Monoceros, but the keeper knows you have been authorized to take them.*
>
> *I must apologize for thrusting Tynan upon you and Master Scrimshander. The situation was a peculiar one, a scheme by my Lord Father which he hoped would help you, me, and Tynan. I do not wish to go into detail about the relationship between Tynan and me, though they are welcome to tell you whatever they wish. After some events that occurred a few months ago, I felt I was unable to be a proper father to them. Due to a geas placed upon my child, they are forced to obey my orders. I wish I could free Tynan from this prison of words, but my Lord Father will not remove the geas. For my own peace, he agreed to let me transfer it, and he said you would be a worthy replacement. Please, be the kind of father toward Tynan that I could never be.*
>
> *Moreover, Tynan wanted to go with you. I don't know why. They said it was for another scheme of my Lord Father's. I trust you to do what is right, Amiere. I will not ask you to follow the law or obey me. Do what your soul believes is the right thing to do. If Tynan asks you to break the law, perhaps that is the right thing to do. So do it. I won't stop you.*

—Lungidus Pavo, Captain of the Godblood Brigade

Tynan had been a big help, so I was not at all upset that they were here to watch over us. Truly, it felt less like we had a warden and more like we had an assistant who could become whatever we needed. When I couldn't open a jar, Tynan was there with wrench-like hands to open it. When I couldn't fix the reeds of my sandals, Tynan was there with a Collembola snout to glue them together.

I read Liesle's letter next.

Mo Ami,

Every night I dream and yearn for you. The pain I feel being away from you is only ameliorated by the thoughts that these years are temporary in the grand scheme of the universe. We will have all eternity together, you and me and Sugar. A few years away in exile or, when the time comes, asleep in Spiritua, is nothing compared to the time we'll spend together in the afterlife. I think of it similarly to how I await seeing Tawny again. We might not see her for one hundred and fifty more years, but what does that time matter in the face of a thousand, ten thousand, a million, billion, trillion years? The ephemerality of our lives is the only thing that keeps me sane anymore.

I spoke to an advocate about letting Fionn spend time with me, and they agreed it would be better for him and me. The advocate convinced a triad of judges that I was suffering for not being with my children, and that Fionn's crisis with self-harming might be managed if he were with the parent he trusted most. Although Hydra Island isn't usually good for kids, the advocate believed Fionn would be fine here. Wynnles are feared here. He would not be bullied like most kids are. He could bring Maika, too. That might be best for all of them, Fionn, the dog, and poor allergic Turquoise, too. The advocate will write to you when arrangements are finalized.

Write back to me if you can. Even if Su has to write it for you, I hope you will sign your name so I can see your beautiful handwriting. I miss you, Mo Ami. I love you. Don't make me wait too long.

—Your Lisi

I could relate to her yearning just for my handwriting. Seeing her handwriting inspired similar feelings in me. It was nice to have a letter from her. I would keep it safe for as long as I could, and certainly, I would write back to her within the day.

Now for Giorvi's letters... Hopefully, just a single letter, if the other was indeed a copy. My stomach lurched like a whirlpool thinking about the contents inside. One on hand, Giorvi was so outrageously kind that I could not imagine him hating me, even after what I did to him. On the other hand, the mere thought of him and his 'sacrifice for the greater good' made me ill.

What sick irony for me to use the phrase 'on the other hand' when I only had one hand...

I considered waiting for Su to join me here before I read these letters. If I were to get too emotional, he could calm me down.

Well, I'd faced much more terrifying monsters than the words on a page. I took one of the letters and opened it, preparing for the worst.

Mr. Lasteran,

This is Beatrice, Daughter of Giorvi Onoretti and Beatrice Iola, writing this. I apologize for sending it under my Papa's name, but I wanted the merchants of mail to treat it with respect. Papa said the merchants have been better about delivering his mail since he complained to them.

I don't know what happened between you and Papa, and I'm very sorry to see that it has ruined your relationship with him. Papa won't tell me, and I don't want to pry into it, either. The reason I'm writing to you is to tell you that I hope you'll still let me and Oboro be friends with Fionn. Please, don't punish us just because you and Papa don't get along anymore. Fionn is our best friend. We love him. I don't know if I'll be able to see him any time soon, but if you are willing to help us stay friends, please give him the address below. Oboro has a mailbox now, since he's a legal adult. I promise I didn't forge Papa's name to get one of my own. If Fionn sends a letter to this box, we can read it privately. Please don't tell Papa. I don't think you will, since you aren't friends with him anymore, but I thought I should ask just in case. He mentioned that he's fine with us being friends with Fionn, but I'm not sure if he really feels that way or if he's just saying it to make us feel better.

I hope you're doing better, too, Mr. Lasteran. When I jumped in front of you, I knew you wouldn't kill me. I know you're a kind, gentle man, and a good father. I didn't want you to do anything you'd regret later. Thank you for not killing me.

—Beatrice Iola

Then below her signature—identical to her mother's—was the address for Oboro's mailbox.

I held back tears, recalling the moment she jumped between me and Giorvi. If I hadn't had control over myself—and not all Wynnles have that degree of self-control when they go berserk—I might have killed that little girl. And if I had, it wouldn't have mattered what the judges decided to do to me, because I would have killed myself in shame.

I couldn't blame her for her father's sins. She deserved to be happy. So did

Oboro. He took off my arm and tail to protect the one man who'd ever been a proper parent to him. I couldn't blame him. Hell, I was proud of him.

I would give Fionn the address, and also advise him to write to them again if he goes to stay with Liesle on Hydra Island since he might have a new address there.

I dared not hope that the other letter from Giorvi was actually from his daughter. I took it out of the envelope next. I saw his seal at the bottom right away, a sure sign it was truly his.

Mr. Amiere Lasteran,

I shall keep this brief and formal, as I have no desire to apologize to you nor to receive an apology from you.
You are required to return all the crystalights that legally belong to the merchants of light. A Domovoi will be by your house soon to acquire them. They will give you the remainder of your wages for labor. They are in the process of collecting Ciu Laan's bones, which we have been allowed to use for our purposes. If you take any of her crystalights, you will be charged with theft. Do not interfere with the Domovoi's business. The courts decided, and Hashma Boura agreed, that you should be allowed to keep the statue of your daughter if it is found. I hope it brings you comfort for the remainder of your days on this mortal plane.
I also hope your healing goes well. May the Gods judge you with fairness upon your death, and may that be many years away, when your children are grown, and perhaps have given you grandchildren. May your path glitter with starlight.

—Giorvi Onoretti, Chief Liaison of the Merchants of Light to the Aloutian Government

Tawny's statue... I could keep it if I found it. I allowed the letter to fall upon the sand, heedless to whether the wind blew it away or not. Let it. I never wished to see that man's seal again. I'd have cursed his very handwriting, but if Beatie needed to copy it to sneak messages to Fionn, I would not have faulted her.

Step by painful step, I marched to the sea, toward the beam of light on the horizon, to the multitude of other lights emerging from Deep Sea where Ciu Laan's bones were laid to rest.

"Deep Sea!" I shouted. "Please! You've taken enough of my despair, now let me have hope!"

The wave crashing at my feet was as indifferent as the mountains, trees, and sky. I waded into him, my one arm swinging. Gods, please let Tawny's statue still be out there, intact and secure.

Deep Sea wrapped a tentacle of pure water around my torso and dragged me beneath his surface. I took a surprised breath and closed my eyes before being pulled under, but the touch of Su's hands on mine made me release my breath.

I could breathe. I had heard of Deep Sea allowing people to breathe within him but had never experienced it. A school of fish fled past me, diving into a nearby garden of coral and sea anemones. Sunbeams refracting from the Demon Lord's skin danced in unpredictable, dappled patterns. The only consistent light came from ahead.

Su... was the most magnificent being I had ever laid eyes on. He wore a stunning, long, billowy purple betta fish tail that swayed with the currents. His hair splayed out, long and luxurious, perfect and Godly. His brown eyes and his brilliant smile, the essence of love, shone with unparalleled joy and... and a real light. A light clutched in his lower hands. Tawny's statue, golden light radiating from her mane and face, specked with her perfect freckles.

"Look, Amiere," he said, voice filtered through the water. "Our daughter has returned, shining with starlight."

I reached for it—for her—and Su put the statue in my hand. He swam around to hug me from behind while keeping one hand over mine. His tail swirled around me, surrounding me in a wall of purple reflecting the exquisite light of Rini Laan's bone. The tears escaping my eyes joined immediately with Deep Sea.

"Amiere, my love," Su whispered most sweetly into my ear. "Down here, only Deep Sea can tell when you're crying, but I'll hold your hand any time you need me. You'll never swim alone in the sea of despair."

Acknowledgements

Thank you to all the friends, beta readers, editors, and artists who have supported me these last few years as I wrote this book. And thank you, dear readers, for embarking on this quest I've poured my heart and soul into. If you enjoyed this book, please rate and review it on Amazon and Goodreads.

About the Author

Erika McCorkle is an avid world-builder and consumer of all things fantasy, whether that be books, video games, or anime. She has been developing the Pentagonal Dominion for over two decades and is publishing novels that take place in that fantastic world. She has a Bachelors of Science in Biology and works as a laboratory technician on the graveyard shift at her local blood bank, which qualifies her as a vampire. She can be found on Twitter @KiraoftheWind1 or on her website authormccorkle.com

Made in the USA
Las Vegas, NV
22 August 2023